Sarah

CW00460819

A Chilling Revelation

Best Wishes

Paul Cude

Paul M Cude

CONTENTS

1 THE SHIFTING SANDS OF TIME

Coarse grains of cold yellow sand trickled over the top of her toes, sifting through her sandals as she sprinted through the dark, narrow passage. Horribly hounded, her acute senses could pick out the individual footsteps, still some way back. From what she could tell, there were an awful lot of them, maybe as many as a hundred. In anywhere but an enclosed space, she could easily have evened the odds, but she'd been tricked into coming in here, and now it looked as though it would end up being her tomb, as well as that of the king for whom it was intended.

Turning a sharp corner at speed, Aviva stubbed one of her toes on a rock sticking out of the sand. Silently she cursed the narrow passageways. There were supposed to be secret entrances and exits throughout the pyramid, but she hadn't found any up until now. A reasonably large chamber would do, just big enough for her to transform into her dragon persona, so that she could fight off the attackers that were hot on her tail.

Stumbling across a flickering torch hanging on the wall, for a brief moment the courageous agent thought about taking it, just to have the comfort of the heat near her small, lithe body.

'No! It would just waste time.' But she knew it might aid the screaming mob baying for her blood, so she pulled it from the wall and rolled it in the sand until the beautiful flames died away, leaving it lying across the cramped corridor. In near total darkness, she accessed her dragon abilities, choosing to concentrate on enhancing her vision. It all happened in a split second and before she knew it she was back to sprinting for her very life.

Scurrying along as fast as the environment would allow, she wondered where it had all gone so wrong. Handpicked by the dragon council especially for this mission, her infiltration skills were renowned throughout the domain, and yet she still found herself in this precarious position. Worst of all, she hadn't managed to get a message off to caution them about her astounding discovery. Of all the regrets she had just then, that was at the top of her list.

Skidding to a halt in the sand, her legs nearly disappeared from under her. In the wall to her left was a door, a frame anyway. It looked as though it had been hastily blocked by a large slab of rock, but it was a door nevertheless, and the first one she'd seen. Studying the entrance, her enhanced hearing picked up the sound of a crowd rubbing against the walls back down the tunnel. Having gained some ground, she figured they were less than a minute behind her. Running her fingers around the edges of the frame, looking for anything strange, Aviva knew it wasn't unusual for openings of any kind inside a pyramid like this to be triggered in a secret manner. Finger holes, the touch of a certain rock, the twisting of a torch, were all means by which, over the past weeks, she'd activated concealed mechanisms to open up blocked routes. Coming up blank this time by searching with her fingers, she scanned the nearby walls beside the door and the corridor behind her.

NOTHING!

It was then that she heard the leader of the murderous

horde, heading her way, cry out in pain, no doubt stubbing his toe in the same way she had, only moments ago. Was it worth continuing further into the depths and leaving this entrance in the hope she'd find another? Or did she risk it all? Every instinct shrieked at her to try to open this door. Crouching down, she put all her strength into pushing against the hunk of rock, taut muscles in her arms glistening with the effort. It didn't budge. Quickly the daring agent moved further along and redoubled her efforts. Noticing it give a little towards the top, reaching up, she felt the slab move just slightly as she shoved it with all her might. Time was running out, the assailants had just fallen over the fireless torch, and were nearly upon her. Instinctively her hand brushed against the hilt of the sturdy little dagger tucked into her belt. Although she wasn't ready to die, she knew that if the moment came she'd take a whole lot of them with her.

Both hands pressed firmly against the top of the heavy chunk of rock, using all her agility, she jumped backwards with her feet, her heels landing solidly against the wall behind her. Knees bent, she began to walk upwards, eventually finding herself some two metres or so above the sandy surface of the passageway, feet pressed firmly against the opposite wall, her palms pushing against the portion of stone behind the door frame. Tensing every muscle in her body, sweating despite the relative chill, the disguised dragon pushed again with all her strength, shifting the slab in one corner, revealing a tiny opening. From her horizontal position above the corridor she was able to note the breach was perhaps big enough for a cat to scamper through. Her body was small, compact, dainty even, but the gap looked impossible for even her to climb through. As this single thought ran through her mind, time ran out. From around the corner came the frenzied mob, all vying to get to her first. Seeing them heading towards her with such hatred, their torches blazing above the leaders' heads reflecting the madness in their faces, was all the inspiration she needed. Using every ounce of strength, Aviva pushed, almost able to taste the stench of their fetid breaths. Quick as a flash, she launched herself at the tiny hole, barely scraping through, ripping the skin off both her ankles in the process.

Perched on the edge of the mammoth stone slab that had now fallen back into place inside the darkened chamber she felt bright, thick red blood ooze down her ankles, silently dripping onto the sand below, all the time catching her breath after what had been a frantic ten minutes. Both her feet hurt like hell, but there was nothing she could do about that just now.

Channelling as much magic as she could into her injuries, she hoped it would be enough. Listening as the crazed mob battered the rocky slab in frustration from the other side, she took in the contents of the totally dark room. Nearly choking on the dust particles hanging in the air, in her previous excursions she'd never come across anywhere that had smelt this musty and old. Not only that, but nearly every single thing was covered in layer after layer of spiders' webs.

'Oh great... spiders,' she thought, shivering.

Weapons and tools clinked and rattled beyond in the corridor, the noise prompting her into action, despite the fact that she just wanted to sit and heal up. Carefully sliding down the side of the slab, leaving a trail of thick blood in her wake, she stepped gingerly onto the sandy floor, her ankles sending agonising waves of pain up her legs as she tried to move. Parting the terrifying spiders' webs that were everywhere, she started to investigate the room, while attempting to ignore the sound of the angry mob.

Moments later, it dawned on her what she'd discovered - a small burial chamber of some sort, and if her normally efficient sense of direction wasn't off, it appeared to be hidden somewhere between the King's and the Queen's chambers within the structure.

'Fancy that,' the dragon agent thought to herself, 'a secret chamber inside Khufu's pyramid.' Under more pleasant circumstances, she'd have been ecstatic about her find, but she had to get out and send a message to the council. It was all that mattered now.

Deciding very quickly that she was bored of the cold and darkness, Aviva searched the pots and jars inside the room for some papyrus. Despite the urgency of her situation, she took great care for fear of accidentally opening one of the canopic jars (containing either the mummified liver, lungs, stomach or intestines of someone extremely important) that surrounded the large sarcophagus which sat dead centre, almost certainly containing a mummy of some sort. The last thing she wanted to do was to disturb any of those. Although knowing on a logical level from her dragon training that the religious tendencies of the humans were nothing more than false beliefs, she still maintained a great respect for them. Reaching into an ornate pot with intricate gold decoration around its base, she found what she was looking for: a tightly wound piece of papyrus. Gently pulling it out, she set about unwinding it. After that the dragon spy (as that's really what she was) retrieved one of the biggest bones she could find from a skeleton that sat propped up against the wall furthest from the doorway. Wrapping the papyrus tightly around the bone at one end, she mentally switched off her enhanced vision and concentrated on producing any sort of flame from her mouth. Not realising how chilly she'd become, it was something of a chore to conjure up a tiny dribble of fire, that hiccupped into life pathetically from between her perfectly formed human lips. Waving the papyrus through the insignificant heat, her heart leapt as the flames took hold and the makeshift torch burned and crackled with intent.

'Thank goodness,' she mused, watching the flickering light play over the dusty surroundings, the tiny source of heat feeling good on her exposed flesh. All she'd had on when she'd entered the pyramid was a tight fitting ankle length dress, with two shoulder straps, and a decorative collar. Regardless of the mind-bogglingly hot climate outside, the interior of the pyramid was incredibly cold. Waving the torch up and down her body, part of her rejoiced at the warmth from its flames. Moments later, she decided it was best to get on with the job at hand: survival. Before doing anything else, she crafted two more torches in much the same way as the first, concerned by the sudden silence of the baying horde that, up until a few minutes ago, had been clawing and scratching at the blocked entrance way.

With the torches made and ready to be lit at a moment's notice, Aviva set about investigating everything else in the chamber, everything except the mummy, that is. Even though she knew exactly what it was, she still had no desire to disturb it unless it was absolutely necessary and her entire existence depended upon it.

It didn't take long to finish her examination. Laid out in front of her, the inventory consisted of a necklace of golden flies, a half used scribe's palette with two used blocks of ink (one red, one black); two adzes (small carpenters' tools, one much more blunt that the other): half a dozen reed pens; two beaded bracelets; a glass container shaped like a fish that smelt of perfume; a polished bronze mirror and a small wooden good luck charm shaped like a man. Not quite sure what she'd been expecting, her hopes had been more than a little dashed.

As the first of her torches started to splutter and die, she lit one of the fresh ones, once again appreciating the heat and light.

After composing her thoughts for a few moments, the disguised dragon knew where to start... well, almost. With the ink she could write several messages in case escape proved beyond her.

'How to get some water though, that's the question.'

Immediately it came to her. Picking up the mirror, she carried it over to the darkest, coldest corner of the chamber. Inhaling deeply, she exhaled onto the chilly surface, her mouthful of air condensing instantly. A few breaths later, any sort of reflection was impossible. Leaving the mirror in the sand, she rushed back to the flickering torch, towering over her pathetic looking inventory. Spending a few minutes circling the crackling source of heat and light, warming her tiny false body, she wove her way back to the mirror. Sure enough, the condensation had started to turn into water, and as she moved the mirror in different directions, small drops ran down its reflective surface. Taking it back to the inventory, she dipped the tip of one of the reed pens into the moisture, before gently prodding it into the red ink in the palette. Repeating the procedure a few times, eventually she had enough runny red ink for her purposes.

Poised with the reed pen in her hand, she stopped to think for a moment. What could she write? Anything too obvious and it would almost certainly be covered up or destroyed by Ptolemy's cohorts. Scanning the chamber for inspiration, she noticed two of the walls were covered in hieroglyphics. Not just a few, but thousands of them.

'This,' she thought, 'could be just what I'm looking for.' It didn't take long for her to realise that everything she required was right here. Screwing her delicate little face up with effort, Aviva visualised the runny red ink. As she did so, whispered ancient words flowed across her tongue, almost hovering in the air before her. Looking down at the ink, she seemed satisfied that the mantra she'd cast had worked. Quietly going about her business, the unerring silence spurred her on. Halfway through she had to stop and light the remaining torch as the previous one spluttered out of existence. Five minutes later she'd finished her message to the council. It had been easy really, she thought, taking in her masterpiece. Using the ink, she'd covered particular hieroglyphs on both walls with the mantra, having altered the properties of the liquid, in effect turning it ultraviolet. Normal humans wouldn't notice anything, but a dragon trained to switch through their different visions would instantly recognise the message:

"Ptolemy attempting to murder Alexander's sons, so he can be king himself - Aviva Longwings."

Having spent too long admiring her handiwork, the human shaped dragon set about removing the excess ink and destroyed the reed pens, covering all traces of her efforts. Her top priority had been a message for the council, now that she knew about the underhand treachery that was afoot, knowing full well that if she failed to report in, they would send another of her kind to investigate. Whoever it was would discover the secret memorandum and hopefully the council would be able to stop Ptolemy's despicable plan before it came to fruition. Now it was time to leave if at all possible and hopefully report back in person. All she needed now was to find a way out.

Standing in the middle of the chamber, next to the sarcophagus, Aviva closed her eyes and once again altered her vision so that she could see in the dark. Mindful to avoid looking at the torch, she took in the rest of the chamber, in particular the ceiling high up above. It appeared to extend to a point, some twenty metres or so up. Two thirds of the way, on one of the walls without the hieroglyphs, was what looked like a small hole. What made the dragon agent think it might be more than it appeared was that the gap itself was perfectly square in shape. During her investigations she'd heard rumours that the humans had added vents to some of the chambers so that the spirit of the deceased could head up to the stars and into the afterlife. Of all the vents she'd heard about, none ever seemed to reach the outside of the actual pyramid itself.

'Still,' she thought, 'it's not like I've got much choice. I just need to figure out how to get up there.'

Aware that the last of her torches was over halfway

through its short lifespan, Aviva had a quick scout round in an attempt to find some more papyrus. Unfortunately, she'd used the last of it, and didn't really want to be without a torch, not so much because of the light, although that was partly it, but more because of the heat. Even a small heat source like that was enough to warm her up and make her dragon abilities easier to access. With nothing else for it, moving reluctantly to the centre of the room, and cautiously, she started to slide the lid off the sarcophagus. It was tough going, even with her enhanced strength. Despite knowing otherwise, there was still something eerie and creepy about revealing the contents. Staler air swished out of the tomb, forcing Aviva to hold her breath as the mummy inside revealed itself. Determined to take only what she needed, she tore off some of the fabric encompassing the remains of the long dead emperor, knowing it would burn well.

With five more torches completed, she reluctantly crept back to the half open sarcophagus, searching for something that had caught her eye when she'd first opened it. Sure enough, poking out from the upper left hand side of the mummy's body was a spectacular, jewel-laden dagger. Nervously, Aviva reached inside and grabbed it by the hilt. An unexpected, full on surge of power raced through her, unlike anything else she'd ever experienced. Wandering over to the burning torch, she studied the weapon in detail in the only light available. Turning the dagger over and over in the iridescent light, brightly coloured rubies and emeralds sparkled beyond belief. That, however, was not its most amazing feature. What had taken her breath away was the fact that with the exception of the jewels, the rest of the dagger had been forged from... laminium! Standing dazed for what seemed like minutes, studying the awe inspiring blade, probing its hidden power, not only had she never seen anything like it, she'd also never heard of anything like it either, and she prided herself on knowing dragonkind history. Yes, there were plenty of rings, amulets, earrings, belt buckles even, but a dagger... impossible... and yet here it was, twisting around in the palm of her hand. Even trapped in this cold dark tomb, she could feel the intense power of the magical metal ignite the supernatural senses inside her. Up until now, she hadn't realised how cold she'd gotten, and just how much it had drained her, not just physically, but mentally and emotionally as well. Quickly the laminium in the weapon changed all of that. Starting to feel totally invigorated, as if she'd just jumped out of a dirty great lava pool in her natural dragon form, with the blade in her possession, she quickly revaluated her situation. Moments ago she planned to split the sarcophagus in two and try to stand the two halves on top of one another, with a view to getting as close as possible to the opening. But now, with her dragon powers magnified by the ability enhancing metal, there might just be another way.

Stalking around the room, she let her enhanced imagination run wild with all the possibilities. Time and again, the same solution presented itself. Walking past the spluttering torch for a third time, her perception caught a sense of something. Stopping abruptly, she ceased worrying about getting out and concentrated on her surroundings.

'There it is again,' she thought. Just on the edge of her perception, a something, or group of somethings, was heading her way, murderous intent driving them on.

Brought back to reality by the crackle of the flame and the acrid smell of smoke, she knew it was time to leave. Discarding her old dagger for the magical laminium one, which she tucked tightly into the belt on her dress, she pushed aside all doubt about what she was going to do. The solution that kept popping up seemed more than a little risky, but with something ominous heading her way, she was more than prepared to take that chance. Bounding over to the sarcophagus, she slid the lid back on and removed her sandals, knowing that for the latter part of what she had in mind, bare feet would be critical.

"Awww," she groaned as she clutched her head in pain, able to feel them now, getting closer by the second. And they had something with them, something that would... finish her off for good, if their thoughts were anything to go by.

'This is it,' she reflected, suddenly exhilarated by the realisation that, one way or another, her fate would be decided in the next few moments. She would either escape or die. Smiling, part of her wouldn't have it any other way. It wasn't her first time in this situation by any means, but each and every time she found herself here, she always swore that it would be her last. Backing up to the cold stone wall, facing the length of the stunningly carved sarcophagus, she took a large, calming, deep breath, knowing they were close, if her enhanced hearing was anything to go by.

With a shake of her head and a wry smile, Aviva opened her eyes and sprinted towards the sarcophagus, dipping into her dragon magic to augment her speed. Five paces in, she jumped onto the ancient tomb, tearing along its entire length. Reaching the end, and with every last ounce of power she could muster, her lithe form leapt as high as it could, up the dark stone wall in front of her. Mid jump, she adjusted her centre of gravity, changing her direction just slightly, aiming to hit the wall full on with her feet. Bending her knees, a moment turned into years as she closed in. Timing it to perfection, she impacted the wall, and with her knees bent, pushed off at an angle that would take her higher up. With a whirlwind of magic supporting her, she shot upwards, before somersaulting over and across to the opposite side. All she had to do now was continue this, three more times. In the blink of an eye, the next two transitions came and went, all perfectly executed in the manner of the first, but just as it was time for the last one, something far below interrupted her concentration, and instead of hitting the wall cleanly and kicking off, she smacked her foot badly, barely pushing off at all. On any of the previous transitions, it would have proven disastrous, but because she was right at the top of the ever narrowing ceiling, there was a fleeting chance to turn things around. Literally only a metre or so from the square hole of the vent, twisting awkwardly, she thrust out her right arm as her momentum tried to take her away. Slapping against the side of the opening, as the dragon agent started to slide down, her fingers scrabbled to grasp hold of the edge. However cold she'd been, sweat now raced down her forehead, back and arms as she dangled precariously over the side of the vent, by just her finger tips.

Ignoring the thick beads of sweat that trickled down her nose, suddenly an ominous 'tick, tick, tick' sound from far below echoed upwards. Turning her head and forcing the thought of the drop to the back of her mind, with her enhanced senses, she could just make out the small gap at the top of the door through which, dozens of tiny fluorescent shapes were now flooding.

'Oh no,' she thought, 'not scarab beetles, anything but those... please.'

Sounding like the best stocked clock shop in the world, the 'tick, tick, tick' continued to assault her ears as the tiny bright blue shapes carpeted the sandy floor below. Knowing it wouldn't be long before they locked on to her scent, if they hadn't already, they would have no problem in scaling the walls and coming after her. Mustering all her concentration, and with muscles burning like an ironsmith's forge, gently, she started to swing from side to side. Even boosting her magic with the laminium dagger did little to ease the pain in her fingers that threatened to overwhelm her. Ignoring the deadly blanket of insects far below, Aviva gave her all. Thirty seconds later, the swinging paid off, and she was able to bring her other arm up and grab the ledge. Pulling herself up so that she was half inside the vent, she paused to catch her breath and give her aching arms time to recover, sweat dripping off her nimble legs, dropping into the darkness below.

Scuttling feet and 'tick, tick, ticking,' jolted her from her rest. Pulling herself fully into the vent, she turned to face outwards, no mean feat in the confined space. Looking down, she could see that the insects had caught her scent and, after completely covering the sarcophagus, were now rushing up the walls on all sides of the chamber. With her only option to retreat, she crawled backwards and waited for them to come swarming over the edge. Sure enough, before she'd backed up three metres, the first wave flocked over the lip. Stopping, she knew that trying to outrun them would be futile. Fingering the laminium dagger, wishing that it would heighten her abilities enough, she closed her eyes, knowing that only one hope remained. Reaching inside, she searched for the feeling that all dragons have, deep down past their stomachs. Brightly coloured scarab beetles trickled towards her on all four sides of the exhaust that she found herself in. Finding her magic, and with a measure of concentration, the feeling coalesced with the deep breath she'd taken. A measure of calm washed over her on realising it was going to work. Blowing out in the same way she would as her alter ego, a mighty stream of flame lit up the vent like a team of university students lighting their own farts.

Aviva kept up the almighty line of fiery death for as long as she could, the stench of scorched beetles attacking her nose, acrid, wispy blue smoke filling the confined space. Out of breath, she opened her eyes. Crispy insect carcasses crackled all around her. From what she could tell, they were all dead. Not wishing to look over the edge to see if there were any more, she shuffled round and began crawling further into the vent, her right hand checking to make sure the priceless laminium dagger was still tucked firmly into her belt.

No more beetles appeared in her wake, despite her constantly checking over her shoulder. The further she crawled, the steeper things got. Air getting staler with every metre, she'd hoped that further progress might mean better ventilation, revealing how close she might be to the outside.

Twisting and turning, there was little choice now but to continue on despite her knees being chafed and sore. During all this she took great comfort knowing that her enemies would assume her dead. Nothing much usually survives that amount of scarab beetles.

A good deal of time passed with numerous stops to catch her breath, before she decided that the air might actually have changed for the better. A sharp turn and an even steeper incline later, she finally caught a glimpse of sunlight shining through the sides of an ill fitting block of limestone. Panting like an exhausted dog, she studied what little of the desert she could see through the narrowest of gaps. Exhaustion threatening to consume her, unable to remember how long it had been since she'd been tricked into entering this godforsaken pyramid, she only knew that the lack of water and the long, slow, tedious crawl had taken its toll. Deciding to wait until it was dark to get out, for fear of being spotted, she curled up against the limestone block, dagger in hand, and promptly fell asleep.

Cold air brushed her neck, raising goose bumps and startling her awake. Shaking off the muddiness of her slumber, she quickly became alert. Night had fallen. Licking her dry lips with what little moisture remained in her mouth, she held the dagger up towards the limestone block, gently inserting it into the narrow gap. Using the priceless weapon as a lever, she gave it everything she had, moments later pulling up short. It had given a little; she'd felt it.

'If this is a vent, then surely this last block is supposed to move of its own accord,' she mused, totally parched. 'Perhaps the lack of water is making me stupid.'

Two more attempts with the blade proved fruitless. Sitting back against the cool rock, shivering just a little, she knew her best chance to escape was during the dark. With a little luck, she could in theory climb down the pyramid and make it to the nearest village without alerting anyone to her presence. How to get past this pesky brick though, seemed to be key to everything. Concentrating fully, ignoring just how dehydrated she was, her mind wandered all over the place, from thoughts of finding the dagger, to being chased by the baying mob in the narrow passages far below.

'That's it!' she thought. 'I bet there's something hidden that will open it.'

Sitting bolt upright, the disguised dragon slipped the blade into her belt and moved over to the block. Gently, with the palms of her hands, she felt its surface. Nothing. Probing the small gaps around the side with the tips of her dainty fingers, hoping to find something out of the ordinary, about to give up, she noticed a small protrusion on the ceiling. It was tiny... not even worth bothering about, but that was probably the point. Engineers constructing the pyramids had been the best around and were extremely crafty, in more ways than one. Reaching up, she gave the protrusion the tiniest of touches with her index finger. A faint rumble off to one side caused her to jump. Ever so slowly, the limestone brick lifted itself up and slid partially into the wall beside it, offering up just enough room for somebody to pass. Momentarily she stood still, in shock. As well as hearing all the gears and gadgetry, she felt as though there was something else, something she was missing because her head was too muddled from lack of water. Coming to her senses, quickly she darted through, out into the cold night air, not knowing how long her exit would remain open, or if in fact it was something that could only be used once.

Perched on the edge of an outside limestone ledge, she was surprised at how high up the pyramid she actually was.

In fact, she was very nearly at the top. Gazing down, she could clearly make out lots of people, villagers and guards alike, around the base, lit up by an array of torches. Remaining as low as possible, she began to make her way around the outside of the huge structure, determined to see if any one side was less populated than the others. A short while later, after covering all four sides which was no mean feat, she discovered everywhere to be teeming with people and sentries. Perhaps there was a religious ceremony taking place, or maybe her enemies knew she was still alive.

Of course the most obvious thing to do would be to turn into her dragon form and fly away. However, that would undoubtedly be seen even in the darkness, and with the dragon council having only recently issued orders about agents not using their prehistoric guises in front of humans at any cost, it was hard to see any alternative other than to climb down and escape, which although time consuming, shouldn't really present too much of a problem given the nature of her clandestine skill set. Although sure those in charge would understand if she had to revert, particularly given the relevance of the information she'd uncovered, the orders had been incredibly specific and had applied to all operatives, so she pressed on in her cold, nimble and determined false human appearance.

All she had to do was make it off the pyramid, flee the immediate area and then with nobody else about, slip into her natural shape and return to the council.

'Simple,' she thought, shaking her head and berating herself for not transforming and flying off.

Gingerly vaulting down, block by block, the cover of night shrouding her movement this high up, the chilly air started to take its toll even with the laminium dagger boosting her powers. On top of that, her feet were absolutely killing her, having been barefoot since she somersaulted up to the vent entrance; it hadn't troubled her too much inside the giant structure which was silky smooth, but now that she was outside, the limestone blocks were rough and very hard going on the soles of her feet.

Abruptly a dark shape appeared further along on the same level as Aviva. Throwing herself down onto the jagged surface, she looked up to see a burly guard carrying a torch in one hand and a sword in the other, nervously looking around, almost as if scared of heights. Feeling for her dagger, she knew she had to take him down quickly and quietly. As he approached, she used her free hand to search for any loose stones or gravel. Grabbing a few small rocks, she lobbed them into the air, over his head. As the guard turned, instantly distracted by the noise behind him, the dragon agent seized the opportunity and leapt, dagger at the ready. Covering the four metres in the blink of an eye, she clamped her hand over his mouth and swiped the blade across his exposed throat. Warm liquid squirted across her exposed forearm, while a brief gurgle uttered from the dead guard's mouth. Slowly, she lowered his still quivering corpse to the ground, breathing a deep sigh of relief. Quickly she removed his outer clothing and put it on. On close inspection she look ridiculous because the outfit was far too big, but in the dark, she shouldn't have too much of a problem fooling anyone from a distance.

Moving the cadaver so that it was lying totally flat, making sure the only chance of it being found was to stumble right on top of it, she grabbed the torch he'd dropped when she'd slit his throat. Using a little burst of flame from her breath, she ignited it and very carefully continued her descent.

After an hour or so, she wasn't far from the base of the pyramid. Instead of climbing straight down at this point, she wound her way around, carefully avoiding prying eyes, trying to assess the best place for her to join the flocking crowds. After biding her time, she found what she was looking for, a throng of people with absolutely no guards.

Casually she made her way down the last dozen or so blocks and into the multitude of people, before quietly extinguishing the torch and discarding it. Moving through the crowd at random, and keeping her head down, she headed for the nearest village where her first priority was to find some water and then a deserted spot to change into her dragon form.

An hour or so later, Aviva had left most of the crowd and the pyramid in the distance, ditched the guard's clothes and was fast approaching the outskirts of the nearest settlement. By now, she was overcome with dizziness through dehydration. All she wanted to do was have a drink. Stumbling through the only undergrowth for miles around, moments later she found herself in the hamlet good and proper. Staggering towards the centre, as that's where the well would be, she struggled to lift one foot in front of the other.

Finally reaching the well, she slid down next to it in a cold sweat, needing to catch a breath before attempting to lower the bucket. Holding her head in her hands, it was all she could do to remain lucid. With her throat as dry as the surrounding desert and with spots starting to appear in the periphery of her vision, she crawled to her feet and started lowering the pail into the well. The faint splash of water from below spurred her on, and once she could feel the weight of the liquid, she pumped the handle with all her might. Strength starting to wane as the bucket appeared out of the darkness, in a frenzy she began pouring the gorgeous cool water down her throat, not caring about the amount that was spilling down the front of her dress onto her bare feet.

Pausing for breath, she wiped her mouth with the back of her hand, wondering why water had never tasted this good. As she did so, the faintest 'twang, zffooofff' ricocheted around her position Mind bending pain erupted from her left leg as she dropped to the floor, spilling the remaining water from the bucket into the sand. Rolling onto her front, she tried to get to her feet, but couldn't. A very primitive wooden arrow had pierced her calf, sending wave after wave of agony up that side of her body. Grasping the side of the well to pull herself up, the suffering she felt was suddenly interrupted by something much more sinister.

A loud, booming, "HA HA HA," echoed through the night air, as Ptolemy himself strutted out from behind one of the adjacent buildings, followed by the archer that had shot her and, to her surprise, two dragon councillors, both in their human guises.

Heart racing with fear at not knowing exactly what was going on, she steeled herself to face the brazen arrivals.

"Ah, brave Aviva," whispered Ptolemy, with just a hint of sarcasm. "My most loyal servant, or so it would seem. These fellows have put me right on that front though, and quite a bit else."

A split second was all that was needed for it to become clear. For a moment, she'd thought that the councillors were here to aid her, but she should have known that really wasn't the case. Carrying an injury, this situation would have been hard enough to get out of, but having these two here made it all but impossible.

'Still,' she thought pragmatically, 'you can be damn sure I'm gonna take one of them with me. And the biggest surprise of the lot is that they don't know about the laminium dagger which gives me more of an edge than they think.'

Screwing up their faces in unison, the two officials gave their best false smiles.

"Aviva, you're so predictable. I bet right at this very moment you're contemplating taking one of us to the grave with you."

Not a muscle moved in her face, so determined was she not to let them know they'd been right. Instead, the courageous agent allowed all the rage and power inside her to build up, waiting to let it explode out when the time was right.

"Anyway, much as this reunion has been fun, I think it's time to get down to the business at hand," began Ptolemy, nodding at the two councillors.

Taking the hint, she knew that the time had come. Faster than the eye could see, powered by her inherent bravery, she grabbed the tip of the arrow poking out of her calf and yanked it free with all her might, ignoring the mind numbing pain that accompanied it. Before anyone had a chance to react, Aviva had thrown the arrow at the archer some fifteen metres away, and hit him straight through the forehead, rendering him instantly dead.

As the bowman crumpled to the ground, and Ptolemy wriggled behind his two companions, Aviva smiled to herself.

'Looks like I'm not the only one to be hit by a surprise arrow today. Karma and irony all wrapped up in one.'

"You said you could protect me. You said she'd be no danger. Do something!" barked Ptolemy at the two traitors from below ground.

Both councillors took a step in Aviva's direction, whilst at the same time muttering under their breaths. Instantly they started to transform.

Pretty sure she knew what would happen, Aviva forced a little sliver of dragon power into her calf to stop the bleeding and uttered a small lightning mantra, throwing some of the extra power from the dagger at it in the process, directing it towards the sand in between them. Tiny, fragmented yellow grains blasted everywhere as the first humungous bolt frazzled into the ground, making it impossible to see more than twenty metres in any one direction. Fully prepared for the outcome, she vaulted over the well and sprinted around behind two of the nearest buildings, ending up next to the river. Panting with exertion, inside her head she whispered the words that would start her own transition, hoping she'd bought herself enough time. A second in, tremendous pain whirled around inside her, something totally out of the ordinary. Quickly it became apparent... her change was taking fractionally longer than normal. Things did not bode well.

Finished, the experienced spy collapsed onto the river bank in her dragon form. Even in the cool night air, she really should have been fit and alert, she thought, struggling to get her huge dragon body to respond. Somewhere in the back of her mind, a sense of danger screamed at her to get up, knowing her enemies were mere moments away. Tottering to her feet, Aviva tried frantically to wash away the fog around her brain. Looking down at her leg, she could see that it wasn't bleeding from the arrow wound. A few more seconds passed before she finally felt some sense of normality. Again, her sense of danger screamed out, this time to take to the air. Not needing to be told twice, and despite the nagging sense that something was amiss, bending her knees she leapt gracefully into the air. As she did so, the building behind where she'd been standing splintered into a million pieces as one of the councillors ploughed through it.

Circling overhead, she breathed a sigh of relief, not for one second letting her guard down. In the distance she could see Ptolemy roaring orders at some of his men that had appeared out of the undergrowth. Suddenly, Aviva remembered the dagger. She didn't have it with her. In her haste to take to the sky she'd forgotten to pick it up and now it lay beneath what was left of her clothes, not four metres from the dragon councillor that had just destroyed the building.

Distracted momentarily, she turned sharply as a rush of cool air brushed her back, just a little too late. Razor-sharp talons raked her spine, as she painfully spun out of the way, only just managing to avoid a vicious jet of flame by dropping into a steep dive.

Head spinning as she hastily charged towards the ground, thoughts of escape had long since passed. On top of everything, she couldn't work out why she felt so strange and underpowered. Maybe the arrow she'd been shot with had been poisoned, but her leg, although painful, showed no sign of any venom and was, in fact, starting to heal up just fine. Noting Aviva's approach, the dragon who'd decimated the building had now leapt skywards to join the fight. Aware that her lifespan could now be measured in minutes, if not seconds, without the dagger, she knew that with it, just maybe she could turn things around.

With one councillor charging up towards her, and one hot on her tail, quite literally, Aviva knew she had to take a chance to get the magical blade back. Using all her supernatural reserves to elicit a burst of speed, she accelerated towards the dragon heading up from the surface, his glinting red scales standing out in the darkness, back lit by the reflective surface of the river behind him. As the gap between them narrowed, she could see his prehistoric jaws twist into a smirk, thinking that there was no way out for his prey. A quick glance over her shoulder confirmed that 'Yellow' (as she thought of him, because of a huge twisted stripe running down one side of his dull, white belly) was only a matter of metres in her wake, bearing the same knowing grin.

Turning to face forward again, knowing that she needed a whole lot of luck in the next few moments, 'Red' speeded towards her, his wings spread, the moonlight glinting off his sharpened talons, opening his jaws wider than it appeared possible.

'This is it,' she thought. 'It's now or never.' Just as Red, hurtling up to meet her, about to snap his jaws shut, she curled up into a massive ball, her toughened frame smacking the councillor right in the mouth with a bone shattering CRUNCH. After that, her trajectory changed dramatically, falling almost like a rock towards the ground. Yellow, had been chasing her so closely, there was little he could do but crash firmly into his comrade. For the second time in quick succession, a resounding breaking of bones echoed over the village, as the two prehistoric turncoats collided in mid-air.

As planned, Aviva's trajectory had her heading straight for her clothes and of course the laminium dagger. Unfurling just before she hit the ground, the wind was knocked fully out of her due to the abrupt landing she was forced to pull off. Stomping over to her discarded garments, she retrieved the blade, slipping it safely into one of the hidden pouches that circled her belly. Contact with the weapon instantly heightened her senses. It was then that it struck her. Something was seriously wrong deep within, not near her calf, although that was starting to throb somewhat. No, something unusual was pumping throughout her system, causing everything inside, including her major organs, severe harm.

Having retreated somewhat to lick their wounds, the two councillors continued circling high above Aviva's position. Whilst their collision hadn't been anywhere near fatal, bones had been broken and scales lost. Of course, with their multitude of magical abilities, a full recovery wouldn't take very long. As Aviva started to wonder why the pair hadn't resumed their attack, Ptolemy returned with a number of his guards, slightly further down the river. Archers appeared in their ranks, causing the dragon agent to recall their previous assault. Anger surged through her, so much so that she let out a ferocious roar in their direction. It had the desired effect; with nearly all the soldiers cowering in fear. Ptolemy though, puffed out his muscled chest in her direction as he took a breath.

"Feeling a little... unwell?" he mocked, knowingly.

Trying to respond, all Aviva could manage was a loud racking cough. The despicable traitor smiled at his prey's discomfort.

"What have you done to me?" Aviva croaked.

Laughter reverberated through the night air, sending a chill up her tail.

"Not me this time, I'm afraid," sniggered the wannabe

King. "In fact, you can thank your friends up there, for that," he said, pointing high up into the sky. "Their little concoction seems to be doing a good job. While I didn't approve of poisoning the whole village just to contaminate the well, it does seem to have paid dividends."

Craning her neck, she gazed up into the sky, before looking back at him, shaking her head all the while. Ptolemy had previous in this department, but for any dragon to do something so dreadful was just outrageous.

'This ends now,' she thought, suppressing another almighty cough. 'But how to do it is the big question? Ptolemy and his soldiers aren't cause for concern now that I'm in dragon form, but taking out the two councillors whilst the poison continues to debilitate me presents much more of a problem.'

With them all having backed off, waiting for the toxin to do its job, she decided to play along and began retching wildly. Overhead, the two dragons, staying well out of the way, shared a smile. Ptolemy and his guards stood nervously waiting for the prehistoric beast in front of them to keel over and die. All the while feigning illness, she combed her memory for anything that would be of use. Aware that she was playing into their hands, given that with every second that ticked by, the closer to death she became, any attempt she was going to make, had to be sooner rather than later. Dropping to one scaled knee for effect, suddenly it came to her.

As well as being a deadly assassin, a member of the elite King's Guard and a trusted ally of the monarch himself, Aviva was also a keen scholar. With regular access to the council's main library and even the occasional supervised visit to the king's private library, she considered herself one of the best educated dragons on the planet, and had read just about everything ever published, dragon and human alike. Now it was time for that information to pay dividends. Buried in one of the tomes in the ruler's repository, there was a tale of a dragon who'd gone up against a horde of evil dark beasts, armed only with a trident. It wasn't just any trident though. It was, if she remembered correctly, one fashioned from steel and plated with laminium. Once read, the tale had seemed more than a little far-fetched, but the interesting part was that the dragon in question was able to take on these enemies because every time he killed one of the creatures with the augmented trident, the mighty weapon infused itself with the magical power from each of the deceased, making its owner more powerful with every single kill.

'If I could destroy just one of the councillors with the laminium dagger,' Aviva thought, 'then maybe I'll be infused with enough energy to carry on and finish off the other, and Ptolemy as well.'

Fully bent over now, dry coughing for all she was worth, from the corner of her eye, she could just see the two councillors sneaking closer and closer overhead, whilst Ptolemy and his soldiers edged ever nearer, weapons raised, ready for action. Pulling in a deep breath, which she knew might well be one of her last, the agent twisted her head in the would-be king's direction and launched a searing stream of fire. Nothing more than a distraction really from her point of view, as they were over fifteen metres away, it did however send them scampering to take cover behind one of the remaining structures.

Pretty sure that between them they could take down one lone dragon suffering from acute poisoning; both traitors were, if anything, coming in lower, playing right into Aviva's hands.

Banging her tail in supposed frustration, she let one of her legs give way, causing her to topple onto the dusty sand. Lying exposed on one side, she could see both officials getting ever nearer. Clutching the dagger in her right hand, hidden beneath her wing, the crafty agent prepared to strike.

Like lightning on steroids, she was up, using everything she had to propel herself into the air. Both councillors were caught off guard, absolutely no idea what to do, Aviva heading towards them in a blur. Yellow tried to double back in an arc, confused as to how their adversary had gone from her deathbed to airborne in an instant. His partner opened his jaws in a full on challenge, angry at the turnaround of events. Concealing the dagger in her hand, bravely she appeared to ignore Yellow and go straight for the challenger. Dropping his guard, Yellow waited to pounce after she'd shot by. It was the last mistake he ever made. Making the sharpest high speed turn possible without ripping both her wings off, she was all over Yellow in an instant, already having located his weak spot, she thrust the dagger into the underside of his belly with all the force she could, whilst whispering the words from the tome, deep within her mind. Much as she didn't want to murder another of her kind, there was simply no way out of this now. It was kill or be killed. None of this had been part of the plan, for which she was very sorry. But given what they'd both done, not just to her, but the villagers as well, she had no doubt they deserved to die.

Red was aghast at what had happened, and although on his way to his comrade, he was far too slow to make a difference... Aviva's strike was well placed, the laminium dagger slaughtering Yellow instantly.

What happened next though, even the courageous agent couldn't have predicted, despite having read the account of the dragon with the trident. Shimmering, Aviva's laminium dagger turned the brightest shade of blue, lighting up the sky all around, as far as the pyramid, more than four miles away. Hovering in place, she was totally blinded by the searing bright light, and she wasn't the only one. So was the other councillor, out to exact revenge for the friend he'd just seen murdered. Unfortunately for him, he'd tumbled around a few times and was now heading in totally the opposite direction, all the time howling in pain.

Overrun with magical energy, the laminium blade

started to heat up. Not just a little, oh no. It became hot like the sun. Maintaining her grip, acrid grey smoke rising from her scorched palms, she knew that if she was going to boost her powers somehow, then the rare weapon was key. Still she held on, despite fearing she might pass out. Abruptly the heat and the pain passed, replaced by an all encompassing serenity. A scorching bright light all around her appeared to get sucked into the rare laminium artefact, and then from it, into Aviva herself. Everything became completely crisp and clear for a split second. In that moment anything was possible, her power unimaginable, even getting a split second glimpse into the future, or futures, depending on how you looked at it.

With the light having dissipated, turned into energy and transferred itself into the cunning female, darkness once again cloaked the surrounding area. Soaring up high, she could just make out Ptolemy, terrified, fleeing with his men, back towards the pyramid. On the far side of the village, Red screeched the most unholy noise as he circled low over the ground, mourning the death of his comrade, blinded and not knowing where he was. Deep inside she knew she had to finish him off and quickly. Despite her training, killing another of her kind was not high on her 'to do' list, particularly one briefly disabled. However, she'd gotten some idea of just how dangerous he could be, and knew it was best for everyone if he died here and now, especially as she had no idea how long her new found infusion of magical power would last, or keep the toxin within her at bay. Thoughts of the entire village being slaughtered by the poison that seeped through her spurred her into action as she sped towards him, determined to make it as quick and painless as possible.

Hovering just above the buildings next to the river, the remaining councillor spurted flame in a wide arc, hollering and howling like a deranged werewolf who'd just stood on a Lego brick. Aviva approached from high above, already having noted that his weak spot was about half way up his back, just off centre. With nothing else for it but to get on with the task at hand, she nose-dived towards the stricken traitor, who seemed to be going more berserk by the second. Tackling him from behind like a professional rugby player, they struggled madly, as he tried to turn around and lock his jaws onto her. Tangled up, they both scrambled towards the river, as Aviva plunged the dagger into his weak spot. Instantly, the mad howling and screaming died out, as the blade glowed ever so slightly with a bluish tint, but nothing like the first time. Striving to take his weight, the councillor's prehistoric body hung limp in her arms. With nothing else for it but to dump the antediluvian cadaver in the river, using all her strength she managed to take him a few extra metres, above the middle of the deep, fast flowing body of water, before finally letting him go. A gigantic SPLASH boomed across the village, as ripples of dark water washed out in concentric circles.

Utterly exhausted, despite her best efforts the poison had done its job, leaving her close to death. Determined to right all the wrongs that had gone on in this place before passing, Aviva was desperate to find Ptolemy. Through the fog that clouded her mind, she recalled seeing him retreat back towards the pyramid. Putting what little effort she had left into heading in that direction, the cool night air washed over her pain racked body causing her to shiver like mad. Flapping one of her giant wings sent spikes of blistering agony coursing through her, forcing her to contemplate simply curling up and dying. But her amazing willpower, which had never before been tested in any of her previous adventures like it was being tested now, simply refused to yield.

Winging her way over the undergrowth that separated the village from the pyramid, she caught a glimpse of Ptolemy, not far from the gigantic stone structure's entrance. Both wings beating in unison, nearly passing out from the pain, she put on one last burst of speed, determined to intercept the scheming would-be ruler before he found sanctuary in the recently completed construction. People in the dense crowd surrounding the pyramid pointed, unable to believe what they were seeing. Panic soon set in, as they all fled in different directions at the sight of Aviva's scaly prehistoric form descending towards them.

Coming in hard, she crashed to the ground right in front of the pyramid's main entrance, stopping Ptolemy and his men in their tracks. On his orders, the guards closed ranks around their master, forming a circle three deep. As Aviva took this all in, her vision started to blur quite badly, able to see three of everything, knowing that her time was nearly at an end. Leg muscles tightened as she tried frantically to move them and walk over to the group, but to no avail. Ptolemy barked out more orders; Aviva could no longer understand them. All her willpower was focused on destroying him and returning the region to some kind of stability, protecting everyone from this murdering, scheming, would-be king.

Suddenly a ring of archers stole out of the night, surrounding the stricken dragon. Letting out a little chuckle, she looked at them, not knowing just how many there actually were due to her failing vision. With inevitable death only moments away, she drew in the biggest breath possible, which was quite pathetic given what she could normally achieve, added as much magic as she had left, and let rip with the biggest stream of flame she could manage, in the direction of Ptolemy and his guards. Unfortunately for her, only a tiny smattering of fire appeared from between her ancient looking jaws, barely enough to warm the archer standing directly in front of her, let alone harm Ptolemy. Spent, she collapsed awkwardly to the ground, the cool golden sand spraying up around her.

Through half open eyes, she could just make out her nemesis walking towards her as the guards ahead of him parted. Fighting with all her might to lift her jaw off the floor to get a better look, she failed spectacularly, too far gone to move even one muscle, let alone her whole head. Appearing only centimetres in front of her, Ptolemy barked out questions she could barely understand, his sickening smile making her want to puke. Wishing with her dying breath for one last surge of energy, so that she could bite his head clean off, the poison finally took hold. As she drifted into nothingness, her last thought was of the laminium dagger.

'Where has it gone? Have I dropped it somewhere or did someone else...'

"Ptolemy went on to become king; both of Alexander the Great's sons were murdered in mysterious circumstances. That was one of the key events in him founding the Ptolemaic dynasty.

And that, young dragons, is yet another example of our kind, good or evil, interfering with the natural development of human evolution. Time and again we see rogue dragons trying to manipulate the populated world above, and time and again, the so called good amongst us are sent after them in an effort to rebalance the scales.

Now, all of you, off to Lava Falls to practise your aerial acrobatics. This year's examination is only a few days away, and I expect you all to pass with... flying colours... ha ha... flying... get it?"

As one, the class groaned at the *tor's* feeble attempt at humour.

Perched on the wall that separated the courtyard of the nursery ring from the main walkway into Purbeck Peninsula, Peter shook his head and suppressed a smile at the thought of the teacher's attempted joke, having only heard the *tor* say that about a thousand times, and it hadn't been particularly amusing on the first attempt.

As the youngsters eagerly scattered, excitedly heading

off to practise their airborne acrobatics, he felt a pang of regret, wishing he were able to join them. Despite more than six weeks having elapsed since his ordeal on the Astroturf with the mysterious dragon Manson, he had still not fully recovered. So much so, that he'd been told by the best dragon doctors that under no circumstances was he to try and take his prehistoric form, at least not until he was fully healed which was, at best, still some way off.

Gingerly shuffling off the wall and onto the busy thoroughfare, he headed towards the monorail station at a sedate walk. Dragons travelling in both directions gave him curious looks, some even daring to smile, at the left arm he currently had bandaged and in a sling. It was unusual to see any of their kind in this condition, because normally they would have been completely healed by magic. His fight with Manson had left him with some bizarre injuries, puzzling even the brightest and most experienced doctors below ground. In the end it had been decided that the best course of action was to let Peter's body heal on its own, something that was taking a seriously long time. Meanwhile, the tale of his heroics had been splashed across the front of the telepathic papers almost constantly. While from a certain point of view, he could see how it could be construed that way, but he maintained now, as he had done at the hospital after the attack, that he had only survived due to luck, and that he just happened to be in the right place at the right time to thwart the dastardly Manson. The papers were having none of it, putting it all down to modesty on Peter's part. So now, everywhere he went, dragons stared, pointed and occasionally smiled. All of it bothered him, nothing more so than the fact that he felt like a fraud, and couldn't shake the feeling that he'd done the least he could at all times and it was only really with the help of his friends... Tank, Richie and Gee Tee the master mantra maker... that the whole situation had been resolved.

Continuing along the narrow path, gazing longingly at

the bright orange slivers of lava shining through the thin cracks in the walkway's surface, to his relief, the number of commuters started to dwindle to barely a handful, a minute or so later. While nothing bad had happened to him through the publicity, all he really wanted to do was go back to his normal life and relative obscurity, something that seemed a million miles away at the moment.

Not due back to work at Cropptech until after Christmas, playing hockey, his favourite sport would have to wait until well into the New Year, due to the severity of his injuries. Richie and Tank had been wonderful throughout everything, visiting him regularly. Pretty sure they'd both been given instructions to do so by the doctors, he was certain they would have appeared anyway.

Over the course of their last few visits though, he'd gotten the impression that something was... not so much wrong, just... going on, and that both of them didn't want to burden him with whatever it was. Tank had been giving Richie some very curious looks. As their friend he always liked to think he could pick up on such things. Clearly the pair didn't want to tell him what the problem was, and after giving them a few chances to do so, he decided it was best to leave it alone, sure he would find out eventually. It couldn't be that important anyway, could it?

Cresting the top of the hill that overlooked the Purbeck monorail station, once again it took his breath away. Not in the same way as say, Salisbridge Cathedral, or the picture perfect water meadows, but still it was a stunning sight. Keeping his head down as he approached the station in the hope that the other travellers might not realise who he was, in his heart of hearts he knew the sling he was wearing would give it away. Glancing up only to see which platform his carriage was departing from, he was glad to see it waiting there for him to step on to as he arrived. Taking his seat, almost immediately the carriage accelerated away into the eerie darkness of the tunnel that led out of the smallish dragon enclave. Fiddling with his sling, he snuck a peek at the rest of the carriage, hoping to find it deserted. It wasn't, but it wasn't full either. Chuckling to himself, he noticed one of the other dragons nearby reading paper from the world above.

'What a typically human thing to do,' he thought, glad that it wasn't just him that had picked up more than a few of their mannerisms.

Arriving at Salisbridge, the monorail was on time to the second. Last to leave the carriage and step out onto the pristine, shining surface of the station, he quickly headed through the crowds, not for the first time today, wishing that he'd brought a jacket of some sort to hide the sling from everybody. Ignoring the delicious aromas of food that wafted across the plaza, he headed for the smallest exit that would take him back to his house.

Moments later he reached the underground entrance to his home, gingerly slipping through the small gap in the wall, before heading up the darkened path and the clumsy looking steps. As he got within reach of the solid block of rock that barred the way, it started to move silently aside, apparently without him having done anything at all.

'Ah,' he thought, 'looks like the 'relatives' are waiting. Hope my dinner's on the table... hmmm... fat chance of that.'

Striding into the dusty cellar, lit only by a cascade of light flooding down from the top of the black ornate circular staircase in one corner, he could just make out a frail old lady, dressed in a cardigan, skirt and slippers, standing off to one side. Huge glasses hung from the end of her twisted nose, small straggly hairs littering her jaw line. She could have been anyone's favourite old grandma. She wasn't. In fact, she was everyone's worst nightmare.

"Hi," ventured Peter, more cheerily than he actually felt. "Thanks for opening the door."

"You've been gone quite a long time," the old woman grumbled in rather a gruff voice.

"Just went for a walk and stopped off at the nursery

ring, that's all."

"Ten more days and you'll be back on your own. No more babysitting for us... thank God."

Sliding silently shut, the rock door behind Peter made some of the cobwebs in the cellar sway as it did so. The old lady gestured for the wounded youngster to go up the spiral staircase ahead of her. He duly obliged, poking his head, and then the rest of his body, through into the living room of his house. Bounding up two steps at a time, the old woman followed. Once they were both through and out of the way, she yanked hard on the Galileo thermometer that sat on top of the light coloured piano. Sliding around in an arc, the beautifully crafted instrument came to a rest atop the entrance to the dusty old cellar.

Across the sitting room, lounging on the sofa, next to a pile of discarded knitting, sat a very similar looking grandmother persona, albeit slightly more colourful. This one wore luminous yellow tights with a bright red skirt, a shockingly blue shirt and a pink tank top. The ever inclusive facial hair once again raised itself, but this time instead of a tickly beard, there was more of a moustache, something the original Magnum PI would have been proud of.

'Nearly all the colours of the rainbow,' Peter mused, looking over her attire. 'I think a unicorn must have swallowed a rainbow and then thrown up all over her.'

Unfortunately, these dear women were experts at reading thoughts amongst other things, and had no doubt picked up on both of these ideas, at least that's what he'd heard was possible.

"There I was thinking I looked quite dashing," quipped Mildred, in a very confused Scottish accent, from the sofa.

"Ohhh... you do dear, you do," replied June gruffly, from behind Peter.

Flashing them his best false smile, he'd become bored many weeks ago with their very strange banter.

Both old ladies (dragons in reality) had been waiting for

him when he'd arrived home from the hospital, a little over four weeks ago. Posing as his Aunt Mildred and her best friend June, the two were in fact highly placed members of the King's Guard, both there in case Manson or any of his cohorts should try to come back and harm him, something he hadn't thought too much about until he'd met these two. Every time he looked at them, all he could think about was his nemesis returning to exact revenge. They were constant reminders of the battle that he'd fought and how his life had now changed forever.

June threw herself down on the sofa next to Mildred, causing the discarded knitting to jump into the air as she did so. Picking up the television remote control, she switched on 'Deal Or No Deal,' their favourite programme, before turning towards Peter.

"Get the tea on then, oh gorgeous nephew of mine."

Giggling hysterically, they turned their attention back to the screen.

'Playing their parts just a little too well,' he thought, skulking off towards the kitchen. 'Ten more days, only ten more days to go... it's going to feel like a hundred, I just know it is. All I want is for things to be back to normal.'

Sitting down at the table, Peter held his head in his undamaged hand, the sound of Noel Edmonds leaking through from the living room.

'It's no good, I have to get out or I'm gonna go insane,' he thought, frustrated. Carefully he pulled his phone out of his trouser pocket, no mean feat using only one hand and having very tight jeans on. Retrieving it, he sent Tank a text pleading with him to help him out. Waiting five minutes, hoping that his friend would respond straight away, after no reply he decided he was probably still working hard at the Mantra Emporium, in which case there would be no phone signal.

Rising from the table, his arm in the sling was noticeably starting to smart. The pain from the wound would generally come and go, but now it throbbed agonisingly. Using his limited dragon powers he tried his best to heal it, but just like all his other attempts, it made very little difference.

Abruptly, a shout from the living room interrupted his healing effort.

"Any closer with that tea yet nephew?" Mildred bellowed over the television, June laughing in the background.

Everything was unexpectedly interrupted by the front doorbell ringing. Immediately June tottered down the hall, as Mildred leapt up from the sofa, signalling to Peter to stay in the kitchen, something he knew better than to argue with, despite the fact that he knew the identity of the visitor. The echo of the security chain resounded up the hall, followed by the creak of the door opening.

"Hello there June," mocked Tank, pushing his way past the old lady's squat frame, patting her on the head as he did so. Snarling viciously at the young rugby player as he passed, she could do little but watch as Peter bounded down the hallway to meet his friend.

"Pete, how are you?"

Rolling his eyes, the home owner hoped he would take the hint.

"Ahh... you know, okay I suppose."

Tank's eyes sparkled just a little, having picked up on his pal's predicament. Then he came out with the words Peter longed to hear more than anything else in the world.

"Fancy coming to the sports club for a drink?"

Injury or not, he nearly wet himself with excitement.

"That would be fantastic."

"Hrrrhhh... hrrrhhh," coughed Mildred from the entrance to the living room.

"What harm can it do... really?" pleaded Peter.

Both old ladies sidled up to Tank, giving him an evil look.

"The first sign of trouble, you call for help, do you understand?"

Tank let loose one of his massive grins.

Without warning, June smacked him around the shins with her dark wooden walking stick.

"Ouch!" yelled Tank, loudly.

"Do you understand?"

"Yeah... um... sure... no problem," he answered, hopping about nursing his bruised leg.

"This isn't some kind of game you know."

"He knows," replied Peter defensively.

Mildred and June, for that's how he thought of them, stared menacingly at the two friends.

"So be it," said Mildred quietly. "But take heed of what we've told you."

Putting his good arm around Tank, Peter checked he had his keys, phone and wallet, before guiding his friend, who was still feeling the pain, out through the front door. Walking down the garden path, Peter apologised for the behaviour of the two specialist guardians.

"It's okay Pete," replied Tank. "Some of those King's Guards can be right nut jobs."

"Sssssssssssshhhhhhhhh," whispered the hockey player. "They'll hear you."

"I don't care if they do," observed his pal, unlocking the car, holding open the passenger door. Before Tank could start the engine, Peter stopped him.

"Thanks for coming round tonight. No really, I mean it. It got to the stage where I'd just really had enough."

"I know mate," replied the big rugby player sympathetically. "It must be really hard with those two clowns around all the time. Anyway, let's go and have a drink and a laugh shall we?"

"Magic," uttered Peter, as Tank gunned the car into life.

Five minutes later they pulled into the sports club. Walking across the car park to the club house in the dark, Peter marvelled at the Astroturf pitch, lit up with footballers playing six-a-side. This was the first time he'd been back since that fateful night and the surface looked as good as new, if not better. It was odd how not even a single scratch remained from the devastating battle that had taken place some six weeks previously.

Tank caught his friend gazing across at the pitch.

"Incredible isn't it? The thing was all but destroyed, and in only a matter of hours they'd returned it to its original state. The really amazing thing is that," Tank touched the side of his nose as he continued walking, "apparently they only had two dragons working on it. In the past, it would have taken over ten dragons to repair something that big in that kind of timescale. Spooky, eh?"

Peter nodded, hoping to be fully recovered soon and able to get back to playing hockey, something he missed like crazy.

Making their way inside the clubhouse, the two friends waited to be served, Peter sucking in the atmosphere even though it was relatively empty. A sudden tap on his shoulder caused him to jump.

"Hi Peter, how are you?" squeaked Janice the barmaid, excitedly.

Tank, ever the diplomat, gave his friend a wink and then shuffled away a little.

"Janice. Good to see you. I'm getting better thanks."

"I heard what happened," declared the blonde bombshell, nodding towards his sling. "You were so brave, foiling the robbery and everything.

For a split second he had to think about what she'd just said.

'Ahh... that's right. The council put the story out that there'd been an attempted theft at Cropptech and that somehow, singlehandedly I saved the day.'

"Well... it wasn't just me," he whispered as she gazed across the bar at him. "There were others there as well, and anyway, it's just part of my job."

Peter didn't know it, but at that very moment he might as well have told Janice that he could make chocolate appear out of thin air. She'd seemed very keen on him before, and that was nearly two months ago. Here and now, in this moment, she was smitten, something that to his horror, Tank had managed to pick up on.

"Pint of bitter please Janice," announced the big fella, trying to distract the dizzy bar worker. "What do you want Pete?"

"Lime and soda please mate," he replied, still a little unsure of what was going on.

Seemingly from out of nowhere, Richie appeared.

"And a gin and tonic for me please," she added, surprising the two of them.

"Hi Rich," said Peter, pleased to see her, as she enveloped him in a huge hug, much to Janice's disappointment.

"Pete, how are you feeling?"

"Much better thanks."

"And a gin and tonic as well please Janice," stated Tank, giving Richie a wider berth than normal.

Janice came back with the gin and tonic, and then Tank paid for the round of drinks.

"Thanks," said the lacrosse superstar, smiling.

"No problem," replied Tank disinterestedly.

Peter couldn't believe what he was seeing. Normally his friends got on like a house on fire, but it all seemed to have changed. While he wouldn't describe things as frosty, which would be a little over the top, there was certainly an undeniable air of tension.

"So," said Peter, knowing it wasn't lacrosse training, "what are you doing here tonight Rich?"

"Just hanging out, shooting some pool, watching the sport on the telly, that's all really."

Tank rolled his eyes nonchalantly in a disbelieving sort of way. Richie seemed to pick up on this and looked none too pleased.

"Anyway, looks like it's my turn on the pool table," she uttered, looking relieved. "Thanks for the drink. I'll see you boys later." And with that, she bounded over to the corner and selected a cue.

"What the hell was that all about?" he whispered to his friend, absolutely astonished.

"You don't want to know." replied his pal, almost a little too sharply.

"I most certainly do."

Tank turned across the bar to face the beautiful bar worker, who hadn't moved very far away, and asked,

"Janice, is there a committee meeting tonight?"

"Oh yes," she answered pleasantly. "They're upstairs right now, and should probably be finishing quite soon."

"Thanks," he said, taking a huge gulp of his drink.

Peter stood looking at Tank, more than a little confused. The strapping rugby player smiled at his friend and said,

"Stick around and you'll see for yourself."

Not knowing what else to say, the two friends stood in silence, nursing their drinks, watching Richie perfectly strike ball after ball from a distance. When Janice wasn't serving, she made a point of cleaning near them, or changed nearby bar mats, not that Peter really noticed at all, he was just too busy feeling happy at being out of the house and away from the overbearing and overzealous June and Mildred.

Twenty minutes went by, during which Peter returned Tank's generosity and bought him a drink, buying one for Richie as well. Smiling briefly when he bought it over, she thanked him and returned to beating some of the rugby players at pool. Wandering back to rejoin Tank, he remained oblivious to the ever so attentive Janice.

Ten minutes later the clatter of feet could be heard trampling down the stairs at the end of the clubhouse, the committee meeting finished, the members rushing for a drink, as was their custom. Tank raised his eyebrows in Peter's direction and mouthed the words, "Get ready." Not quite sure what to expect, Peter put his drink down on the bar and kept a beady eye on Richie. Sure enough, moments later, he had the answer to everything, his friend rolling her pool cue onto the table conceding the game which she'd clearly been winning, unusual in itself, but the best was yet to come. Vaulting over a chair in her path, she rushed madly over to the bottom of the stairs, and to Peter's utter amazement, threw herself into the arms of a man he vaguely recognised. Catching the lithe, young lacrosse player in his arms, he lifted her off the ground and kissed her passionately.

Open mouthed, Peter turned and looked at Tank, not knowing what to say. Sighing, the plant and animal lover just shook his head.

'This is it. She's finally gone too far,' Peter reflected. 'The dragon council are gonna go spare.' Continuing to watch his friend, all these opinions about dragon officaldom and her fate whizzed around his head. The really strange thing though, was that they both looked unbelievably happy, almost as if they were made for each other, which given that they were two totally different species, really didn't add up. Suddenly an evening with Mildred and June looked better and better.

Janice stuck her head across the bar between the two friends, noted what they were looking at and said,

"Don't they make a lovely couple?"

Peter swiftly replied,

"They most certainly don't."

A miffed expression on her face, the normally cheerful bar worker ducked back out of the way. Oblivious to Janice's hurt feelings, Peter supped his drink, while Tank, a devotee of human behaviour, just shook his head.

As Richie and her new love headed their way, the big fella let out a sigh and turned away to face the bar, pretending desperately to study all the different spirit bottles lined up on the shelf behind it, just below the crystal clear mirror.

As they approached, Peter remembered the guy's name.

'Tim Simms, of course,' he thought. 'Plays hockey for the first team but got badly injured and had to miss the rest of the season as a result. If I'm not mistaken he's also the treasurer of the sports club.'

Arm snaked around Tim's waist, Richie approached.

"Peter, I'd like you to meet Tim. Tim, this is my friend Peter."

Tim thrust his hand out and said,

"Pleasure to meet you. I've heard all about you."

A startled Peter shook the proffered hand, hoping that he hadn't really heard all about him.

"It's nice to meet you Tim. Any friend of Richie's is a friend of mine," he mumbled, noticing Tank's expression from the reflection in mirror behind the bar.

Turning towards Richie, Tim whispered,

"Ahhh... he is as sweet as you said."

Instantly, the hockey playing dragon started to blush, and turned towards Tank who was still facing away, for some support.

"And of course you've met Tank before," prompted Richie, coldly, gesturing towards the strapping rugby player with her arm.

"Nice to see you again Tank," declared Tim cheerily.

Tank just turned his head and nodded, provoking a look from Richie that nearly turned him to stone.

"Anyway, can't hang about I'm afraid," put in the lacrosse superstar, all smiles. "We're off for something to eat. Nice to see you out and about again Pete, and of course we must catch up when you're back at work."

"That would be great," he replied, nodding.

"Good to see you both," stated Tim pleasantly, as Richie quite literally dragged him towards the exit.

Tank hung his head low and said nothing, as the happy couple swept through the double doors, out into the cold night air. A very difficult silence enveloped the two pals back inside. Peter had no idea of what to say. It had all been such a surprise. As both drained their glasses dry, eventually he piped up,

"Why didn't you tell me?"

"Could it be any more awkward?" huffed Tank. "I wanted to, of course but I didn't know where to begin. And I most certainly wouldn't have brought you had I known she was going to be here. Do you have any idea of the trouble she's going to be in?"

'That,' thought Peter, 'is the million dollar question.'

To be honest, he could have done without all this at the moment, but part of him was at least glad that he'd found out what Richie had been up to. In a way, it was better to know than be kept in the dark.

Suddenly turning to Tank, checking that no one was in ear shot, Peter declared,

"Oh God, what if June and Mildred find out about her?"

Tank's forehead creased in confusion.

"How would that happen?"

Leaning in close to his friend, so that he could whisper really lightly, Peter said,

"You must have heard that some of the King's Guard can read your deepest thoughts telepathically?"

Tank let out a great big belly laugh that attracted the attention of the few people remaining. After a couple of moments to catch his breath and wipe away some tears from his eyes, he turned back to his very disappointed buddy.

"It's a myth. Something the King's Guards put around to keep everyone on their toes."

"How can you be so sure?"

"While it's possible to share your thoughts with someone that way, the key word here would be share. Another of our kind cannot just roll in and extract a stranger's thoughts without their consent. It's simply impossible. Trust me Pete. You do remember who my employer is, don't you? If he's told me once, he's told me a million times."

Feeling a little better on hearing that the master mantra maker had endorsed what Tank had just said, he still wasn't a hundred percent sure and knew that dropping off to sleep tonight and leaving his mind unguarded was going to worry him senseless. The sooner the disguised pair of old women left, the better, even more so than before, now that he knew about Richie's secret indulgence.

Both returned their empty glasses to Janice, who seemed to be getting more disappointed by the second that Peter had taken more notice of his female friend than he had of her. Tank dropped his pal off at home, with neither of them mentioning Richie on the journey back. Having waved Tank off, Peter trudged up the path to his front door, trying not to think about his lacrosse playing friend getting it on with a human, for fear that either of the crazy old women waiting up for him would sense it. As he put his key in the lock and turned it gently, one thought echoed around inside his head.

'It's going to be a long ten days.'

2 ICE BREAKER

Clapping his black, top-of-the-range gloves together in an effort to keep his hands warm whilst pulling another bitingly cold breath of air reluctantly into his lungs, he watched, fascinated, as even bigger icebergs floated into view. Not at any point during his long life had he experienced cold like this. Even with all his expensive thermal equipment, he still shivered painfully almost all the time. The most depressing thing was that he was still well over one hundred miles away from his destination, meaning that it could only get chillier still. Knowing he should go back inside; it would be warmer of course, but the other passengers were driving him mad. Also, he had to acclimatise to these barbaric conditions and quickly. As well as a physically prepared body, he would need his wits about him, at least that's what he told himself as his crisp breath appeared in front of his face as he exhaled and drew in another distressing lungful of freezing air.

Looking over the side at the decidedly beautiful but deadly dark blue sea, he cursed his luck for being given this of all assignments. What was the council thinking? Did they not realise what a waste of his valuable skills this was? Briefly, anger welled up inside him as he considered being sent to look for some lost scientists.

"Oh and by the way," they'd said, "if you see any sign of the mysterious and long lost naga community on your travels, could you report back immediately." Banging the wooden rail in frustration, his hand throbbed through the expensive gloves. So now he was a diplomat, as well as a glorified scientist babysitter. Pulling his furry hood closer around his stubbly cheeks, he sighed in frustration, almost ready to go back inside.

'All my infiltration, fighting and weapons training and it comes down to this,' he mused, taking one last look over the rail. 'Where did I go wrong? Have I offended somebody? If I have then no one's ever said anything to me about it. I've always carried out my missions with dedication, precision, and never failed at a single one. I can't believe I'm stuck here at the arse end of the world doing this,' he reflected, walking up the deck to the nearest door that led inside, before going through. 'The sooner I unearth the missing boffins the better, and boy, am I going to give them a hard time when I do find them, for dragging me all this way, in these atrocious conditions. Not even allowed to travel by plane, because of my cover and the equipment I'm carrying,' he thought, closing the metal door behind him as the much warmer air wafted across his exposed face.

Born Dendrik Ridge, just about everyone called him Flash. Having joined the King's Guard straight from the nursery ring, which in itself was quite unusual, he'd found out the reason he'd been selected from one of his instructors much later on, who on his death bed had confessed that they'd gone through a phase of recruiting young dragons with behavioural difficulties, particularly ones with short tempers who had a tendency to use unnecessary violence. Astonished to learn all this from his former tutor, and after a prolonged period of mourning that hit him pretty hard, Flash redoubled his efforts at the training, vowing to channel his volatile attitude into his work, coming out top of his class, enabling him to eventually be offered a place in the very secretive Crimson Guards. While the King's Guards were considered to be the most elite troops in the dragon world, answering only to the council, the Crimson Guards were one step above all that again. In times gone by, the monarch would have a number of agents that would carry out missions on his behalf, some sanctioned by the council, some not (so called 'shadow missions'). Throughout the previous seven decades or so, that had all changed. On the ruler's orders, the anonymous Crimson Guards had been brought into being by one of these former agents; the dragon in question had been lost on a mission many decades ago, or so rumour had it. Flash had been part of the Crimson Guards for over forty years.

Flash's current mission was to recover the scientists that had gone missing on not one, but two, previous expeditions to Antarctica. They'd been working for the Australian Antarctic Division (AAD) at a base called Antarctic Station Casey, one of four permanent headquarters Australia had in the area. Their cover story included studying the effect of climate change and its impact on the wildlife and vegetation in the immediate surroundings. Little had been known about their disappearance, only that both parties, on separate occasions, had gone missing in bad weather, and contained only dragon members, not that the humans of Casey Station knew this. With the frigid Antarctic climate varying between 9.2°C and -41°C with winds gusting around 100kph, occasionally reaching 160kph, the two troupes disappearing in bad weather wasn't as far-fetched as it seemed. However, for both to go missing, a month apart, containing only members of their race, was... odd! Of course the dragons would be limited by not being able to use any of their magical abilities due to the extreme cold, so from that point of view it could be possible, but still... it was ever so unlikely.

Like every other of his kind, Flash knew a great deal about Antarctica. As hostile, remote environments go, it was like no other, being the coldest, windiest, highest continent on earth. As well as containing seventy-five percent of the world's fresh water frozen in its ice caps, the South Pole is twice the size of Australia. Anyone exposed to the elements here could expect blizzards, frighteningly high winds, frostbite and exhaustion, all of which would be child's play, if he could access the dragon powers locked away in his human shaped body, but because of the extreme temperatures, just like the lost scientists, he couldn't.

Since Casey Station was the last place the missing scientists had been seen alive, he'd made sure to read up on it. One of four Australian permanent garrisons, the present day site was opened in 1988. Built from a metal frame on concrete foundations, covered with an external skin of steel clad polystyrene foam panels, the base consisted of sixteen buildings, all painted in bright, bold colours. Situated on the Windmill Islands in the midst of Wilkes Land in East Continental Antarctica, it lies near the Law Dome, a small ice cap, 1300m high, 200km in diameter, and also the Nanderford Glacier, which is the major ice outlet at the southern end of the region.

The facility itself boasts all the usual things you'd expect to find somewhere so isolated, as well as a living area in the Red Shed that includes indoor climbing, a home theatre, gym, a well stocked library and communal sitting areas. There is also a bar called Splinters, where the hard working community spend a lot of their free time. Flash was surprised to learn that part of the station was devoted to a special hydroponics building, where they are able to grow such things as lettuce, tomatoes, green vegetables and fresh herbs. All in all, it's quite a setup for somewhere well off the beaten track.

Some thirty-six hours later, the ship Penguin Emperor came within sight of the Windmill Islands, nearly at the end of its 3835km voyage from its starting point of Perth, Australia. Approaching the frozen land mass, huge icebergs the size of houses littered the horizon like popcorn on a cinema floor. Like most of the other passengers, the dragon agent had come out on deck, despite the flurry of snow, to witness the ship's arrival. In the distance he could just make out the different coloured buildings, brilliant gold, green, yellow and red looking amazing against the all white background. Other passengers were pointing, some waving at long lost friends. Most were scientists, like Flash's cover, with the exception of an engineer and carpenter, all of whom the Crimson

Guard had talked to whilst trying to gain any insight into his covert investigation. Every single one had bored him senseless. It was all he could do to remain in their company for more than a short while.

Two more hours passed before they started unloading the equipment. Like the others, he pretended to be over protective when it came to all the gear he'd brought aboard. It was all cutting edge stuff, and he'd been thoroughly briefed on what it did and how it worked. However, he had to be careful not to be caught out by anyone on the base. There were some incredibly smart people out there, and although little was known about the type of work he was supposed to be doing, he wouldn't put it past some smarty pants to know enough to catch him out. After all, his primary mission was to recover the scientists, or at least find out what had happened to them.

He'd thought being on the ship and practising his breathing would prepare him adequately for his arrival at Casey Station. How wrong he'd been. Nothing he'd done so far came close to readying him for the biting cold that assaulted his very being, as he helped move the equipment from the dock to the main base. Wind battered his semi-exposed face, while huge blobs of wispy snow burnt him, at least that's how it felt.

After what seemed like two lifetimes, the last of the apparatus was finally unloaded. Completely exhausted, never in nearly one hundred years had he ever felt so wasted, the cold having taken its toll. Heading for his quarters, which he'd been shown earlier when he'd unloaded all his personal stuff, all he wanted to do when he got there was sleep, but by the time he'd slipped off his outer layers, he'd changed his mind, deciding that a shower was way more important. Strolling back from the washroom that he was expected to share with two other people due to the limited space, he caught sight of a card that had been tucked under his door. Bending down wearing just a green towel, he picked it up and turned it over. It read:

Greetings Party at Splinters Bar 19.00... be there!!!!!

Shaking his head in dismay, as the last thing he wanted to do was meet lots of new people, he checked his latest wristwatch, one that he'd procured and modified especially for this particular mission. It was a magnificent piece of engineering from the humans, enhanced even further by himself, with the help of a few very select and secretive mantras. The timepiece was a Polar Surveyor Redesign by Kobald, the choice of most discerning Arctic explorers. Incredibly crafted, designed to perform in the harshest of environments, the normal watch itself was magnificent. Flash's upgraded version saw it equipped with eight toxic darts, titanium tipped, each one capable of felling an elephant almost instantly, a microscopic GPS transmitter and the ability to cause quite a large explosion, if needed, but that particular function would mean sacrificing the item itself. All in all, it was very 'James Bond.' The time showed it was 15:51, so Flash decided to grab a couple of hours of sleep, before heading on over to Splinters. If nothing else, it would at least give him a chance to check out quite a few of the other residents, telepathically, to see if they had anything to do with his missing targets.

Much later that night, the Crimson Guard in his disguised human form staggered back to his quarters, through the deserted labyrinth that was Casey Station.

'Boy,' he thought to himself, 'these guys sure know how to party.' He'd thought he was tired earlier, but now he could barely stand up due to fatigue. Reflecting on the evening, he thought of it as a partial success, having managed to convince everyone that he was a lonely scientist, slightly nerdy and introverted. In all honesty, they didn't need much convincing. He'd been one of seven new arrivals, all of whom had to take part in a series of challenges, most of which had involved alcohol as a forfeit in some way, shape or form. Thanks mainly to his dragon constitution, he'd remained relatively sober, even though he'd had to pretend to be rather drunk, not really a problem for him, as blending in was one of the many skills he'd mastered over the years. Throughout the evening he was able to telepathically scan just about everybody present, with only half a dozen members or so missing due to being on duty, and had come a lot closer to understanding the environment he was in. Ruling residents out of having something to do with the disappearance of the missing scientists was in fact much easier than having to covertly chase shadows in the dark.

Slumping onto his mattress, although part of his mind was screaming at him to get undressed and get into bed, he was just too tired. Instead, he closed his eyes and thought that falling asleep fully clothed was in character with someone who'd consumed too much alcohol. Seconds later, he was snoring like a pig with a sinus problem.

Days passed with most of Flash's time spent within the confines of the station, setting up his state of the art equipment. Longing to get outside and begin his search proper, he knew appearances were important, and that he must not arouse too many suspicions. So he played his part to a tee, working hard, seeming nerdy, geeky and not being a threat to anyone. In the meantime he'd telepathically scanned those who hadn't been at the party, finding nothing out of the ordinary. From this he concluded that no one on the base had anything to do with the disappearances; the guilty party, or parties, had already shipped out, if indeed they existed at all. Either someone living in the area but outside the base had something to do with it all, or indeed, it may just have been what everyone thought, that there had simply been two unconnected accidents in the harshest environment on the planet. He found it easy to believe that everyone at Casey was completely above suspicion; the possibility of someone here previously having some involvement and then leaving in the meantime was very real, however. In the hope of retrieving details of everyone who'd left over the last few months, he would have to try and gain access to the base's mainframe. As far as believing that somebody could survive out here, but not on the base, that took more than a little imagination. Difficult to rule out entirely of course, something about it just didn't ring true. Two separate catastrophes were looking increasingly likely, but the more he thought about it, the more something at the back of his mind screamed, "NO!" Over time, he'd learned to trust the little voice inside him, because it had been right in the past, almost all the time.

Two days later, after proving that he was qualified on all the station's vehicles and passing a very simple health and safety course, Flash got his wish. Opting to take a skidoo with a heavy field sledge for his equipment, rather than one of the much smaller quad bikes, he packed up early and was ready to leave before most of the residents had even begun to start their day. In advance of setting off, he checked that he had all his equipment. Not the scientific stuff of course. No, his personal gear that he'd specially prepared for this particular part of the mission. His watch was fully functional, with not even a hint of it icing over in the harsh temperatures, and was topped up with eight toxic, titanium darts, with two more clips each with eight darts hidden in his belt buckle on his trousers beneath the cold weather attire that he wore. The darts in his extraordinary timepiece were activated by his pulse, which in turn was constantly monitored by an ingenious bit of technology mounted into the underside of the wrist strap. If needed, he could unleash all eight in under three seconds, and they could pierce just about anything on the planet. It did give him a little extra reassurance, on top of all his training and special talents.

Scrolling through the watch's functions, he checked the GPS transmitter was working properly, and that the self destruct checked out. Bending his left knee, he lifted his boot up behind him and tapped the smallest looking irregularity in the sole, once. Out shot the meanest looking knife in the world, a gift from... a friend. Glinting in the bright Antarctic sunlight, deadly barbs adorned one side, with a razor sharp edge traversing the other. Feeling its comforting weight in his gloved hand, Flash tossed it lightly into the air, catching it by its handle as it came spiralling back down. Slickly he hid the blade back in its housing, concealed in the bottom of his boot. Last, but by no means least, he confirmed with his left hand that he had his necklace on, and that the ring on the index finger of his right hand was still firmly in place. There was no reason why either of these wouldn't be there, his body would have told him if they weren't, because both were made from laminium, and were the most valuable items that he owned. Checking them physically with his hand was more of a ritual than a necessity, but he hadn't gotten this far in his career without looking out for the small details.

Confident that he was ready to go, he stepped up to the bright yellow skidoo, gave a hard yank on the starting cord and listened to the pleasing sound of the harsh petrol engine kicking into life. Donning his shiny, black crash helmet, he mounted the throbbing vehicle. Knowing that there might be residents watching his departure, he sedately headed out of the Station and into the frozen wilderness, heading directly towards Law Dome, the nearest small ice cap.

As soon as he was beyond visual range, he opened up the throttle, gunning the poor vehicle for all it was worth. Even with his enhanced dragon abilities, which were severely limited by the freezing temperatures, riding the machine at high speed was a life threatening risk in this environment, with its steep slopes, rough hidden rocks, jutting peninsulas and detritus filled valleys, but he just couldn't resist. Jeopardy and thrill seeking were simply part of his nature, as much as a three metre tail, brown shiny scales and teeth that a crocodile would die for, were part of his natural form.

Every twenty minutes or so, he would stop and take in his surroundings, using his limited supernatural senses to see if he could detect any sign of the missing boffins. By his third stop he'd had no luck whatsoever, but told himself that it was early days yet as he still had many hundreds of square miles to cover, and that was just the area they were known to have been in.

Carrying on in the bright sunlight through the untouched powdery snow, Flash focused purely on the task at hand; his dedication to the mission was unparalleled in both dragon and human worlds.

After five and a half hours, he stopped the skidoo abruptly in the thick fresh snow, convinced that just for a moment he'd felt something recognisable. Undoing his helmet and placing it on the vehicle's seat, he trudged through the knee high snow, the only sound accompanying him the sharp 'crunch, crunch, crunch' beneath his boots. Opening his mind to the harsh surroundings, he tried desperately to use the laminium in his ring and necklace to augment his flagging abilities, the brisk wind all the while clawing at the exposed parts of his unshaven face.

'There it is again,' he thought. 'There's something close by, but where...?'

Standing on the edge of a steep, rocky slope on one side, a valley laden with thick, fresh snow on the other, there was nothing he could see that led him to believe there was anything of importance here. About a hundred metres away stood a snowy, ice encrusted overhang, something he'd seen about fifty of already today. Still, his senses were telling him there was something here. Knowing only too well that he could search this area for a week with all the fresh snowfall and not find a thing, he had to at least try. After wandering carefully through the lower part of the rocky slope for about an hour, figuring that he was more likely to find something there rather than in the deep, fresh snow field, frustrated he returned to the skidoo and procured a ration bar and a drink of water from the heated bottle in his pack. Opting to walk around the area as he drank and ate, his mind wandered, having not found what he was searching for. Before he knew it, he'd meandered up to the icy overhang that resembled something like a giant frozen wave. The snow had built up against its base, while delicate icicles hung like vicious looking needles from the outcrop itself. In the brilliant bright sunlight, it sparkled like an expensive jewel. Even Flash, not known for his appreciation of any sort of beauty, thought that it looked magnificent. The perfect silence all around was abruptly shattered by the radio attached to his jacket.

"Casey Base to Foxtrot Two, come in... over," crackled throughout the air as Flash struggled to retrieve the handset.

Setting down his water bottle and stuffing the rest of his ration bar in his mouth all at once, he held down the long black button on one side.

"Casey Base, this is Foxtrot Two... over," he shouted above the harsh wind.

"Just checking up to make sure you're okay doc," came a squeaky voice through all the static.

"Thanks Casey," replied Flash, strangely comforted that these people he barely knew were concerned for his wellbeing. "I'm just checking one more site, and then I'm heading back... thanks."

"Okay doc, good luck, see you when you get here. Don't forget the darts tournament at Splinters tonight... starts at 20:00."

"Thanks Casey, I'll try and make it... Foxtrot Two out."

Relative silence returned to the valley, apart from the whistling wind that had started to whip up the soft powdery snow a treat. Bending down to retrieve his water bottle, the tiniest glimpse of colour caught his attention from the corner of his eye. Blinking in astonishment, for just a moment he could have sworn he'd seen the tiniest patch of crimson at the bottom of the solid wall of ice that made up the overhang he was now standing under. Striding over to the wall and crouching down so that his entire lower half sunk into the powdery build up of snow, he rubbed at it with his gloved hands, clearing away the beautiful flakes in front of him. It wasn't until he'd rubbed away a decent sized portion of the wall that it hit him.

"Dear God, it can't be," he muttered only to himself, his breath freezing in the cold as he did so. Beneath the thick ice of the wall making up the overhang, was a crimson coloured wing. The mighty membrane and wiry sinew could be seen clearly now that he was up close. He knew exactly what it was, well... not what, but who... Professor Rianne Pilkington, to be precise.

Crouching in the snow, inspecting the frozen body of the lead scientist, his pulse raced. A million questions zipped around his spinning head, chief amongst them was: why on earth is she in her natural prehistoric form? No dragon in their right mind would transform in these conditions. They wouldn't last more than a couple of minutes at most, before they died horribly. It made absolutely no sense.

'There's nothing in the world that would make me return to my natural state here. Nothing, he thought, tears streaming down his face, threatening to freeze to his skin.

Then, the most unbelievable thing in the world happened. A loud laugh pierced the howling wind, from just behind him. Standing up and turning around all at the same time, he struggled to comprehend the vision before him. Two medium sized nagas, one very nearly gold all over, the other a purple bluish colour, stood not seven metres away, grinning wickedly in his direction. The nagas were quasi-humanoids, with snake shaped bodies and a top half resembling a scaly, reptilian human. Both had tails about five metres long, rippling with muscle. Nearly two and a half metres tall, they both swayed from side to side like deadly cobras. Flash's first thought was that he was dreaming, and that perhaps he'd suffered some sort of trauma, maybe falling and knocking his head. Deep down inside though, his little voice screamed, "DANGER!" over and over, as loud as it possibly could. The golden tinted naga shook his head back and forth, before letting out a low rumble and grinning.

"Ahhhhh... it seems they've sent another one."

His partner smiled at that.

"When will they start to learn?"

Flash couldn't work out where they'd come from, how it was that he couldn't sense them telepathically, or why they were behaving like this. Putting on his best smile, in the name of diplomacy of course, he addressed the golden beast who seemed to be in charge.

"Please let me extend greetings and honoured intentions directly from the dragon king himself, clan of the mysterious nagas," he shouted calmly over the wind, phrasing his words in much the same way as he'd heard the ruler do on numerous occasions.

Both beasts' expressions turned serious, their wicked grins disappearing, reinforcing Flash's belief that he'd made an impression.

'This diplomacy thing is a doddle,' he mused, hoping that the two snake-like monsters would consider helping him recover the bodies of the missing scientists, which could prove unbelievably difficult if they were all in dragon form. As both beings slithered forward, friendly smiles adorning their scaly faces, the Crimson Guard breathed a sigh of relief, bending down to retrieve his discarded water bottle for a second time. Distracted for a split second, he had virtually no time to react when both of them spun around simultaneously, their long, scaly tails heading straight towards him at high speed. Pushing himself back against the icy overhang, Flash tried desperately to bring his right wrist around to unleash the toxic darts in his watch, but knew almost immediately that he was too late.

As the pain from the impact rippled through his body, and darkness started to claim him, his last thought was,

'What the hell is going on?'

3 IN THE FREEZER

Not far from where Flash had been captured, at least not far as the crow flies, crude electric lights flickered and spluttered in a vast underground cavern looking, not for the first time, like they were about to plunge the whole place into total and utter darkness. Chained side by side along a vast icy partition were four prisoners, all from very different eras and all, despite appearances, anything but homo sapiens. The first, a human shaped dragon, sat on the wet icy floor, clad only in a dark, all-in-one thermal under suit, shaped much like a pair of wild west long johns, only much more up to date, made from heat insulating material. Hands manacled to the frozen wall above his head, forcing his arm muscles to stay taut all the time, his cover was that of a scientist, at least while he roamed the surface, disguised as one of them. Despite his thermal clothing he was bitterly uncomfortable. Ice and moisture on the ground seeped through his suit, attacking his delicate human inspired flesh. Because he was a dragon, he was more susceptible to the cold than any other being on the planet. The biting pain from the ice, moisture and the sub zero temperatures caused him to keep on passing out. Each time he came round, all he would know once again was total and utter agony. This is how it had been since he'd been captured and taken there, more than two months previously. Occasionally, from a long way away, he caught the odd glimpse of human shapes that seemed to have some sense of authority, but the only person or thing that came anywhere near him was a mean, looking human, resembling a smelly and scruffy tramp, dressed in clothes and rags that looked to be decades out of date. Arriving every few days, he would kick and beat each of the prisoners until the amusement wore off, before tossing scraps of rotten fish to each of them. Other than that, they saw no one in the vast, desolate, freezing cold cavern.

Captive number two was manacled to the slippery, white ice in much the same way as the first, some twenty metres or so further along. The big difference though, was the fact that this one was a... naga. Although the naga in question looked haggard and filthy, clearly this was anything but an ordinary specimen of their race. Still looking magnificent and regal, despite his captivity, shades of blue flickered in the twinkling light along his entire body, right to the very tip of his tail which was the darkest shade imaginable, standing out abruptly against his icy white confines. Further up, the scales gradually lightened, almost in concentric circles, until the very palest sky blue beset his head and the ever moving gills off to one side. Clearly his captivity had taken its toll, but anyone who observed closely and knew what to look for would have recognised the keen glint in his eyes, realising that this was an exceptionally intelligent creature, far from broken. In fact, this stunning looking individual was the single most important in its entire race... he was the king of the nagas and had been imprisoned against his will for decades.

Sixty metres or so further along sat the most remarkable sight of all; an ancient dragon lay curled up asleep against the icy mass, as moisture dripped onto its head from a set of stalactites, high up on the vast ceiling. Looking as though it were on its deathbed, all across the beast's body, scales were missing, hanging off or just ragged around the edges. Holes through the membrane in its wings stood out like windows into another world. Outlines of bones beneath its scales were visible all over. As it slept, its breath wheezed in and out, like some kind of nicotine ridden pensioner, while all the time its entire frame shivered and mumbled incoherently, not at all like the mighty monster it had once been. Littered all around it were signs of the abuse it had suffered over a seriously long period of time: dark claws that had been plucked out, along with shattered, shiny, white tooth fragments, lay frozen for all to see. Worst of all though was the tip of the dragon's tail. The last metre or so had been hacked off in some dreadful deed, and stood point down, embedded in the ice, just out of the creature's reach.

Further along, in the darkest recess, was another human shaped dragon. Naked except for a hole littered, shredded pair of raggedy trousers, shivering against his cold, metal manacles, he squatted in the darkness, occasionally flexing his taut, honed muscles. Long, dirty, scraggy hair flowed halfway down his back, frozen solid in places from the extreme temperatures. His toned body looked like that of a boxer, with a noticeable blue mark that looked like a tree of some sort adorning the left side of his chest, right over where his heart would have been, if he were truly human. Unlike the other human shaped dragon, this one kept his counsel, not having uttered a word in all his time here, much to the disappointment of his captors. Horrific torture of every kind had been used against him on a regular basis, but had long since proved fruitless, as had the abuse by the guard who appeared infrequently, delivering scraps of foul food. Currently he was sporting the mother of all black eyes, a broken finger and what felt like two broken ribs. Numerous other minor bruises and cuts littered his body, but despite this, he still flexed the muscles he could, biding his time in the hope of returning to the life he'd once known.

Of the four, the scientist was by far the most nervous, constantly wailing and crying, begging to be released by his invisible tormentors. Although seemingly resigned to his fate, the naga king was clearly on the lookout for the right opportunity to escape. The dozing dragon just looked like it was just waiting to die, whilst the prisoner in the darkest recesses constantly exercised in silence, as much as his bonds would allow.

Against the backdrop of the captured boffin's wailing and pleading, and the sleeping dragon's rattling breath, the constant sound of running water from a deep and chilly underground stream, not thirty metres away, echoed throughout the cavern. It never stopped. Twenty four hours a day it gurgled and spluttered, tormenting the four captives in an entirely different way to their jailers.

Somewhere above the freezing dungeon, inside a gloomy cave carved into the side of Law Dome, Flash lay on the cold, rocky floor, hands bound crudely behind his back. A few minutes earlier he'd regained consciousness, but was currently trying to make out that he hadn't, whilst taking in his situation. Blurring his vision, his head rang like a bell, presumably from being hit by the nagas' gigantic tails. Despite being sheltered from the worst of the weather, the cold tore at him in ways that he couldn't previously have imagined. His outer clothing had been taken, leaving him in only the black, thermal base layer that he'd donned earlier on in the day. Also his boots were missing, but his thick socks, despite being damp, still covered his feet. The only thing in his favour so far, was the fact that his watch still clung to his freezing cold wrist, the metal strap burning his aching skin. Unfortunately his attackers had stolen his laminium ring and necklace.

So far he'd managed to gain a limited amount of information, lying curled up on the hard floor of the cave. From what he could tell, he was right up against the back wall of the narrow cavern, which in itself looked to be about one hundred and fifty metres long. Through its entrance, he could just see a torrent of snow steadily accumulating outside. Between him and it was a comforting fire, flickering and crackling as it danced towards the high ceiling, the smoke blanketing the cave, blown inwards by the howling gale outside. It was all he could do not to cough violently. Sitting either side of the flickering orange and yellow flames were the gold naga from earlier, and a human wearing his missing clothes. Having studied the tracks on the ground from a distance, he assumed that the latter had to be the purple and blue slippery serpent, because the markings on the cave floor at the entrance showed what looked like a huge trail shape abruptly turning into a set of footprints. The surrounding snow was a little scuffed up, leading Flash to think that the naga had changed into human form, and slipped on his precious clothing. Carefully, he fiddled with the restraints behind his back, trying hard not to make any noise and alert his captors to the fact that he was awake. Abruptly he stopped, hearing the two of them talking. Try as he might, he couldn't make out what they were saying over the crackling of the fire, and the ringing in his head. Opening his eyes just enough to look through his long eyelashes, he could just see the two of them arguing about something, through the thick, blue tinted smoke.

Racking his brain for a way to escape, the problems he had were two fold. With his hands restrained behind his back, he had no way of being sure the poison darts from his watch would hit their intended target. On top of that, it didn't seem likely to him that the darts would pierce the nagas' thick scales. They would almost certainly deal with the human shaped one, but the other in its natural form probably wouldn't be affected at all. Desperately wishing the pounding in his head would stop because it was driving him to distraction, he needed his wits about him, in case an unexpected opening to escape should present itself.

A tinny laugh bounced around inside the cave.

"We know you're awake... dragon!"

Accepting it was pointless to pretend any longer, he rolled over, trying unconvincingly to sit up against the back wall, causing the ringing in his ears to get worse, his brain feeling as though it was being pummelled by a hammer on a building site. Feeling the coolness of the rock on the back of his head, forced him to open his eyes and look at his two captors.

Smiling at his detainee, the human shaped one tugged the collar of Flash's stolen jacket tighter against the cold as he did so.

"What's the matter, not coming up to join us by the... fire?" mocked Gold, the gills on the side of his head contracting furiously as he did so.

Flash continued to stare ahead.

"You'd think, being a dragon, he'd want to come and appreciate the warmth a bit more," chuckled the human shaped naga.

Flash's mind was full of a million questions he wanted to ask, but he bit his tongue. Decades of training told him he'd get nothing useful out of these two, and if he started to talk, just maybe he'd let slip something important that could aid them, due to the cold and the ringing in his ears. Resting his head back on the icy wall, he closed his eyes, albeit not fully. As he listened to the crackle of the fire, savouring thoughts of being warm in the past, he tried to puzzle out what on earth was going on. Missing scientists, dragons turning back to their true form in the Antarctic, nagas, being captured... none of it made any sense.

Making his way over towards the hostage, the homo sapiens shaped monster clapped his hands together inside the stolen gloves, as Flash remained perfectly still. Leaning down, the naga grabbed the dragon agent and pulled him up by the collar of his thermal top, so the two were face to face. Opening his eyes, he stared directly into at the human figure before him as the overpowering stench of rotten fish from the naga's breath threatened to overwhelm him. Fighting back the urge to throw up, the Crimson Guard wondered what was coming next, as the disguised beast opened his mouth, an even sicklier smell wafting out.

"Your freedom is forfeit. You'll be spending a lot more time in captivity, and believe you me, the accommodation won't be nearly this luxurious," he rasped, in a distinctively tinny voice. "As soon as the storm passes, we'll be on our way to your new home."

From the pit of Flash's stomach, erupted the worst feeling in the world, and this time it wasn't the urge to be sick from the putrid smell cloying at his face. It was something all his years of training had never prepared him for... fear, deep down, genuine fear, with a capital F.

4 KNITTING NUTTINESS NULLIFIED

Finally the day had arrived, and not a moment too soon, as far as Peter was concerned. June and Mildred were leaving, packing their bags right at that very moment. Rubbing his hands in glee, he stood in the kitchen looking out of the window into the back garden. Much as he appreciated the dragon council's fear that Manson might come back to try and take revenge by striking at him in his own home, having the two guards there for not far off two months almost seemed like a crueller punishment. With his injuries all but healed, he knew he could cope, and with the new security arrangements that had been installed, felt confident that he would survive, even if the vengeful supposed ex-army major did reappear.

The new fangled security had been put in place long before he returned home from Salisbridge hospital. When he'd got back from his prolonged stay (two and a half weeks is mighty prolonged in dragon terms) June and Mildred were there to greet him and explain what had already been done. Firstly, the old front and back doors of the house had both been replaced by nice new, solid feeling, double glazed ones that kept the cold out a treat. Similar windows had also been fitted throughout the building. Of course there was more to these new features than at first met the eye. Components inside them had been imbued with special protective mantras, very similar to the *alea* that Peter had inherited from Mark Hiscock and now kept permanently around his neck, only much more stable, with absolutely no chance of any unexpected side effects. If he didn't unlock the doors with the key, from either inside or outside, then there was absolutely no chance of them being breached. So powerful were the spells, that even a dragon in its natural form, using all its strength and abilities, would not be able to break in. Also, a spy feature was added to the new front door, so that he could vet any potential visitors.

Secondly, the whole area underneath the house, where the secret entrance spilled out into the dragon domain, had been imbued with specialist magic that would capture any being lingering there for longer than a minute, contacting the King's Guard at the same time. Aware of his predicament, those in charge had special pre-programmed numbers set up on his mobile and home phones that would contact them and have them at his house in under two minutes.

The last, and as far as Peter was concerned, most scary addition, was a series of tiny interconnecting pipes that ran throughout the old property, having been installed by the king's own dragon specialists. All the ducting contained a potent anaesthetic, so powerful in fact that it could take down a dragon in its natural form. If someone unwanted should break in, Peter could flip a telepathic switch that was hidden deep inside the walls, triggering the anaesthetic and rendering everyone in the building unconscious. If it should ever be used, once again, the King's Guards would be on their way in seconds. It was of course only a last resort. Every time he thought about the powerful sedative, it made him incredibly nervous, and took all his concentration and willpower not to think about the hidden switch, which could so easily be set off by one of his stray thoughts. An elephant in the room had nothing on this. All these additions had taken place secretly, and Peter had been specifically instructed that he wasn't allowed to tell anyone else about them, not even Tank or Richie.

A sharp creak had him turning around from the window, as Mildred and June made their way down the stairs, their suitcases on wheels dragging behind them, thumping as they hit each step. Peter walked out into the hallway to meet them. Both King's Guard dragons reached the bottom just as he arrived.

"Right then Bentwhistle, don't forget what we told you," bemoaned June gruffly.

He could only nod in reply.

"Anything strange at all, don't hesitate to get in touch. These security measures are the best our race has to offer. Don't waste them. Understand?" urged Mildred, in a much better Scottish accent than when she'd first arrived.

"I won't take any unnecessary risks," he confirmed.

"Hmmmmmmm," muttered June. "You seem to forget that most dragons' minds are like open books to us."

Peter winced, certain they had both read his thoughts. Frowning a little, and with two old ladies staring intently at him, he thought about their words. He'd meant what he said; he wouldn't take any unnecessary risks. How could they be reading his mind and get it so wrong? Of course, they couldn't actually do it, just as Tank had said. A huge smile broke out across his very ordinary face.

"Tell me what I'm thinking now," he implored, certain they'd been bluffing for weeks about their telepathic powers.

"We don't do parlour games sonny," barked June harshly.

Once again he nodded, his curiosity satisfied. It had all been one long con.

The sound of a throbbing engine pulling up outside, caused him to turn.

"Must be our taxi," stated June.

"You know what I'm going to miss the most?" announced Mildred.

June screwed her wrinkly old face up for a moment, before a smile appeared, a light bulb switching on inside her head.

"Deal Or No Deal!" she spouted, pleased with herself.

Mildred burst into uncontrollable laughter.

"Of course," she replied through the hilarity.

Peter shook his head, pleased the two of them were leaving.

Both elderly women walked past him on the way to the front door. Before they reached it, both turned and looked back.

"A goodbye kiss for your aunt?" Mildred enquired, puckering up, her Magnum PI moustache doing a little jig of its own as she did so.

"I'd rather kiss a human," he remarked.

Both old ladies simultaneously burst into laughter again.

"Very good," said June, turning the handle on the front door, still chuckling.

Mildred gave Peter a sly wink and followed her friend out through the door, making their way down the garden path to the waiting taxi. The driver had already got out and was halfway through putting June's suitcase into the boot of the car, June constantly blabbering in his ear. The look on the driver's face made Peter smile. It was a picture, as he turned to find Mildred approaching, dressed in clothes that only someone colour blind could fully appreciate.

Both elderly women clucked around their chauffeur, and then argued about who was going to sit where, before taking an age to get in. Sitting in the front shaking his head, the cabby cursed his luck at being called to a fare like this. As the engine thrummed into life, Peter smiled and waved the two of them off, mainly to show anyone that might be watching that all he was doing was waving goodbye to his aunt and her friend after a prolonged stay. June and Mildred returned the waves as the car sped off up the street. Breathing a sigh of relief, he shut the front door. To keep up the pretence, it was thought to have been better for them to take a taxi to the railway station, where they would catch a train and then make their way back to the underground world somewhere further up the line.

Wandering along the hall and back into the kitchen, he switched on the wonderful new black DAB radio that Richie had bought him for Christmas. The quality was great, and having put it in the kitchen, he could now listen to it as he ate his breakfast every morning. An upbeat song sprang into life with crystal clear quality as he delved into the fridge to get a yoghurt before sitting down at the table, tapping his spoon to the beat of the music. Halfway through the yoghurt, he decided to retrieve a copy of the Daily Telepath, something he hadn't done for a few weeks.

THE LATEST HIGH MINERAL, HIGH PROTEIN, LOW CARB, HUMAN FREE DIET TODAY...P9

The Daily Telepath

Britain's Oldest Telepathic Newspaper   Issue No

Snakes Alive!
By Mike Frame

Historians think they may have stumbled on to some vital clues about the possible whereabouts of the long feared extinct Basilisks, thanks to a group of explorers, deep in the Amazon rainforest. The explorers have sent back their preliminary findings on a group of long lost temples. At first glance it seems that this might have been the Basilisks last refuge. Ancient texts, a collection of scales and fully formed skeletons are rumoured to reside inside.

A Brief Encounter
By Rainbow Swan

A devastating tornado ripped through Tornado Alley in the USA yesterday. Originally the extent of the tornado was described as 'off the scale', when it first formed, and would to have dwarfed every other tornado ever recorded. Lucky or not, a plucky dragon by the name of Elgar Moss was in the exact area, visiting friends, just as this extreme weather unleashed this ferocious beast. Dragon onlookers describe Elgar Moss leaping forth into the heart of the tornado, determined to try and stop it. There's no doubt that whatever Elgar did, it most certainly had an effect. The tornado reportedly reduced in size, to less than a quater of what it had been, in a matter of only a few seconds, after our brave dragon entered. However, Elgar, through no fault of his own, was left exhausted and unable to either contain the remaining storm, or protect himself. His broken and ravaged body was found amongst the devastation much later on. Dragon surgeons are currently treating him for life threatening injuries at the underground Oaklohoma medical facility.

A Concert For the King, By The King...AHAHA!
Arts Correspondent Angela Crab

For one night only, Elvis has promised to come out of retirement and take up his human form, something that he'd said previously, he'd never do. A planned concert by John Lennon aims to convince those artists that have shedded their famous identities to come back and appear for one night only, in aid of our beloved dragon monarch's birthday! John said from his underground New York apartment "I'm hoping to persuade as many of the guys as possible to perform. I'd like to say it would be a Beatles reunion, but undoubtedly, Paul will already be booked up."

The Core Of The Matter
By Colin Carp

A sucessful test bore that travels through the Earth's core has been completed. While nothing has travelled through it as yet, plans to send an experimental carriage into the depths, progress steadily. The bore hole originates in Rouen in northern France and terminates just outside of Mandurah, in western Australia. Currently a few heat and geological problems are being wrestled with, but I'm assured the engineers are confident of a solution soon. If sucessful, the transworld link will make travelling to the othernide of the globe common place. It is believed scientists feel that our planet could accomodate up to six of the direct links, without comprimising the structural integrity of the Earth.

Sandskimming Added To Aerialympic Line Up
By Chief Sports Correspondent Mike Meson

After over forty years of campaigning, Sandskimming is finally destined to become an Aerialympic sport. The panel of eight distinguished dragons returned their verdict late last night from Aerialympic headquarters beneath Athens, Greece, after months of furious debate. The inclusion comes at a price........... dragon polo will drop out to make way. A representative from the dragon polo world governing body described the decision as 'outrageous'

and confirmed they would be looking at launching an appeal.

Burton Upgrade
By Vedran Hale

The underground enclave of Burton-on-Trent has been announced as the winner of a tendering process to the dragon council's 'Pride of England' competition. Burton representatives managed to demonstrate to the council their need for redevelopment and show exactly what they would do to improve their enclave and its surrounding area. Proposals include the development of derelict buildings, much improved transport links, an urban relaxation area, an upgrade to the outdated geothermal heating system and a high ceiling flying range, that will be able to accomodate beginners through to advanced aerial combatants. Four runners up include Lowestoft, Worthing, Torbay and Basingstoke will all receive mini makeovers, alongside improvements to their monorail stations. Burton's manager, Burty Bradstock is said to be delighted by the news.

Anger At VIP Suites
By Jessica Pitard

Some council members are under fire for lavishing a huge amount of money on corporate hospitality during a recent laminium ball match. The councillors in question enjoyed the run of the plush 'Excaliber' suite during a recent game at the 'Asphalt' Arena in London, between the Cardiff Corkscrews and the Tower Bridge Titans.

The extravagant costs included gourmet food such as lobster deep fried in charcoal, a tasty selection of British charcoals, gammon and Gressingham duck carveries as well as a free bar. News of the latest 'jolly' was met with disbelief by the (O.D.A.) Ordinary Dragon's Alliance. A spokes dragon was quoted as saying "It is outrageous that hard-pressed dragon families are struggling to get by in these times of austerity, when councillors are out doing this sort of thing."

King Feeling The Heat After Votes Go Against Him
By Chief Political Correspondent Danny Ingham

It has been revealed through the the king has been on the losing side in twelve out of the last seventeen council votes that have been held. While not a total disaster, it is still the second lowest win percentage rate of any monarch since records began in 1781. The king's spokes dragon refused to state whether the king always applies his vote in whatever direction he considers best for the dragon community, whether locally or globally.

Scorching New Talent
By Woody Bile

Dragons on the latest series of 'The Flame' have exceeded all expectations exclaimed one very happy judge. Dr.A.Gon.I.B. world renowned combatant and record holder for the hottest continuous flame over a fifteen minute period, told the D.B.C (Dragon Broadcasting Company) that the new talent in the upcoming new series would quite literally 'blow your head off'. The new show starts at 8pm on Saturday night.

JOIN OUR REWARDS CLUB AND COLLECT SCALES TO WIN PRIZES.........P22

Having read the paper and finished his breakfast, he

decided to go and tidy the bedroom that June and Mildred had been staying in. Climbing the stairs and turning the corner on the landing, he reluctantly pushed open the door to the room that he hadn't been allowed near since the two crazy King's Guard dragons had arrived. The space, with two single beds in it, was a complete and utter mess. No teenager's room in the world had ever looked this bad. Hundreds of sweet and chocolate wrappers besieged the crumb ridden floor. A square coloured pattern was supposed to be visible on the carpet, but there was absolutely no way to make it out through all the chaos. Peter's stomach gurgled in disgust. Storming back downstairs, he retrieved the vacuum cleaner and a roll of black plastic bin bags, spending the next three hours tidying it all up to his satisfaction. Once finished, only the bare frames of the beds remained. Much to his frustration he'd had to throw away both mattresses as they were worn and dirty beyond belief. Five big bin bags of rubbish waited outside. Both guards had most certainly done a job.

'The bin men are going to have a hissy fit when they see the amount waiting for them this week,' he mused, gazing at the now tidy space.

Deep clean finished, he spent a little time on his computer, before grabbing a bite to eat and then having a relatively early night. The next day was his first back at work since the fight with Manson on November 5th and he had no idea what to expect, or what had gone on in the meantime. Hopefully he could just slot back in without any fuss and pick up from where he'd left off. Drifting off to sleep, content to know that in the morning he'd be back in the job he loved, all the time he felt happy to be rid of those two crazy King's Guard dragons. The sound of knitting needles clacking at all times of the day and night had, he was sure, driven him to the brink of insanity. Silence and darkness claimed him as his eyes closed and he started to snore, ever so slightly.

After the best night's sleep he'd had in months, he

wolfed down a leisurely breakfast, grabbed his packed lunch from the fridge, strolled purposefully through the hall to the new front door, checked he had his phone, wallet and keys, before strolling outside and heading to his car, which for once was parked in front of the house.

Hopping in, he found himself feeling rather nervous for some reason, his stomach turning somersaults and legs having that turned to jelly kind of feeling. Desperately he tried to tell himself that it was just like any other day, despite the fact that he hadn't worked for nearly two months and that the last time he was there, he'd been escorted off the premises in front of the whole company, by two gun toting maniacs.

Too nervous to turn the radio on, he made the short journey in complete silence. All too soon the turning for Cropptech came into view, the red and white barrier of the security checkpoint standing out, moving up and down to let the darting line of cars through, one by one. He queued for thirty seconds or so before he reached the barrier, while other cars ahead had only waited a couple of seconds or so before it had been raised. It felt as though he'd been waiting for an age.

'Perhaps it's been so long since I've been here, that they don't recognise me,' he thought, more than a little worried.

Up until now the gate guard had been leaning through the window, into the security lodge, with his back to Peter. As he turned around, the young hockey player was pleased to see it was his friend Owen, the one person who'd stood up to Manson's gun toting goons, and had brought just a tiny sliver of hope to him when he was forced to leave last time. Owen just stood watching Peter in his car, a huge beaming smile spreading across his clean shaven face. Still unable to fathom why he hadn't been let through yet, he could see the traffic building up behind him in his rear view mirror. Just as he was about to turn off the ignition and step out, the white double glazed doors of the security lodge sprung open, revealing a line of staff who exited into the frosty morning air. Still, he had no idea what on earth was going on. After every single member of staff had stepped out into the cold, they all formed a single line on the pavement and then, as one, gave him a huge round of applause, led by the burly Owen. Peter blushed, as cars all around honked their horns in appreciation, provoking a sheepish smile for what he considered unworthy praise. Thirty seconds later, the staff all gave him a quick wave, before disappearing back inside. Owen smiled at him, gave him a mock bow and then raised the barrier. Grinning back as he pulled away, he went off in search of the nearest car park.

On the way to his office, he passed numerous Cropptech employees, most of whom he didn't recognise, but nearly all of them gave him a smile and a nod. They'd clearly all heard that he'd played a big part in recovering the stolen laminium and thwarting Manson's attempted heist.

Entering his office, eager to escape all the attention, he shook his head at the sight that greeted him. His workspace was inundated with cards in all shapes and sizes covering just about every free space available. Picking one up at random, it read: *'Thank you so much for the heroic effort you put into getting the company back on its feet.'* It was signed by someone he'd never heard of in the accounts department. Intrigued, he picked up another. *'Good job getting the company back on track. Hope you feel better soon.'* Again, it was signed by a stranger, in logistics this time. Reading another dozen or so, they all appeared pretty much on the same theme as the first two. Sighing as he flopped down into his comfy leather chair, it was all a little bit too much, he thought as he booted up his office workstation. Leaning back, waiting for the computer to come online, he spied something hidden amongst the stack of cards on top of the bank of security monitors. Reluctantly getting up, he made his way around the desk and delved into the group of cards.

Pulling out a wrapped up package about the size of a large board game, he tore the blue bow and silver wrapping off in one go. To his delight, the biggest box of chocolates he'd ever seen materialised. A little card was taped to the box. It was from Doctor Sheridan Island, the scientist who'd been forced out of the company so brutally by the dreadful Manson, while he held sway over Al Garrett. The note simply said, *'Peter, heard what happened. You've changed things for the good for so many people. Feel free to pop over to the lab any time you like for a coffee and a chat. Regards, Sheridan Island.'*

Taking the chocolates back to his desk, Peter was stunned.

'All this attention is so unwarranted,' was all that he could think. With his computer fully ready to go, he put down the sweet treats and cut through the haze of thoughts swirling around his head, ready to get on with his job.

Time flew by as he got back to grips with things. It was like he'd never been away, with one exception... his email inbox. When he'd first opened it, he was barely able to believe his eyes. He had one thousand, nine hundred and eighty five unread emails. Where do you start with all that?

Dead on half past ten, his phone rang for the third time that morning. Picking it up while continuing to type, determined to make some headway on those outstanding emails, he instantly recognised the voice on the other end.

"Hello Mr Bentwhistle," whispered the individual softly down the phone. "It's Mr Garrett's personal secretary here."

Immediately he stopped typing and did a double take... Mr Garrett's personal secretary. The same fire breathing (not like that) personal secretary as last time, able to turn you to stone with just a look, the one who'd constantly denied him access to the top floor, and only reluctantly let him pass when he'd tried to use the antidote to the poison Garrett had been affected by. It can't be the same woman, surely... can it? All this buzzed through his head in a split second. As if to answer his query, the voice on the end of the phone continued.

"Mr Garrett would very much like to see you at eleven o'clock if that's convenient?"

"Of course, eleven o'clock would be fine," replied Peter, preparing to put the phone down.

"Uhhhhhh... before you go Mr Bentwhistle... I... I... um... I... um would like to say... sorry."

"I'm not sure I understand."

"I'm sorry for treating you so badly, you know... before."

'Ahhhhhh,' he thought, 'it is her.'

Mr Garrett's secretary continued, clearly finding it very difficult, judging by the sound of her shaky voice.

"I know it's no excuse, but that, that Manson fellow, some of the things he said, and the way that he said them, well... it was all so... believable. I hope you will accept my heartfelt apology."

Not surprised to hear that the ex-army major had been bad mouthing him, he supposed that he should have realised earlier exactly what had been going on.

"Apology accepted," he mumbled down the phone before the secretary could burst into tears. "Let's just put it all behind us."

"That's very kind of you Mr Bentwhistle, we'll see you at eleven o'clock," she replied with a sniff, before hanging up.

Peter's face lit up with a small grin, wondering whether the day could get any weirder.

At exactly 10.55, he put on his jacket and headed towards the nearest stairwell, on the way to Garrett's office on the top floor, not wishing to be stuck in a lift with anyone due to all the unwanted attention. Bounding up the stairs three at a time, he straightened his tie before going through the door at the top. In front of him, in the middle of the corridor, on the thick plush carpet, at her desk, was the secretary who he'd only spoken to a short while ago.

She nodded and smiled at him as he walked past.

"Go straight on in, he's expecting you," she said softly.

Striding past the desk he noticed a wicker bin on the floor, full to the brim with used tissues, next to a very shiny yucca plant. Silently he hoped that she hadn't been crying on his account, but from the sound of her voice on the phone, he thought that perhaps she had.

Walking up to the oak door, he knocked twice and waited.

A soft, "Come in," floated through the door. Turning the brass handle, he walked through. Sitting at his desk, beaming away, paperwork in hand, was Al Garrett, fit and well, in fact looking decidedly more healthy than Peter had ever seen him, even appearing to be sporting some kind of tan, with his normally pale skin looking a lovely shade of golden brown. With a wave of his hand, his boss guided Peter to the chair opposite.

"My boy, it's so good to see you," remarked the bald eagle jovially, putting down the paperwork he'd been perusing.

"You too, sir," replied Peter, vividly recalling the last time he'd been in that office, when Manson had appeared unexpectedly, foiled his clever plan, sacked him on the spot and had him led from the building by armed guards in restraints. Perhaps not his finest hour.

"Less of the sir, Peter. Please call me Al as you have done in the past."

He nodded agreeably.

"Before we get into anything else, I have to ask, how are you? Have you fully recovered from your heroics? I was led to believe that you may still not be fully fit."

"I'm fine sir, um, I mean Al. I have only really recovered in the last few days, but I feel as fit as a fiddle now, and I'm so glad to be back."

"That's good to hear my boy, we've sorely missed you."

A warm, fuzzy feeling coursed through the young dragon's false body on hearing this, not realising how much working at Cropptech meant to him until he'd been injured and unable to return. It was just like one big happy family. Since leaving the nursery ring and working above ground, he'd spoken to so many of his kind in the same position. It was quite staggering the sheer number who thoroughly hated the cover jobs they'd been thrust into. It had taken him a long time to piece it all together... that there were jobs, good and bad, in exactly the same way as there were below ground. Fortunately he'd hit the jackpot when being assigned to Cropptech, something he appreciated now, more than ever.

"I do have to offer you my most sincere apology for what you went through at the hands of that c... c... c... cad Manson. I can't begin to imagine what it must have been like for you. We all, particularly myself, owe you so much."

Peter got as far as opening his mouth to protest before Garrett waved his finger, signalling for him to remain silent.

"Also I understand that Mrs Green, my secretary, treated you rather badly during that period.

Still not sure if he was meant to speak, he gave an awkward little smile, one that Garrett assumed meant yes.

"You have to understand that during the time Manson was here, I had very little control over what I was thinking or doing, Looking back, the whole thing seems to be just one long, continuous blur. I don't remember eating or sleeping, only being in this damned office, doting on every word he said, and believing it without question. I can't even recall hiring the damned man. I'm told that I did though, through a friend of a friend, who'd had a recommendation from someone in the army. But alas, I can't dredge up a single recollection. While I know now that I was under the influence of some very new and powerful drugs, thanks to the people at the... at the... now what were they called? Oh yes, that's right, the Illegal Appropriation of Precious Metals Bureau, which incidentally I believe you know, as they were the ones debriefing you and overseeing your recovery."

Feeling himself getting hotter and hotter, clearly the bureau to which Garrett was referring was the dragon clean up squad, straight out of the King's Guard.

"Um... yes, they seemed extremely knowledgeable, and have looked after me very well," lied the youngster, hoping that the line of questioning would move on quite quickly.

"Anyway, back to Mrs Green. I hope, Peter, that you can find it in yourself to forgive her. I know that it was only me under the influence of the drugs, but she was constantly bombarded by information from Manson, backed up by his smooth talking. While it's no excuse for her behaviour towards you, I'm absolutely convinced she only acted that way because she thought you were out to harm me. Ludicrous to believe now of course with hindsight, but not so at the time."

Garrett indicated with the crook of his finger for Peter to come closer, and then looked around the empty office suspiciously to make sure no one was about.

"To tell you the truth, the reason she acted that way was because of her feelings towards me. We, that is, Mrs Green and I, have a very complicated and unusual relationship. More than that, I really can't say."

Peter sat there agog.

"Anyway, I hope you can see your way to forgiving her, and everyone else that may have treated you badly during that period."

"I think I can," he replied, nodding.

"Good lad," ventured the bald eagle, shuffling through the papers on his desk. "Now what was next on the agenda? Ahhh that's right, I remember now."

Fiddling with a loose thread that had come away from his black trousers, he twisted it with two fingers, trying to belie the nervousness he felt sitting in front of his boss.

"Protecting the laminium like you did, saved the company and myself a whole lot of money. More than you could ever know. If Manson had got away with everything that he planned to, then almost certainly the insurance wouldn't have covered us, which may even have resulted in the corporation going out of business."

Shocked, he hadn't realised the situation had been so finely balanced. Garrett continued.

"Anyway the fact of the matter is that Manson only stole a very insignificant amount of laminium."

'Not insignificant in the dragon world, I can assure you Mr Garrett,' he thought.

"And the company itself is now as sound as ever. All this is down to you young Peter. So... I feel the need to ask if there's anything I can do for you, anything at all?"

He wasn't sure he'd heard Garrett right.

'What is he trying to say?'

'Bald Eagle' sat stock still, gazing keenly over his glasses at his employee, who didn't know what to say, still not quite sure what Garrett was offering. After an uncomfortable thirty seconds or so of total silence, Peter felt compelled to speak up.

"I'm not quite sure what it is you're saying sir... um, I mean Al."

Garrett smiled across his desk.

"What I'm saying son, is that your actions alone have saved this company millions of pounds and that I want to reward you. Would you like a new car, your mortgage paid off, the holiday of a lifetime, a lump sum of money? You name it."

Unable to believe what he was hearing, he wondered what to do. All he'd done was his job... his dragon job anyway. And he certainly didn't feel that he was owed any sort of reward, let alone the kind Garrett was talking about. But if he didn't accept something, then maybe it would look suspicious. What exactly should he do?

Sitting across the desk from Peter, Garrett could sense his employee's turmoil.

'This young man,' he thought, 'is unlike most ordinary young men. Anyone else in his position would have already grabbed the cash, yet he seems almost reluctant to accept anything.'

"Perhaps you need a little more time to think about it? There's no rush of course. When you've made up your mind, or think of something, then just come and see me. A decision like this should be well considered."

"Thank you... Al," he whispered.

"Now," said Garrett, moving on. "Is there anything I can do for you at work? Any equipment or staff you don't have to do your job effectively? If there's one thing you've shown, it's that you know what you're doing when it comes to protecting this company. Anything you need, you just have to name it."

Momentarily, Peter considered what his boss had just said... carefully. Part of him was once again blown away by the generosity of it all. The sensible side of him knew that this might be his one chance to make the company's security as good as it could get, and prevent anything like the Manson fiasco from ever happening again. Thinking hard, he tried to come up with anything that would make a difference on top of all of the state of the art equipment and great personnel they already had, but found with his boss staring at him from the other side of the desk, that his mind had turned to mush and all he could think about were the armed goons that the ex-army major had used to do his bidding, and he certainly didn't want to go down that route.

"Is it possible for me to think about this and get back to you... Al?" he said, a little sheepishly. "It's just that nothing springs to mind right now."

"Of course," replied Garrett sincerely. "Take as long as you need."

As he breathed a sigh of relief, something did spring to mind. Something the bald eagle could in fact do for him.

"Sir... um... I mean... Al, there is something I'd like to ask for," Peter stuttered awkwardly. Garrett leant back in his chair, eyes wide in surprise.

"Go ahead son."

"Well, uhhhh when all the things with Manson were going on, and I was sacked and escorted out at gunpoint, one of my men stood up to them. He didn't have to, but he just did, totally out of nowhere. Not only was it great judgement on his part, but at the time it gave me comfort and a certain amount of hope, perhaps even spurring me on into coming back. I was wondering if it was possible to see your way to offering him a... promotion."

"And just who would this be?"

"Owen Brown."

"Ahhh," sighed his boss. "The big burly fellow who's normally on gate duty in the mornings."

"That's him."

Garrett sat back in his chair, scratching his chin. Just as Peter started to wonder if he'd overstepped a boundary, the old man cracked a smile and nodded.

"Sure, why not. Might as well make it two promotions instead of just one."

Peter screwed up his face, not really understanding what he was saying.

"Two promotions si... Al?"

"Of course my boy. You'll take over as departmental head, responsible for security throughout the whole of Cropptech. Owen can then step up into your current role. How does that sound?"

Not knowing what else to do, he nodded his agreement.

"Good, good," mused Garrett. "I'll make the necessary arrangements, and hopefully everything will be in place by the end of next week. Is there anything else Peter?"

"No Al," he replied, shaking his head.

Garrett thrust out his hand and shook Peter's, as they both stood up.

"Don't forget son, think about both of those things we talked about. My door is always open to you. Have a good rest of the day."

With that, the old man sat down, picked up the white phone on his desk and started dialling. Turning around, Peter made his way out of office, and back into the plush corridor, all the time in a kind of daze. Smiling at Garrett's secretary as he made his way to the lift, he pinched himself on the wrist, as he pressed the button to go down, wondering if it had all been a dream. The 'ding' of the elevator announced its arrival and proved that it wasn't. Stepping in, he pushed the button for the ground floor, silently staring at his reflection in the mirrored walls as the doors slid shut behind him. Instinctively, he adjusted his light blue tie, straightening it ever so slightly. Continuing to stare at himself on the short journey, for the first time since he'd taken human form, he decided that he needed a... haircut. His long, dark, wavy hair, flowing down just beyond his shoulders didn't really fit in with the post he now held, and it certainly didn't suit his promised promotion. On the walk back to his office, he thought about having a haircut, particularly whether he should let a human hairdresser do it (a lot of dragons do it this way) or whether he should see if Gee Tee had a mantra that could help. Opening the door, he stepped inside.

"BOO!"

Nearly jumping out of his skin, he whirled round, ready to fight if necessary. Richie stood, arms folded, behind the door, a huge smile lighting up her delicate features.

"You nearly gave me a heart attack," he exclaimed, relieved.

"Some head of security you are... Bentwhistle!" she replied, walking over to him and enveloping him in the mother of all hugs. "Anyway, Scared of Salisbridge, I'm here to take you to lunch."

Peter glanced down at his watch.

'It can't be that time yet,' he thought. But it was two minutes to twelve, and the staff restaurant always opened dead on the hour. 'I had no idea I was in Garrett's office for that long.'

"Come on," she ordered, offering out her hand.

Patting his trouser pockets, he checked he had his phone, and more importantly... wallet, and then took her hand.

"You're in a very good mood," he said as they walked down the brightly lit corridor.

"Cheeky!" she cried, slapping him playfully on the bum, which caused him to blush profusely. "I'm always in a good mood, I'll have you know."

"Hmmmmm," he sighed sceptically.

Richie raised her eyebrows.

"Want another slap?"

"No," he replied, covering his bottom with both hands. "Anything but that."

It was then that they arrived at the double doors of the staff restaurant, which strangely seemed closed. Normally, they would be open wide with a queue extending out of them.

"What's going on here?" he asked with a puzzled expression.

"Let's find out," remarked his friend, giving him a great big shove into both doors. Flying clumsily through them, Peter tried hard to maintain his balance, and not fall on the floor as he did so. Total darkness suddenly turned into an explosion of bright light. Looking around, he found himself the centre of attention in a very full restaurant. A round of applause started, softly at first, building to a full on thunderclap after thirty seconds or so. With little else he could do, he stood, blushing all over again, as even Richie, off to one side, now joined in.

Eventually the clapping subsided. It was then that he discovered he was the guest of honour at a lunchtime celebration arranged by Al Garrett. Richie, of course, had been in on it all along, and Peter wouldn't have been too surprised to find out that it was originally her idea.

The lunch, if that's what it could be described as, went on for just over two hours. By the time it was all finished, the youngster was stuffed to the eyeballs. Great pleasure had been taken by the chefs in dishing out all his favourite foods: roast beef, fajitas, fish and chips, and not just one portion either. Never had he eaten so well, or so much. Staff from numerous departments came over and shook his hand, clapped him on the back, or just said thanks. All the time, Richie sat opposite him, grinning away, amused beyond belief.

Although he didn't relish the attention, surprisingly, he had a wonderful time. Everyone was so friendly. It made everything he'd been through seem totally worthwhile. As the last of the staff filed out of the restaurant and the staff started clearing away, only the two friends remained, having both been told by Al Garrett to relax and soak up the atmosphere.

"You sneaky git," accused Peter, leaning across the table towards his friend.

She shot that famous Richie smile right back at him.

"Would you have agreed to come if you'd have known?"

Carefully he considered the question.

"No," he admitted truthfully.

"There you go then."

"That's all you have to say?"

Shaking her head, Richie said,

"It wasn't all just about you, you know."

"Do tell," he replied sarcastically.

Richie's beautiful smile faded as she sat back in her chair, considering her next words.

"Manson being here, and what he did, affected nearly everyone in the company. From ordinary workers being intimidated and bullied by those gun wielding idiots, to Dr Island being sacked. I guarantee you that everyone here knew someone who'd had a bad experience. You've seen what this place was like before Manson, much like it is now. Everyone, and I mean everyone, is so pleased that the company and its leader are back to normal. They all wanted, needed even, to be given the chance to put everything behind them. Also, they all feel they owe you a great debt for playing such a vital role in returning it to what it was. For them to be able to come and thank you, pat you on the back... it may seem an embarrassment to you, but it's a vital part of the healing process for each and every one of them.

None of those things had even occurred to him. Now that she'd explained it though, it did all seem to make perfect sense. Never before had he considered looking at things from this point of view.

"You see?" asked Richie, having let her words sink in.

"I think I do," he replied. "When did you get so smart?"

Letting out a little chuckle, she tried to explain.

"It's simple really Pete. All you need do in any situation is put yourself in the other person's shoes. Think what things look like from their perspective. If you do that, you get a much more balanced idea of what's actually going on. One or two of the more rounded humans on my team do exactly that, nearly all the time, and do you know what? They're far better at their jobs, and far happier in general, than the ones who don't. Speaking to them about it, they claim that it's a mixture of growing up in a happy and loving environment, along with maintaining good manners and a high regard for others. One of the other things that's very noticeable about all the same people, is that in their words, they treat others how they hope to be treated themselves. Admirable in design, impractical in the real world, as it doesn't often pay off, but something that everyone should strive to achieve."

He was impressed, having never heard her talk this way, and marvelled at how passionately she spoke about it all.

"Well, there you go. Not just for your benefit, but for the good of everyone. Anyway, time to get back to work," she said, smiling, scraping her chair across the mezzanine floor as she got up.

Peter stood as well, having thoroughly enjoyed his very long, and delicious lunch. As the two left, he gave Richie a peck on the check..

"Thank you."

"You're very welcome," she replied, about to go off in the opposite direction.

"Before you go Rich, can I ask you something?"

"Sure."

"You seem really, really happy. Can I ask why?"

Richie let out a soft chuckle and whispered into his ear.

"If you had with Janice, what I have with Tim, you'd have a constant smile on your face." With that, she turned and walked off towards her department, waving over her shoulder as she did so.

Standing in the middle of the corridor, outside the large double doors of the restaurant, he buried his head in his hands at what he'd just heard.

'A relationship with a human, that's what we all need. This is going to end so badly, for everyone... I just know it.'

5 FROZEN SCALES WEIGH IN

It had nearly stopped snowing outside the cave. Unusually for him, Flash wasn't sure exactly what to do. Even with his fancy watch, he figured he stood virtually no chance against the two nagas. On the other hand, the two of them were very confident about taking him to his 'new home,' as they put it, somewhere he knew without even seeing, that he really wouldn't like. Not for the first time his life hung in the balance, dependant on whether he could exploit the right window of opportunity, should it even exist.

Pacing up and down in the entrance to the cave, the human shaped naga occasionally glanced over at his gold partner, the crunch of the snow echoing from beneath the soles of Flash's stolen boots.

"It's nearly stopped," remarked the fake human, as his cohort delicately flicked some more wood onto the smoky fire, with his long, muscular tail, compelling the flames to crackle and spit as tiny flecks of timber exploded out at all angles.

"You know as well as I do that it has to end fully before we try to ascend. On our previous attempt in even a little snow, we nearly fell down that crevasse and died."

Staring forlornly out into the distance, the falsehood human thief shared his feelings in a rare moment of clarity.

"I just want it to be over. I'm tired of doing their bidding. All of this... kill these, capture those, bring these ones back here. It makes me sick to the stomach."

Slithering over to his friend, the gold, snake-like beast stopped short of the entrance itself.

"I don't like it any more than any other of our kind. But it's not like we have much choice at the moment. There will come a time when we get him back, and let me assure you, when we do, there will be hell to pay. We will take our revenge on their kind, mark my words," he spat, venomously.

"But they've had him for so long. Why should we believe they'll let him go at all?"

"A fair and good question, for which I don't have an answer. Those higher in the chain of command believe this is all coming to an end, and that HE will be freed shortly. Whether that is actually the case remains to be seen. Given what we've been promised in the past, I'm more than a little sceptical."

Remaining at the back of the cave, firmly against the wall, Flash listened intently, able to hear everything the two said, because they were practically shouting. Whether it was because they knew he could enhance his hearing, or because they truly believed he was their prisoner and had no way of escaping, he just couldn't be sure. Once the snow stopped, they would attempt to move him. Where to, God only knew, but his experience and training screamed at him to wait until the journey began before trying to escape. That in theory, should present the best possible chance, particularly if the minds of the nagas were focused on other things. Whatever was going on, it seemed to be very important to both of them, he thought, waiting for the shimmering snowflakes to cease falling from the grey and white sky beyond the cave's entrance.

Another three hours passed before the snow finally stopped. With one flick of his giant tail, the gold shaded naga destroyed the smouldering remains of the hastily built fire. Flash could feel his stomach twist and turn as his kidnappers approached. Unsure of what to expect, he hoped that if he was going to be frogmarched up the mountain, then at least they might give back his stolen clothing. That in itself would be an added bonus.

"On your feet," commanded the human form.

Instantly he stood up, wanting to at least appear compliant and resigned to his fate. A smoky, ashy smell wafted over him as 'Gold' came in close. Flash studied its head closely, on the lookout for any potential weak spots, should it come down to using the lethal darts in his watch.

For his part, the naga just stared back, moving its head lazily from side to side as if in some kind of trance. Flash's fear started to get the better of him, but he remained steady and still, putting on a brave face, as the humans would say. Inside, he was absolutely terrified, something that was very much a new experience for the talented Crimson Guard. Trapped against a sheer wall, facing two deranged nagas, one in human form, the other resembling a giant serpent, both with absolutely no regard for his life, it seemed things could get no worse. The moment he blinked, he realised just how wrong he'd been.

BAM!

Gold swung round in an instant, smashing him against the cold, hard, rock wall. Desperately he tried to breathe in, the blow having knocked all the air out of his lungs. Gulping frantically, all he could manage were small, short breaths, over the pain which was tremendous. Figuring the strike must have broken at least two of his ribs, as spots started to appear around the periphery of his vision, using all his willpower, he concentrated on channelling some of his dragon magic into the damaged area, but with the cold biting at him and both beasts dragging him across the cave floor, he seriously doubted it would do any good.

With his head bobbing up and down like a yo-yo, bouncing off the solid rock, something cold and slimy started to curl itself around his prone body, constricting as it did so. Waves of pain that came with the squeezing nearly rendered him unconscious. It was all he could do not to fade away. After forcing more than half a dozen short breaths into his weary body, he managed to move his head a few centimetres to see exactly what had happened. It was as he'd thought. Gold had wrapped his long tail around Flash's entire body, so much so that he could barely move. His view was suddenly blocked as the human shaped naga wearing his stolen clothes hovered into view. It started to mumble words, most of which the Crimson Guard failed to recognise, which in itself was deeply disturbing given most dragons have a basic understanding of just about every language on earth, past and present. Flash certainly wasn't most dragons, and due to his training and diligence, was pretty sure he knew every tongue that had ever existed, to quite a high standard. A language with words that he didn't recognise, he reflected, could mean nothing good in his current predicament.

The words, as it turned out, had been the naga equivalent of a spell or mantra. This magic was designed to keep their prisoner warm and unaffected by the Antarctic wind and cold that he was about to experience.

Leading the way, the human shaped naga, his boots crunching in the snow, climbed up the steep slope. Flash, wrapped in the other naga's giant tail, slid over the ice and rock, occasionally feeling a bump from the rough ground below. Looking back down the slope into the valley, he could just make out the handlebars of his skidoo, sticking out in the freshly fallen snow. It seemed such a long time ago that he'd arrived there. Would Casey have sent people out to search for him? Probably not in the storm, he decided.

The going was slow, as the higher up the slope they got, the more obstacles they encountered. Boulders changed from small ones that could be stepped over to monstrosities that had to be circumnavigated. Fresh flurries disguised deep trenches and lethal holes, two of which the human shaped naga had nearly fallen into.

Feeling like closing his eyes and drifting off to sleep, Flash was exhausted, not having had any food or drink for some time, combined with the injuries he'd suffered. Despite all this, he knew he had to fight to stay awake with all his strength; his life, quite literally, depended upon it.

After one more narrow escape in which all three of them nearly plummeted down a gaping crevasse, the group appeared to arrive at their destination.

Managing to turn his head slightly, the Crimson Guard tried to view exactly what was going on. Nearby he could just make out the steady stream of running water.

"What do you think?" asked the false human form. "Want to keep him like that all the way there?"

On hearing this, Flash panicked, barely able to breathe, let alone make a bid for freedom, his heart racing at the thought of being trapped like this all the way to their final destination.

"I think it's probably best," answered 'Gold.'

Wandering over to where the captive lay entwined amongst the scaly tail, the homo sapiens shaped beast once again leant over and uttered another series of unrecognisable words. Fearing the worst, Flash channelled every ounce of strength and magic he had into breaking free, having had enough; he just wanted to fight to the death if necessary. But it did him no good. Gold's massive muscular tail didn't budge. Offering up a sadistic grin as he finished reciting the unusual words, the male form disappeared from Flash's field of vision, leaving him to wonder whether anything had been cast at all. Feeling absolutely nothing, as far as he could tell there was no difference at all. This worried him more than anything. Were they going to render him unconscious? Was it all about to end here? Two questions of many that darted around his very full, and scared, brain.

Gazing up into the distant sky which, now that the storm had subsided, had turned a warm and loving shade of blue, he wished to be anywhere else. With absolutely no warning at all, 'Gold,' shot forward at breakneck speed. In that fraction of a second, Flash braced himself, for all the good it would do, figuring perhaps a sharp drop on a steep downward slope was coming. Imagine his surprise when a loud SPLASH bombarded his ears, before he found himself thrust into the coldest white water imaginable. Writhing in pain from the iciness assaulting his body, which strangely the first mantra did nothing to protect him from, he desperately tried to fight the urge to open his mouth, knowing full well that death by drowning was particularly unpleasant. A few seconds after the initial shock, and despite the agony washing through him, he opened his eyes and looked out in front of his face. A small pocket of air completely encased his head. Reluctantly, he opened his mouth and tried to breath normally. Marvelling at the magnificence of the magical deed, all he could think was that it would have taken an age for a dragon to achieve the same result, if that was indeed possible. It was so... simple, yet so complicated at the same time. As all this zipped through his mind, he zoomed along beneath the water of the underground stream, with great speed and purpose, gripped by the naga's strong tail. Through the bubbles and swift flow of water, he could see the human shaped naga, still sporting his stolen clothes, swimming clumsily behind them, also with a pocket of air surrounding his head. The blistering cold continued to batter his already worn body, so much so that he'd already resigned himself to whatever nightmare fate awaited him at the other end.

All three of them continued to be carried on by the fast flowing icy water. Sharp twists, turns and descents would occasionally force Flash's stomach to do backflips, but overall, despite the bone biting cold of the swiftly running stream, the journey was remarkably comfortable. Flash knew that they were now somewhere deep inside the ice cap Law Dome. Escape now seemed utterly futile.

'Still,' he thought, bumping his head on an icy ridge, 'perhaps at the very least I can take a few of them with me.' With that in mind, he settled back and began to make plans.

Deep within Law Dome, the four prisoners' wretched incarceration continued. The human shaped scientist, along with the ragged, emaciated dragon, slept uncomfortably on, hanging on their secure chains. Staring blankly at his surroundings, whilst listening to the running water that just seemed to go on and on, intelligence flickered behind the naga king's serpent like eyes. Squatting against the cold, icy wall, having long since lost all feeling in his back, the half naked human shaped dragon continually flexed the toned muscles in his arms and legs, doing so with a faraway look shrouding his face, almost as if he were there physically, enduring the tortuous existence, but mentally somewhere else entirely.

Abruptly the cold, colourless, icy prison gurgled into life. Remaining asleep, the skin and bone dragon let out a loud, painful snore, while the human shaped scientist hung almost lifeless, too exhausted to wake. The naga king and the finely honed dragon disguised as a human exchanged the tiniest of glances. Someone, or more likely, something, was coming, they were almost certain, because that's how it had happened before, with the scientist and many others. They always arrived via the water, and it always started with the sound they'd just heard.

Like a bath tub emptying, the gurgling continued. Strangely, the ever present noise of the running water decreased, just slightly. It would have been barely noticeable to anyone else, but spending day after day, week after week, month after month, year after year in its company, the two detainees could sense even microscopic changes in the fast flowing water's characteristics. Thirty seconds later there was a huge SPLASH, followed by a brilliant gold naga slithering out of the stream and onto the icy plateau next to it. Curled up in its tail lay a human, looking more relaxed than any being ever had a right to. Suddenly there was a much smaller spray of water, and a fully clothed human flung himself up onto the chilly table.

Both the naga king and the half clothed prisoner could sense what stood before them: two nagas, one human shaped, fully clothed, and a dragon in human form, who was only now being untangled from the naturally shaped naga's tail.

Shaking some of the water from his shivering, frozen

body, Flash's eyes started to adjust to the light in the icy prison. Rubbing his hands and legs together on the cold, wet floor, he took the biggest breath he could, now that he wasn't restricted by the giant tail of 'Gold.' Straining his head to look up, he caught sight of the ragged group of captives chained to the icy wall.

'So that's what fate awaits me,' he thought, trying to get to his knees.

With unwarranted brutality, the human shaped naga slammed his foot into the middle of Flash's back, forcing him back down on to the chilly, wet floor. As Flash's damp hair started to freeze to his scalp, a nagging sensation blossomed into life, right behind his eyes. At first he thought it was the pain from the cold and the shock of being immersed in the stream. But the sensation started to get stronger, almost like a knocking, but from the inside. With the naga's boot planted firmly on his back, preventing him from getting up, recognition finally bloomed within him.

'Someone's trying to speak to me telepathically,' he thought.

It was an outdated method of interaction, even by dragon standards, something akin to using line of sight communication in the human world. Opening his mind, just a little at first, fearing some kind of trap, he caught a momentary sliver of recognition from the semi naked, human shaped prisoner, the one with the glistening muscles. Deliberately he buried his face in the icy cold of the ground he was lying on, something that cleared his mind, startling him wide awake. Opening up fully, he listened intently.

"Can you understand me?" asked a weary voice.

"I can," Flash replied carefully.

"We have little time. You have to listen to what I tell you without interruption. Understood?"

Lying as still as he could in the circumstances, so as not to give the two nagas a clue about what was going on, he replied,

"Okay."

"If you don't act quickly, you, like us will end up trapped here. Do you have any way of taking out the human shaped naga?"

For an instant, Flash wondered again if it was a ruse, designed to make him reveal his true identity. As quickly as that entered his head though, it disappeared. His gut instinct told him this was for real, and that he would indeed be ensnared here if he didn't listen to what he was being told. Quickly he replied,

"Yes."

"Good. Once you've taken him out, you need to get straight back into the stream and follow its course."

"You're kidding me, right?"

"If you don't do exactly as I say... we're all dead. Do you understand? I realise it's about the last thing you want to do. But look around. Do you really want to end up like this? We take a great risk to give you this opportunity. Use it well."

"Sorry," said Flash, meaning it more than at any other time in his life.

"When you reach the point where the river branches in two, you must take the left hand route. It is the only way out. The right hand route will take you further into the mountain and to certain death, while the left hand route breaks the surface towards the bottom of the icecap. You must hurry before the breathing mantra they've cast on you wears off. Understand?"

A thousand questions bubbled to the surface of Flash's intelligence. Instantly he filtered them all, leaving only the most important.

"What about the gold-coloured naga? I can't possibly handle him."

"We'll take care of him. You just manage the human shaped one, and get ready to cover your ears."

"There are so many things I want to ask."

"You have to go now. It's the only opportunity we'll have. The naga prisoner you see here is their king. They can't free him, that's why they are co-operating with these... scum. You must get help and liberate the naga king; the fate of a lot more than just the dragon domain depends upon it. Now go, or it will be too late for all of us."

Flash felt the foot of the human shaped naga step off his back as his stolen jacket was thrown to the floor in front of him. Immediately poised to strike, knowing that every moment he delayed might cause him to fail, the chance of getting some of his clothing back was just too great to pass up. Boots were tossed on top of the jacket, followed swiftly by his leggings. That was it. Channelling every bit of magic he possessed, he rolled over onto his back and sprang to his feet, virtually on top of the human shaped serpent. A puzzled grin crossed the face of the naked naga, as Flash pumped the entire contents of the watch's poison darts into the surprised monster. For a split second, he thought that it hadn't worked for some reason. That was until the human form crumpled to the ground in a heap, wearing just his stupid grin.

Gold glanced across at Flash menacingly, his look alone causing the Crimson Guard to have one of his epiphanies, the ones he only had when he was a hair's breadth away from death. He needn't have worried though. Before the naga had a chance to exact revenge, a wave of high pitched sound came screaming towards them. Flash scrambled to bring his hands up to the side of his head as the wave knocked him off his feet. Feeling his ears leaking blood, he glanced over to where Gold had been. The seemingly unstoppable creature was writhing around on the icy floor, screaming incoherently, its gills expanding and contracting at an alarming rate. A voice deep within Flash's psyche told him it was time to go. Unable to work out whether it was his own, or the other dragon's, slipping on the leggings, boots and coat, he turned and looked back at the prisoners one last time.

"Go!" commanded the other dragon.

Having now stopped producing the sonic wave that had rendered Gold useless, the naga king looked directly into Flash's eyes.

As he did so, the courageous Crimson Guard heard a very different voice inside his head. A dreamy, screeching kind of sound that said,

"Youuuu muuussst geeeet heeeelp, to freeeeee ussssss aaaalllll. Only theeeen wiillll my kiiiind deeesist."

With that, the naga king turned away. Flash knew his time was up. It was now or never. After one last look at the semi naked human dragon, with great reluctance, he turned and flung himself head first into the icy flowing water.

The magic that had been cast on him still held was his first thought, as he tried not to pass out from the shock and pain assaulting him once again. His second was that it hurt more now, entering the icy torrent a second time around.

Light from the cavern subsided as the stream became fully enclosed underground, quickly leaving Flash encased by raging white water and tiny bubbles of air, unable to see further than a metre in front of his face. How on earth was he supposed to see when the stream separated into two? Kicking his feet and flailing about with his arms, he tried as best he could to stay over towards the left of the channel, scraping himself along the wall of ice as he did so.

A sharp right hand bend, followed by a steep drop sent him tumbling head over heels as the freezing torrent numbed his exhausted body. As he came out of the roll his face smacked violently into a solid, vertical piece of rock, right in the middle of the subterranean watercourse.

'Oh my God,' he thought. 'This is it! This is the point at which it separates. Scrabbling with his fingers, he managed to get a handhold on part of the solid rock that he'd just banged his face on, realising belatedly that he'd tumbled over to the wrong side of the stream, and was now perilously close to plunging down the right hand side, almost certainly to his... DEATH!. Holding on for all he was worth, despite the fact that he could barely feel his fingers or hands, fast flowing water continued to pulverise his body as he flailed about, all the time knowing that the longer he remained this side, the more likely it was that he would be carried to his doom.

Digging his fingernails into the stone, he used every muscle in his entire body, willing them all to work, ignoring the agony he felt in each and every one of them. Slowly, it started to work as his head became level with the top of the partition. All he had to do was pull himself up just a little higher and then he could get one arm over the other side and drag himself into the left hand current. Concentrating hard on pulling himself up, he failed to notice the tiny slivers of water that had started to seep through the magic that was keeping his head dry and surrounded by air. The surprise at feeling the ice cold water running across his face nearly caused him to lose his grip. Opening his eyes, for they'd been closed as he'd willed his muscles on to greater things, he saw that the water had started to leak around nearly every part of his face.

'The mantra must be wearing off,' he thought, totally terrified. 'I'm going to drown in only a matter of moments.' It was this thought, and this alone, that gave him all the motivation he required. Scrambling up the rock, he threw himself into the flow on the other side, zooming headlong into the rushing white water, concentrating on what was in front of him and the leaky pocket encasing his head.

Tiny rivers had started to flow around his face now, so much so that he'd swallowed a couple of mouthfuls accidentally, and had taken to spitting some of the water back out and away, which hadn't worked out as well as he'd thought. As the channel started to widen, the stream began to slow, the icy white sides becoming smoother, a bit like an underwater bobsleigh run. Hoping that the changes were indicative of reaching somewhere outside the mountain, a point where he could exit, still the water leaked in around his freezing, throbbing, bleeding head.

'Must have been where I hit the rock,' he mused, spitting out blood along with a mouthful of icy cold water. Tongue and teeth burnt from the cold, his hope that the river would be leaving the mountain and coming out above ground seemed to have been dashed. The much slower flowing water was still firmly trapped in a dark, icy warren, punctuated by only a few random eruptions of bubbles from the stream bed. In that moment he knew that time had nearly run out. Only a small amount of air remained around his face, air that he knew could disappear any time. Desperation forced him into action as he started to swim as fast as he could, all the time taking deep breaths, knowing that any one of them might be his last. Rounding a huge corner in what seemed like the widest part he'd come across so far, he pushed on, forcing his legs to move for fear of drowning.

Moments after taking another gargantuan breath, the remaining air surrounding his head bobbed away, with the magic having totally died, leaving him terrified and exhausted. If he could have done, he would have cried. The irony of being surrounded by this much water and wanting to add more in the form of tears nearly made him laugh. As the current carried him along, he held his breath and looked back on what had been quite an adventurous life. A dozen or so thoughts and images whizzed past him, but instead of lingering on what had been, he was jolted into action, not wanting to end it all here and now, with nobody knowing his fate. He wasn't the sort of being that calmly laid down his life and surrendered. Alright, given the choice, he probably would have opted for an all-out fight to the death, with amazingly bad odds and just a hint of glory.

'Well,' his mind reflected, 'I haven't been given the choice but that doesn't mean I'm just going to give up and drown.' Urging his legs on, he kicked as hard as he could, his muscles burning with pain. Knowing that at best he'd have another minute or so before he was forced to expel the air inside him, he was determined to fight to the very end, albeit in a very different way from what he'd have preferred. Swimming for all he was worth, he seemed to be moving faster and faster.

'The current is increasing again,' he mused, ploughing on. Soon wave after wave of bubbles obscured his vision, as he zipped through them at unerring speed, much like a torpedo locked onto its target. As his cheeks, with the remainder of his air, were battered and bruised by the rushing, effervescing water, wanting nothing more than to expel his last breath, coordinating his arms and legs became vastly more difficult. Concentrating hard on not opening his mouth, as he pitched through another curtain of rippling white foam, a fast flowing torrent engulfed him, dragging him round a bend and into an almost vertical drop. Fighting not to open his jaws, while wanting to scream, he hit the bottom of the river bed hard, jarring his right knee and elbow, both at the same time.

Only a few seconds away from drowning now, he could feel his mouth about to open of its own accord, knowing he could do absolutely nothing to stop it. Unexpectedly, a haze of light appeared through the bubbles up ahead. Clamping his lips firmly shut with all his might he surged forward. Black spots started to cloud his vision, but he pushed himself on. Rising upwards towards the light, he had no option but to open his mouth. As his body continued to potential salvation, the freezing water raced down his throat, filling his lungs. Amazingly, he broke the surface of the stream, out into the bright Antarctic daylight. The spots before his eyes were getting worse; only tiny openings in his vision remained. With both his arms outstretched, he pulled himself for all he was worth out of the freezing stream, and flopped onto the snow covered bank. Rolling onto his side, his body started to expel all the water it had swallowed, the cold continuing to nibble at his soaking wet body, paradoxically piercing him like a red hot poker. With the excess water having left his body, he passed out, only a metre or so from the bitter waterway that had so very nearly cost him his life.

Barely five minutes later, his built in survival instinct kicked in, and in a staggering display of stubbornness, he awoke, wishing with every part of his body that he hadn't. Feeling worse than an alcoholic's hangover, and shivering on an international level, he knew that he had to get back to the dragon domain and warn the king. Nothing else existed, only that one thought. Stumbling to his feet, he staggered slightly, before dropping back down to his knees, his head so muzzy he couldn't concentrate. Two deep breaths later, he was back up, knowing he had to get a grip, get his bearings and find a way out of this hellhole and back to the dragon world. Glancing round at the body of water he'd just come out of, he found that the stream only broke the surface for perhaps twenty metres or so, before disappearing back underground. The bank and the surface of the waterway were shielded from the normal roaring wind by a wicked looking rocky outcrop that hovered menacingly over him right at this very moment. As he took all this in, a little voice in the back of his head screamed,

"They'll come after you. As soon as they've recovered, they'll come."

Instantly, he knew what he had to do. Shivering violently, he removed his precious watch, noted the time and GPS location of where he was, and then set it down in the snow. Rubbing his hands together in an attempt to get some feeling back into his fingers, he set about turning the watch into a bomb. Of course he knew how to do it, and under normal conditions it would only take a few seconds, but his frozen digits made it hard for him to depress all the small buttons in the right order. At the rate he was going, he'd be lucky not to blow himself to smithereens.

Eventually, after lots of fiddling and a large amount of luck, he managed to set the proximity detection function. Setting the countdown to sixty seconds, so that he had enough time to get out of range, he depressed the button, leaving the watch on the icy bank, pressed into the snow. After the timer had counted down, any movement at all in a radius of thirty metres would set off the explosive device. Turning away from the extraordinary timepiece, he started to jog slightly, buoyed by the knowledge that he had once again escaped certain death by the skin of his teeth.

A few paces in, a thunderous splashing noise erupted from the stream, forcing him to turn round. A vision from hell appeared, dripping wet, on the water's edge... the golden scaled naga who'd captured him previously, the one that he'd last seen flailing around on the floor of the icy prison, barely conscious, stared at him from fifteen metres away. Flash couldn't believe what he was seeing. Another forty seconds or so and the beast wouldn't have been a problem, because the explosive he'd just planted would have gone off, either killing the naga, or trapping it below the surface for good. Fighting off waves of exhaustion that were just begging him to lie down in the snow and call it a day, he couldn't begin to comprehend that he'd come so far, avoided death by a gnat's... well, whatever it was, only for it to end like this. If it weren't for the deadly seriousness of it all, he'd be laughing his head off.

Cocking its head to one side, the naga's gills expanded and contracted briskly. Bright yellow fluid dribbled out of both its tiny little ears, dripping down the scales on the side of its head.

'Of course,' he thought, 'I bet it can't hear a thing after being hit by that sound wave. If I can string this out a little longer, maybe I'll get out of here yet.'

Flash and his enemy, Gold, were both standing well within the blast radius of the explosive that was about to go off. The only difference was that Flash was fully aware of this, and the very deaf naga was most certainly not.

With two seconds to go, the alarm on the watch would beep constantly, priming the proximity sensor. After that, anything that moved within range would set off the charge, which in turn would bring down the rocky overhang above.

Pure evil and malevolence gripped the naga's face. If ever the phrase 'murder in his eyes' was apt, it was here and now. Flash knew he had to play for time, keep the monster in the blast radius, and avoid being killed. Feeling like a juggler entertaining an audience, at least the adrenaline pumping through his near perfect replica of a body made him forget about how cold he was. Letting a panicked expression envelope his face, he waved his arms about in the air, pointing in different directions, all the while mouthing gibberish at the slippery fiend. More than a little suspicious, given how he'd been fooled once already, the beast watched Flash fall to his knees in the snow, looking vaguely injured and much less threatening. From the Crimson Guard's point of view, it appeared to be working, with the naga not having moved from its spot next to the bank. Continuing with the gibberish, he watched as the serpent-like monster turned its head in an effort to rid some of the what he could only assume was blood from its ears, and find out exactly what his prey was trying to say. Very soon, time was going to run out. Flash's best guess told him that there were still about twenty seconds remaining, and it looked very much like the naga's patience had just expired.

'Perhaps if I surrendered,' he thought, clearly as desperate as ever. Ever so slowly he unzipped his jacket and tossed it into the snow. Carefully, all the time watching the gold, he raised his hands in the air, to signal that he'd indeed given up. Once again, he mouthed absolute rubbish, hoping to keep him off balance and buy himself that extra bit of time. A strange smile crept across the scaly face of the naga as Flash raised his arms and surrendered, a smile that turned to confusion when it couldn't understand what his adversary was mouthing.

'Whatever it is,' thought the snake-like beast, 'it seems to be important.'

Shaking its whole body, flicking off a mound of snow from its tail in the process, the naga zigzagged towards Flash, its gills pumping furiously. A calm sense of acceptance washed over the Crimson Guard as he stood motionless, arms high above his head. Abruptly, the naga stopped, staring down into the snow where the watch lay, only two metres away from him. It was then that it started to beep continuously, and the lights on its dial flared into existence. A look of absolute horror crossed the monster's ancient face as it realised once again it had been tricked. Flash's eyes locked onto the naga's just long enough for him to mouth the word, "Sushi," before he turned around and threw himself for all he was worth in the opposite direction. All of this happened in roughly two seconds. The naga tried to flee.

BOOM!!!!! Flash's timepiece exploded, shattering the peaceful expanse. Thrown about fifteen metres in the air from his prone position, the inventive dragon agent landed face down in the fresh snow. Huge slabs of rock came raining down on top of the stream itself, each sounding like a little explosion. Dust, snow, rock and ice filled the air. After a thirty second period of wishing he were dead, the Crimson Guard staggered to his feet, choking on debris in the air all around him. Covering his mouth with one hand, he stumbled back towards the blast's epicentre. Trying to clear the dust, snow and ice in his path, to see exactly what had happened, suddenly he trod on something... squidgy, and most certainly not snow. Glancing down, he recognised that he'd trodden on a thick section of golden naga tail.

Instantly he became ready to fight, that is until he looked along its length. Some two metres or so from the tip, the part that Flash had inadvertently stepped on came to an end, cut brutally in half by the explosion. As the debris cloud started to settle, he could just make out the rest of the golden naga's body, twenty or so metres away from its severed tail, embedded in the snowy plateau. Kicking the appendage as he moved past, he made his way over to the main part of the beast's body. Even from where he was, he knew the fiend was no longer any sort of threat. Reaching the torso, the monster's eyes fluttered furiously as it attempted to draw breath. Throughout his lifetime he'd seen beings die before and was pretty sure that this one was very close to death itself.

Slumping down in the snow beside it, the events of the last hour or so started to catch up with him, noticing only now that he was shivering from the cold. The jacket that he'd taken off when falsely surrendering had been destroyed in the blast, and he couldn't see how he was going to survive for even a small period of time in this harsh environment. Beside him, the serpent-like brute started to cough and gag, in the last throws of death. A dejected Flash thought he might as well curl up beside him and wait for the dark embrace to come and claim them both.

'That's it!' he suddenly thought, a sneaky smile crossing his face for the first time in days. Quick as a... flash, he bounded to his feet, towering over the dying naga. Searching his near perfect memory, he knew he didn't have long to find what he needed. Ten seconds passed... fifteen... twenty... and then it came to him. It was something he'd been taught when he first joined the Crimson Guards, many, many years ago. At the time, he'd thought it a total nonsense, a mantra that he'd never get to use in a million years. Here, in the freezing cold, with little or no option but to trek tens of miles in one of the harshest environments on the planet to save himself, and possibly the dragons and nagas as well, it didn't seem quite such a waste of time.

All those years ago, he'd learnt a mantra that was positively ancient in design, known only to a select few, as well as being highly controversial. It was, after all, designed to suck all the magical energy out of one creature, and then channel it into another. It could only be achieved when the being on the end of it was at death's door so to speak, because just a little willpower could interrupt its effect. Never having actually used this particular spell before, not ever having been in a situation where he'd needed to, his Crimson Guard instructors had cited this mantra as something that could be used in the heat of a pitched battle, when a fallen comrade or enemy had been fatally wounded and you, the user, had exhausted nearly all your magical reserves. It would, if used correctly, replenish all the exhausted magic, maybe even giving the user more than he or she would normally have in the first place, for a brief time anyway. Something else about it set it aside from nearly all other enchantments. Physical contact had to be maintained throughout, which was most unusual.

Reaching out towards the naga's scorched forehead, his fingers almost blue with cold, so much so that he could barely feel the touch of the sticky, scaly skin, the beast rippled and convulsed with fright, trying desperately to pull away, but without its tail, it had no hope. Touching his numb fingers to the monster's face, he could sense all its magic bubbling beneath the surface. Closing his eyes, trying very hard not to let sleep consume him, he sought out the words he needed.

"Exsisto procul pacis quod sileo facile pro totus infinitiol.
Permissum quis eram quondam vestry iam exsisto mei."

Reciting the text, his mind simultaneously did a rough translation, which was something like this:

Be at peace and rest easily for eternity.
Let what was once yours now be mine.

Still touching the naga, Flash's eyes flew wide open in surprise as the floodgates quite literally opened. Huge amounts of ethereal energy, with a very different kind of 'taste' to it, flowed into him, overwhelming him in almost every sense. The exhaustion that he'd felt so heavily only moments before was washed away, his numb extremities becoming instantly recognisable to the rest of his body. It felt as though he'd been transported from this cold, bitter wilderness onto a tropical beach with the sun beating down. Warmth, energy and happiness consumed him. Then, something very odd happened... memories. Tiny glimpses of a different world, strange lives, unusual ideas, dissimilar... everything. Recollections started surging into him from the naga's childhood, swimming beneath the icy ocean, parents, children... a huge family... Using all his mental fortitude, Flash tried to pull away, break contact and stop the transfer, but he couldn't, and wasn't able to move at all. More memories assaulted him, fresher, clearer... more recent. There was a threat, a threat to all nagas. Their king had been captured by a group of... dragons! A meeting, no, a summit had gone disastrously wrong. Nagas had been killed trying to protect their ruler. Dragons had demanded things from them. Missions, intelligence, all sorts of information.

"Aaaaaaahhhhhhhhh!" he screamed, as the reminiscences consumed him. Instead of the joy and exhilaration that he'd felt at first, intense pain threatened to render him unconscious. He had to find out what on earth was going on, he realised in the back of his mind, the part that was still under his control.

New images overwhelmed his psyche. Nagas disguised as humans, all across the world. A shadowy figure in the background, one of his kind, a really old dragon. Transporting dragons in human form out of a mountain. A councillor somehow involved. Flash couldn't quite make out the darkened image that appeared with this thought, much as he tried. Nagas disguised as humans at Casey station... killing the dragon scientists who'd come to investigate climate change, the prisoners that he'd seen briefly. Waves of sorrow and regret flooded through him with these last images, so much so that he passed out on top of the dead fiend, remaining there for over an hour.

Wafting around on the icy breeze, the rotten stench of decaying flesh startled him awake. Jumping up off the corpse pretty damn quick, in a split second he took in his situation and the events leading up to it. Magic from the naga coursed through his body, invigorating him, making him as sharp as he would have been in warm surroundings. Remembering the GPS coordinates he took from his watch before he set it to blow up, his mind quickly told him that he was a little under ten miles away from the station itself. Despite his lack of clothing, the extreme cold, bitter wind and snow laden ground, he knew getting back there while he had this amount of raw energy available would present little or no problem. What was an issue was the fact that the naga's intrusive memories had provided an insight into some of the things going on, and from his point of view at this time, chief amongst those was the fact that there were three nagas living and working at Casey Station, disguised of course as humans. They would no doubt be aware of his escape by now and would almost certainly attempt to recapture him. Above all he needed to get back to the dragon domain and report everything he'd discovered to the king himself. How, though, was the question he asked himself, as he set off through the snow in the direction of Casey Station. And that was the thought that circled his head constantly, like a chugging train, for over an hour as he headed towards the other nagas and hopefully what he considered civilisation.

Meanwhile, far beneath Law Dome, retribution had been visited on the four prisoners for their part in Flash's escape. Wailing and screaming like a banshee which in itself was nothing new, the human shaped scientist this time had good reason, as his left leg had been brutally broken in two places with an iron bar, by the very angry jailer, the mean young human shape who visited occasionally with the rotten food. The boffin wasn't alone in his torment. Not asleep anymore, the ancient dragon in its natural form that was more bone than body whined and howled in pain further along the icy wall, having had his left wing pierced with a specially designed stalagmite that had been sharpened with great care and precision, designed to inflict maximum pain. At the end of the wall, the half naked human hadn't fared much better, having been beaten, at first by the filthy young jailer, and then by the human shaped naga who was still recovering from the poison darts that Flash had pumped into him from point blank range, with his partner, the golden naga, having cast healing magic in his direction before leaping head first into the fast flowing freezing water of the underground stream after the escapee. When he came round, the human shaped naga had been seething, taking his anger out on the nearest being possible... the semi naked human shaped dragon. The jailer had already beaten him once, and was just in the process of thrusting the stalagmite into the old dragon's wing, when the human shaped serpent set about beating the prisoner. Relentless in its ferocity, the naga pummelled and punched the dragon until he bled all over, splintered bones protruding from his hands and arms, while his feet lay at excruciating angles. While the dragon's healing abilities would eventually kick in, albeit rather slowly in this bitterly cold prison that he was incarcerated in, the raggedy young guard had to go over and pull the naga away, for fear that he would take things too far and unintentionally kill the captive, something the beings in charge certainly wouldn't want. Of the four, only the naga king remained untouched, standing manacled to the thick white wall, staring straight ahead, defiant. More than anything, the jailer wanted to attack him, teach him a lesson, for there was no doubt that he'd played an integral part in the escape. But he'd been given very strict instructions not to, on pain of death. Instead, he wandered over to the monarch, just out of reach of the defiant naga, for he knew from experience that to get within striking range was just asking to be dealt a fatal blow, a lesson his predecessor had neglected to learn. Stepping in front of the naga's unblinking field of vision, the jailer smiled his sickly, perverse smile, straight at the naga king. Continuing to stare straight ahead, the monarch showed no emotion whatsoever.

"You'll pay for what you did... you will," spluttered the jailer, whilst poking out his tongue, hoping to provoke some sort of reaction.

Continuing to stare, unblinking, the captive took no notice.

"They've gone to find some of your kind... to punish them for your lack of cooperation."

Despite wanting to beat the disgusting monster of a jailer to a pulp, the naga king remained unmoved, determined not to give the jailer the satisfaction of knowing the one thing that bothered him was the health and wellbeing of his subjects. After a minute or two of just staring at each other, the jailer gave up, but not before spitting in the detainee's direction, and cursing all naga kind.

For three hours now, he'd run through the knee deep snow. There was no doubt it had been slow going, and more than a little luck had been involved in not breaking a leg or falling into a crevasse. But now he crouched on a rocky outcrop watching Casey Station from a distance, catching his breath, reluctant to go straight in because of the questions he would struggle to answer truthfully, but more importantly, it would alert all three of the human shaped infiltrators. Regardless of the fact that he was still fully charged, in magical terms anyway, and despite the fact that he'd run over nine miles in just thermal base layers or Antarctic underwear to you and me, he still didn't think he could take all three at once. If he was going to escape, then he was going to have to try and whittle them down one by one. When the golden naga's dying memories had overwhelmed him and he'd realised there were nagas at Casey Station, he didn't get any sense of who they were, not even whether they were male or female. This presented a huge problem because he'd already come into contact with everyone in the facility and hadn't been able to sense anything unusual in any of them. If he couldn't sense them, he needed to find some other way of weeding them out, and all he could think of at the moment was to watch the base from a distance and see if anything out of the ordinary turned up. Maybe later he could try to sneak in and use the communication systems to get out a message for help. That thought made him chuckle. In his entire career, he'd never before had to request assistance. The other Crimson Guards would have a field day with him about that.

'Still,' he mused, 'I'm getting a little ahead of myself. There are still three dangerous nagas to be dealt with, before I can even think about getting back to the dragon world and be laughed at by others of my kind.'

After about an hour of watching the base with nothing out of the ordinary happening, he started to get impatient, wanting to sneak in and issue his call for help. Waiting out here was getting him nowhere and was just giving his enemies more time to organise themselves. Despite this, the little voice inside his head that he listened to more often than not, told him to remain patient and continue to watch so, reluctantly, that's what he did.

An hour and a half later, his patience paid off. Three figures came outside together, one clearly issuing orders to the other two. In the hours that Flash had been watching, he'd seen only a handful of people outside, and all of them had been on their own, doing the normal, day to day things that you would come to expect on a station like this. Three people together was suspicious, even without the information he possessed. Taking note of them from his prone position on top of the outcrop, he could see they all wore different coloured clothing. One was dressed all in black, from his boots through to his leggings, up to and including his jacket, and it seemed appropriate that he was dishing out the orders. Of the other two, one wore a thick red jacket with silvery leggings and brown boots, while his friend carried off a light blue coat with a fur lined hood, matching leggings and white snow boots. Currently, all three were crowded around a heavily packed skidoo. The leader, all in black, was still issuing instructions, getting quite animated about it as well, pointing in the direction that Flash had come from, before waving at the base itself. At this, the two figures in red and blue nodded, with one getting onto the front of the skidoo, while the other yanked the cord to start the engine. Watching intently, Flash thought it looked as though the snowmobile would be heading in his direction.

'They can't possibly know I'm here, can they?' he wondered, as the sound of the vehicle's harsh engine leapt into life, echoing across the desolate landscape in his direction.

Trying to ignore the thousand thoughts running amok inside his head, he scrambled back down the slope to the far side of the rocky outcrop. If the skidoo was headed this way, then almost certainly it would come within metres of where he was concealed. Did he try and take out whoever was on it as they came past? Did he sneak into the base and go for the leader? A lot rode on him making the right decision here and now. His little voice screamed at him to take out the skidoo driver. Rushing around two huge boulders, climbing on top of the slightly smaller one, he waited for the snowmobile to come around the side of the outcrop. In theory at least, the machine and its rider should come close to his position. If not, then he would have to stay concealed and let it go on its way. Pulling in a wheezing breath, he hoped that the three nagas had been suckered into being over confident. After all, they should be searching for an exhausted, semi naked dragon with virtually no power, cold, hungry, utterly demoralised and, most importantly of all, a very long way from here. Only managing to get there so quickly because of the magical energy that he'd leeched from the dying naga, he was certain this was something his enemies should have absolutely no idea about.

'That,' he thought as he waited silently, 'should give me the advantage that I need against them.'

Resounding across the ice, the noise from the skidoo's engine started to get closer. He knew what he had to do: be totally and utterly ruthless and kill the driver. Of course, he'd murdered in cold blood before, when the need had arisen. It wasn't something he particularly liked, unlike some in the Crimson Guards who seemed to get a kick out of it. But it was something he knew that, on occasion, he had no option but to go through with. This was one of those times when nothing else would do, because he simply couldn't afford to leave one of them alive. Too much depended on it. Taking them down one at a time, with the amount of magical energy that currently topped up his body, should present little or no trouble. Of course he could, like most of the Crimson Guards, cast mantras that could kill instantly. They were amongst the most highly magical spells in the dragon world, and were mana intensive, draining all but a little of the supernatural energy the caster possessed. Even in his highly charged state, he knew better than to begin with something so taxing, and figured on taking the first two down with his bare hands, thus saving the magic in case he needed it against the third.

The 'putt, putt, putt' of the skidoo's engine was nearly on top of him now. As he crouched, ready to jump and strike the naga at the controls, a flicker of movement appeared from around the rocky corner. His muscles contracted, ready to let loose. Rushing through at quite a speed, the vehicle presented little problem for Flash who was able to use all his dragon abilities, and could time his jump to within a thousandth of a second if need be. At exactly the right moment, he launched himself off the rock, his timing perfect for making contact with the driver. However, as he soared through the frosty air towards the fast moving machine, his brain registered an almighty problem with his plan. He'd made a big mistake, one that potentially could prove fatal. There, sitting right behind the driver in the red jacket, was his colleague in the all blue outfit, with the skidoo carrying two of the three nagas, not just the one he'd assumed, as he soared through the air towards them.

Instantly his brain reverted back to his body tumbling through the biting wind. Stretching out with his bent right arm, he took the driver around the neck as he swept in from above and to the side of the skidoo. Flash and the naga crashed to the ground as the pilotless vehicle made a sharp turn, too sharp in fact, as the driver's legs had smashed into the handlebars when he'd been dragged off into the snow. Rolling over onto itself, the heavy equipment pouches attached to either side of the snowmobile spilled open, littering the fresh flurries dotted all around with their contents. With no time to think, the Crimson Guard acted instinctively, leaping on top of the strewn driver, who was face down in the snow. Putting both hands around his chin, getting ready to twist his neck and break it, the driver, still with his helmet on, brought his head up faster than Flash could ever have anticipated, catching the dragon full in the chest, causing him to fall to one side, winded momentarily. The red jacketed naga wasted no time. Rolling over, he thrust himself through the snow and on top of Flash, scraping a big handful of the frozen water into the Crimson Guard's face. Blinking furiously as the naga pounded on his already sore torso with his gloved fists, anger welled up inside him.

It had all been going so well, and now... this! Red Jacket had managed to pin one of Flash's arms to the ground by the time he'd cleared the snow from his eyes, and had one arm around his throat, while the other fended off the dragon's free limb. Something inside him snapped as his rage got the better of him. Over the last few seconds, he'd felt the overwhelming supply of magic call out to him, urging him to use it. As the helmeted attacker hovered over him, he caught his own reflection in the mirrored surface of the dark visor. Instantly Flash cast a silent mantra, designed to heat anything that he focused on and turn it molten in a matter of moments. Targeting his attacker's helmet as the hand around his throat tightened, darkness formed on the periphery of his vision. Abruptly he felt both his aggressor's hands withdraw, so he used the moment to breathe deeply, instantly returning his vision to normal. Rolling off, his assailant landed in the soft unbroken snow with a thud, kicking and screaming, all the time clutching the smoking hot helmet that covered his face. Jumping to his feet, Flash kicked the brute in the chest, forcing the wind out of him as the muffled screams echoed from inside the twisted headgear. Leaning over, he prepared to get a grip on the dark helmet with a view to breaking his attacker's neck.

Before his hands even touched the shiny head covering, from which a sickly smelling smoke was now oozing all around the visor, a blistering pain seared across the Crimson Guard's back, forcing him to his knees. As he fell, his brain screamed for him to react, knowing that something bad had just happened, almost certainly in the shape of the other naga. Hitting the snow face first with a THUD, he ignored the fiery pain that crisscrossed his spine and instead feinted to roll one way before quickly rolling the other. On doing so, he saw the glint of a razor sharp dagger land just where he would have been, had it not been for his outrageous dummy. Knees nearly buckling from the searing agony, he turned to face the threat that had ambushed him. It was of course the other beast, standing there helmetless, blood streaming down both sides of his face from two deep wounds around the top of his head, his blonde shaggy hair matted and stuck to his skull. Flash realised that the man he was facing was one of the base carpenters, O'Brien, if his memory served him correctly. Distinctly, he remembered having a drink with the guy at Splinters, after a closely fought darts match. Evidently he'd been hurt quite badly when the skidoo had turned over at speed. Facing each other, both panting frantically, the helmeted naga rolled aimlessly in the snow only metres away, while the dagger that had been thrown just moments before stuck out of the snow invitingly, about halfway between them, glinting in the bright sunlight.

"Save yourself the trouble and come quietly," O'Brien spat, wiping the thickening blood from his hair with his gloved right hand.

Flash's face creased with agony as the pain in his back felt like every nerve ending there was being attacked simultaneously. O'Brien smirked at his discomfort, making him more determined than ever to take him down. Briefly he considered diving for the blade, but knew he couldn't get to it before O'Brien got to him. Disappointingly, his magical reserves were lower than he would have expected. The mantra he'd cast on the naga's helmet really shouldn't have taken so much out of him, but he felt positively drained, so casting something on this one, even to slow him down, seemed out of the question. Before he could come up with a plan, his hand was forced. O'Brien moved as fast as lightning, on him in an instant, gloved fists smashing into the side of his face and chest. Trying unsuccessfully to block the withering blows, Flash felt his nose break during one particularly vicious onslaught. Falling back on to the ground he noticed the very prominent splattering of bright red blood, from his nose he assumed, standing out against the pristine white carpet of snow. O'Brien kicked Flash in the ribs, causing him to howl with pain. Before he had a chance to recover, the carpenter's powerful arms wrapped around his upper limbs, hands pushing hard on the base of Flash's neck. As the most amazing pain coursed through his broken body, the Crimson Guard knew that he was in no condition to fend O'Brien off.

'He's trying to kill me,' was all he could think. Starting to succumb to the being's superior strength, Flash's only thought was that perhaps death was a preferred option to being captured and spending all eternity in that... hellhole of a prison.

Sunlight dazzled him as it reflected into his eyes off the dagger in the snow, some five metres away.

'If only I knew a mantra for calling the dagger over to me,' he reflected as the pressure on the back of his neck became almost unbearable. 'It's just what I need right now. I could gut him like a fish.'

As his vision faded around the edges once again, the feeling of stupidity overwhelmed his every thought. Learning his lesson while he was still alive to do so, he tapped the back of his right boot on the front of his left, forcing the chamber with the hidden blade to spring open. With renewed hope, he slipped his hand out from his aggressor's grip, dislocating his shoulder in the process. O'Brien ignored Flash's free arm, knowing that in only a couple of seconds he would succeed in snapping the Crimson Guard's neck. Fortunately for Flash, he needed less time than that. Grasping the hilt of the razor sharp weapon, he thrust it into the disguised naga's meaty thigh. Shock from the pain caused O'Brien to lose his grip on Flash's neck. In the blink of an eye, the Crimson Guard had turned round and carved open the pretend carpenter in a fitting display of blade mastery that would have put Zorro to shame. The murderous monster's human disguise stood wide eyed for a split second, before slumping to the ground.

Dagger in hand, Flash knelt over him, checking he was dead. He was. Only metres away, the other naga lay still in the thick, deep snow. Crossing over to him, blade shaking in his hand, Flash thought about plunging the weapon directly through the beast's heart, but hesitated. Being as careful as possible, fearing the naga was just playing dead, he prised open the visor on the dark helmet. Flash jerked back and let out a yelp on seeing what lay beneath. There could be no doubt now that both were entirely deceased. Judging by the state of him, the naga with the helmet on had been poisoned by the fumes. Flash was glad he hadn't plunged the dagger through its heart: it would have ruined his thick outer jacket, something he could now procure in an effort to stave off the cold. Gingerly, he removed the coat and slipped it over his shivering body, knowing that he should steal the trousers as well, but somehow thinking of that as crossing a line. So many lines had been crossed today, they all seemed in his mind to have blurred into one. Wanting to get it over with, he untied the monster's boots, throwing them over his shoulder as he did so, then removed the trousers and put them on. Whilst doing the laces up, he cleaned the bloodied dagger, before replacing it in the hidden compartment. Sitting down, he grabbed a huge handful of fresh snow and began to shovel it in his mouth, ignoring the burning sensation around his tongue and teeth, surveying the surrounding mess.

'Two nagas down, which in itself is good. But I really can't leave things here like this for someone to stumble across, which they surely would. It's just a matter of time.'

Finishing his extremely cold drink, he rose to his feet and wandered over to the rocky face he'd jumped from. Once there, he threw his dislocated shoulder against it with all his might. A loud CRUNCH later, his bones painfully slipped back into place, as a roiling wave of torture hit him like a steamroller. Trying to ignore it, all the time struggling for breath, it felt as though someone was waving a blowtorch up and down his back. After a minute or two of not being able to move, the blazing ache finally receded, disappearing almost as quickly as it had ignited. Moving slowly for fear of the new found pain returning, he trudged over to the naga's knife that lay embedded in the snow. Picking it up carefully by the handle, he examined it, particularly the blade. As he'd expected, it had been laced with some kind of venom. When the naga had sliced into his back, as well as making a deep cut, the edge had poisoned him. Without the time to find out exactly what with; he would just have to cast a general toxin combating mantra and hope for the best. This he did instantly, not even bothering to say the words out loud, just whispering them in his mind while reinforcing them with all the belief he could muster. Feeling the tingle of ethereal energy washing over him, he expected his back to return almost to normal. When it didn't, and he could still feel a burning prickle in the background, he became slightly anxious. Shaking his head, he knew that his injuries would have to wait until much later. Getting on with the job at hand was his number one priority.

Wandering over to where the skidoo had come to rest, its handlebars bent almost beyond recognition, certain it was well past any repair he could instigate here and now; besides, he knew better than to waste what little magical energy he had left on something like this, especially with the other naga still on the loose. Trudging back through the vehicle's path in the snow, he started to gather up everything that had spilled out onto the ground. The things he picked up shocked him, but he supposed they shouldn't have: clips of bullets, a rifle with a telescopic sight, four handguns, a twin set of radios, two mobile phones and most amazingly of all, a rather large amount of explosives.

'These two,' he thought, 'could have started their own war.' After gathering up everything he could find, he piled it up next to the broken skidoo, taking both mobile phones and slipping them into his jacket pocket. For the moment he'd stopped shivering, due mainly to his newly acquired clothing, while the shaking from the shock of having to fight, and having killed, was also beginning to subside. Despite his vast training, it still affected him deeply. Perching on the skidoo's comfortable saddle, about the only thing that hadn't been damaged in the crash, Flash's stomach growled with hunger, having not eaten anything for what seemed like an age. Typically, there had been no food in any of the equipment pouches, and he'd searched both nagas for any sign of anything to eat, but had come up empty. Clapping both his gloved hands together, he decided that whatever he was going to do, he'd better get on with it, having already wasted too much time. Probably, if the nagas were as professional as their equipment suggested, they would be expected to check in regularly with their leader back at the station. The longer he waited, the more chance there was that their chief would realise something had gone wrong.

Flash knew what he had to do. He couldn't leave the area like it was; two dead humans would cause a riot, particularly the way that they'd died. On top of that, if the base carried out an autopsy, which they most certainly had the equipment and facilities to do, they would find out that both humans were nothing of the sort and were, in fact, an entirely different species. Using the explosives to blow everything to hell was really the only logical choice. That could just about cover things up if he did a half decent job. The problem was that he would probably alert the naga leader at the base to what was going on. He or she would never believe in a million years that an accident had occurred. One of the last things he wanted to do was to forewarn the leader of his presence, but it seemed as though he had little or no choice. He really couldn't leave things as they were. Slipping off the saddle, a devastating wave of pain again crisscrossed his back, forcing him to his knees. Clearly the poison combating mantra was having little effect against whatever had been on the naga's knife, he thought, catching his breath before getting back to his feet. Slipping off both gloves, he pulled out one of the mobile phones and powered it up. Not surprisingly, it asked for a code to be input. Shaking his head, he tried the other. The same thing happened. If he'd still had his watch, it would have defeated the code in mere moments and he would have been able to get out a message for help.

'Two phones and I can't get either working. Perhaps I can run a course for the Crimson Guard new recruits when I get back. It could be entitled, 'How not to be a secret agent by Dendrik Ridge, aged three and a half'.'

Cursing under his breath, and then wondering why as there was nothing, not even any animals, for nearly a mile, he began to put the phones back in his pocket, only to suddenly stop, and have a good look at one. A plan started to form in the back of his mind. Opening one back up, he started to power it on again, only this time he paid much more attention. Before it got to the point where it asked for the code, the option for flight mode appeared. Flash pressed the button to enter that particular setting, designed to be used on board a plane or in a hospital where all the functions of the phone could be used, except incoming or outgoing calls or messages. Checking out all the handset's functions, it had just what he was looking for: an alarm, set on a countdown timer. It was then he knew just what to do.

Thousands of miles away in a small, terraced house, deep within the city of Salisbridge, Peter had just finished a snack, not wanting anything more because for the first time in ages he was going hockey training. While he wouldn't say that the injuries he'd picked up in the fight with Manson on that fateful bonfire night had healed entirely, he did feel much better, so much so that as well as going to work, he felt he could manage a session on the Astroturf, and show his face there for the first time since the events of November 5th.

Gazing at his empty plate, with an hour to go before he

had to leave, he decided to grab today's copy of the Daily Telepath, not having seen a dragon paper for a while, and more to the point, the laminium ball league season was less than a week away from kicking off. With barely a thought, his consciousness disappeared off to find the latest copy. Sitting happily at home as his mind flew across rooftops, swooped down alongside the river and headed for the tree on the small island in the waterway that runs through the fantastic park adjacent to the water meadows, he blinked as his intelligence disappeared straight up into the branch. This always happened, however hard he tried to resist. Sometimes he sat and tried with all his might not to, but not once had he ever succeeded.

Sifting through all the previous copies of the paper, his consciousness grabbed hold of the latest one and gave it a tug in the direction of the exit. Wondering how hockey training would turn out, he was abruptly jolted from his thoughts as a giant purple trident zoomed out of nowhere and pierced what his psyche was holding onto. His awareness and the copy of the paper wobbled horribly in mid air. Back in reality, he fell off his chair, landing with a bump on the tiled floor. Standing up, he felt a little head rush as he scrambled back into his seat. What on earth was going on?

His consciousness remained where it was, somewhere high above the filing cabinets it had retrieved the paper from. Closing his eyes, Peter used all his concentration to catch up with that part of his mind. When he did so, he was surprised to find it firmly wrapped around the paper, trying to pull it out of the huge telepathic storage repository, the gigantic trident currently stuck right through the middle of it, giving off occasional wisps of thick purple smoke. Trying to jerk back out towards the exit, he hoped to pull it away from the trident, even if he broke the paper, after all, he could just return and pick up another copy. It had no effect whatsoever. Frustrated, he tugged some more. Nothing happened. For the first time, he zoomed in on the weapon, studying it properly. A long strand of purple smoke hung inconspicuously from its end. Written along its length were the words, 'Pull to unravel.' Carefully, he gripped the strand with his mind and then yanked a little. Slowly, the thread began to unwind, soon getting faster and faster. Before he knew it, the whole thing was a whirlwind, his consciousness hovering in mid air, mesmerised by what was happening. It looked like the kind of knitting project that NASA, the American space agency, might undertake, if indeed it decided to take on a mission of that kind. It was... mad! Just as he considered leaving without the paper, the trident and the mess surrounding it burnt themselves out, leaving a giant face formed from purple smoke, staring straight at him. It was one he recognised instantly, one that had featured more and more in his dreams of late, and one that most of his kind would perhaps struggle to recall, despite the fact that this being in his dragon form was one of, if not THE most famous on the whole planet. It was the... KING! As Peter noticed other dragon wills stopping all about and staring, the smoky face broke into a smile and started talking.

"Hello Peter," mouthed the monarch's foggy visage. "I hope you and your friends are well and that you've sufficiently recovered from the injuries sustained in your... bonfire night escapades. I'm sorry I haven't been in touch sooner but as I'm sure you can appreciate, I've been exceptionally busy of late. Anyway, I've managed to juggle my commitments so that I have a whole morning free this Sunday. I'd rather hoped that you and your companions would join me at my private residence. I have some fascinating things that I'm just dying to show you all. Perhaps you'd be good enough to extend the invitation to our mutual mantra making friend as well, as long as it's alright with you. I haven't seen the old dragon for what seems like a lifetime and I'm sure he'd love to poke around the private library here. Anyway, let me know if you can't make it by sending a message to the council building in

London. Otherwise I'll expect you and the others around 9am on Sunday. Regards George."

With one giant puff, the massive, purple, misty face dissolved into nothing, leaving Peter's consciousness floating alone with his copy of the Daily Telepath. All around, the other minds that had been eagerly watching the exchange, whizzed off in every different direction, some delving into filing cabinets, some heading towards the exit at high speed.

Back at the house, Peter's eyes shot open to the sight of an empty plate on the table in front of him. Immediately he willed his consciousness back. Thirty seconds later it arrived with a copy of today's Daily Telepath. Filing it in his mind, receiving the message from the ruler had made him lose interest in reading it at the moment.

'Wow,' he thought. 'I get to go and meet the monarch at his private residence. How cool is that?' Not caring that it was a slightly childish thing to do, he danced around the kitchen like a pop star on the way to putting his plate in the sink. All he could think about was going to see the sovereign and taking his friends with him.

'It will be absolutely fantastic,' he mused, bounding upstairs to don his hockey kit.

Training itself turned out to be pretty uneventful. Only just managing to take part in all the exercises, at the end he'd been absolutely exhausted. Judging by how he felt, his injuries, despite their physical appearance or lack of it, had nowhere near healed. Throughout the session, his teammates all told him how good it was to have him back, along with a number of players from some of the other teams, with him almost constantly being patted on the back and cheered in some way, shape or form. As he entered the bar afterwards, he was bombarded by people wanting to buy him a drink. As it was, Andy, the second team captain, had already done so, and handed him a pint of diet Pepsi, seemingly before he could even catch his breath. Thanking his captain, he scanned the bar for any sign of his friends. Unable to see either, he did catch sight of Janice, grinning inanely at him. Smiling back, he caused her to blush and turn away sharply. His stomach started doing somersaults.

'What's that all about?' he pondered. Spotting Tank standing up from a table full of boisterous rugby players, he waved at his pal, who headed immediately in his direction. Weaving through the increasingly crowded bar, the big rugby player clapped his friend on the back and smiled.

"Evening Tiny," he mocked, raising a pint of lager in Peter's direction.

Gazing up into the ever grinning face of his friend, Peter asked,

"How was training?"

"Ohh, you know, the same old thing. Some bugger kicked me right in the..." Tank paused as a whole gaggle of lacrosse ladies walked straight past them, "... box," finished Tank, altering what he was going to say, not wanting to offend anyone nearby. Peter chuckled at his friend's manners.

"Don't worry," whispered the big fella slyly. "I got my own back in the scrum. Bet you can't guess which bugger it was?" he said, gesturing with his head over towards the table full of rugby players. Peter scrutinised the table, coming up blank, that is until a tall, wiry, brown haired player that he'd never seen before turned round to answer somebody's question. The player was sporting the biggest black eye he'd ever seen. If there'd been any female pandas in the vicinity, they would most certainly have considered him mating material. Shaking his head, he turned back to his pal.

"Not very sporting," he remarked, raising his eyebrows.

"Believe you me," replied Tank, "his strike was about as deliberate as they come. I think if you join a new club, coming in kicking and screaming with an attitude like that, you deserve everything you get."

Peter nodded. his agreement. Just as he was about to voice his approval, he got a sharp, playful, smack on his arse. Knowing full well who it was before even turning, he shook his head and turned to face the third of their trio with his tongue poking right out. Richie ignored her friend's outstretched body part.

"Hello lads. Holding your own committee meeting?"

"Very funny," answered Tank, taking a great big slurp of his drink.

"Hi Rich, how are you?" Peter managed to babble with his tongue still fully extended.

"Put it away will you. How old are you?"

"Nearly fifty three," he murmured softly.

All three of them laughed simultaneously.

"Guys," whispered Peter, conspiratorially. "I've got something really important to tell you." This captured their attention. "Let's sit down first," he put in, guiding them to an out of the way table in the corner of the room. Taking a seat, they all leant into the middle to hear what was so significant.

"I received a message from the king earlier." Huge gaping mouths and wide eyes were the order of the moment for both of the other friends. "He's invited us all to his private residence on Sunday morning. How amazing is that?"

Tank's face lit up like a bonfire dowsed in petrol.

"That's just brilliant," he replied jubilantly.

Richie's face remained stoic. Peter couldn't read her at all.

"What do you think Rich?"

"I'm really sorry, I can't make it. I have something else on I'm afraid."

Peter shot back so fast, he nearly fell off his chair.

"WHAT?" he practically shouted. Half the huge bar suddenly stopped at his sudden outburst. Instantly embarrassed, he quietly apologised and turned back to face his friends, as the noise in the bar returned to its previous level.

"What do you mean you've got something else on? You're kidding... right?"

"Sorry," she responded, quietly. "I've already made plans with Tim I'm afraid."

"Can't you change them?"

"Sorry no. You boys go, I'm sure you'll have a good time without me," and with that, she got up and left, rejoining the lacrosse girls she'd been training with.

Peter sat open mouthed, while Tank let out a long breath, before wrapping one of his big arms around his friend.

"Don't worry. It'll be alright."

"Who wouldn't want to go and meet the monarch at his private residence?"

Tank pointed out,

"You already know why."

"Tim."

"Hmmmm," Tank agreed.

Taking a huge gulp of his drink, the hockey player tried to let go of his disappointment, instantly brightening up when he realised he hadn't told his buddy everything.

"Uhhhh Tank."

"Yes."

"There was something else in the message."

"Go on."

"The invitation is for Gee Tee as well."

"Really?" commented the plant and animal loving dragon, a little taken aback.

"Do you think he'll want to go?"

"Can dragon poo reach speeds of over four hundred and fifty miles an hour?"

Peter knew the answer to this. It was definitely YES!

"Of course he'll want to go! Ever since I recounted what happened at your bedside at the hospital, and extended the sovereign's thanks to him, all he's gone on about is the king. He'll be tickled pink, purple, indigo and blue, I should think."

Peter was relieved. Explaining that Richie had turned down his invitation was one thing, telling him that Gee Tee wasn't going either was something he just didn't think he could cope with.

"Well, we all need to be there at 9am on Sunday."

"No problem," stated the rugby player. "I'll go and collect Gee Tee and make sure he gets there on time. That way I can make sure he's taken all his medication, and looks as smart as possible."

Peter smiled at the thought of Tank hurrying Gee Tee along and trying to make him look respectable, almost believing he had the easier job of telling George that Richie had turned his invitation down, rather than get Gee Tee anywhere on time.

Continuing to talk about their respective sports for another ten minutes or so, the two friends then decided it was getting late, and was time to head home. Grabbing their empty glasses, the young hockey player returned them to the deserted bar. Suddenly Janice appeared from beneath, having been stocking up some of the empty shelves.

"Thank you," she announced, in a high pitched, squeaky kind of voice, as Peter put the glasses down.

"You're welcome, he replied smiling. "Anyway, see you later," he said, about to turn and head towards the exit.

"Ummm... Peter?" giggled Janice, squeakily.

"Yes," he replied, turning back towards her.

Tank shook his head, not believing what he was seeing.

"I'll see you both later," he said, patting his pal on the back as he made his way out of the clubhouse.

Peter waved his friend off, bemused, before turning back and facing the bubbly blonde behind the bar, who was smiling radiantly at him.

"I... um... don't... suppose you would like to go to... go to the... cinema to catch a film some time, would you?"

asked the gorgeous young bar worker, nervously.

'There's that feeling again,' he thought, as his stomach started putting on its own gymnastic display, while at the same time both his legs decided to turn to jelly. 'How odd,' he contemplated, gazing straight into her beautiful face.

"That would be great," he replied, more confidently than he felt.

"I'm not working this Friday," she announced sweetly. "How about then?"

"Sure," he answered, still concerned with what his false body was doing, and more importantly, why.

"Shall I meet you outside the cinema at say... 7pm?"

"That would be great. I'll see you then."

"It's a date," announced Janice, before scooping up the empty glasses and scuttling off behind the bar somewhere to wash them.

Turning and heading out into the car park, the freezing cold air hit him like a champion boxer's punch. Climbing into his car, his stomach continued its acrobatic routine all the way home, gradually fading sometime later. Falling into bed after having a shower, he drifted off thinking about his misbehaving form, his last thought reflecting on whether or not it was somehow faulty. Then the darkness claimed him, until morning anyhow.

Sprinting as fast as he could through the snow as it crunched softly beneath his feet, Flash had no time to spare now. Quite literally he was on the clock. Having squeezed himself through a narrow gap in the rocky overhang, he was approaching Casey Station from a very different direction to the one where the damaged skidoo and the bodies of the nagas lay. Wearing the light blue matching coat and thermal trousers from one of the despicable beasts, alongside his own boots, he'd found a pair of reflective snow goggles attached to the damaged skidoo before he'd fled. Despite the fact that he was moving quickly, he was still being as careful as possible because he wanted to try and approach the station without anyone spotting him, thinking he might be able to do just that, even though he stood out more than a little in his all blue outfit. On top of the rocky overhang earlier, waiting for anything unusual to happen, he'd noticed that the station itself appeared to have a bit of a blind spot off to one side. At the time he hadn't thought too much about it, but at the moment he was hoping that it would help get him back inside unnoticed. If he was to take down the last remaining naga, surprise was going to have to play a big part, particularly with the way he was feeling right now. His back constantly caused him pain, and intermittently, a wave of additional, unexpected agony would hit like a steamroller, causing him to drop to his knees and cry out. As every second passed these waves became stronger and more frequent. In trying different mantras he'd wasted more of his valuable magical energy reserves, but none seemed to have any effect on the debilitating wound.

About two hundred metres out, right on the perimeter of the base, he wondered what he was going to do if he came across any of the station's staff. Certainly not wanting to kill or even harm any of them, as they'd only shown him kindness, his mission had now taken on much more urgency, with his priority being to get a message out to the dragons, ideally to the king himself, especially as there may be a traitor within the ranks of the council. Whatever was going on needed to be investigated urgently. A sudden wave of pain blossomed out from the centre of his back, like ripples in a pond dropping him like a stone. Concentrating on staying conscious, while flailing about in the fresh snow, after a minute or so the episode passed. Sitting up, his head spun out of control. Momentarily he wished he hadn't. For the first time, he realised he was sweating profusely and had a high fever. Whether it had been there all along and he'd overlooked it, or perhaps it had just come to the forefront of his body during the last attack, he had no idea. What he did know was that time was running out, and he had to deal with the remaining naga with a view to getting out of this frozen nightmare.

Pulling his goggles above the furry lining of his jacket, he took a handful of snow and covered his hot sweaty face with it, for once relishing the delight of the cold. Grabbing another handful, he forced it into his mouth and down his throat, not before it had sent unbelievable spikes of pain surging along his front row of teeth. Breath freezing in the cold air, he cursed out loud. Beads of ice cold water streamed down his neck and chest beneath the layers of clothing he wore, forcing him awake, making him carry on with his mission. Continuing to march through the snow, he made it to the back of the nearest building without any trouble. Carefully peeking around the corner, he found he had a clear view of the base. At the moment, no one was outside, but he still had to make it across a large open area to reach the nearest entrance that would take him into the accommodation block. In his room were a few other things packed away that might just help him. It was probably too much to hope for that the nagas hadn't searched all his kit thoroughly, but they might just have missed what he was looking for. The downside in going back was that the leader might well be watching, in case of such an event.

'Still,' he thought, patting the two outer pockets of his snow jacket, 'at least I've got the two pistols, as well as all the ammunition, and one of them has a silencer on it, which might prove more than a little handy the way things are going.'

Taking the second of the two phones out of his jacket, he checked the timer that was counting down. Seven minutes until the naga found out he was close by. Slipping the handset back into place, he decided that the best way to cross the open space was to just walk casually, as you would if you were a normal member of the station going about your business. Setting off at not quite a walk, but not a run either, he was supposed to look like another person keen to come in from the relentless cold. Rubbing his gloved hands together, he made sure before he started that the combination of reflective goggles and fur lined hood concealed his identity fully. Reaching the entrance without incident, he passed through the thick door as quickly and quietly as he could. Once inside he stopped, leaning against the wall, catching his breath, letting his body be assaulted by the warm, circulating air, which felt so good against his exposed skin. It seemed like a lifetime since he'd been out of the cold. Without any warning, his back went into meltdown once again. All his gathered strength prevented him from crying out as he slid down the cream coloured wall and the tears started to fill up the reflective goggles. Silently he prayed that nobody would stumble across him while he was in this state, or the secret about him being back would be well and truly blown.

Two minutes later he climbed to his feet, peering around the corner that joined the adjacent corridor which led to his room. With the furry hood on his jacket lowered and his goggles resting atop his sweaty hair, he walked confidently down the corridor, all his senses alert for anything out of the ordinary. Having no idea who the leader was, only that he or she was most certainly on the base, gave Flash the creeps, with him finding it hard to believe that his room wasn't under surveillance, in case of an unlikely return. A beep from the phone in his pocket caused him to quicken his pace. Whipping it out as he stepped through the open door and into an alcove that had three rooms attached to it, he looked down at the timer as he stood just outside the closed doors. With the display showing 48 seconds, he knew that the mess he'd made out by the rocky overhang was about to be cleared up. In less than a minute, a diversion of devastating proportions was about to present itself, all of Flash's own making.

Before leaving the site of the ruined skidoo, he'd piled up all the equipment he couldn't use or carry, along with the bodies of the human shaped nagas, around the ruined vehicle. Siphoning as much petrol as he could from its fuel tank, he'd covered the immediate area before priming the explosives the nagas had been carrying. Attaching some of them to the face of the overhang for greater effect, knowing that when they went off, it would bring down hundreds of tons of rocks onto the skidoo itself, he covered any trace of what had really gone on, with the petrol residue helping to make a half decent explosion, that combined with the rock itself should devastate the whole area. Because it wasn't that far out from Casey Station, it should, if everything went to plan, cause a very nice diversion. While doing all this, he'd had to use up more of his magical energy, casting a mantra that would link the timer on the phone and the primer on the explosives. The mantra itself was relatively simple and foolproof; any dragon with a year's worth of mantra training would be able to cast it successfully, with the only weak link in the whole thing being the timer. If for some reason that failed, then the phone wouldn't pass the small charge from itself to the primer and the explosives would fail to detonate. Flash glanced down at the phone in his hand before returning it to his pocket. In less than ten seconds he'd know whether or not it had worked. With his hand poised on the handle of the door to his room, his human shaped heart thumped just that little bit harder in his ears.

Seconds later, he wasn't disappointed, the sound of the explosion impressive to say the least. It echoed throughout the whole facility. Turning the door handle silently, he moved swiftly through, one hand on the pistol with the silencer in his pocket. A quick look confirmed there was no one lying in wait for him; the room appeared to be exactly as he'd left it, but he didn't believe for one minute that one of the nagas hadn't been through it at some point. Pulling one of his giant kit bags out from beside the bed, he could hear chaos in all the adjoining parts of the base. An alarm was ringing somewhere close by, with plenty of footsteps running down the main corridor. Breathing a sigh of relief, he opened up one of the side zips. Delving into the deepest recesses, he felt what he'd come back for. Pulling out the small, black, zipped bag, he swiftly opened it up to check that it hadn't been tampered with. Inside the bag was a seemingly brand new blood sugar monitor that diabetic humans use to help them control their condition. In the middle of sat the monitor itself, alongside a sealed container of test strips and most importantly of all, the lancet pen that contained sharp needles to pierce the skin so that a drop of blood could be obtained for the test strips. So convincing was the kit, that it would easily fool any human diabetic, or specialist doctor or nurse, come to that. All was not as it appeared though. It was in fact, something the geniuses at the equipment development lab had set up specifically to support the Crimson Guards, just like the watch he'd been wearing when he'd arrived. The lancet pen was in fact a specially disguised storage device. Not just any kind of storage device, it has to be said, but one for compressed magical energy, mana, ethereal energy, whatever you like to call it. Used correctly, the pen could take reserves from a dragon at a time when they had no need for it and felt full to the brim, and store it indefinitely until it was required. Flash always made sure the pen was topped up and ready to be used before every mission. By turning the top, a certain combination would allow the compressed magical energy to become attached to one of the needles, and instead of pricking a finger to extract a small amount of blood, the device would instantly inject the user with all the compressed mana it held.

Perched on the edge of the unmade bed, he fumbled with the lancet pen, his hands shaking from the day's events. Just as he finished twisting the top in the correct combination, his back erupted with yet another painful seizure, for what seemed like the thousandth time. As the pen cartwheeled to the floor, Flash fell back on top of the bed, writhing in agony as wave upon wave of excruciating pain zigzagged over him. Heat rushed through his comparatively frail human shape. Normally there's nothing a dragon likes more, but this was different, almost evil in its intent, shooting upwards from his back, bathing his head and neck, causing sweat to break out. It took all his willpower not to throw up as he rolled about on the soft mattress. With the blistering agony and heat battering his already weakened form, he could have been forgiven for not hearing the door to his room open quietly and then close again in exactly the same way. Burying his head in the sweat covered pillow, he breathed deeply as the torture started to subside. Lying face down, as this seemed to cause him slightly less pain, his thoughts darted back to the lancet pen and recovering all the magical energy he'd already lost. Draping his right hand over the side, he scrabbled about on the floor with his fingers, trying to find it, without any luck. Abruptly, a rapturous, throaty laugh enveloped the tiny space. Very slowly, he rolled over. Standing at the foot of his bed was a tall, blonde female scientist, Dr Alison Manilow, if his near perfect memory served him correctly. She was holding the primed lancet pen in one hand, a pistol with a silencer in the other.

"Looking for this?" she enquired glibly.

Flash considered his options in all but a split second. He needed the pen. If he could get to it, taking her down shouldn't present too much of a problem. Without it though, he was almost certainly destined to die here and now.

"You've caused us no end of problems today," she sneered, a hint of steel in her throaty voice.

Not knowing what else to do, Flash just gave her the biggest, toothiest smile he could muster, hoping it might anger her enough to get distracted.

"You'll no doubt be pleased to hear that we won't be taking you back to the dungeon."

Knowing she meant it, and that she fully intended to kill him, strangely, a small part of him was pleased to hear this. Death was much better than living out his days in the same way as the other prisoners that he'd briefly glimpsed, of that he was certain. And having seen all that for himself, if he hadn't been sure before that they were going to kill him, he knew only too well that he'd seen too much to be left alive. He was out of time and options.

Feigning the start of one of his back spasms, he moved with all the speed and agility he could muster. Quick wasn't really apt, in human terms you understand. Unfortunately a naga's idea of fast was very much like that of a dragon. They had outstanding reflexes and speed of thought, much to the Crimson Guard's disappointment. Rolling across the bed, he then sprung head first at the naga, who remained as still as a statue. She shot him twice from the hip with the suppressed pistol, piercing his shoulder and abdomen. Trying to use his momentum to continue forward, the shots slowed him right down. Smiling wickedly, Dr Manilow let go a swift kick with one of her perfectly formed legs, catching him straight in the unmentionables, causing him to curse the fact that his human shaped body had been so accurately formed. Grabbing him by the throat, as blood raced from his bullet wounds, the beautiful doctor, a sneer on her face, did the stupidest thing she could have done, the one single thing that would enable him to win. She stabbed him right in the eye with the lancet pen. Automatically he howled in pain and terror, continuing to do so as the compressed magical energy rushed into his body like an out of control freight train. Within a thousandth of a second he'd cast two mantras with his mind, one to heal the gunshot wounds he'd already suffered, the other to protect him from any more bullets. With the doctor gazing straight at him from only an arm's length away, he quit screaming and very carefully pulled the lancet pen out, flooding the area with magic as he did so. Dr Manilow's sneering expression of victory disappeared faster than an MP rushing to claim their expenses. She moved her arm slightly, to aim the silenced gun at his head, but he disarmed her in a fraction of a second with a sharp kick to her right knee, followed by a speeding punch to her solar plexus and then a pivoting strike to remove the gun from her hand. Regaining her composure, Dr Manilow came at him faster than he would have believed possible. Kicks and punches rained down as the human shaped naga put everything she had into the attacks. Boosted by the magic, it was as if time had slowed right down. Not only able to anticipate the chilling violence, but formulate a strategy and then implement it before the assault had even reached him, the shock was evident on the female's face. After the fifth such strike from the, by now flagging doctor, Flash made a block with the underside of his right arm and then returned the poorly implemented show of aggression with a sharp kick to the doctor's left knee, instantly rewarded with a sickening CRUNCH, as she dropped unceremoniously to the hard concrete floor. Knowing things had to end now, in one smooth motion, he grabbed the suppressed pistol and pumped the entire round of bullets into her forehead. With a THUD, her blood splattered corpse slumped back to the ground, motionless.

Wiping the sweat from his forehead with the back of his right hand, still gripping the pistol tightly, he sat down on the bed, breathing heavily from the exertion of the fight, his whole body shivering violently. Closing his eyes, he fully expected his back to spasm and waves of pain to overcome him. But it never happened. A feeling of nausea and bone weary tiredness swept through him, but he knew he had to push on, or everything he'd been through would be for nothing. With his legs feeling as if they'd turned to lead, willing them to work, knowing that he had to return to the dragon domain as quickly as possible, a plan that had been in the back of his mind all along became a distinct possibility, now that he was aided by a reasonable amount of magical energy. First of all though, he needed to clear up the mess from the fight, starting with the good doctor.

All Crimson Guards were equipped with just about every mantra that had ever existed. From the simplest to the most intricate, nothing was beyond the capabilities of their agents. Mostly, it was just a case of knowing the correct one for the corresponding occasion, whilst maintaining a reasonable supply of magical energy. While most situations could be dealt with by rather vague, powerful, blanket mantras, they were by their very nature magically intensive. It was little or no use to an agent to constantly use these intensive spells, only to find themselves in a life threatening situation shortly after, with virtually nothing left to draw upon.

Taking a few moments to consider his situation, he knew that for his plan to work, he would most definitely need to retain some of his mana for later. If not for his debilitating back injury, he would normally just cast a high intensity blanket mantra that would restore the room back to normal, clearing all the blood, DNA and broken items away as it did so. Not having enough magical energy to spare, he pulled off the top blankets from the rather messy bed and set about the grisly task of wrapping Dr Manilow's body up in them. Pulling one of the pillow cases free, he then did his best to wipe away all traces of blood.

'It probably isn't perfect,' he thought, 'but all I have to do is fool people long enough to be far, far away.' Finishing with all the bodily fluid, he stripped off the stolen jacket and trousers, making sure the pistols and ammunition were tucked away firmly in the pockets, and added them to the bundle that encased the deceased doctor. Once done, he shoved the wrapped up body as far back underneath the bed as it would go. Reaching out, he let his index finger gently rest against the gruesome package. Closing his eyes, he let the words he'd used hundreds of times before, flow through his mind.

"Blend into the scenery that sits all around,
Invisibility and stealth to you shall be bound.

Only a mantra of power so strong,
Will knowingly undo all that is wrong."

Immediately, the wrapped up bundle disappeared. Pulling his finger away, he then thrust it back out towards... nothing. Sure enough, it hit something solid and invisible. Satisfied that the mantra had done its job in turning everything invisible, he slid out from beneath the bed and got painfully to his feet, still able to hear voices and running feet from the main corridor, but they seemed less chaotic and more measured. Not knowing how much longer he could go without being discovered, he swiftly retrieved the spare leggings and jacket out of his kit bag, shoving them on as quickly as possible, not needing any gloves or goggles for what he had planned, quite the opposite in fact. Zipping up the bags, making the room look exactly as it had before, with the exception of some of the bedding, he very carefully headed back towards the corridor and the same exit he'd used to re-enter the base. Using his enhanced hearing, he waited in the alcove until he knew it was clear. Sprinting for all he was worth, he made it to the exit unseen. Checking to make sure no one was visible outside, he carefully let himself out into the snowy wilderness, hoping he had enough magical energy to cast the two remaining mantras his plan called for. If he hadn't, it would all be over.

Standing just outside the door, he closed his eyes and once again found the words he needed, putting just enough belief and magic behind them to achieve his goal.

"Cover my tracks mighty wind and air,
Impossible for anyone to follow me there.
Leave not a single trace of my being,
So that no one knows in which direction I'm fleeing."

Standing in the snow outside the thick door, he had to make sure that the mantra he'd just cast had taken effect. So he took two steps forward, the white stuff crunching under his boots as he did so. Twisting his head over his right shoulder, he gazed back at the spot he'd been standing in. His two dirty great footprints were about ten centimetres deep, but as he watched, something quite literally magical happened. A swirl of wind, about the size of one of his boots, appeared from nowhere, directly over one of the footprints. Gently it lowered itself into the print, causing the beautifully formed, crystalline snowflakes to flutter about briefly, before settling back down. The footprint had been wiped away. Moving across to the other, the small swirl did exactly the same again. Smiling at the simplicity of it all, he felt confident he wouldn't leave any tracks, and so very quickly and carefully started to make his way around the station, to the opposite side to that of the explosion. As he'd hoped, the disturbance had drawn people towards it, and with the exception of one very close shave with one of the base's engineers who was retrieving materials from one of the outbuildings, he completed his journey without being spotted. As sure as he could be that nobody was watching, he put on a burst of speed so that he ended up about five hundred metres away from the nearest outlying building. In his mind, he cut off the tiny trickle of magic that was constantly being drained in covering up his tracks. Widening his footsteps ever so slightly, as if to signify a stagger, he headed directly for the base, still making sure he wasn't being watched, This, he thought, was where it would hopefully all come together, if, and it was a big if, he still possessed enough mana to cast the final mantra and make everything fit together. Deep inside he knew it was going to be close.

Still staggering towards the main building, he opened his jacket to about halfway, picked up a handful of snow and rubbed it into his hair and face, while at the same time, in his head, searched for the spell that would ultimately get him back to civilisation and the dragon domain. Knowing what he was about to do was dangerous, in oh so many ways, it was the only thing he could think of that would get him back really quickly. Trying to think of the words he needed, he could feel the heat and pain in his back start to build up. Silently, he cursed, knowing that he needed to cast the mantra now. If he could, it wouldn't matter if his back went into total meltdown, in fact, as much as he didn't like to think it, it might just make the whole thing more realistic. Unfortunately the words wouldn't come. For some reason they seemed hard to find, and the heat and the pain were starting to become a distraction. Finally he recalled them, and accessing the remaining magic available to him, closed his eyes and began to concentrate.

"My skin and body, make them old,
Hard, pale tissue, blackened by cold.
My body overwhelmed by serious frostbite,
Looking like I've been abandoned for many a night."

Just as Flash finished casting the mantra and it began to take effect, his back erupted with fiery slices of pain weaving up and down, left and right. Instantly he dropped to his knees, eventually falling face down into the crunchy, wispy, white snow. In a strange way he stifled a laugh. Although he hurt more than he thought possible, the changes the mantra were adding to his human shaped physique were undoubtedly more painful.

'Ha... the agony from the mantra is taking my mind off the pain in my back. How ironic is that?' was his last thought before he blacked out, face down. As he lay there, the spell he'd cast followed its instructions to the letter, changing Flash's body and using up the last of the residual magic inside it. Mantra makers across the dragon kingdom would have been proud of the results of this particular beauty, even the famed and hard to please... Gee Tee. All across his form, the previously pristine flesh had been replaced by hard, pale skin, blackened dead tissue and horrifying blisters that would put even the most ardent marathon runners to shame. His hands, feet, nose and ears were the worst hit areas, as they would have been if he were genuinely human and had been stranded in the freezing wilderness on his own for a long time. As well as replicating the frostbite down to the last detail, the spell would also make him appear weak, confused and disorientated. Once he was found, he hoped it wouldn't take the staff at the base too long to figure out that he needed expert medical attention that he could only receive somewhere else... rather a long way away. That was the hope.

He awoke in debilitating pain. Despite the fact that he was supposed to be clear headed and cool underneath all the symptoms of the mantra, clearly the wound on his back was playing a massive part in things, because he felt worse than ever. Managing briefly to get to his feet and stagger some twenty metres or so, before once again blacking out, this round of events continued another four or five times, over the course of how long, he had no idea. Midway through his last excruciating stagger, he heard a scream off to one side. Dropping to his knees, he saw two figures in his peripheral vision running towards him, his life, he thought, was very much in their hands.

Every now and then he'd regain consciousness, vaguely able to remember bright lights overhead, people, lots of different kinds of voices, and wires and tubes poking out of his damaged body. Eventually he'd lose consciousness, this twisted routine repeating itself over and over again.

The sounds weren't getting any clearer. Somewhere inside, a little thought poked at him, telling him that he really should be able to comprehend what they were. His mind continued to ignore the thought and hide in the dark recesses that it had made its own. Although he couldn't recognise the people the voices belonged to, he did start to understand the urgency with which they spoke. Urgency was good, he thought. Urgency would get him out of this frozen hellhole and back to somewhere he could slip into the dragon domain from and board the monorail back to London.

Tiny, intricate flakes of snow fluttered past his face, the

next time he came round. Panic gripped him. Were they taking him back to the prison? Had he played right into their hands? Before he could find out the answer, he blacked out.

Realising he was somewhere different, he steadied the rising panic within his mind, so that just an underlying nervousness accompanied him. Looking up at a dirty white, narrow ceiling, he could just make out someone barking instructions but they were all but drowned out by an incredibly loud whirring noise that seemed to be everywhere. The sound of a door slamming shut close by made him jump, causing his back to spasm once again, just as the whirring got louder and his body felt the sensation of movement. He was in some sort of vehicle, he thought fuzzily as his mind struggled to cut through the pain in an effort to make sense of it all. And then, with the sound increasing tenfold, it all became startlingly clear.

'I'm in a plane.' As the comforting feeling of the aircraft powering into the sky tickled his body, a small tear ran down the side of his face.

'I'm going home,' he thought. 'I'm going home.' Once more the darkness took him.

6 AND TODAY'S DATE IS... JANICE!

Deciding to walk into town to meet Janice, he hoped it was far too early to be full of drunken lunatics despite it being Friday night. Feeling more and more tired as the week had gone on, being back at Cropptech was fantastic, and he couldn't have been happier, but he was absolutely beat. His injuries, despite looking fully healed, were anything but, and the more he thought about it, the more it bothered him. Would they ever mend, or would he stay in this continued state of tiredness for the rest of his life? Would his life expectancy be affected in any way? These were just a couple of the questions that played on his mind regularly.

In spite of his fatigue, he'd found himself buoyed by the thought of meeting Janice and going to the cinema. At first he thought he would call and cancel because of the way he felt, but the closer it got, the more he was looking forward to it, and besides, he didn't have her number, and phoning her up at the sports club didn't sit with him very well. So here he was, strolling through the cold evening drizzle, dodging the potholes in the roads and the cracked and uneven pavements, going to meet a human girl, who he didn't really know that well, to spend the evening with her. Oh he knew what Tank would have said, that he was just the same as Richie. Please... it was nothing like her situation. All he was doing was going out for a nice evening in the company of someone new. If he hadn't been doing this, he'd just be stuck at home on his own. And after all, part of his mandate was to blend in and act like any other human. So that's just what he was doing.

Glancing down at his watch, he could just make out the time in the soft, yellow street light. He had a few minutes before they were due to meet, but he liked to arrive early for almost anything he did and so picked up the pace a little. He hated anyone being late. It drove him mad. Tank was always exactly on time. Richie on the other hand was almost invariably late. Not by much, the odd minute here, thirty seconds there, but never on schedule. It drove him bonkers. Secretly he thought that she knew this, and that's why she did it. The thought of asking her had never crossed his mind, but the next time it occurred, maybe he would.

Stepping out into the road to avoid a group of rowdy youths, he turned the final corner. In the distance, he could just make out lots of people waiting outside the cinema, but whether it was a queue or individuals that had just exited a screening, he really couldn't be sure. As he approached, the crowd thinned and he spotted Janice, dressed in light boots, lovely blue jeans and a light brown leather flying jacket.

'She looks gorgeous,' he thought, suddenly realising that it was quite an inappropriate thought. After all, he was a dragon, and could get into serious trouble for such things. By the time all this had gone through his head, she'd spotted him and let loose one of her radiant smiles, one he returned as best he could.

"Hi Peter," she remarked happily.

Before he had the chance to return the greeting, she leant up and planted a small kiss right on his cheek, beaming beautifully as she did so. In his life he'd never felt so flustered and confused. Straight away his stomach started doing loop the loops, his legs turned weak, and worst of all, he could feel himself start to blush.

"Hhhhhhi Janice," he managed to stutter. "Hoooow are you?"

"Wonderful thanks," she replied, completely oblivious to his discomfort and awkwardness. Peter could almost hear the drizzle drop in the uncomfortable silence that followed. Janice was first to break it.

"Which film would you like to watch?" she asked sweetly.

Trying his best to get a grip on his misbehaving body,

he took a deep breath.

"I really don't mind. It's been so long since I've been to the cinema. Why don't you choose? I'd be happy to watch just about anything."

Creases appeared on the young bar worker's forehead briefly as she thought about what he'd just said, as he gulped, concerned that she would be offended by him not having decided. Luckily he needn't have worried, as a familiar grin soon blossomed across her face.

'He must be here for the lovely company,' she thought, grabbing his hand and pulling him through the ancient wooden doors and into the reception area. Marvelling at the high ceiling, the massive wooden beams that arched overhead and the long medieval hallway that led further into the depths of delightfully crafted old building, he knew the place itself was hundreds of years old, but despite being used as a cinema, much of the ancient building remained exactly as it had been originally. Turning his attention back to the queue of people he found himself in with his new found friend, he suddenly realised they were about to reach the cashier. Now he didn't know much about going out alongside, or even with humans, but his trips into town with Richie and Tank had taught him a few things and he was determined to pay for both his and Janice's tickets. As the couple in front moved away, he swiftly pulled out his wallet and whipped out a twenty pound note before the beautiful blonde could even bat her long eyelashes at him. Turning to her, he smiled and asked,

"Which film would you like to see?"

She duly told the cashier the name of the film, he handed over the money in exchange for the tickets, and they both headed off down the corridor towards the foyer.

"Thank you," she whispered in his ear, as they weaved in and out of other people.

"You're welcome," he replied.

"Shall we have a drink and some sweeties?"

Knowing full well that if he'd been here with Tank or

Richie he'd load himself up with sweets and snacks, so much so that he'd probably struggle to carry it all, something inside him, he wasn't sure what, but he felt it may have been connected to all the strange things playing up inside his body, told him that perhaps it wasn't the best idea to go mad on the food front.

"That sounds great. I'll just have some popcorn if that's okay."

"Cool," said Janice. "Something we can share."

Startled, he managed to hide his look of horror.

'Share?,' he thought. 'She's kidding... right?'

Janice went off to grab some pick and mix sweets, while Peter got some popcorn and a drink, making sure to get the biggest size available. Just as he was putting the lid on the drink, and picking up a straw that seemed like it could double as a hosepipe, he felt a sharp fiery sensation on his bottom. Gobsmacked that she would do such a thing, he turned around indignantly, only to find... Richie!!!

"Hellllooooooo lover," she announced cheekily.

"I might have known it was you."

"Who else would it have been?" his friend replied inquisitively.

Peter shook his head nonchalantly, or so he thought, but by now, the lacrosse superstar could smell blood. Pointing at Peter, and leaning her head to one side, she frowned, deep in thought.

"Hang on a minute. Tank's at the sports club helping run a training course. Exactly who are you here with?"

Wishing the ground beneath his feet would open up and swallow him whole, just when he thought things couldn't get any worse, a petite arm linked through his, causing him to turn.

"I've got some sweets. Shall we go and pay for it all now?" Janice asked, not having noticed Richie yet.

"Ahhh... sure thing. Before we do though, there's someone I'd like you to meet."

Janice squeezed past Peter and found herself squaring

up to the lacrosse captain in the crowded foyer. She did not look at all pleased.

"Uhhh... Janice, this is my friend Richie. Richie... Janice," announced Peter awkwardly. Richie carried her normal self assured grin, while Janice looked distinctly unimpressed. Bowing her head down just slightly and nodding, Richie said,

"It's a pleasure to meet you."

Janice nodded.

"Likewise Richie."

The awkwardness was suddenly interrupted by an arm slinking its way around Richie's waist.

"Nearly ready sweetheart?" asked Tim, extremely smoothly.

"Oh, hi Peter," ventured the treasurer, finally noticing the couple.

'That's what Richie's doing here. She's with Tim,' he thought, a little slow on the uptake.

"Hi Tim," uttered Peter. "Good to see you again."

"And you."

"This is Janice," announced Richie, once again smiling.

Tim offered out his hand.

"Pleasure to meet you."

"You too," replied the bar worker politely. Clearly Tim appearing on the scene had pleased Janice no end, as she had not been impressed with Peter running into his female friend.

As silence once again threatened to envelop the group, Richie was the first to speak.

"Which film are you guys going to see?"

"The one in screen three," answered the blonde bombshell.

"Ahhh... the romantic one, that's nice," replied the lacrosse player, trying to make Peter feel as awkward as possible.

"Anyway," stated Tim, ever the diplomat. "We're in screen one and it's about to start, so we'd better get

148

going." With that, he scooped Richie along with the one arm that was still wrapped very much around her lithe waist, heading through the crowd to the stairwell which led to their screen. Richie waved goodbye over her shoulder, all the time laughing at Tim having to drag her away.

Turning to Janice, not knowing what to say, Peter realised something strange and unsaid had gone on between the two women. Not sure what, he knew it had something to do with him.

"I'm really sorry about that," he stressed. "I had no idea they were going to be here."

"It's alright," she said, clutching her bag of sweets. "Let's just pay for the snacks and go watch the film."

"Sure thing."

Having paid, the two of them headed into the screen, grabbing two seats in the middle right at the back. Peter marvelled at how quiet it was. The relatively tiny screen was almost deserted, with most cinema goers clearly choosing one of the blockbusters in the other, bigger screens. It had to be said, he much preferred it this way. As the previews played, the two of them munched their snacks, occasionally sharing a slurp of the huge fizzy drink with the hosepipe for a straw. Once the film started, Janice snuggled up against him. It was a good job it was dark, otherwise she might have noticed the look of fright on his surprised face. Not ten minutes later, that look had been replaced by one of contentment. Curled up together, the two of them laughed at the same parts of the film, sighed at the same parts, but he drew the line at joining her in crying at the ending. It was sad, even he had to admit that, but he pushed all his emotions to one side, only then understanding he'd been doing that for most of the night. Janice had a good weep at the tear jerking finale, but you couldn't tell that she had by the time the lights flickered into life.

Leaving together, the petite blonde bar worker clutching Peter's hand and him, surprisingly, not minding, they reached the foyer as all the films finished at once. Swarms of people swept out from doorways on all sides, heading for the long ancient hallway that led back outside. Hoping against hope that he wouldn't bump into Richie again, he wasn't sure he could cope with that, especially as he'd had such a wonderful time, but he needn't have worried. Janice had a similar thought, and in one swift move dragged her date into the flow of people, heading quickly for the exit. Once outside, she hauled him off round to the left of the building, in the opposite direction to the throng of cinema goers. Most were either turning right or queuing for the last of the late night buses right outside the main entrance.

In the quiet recess of a deserted shop doorway, the two turned to face each other, as they sheltered from the drizzle.

"Thanks for a lovely evening," she whispered, the condensation from her breath brushing Peter's face.

"You're welcome," he replied. "I've had a great time."

The two of them just stood there smiling at each other. Once again his legs turned all flimsy, his arms went weak, and his tongue felt as though it had tripled in size. He didn't know what to do or say next. Luckily for him, he didn't have to do or say anything. Gazing up into his eyes, the diminutive Janice stroked his cheek gently, and then kissed him passionately on the lips. His whole body exploded. Inside his head, the biggest firework display imaginable played out. Bright colours, explosive noises, everything. The kiss seemed to last forever, Peter lost in its wake. Eventually she pulled away, at least, that's what he guessed had happened, as he'd had his eyes closed the whole time and still hadn't opened them. With the fireworks still going off, he forced his eyes open. Janice stared up at him, with the same smile he was pretty sure he was wearing.

"Are you okay?" she asked.

"Oh yes," he sighed contentedly.

Janice wrapped her arms around him, as he did the same to her. With her silky blonde hair nuzzled against his chest, he didn't have a care in the world. Everything just seemed to melt away into nothingness. She gazed up at him after about a minute or so.

"I really should be getting home. I've got an early shift at the sports club tomorrow, sorry."

"That's okay. I understand. Can I walk you back?"

"It's in totally the opposite direction for you."

"That's okay," he whispered. "It's just I'd worry about you getting home safely otherwise. Just let me walk you back... please?"

She smiled.

"You're very sweet. Okay."

The two of them headed towards Janice's house which was in exactly the opposite direction to Peter's, although about the same distance out from the centre, about a ten minute walk.

Accompanying her to her front door, he thanked her once again for a good time, kissed her goodnight, and promised to see her the following day. Then he set off into the, by now, pouring rain, heading home. Within seconds he'd taken the decision not to walk back through the city centre, the most direct route home, because he knew that it would almost certainly be full of drunken idiots. Instead, he thought he'd go through the suburbs, knowing that it would probably double the time, from twenty minutes to about forty, but he didn't really mind, in fact he was sure the walk would help him clear his head. He had an awful lot to think about.

Five minutes after leaving Janice, he found himself walking briskly down a quiet suburban street, contemplating the evening's events. He was so lost in thought he failed to notice the car that had slowed right down and was pacing him, that is until the driver wound down the window.

"Oi... Shorty! Want a lift?"

151

Peter ducked down and glanced inside. It was Tank. With a big grin on his face, he grabbed the door handle and leapt in.

"Hello mate, fancy seeing you here."

Tank shook his head as Peter fastened his seatbelt, and then slammed his foot sharply onto the accelerator pedal.

"What are you doing out and about at this time of night?" asked the hockey player cheerfully, glad to see his pal.

"Just finished a coaching course at the sports club and it ran a little later than expected."

"Ahhh," he sighed, remembering that Richie had told him that. "Still, this is a bit out of the way for you... isn't it?"

Tank looked across at him disapprovingly.

"It's not like I've been cruising the streets all night. I know how you think. I knew you wouldn't walk back through the town centre, alright."

"So you were spying on me?"

"Not spying, just... concerned. That's all."

Peter was less than impressed. Not for the first time this evening, an awkward silence developed, broken only by the sound of the occasional gear change. Tank pulled up outside the hockey player's house after only a few minutes, preventing him from getting any wetter, saving him over half an hour's walk.

"Thanks," he said, grumpily.

"You're welcome," replied Tank, switching off the car's engine.

Both friends just smiled at each other.

"Well," asked the big fella. "How was it?"

Peter held his head in his hands, something that deep inside, delighted his friend. However, he'd yet to hear the full story.

"I'm really sorry, and I'm sure this is probably the last thing you want to hear, but it was... fantastic, amazing, just... brilliant."

Tank banged his head on the steering wheel in frustration.

"Do you have any idea what you're doing? You and Richie are going to get into soooooo much trouble... really."

Peter leant back in the passenger seat and let out a big sigh.

"It was like nothing I've ever experienced in my life," he announced. "Imagine the first time you took flight. It's the most magical thing in the world, isn't it? Warm air caressing every scale, the wind rushing around your legs, over your wings, along the tip of your tail, nothing binding you to the ground, total and utter freedom. Imagine that, only... more powerful, more intense. I can't believe I'm saying any of this."

Tank playfully punched Peter in the shoulder.

"Don't worry, I'll come and visit you both regularly when the King's Guard lock you and Richie up in the dungeons beneath the council building."

Peter smiled, glad his friend could joke about such a serious situation.

"Promise?"

"I'll even bring along some of those delicious charcoal fajitas that you love so much."

"Great," replied Peter, his thoughts turning to food.

"And let you smell them through the bars in the cell door before I wolf them down," declared Tank, starting to laugh. Peter joined in.

"You have a knack for bringing me back to reality with a sharp bump."

"Somebody's got to. Seriously though, Pete, be careful. Those rules were made for a reason. Also, it's one thing Richie doing it - she seems to have an inexhaustible supply of luck when it comes to anything that could go wrong. You, on the other hand, perhaps not so much."

"Thanks bud," he said, patting his friend firmly on the shoulder, "for the lift and the chat. I look forward to those fajitas. See you tomorrow at the sports club."

Getting out, he slammed the door shut. Both pals waved to each other as Tank disappeared off into the cold, drizzly night.

Peter went to bed contented, his dreams a confusing mix of ancient dragons making complex decisions and a blonde haired goddess professing her love for him.

7 A FEW KANGAROOS LOOSE IN THE TOP PADDOCK

Forehead burning like the raging sun itself, sweat trickled down his neck, onto his chest, dribbling down his side, soaking his clothes. Aware of all these little things, he couldn't seem to focus on the much bigger picture, no matter how hard he tried. Suspecting he was still on the plane, if it even was a plane, it may have already landed, but he thought he would have felt it touchdown and to his knowledge, he hadn't. White hot pain in his back sizzled through him regularly now, forcing him to cry out and squeal like a pig trying to avoid the bacon slicer, before unconsciousness washed over him. On occasions, the same two faces would swim into view, whispering kind words of encouragement, words that, no matter how hard he tried, he just couldn't seem to hear over the ringing in his ears. From all this he knew that he was in a bad shape.

After blacking out at least twice more, Flash awoke to find that something was clearly going on. He'd been strapped down to whatever was holding him, and just out of the corner of both eyes he could see the two people looking after him, both seated, which he couldn't remember happening before. The ceiling of what he assumed was an aircraft swam in and out of view, making him think that they might be coming in to land.

'If that's the case, then we should be somewhere with access to the dragon domain and the monorail,' he thought drowsily. Moments later his hopes were confirmed as the sharp bump of touchdown vibrated throughout his whole body. As the plane taxied to the end of the runway, he knew he had to shake off the effects of the poison and work out a way to escape back to the underground world. At least there he could be cured of his affliction and warn the king about everything he'd discovered.

Feeling the plane come to a halt, one of the doors opened immediately, letting brilliant sunshine spill in. Lying back, he tried desperately to access the magic dormant within him and listen to the muted conversation that was going on only a metre or so away. Try as he might, he wasn't even close to being able to use any of his abilities. The best he could come up with in his fevered state was that the toxin seemed to be affecting him on a sub atomic level. Something he hadn't noticed before, but was quite obvious now, was the fact that his magical energy reserves were not recharging, which was a worry given his current state. Normally, when one of his kind isn't using their magic, or using just a little, the supply would automatically replenish until it reached the maximum capacity that particular being could hold, something unique to each individual. Different dragons have different magical energy capacities, as well as needing to use varying amounts of ethereal energy to cast the same spells. Those such as Flash had been honed and trained rigorously to enable their bodies to have an even bigger capacity than most normal dragons, as well as having the fastest recharge rate possible. For his body not to be refilling at all, something had to be seriously wrong. It could only be that the energy that should be recharging was instead warding off the effects of the naga poison. If that were the case, then he was in even graver danger than he'd first thought, and needed to get to a healer fast. The only problem now were the humans who, at this very moment, were carrying him out of the plane on a stretcher, with a view to operating on his very bad, very superficial, and very self inflicted frostbite.

A nurse carried a drip above him as she ran alongside the fast moving stretcher. Focusing all his concentration, he managed to sweep aside some of the fog that had clouded his brain. Lifting his head a fraction, he could see an ambulance, back doors splayed wide open. Three people climbed in beside him. A very kind nurse mopped his fevered brow, for which he was unbelievably grateful. Only a small kindness, but given exactly how hot he felt, just a moment's relief felt like a lottery win.

Shortly, the vehicle arrived at its destination, with Flash quickly being taken to the emergency room. Hushed conversations nearby sounded urgent, despite the fact that no details could be heard. All of a sudden, a different nurse appeared over him.

"Don't worry son, the doctors are on their way. They're some of the best in the country, and when they get here, I'm sure they'll give it heaps."

Through the fog clouding his mind he started to become concerned, not at the thought of them operating on the frostbite; the mantra itself, he knew, would have created near perfect replicas of frostbitten human fingers. Even if the doctors amputated them, they wouldn't find anything unusual that would lead them to suspect that he wasn't really human. His big worry was that they would use a powerful anaesthetic, one that would only hinder his body's fight with the poison, a battle that wasn't going too well at the moment. Bringing his right hand up, he tried to catch the attention of the two nurses standing in the corner. Eventually, one of them came over.

"I need the... toilet," he asked huskily, his throat raw from the cold and everything else that he'd been through.

"I'll get a catheter," replied the medical professional politely.

Lifting his head up, Flash shouted after her.

"I think if I can get up, I'll be alright to go by myself."

Both nurses burst into laughter.

"I think you must have a few kangaroos loose in the top paddock, thinking you can go on your own. Have you seen the state of your fingers? All of them are seriously frostbitten. And that's before we've even looked at your... wedding tackle."

Shaking her head, she wandered off with the other nurse to find a catheter, leaving the Crimson Guard needing a new plan to free himself and get back to the dragon domain. Mulling things over something else occurred to him, something he hadn't thought of before.

'I got rid of all the nagas at Casey Station, but what if there are more here, disguised as humans?' Knowing he wouldn't find out until it was too late, he had to escape, and he had to do it now.

While dragons in general know about most, if not all, of the entrances and exits to their underground world in or around where they live, specialist dragons such as those in the King's or even the Crimson Guards that Flash belonged to, need a much broader scale of information, mainly because they have no idea where exactly their missions will take them. Fortunately for him, he was back at the point where he'd started the mission: Perth, Australia, and he was after all, like any good boy scout, always prepared. Assuming that he must have been admitted to the Royal Perth Hospital, as it was the best in the region and one of the best in the country, accessing his near perfect memory, he found it a lot slower and harder to retrieve the information he needed, than it would have been normally. Eventually, he found what he was looking for. A bare bones, emergency kind of... list! There would in fact have been thousands of entrances to the dragon domain, if not tens of thousands, in and around the city itself, but he didn't really think he could start breaking into houses on the off chance that they were dragons, asking to borrow their secret entrance. Standing out in his head, the list included the Swan Bell Tower. Built for the millennium, it stood 82.5 metres high and was home to twelve bells from the historic St Martin-in-the-Fields church in London, together with six new bells. The entrance here, he noted, was in one of the visitors' toilet cubicles. By pressing a certain sequence of tiles on the wall and then flushing it while sitting down, the toilet would flick the occupant up and over, through a gap in the wall behind that would appear for a very short time, and onto a steep, spiral slide, that eventually enters the dragon domain, deep beneath the stunning city.

Also on the list was the Old Perth Observatory, a stunning historic building dating back to the late 19th century, incorporating impressive architecture and fantastic period features, on which this particular entrance was dependant. To use this death defying drop, a dragon first had to make their way around to the very back of the building, where a series of beautiful flower beds skirt the outside, below and adjacent to the walkway. One of the features of the paths is the intricately carved handrails and spindles that run below them. To activate the entrance, a dragon must stand at a particular point between two of the flower beds, facing the walkway. With the spindles now at chest height, and preferably with no one looking, two of the spindles, three apart, need to be yanked back as hard as possible. All are sprung loaded, and leap back into place immediately. They do, however, need a lot of force to make them work. Once done, a small covering of grass disappears momentarily, just enough time for a human shape to disappear beneath the surface, with gravity playing a pivotal part in the whole equation.

Other entrances on the list include Perth zoo, only five minutes from the city centre and the Perth Mint, established in 1899, and Australia's oldest mint still in operation today.

Plumping for the closest, only half a mile away from where he currently lay, at least that's what he assumed, letting his head be enveloped by the soft, squishy pillow that had delicately been placed under his head by one of the nurses, he tried to recall every part of his journey on the stretcher since he'd left the ambulance. Images of a reception, patients sitting hunched on chairs waiting to be seen by incredibly busy doctors, brightly lit corridors and a quick trip in an expansive lift all swam by in an instant. Now sure that the room he lay in was in the south block of the hospital, adjacent to Wellington Street, catching his breath, sweat running down the side of his head, he knew the entrance he needed was so close he could almost smell the dragon poo from where he was. It was going to be tricky though, but desperate times called for desperate measures, and just hopefully a contingent of King's Guards could sort out the mess after he got back and revealed the information he carried to the head of state.

After another prolonged attack on his back, Flash noticed that neither of the nurses had returned from rushing off to find him a catheter. Part of him was truly thankful for this. While he was a dragon and always would be, whatever form he took as a disguise, he still managed to feel very much how he assumed a human would in these situations. The very thought of a young woman inserting equipment... there... made him feel embarrassed, scared, ashamed, and yet it shouldn't have bothered him. After all, it wasn't really his body, was it? It was just pretend, or at least it should have been, but it never really worked like that, no matter how hard he tried.

Gingerly sitting up for the first time in many hours, he wiped the sweat from his brow. After only a few seconds, the dizziness that he'd felt vanished. And then it hit him... he was actually starting to feel better. Not better as in all of his dragon abilities had returned, but just... improved. Inside, he could just make out the tiniest sliver of magic, waiting to be cast, and his fever felt as if it was about to break, so good in fact, that he could probably get off the raised bed without any help.

'If I could use that little bit of magic to reverse the frostbite mantra, then just maybe I could walk to the entrance, plain and simple,' he thought, looking around to make sure no one else was lurking anywhere in the big, sterile room. Sure it was clear, he closed his eyes and with his mind, delved deep inside the human shell he currently found himself trapped in. Marvelling at the complexity of the mantra that held his DNA together, he soon found cause for concern, stumbling onto the true extent to which the naga's poison had ravaged the body which at the moment he called his. From what he could tell, the toxin was slowly attacking his DNA, changing it, damaging it and if left unchecked for much longer, probably destroying it.

Pure determination and will took over. Banishing any thoughts of failure, he found the words in his mind to reverse the frostbite mantra, and putting as much belief behind them as he could in his worn down state, he whispered them under his breath. A sharp prickling sensation overwhelmed his extremities briefly, and then it was done. Looking down at his hands, he found them... soft, smooth, nicely pink, almost brand new. Pulling his legs out from under the rough covers, he slung them over the side and dropped to the floor. His newly reformed feet sensed the cold of the mezzanine floor, and while he couldn't be described as in tip top shape, he felt better than he had in a while, ever since he'd been poisoned by that damn naga.

'Anyway,' he mused, 'no time to dwell on previous events. I have to leave as quickly and quietly as possible.' Checking the room for anything to wear, typically he found nothing. Remaining in his thermal base layers, a black skin tight top that had been cut off with a pair of scissors around the elbows, and black leggings that again had been cut off just below the knees, he looked like a ninja that had been in a fight with a combine harvester.

'Not inconspicuous at all,' he thought, allowing himself a brief smile. Sneaking a peek through the tiny panes of glass in the heavy wooden, double doors, he couldn't see a single person. Knowing that if he was caught now, the game would be well and truly up and he would almost certainly be detained by a huge number of medical staff, all wanting answers he couldn't provide, opening the door as far as he dare, he moved as fast as he could along the corridor, on the lookout for any sort of disguise. Suddenly, he heard voices from close by. Instinctively, he dived under one of the queue of unused beds that littered the wide walkway.

"Anyway, today's supposed to be another scorcher."

"Great, and here we are, stuck on theatre duty."

"Well, I for one can do without seeing anybody kark it again."

"Let's go see if we can prevent that, shall we?"

The two doctors, at least Flash assumed that's what they were, wandered down the corridor in the direction that he'd come from, their voices trailing off. Checking for any legs heading in his direction, he jumped out from under the bed and slipped into the room the doctors had come out of. Pumping his fist in triumph, he'd stumbled across a changing room, clearly used by the medical staff about to go into surgery; there were lockers, gowns, masks and special sandals. It was a positive treasure trove. In under thirty seconds he was kitted up in a green gown, a mask around his forehead, sandals on his feet, and a stethoscope for good measure that he'd found on top of one of the lockers drooped around his neck. Knowing that time was of the essence, he exited at a quick walk, heading away from the theatre and back to what he assumed was the main through route of the hospital. In his mind's eye he could see a very rudimentary map of its layout. Reaching the waste disposal area, which was located on Moore Street, a stone's throw from McIver train station, was his goal. The map inside his head told him he needed to get from the south block to the north block, which he could do on foot, via either Lord Walk, or Victoria Walk. His disguise should certainly hold until he got to the north block; after that, well... he wasn't so sure. He'd have to exit the northern precinct, head up Moore Street, and then cross it, quite a busy road at the quietest of times, and then reach the waste disposal centre. Dressed as a surgeon, he might stick out like a sore thumb for the last part of the journey, but he'd cross that bridge when he came to it.

Strolling purposefully into one of the main corridors,

he was relieved to see everything clearly and concisely signposted. Following the notices for the northern precinct, he tried desperately not to look as though he was unsure of where he was going. As he approached the Victoria Walkway on level 3, that would take him across Wellington Street and into the northern precinct, some sort of commotion broke out back in the direction that he'd come from. Still trying to look self assured, he stepped onto the walkway and glimpsed down at the traffic below him. On glancing back up, he spotted a big, burly security guard heading down the narrow, jam packed corridor towards him at full tilt. Within ten metres there were two beds with patients being pushed, as well as someone in a wheelchair, three nurses, two elderly couples and a porter. This was the very last place to make a stand and fight. Also, despite feeling better than he had, he was pretty sure he wouldn't last long in that department, against anybody. That and the fact that he was also out of tricks made him truly fearful of what was going to happen next. With the two nurses and the porter having moved swiftly aside, the guard was nearly upon him. From the look of the size and determination of the security officer, he knew instantly that he didn't stand a chance. Deciding not to make a stand, as this really wasn't the place for it, too many innocent people would get hurt, he opted to find another way to get the information to the king. Offering up his best smile, he put his arms harmlessly by his sides, opened palmed, and gave up. On doing all this, he realised just an instant too late that the guard had no intention of stopping, and was going to take him down the hard way. Closing his eyes, he braced for the oncoming impact. At the last instant, the man altered course, keeping up the same breakneck speed, catching Flash a glancing blow on the shoulder, sending him spinning to the ground. Sitting up on the cold, hard floor, he looked over his painful shoulder to see the man continuing on his run at top speed.

"Sorry... emergency," he shouted back over his shoulder, puffing frantically.

Shaking his head in wonder, he got to his feet.

'What are the chances...?' he wondered, as one of the nurses came to see if he was alright. Nodding to all the patients and staff, desperate not to attract any unwarranted attention and without looking at what commotion the guard was running towards, despite wanting to, he pressed on in the direction of the northern precinct, finding himself there in only a matter of moments. Skirting into the nearest stairwell, he knew he had to hurry. Part of him was convinced the commotion was all about him being missing and that it wouldn't take long for the guard to realise he was who they were looking for, once the nurses dished out his description.

Dashing down the stairs with as much speed as he could summon, he raced towards the nearest exit, having ditched the mask and stethoscope behind him. Casually, he walked past the reception desk, and through the sliding glass doors, which parted neatly at his approach. Inside, he felt dizzy and confused, but knew he couldn't let on, not here of all places. It would attract attention, with no doubt a hundred well intentioned nurses just waiting for him to show any kind of symptoms and escort him back into the building. Willing each foot to plod ever forward, he drew in a deep breath of cool, fresh air and tried to figure out where exactly he was. To his right was a huge car park that exited into a main road. Hoping to hell that the main road was Moore Street, he crossed the car park, every now and then peeking back over his shoulder. As he got closer, he could see a sign about halfway up one of the buildings. It read Moore Street. Buoyed by the thought that he was nearly there, another quick glance over his shoulder told him that it wasn't going to be quite that easy. Outside the hospital entrance, a young woman was pointing in his direction, while talking animatedly to a group of guards. Ripping off the surgeon's gown, and kicking off the sandals, he hoped that being in just his torn thermal base layers might buy him a few valuable seconds.

As a strong gust of wind blew the gown down the street, like tumbleweed in a Western, Flash leapt into the busy flow of oncoming traffic, not having time to make for a crossing or wait for an appropriate gap. Cars slammed on their breaks, tyres squealed, horns honked in dismay at his outrageous attempt to reach the other side. Weaving in and out of the vehicles and their irate drivers desperate to reach the waste disposal centre, he knew there was no point in looking over his shoulder, his vivid imagination already picturing a dozen or so burly men closing in, which in itself was spurring him on to greater deeds. In fact, he was almost at full sprint, and considering his condition, that was something of a feat.

Heart racing, his head thumped, while his legs pounded as he ran straight for the nearest door. A man was just exiting, and had opened the door right at the perfect moment.

"Hey!" he shouted. "You can't go in there. It's off limits to all but staff."

But Flash had already darted through and disappeared around a corner.

Three bulky guards pursued him into the waste disposal centre. Not quite sure why they were chasing him, they figured he must have done something wrong, that and the fact he was now inside a deeply restricted area and clearly running from them.

Meanwhile, the Crimson Guard was on the lookout for a huge industrial incinerator that he knew existed somewhere inside the facility. Buried deep within it was the emergency entrance to the dragon domain. If he was right, he was searching for an innocuous looking plate, that, if touched correctly, would move for just the briefest of moments and allow a human shaped dragon back into the underground world. Undoubtedly, the inside of the incinerator would be extremely hot and dangerous, no doubt full of toxic gases, contaminated needles, and other hazardous medical waste. These things were why this particular entrance was regarded as an emergency only access, at least that was his understanding. Very few of these existed, because there were so many other ways of returning back underground. But some did, thank God. He'd never really given it much thought before, but he did today, and wouldn't have made it to another safer one, that's for sure, and so this one, if he ever found it, might just save his life.

A dark haired woman wearing a lab coat and holding a clip board stepped out in front of him from an office off to one side. Her frown quickly turned into an angry look as she pointed at his chest with her free hand.

"Who are you? What do you think you're doing?" she asked snootily. "You're not allowed in here, you know. Remain where you are while I contact security," she ordered.

In a strange way, Flash was impressed. Even in his weakened state, he was a good deal taller than she was; his strength must have been obvious, as his bulging muscles were clearly visible through the ripped sections of the thermal base layers he was wearing, and yet here she was, fierce and defiant, ordering him to keep still and wait.

'Impressive indeed,' he mused, standing only a metre away. In different circumstances, he might have sought her out, got to know her. Unfortunately he really didn't have time for any of this, and much as it pained him to do it, and it really did, he had to take her out of the equation, now. Because of his training, he knew everything there was to know about human physiology. Every nerve, every muscle, every blood vessel, he knew them, more so than any other dragon, and even they knew an incredible amount. They had to, to perform and maintain the convincing mantras that held their human disguises in place. But Flash and his fellow Crimson Guards had an altogether different knowledge, about where to strike to kill, maim, incapacitate or inflict the most pain possible. Humans across time had done all these things to each other, different factions claiming that they had more knowledge and were better at it than others, but the truth was, the understanding Flash had gained throughout the years was far more intricate, detailed and dangerous than anything that had gone before it.

In the blink of an eye, the Crimson Guard decided what needed to be done, based purely on necessity, the little voice in the back of his mind playing its part as well, urging him not to hurt this fiery little human too much. Quick as a... flash, he let go with the sharpest and strongest punch he could. It connected with the dark haired woman just below the temple. Before she hit the floor, Flash caught her in his huge arms. Lowering her gently to the cold, hard surface, he rolled her onto her side and checked her breathing, before deciding to procure her lab coat. Quickly whipping it off her, slipping his arms through the sleeves as far as they'd go (not very far), he then sprinted off further into the heart of the disposal centre. It was a reasonably sized place, and he was just guessing where he had to go, following his gut feeling if you like. Reaching a junction in the corridor, he stopped momentarily. Pausing to catch his breath and estimate which direction he should go in next, he felt the hot stabbing pain of one of the spasms, start to creep up his back. Knowing time was of the essence, he darted left, the stolen, ill-fitting lab coat flapped about in his wake.

Meanwhile, the flurry of guards in hot pursuit had found the unconscious woman on the floor of the corridor. A brilliant purple nebula bruise had just started to blossom out below her temple. One of them stayed with her, while the other two continued to give chase.

Flash found himself in a corridor that was considerably darker than all the others. Through a series of glass windows, he could make out a room up ahead with a lot of computer monitors in. If he was right, and he hoped to goodness that he was, this would be the control room for the incinerator. Slowing to a walk, he crept along one side of the passage, sticking to the shadows, determined to confirm whether or not it was what he was seeking before he entered. While he could see some of the screens from where he was, a large part of the space was still obscured. Assuming there were people working in there, how many, he just didn't know, pressing his sweaty head up against the glass, he looked at the bank of monitors nearest to him. It took only a few seconds to comprehend that this was indeed the control room, and by the looks of things, the incinerator was just cooling down from having been used.

'Perfect,' he thought, turning his back on the glass. 'There should be some sort of access in there to the incinerator, even if it's just a maintenance hatch. All I have to do is overcome whoever is in the way, use the hatch, and then BAM, I'm back in the dragon world.'

Taking a deep breath, pushing the nagging pain in his back aside, he decided to stride purposefully into the room, size up the situation and then act... quickly, relying on the element of surprise and the fact that he could respond to the situation much faster than a roomful of human technicians. Keeping his head down, he strolled quickly down the corridor, turned right into the space, all the time poised to act. On entering, he found two people slumped over their keyboards right in front of him. Before he had time to figure out exactly what was going on, a rasping voice drifted out from behind a bank of computer servers that he'd already passed.

"I knew you'd head for this place. You dragons are so... predictable, just like the silly little humans."

Instantly, he whirled round, all the time aware of the nagging pain in his back. There, standing across from him, was a large, bald headed human, very tall and very strong from the looks of things, dressed in a green surgeon's gown similar to the one Flash had discarded earlier. All hope of returning to the domain with the information he'd gleaned, seeped out of him. Clearly the human in front of him was no such thing, and was instead almost certainly a naga, here to destroy him.

"I thought from what I'd been told that you'd be so much... more," rasped the naga, chuckling just a little. "Apparently you've caused a significant amount of trouble, even killing some of my race; no mean feat. And yet here you are before me, weak and pitiful. No match for any of us really. It must have been luck. What do you say?"

For the first time in his entire life, Flash was speechless; he had no remarks, no witty comments, no famous last words... nothing! All he could think of was how close he'd come to returning with the information, and how he would never find out what was really going on.

Without warning, the disguised shape sprinted towards him, diving at the very last moment. Despite all his training, the Crimson Guard couldn't avoid the collision. It was as though he were wading through the thickest, most viscous syrup, his arms and legs barely responding to his brain's commands. All he could do was make sure it was a glancing blow, rather than the full on contact the naga had hoped for. Gracefully, the disguised serpent rolled up onto its feet, while the contact sent Flash flying into a desk, smashing his head onto a large monitor that had subsequently fallen to the floor. Grinning confidently from across the room, the vile beast laughed.

'Do they all do that?' Flash thought, starting to get really disappointed.

Picking up one of the office chairs that littered the room, the naga hurled it at the Crimson Guard and then raced after it. At that exact same moment, the pain in the dragon agent's back flared up, attacking every nerve, every sinew, every muscle. Immediately his legs gave way and he crumpled to the floor, which in a way was good, as the flying chair missed his head by about a centimetre, smashing loudly into the wall behind him. His right knee cried out from the awkward landing, but with the pain in his back threatening to knock him out, he could devote it no attention. Then... his adversary was upon him, straddled across his chest, raining punches down onto his face. Automatically, he flailed about, trying to deflect the onslaught of blows, but any concentration that he may have had was constantly interrupted by the excruciating agony inundating his back. At most, he was only a few seconds from death.

As the monster continued to pummel Flash, two bulky security guards careered around the corner, determined to intervene. With a bloody, bruised and barely conscious Flash lying in the middle of the floor, the naga turned its attention to the two new arrivals. Leaping up, the beast planted an expertly placed kick right into the kneecap of the first guard to challenge him, forcing the guard to cry out in pain as a loud crack reverberated around the room. As he doubled over, the naga followed up with a roundhouse kick that was so powerful it took the man fully off his feet, throwing him over three metres into the air, smashing into one of the room's computer servers housed in a glass case in the corner. Breaking glass exploded as brilliant blue electrical charges zapped across the floor and the dead guard's body. With one down, the naga now turned its attention to the other, who had remained by the entrance to the room as it fought his colleague. Seemingly enjoying itself beyond belief, it beckoned with four fingers for the guard to bring it on.

Through all of this, Flash had only been able to catch glimpses of what was happening from his prone position on the floor, all the time wishing to God the pain in his back would subside, but it seemed to be worse than ever, showing absolutely no sign of abating. No matter how much he wanted to, and he did, he just simply couldn't move, and had resigned himself to watching yet another innocent human lose their life.

A terrified expression seemed ingrained on the guard's

face, understandable really when you consider what he'd just witnessed, his friend and colleague tossed around like a rag doll, killed in cold blood. Running wasn't really an option, something the naga seemed to sense. Another short fight appeared inevitable.

Lying on the cold floor, the pain in Flash's back lessened just a touch, enough for him to experience the hurt from the other injuries he'd suffered. Blood poured from his broken nose and a cut above his left eye, flowing down the side of his face, pooling beside him. Despite his cheeks being cut and probably broken, a familiar sensation prickled at his senses, nagging away at him. It was taking all his effort to stay conscious, but there was something about this, something important, something that could change everything.

Cautiously the security guard approached the very dangerous human being, a naga in disguise, who'd just killed his friend, baton in hand, ready to use. Laughing mercilessly at the pitiful weapon, and wanting nothing more than to get back and finish Flash off, the naga made the conscious decision to get this over with... quickly.

'It may take up to ten seconds,' the beast thought arrogantly as it prepared to strike.

And strike it did. Using all its power and speed, it launched itself at the terrified guard in one all out, deadly assault. From his position on the floor, even Flash had difficulty in keeping up with the action. Lamb to the slaughter, the petrified human had absolutely no chance. As the Crimson Guard forced himself to watch, sick and tired of all the bloodshed he'd seen on this mission, the single most bizarre thing happened. With the naga mid flight, about to tear his enemy in two, the expression on the guard's face abruptly changed from terrified to... smug.

'Odd,' wondered Flash through the incredible pain. All of this happened in roughly three hundredths of a second, and while the prostrate Crimson Guard had no real love for what humans called Grand Prix, in that instant, he did at least appreciate how things could go from good to bad and vice versa in such a small amount of time.

Not having spotted his supposed victim's facial expression, if the beast had done so, maybe it would have altered its tactics or at least felt a pang of fear. As it was, neither happened. If either had, it may have given the naga some kind of chance.

Hundredths of a second before it was about to make contact, the guard moved faster than any naga in history, bringing round his baton, and with the force of a small car, caught the monster full on in the throat, sending it spinning head over heels across the room. The sound of the impact sent shivers racing down Flash's spine as he lay on the ground, agog. It was a noise that would have given him nightmares for years had he been human. Before the naga could even sit up, the guard, or as Flash had finally come to realise, the dragon... in human form, was on it. Much in the same way as the naga had pinned Flash down and pummelled him senseless, the guard was returning the favour. Flash breathed a sigh of relief, not just because the pain in his back had started to become manageable, but at the sight of one of his fellow dragons. Once the guard had beaten the naga unconscious, he bound its hands and legs with plastic binders from his belt. Only then did he cross the room to Flash, by which time the Crimson Guard had managed to sit up, albeit rather unsteadily. He looked a right state, blood covering his face and clothes, with bruises and cuts all over.

In the spirit of friendship the disguised human offered out his hand.

"Sorry that took so long and that I didn't arrive earlier. I was on the far side of the complex when I got the call about it. It wasn't until you left the north precinct that I realised you were... one of us. By then you were nearly here, and I had company in the shape of the other two. Anyway, I'm Simon Stock, King's Guard."

Flash grasped the offered hand lightly.

"Pleasure to meet you Simon," he said, clearly struggling with the pain. "Dendrik Ridge, Crimson Guards, thanks for the save."

"No problem," replied Simon. "Wanna tell me what's going on?"

Silently, Flash contemplated what to do. He couldn't tell Simon everything and yet he needed to know exactly what he was dealing with, and after all, had just saved his life.

"All I can really tell you is that our psychotic friend over there is a naga, a very dangerous one by the looks of things, and part of a much bigger picture, if you get my drift. It needs to be locked up... securely, with as few dragons as possible knowing about it. This is as important as it gets and I'm sorry I can't say more, but everything I've told you is in the strictest of confidence. I don't doubt the king will be in touch over the next day or so with instructions as to what to do with it. And now, I really have to get back below ground. London beckons. I need to meet with the monarch as soon as possible."

"I understand, I really do," Simon added, wondering quite where he was going to secure the naga. "If you sit still for two minutes, I'll fix your injuries."

"How long do we have before anyone else arrives?" Flash asked nervously.

"Could be any moment really, but don't worry, I'll sense them before they get too close."

"I need to get below ground... it's important."

"Let me sort the worst of it out and we'll get you into the incinerator. It must be important if you're trying to use this entrance?" he enquired.

"More than you could ever begin to know," ventured the Crimson Guard, as Simon started to cast his healing mantras.

Flash could feel the wounds on his face healing right up, the bones in his nose and cheeks knitting back together, the swelling above and around his eyes returning to normal, and the cuts that littered his lips and forehead binding, so that not even a single sign of the battering that he'd taken at the hands of the naga remained. Despite all of this, he felt absolutely rotten. Rather than coming and going, the blistering pain in his back was constant, and felt like a raging fire. Worryingly, that sensation had started to spread to other parts of his body, namely his arms and legs. As well, he just had no energy. I don't mean no energy to run, jump or swim. I mean he simply wanted to concede defeat, curl up in a ball, never stand again, never take another pace, not possessing either the physical or mental strength to go on. Simon seemed to sense all this as he continued his efforts, and as well as healing all his wounds, offered up a significant amount of magical energy, something Flash gladly accepted, startling him out of his morbid thoughts, and producing a faint smile.

"Thank you," he whispered.

Abruptly, Simon stood up.

"They're coming," he uttered, a far off expression on his face. "We have to hurry."

Taking Simon's proffered hand, Flash let the other dragon help him to his feet and then followed him over to one side of the room. Pulling one of the undamaged computer servers aside, Simon revealed what looked like an old maintenance hatch.

"It'll get you in there okay," he added. "Just watch out for all the medical waste on the floor once you're in."

"Thank you."

"You're welcome," replied Simon. "Don't worry about naga boy here, we'll await the king's instructions and make sure he's totally secured. Oh and by the way, you should get somebody to look at the damage to your back, pretty damn quick."

Flash turned inquisitively to face him.

"Field medic, that's my normal role," said Simon, answering Flash's unasked question. "It needs attention, soon."

"I'll get it sorted," announced the dragon agent, climbing into the cramped maintenance tunnel.

"Good luck," shouted Simon, before securing the door back in place, and moving the computer server back to its original position. The other guards were only seconds away from the control room now.

'Aah, to use my imagination, and explain all this away. There are just some parts of my job I really hate,' Simon thought, still slightly in awe of meeting one of the legendary Crimson Guards.

Meanwhile, Flash had crawled steadily along the tunnel, passing through two more doors, following its mazy path until he dropped down inside the incinerator itself.

'Simon was right,' he reflected, looking across the floor that was scattered with all sorts of medical waste, despite the fact that it had been recently used, given away by just how hot it was. Scrabbling away through needles, syringes, rubber gloves and all sorts of glass and plastic, he eventually found what he was looking for. The metal plate didn't look very special at all, quite the opposite in fact. Shoving everything around it out of the way, he sought in his mind the instructions on how to act. In doing so, he became aware that the magical energy Simon had shared with him was being consumed at an alarming rate, his body clearly struggling in the fight against the poison. Urgently, he read the instructions in his mind, pressed down on the edges of the plate in certain places and waited to see if he'd done it correctly. Sure enough, a second or so later, a human sized hole opened up. Relief washed through him, taking away some of the pain temporarily, as he jumped feet first into the darkness, and began sliding to what he hoped was the conclusion of this nightmare mission.

8 MY KIND OF SCRUM

Just after lunch, Peter arrived at the sports club. Today his hockey team were playing away, but he'd come for a totally different purpose, here first and foremost to see Janice, but also to watch Tank play rugby and Richie play lacrosse. As he walked into the half full bar, he knew it would become busier as the day progressed, culminating in chaos at about 5pm when all the rugby, hockey and lacrosse teams that had been playing at home would come in along with all their opponents, as well as some of the away teams returning from their matches.

Standing at the quiet end of the bar, his fingers tingled, arms and legs weakened and his stomach auditioned once again for the Olympic gymnastics team. Lately, he tried to pay close attention to all the things going on within his pretend body, and today he'd found out something startling. After leaving home, the closer he got to the sports club, the more powerful the sensations had become. Now that he was standing there, it was all he could do to remain upright, the feelings were so overwhelming.

'Nothing makes any sense,' he mused, trying to catch a glimpse of Janice. Smiling to himself, he knew what Tank and Richie would say. At least he thought he did. The big fella would tell him to obey the strict dragon rules and leave all this behind. Richie would undoubtedly convince him that he'd fallen head over heels in love, hence the strange goings on within his body, and that he should follow his heart. For goodness' sake, he was a dragon, he had no heart, well he did, it just wasn't real, belonging to another race altogether. It was all so complicated, he felt like banging his head against a wall.

Suddenly soft hands swept around from behind and covered his eyes.

"Guess who?" whispered a squeaky voice in his left ear.

Feeling his heart rate quicken as a weak and wobbly

176

feeling shot upwards through his entire form, he responded with the first words that came into his head.

"Tank, how do you keep your hands so wonderfully soft?" he asked playfully, knowing full well it was Janice.

Before she could remove her hands, he grabbed them, turning around quickly to face her.

"Just kidding," he whispered, before she had a chance to be offended. "Hello gorgeous."

She popped up and kissed him slowly on the lips.

"You're cheekier than a field full of nudists."

Peter smiled.

"Thanks for a great night last night," he stuttered.

"Hmmmm... it was good, wasn't it?" she replied dreamily.

Slowly, she pulled away.

"Sorry, I've got to get back to work. They don't like members of staff fraternising with the customers, not when they're on duty, anyway."

"No problem."

"I finish at five, so what about a drink then?"

"Sure. I'm going to watch the ruby and the lacrosse so I won't be very far away."

"See you at five," she said, winking as she picked up some empty glasses before heading on through to the kitchen.

Realising that once again his stomach had gone somersault mad, his legs even weaker than before, he knew he needed to sit. Heading over to a table by the window, he flopped down and took a deep breath. Inside, he knew that he really shouldn't be doing any of this, but it just felt so... right.

Perched there mulling things over, he pulled his chair in as somebody moved into the seat directly behind him. That person leant back and bumped into his chair... twice. He ignored it.

'Some people are just so rude,' he thought. After a few more seconds, whoever it was did exactly the same thing again. Never normally able to say 'boo' to a goose, he'd had enough, and was about to tell the banging chair person exactly what he thought. As he whirled round, a grinning face greeted him, causing all his frustration to just melt away.

"She's soooooo pwettyyyy," teased Richie in a silly voice.

"Don't start," replied Peter firmly.

"But she is."

Peter just shook his head.

"Shouldn't you be getting ready for your match?" he asked, trying to change the subject.

"Unfortunately the opposition had to cry off."

Deciding not to make a joke of things, he had some idea of just how frustrated Richie would be.

"Sorry Rich, that's not very good."

"Oh well," she said rolling her eyes. "Just means I have to keep you company while we both watch Bulging Biceps over there do his thing," she added, nodding her head in the direction of the window.

Glancing out to see the home rugby team warming up together, Tank stood out like a sore thumb, his giant frame dwarfing most of his teammates, who were by no means small themselves. Richie leant back in her chair, put her head next to Peter's and quietly whispered into his ear.

"Right at the moment, how much does he look like the true Tank we've come to know and love?"

Gazing out at his pal, Peter recognised just how right she was. Standing amongst his teammates, stretching, flexing his muscles, socks rolled down to his ankles, Tank looked magnificent as he exhaled a frozen breath. With the bright sun glinting off his receding hairline, he looked incredibly similar to the giant dragon that they'd come to know as their friend.

"He could almost be atop Lava Falls, ready to leap off."

"Indeed," agreed Richie. "Anyway," she quipped,

standing up, "are we going to watch him play, or are you going to sit on your scaly backside for the rest of the afternoon?"

Grabbing drinks, the pair proceeded outside with their plastic glasses, taking their place in the small crowd of spectators already there. Propping themselves up against the metal railings that surrounded the muddy pitch, the friends' timing couldn't have been any better as the shrill sound of the referee's whistle got the match underway.

Sipping regularly from his drink, inundated with huge cubes of ice, something quite ironic given the temperature, he marvelled at the action going on in front of him. When Richie had encouraged both of them to try different sports, she must have had some inkling of which ones would appeal. Of course he'd taken to hockey like a dog to sniffing bottoms, Tank likewise with rugby. Looking out across the pitch at his friend, already covered from head to toe in mud, despite the fact that the match was barely a few minutes old, it was evident that the plant and animal loving apprentice was a natural player, and obviously felt the same about rugby as he did about hockey.

The first scrum of the match jolted Peter out of his musings. Tank, as prop, took his place in the front row, his big strong arms wrapped around his teammates, before the two sides slammed into each other. Unconsciously, Peter winced at the thought of being in the scrum, despite knowing his dragon physiology would offer him some protection. Quickly, he scrolled through the variety of different visions available to him, finally settling on the one used to detect even a hint of magic. Glancing across at his giant friend who, right at this very moment, was pushing the scrum forward almost singlehandedly, he was bowled over by the heroics on offer, his mantra vision confirming beyond any doubt that no secret abilities were involved at all. Switching his sight back to normal in the blink of an eye, he turned to look at Richie who was staring intently at him.

"It's okay," she said. "We've all done it."

"Done what?" he replied innocently.

"Checked to see if everything's... dragon free."

"Ohhh," he sighed. "It's not that I don't trust him," whispered Peter, nodding in Tank's direction.

"I know," confirmed Richie, rolling her eyes. "Remember that hockey match you played against Manson?"

A rolling wave of nausea threatened to engulf him momentarily. Quickly he shook it off.

"What about it?"

"I checked you out with my mantra vision while you were still playing."

"Really?"

"Of course."

"And?" Peter asked indignantly.

"Oh come on Pete, don't go all grumpy on me. You know full well I didn't find anything amiss, because it would never occur to you to cheat and use your..." Richie leant in a little closer, "...differing species abilities."

Chuckling at the way his friend chose to phrase her words, he let her continue.

"Besides," she said, a stern look on her face, "don't try and pretend you haven't at least once checked up on me to see if I was abusing my... position."

Feeling he had to come clean, he knew he'd never fool her anyway.

"Maybe just... once," he uttered sheepishly.

She laughed, before taking a huge gulp of her frothy lager from the flimsy looking plastic glass she held. Having turned his attention back to the rugby, Peter could see that the scrum had turned into a ruck, or as he preferred to think of it... a mud covered skirmish. How there weren't more serious injuries in the game, he had no idea. Both teams were going at it hammer and tongs, crunching tackles on players who'd just released the ball, thundering charges, players diving over the ball into an oncoming mass of opponents. Finally the referee blew his whistle to signal a penalty to the opposition, much to Peter's relief, as it was only then that he realised he'd been holding his breath, the action had been so compelling.

Hearing the referee explain to the Salisbridge players that the penalty had been for an offside to the blind side, much to the disagreement and disappointment of them all, he looked on as the away team quickly took the penalty, trying a cheeky chip over the top, but the Salisbridge defenders were all switched on and alert to the danger, negating the threat posed, starting their own sizzling counter attack in the process. Both friends watched in awe as the odd shaped ball was played out wide on the far side of the pitch, the winger eventually being forced back inside, well into the opposition's half. Having weaved and dodged with outstanding dexterity, the winger finally succumbed to a well timed tackle by a very tall and thin opponent, with the play again breaking down. Through the crowd of players, he could just make out Tank's considerable bulk piling forward. With the tackled player having just released the ball on the ground, Tank was first to reach it, scooping it up with just one of his giant hands, pulling it into his chest and vaulting over the downed winger. Opponents converged on him like ants on a sticky sweet, stuck to the pavement. Still he remained upright, the ball clutched firmly to his filthy chest. Richie pumped her fist in the air, careful not to spill her drink, and shouted,

"Go on Tank, show them how it's done."

Peter shook his head, and then quickly buried it in his thick, warm coat, embarrassed by his friend's outburst.

Meanwhile their huge pal had managed to palm off a few opponents, while at the same time shaking free the one on each leg. With the burden of clinging rivals relieved, albeit temporarily, he broke into a sprint, determined to score a try. Unfortunately for him, one adversary remained firmly planted in his way. Tank dropped his broad shoulders, in an attempt to sell the dummy, but the defender was having none of it, and tackled the man mountain of a Salisbridge player with all the ferocity of a great white shark with a sore tooth. Fortunately, just as the disguised dragon realised his bluff hadn't come off, he spotted one of his teammates out of the corner of his left eye, just slightly behind him. Instantly he unfurled the ball from his chest and managed to offload it to his colleague, just as the opponent ploughed into him with a sickening crunch.

On the sideline, Peter once again winced, and then tried to peer through numerous bodies to see if his friend was okay, but to no avail. The pass that Tank had made had been gathered in by his teammate and converted into a try, as the big fella continued to lie in a heap with the defender in the mud, seven metres from the try line. Eventually the bodies in the way cleared just long enough for Peter and Richie to see the defender stagger to his feet, a smug grin etched across his dirty, deformed and beaten face. Peter, who'd been holding his breath again, exhaled into the cold winter air as his pal finally rose up, albeit slightly dazed and confused. In an instant, the Salisbridge physio was by his side, checking out not only his vision, but a huge lump that had appeared on the top of his right cheek. Although he knew it was nigh on impossible for Tank to be seriously hurt, Peter remained deeply concerned for his friend, even after the physio left the pitch and play resumed with Salisbridge successfully kicking the conversion to go 7-0 ahead.

As the sides took their positions for the restart, Peter glanced over his shoulder at the hockey match taking place on the Astroturf, just beyond the frozen lacrosse pitch. A disconcerting shudder rattled down his spine. Images from the horrific, icy cold, November evening he'd spent as Manson's prisoner flashed before his very eyes. As the terror filled moments in which he'd almost died replayed in his head, it was all he could do to hold back the tears. Immediately a comforting arm slinked around his shoulders, pulling him in close.

"It's alright Pete, it's over. Manson's gone, never to be seen again. You know that," she whispered, understanding exactly what he was feeling.

Wiping his eyes with the back of his hand, sniffing as he did so, he felt so... embarrassed... ashamed... frightened. Knowing he'd caught the attention of the other spectators, he decided he just didn't care.

"Sorry Rich," he finally managed to splutter. "Seeing the pitch again like that, on a Saturday, just brought everything flooding back."

"You don't have to apologise Pete. It frightens me to think back and realise we could have lost you that night, despite the fact you were only a stone's throw away from both me and Muscles over there. Looking back on things, it makes me feel weak, helpless and vulnerable, knowing there was nothing I could have done to stop you going through all that. I've felt for a while that it should be me apologising to you, for not knowing you were in danger. Despite all Manson's special talents, I still should have been there. I'm pretty sure Tank feels the same way."

Peter wiped even more tears away from his wet, chilly face.

"It's like a nightmare Rich. I thought I was over it. I had a few bad dreams for a couple of weeks afterwards, but since then, I've not really thought about it, but just seeing the pitch again was enough to trigger a reaction. Everyone keeps reiterating that it's over and that's the end of it for me, but is it really? Somewhere in the back of my mind there's a little niggling voice that keeps telling me I'm still in some way connected to it all and that I might get dragged back into whatever's going on. Sometimes it makes me want to go and live wholly underground, and I never thought I'd hear myself say that."

Richie pulled back, flabbergasted.

"My God Pete, I hadn't realised it was that bad."

He just nodded, not knowing what else to say or do.

With more warmth than the hottest of dragons, she embraced him, pulling him in close to her with both arms. As she did so, she whispered very quietly into his ear.

"It WILL be alright. You will ALWAYS have Tank and I, and the way things are going, I'd say a human girlfriend... result!"

A smile spread across his sad face, all thoughts of his ordeal banished, for now at least.

"You always know the right thing to say," he declared with a wink.

Richie nodded, before both friends returned their attention back to the third member of the trio, eager to see how the rugby match was panning out.

It didn't take long to figure out that the whole match had been turned on its head. Salisbridge were very much on the back foot, with Tank limping as he ran to catch up with the ball, Peter noticed, sorry for the interruption his outpouring of emotion had caused. Richie leant over and chatted to the spectators further along, returning to inform him that the score was now 7-6, with the opposition having scored from an open play drop kick, as well as a penalty kick. On top of which, they'd been using some very underhand tactics apparently. Both friends continued to watch the Emporium worker hobble about, knowing that not only was he suffering with an injury to his leg or ankle by the looks of things, but that he was almost certainly outraged at the opposition resorting to a whole catalogue of dirty tricks. They both knew he would give everything he had to turn things around on the pitch, much as they would in either of their respective sports.

With the opposition having a clear foothold in the game, the home side seemed to capitulate more and more as the half wore on. Tank found himself on the end of a couple of nasty uppercuts from the opposing prop while in the scrum, twice in succession, both of which were missed by the officials. Peter shook his head when the score reached 7-20, barely able to watch the action, if that's what it could be called. Thankfully for the players and spectators alike, the referee finally blew for half time, allowing the home side a much needed rest and revision of tactics, whilst the freezing spectators found respite from the cold and were able to top up their drinks.

Staring out through the windows of the cosy clubhouse, queuing at the bar with Richie, Peter watched as the bedraggled band of Salisbridge rugby players got a right royal rollicking from their coach. Deflated was the only word he could think of to describe them right now. To a man, they all looked ready to throw in the towel, even his man mountain of a friend, who was usually the most optimistic and upbeat person he'd ever met. Part of him couldn't blame them... freezing cold, covered from head to toe in mud, bleeding from legs, arms, head, fingers, etc. They were a mess. Peter, very selfishly he realised, didn't particularly want to go back out to watch the second half and witness the beating, not just in terms of score, which was so obviously coming his friend's way.

Tapping him on the shoulder, Richie handed him a fresh drink.

"Thanks."

"You're welcome. Better watch out though, babe magnet," mocked Richie, nodding in a certain direction.

Turning to follow her look, he had but one thought.

'Ah Janice.' Richie stepped back a little as the gorgeous bar worker nuzzled up to Peter, whispering to him as she carried a near impossible stack of glasses.

"Still okay for later?"

"Of course."

"Good," she added, smiling profusely, before pecking him on the cheek and disappearing into the crowd.

Just as Richie opened her mouth to say something, he beat her to it.

"Not a word, not one single word."

Grinning from ear to ear, she was just pleased deep down to see him happy. Both of them joined the rest of the supporters and headed back outside, sensing more than a little pessimism amongst the crowd, mainly made up of home fans. So wanting Tank to do well, realistically Peter just couldn't see it happening. As the chaotic horde slowed up to squeeze through the double doors that led outside, a very grumpy and stressed looking figure forced his way through from the outside, bumping into people heading in the opposite direction, spilling a couple of drinks without even a hint of an apology, showing absolutely no manners whatsoever. Peter could see Richie about to take the rude man to task. Instantly, he grabbed her and stopped her from doing it, allowing him to pass unhindered. She was not happy at his intervention.

"What exactly do you think you're doing?" she demanded.

"You can't just go off at him. Do you know who he is?"

"Yeah," she replied angrily. "He's the chairman of the sports club. So what?"

"I don't think letting him have it with both barrels is a very good idea. Do you?"

"He shouldn't be immune to showing some manners, quite the opposite in fact. If you hold a position of responsibility like that, then you should carry yourself with some dignity and pride. This place is always full of kids and teenagers and I don't think anyone should act that way and get away with it. What sort of role model is he to the youngsters, eh?"

As they both hit the bitingly cold air outside, Peter carefully considered her words.

"Sorry. You're right of course. Want me to come with you to find him?"

"I don't think that's really necessary, do you? If you stop me like that again, I'll snap you like a twig," she joked.

"Understood," he replied, knowing when he was beaten.

Leaning against the barrier, the two friends found

themselves in pretty much the same place they'd been for the first half, as they waited for the ref to restart the match. It didn't take long.

Salisbridge were out of the blocks like a jet fighter fuelled on pure adrenaline. Whatever the coach had said to them at the break had certainly got them going. As he witnessed yet another ferocious tackle from one of the home side's players, Peter wondered how long they could keep up this high tempo, and whether they could all remain injury free. Looking on, he could see that each and every one of Tank's teammates were focused only on getting the ball, performing to their maximum and getting themselves back into the match, and he knew from playing hockey that you were more likely to get hurt going in for a challenge half heartedly than going in fully committed. It was almost as if the Salisbridge players were reborn, they were so totally different from their first half display and leading them by example, throwing himself in harm's way almost constantly, was the big fella, their friend. Watching his pal, back to his normal self, a steely glint in his eye, he knew at that precise moment that his prediction about Salisbridge losing the match couldn't have been further from the truth.

Right now one of the opponents had the ball, looking to kick it long. With a Salisbridge player bearing down on him, he must have panicked just a little because he sliced his kick wildly. One of the home side's wingers was on it in an instant, gathering it in and charging off down the pitch, taking out half of the opposition in one swift move. The rest of the side gave chase, hoping to offer support, but he was miles ahead of everyone, everyone except Tank. With only two opponents to beat, the winger dropped his shoulder one way and speedily swerved the other. Not having been totally fooled by the dummy, his opponent managed to recover enough to grab hold of the winger's ankle, just as he'd thought he'd got past. As he started to stumble to the ground, he just about managed to offload the ball to Tank who was motoring along just inside him. Keeping his eyes on the ball, despite it spinning wildly, the plant and animal loving dragon gathered it in cleanly as he ran, avoiding the flailing opponent on the floor as he did so. Clutching the ball tightly to his chest, he glanced over his shoulder, pleased to see that no one from behind was in a position to catch him. Turning his attention to what was ahead, he had a sudden feeling of déjà vu. Standing in his way was the opponent with the smug grin, the one who'd injured him in the first half and the one that had punched him twice in the scrum. As Tank approached like a huge out of control runaway boulder crashing down the side of a mountain, his opponent still wore the same smug smile.

Tank had already decided on a course of action, pouring on as much speed as he had left, the muscles in his legs burning with pain from the effort. As the distance between them closed, the opponent's grin wavered. Not sure what to do, the opposing defender mirrored Tank's moves, jinking first left, and then right, before going left again. Knowing the defender was more than a little off balance, Tank put his head down and, wrapping both hands tightly around the ball, pumped his legs as fast as they would go, gasping for breath as he did so. An instant too late, the defender cottoned on to what was about to happen, but being just slightly off balance there wasn't a chance of him doing anything about it. Tank ploughed through the defender, catching him full on in the stomach, sending him some two metres into the air. A splintering crack, like the sound of a gunshot, echoed across the pitch as the two collided. Crossing the line, the disguised dragon placed the ball down on the turf directly beneath the posts, the welcoming squelch of the defender landing awkwardly in the mud brought a smirk to his face. Raising his hands above his head in delight, the young dragon lapped up the applause from the small crowd, including both Richie and Peter. By now his teammates had caught him up, enveloping him as a group, patting him on the back and ruffling what little hair he had left.

'None of this kissing and cuddling here,' Peter thought, 'unlike in all the football on the television.' Why footballers who know they're going to be filmed celebrate in quite the way they do, he just didn't know.

Causing a five minute delay to proceedings, the smug defender had to be helped from the pitch by two of his team's substitutes and their physio. The match resumed with Salisbridge putting away the conversion, much to the delight of the spectators, who now had something to cheer about. The home side were now very much in the ascendancy with the score at 14-20.

Play continued with Tank's team trying their hardest to break down the opposition and gain the much needed points they needed to win, but without much luck. They had a few drop goal attempts, which didn't really trouble the posts very much, along with two penalty kicks, both within range, each going agonisingly wide. The crowd, along with the two friends, were becoming frustrated in much the same way as the players. If it hadn't been for the smug defender crying like a baby as the physio escorted him into the changing rooms, they would have had nothing at all to smile about.

Both sides having made their final substitutions with ten minutes to go, the match became even scrappier, to the disbelief of the onlookers. Peter and Richie drained their plastic glasses dry, both tossing them over three metres into the air, landing them squarely into a bright blue bin set up beside the pitch, much to the amusement of several bystanders. Both smiling at each other, each with but one thought.

'If only they knew everything else we were capable of.'

Turning their attention back to the muddy skirmish, the two friends shouted encouragement in Tank's direction, but whether or not he could hear it was something else entirely.

Towering high into the air on the halfway line on the opposite side of the pitch, the fancy new electronic timer showed that only three minutes remained. It looked as if time had run out for the home side to get anything out of the game, thought Peter, shivering ever so slightly, all the time rubbing his hands together. Feeling for his buddy, knowing that he'd be gutted to lose, particularly to such unsporting opposition, all he wanted to do at the moment was go and warm up inside the club house; he really didn't care who won or lost at this point. Tank, it had to be said, had other ideas. His body ached beyond belief. In all the time he'd played this action packed, adrenaline fuelled, mightily addictive sport, he'd never hurt this much. NEVER! He knew he'd done something bad to his right ankle and really wasn't looking forward to taking his boots off. On top of that, his left shoulder felt badly bruised, and as for his left ribs, well he struggled to pull in a full breath, and couldn't stand upright without nauseating waves of pain pulsing through them, not to mention the cuts and almighty bruises lining his face and the huge lump on the top of his right cheek.

'All in all,' he reflected, 'not one of my better days.' Catching his breath in the momentary respite before another line-out, he decided there and then that these dirty, cheating... opponents (even in his mind he couldn't say the word that most others would have used to describe their antics), weren't getting away with it, not while he could still stand, even if he had to tear up the entire pitch and bring the try line to the ball. They were simply not going to win, there were no two ways about it. However he did appreciate that with a little under three minutes left on the clock, it would need something very special to turn the match around, and would probably involve a huge slice of luck. Straightening up, ignoring the mind numbing pain that came with the move, he wandered over and assumed his place in the line-out, focused solely on getting a hold on the ball.

Right hand gripping the ball like an eagle clutching a fish, the Salisbridge hooker was poised to throw it straight down the line of opposing forwards, but as he drew it back behind his head, he gave Tank a little wink. Immediately the disguised dragon knew this was it, the chance he'd been looking for. As the hooker released the ball straight down the line, at exactly the height Tank had been expecting, having practised this over and over again, the man mountain of a dragon wrapped in a human body jumped with all his might, one of his gigantic hands plucking the beautiful oval out of the air, before falling back onto the muddy surface, his damaged ankle nearly giving way with the bone shuddering impact. Holding one opponent at bay with his free hand, he sprinted for all he was worth around the back of the forward line, shaking off the opponent and headed deeper into the middle of the muscle sapping pitch. On doing so, he found himself directly level with the electronic timer. It loomed over him like a dark, prehistoric dinosaur about to strike, the brightly lit numbers standing out like piercing, fluorescent eyes. In a fraction of a second he read the display, his mind registering that he had less than ninety seconds to turn defeat into victory. Ignoring the agony slicing through his body, he found solace in noticing out of the corner of his eye that his friends were still watching him from the sideline. Stretching the huge muscles in his neck, he put his head down and charged for all he was worth past a row of his own players, determined to score and win the game for his team.

In the few seconds since the line-out, Peter and Richie suddenly became more alert, and less interested in going inside to get warm. Both of them sensed simultaneously that something had changed, and that things were about to get very... interesting.

Head down, running at full tilt, Tank had already thundered two members of the opposition out of the way and was busy weaving between the next two, the rest of the home team in hot pursuit.

Leaning against the metal rail that surrounded the pitch, the very last thing Peter currently felt, was cold. Nervous, excited, hopeful, barely able to look... he was all of these things, but most definitely not cold. Tank was brushing off opponents like they were children, and had everyone watching, spellbound. The crowd had collectively inhaled, and were now holding their breath, waiting to see how things would pan out.

Tears streamed down the big fella's face as one of the opposition grabbed his damaged ankle. Gathering all the pain up in his mind, he sealed it in a brightly coloured box deep inside his psyche, something dragons were taught to do in the nursery ring at a very young age. Still within his mind, he tossed it into the furthest recesses, watching it disappear off into the darkness, and then back with his body, wriggled free of the defender. Continuing his selfless charge towards the try line, he was careful to make sure that none of his dragon abilities bubbled to the surface in an effort to help him, so while he'd been taught that little trick with the pain during his youth, he didn't consider it part of his array of magic, or a particular dragon feature that would give him an unfair advantage. Like his friends, he was as honest as the day was long when it came to any kind of cheating within his chosen sport.

Richie and Peter had seen their pal do astonishing things whilst growing up, but the display he was putting on here and now made Peter wonder if he'd seen anything from his friend that was quite so amazing.

Things had started to blur around the edges of Tank's vision.

'Not a good sign,' he thought, as he pushed ever further into the opposition's half. The good news was that some of his teammates had nearly caught up with him; the bad news was that nausea washed over him in giant waves, so badly that he feared he would pass out at any second. But he knew if he did, any chance of winning would be lost forever. Suddenly his brain registered that he was in a lot of trouble. Three opponents were converging on him all at once, with absolutely no way to avoid being tackled. Bringing his head up just slightly, he glanced over his left shoulder. Sure enough, Speedy Ian, the Salisbridge winger, was galloping down the flank like a racing thoroughbred. Tank waited until he could see the whites of his opponents' eyes, something made even harder by the problems with his vision. The three of them knew that the hulking great opponent had nowhere to go, and were oblivious to anything else around them. All they knew was that they were going to take him down... BIG TIME! With them all just fractions of a second away, Tank, without looking, threw the ball high up into the air over his left shoulder, and then dived down onto the churned up ground. All three opponents were left stunned as they helplessly watched the ball fall directly into the path of Speedy Ian. Worse was to follow, as they all tripped over Tank's prone body at speed and at exactly the same time, causing them all to pile up into each other with bone chilling thumps.

On the ground, Tank wheezed in pain from the falling opponents, all of whom had made contact with his ribs and back to one degree or another. With a Herculean effort he forced himself to his feet, determined to see it through and make sure his team got the try their hard work fully deserved.

On the sideline, the spectators still collectively held their breath, waiting to see if their side could do the impossible with only seconds remaining.

Willing his battered and bloody body to move, Tank took off after Speedy Ian and the rest of the Salisbridge attack. Through his ever diminishing eyesight, he could just make out the winger being tackled, with the attack turning into a ruck about three metres short of the try line. His body moved on autopilot as he joined his teammates in what he knew to be the final seconds of the sporting skirmish. The ball came fizzing out of the ruck quicker than he would have thought possible, back to one of the forwards who, surprisingly, rather than run towards the line, threw the ball straight back to him. Clearly the forward's brain must be addled, because if he looked only about a tenth as bad as he felt, then no one in their right mind would have passed him the ball. Tank's bloodied, numb, frozen fingers seized the glistening odd shaped oval, before his mind even registered it. Unable to take a painful breath, something grabbed him around the neck, forcing him to the ground. Above the impact of smashing into the soggy grass, and the subsequent face full of mud, Tank heard the referee's high pitched whistle nearby. In an attempt to win the game and waste time, their opponents had given away a deliberate penalty. Rolling over, trying hard to make his giant, tree trunk-like legs work, Tank glanced over towards the electronic timer. The fluorescent numbers dazzled his broken eyes. There were eighteen seconds left, eighteen seconds to do the impossible. Staggering to his feet with the ball on the ground in front of him, he took everything in. He was standing off to the left hand side of the pitch, some five metres away from the try line that he so desperately needed to get to. Glancing around, his teammates looked worse than he felt, which was saying quite something. To a player, Salisbridge had given their all. More to the point though, was that they looked as though they'd already lost, a feeling that was creeping up inside him. That is until he looked up into the faces of his opponents between him and the line, all looking like they'd... won. A primal, unjust rage roared from somewhere deep inside. It powered every muscle, every sinew, and wrapped itself throughout his broken body, as it screamed,

"I will not be defeated by you!"

Instantly Tank picked up the ball and kicked it to himself. Clutching it to his well defined chest and gritting his teeth, he picked his path and started to run. Most of the opposition were busy slapping each other on the back, having already mentally prevailed. Only a handful were aware of what was happening, and all of them closed in on the disguised dragon, eyes filled with malice for what he was about to attempt. The Salisbridge players watched aghast at what the young dragon was trying. What else could they do? There were just a handful of seconds left now; the game, for all intents and purposes, was over. While he hadn't achieved quite enough momentum to reach what he considered to be his full speed, he was certainly moving quite quickly, something the first opponent to reach him found to his cost, as he bounced clumsily off Tank's right shoulder. As the primal fire burned brightly within, he could just make out the try line through the mass of bodies and limbs that stood in his way. Able to identify every blade of grass, every tiny fleck of paint, through just the centre of his eyes, his peripheral vision was just a dull blackness. A tiny smile stretched across his beaten face, as he knew in mere moments he was going to smash the ball down on that wonderful scuffed up piece of turf. Deep inside his head his mind screamed at him,

"NOW!"

As everyone watched, he knew exactly what he had to do.

Mid run, he put all his effort into jumping, and leapt for all he was worth, his knees protesting beyond belief, but they held firm and helped him get the launch he needed. Not a light fellow, quite the opposite in fact, he did have muscles made of his favourite laminium ball player... STEEL! And when he wanted them to work, boy did they do just that. With opponents rushing towards him, even they were too shocked to react as he sailed between their heads, ball held firmly out in front of him, concentrating on nothing more than putting it down across that sacred line. Time stood still for Tank, who savoured the shocked and distressed faces of the unscrupulous players he and his teammates had been battling against for nearly eighty minutes. Abruptly, things speeded up as he found himself hurtling towards the ground at quite a rate, knowing beyond any doubt that his landing was not going to be pleasant. How right he was. The ball, followed closely by the big fella's all but numb fingers, and then the rest of him, hit the grass just the other side of the try line. Tank tumbled head over heels, his body having finally reached breaking point. As his eyes started to close, he could just make out the referee's whistle shrieking through the air and knew that it had all been worthwhile.

Along with all the other home supporters, Peter and Richie screamed their heads off as the referee blew his whistle, signalling that Tank had scored the try of his life. To a man, the home side went mad, jumping up and down, hugging each other, high fives, fist bumps... the lot. That is until they realised that Tank hadn't moved since he'd hit the turf. Instantly the physio was at the man mountain's side, hurrying his teammates out of the way. Richie and Peter looked on anxiously, worried for their friend. While all this happened, the official in charge blew his whistle for full time, but the match was not finished yet. With Tank's try, the game stood at 19-20, but if Salisbridge managed to kick the conversion, they would win 21-20. It was a nail biting finish to a very unusual game. After the most tense three or four minutes both teams had ever experienced, Tank was finally helped to his feet by the physio and three of his teammates. With his arms around their shoulders, he managed to get back to the home side's dugout and sit down. Silence enveloped the pitch, the crowd and the players, as Hatchet Hammond placed the ball on the ground, directly in front of the posts. Tank knew the kick should be a sure thing, but with all the waiting around, even he could feel the pressure his teammate must have been under. Having taken a few steps back, Hammond made his run up, kicked the ball cleanly and watched it fly straight between the posts. Turning around towards his own dugout, he took a bow. With the exception of Tank and the physio, the whole team sprinted over to Hammond and mobbed him. Peter, Richie and the rest of the crowd cheered wildly as the ball sailed between the sticks, the referee signalling the conversion had been good, with the game finishing 21-20 to Salisbridge.

Taking a very shallow breath, as that was pretty much all he could do, a deep seated satisfaction washed over him as he observed the opposition trudge off towards their dressing room. All he could think was that they got exactly what they deserved. Gingerly he got to his feet, and with a little help from the physio, he followed the rest of the squad into the changing rooms, hoping that the celebrations which he knew would follow, would not be beyond him. As he left the pitch, Richie and Peter waited anxiously by the door to the building, determined to check on their friend's wellbeing. As Tank approached, he shook off the physio and hobbled over to them. Richie opened her mouth, but before she could utter a word, the big rugby player waved away her concerns.

"I'm fine guys... honest," Tank puffed, looking like he'd been thrown to the lions.

Richie looked up into his wreck of a face, examining each and every bruise that crisscrossed it, before leaning close and whispering in his ear.

"Do you want me to cast a quick healing mantra?"

Tank shook his head, surprised by the level of pain the small movement sent shooting down his back.

"Thanks for the offer Rich, but I'll struggle through for now and then cast one on myself when I get home."

"Sure?" she asked.

"Sure," he replied, managing the faintest of smiles.

Tank looked across at Peter, who stood, arms folded, next to the door, unconvinced by his pal's claims of being fine.

"As you know, I'm not really a rugby fan, but that was... FANTASTIC!" he announced.

"Yeah," replied Tank dreamily. "I can honestly say I've never played in a game quite like it."

Peter smiled, recognising in Tank the same dedication that both he and Richie had to their respective sports.

"Anyway," said the big fella, clutching at his clearly painful ribs, "you'll have to excuse me, I desperately need a shower, and a beer afterwards. So I'll see you in the bar shortly." With that, he turned and limped off.

Both friends made their way through to the pleasantly warm interior, with the rest of the evening turning into a pretty much normal Saturday for them. Of course, it was normal for when Peter was playing hockey, something he hadn't done in months, and was more determined than ever to return to full fitness and participate in the remaining games of the season for the second team. It wasn't long before the three friends ended up playing rowdy games with the rugby teams, with Tim and Janice joining in for a short time. Peter found that for some reason, he was uncomfortable with Janice in front of his friends, something he hoped she hadn't picked up on. Whether or not it was the whole dragon relationship thing, he really didn't know, but vowed to think long and hard about it. Later that evening, they all left the sports club together, Janice heading home in her cherished pink mini, giving Peter a passionate kiss goodbye. Tim and Richie headed off in his BMW, not before Richie instructed Peter to make sure that Tank had cast that healing mantra on himself. Peter helped his huge friend climb into his car, rugby kit and all, and headed back to Tank's house to drop him off. During the journey, the rugby playing dragon cast a healing mantra that the hockey player had never heard of before, one that seemed to have amazing properties. While the bruising and damage to his face remained, Tank seemed to be well on his way to being healed, as he jumped out of the car, able to sling his rugby kit over his giant shoulders, something he certainly couldn't have done before. Waving his friend goodbye, watching him skip up the garden path with the huge kit bag, Peter smiled to himself, started the car, and headed for home, bowled over by the wonderful time he'd had in the company of not only his two best friends, but these thrilling humans as well.

9 PLANTING THE SEEDS OF DESTRUCTION

Climbing down the rusty ladder, the stench of waste assaulted his nose once more. Every time he did this he always found himself surprised that he hadn't yet got used to the smell.

'If I haven't by now, then obviously I never will,' he thought as he shut the hatch above, leaving him alone in the dark. Flicking the switch on his helmet, the bright white light from the lamp on top leapt into life. A brief rush of fear gripped him momentarily. It was the first time in the eleven years he'd been doing this that he'd been down this far alone. Normally, there'd be at least one other person with him, probably more. Not tonight though. Reaching the bottom rung of the ladder, he jumped the last metre, landing with a splash as his rubber boots hit the flowing river of waste. Taking a short shallow breath of the rancid air, he checked the backpack he carried to make sure it was secure. It was, thank goodness. Part of him was appalled at what he was doing, knowing full well that people would almost certainly die at some point in the future because of him. Unfortunately, a much bigger part inside really wasn't bothered. Nobody in this city liked or cared for him very much. His wife had left him for another man, and was living quite comfortably in a wealthy suburb even now. As he trudged along the murky sewer, even darker thoughts strangled his mind. His colleagues were... bullies. Not a day passed when he wasn't ridiculed or forced into doing something humiliating and for that he hated the lot of them. And with the money he'd collect for placing this... package, no not package... bomb, as that's what it was, the money would allow him to start a new life a long way from the city above his head... Chicago. In a few days he would hand in his resignation, leave for greener pastures, and know that he himself had played a small part in the new world to come.

Arriving at an intersection in the maze of sewers, he turned left, knowing that he'd nearly reached his goal. Ducking his head to avoid a cluster of smaller pipes running across his path, out of nowhere a huge lump of goodness knows what plopped onto the shoulder of the rubber suit he was wearing. Wearily wiping it off as he walked, no longer disgusted by it, just sick to the teeth of the whole damn sewer system, he finally reached his destination. Turning the light on his helmet towards a seemingly innocuous part of the wall that lined the tunnel, he rubbed his gloved hand along it until he found exactly what he'd been looking for. There it was, a brick amongst bricks, looking just like any other. But he'd found this one ten days before and it would bring him a new life, a chance to start all over again. It was a brick that would bring destruction raining down on this rotten city, one that somebody, only last month, had asked him to find. Reaching round into the side pocket of the backpack, he carefully unzipped it and pulled out a small, flat bladed screwdriver. Wedging the tip into the mortar around the brick, he started to wiggle it just a little, before doing the same on the other end, little by little, moving it out from the wall. Taking it nice and slowly, alternating ends, he made sure not to damage the mortar or leave any obvious marks on show.

For a month now he'd been on the hunt for exactly this, since the night he'd been drinking and chatting in a bar with a stranger, a red headed woman who'd bought him drinks all evening long and listened to his tale of woe. When he mentioned that he was a sewer worker, he got the distinct impression that she already knew. It was then that she offered him the deal, on behalf of someone else, allegedly, but he wasn't quite sure. Oh, not about accepting, but about it being on behalf of someone else. She looked troubling, no not troubling, but like...

TROUBLE! Anyhow, he didn't even have to think about the offer. With all that money, he'd be able to start afresh, with the added bonus of giving back to the city everything and more that it had dished out to him.

Nearly free now, carefully he grasped the brick with his gloved hand, and pulled it the last part of the way. Gently resting it down on top of his rubber boot, mindful of it being there, he placed the screwdriver back in the backpack and then retrieved from a bigger pocket the package that he'd come down here to plant. Very carefully he pulled it out and brought it round in front of him. Shining the light from his helmet onto it, he gently removed the plastic bag that he'd wrapped it up in. Its rustling echoed down the deserted tunnel making an eerie sound that mixed strangely with the constant dripping and the gentle flow of sewage beneath his feet. Reaching out to place the package in the gap behind the brick and complete the job he was being paid handsomely for, he hesitated just a little, not because of the consequences, but because he was desperate to see inside the box just one more time. Lifting its well worn lid, he was rewarded with a shiver of excitement that curled up and down his spine as he gazed down at the contents. Another box, this one black, metallic and waterproof, with a clear reinforced window, stared up at him. Through the tiny pane, glowing red numbers shone out like the bat signal on a cloudy night, in the dark, dank tunnel that he stood in. His fingers developed a strange tingle as he watched the red numbers slowly count down, able to imagine what would happen when they reached zero. For sure, he certainly wouldn't want to be anywhere near this place. His attention moved across from the ever changing numbers, past the coloured wires, and focused, as it had time after time, on the glowing ring of shining metal that sat at the very left hand edge of the device. That particular part was mesmerising, captivating, hypnotic almost, he could have looked at it all day long.

Letting out a small sigh, he closed it back up and very, very carefully slid it through the gap where the brick had been. With the box firmly nestled behind the wall, he set about carefully replacing the brick, determined not to leave any trace that it had ever come out.

'Nobody will find out what's coming to this city,' he thought, as he worked methodically at putting it back in place. It was only when he'd finished the job and stood admiring his handiwork in the light provided by his helmet, that he realised quite how nervous he'd been; his skin and hair were both caked in sweat and the rubber boots he wore were nearly full up from the inside. Satisfied that the brick looked no different from the millions of others running through Chicago's sewers, he trudged back the way he'd come, the thought of the biggest shower in the world waiting for him back at his apartment. All he had to do now was pick up the money. Everything was in the bag, so to speak.

On a small boat, aptly named 'Dragon's Destruction,' moored at a pontoon in Montreal, Canada, the sole occupant left the comfort of the cosy cabin where he'd been reading the local daily paper and headed aft, into the biting rain and cloying night air. It was 3am local time, and the moment had come for him to carry out his mission. He'd acquired the boat two months ago from a very shady fellow, who had unfortunately met an unsavoury end involving some plastic restraints, a gag and about a million hungry crabs. Shrugging his shoulders as he recalled the incident, he merely thought of it as poetic justice; after all, the guy in question was a smuggler and had been using the sea, and this boat to transport all sorts of illegal items into the United States for many years. The fact that the ocean and its inhabitants had got their revenge, merely amused him. Of course, he'd been instructed to buy a vessel capable of doing the job, but what was the point in that?

So he'd very casually helped the crooked individual into the sea with the crabs, watched for a while, acquired the boat and pocketed the money he'd been given. Of course he'd spent some of it on having the vessel re-sprayed and changed so that no one would recognise it, particularly the coastguard. It was a pretty good bet that the United States authorities in some capacity would have a record of this particular ship as it had been, and that would prove a major inconvenience if they should happen to interrupt this particular assignment. So now it was unrecognisable from the craft it once was, even the name, which he'd thought of himself and was quite proud of. One feature had been kept though: the smuggling compartments that the shady character had fitted. They were magnificent and the reason why this ship was the one he'd needed.

Wiping the rain from his eyes as he walked along the slippery deck, he glanced over at the deserted pontoon and quayside, hoping that it would remain that way. Reaching the back of the boat, he lifted the hatch that covered the entrance to the engine room, and mindfully climbed down the old wooden ladder. Closing it behind him, he flicked a switch on the wall and watched a tiny bulb to his right buzz into life. Strolling across the enclosed space, careful to avoid getting any oil or grease from the exposed machinery on his fashionable jeans and sweatshirt, he reached up and carefully pulled down the faded, black wetsuit and scuba gear that hung on the wall. Much as he knew how to use them, they would only slow him down tonight, and in any case they were more for show than anything else. Part of his cover was having a history full of diving experience. It would look pretty odd to the authorities if he was boarded and they discovered there was no diving apparatus aboard. Moving the equipment from the wall into the far corner only a metre away, he turned his attention to the oil stained, faded white wall behind where it had hung. Pressing each thumb to oil stains about a metre apart, he moved them along both blemishes simultaneously, one going up, one going across, all the time pressing down firmly. A tiny click, followed by a low sounding rush of air, preceded an invisible panel sliding out from the filthy partition, revealing a small, cushioned compartment. Reaching in, he pulled out a small metallic box, with a see through window, red numbers visibly counting down beyond it. Touching the end of the panel that had slid out he watched it dart back into place, hiding in plain view. Gathering up the container, he thought momentarily about replacing the scuba gear and wetsuit on the wall, but knowing that time was now of the essence, decided against it. In the cramped cubicle he stripped off all his clothes and placed them atop the wetsuit. Flicking off the light switch, he climbed the ladder in the dark, all the time clutching the oh so important package. Taking a moment to listen for anything unusual outside, quietly he lifted open the hatch and poked his head out to look around. With the coast clear, he vaulted up the last two steps onto the rain soaked deck, his naked body remaining entirely in the shadows. With a firm grip on the box, and a last check to make sure no one was watching, he sprinted to the rail and dived head first over it into the freezing ocean.

Sub-zero sea water assaulted every pore of his naked body in the murky, lightless environment, as he swam deeper into it. Reluctantly, he released his grip on the box, watching it tumble away towards the hidden depths, the bright red numbers shining for mere moments before becoming obscured by the dark.

Pulling his mind away from the pain cloying at his misshapen body, he sought out the necessary bonds that held his DNA in place, releasing them, feeling the rush from the change that followed. His awkward, human shaped body shimmered like a school of fish under attack as the genetic material inside him looked to find its true guise. In mere moments, it had. Awkward turned to sleek, sleek like a... naga. Gills pumped as he torpedoed his way through the water towards the very valuable container, which had not quite reached the bottom. Senses dampened down when he was in human form kicked in with a vengeance, allowing him to know exactly where it was in relation to everything in the ocean, for miles around. Two metres before tumbling to the rocky bottom below the pier, the pale green naga swept in and grabbed the water resistant case that held doom and destruction for so many.

Swimming like a menacing eel in and out of the limpet encrusted pylons that supported the wharf, he searched with his fishlike senses for the perfect place to plant the ticking time bomb, knowing that if he found the right one, it would be all but impossible for anyone but another naga to stumble across. Ten minutes later, he had it. Inside a long slender recess that wove up beneath the massive jetty itself and had a tiny air pocket halfway along, he found an uneven concrete ledge, which he deemed perfect for his purposes. Propping the box up so that it remained out of the water, he swam back to the sea bed, gathered up some weed, which he draped over the box, to disguise it in the unlikely event that anyone should actually find themselves in the claustrophobic recess. Happy with his night's work, he headed back towards the boat, considering a celebratory swim, letting loose all his natural instincts. It took him only a split second to decide not to. After all, he was a consummate professional and knew that deviating at all from the plan could have unexpected and maybe even fatal consequences. Unhurriedly, he swam back to the boat, and just as he could make out the street lamps of the pier from beneath the surface, triggered the same bonds within him that he had earlier, only this time it was anything but a natural regression. He had to really concentrate, forcing the DNA to do his bidding, unlike the ebbing and flowing that had taken place only minutes earlier. When the human form had settled into place, he broke the surface and quietly gulped in large mouthfuls of air. Paddling noiselessly to the aft of the vessel, he climbed the steps leading out of the water, and using the shadows for cover, slinked over to the hatch, making his way inside once more before closing the cover, safe in the knowledge that he'd completed another task, another in a long line that would eventually free his leader, or at least that's what he'd been led to believe. Happy he'd planned everything down to the final detail, it was only when he flicked on the light that he discovered he'd left out one very important thing... to bring a towel. Dripping wet and shivering insanely, he snorted with laughter at his own inadequacy, long into the remaining night.

In the small village of Wang Chan, Thailand, a local cattle herder stopped along the edge of a disused paddy field, gently placing his bike on the ground, before retrieving a badly wrapped parcel from the back of it. A tattered string encompassed the torn, faded paper that covered whatever was inside, many times over. Desperately wanting to unwrap it and check out the contents for himself, the trader who had given it to him, along with more money than he would normally earn in two years, had been quite specific. It wasn't under any circumstances to be opened, and if by any chance that happened, some very bad people would know about it and come looking for him and his family. Pushing his curiosity aside, the herder waded out towards the centre of the field, mindful of the fact that he knew the area to be riddled with snakes. Going as far as he dared, he dropped the parcel into the water and watched as tiny bubbles floated to the surface all around it as it sank to the bottom, before quickly wading back towards his bike. As he swashed through the warm water, he could just make out some of the workmen hanging from a giant crane in the distance, putting the finishing touches to the nearly completed industrial facility that would shortly be opening. Many of the villagers were ecstatic about the complex, particularly those who had gained employment there, but he wasn't one of them. As far as he was concerned, the whole fabric of the area had been ruined by it. His beasts were often frightened by the loud noises from the construction that seemed to go on around the clock, and it clogged up the once beautiful landscape that had dominated for millennia. Every night, just before he got into bed, he cursed that dreaded Cropptech and everything the industrial complex stood for.

10 LAVAPOOL FC (FATALLY CAUTERISED)

Afraid and more than a little concerned, especially at the speed he was travelling, his entire body hurt, particularly his head. It occurred to him that his vision was blurred but he didn't know why, given just how dark it was. Sitting on a massive leaf the size of a sofa, he cursed quietly as it hit a slight bump in the smooth rocky surface. Again he didn't know why he did it quietly; it wasn't as if there were anyone else about, here deep beneath the earth. Gripping tightly to the edges of the leaf, his back roared once again in the most agonising way possible, as he tried to convince himself that in some way he controlled the direction he was travelling in. Grip faltering as the pain overtook him, instantly he fell back into the middle of the giant green leaf, flapping and flailing uncontrollably, his throbbing head nestled in between the thick ridges and veins that crisscrossed its entire structure.

Continuing on its pre-programmed course, now deep below Australia, the vegetation was singularly unaware that its rider lay unconscious on top of it. After everything he'd been through, now was a very bad time for Flash to black out. Flying around another hairpin bend at breakneck speed, the organic transport slipped halfway up the side of the tunnel wall as it wove its way towards its final destination. Flash's body rolled to one side, brushing against the turned up edge of his unconventional ride, only centimetres away from the shiny rock face that zipped past at an alarming velocity. As the leaf came out of the bend and on to another straight, his entire form rolled back a bit towards the relative safety of the centre.

The leaf onto which he had dropped only minutes earlier, had already travelled over six miles, not directly down of course, that was more like three or four, but was now starting to near the end of its journey. Flash still wasn't awake.

A tightly wound spiral was the last part of the descent, with the leaf having just entered the extraordinarily sharp bend that signalled the start, violently throwing the Crimson Guard onto his stomach, his feet at the bottom of the leaf, his head, face down at the top. One of his arms flapped over the side, his hand brushing against the fast moving rocky surface, causing his fingers to become a bloodied mess. Even this wasn't enough to wake him. A hint of light shone up from the bottom of the corkscrew as the amazing plant life neared the end of its journey.

Speeding out of the final spiral of smooth rock, very much like an attraction at a water park, the exotic, organic ride splashed down into an outlandish, waist deep pool of lava, something that most dragons would love. Flash dropped from the leaf like a stone, entering the wickedly bubbling molten magma with a spectacular belly flop, as his transport disintegrated into nothing but tiny wisps of smoke. In the meantime, the Crimson Guard had sunk to the bottom, still no nearer to waking up, but a whole lot closer to dying.

With a vengeance, the heat from the awesomely hot magma attacked his human skin, probing here, attacking there, trying to overwhelm the dragon DNA inside him that fought back with all it had which, due to his naga induced injuries, was not quite what it should have been. Something ingrained within the scorching hot lava knew that it was just a matter of time before his primordial defences were breached. It had a kind of memory, something elemental, other worldly. It knew it had done this before, and that it would only be minutes at most, but more likely in this case mere seconds before it destroyed this individual's resistance and added him to its heated core. As it happened the lava turned out to be right. Another dragon, a fit and healthy one, might have lasted minutes, but not Flash, not today. With the injuries sustained in Antarctica consuming all but a tiny part of his magical ability, he had nothing left to give, nothing left to fight with.

As the first tiny molecules of his dragon DNA yielded, giant wings plunged into the lava around him, pulling his wreck of a body out of the swirling, bubbling pool and onto the raised walkway that ran alongside it. Orange, yellow and red molten magma sparked and flared as it dripped off Flash's prone body. Using his wings and a very basic mantra, the dragon who'd pulled Flash free forced the lava off the path and back into the pool. Smoking hot magma smouldered beneath Flash's nose and all around his mouth, causing his pale looking skin to turn black and crispy. As the dragon waved away the last of it, he silently mouthed another spell, putting the full force of his strong willed mind behind it. Instantly the molten magma that Flash had imbibed came rushing out of his nose, ears, mouth, slivers flowing out of his tear ducts, and well, since he was totally naked (the lava having destroyed every last fibre of his clothes on impact) it came gushing out of his... planet... you know. Not Mars, Venus, Jupiter or Saturn. The other one.

Gently, the prehistoric Good Samaritan lifted the Crimson Guard's head up, inspecting him physically, whilst at the same time probing his mind with magic. By chance, he was a healer of vast experience, on his way to a conference. Concerned and intrigued in equal measures by this unconscious conundrum of a dragon, disguised as a human who, but for him, would now be dead, he glanced along the walkway for any sign of help, but knew this was a little known route, rarely used, so it came as no surprise that it was totally deserted for as far as he could see in both directions. Of course he could call for assistance telepathically, but he wasn't sure who he should contact, or even if the unconscious dragon would last until anyone arrived. Supporting the Crimson Guard's head, the healer gently turned him on his side, to aid his sporadic breathing.

As he did so, he coughed and spluttered in surprise, two tiny jets of flame spurting involuntarily out of his nostrils, as the devastating wound on Flash's back became apparent. Making sure his patient was fully supported, the healer leant closer to look at what appeared on first inspection to be an almost impossible injury.

As well as being one of the most prominent physicians in the southern hemisphere, the dragon who'd found Flash was one of the few who took any interest in their race's history. While it was more of a hobby for him and he had nowhere near the kind of expertise that the renowned dragon historians had, he was very dedicated and knowledgeable in a few specific topics. One of the areas he considered amongst his strongest was the relationship between his race and the others that had thrived so long alongside it. As he intently studied the infected gash that crossed Flash's back, part of him was bowled over by the wound that could only have been inflicted by a naga. If he wasn't mistaken, and he was pretty sure he wasn't, the dragon lying on the path before him had been the recipient of what is known by their kind as *'pulsus of dolens nex,'* roughly translated as the 'blow of painful death.' It was something that had fascinated him when he'd read about it on one of his trips to the dragon repository in Rome, a journey he embarked on for a month once every decade, much to his wife's (yes... his wife, and not mate) disappointment. The ancient text that he'd read so long ago, which thanks to his eidetic memory stood out in his mind, right at this very moment, described how the nagas have an inbuilt supply of deadly venom deep within their bodies, that only becomes accessible to them in a heightened state, either in a mating frenzy, the heat of battle or when they know that death is imminent either from disease or a fatal blow. When the toxin becomes available, it pumps up through the naga's body into tiny receptors beneath their fingernails, through which they can disperse it into an enemy with a simple slash, punch, or even coat a weapon with it, if they act quickly enough. Known as the 'painful death' because the venom, whilst deadly, with no known antidote, can take an incredibly long time to take effect, during which it inflicts the most horrendous pain, so much so that most beings take their own lives long before it kills them.

'No wonder,' thought the healer, 'that this one's unconscious, with a wound of this sort. By the looks of it, he can't have long left to live. What should I do?' It wasn't often that he found himself at a loss like this. His healer training, experience, historical knowledge and great gut instinct all had a profound impact on him, making him more of a leader than most he knew. So much so that other dragons around him were always asking his advice, even those in positions of higher authority with much more understanding and know-how, something that always forced a grin onto his very serious face. But on this occasion, he really didn't know what action to take. Here and now, the very life of this one depended fully on the choices that he made, and nothing about this situation made any sense at all. Convinced his prognosis was right, that indeed it was a naga inflicted wound, coupled with the fact that the dragon had clearly gone to great lengths to get back here, he wondered if he should drag him out of unconsciousness telepathically, something he was more than capable of doing, but something that with the extent of the wound, could end up killing him in a very short space of time.

As vital seconds ticked by, he made his decision, for good or bad. Grabbing Flash by his ears, the healer leant in close, his fierce looking jaws almost touching the Crimson Guard's burnt and cindered mouth. Reaching out with his mind, the healer sought out the consciousness he knew had to be hiding deep within the mind of the creature before him. Not something especially new to him, over the centuries he'd done it literally dozens of times. None of which prepared him for what he found inside this peculiar individual.

Under normal circumstances, finding another of his kind's consciousness, or mind, was for the most part pretty straight forward. Even if they'd fled to the darkest recesses of their psyche, they would always leave a visible trail, easy to follow, ending up with a few mental barricades that they had to be coaxed into letting down before the gradual process of helping them regain control of their body could begin. What the good healer encountered on entering Flash's mind was something altogether different, as he hadn't fled, quite the opposite in fact. He was holed up right in the very centre of his consciousness, sticking out like a hot dog in a vegetarian restaurant. What shocked the physician the most were the barricades that had been erected. In his experience, most dragons surrounded themselves with things they associate with happiness, items that make them feel comfortable and safe. It could be anything from a river of lava, bright hot sunshine, a fort made of charcoal, a roaring circle of wind, a particular nursery ring teacher, a parent or an imaginary laminium ball team. Over the course of his working life, the healer had encountered all of these and they'd all been relatively easy to remove, with just a little encouragement. Flash, unsurprisingly, was nothing like anyone he'd ever encountered before. As the healer's consciousness settled down to take stock, the biggest, scariest looking castle with manned battlements, trebuchets and a huge keep that rose out of view, formed the picture in front of him. A giant moat surrounded it all, with some very ominous things swimming in it. Strangely, a portcullis sat directly across the moat from him, but there was no drawbridge, behind it just the stone wall of the castle. Evil looking vultures perched atop the crenellations that crisscrossed the outer walls and long arrow slits littered the dark stone, making it look from a distance like the castle had chickenpox. Dark, forbidding clouds circled overhead.

'This is going to be... interesting,' he thought, taking it

all in whilst pondering his next move. It was a good job that all his concentration wasn't focused on what was to come. Movement behind the slits in the walls caught his attention. Moments later a barrage of arrows sailed through the sky towards his consciousness, something that in all his time he'd never seen or heard of. In a fraction of a second he'd made the decision to retreat out of range, back right to the very edge of Flash's mind. Heart beating double time back in his dragon body next to the lava pool, the arrows struck the muddy ground in front of him with a solid thwump, deep inside the Crimson Guard's consciousness. Taking a few seconds to regain his composure, he tried to understand what had just gone on. It had happened so quickly that he'd just acted automatically, but the more he thought about it, the more it scared him senseless. How would things have turned out if he'd been hit by one of the arrows? Would any harm have come to him? Would he have... died, here in someone else's psyche? All these questions and more wriggled through his brain as his consciousness cowered in the darkness, the castle with all its dangers towering over everything in the not so far away distance. Knowing that every second here was a second closer to death for the dragon whose mind he'd invaded and maybe even himself, he vowed to do everything in his power to help.

Keeping his wits about him, he very carefully, and very obviously, came out of the shadows walking slowly and surely towards the thrashing waters of the moat, all the time projecting as much calm and serenity as he could muster in the direction of the imposing castle. Briefly clearing his throat, he threw his voice out, hoping it would catch the attention of the individual within.

"Erm... hello," he shouted, mindful of the danger all around him.

"HELLO," he shouted once again. "Could we possibly talk? I mean you no harm, quite the opposite in fact. I'm here to help."

"Get lost!" shouted Flash's mind, loud enough to startle all the vultures into flight.

Cautiously edging backwards, the healer half expected another volley of arrows. Fortunately, they never arrived. Buoyed ever so slightly, he decided to try again.

"I don't know who you are, but you need assistance. Let me help you please... I'm a healer."

A wavering, "Just leave," echoed down from somewhere up high.

A tiny glimmer of hope sparked within the physician, helping him to press on and save this very unusual individual.

"Your body is in bad shape you know. I can help... honest. But you need to come out... now. Every second you delay puts you in more danger."

Silence enveloped the whole vista; even the returning vultures resembled statues. Waiting patiently, the healer noted that whatever lurked in the moat, had for the first time stopped splashing and biting at nothing, while the clouds above were definitely changing from menacing dark, to a much fluffier shade of white.

Out of the blue a sickly looking dragon figure popped his head up from beneath one of the battlements about halfway down one side of the keep.

"Why should I trust you?" croaked Flash.

"Do you know where you are?" asked the healer softly.

Flash leant against the wall of the keep, exhausted, and shook his head in reply.

"Your body's in the dragon world beneath Perth, Australia. I was on my way to a medical conference, walking along a little used path, when I saw you crash into a pool of lava from one of the emergency entrances above. I've dragged you out of the pool and removed all the magma in and around you. But you've got this... this... wound, on your back. It's like nothing I've ever seen before, but I've read about something that it... resembles." He knew then that he had the Crimson Guard's full attention, and could see that he was in a seriously bad shape. Having no idea what would happen if he lost consciousness here, in his mind, would the dragon die? Would they both die? It was impossible to know, and all the more important to persuade him to lower the barricades so that he could be helped. Quickly he decided to continue on, hoping to gain the dragon's trust.

"Your wound looks like it was inflicted by a... naga."

Flash's exhausted prehistoric shape leaning against the keep wall immediately became alert, looking suspiciously across the castle walls and moat, towards the newcomer.

"How would you know that?" he demanded.

"We really don't have time for all this."

"Humour me."

"I study history... in my spare time."

"Really?"

"Look, everything I've told you here is the truth. I don't know who you are, but judging from the defences you've erected around yourself, you're anything but an ordinary dragon. If I had to guess, I'd say you were one of the King's Guards, or perhaps even a councillor or something. Either way, you're in bad shape, not just here, but back on the walkway where both our bodies reside. You need to lower your defences and let me guide you back to where you can take control of your own body and wake up in the real world. Then we can think about doing something with the wound. Nothing I've told you here is a lie. You need to act now. Time is running out."

Flash considered the stranger's words. It did all kind of ring true. Vaguely he remembered something about entering an emergency entrance of some sort, but the details eluded him at present. A pressing need to... go somewhere... to tell someone something, continually exerted itself on him. It weighed down on his mind as if he were deep below the ocean, with the pressure of all that water above him. Barely able to stand now, Flash knew that he really had no choice but to trust this stranger. As he started to lower the mental defences that years of training in the Crimson Guards had taught him, he hoped he was doing the right thing.

Standing stock still, the healer watched in amazement as the scene before him started to change. Arrow shafts protruding from the muddy ground shimmered briefly and then abruptly disappeared. The moat's water receded, its inhabitants vanished and the keep shrunk, slowly at first, but picking up speed as it got closer to the ground. Eventually the giant castle, vultures and everything else within, wrapped itself all into one, and transformed into a beautifully thatched cottage, wild flowers surrounding the bright white walls, with a wonderfully engraved oak door at its centre.

Suddenly the wooden door swung silently open, revealing Flash, doubled over, looking like hell. Sprinting over, the healer wrapped his consciousness around him, catching hold before he fell on the neatly mown front lawn. Flash smiled gratefully, knowing that he'd made the right decision, cursing himself for having wasted so much valuable time. With the healer as his guide, he hung on as he was taken on what seemed like a whirlwind journey through parts of his mind he didn't even know existed. Very much like a mental maze, with the stranger turning this way and that, sifting his way through Flash's memories, occasionally heading down a dead end and having to turn round, all sense of time was lost. The journey could have taken seconds or hours. Nothing made sense, which was odd considering they were inside his own head. Eventually they arrived at the centre of the mental maze. There, in the middle of another freshly mown lawn, underneath a swaying weeping willow, was a three metre wide hole with smooth sides and absolutely no sign of how deep it was. It could have been eight metres, it could have been eight miles.

"There it is," ventured the healer. "Your way back."

Flash stepped forward, reluctantly peering over the

edge.

"You're sure?" he asked, swaying gently back and forth.

"I'm sure it will return you to your body. What we'll find when we get there, I'm afraid I have no idea. Because I've been here so long, I've lost all track of time."

Flash nodded.

"Well... if it turns out badly, thanks for trying anyway."

The healer nodded in return.

"It'll be okay. I'll meet you back by the pool."

With that, the healer's consciousness gathered itself up and shot off back through the maze, disappearing almost immediately. Flash stood alone, gazing down into the gaping hole. Sweat flooded down his gigantic dragon head, rolled off his scaled jaw and dripped down onto the identical blades of grass beneath his feet. More than anything he didn't want to jump. He felt safe here. Still, the never ending pressure hovered all around him, a constant reminder that he was supposed to do... something, something important, something... in the other world, back where his body resided. Finding the centre of calm that had so often saved him, he closed his eyes and leapt feet first into the hole. Cloying darkness took hold.

Elsewhere, the healer had managed, with a great deal of difficulty, to find his way out of the maze that was Flash's mind, and was just waking up in his own body.

'No matter how many times I do that,' he thought, 'I don't think I'll ever get used to it.' Lifting his entire mass up off the path beside his sickly looking patient, he leant over the naked, raggedy human form, looking for any indication that he was about to wake up. While he waited anxiously, he tried to work out how long he'd been inside the Crimson Guard's head. Concentrating furiously for a few seconds and reaching out telepathically into his surroundings, he eventually settled on minutes rather than hours. If he'd had to take a guess, he'd have said about twenty, but it was impossible to be any more accurate than that.

With more of a splash than a bump, Flash landed. Just when he thought things couldn't get any weirder, he gradually started to sink. Struggling with as much strength as he could muster, he tried to escape, but the more he fought, the more submerged he became. Moments later, a familiar feeling overtook him. It was only then that he recognised what he'd fallen into. It was his body, and he'd been gradually seeping back into it. As he dropped deeper and deeper into the sticky goo that had broken his fall, he started to feel all the different aspects of it, not really caring very much for the sensation. It was a little like putting on a rubber glove to do the washing up: lots of fiddling and stretching, with it never really feeling quite right: the odd loose bit here, a bit too tight there.

Reaching out in the rubber glove that was his body, he opened his eyes, taking in a deep breath as he did so. At least, that was the idea. Instead, he found himself coughing violently, the fumes from the nearby magma pool searing his lungs. Panicked, he slapped at the burning sensation eating away at his face, but to no avail. Immediately a soothing presence was beside him, the same one he'd heard from beyond the walls of the castle in his mind only a short time ago.

"It's okay son, I'm here, just relax."

Flash fought hard to push away the pain, but it only made things worse. Then everything came flooding back in high definition. Automatically, he sat up, almost like a human jack-in-the-box, instantly wishing he hadn't. The healer wrapped his giant wings around him.

"Go steady little one. We need to get you to a med centre."

"No... no... no... no you don't understand. I have to get to London... NOW!"

"I don't think there's any chance of that at the moment. You urgently need medical attention. I'm sorry."

Burying his head in his hands, Flash tried to think over the pain that ran through his body.

'It's no good, I'm going to have to tell him,' he thought. 'There's simply no other way.'

Turning and looking at the healer for the very first time, he felt in awe of the impressive member of his species that knelt beside him. With his vast experience and training, he knew a thing or two about his kind: ordinary ones, devious ones, powerful ones and extraordinary ones. This one, he knew without a doubt, came into the latter category. Wisdom and a kind demeanour positively radiated off him, and although he looked slightly frail around the edges, Flash sensed more than a little steel inside him.

'He would be much harder to fight than he looks,' he thought.

With no other option left open to him, the Crimson Guard told the healer who he was, and a little about the mission he'd been on, leaving out most of the important details, as they were only really for the king's ears. When he'd finished, he sat on the cool stone path, head in hands, waiting to see what the physician would say, and if he'd help him get to the monorail, and then onto London.

Well, well, well," repeated the healer. "A Crimson Guard, whatever next? I thought I'd seen it all, but apparently not yet."

"Will you help me?" Flash asked urgently from beneath his hands.

"Of course," he boomed. "Who on earth wouldn't help you?"

Flash looked up at the huge prehistoric face smiling back down at him.

"Thank you so much, you have no idea what it me... aaaaaahhhhhhhhh!"

Crying out in agony, before blacking out, the healer caught his head before it hit the ground. Pulsing with evil, the wound on Flash's back oozed a sickly white pus that dribbled down the length of his spine. Watching for a few seconds, knowing full well that what he was seeing was almost certainly going to prove fatal to the young dragon, the healer knew there and then that there was nothing more important than getting this courageous Crimson Guard back to the monarch in London. Scooping up the naked human form, careful not to touch the deadly wound, he felt a pang of regret. Every atom in his body screamed at him to head for a med centre, in case there was just the outside chance that a cure could be found. But he knew the information this dragon carried was not just vital, but critical, and had to be brought to the monarch as soon as possible. Everything he'd heard had convinced him of that, and he knew full well that the brave agent had left the most important, and sensitive bits out. Plodding off down the walkway in the direction of the nearest monorail station, part of him hoped not just to get the dragon to the king, but to save his life as well. Over the years he'd seen so much pain and suffering, and he just wanted it all to stop. Somehow he couldn't quite believe it was just fate that their paths had crossed. It was going to be a very interesting day.

Flash awoke to excruciating pain racing around inside him. Cursing in his mind, unwilling to open his eyes just yet, one thought dominated all others inside his confused and befuddled head: he must tell the king what he knew, immediately. As he willed the agonising ache away with a view to opening his eyes, the slightest hint of vibration caught his attention. He was lying down, that much he knew, on something comfortable, which made a pleasant change, but there was a familiar feeling... Opening his eyes, he sat up swiftly. Hope jumped up and down within him, as he realised where he was. It was almost too good to be true. He was on the monorail. Looking up from his paper from across the carriage, was the healer who'd rescued him from the lava pool.

"How are you feeling, son?"

Flash was about to describe the pain and writhing agony that seemed to go on forever, when he stopped to think about it for just a second. Something was different, unusual, inside his body. Pushing the fuzziness that surrounded his brain to one side, he concentrated on what was going on within. While the ache from the wound echoed around in the background, just about every other part of his body felt... okay. Not good, or great, but okay. There were no bruises, broken bones, aches or pains. Raising his hands, he felt around his mouth and nose, remembering that they'd been chargrilled by the lava. Nothing... it was all back to normal. Looking across at the healer who straight away smiled back at him, he asked,

"Your doing?"

Folding the paper up in his lap, he nodded.

"I'm really sorry," uttered Flash, "but I have to ask. What is it that you're reading?"

"The Daily Telepath of course," he replied, a big grin spreading across his face.

"In paper form?"

"You have to know where to get it from, but yes."

"But why?" asked the Crimson Guard. "What's the point when you can just download it to your mind and read it whenever you like?"

With a look much the same as an experienced adult would give a child when they asked a question that made little or no sense, the healer smiled before replying.

"Do you spend much time on the surface?"

"A little, usually when I have to."

"Next time you do, and you have a little free time, go and visit a book shop. Any one you like, but something small and private would be ideal. Spend an hour in there browsing, just looking at all the wares, take everything in. Even buy some if you're keen, but you don't have to. Think about that experience for a couple of days afterwards, and then use that internet of theirs download a book and read it, if at all possible, one of the ones you bought. If you do all of that, you'll understand immediately why I choose to have a physical copy," he said, waving the paper in his hand.

Flash thought about what he'd just been told for a few moments, before agreeing to do exactly as suggested, providing he ever had the chance again.

About to ask another question, the darkened carriage started to brighten up. It was then that he realised they were pulling into a station. Gazing out of the crystal clear window, he was pleasantly surprised to see that they'd just arrived at Bali. As the monorail drew to a complete halt, the only other dragon in the carriage stood up, moved over to the doors and stepped through them as soon as they slid open with their customary whoosh. Seconds after the dragon had left, others came streaming through, some in human form, some not, but all, for some reason that he couldn't fathom, looking strangely at him. It was all the healer sitting opposite could do, not to laugh. It was only when the monorail started moving again that the Crimson Guard realised what was going on. There he was lying across one of the dragon form seats, wearing nothing but a fluorescent pink and yellow dragon cloak. Quickly he turned to the healer who by now was guffawing away, tiny clouds of smoke rising from in and around his nostrils.

Normally something like this would have set off Flash's mighty temper, but instead of getting upset or feisty, he just joined the healer in seeing the funny side, and it wasn't long before tears were running down both their faces. Now each of them were getting strange looks from the other passengers, but neither cared very much. This was very much a new experience for the Crimson Guard, both laughing, and having someone to share the amusement with. Once the fit of fun had died down, Flash turned in the healer's direction, opened his arms wide out in front of him to show off the cloak, and asked,

"Why?"

Shrugging his scaly shoulders, the healer answered,

"It was all I could find at short notice. I thought you said you had to get to London as a matter of urgency. If you're that bothered we can stop off at Hong Kong and get you something tailor made."

Flash pretended to think about it before replying.

"No, it's fine. Gets a lot of air to all the important bits that need it."

Sitting up, careful not to put any pressure on his back, he leant over towards his new found friend, although he didn't really know why (however low he whispered, the other dragons in and around would still be able to hear him if they so wished) he said a sincere,

"Thank you."

"You're welcome youngster. I'm just sorry I'm not able to do more. If not for the injury to your back, you would be in perfect health. I really don't know anything else that can be done I'm afraid."

Flash looked on stoically. Part of him had accepted that he would die, sooner rather than later, but as long as he delivered the information into the hands of the king, it wouldn't matter, knowing he'd done well to get this far, and all would have been lost but for the very kind, very intriguing medical professional sitting opposite him.

"I'm extremely grateful for everything you've done, and I'm sure the monarch will be as well."

"Let's just hope it's enough, and with the resources available to him, hope that he has something that can rid you of that ailment," ventured the physician, sitting back in his chair, turning to watch the rock face outside, whizz by.

Letting out a deep sigh, Flash lay down on his side on the oversized dragon seat, the gaudy cloak wrapped around his naked human body. He'd never thought it would end quite like this, always assuming it would be a magnificent battle in a blaze of glory, fighting for good, saving the king's life. Resting his head beneath his hands, he tried to conserve what little energy he had left, knowing full well that he'd probably need every ounce of it just to survive the day.

Having gathered up all the things he needed into his briefcase, the old man walked around his mahogany desk and reached up to the rather splendid picture in the golden frame on the wall. Inside was an oil painting that had been given to him by a client, oh a long time ago, more than thirty years in fact. Having fallen on hard times, the client had practically begged for his services. In the end, he'd conceded and worked for a pittance when nobody else would have taken on such a hopeless case. Of course he'd won, pretty much the same as always in those days, but once the client had got rid of the cloud hanging over him, all talk of monetary reimbursement had been long forgotten. So it came as something of a shock when, some eight months later, a package arrived. After having signed for it, he clearly recalled untying the pristine white string and ripping open the brown paper to find the exquisite piece of art tucked securely inside. Puzzled, he searched carefully around the base of the painting, moments later finding a small hand scrawled note that read:

Thanks for the great job you did in the courtroom. Sorry I couldn't pay you at the time, but hopefully this will go some way to recompensing you. Regards T.'

He scratched his neck as the picture evoked the same memories now as it had done back then. The beach scene sent him right back to his childhood, of growing up by the sea, all those years ago. Both children in the picture bore a startling resemblance to him and his sister Evlyn.

'Oh Evlyn, how I miss you,' he thought, gazing one last time at the boy and girl frolicking in the surf, a red bucket and spade strewn amongst the sand dunes in the foreground.

Pushing the heart wrenching memories to one side, he got on with the job at hand. Reaching up to the picture, he brought his right index finger just underneath the heavy golden frame, in the bottom left hand corner. Lifting the tiniest of latches, he allowed it to swivel out towards him, revealing a very old and heavy safe. Peering over his shoulder across the desk towards the opaque office door, something that was a time honoured force of habit rather than a necessity, once sure the coast was clear, he carefully rotated the big black dials with faded intricate white markings, into their correct positions. Sure enough, he was rewarded with a tiny click. Turning the silver handle, he pulled the incredibly heavy door open towards him, using up every bit of strength he possessed in the process. Inside lay pile upon pile of documents, some held together by flimsy elastic bands, a couple of memory sticks containing valuable information about former customers, and a small stack of money. As he glared at it all in the dull office light, he couldn't have been less bothered, something that in a way shocked him, as it had been his life and soul for the best part of half a century.

Looking back across his desk, he took hold of his briefcase and turned it round to face him. With a feeling of regret, he took out the package that he'd been given and very carefully placed it on top of everything else in the safe. As he pulled his frail fingers out for the very last time, his thoughts turned to what he was doing. It was strange really. Not knowing all the details himself, he could only try and fill in the missing parts, but apparently one of his grandsons, the eldest one of three, had got himself into some kind of trouble. Unsure of what, he only knew that it was something very unsavoury. Of course he'd tried to find out more, but he didn't wield nearly the kind of power or influence now that he had done several decades ago. Anyway, the long and the short of it was that whatever Chuck had gotten himself into, there was no clear cut way out. Or there hadn't been, up until very recently. The boy had been contacted by some of his associates, and offered a way out of everything; all he had to do was get his grandfather to do them a little 'favour.' Whether Chuck wanted to do any of this was anyone's guess, but, yes you've guessed it, that kid was always his grandfather's favourite. Well, the little 'favour' that Chuck's associates wanted was quite bizarre really, something that made it all the more worrying in his experience. All he had to do, for his grandson to be free of any sort of debt, was to take delivery of a package, put it securely in his office safe, and take a holiday for a month. No going back to his office, no going in or out, even to clean it, for the entire duration. It was almost too good to be true, and there had to be a catch somewhere, he just couldn't understand what it was, and knowing that Chuck was now out of the country and safe in the hands of some overseas relatives meant that he didn't really care. He did, however, have a seriously bad feeling and those things, in his great experience, never boded well. Resisting the temptation to open the package, he pushed the door shut, whirled the black dials for all they were worth, and set the painting back in place. Closing his briefcase and snapping the locks shut, he picked it up and wandered over to the coat stand, but not before glancing out of the window at the wonderful view, one last time. Marvelling at the changes he'd seen from this window throughout his career, the skyline looked almost totally different, but then it seemed to him as though Seattle didn't stand still for more than a week, let alone the number of decades he'd been working there. With a tear in the corner of one eye, he grabbed his raincoat off the old wooden stand, folded it across his arm and walked out of the office. Making sure the door was secure, he strolled over to the nearest elevator and pressed the down button, never ceasing to be amazed at the number of people flitting around the building, even though he'd have thought most would have finished long before 8.30pm.

'Still,' he mused, as the elevator doors pinged open, 'it has pretty much always been that way in the Smith Tower.' Riding down to the ground floor amongst the throng of workers, he thought about the history of the magnificent building he'd worked in for so long. His last sentiment as he strolled through the lobby and out into the street, was,

'The oldest skyscraper in Seattle. I sure hope it stays that way until the end of time.'

If only he had acted on that bad feeling.

11 A KING'S RANSOM

Awaking with a yawn, his very first thought was of Janice. Although he was alone, snuggled up under his favourite duvet, he imagined wrapping his arms around her and falling asleep against her gorgeous body. A vision of the dragon council hauling him off to the deepest darkest depths underground shocked him awake. Knowing what he was doing was wrong, as Richie did, he couldn't help but feel at the same time it was so... right. Running his fingers through his long, unkempt hair in frustration, reluctantly he swung his feet onto the floor, wondering why things had to be so complicated. Sure a day of misery lay ahead of him, it was then that he remembered.

'I'm going to see the king, with Tank and Gee Tee.'

That cheered him up. With all thoughts of Janice and his highly illegal relationship banished, he scooted off to have a shower, singing happily as he did so. Twenty minutes later he was pristine and had finished his breakfast. During all of this, it had suddenly occurred to him that he had no idea about what form he should go in to visit the king. In theory, he supposed he should take his natural dragon form; certainly Gee Tee would, and he supposed that meant Tank could well be. But, while he still felt a thrill being in his prehistoric natural guise, he was much more comfortable in the human form that he spent so much time in. Ironic really. Still in two minds, he headed for the piano in the living room, yanking back the tall, glass, Galileo thermometer that stood atop it. Silently, the instrument swivelled out to reveal a dark segment in the floor, through which the top of an intricate, black metal staircase could just be made out. He'd thought he'd been fighting with the decision on which form to assume, but as it turned out he hadn't. It was human guise for him all the way and he was sure the monarch wouldn't mind and would want him to be comfortable, especially spending so much time himself in that particular disguise. Bounding over to the gaping hole, he stepped through into the darkness just as the piano started to swivel back into place.

A short while later he found himself heading away from Buckingham Station towards the council chambers for his rendezvous with Tank and Gee Tee. Looking at his watch, he realised he'd done his normal thing of being early, only this time it was by nearly quarter of an hour. Knowing that the chances of his friend being able to hurry the old mantra maker along to get to the chambers on time were remote, he settled in for a bit of a wait.

'Oh well,' he mused, stopping for just a second to take in all the tall and opulent buildings, something he considered absolutely staggering. Continuing to stroll pleasantly down a side street, waiting to be met by the sight of the stunning council building, he turned a corner only to be greeted by something far more surprising. There, standing halfway up the steps to the council building, stood his rugby playing pal in his human persona, alongside Gee Tee who looked absolutely majestic in his dragon form, a far cry from the normally frail old shop keeper he was used to. Tank waved, having spotted Peter as soon as he'd turned the corner. Returning the gesture, all the time watching the master mantra maker, who seemed to be captivated by the lava pools on either side of the steps, Peter rushed on over to the plateau they stood on.

"Morning," greeted Tank, slapping his buddy on the back.

"Hi," offered Peter, a little out of breath.

"Hello young one," announced Gee Tee, watching his reflection dance across the bubbling pool of lava.

"Hi Gee."

"So," said Tank, "How are you feeling Pete? Excited about seeing the king again, I bet? I know I am."

Nodding eagerly, he agreed with his friend.

"A small part of me's nervous of course, but I can't wait to see him and find out more about my grandfather."

"And don't forget," added his friend, "he's got some stuff to give you as well. You know, everything your grandfather left you."

"Oh yeah," the youngster replied, "I'd almost forgotten all about that. I wonder what on earth it could be?"

Poking the lava in the pool with one of his well worn talons, the master mantra maker continued listening to the two of them.

"Anyway, now that we're all here, shall we proceed?" boomed the old shopkeeper.

Peter looked nervously at his watch.

"Ummm... it's not really time yet. We're still more than ten minutes early. I wouldn't want to catch the king unaware."

Gee Tee let out a loud chuckle, all the time stirring the lava pool.

"Poppycock child. It should be impossible to catch the monarch unaware, as by his very nature, he is in charge. Anyway, I think you'll find he's already aware of our presence. Let us proceed without further delay." With that, the old dragon grabbed a huge handful of lava and to the surprise of the other two, splashed it all across his giant scaly face. Instantly Tank bolted forward, stopping a moment or two later, after seeing how much Gee Tee enjoyed the experience, so much so that he was shaking his head and roaring with delight, much as a dragon half his age would. Turning, the master mantra maker looked at the two youngster's gobsmacked expressions.

"It's good for the complexion, you know?" he announced, before letting rip a great big belly laugh and stomping off up the steps towards the building's entrance. Sharing a look, not knowing what to make of what had just happened, both friends broke into smiles, before deciding it was best to catch up with him before he had a chance to make any more mischief.

Located directly behind the shiny new council building, the king's private residence could only be accessed through a newly built link bridge. By the time Peter and Tank caught up with Gee Tee, he'd just made his way into the lobby, tutting at this, huffing at that, nearly starting a fight with one of the King's Guards who were stationed throughout the building in abundance, for something he'd uttered under his breath. Quickly apologising, the apprentice led his boss back towards the reception desk, where they all explained who they were and that they had an appointment with the sovereign. Unsure at first, the reception dragon checked the state of the art computer, confirming that they were indeed expected, and then sent them on their merry way, the brightly lit floor panels in front of them guiding them to their destination. It didn't take too long for the master mantra maker to start moaning about that either, much to the pair's amusement.

One of the oldest buildings in the whole domain, the king's private residence was also one of the grandest. It had been the biggest landmark in and around Buckingham up until the new council building had been erected directly in front of it. Although the council building had only been up and running for the last year or so, the planning and building work for the spectacular structure had been going on for the best part of five years. That doesn't sound much, but in dragon terms that's a huge timescale, particularly when you think of the way in which their mantras can create, modify, warp or destroy pretty much anything, in very much the blink of an eye. When in the planning stage, the council building had been intended to be on a totally different site. It was only after dozens of meetings that the present location was discussed as a possibility, and even then, only as an afterthought. But the more the dragons responsible for security, thought about the idea, the more momentum it seemed to gather. Eventually, with the king's reluctant approval, the new building came into being, right, smack bang in front of the king's private residence, with the only way now in or out, through the lobby of the brand new structure. It had been chosen this way purely for security reasons; in the unlikely event that the ruler was ever in danger, one way in and one way out was a lot easier to defend, and the council building's defences, although they didn't look like much, were the toughest in the dragon domain.

Peter, Tank and Gee Tee continued following the brightly lit floor panels, on a route that really made no sense at all. All three of them could tell that from a directional point of view, they'd doubled back on themselves three or four times already. By now, the old shopkeeper was getting very... disappointed.

"This is beyond ridiculous," he snorted.

"I agree wholeheartedly," added Peter. "It really doesn't make much sense at all."

Tank paused to think for just a second.

"I think I've read about this somewhere," he said quietly to the other two.

"And just where would that be?" enquired his bad tempered boss. "In a holiday magazine. A few hours in the council building will seem like a week, because that's how long it will take you to find your destination."

Ignoring the aforementioned jibe, the youngster continued.

"If I'm not mistaken, the computer guiding us is designed for security reasons, to never follow the same route twice, in any one day, all for the protection of the king, of course."

"I should have thought the monarch would have been able to protect himself," huffed the master mantra maker, his breath getting shorter all the time due to all the walking.

Just then the three of them turned a sharp corner and stood at the entrance to a raised walkway, known affectionately as the link bridge. Simultaneously, they all gasped at the view. Below them, dragon kings from ages gone by were carved into the rock that supported the private residence; the attention to detail was staggering. Stunning white pillars ran down each side, some at least a quarter of a mile long. Arches made from the same bright, white rock towered overhead. Inscriptions circled the white pillars, while dragon faces stared out from the deep set arcs. The walkway ran across what appeared to be a bottomless chasm, separating the brand new council building from the historic private residence. In many ways it seemed a shame that the council building had been built right in front of the magnificent structure that housed the king in his free time. And Peter wasn't the only one to think so, with many members of the dragon community at large having kicked up quite a fuss during the planning stage. But security had won the day, trumping aesthetic beauty as it normally did here in the underground world. Of course he could appreciate that from a defensive point of view, it was indeed very well protected. But protected from who? There had been no wars for a very long time, and unless the king knew something that nobody else did, then it all seemed a bit like overkill to him.

Leading the way across the link bridge, Peter nervously glanced down into the chasm. It made no sense of course, a dragon, even in a human body, being afraid of heights, but that's just how he was. Tank followed closely behind, with Gee Tee scraping his tail along the floor at the back of the group, amused by Peter's fear of the chasm they were now crossing.

Once on the other side, the trio strolled beneath a large, white stone arch where, much to Gee Tee's relief, the guiding lights on the floor vanished. Continuing along the path they were all on, as there was nowhere else to go, the three remained totally silent, each in awe of the great building they found themselves in. It was rare for anyone to visit the king's private residence. Most of his business was carried out in the council chambers: council meetings, press briefings, bestowing honours, they were all worked through there. Only the monarch's closest allies, friends and family were ever invited into his personal abode, something all three of them were aware of now more than ever.

Slowing, a cooling breeze ruffled Peter's shoulder length hair in a rather pleasant sort of way, as he adjusted his eyes to the much brighter environment. A huge cone of flame swept its way out of Gee Tee's mouth in a moment of surprise at the amazing space they found themselves in. Tank, who'd been standing directly in front of the master mantra maker when it happened must, Peter thought, have experienced this from the old dragon before, as he reacted with super speed, throwing himself forward and then rolling off to one side, all in one silky smooth motion. Peter was impressed, both by Tank's quick reflexes and the heat from the flame that Emporium owner had generated. Most of the cone had been a searing blue, with a touch of white hot flickering orange and yellow around the edges, which was impressive for a normal dragon, but doubly so for one of his supposed age. For a split second, he wondered if the old shopkeeper had been at the Peruvian ink, but was pretty sure he hadn't. Despite all the shopkeeper's bluster and bravado, the hockey player knew he was as keen as anyone to visit the king, in this of all places.

The space all three of them found themselves in was... HUGE! Not just the height either, but the diameter, and it WAS diameter, as the area they'd entered was completely circular in nature with massive wide oblongs stretching off it in a couple of directions. A light marble floor with ancient text smattered amongst it set off a giant stone plinth, smack bang in the centre. Marble railings of the same colour looked down upon them from half a dozen floors above. On top of all of this, the room had a sense of... destiny to it. There was definitely something special and it echoed throughout the entire level. You could feel it in the air; it was everywhere.

"Ahhhhhh, you made it I see," boomed a familiar accent from somewhere up above.

As one, the trio looked up, scouring the balconies for any sign of the voice's owner.

"Sorry to confuse you all. Over here."

Turning round, all three were greeted by the sight of the king descending the elegantly curved staircase, made from the same kind of marble as the floor. Peter and Tank immediately dropped to one knee. Gee Tee chuckled from behind them.

"You can cut that out for starters," the monarch ordered, from the bottom step. "Get up at once and stop being so silly. You're my guests, not loyal subjects today. You could do worse than to take a leaf out of this dragon's book," he urged, motioning to Gee Tee. "He doesn't bow or kowtow to anyone. Am I right?"

"You would be correct... sire," replied the master mantra maker, grinning.

"Oh... very funny," replied the ruler, breaking into a broad smile, patting Gee Tee on the shoulder, having to stand on tiptoes in his human form to do so.

Peter and Tank got to their feet.

"It's good to see you again... shopkeeper. I'm sorry it's been so long."

Peter was glad to see the king had assumed his human guise, and was happy that he'd chosen his own preferred form as well. Despite having spent days thinking and dreaming about coming here, he still felt a little overwhelmed by the situation. Maybe it was the magnificent cane the ruler carried that made him instantly recognisable, looking both strong and flexible at the same time, with that sparkling purple trident carved into it that pulsed away regally. Or perhaps it was the fabulous ring that adorned the middle finger of the monarch's right hand, although as he'd previously found to his cost, it didn't always choose to reveal itself to everyone. Pushing all thoughts of power and position right to the back of his mind, in order to enjoy the day and learn as much as he could, a shiver ran down his tail, despite the fact that he wasn't even sporting it at this very moment.

"It's good to see you to little one. It has been a very long time indeed," rumbled the master mantra maker, from a metre or so away. Sighing visibly, the king added,

"I'm sorry. I really should have invited you here before."

"Yes you should have."

Both friends froze on the spot.

'Oh my God,' thought Peter, 'the king's going to go absolutely spare. We're all going to get chucked out.'

Scrutinising the Emporium owner for what felt like a lifetime, while the two young dragons looked nervously on, finally the monarch clipped the master mantra maker across the wing, and they both doubled up with laughter again. Peter breathed a sigh of relief as the potentially awkward moment passed, turning into nothing more than larking about.

Backing off from Gee Tee a little, as he was the only one in his natural form, the king addressed all three of them.

"I'm glad you could all make it today. It's really good to see each and every one of you. I so rarely get any visitors, well... any that I look forward to. But isn't there someone missing?"

Peter's heart skipped a beat, having known full well the king would ask, and was absolutely dreading having to answer.

"Umm... well... Richie had some... human stuff that she just couldn't get out off, I'm afraid. She sends her regards."

Nodding knowingly, George paused to think for a few seconds.

"Well, shall we start the grand tour?" he asked, flinging his arms open wide. "It's quite the place you know," he added, turning and heading back towards the spiral staircase. Following quickly on his heels, Peter went first, with Tank bringing up the rear, cajoling the old shopkeeper along. For his efforts, the apprentice was quickly shooed away with a flea in his ear, the master mantra maker letting him know in no uncertain terms what he would be transformed in to, permanently, if he tried to mollycoddle him again. Tank raced to catch Peter up, walking alongside him, just behind the king, as they reached the first floor.

"Here are just part of my personal chambers. It's where I eat, sleep, keep all my private belongings and bathe," he announced wistfully, before continuing on up the staircase.

Glancing back over their shoulders, Peter and Tank watched as Gee Tee reached the landing of the first floor. Both knew better than to ask if he needed any help. Heading up after the head of state, albeit at a much slower pace in an effort to help the old shopkeeper, Tank leant across to his pal, and very, very quietly whispered,

"I don't think he believed you about Rich."

"I don't know about him, but I didn't believe me."

Tank shook his head as he turned to check on his boss's progress behind them, before wishing he hadn't, after the look the old dragon threw him.

Catching up with the king on the landing of the second floor, they waited patiently for the old shopkeeper to reach them. It didn't take long.

"This, my friends," announced the ruler, "is my private library."

As Gee Tee let out a long snort of flame, Tank quickly pushed Peter to one side, saving his friend from being scorched by the wicked looking jet, the king eyeing the three of them suspiciously.

"Anyway, as I was saying, this is my repository, and the finest on the planet, more complete than Rome's and with tomes, mantras and magical artefacts that they could only dream of."

Peter stood, amazed. Up until he'd met the king in

hospital he hadn't realised that he'd even had a private residence, let alone complete with its own library. Thinking back, it had probably been mentioned during his time at the nursery ring, and yes he had an eidetic memory, but there'd been so much information to process and store, it was easy to miss out the odd thing or two. A fleeting look at his friends showed that they were not the least bit surprised. Tank looked nonplussed, while the master mantra maker had a look of... hunger in his eyes. What was going on?

"Well, I'm sure you wouldn't be interested in viewing the library itself, so perhaps we should move on to the next level, and view some of the plant species in my arboretum?" observed the sovereign matter-of-factly.

A look of absolute horror crossed Gee Tee's face, with Tank going pale at the thought of missing out on the library, but barely able to contain his excitement about there being an arboretum. Just as the old shopkeeper was about to speak, he was interrupted.

"Just kidding," George laughed. "Now the only rule I have is that you really shouldn't try out any of the mantras that are here. If there is one you want to test, bring it over and we'll do it together, as long as it's not something too dangerous. All the artefacts are quite safe, but I would ask you to be as gentle as possible with the tomes as some of them are really quite old."

Smiling at the king, Peter wondered exactly what he'd let himself in for, as Gee Tee shot off at an unbelievable pace, belying his age, clearly determined to make the most of this rare opportunity, Tank continuing casually in his wake, but Peter could tell his friend was almost as excited; the little skip in his step and the not quite beaming smile on his face told their own story.

Falling into step alongside George, who, on noting the speed with which the Emporium owner had left them, had decided he just might need to be on hand rather quickly, just to... oversee things, Peter finally felt relaxed and happy to be there.

"It's good to see you again my boy," prompted the king. "I'm sorry I haven't been in touch to see how your recovery's been going, but things have been a bit... manic."

"I understand," the youngster replied. "I bet you hardly ever have a moment to yourself, being in charge of... everything."

Letting out the biggest belly laugh in the kingdom, the two of them turned the corner into the library proper, to be greeted by row upon row of shelves, thirty metres high, that seemed to go on as far as the eye could see.

"It does often seem that way my young friend, but it has its own rewards. I get to directly influence the future of our kind, leave my mark on history, and," he whispered quietly, "I get the finest charcoal imported directly from Japan. What more could any dragon wish for?"

Despite the fact that he was grinning broadly, Peter got the impression that the monarch really wasn't as happy as he claimed. It was nothing that he could put his finger on, more like instinct, or a gut feeling. There and then he vowed to himself to find out more should the opportunity arise.

Far off in the distance, Peter could just make out Tank, scanning a shelf of tomes intently, and also hear Gee Tee's giant footsteps padding about from somewhere much further away.

Sweeping his arms in one long motion, the king indicated the library as a whole.

"Go and explore; we've got plenty of time, and not many dragons ever get the chance to wander through this place."

Not needing to be told twice, he turned in the opposite direction to his pal and set off down one of the aisles, looking up towards the top of the shelves as he did, dumbfounded at some of the things he noticed straight away. There were plenty of rolled up scrolls bound with ancient pieces of twine, mixed in with dusty old books and tomes that looked as though they hadn't seen the light of day in centuries. Coming to an abrupt halt only a few metres into the aisle, he reached up as high as he could, and very, very carefully, pulled down a brown, ragged, dust encrusted book. On the spine it read in gold italic, 'Designs and mantras intended to aid in the creation of submersible crafts by Leonardo da Vinci.'

Blowing the thick covering of dust off the front cover, he began turning the delicate sheets very gently. Page after page of drawings, sketches and writing flew by. There was hardly any space on the paper that hadn't been used. Writings and equations littered the margins, doodles danced around the headings, all of them wondrous. There were mantras that made things air tight, kept pressure at bay, and drawings of great mechanical arms that held all sorts of equipment, from nets to catch sea creatures, to intricate metal grabbers that would pick up rocks and minerals. It was fascinating and he couldn't resist tracing his finger over some of the drawings and the fantastic script, trying to imagine what it must have been like to work with someone as great as da Vinci. From an early age the young dragons were all taught about him with stories that amazed and astounded, not only about his dragon life, but about everything he achieved on the surface... he was one of the truly unsung dragon heroes. Brought out of his thoughts by the sound of the master mantra maker stomping about somewhere not that far away, carefully he closed the ancient book, slipping it back into the gap that he'd taken if from. Slowly and steadily he continued to make his way down the row of shelves, ensuring that he looked at as many books, as he could.

On his achingly slow journey, he came across volumes about alchemy, plants, witchcraft and creatures that he was sure were mythical, but by the looks of it had, at some point in history, existed. Scrolls and weathered tomes about underwater cities and jungle islands that contained dinosaurs that had avoided extinction took up shelf after shelf, with titles such as 'Less skull leads to a healthier bowel' and 'Jazz up your mating ritual; ten sure fire ways to decorate your scales with human remains to make you irresistible'. It seemed to him that everything ever written by, or about, a dragon existed here somewhere on these shelves.

Continuing on, he stumbled across a small alcove that contained a massive glass case. A document sat on view, framed and backlit. Intrigued, he wandered over to get a better look. Ancient paper looked perfectly preserved, on which read a surprisingly modern day text in English. Realisation hit him like a herd of stampeding buffalo as he continued to read. This wasn't a prophecy, this was... THE PROPHECY! The one in which...

"Ahhhhh," sighed the king. "I figured you'd be the one to find it."

"This is the, the..."

"Yes, the prophecy, where it all began. I know."

"But... it actually exists?"

"It does," he replied. "But you already know what I'm going to say next. You can't tell anyone. There are reasons why dragons aren't supposed to know."

"That's why in the nursery ring we were taught that the prophecy and the agreement were never actually written down, but were magically agreed, verbally," Peter suggested.

"That's right," observed the king. "They were settled orally, with a binding magical agreement, so what is taught is strictly true. But they were written down as well, so that in time to come, a record would be held for all to see, evidence of what we as a race agreed to, and why. This, my young friend, is all that remains of that testimony."

Fascinated, Peter nodded before going back to studying the document in its glass case, as his host hovered over his shoulder.

"Why is it written in modern day English?"

Much to Peter's disappointment, the king guffawed

again.

"Both the agreement and the prophecy were originally written in ancient Hebrew, and that's what you see before you, part of the original document. The reason it stands out in modern day English to you, is that part of the binding magical enchantment translates the text into whatever language the reader is most familiar with. This, I am led to believe, was the only way at the time that the Basilisks, the Hydra Queen, the Manticores and the Heretics of Antar would all agree to sign up to such a thing."

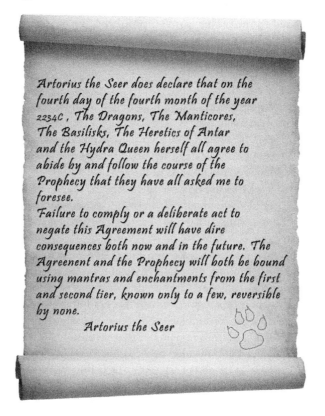

Artorius the Seer does declare that on the fourth day of the fourth month of the year 2234C , The Dragons, The Manticores, The Basilisks, The Heretics of Antar and the Hydra Queen herself all agree to abide by and follow the course of the Prophecy that they have all asked me to foresee.

Failure to comply or a deliberate act to negate this Agreement will have dire consequences both now and in the future. The Agreement and the Prophecy will both be bound using mantras and enchantments from the first and second tier, known only to a few, reversible by none.

Artorius the Seer

Astonished at the antique document, he couldn't begin to comprehend the complexity of the magic that had gone into the translation process, let alone about the part making it binding. It was truly staggering to behold.

"The... ah... ah prophecy itself, was it all about guiding and protecting the humans?" he asked sheepishly.

Considering Peter's question with a much more serious look on his face, the king leant to one side, and while scratching his chin, replied,

"I think you know I'm not at liberty to answer that question. But if it's any consolation, then if I could tell anyone what I know, then it most definitely would be you."

At just the mention of the word 'prophecy,' the words ingrained in the king's head threatened to overwhelm his memory, appearing as if on a chalk board right in front of his face. Becoming instantly alert, the ring had its power ready to be called on, aware of the importance held within the text. As Peter continued to study the ancient record, the king studied the words floating inside his mind.

"Millennia from now, when today's apes have evolved to be more civilised, a dark shadow will fall across the world. Enemies old and new will form a powerful alliance, their goal: total domination.

With the planet ravaged, scorched, on fire, only the pure white brilliance of a dragon can free it from the devil's grasp. Or so it would seem.

In our most desperate time of need, one stands above all others. An ape evolved, or is it something more?

Humanity, as it will become known, is to be guided, protected, nurtured and cherished. All of our destinies depend upon it."

Whenever he thought about the prophecy, the same series of questions always assaulted him. When would it happen? It had been over twenty thousand years since the agreement had been reached, and there was still no sign of it coming true. Who was The White Dragon? In the history of their race, not one single all-white dragon had ever been conceived... NEVER! Of course there are some that are partly white, but not fully. Would it ever come to pass? And just why was it so important to protect and guide the humans of this world? What part did they have to play in all of this?

Opening his eyes, not realising that he'd even closed them, he tried to shake away all the negative thoughts. So much about the prophecy bothered him, as it had no doubt the monarchs before him. He'd always just supposed that things would unravel as they were supposed to, if indeed The White Dragon ever made an appearance. Brushing aside the pointless thoughts, he offered the youngster with him the most encouraging smile he could.

Peter returned it with interest, feeling all warm inside as he thought,

'Things just keep getting weirder and weirder. Here I am in the most amazing and secret place in the entire kingdom, alongside the king, who, by his own admission, wants to confide in me. Four months ago I was just normal, now all of a sudden I'm involved in this. I just can't get my head around it.'

Patting the youngster on the back, the ruler suggested they move on. Continuing on up the aisle, they stumbled across a huge bookcase with literally hundreds of noses carved into it. Craning his neck to look up at the very top, the hockey player could just make out the words 'Aroma Therapy'.

Unable to pass it by, he just had to stop and take a look. Hanging back, the king, had anyone been there to notice, had a smirk which definitely had the potential to become a giggle, and maybe even blossom into a guffaw.

Adjusting his head slightly, Peter looked at the title of the first book in the section, shaking his head as he did so. It read 'Ahhhhh Bicester!!!'

Unable to resist, he reached up as high as he could and

wriggled the book free, blowing about a barn's worth of spiders' webs off the front cover, once it was down. With great care, he opened it up somewhere in the middle, nearly dropping it when a mushroom cloud of golden dust exploded out from its pages, encompassing his entire top half as it did so. Coughing, he spluttered, blinked and shook his head furiously from side to side, attempting to rid himself of the stuff. It just seemed to stick though. All the time George stood, watching with interest, eager to see just how things would unfold.

Golden dust stuck to Peter's face like rusk on a baby's cheeks, his eyes started to water and he felt as though he was going to sneeze. A short cough brought the urge under control. As it did so, a mysterious scent assaulted his olfactory sense, something he couldn't make head nor tail of. After a few seconds, however, the smell, or smells as he'd now come to realise, had started to separate out, inspiring a series of different images to course through his brain. Horses became a theme, lots of horses being... hmmm... he wasn't sure. Next came a perfect picture of the biggest and hottest roaring fire in the world. Shivers of excitement rippled up his body at the thought of the enticing heat. As the blazing fire faded just a little, he could just make out hot metal being worked by two very large, very strong, sweaty men. It was a... blacksmith's forge from a long time ago, he realised, trying hard to understand what an earth was going on. Abruptly there was a tiny pop from the open book still in his hands, and a much smaller shower of golden dust blew up into the air, like a miniature fireworks display, bursting open at its apex to form the phrase 'Industries of Victorian Bicester'. Seeming to have some sense of what was going on now, he picked some pages at random, only to have the same thing happen again and again, smells from many different eras, from the medieval and dark ages through to Tudor, Georgian and Victorian times. It was, he thought... absolutely brilliant! Books that told their story by... odour!

Slipping 'Ahhhhh Bicester!!!' back into its rightful place on the shelf, his gaze wandered along the rest of the section, intrigued to see what else existed in this truly remarkable genre. Meanwhile the king dabbed his cheeks with a multicoloured handkerchief that he'd pulled from the top pocket of his shirt, tears of laughter racing down his face, watching the youngster comprehend this part of the library. Deliberately hanging back a little on purpose, knowing that it might have some sort of amusing twist, Peter's expression had caused him to laugh more than he had in ages. So bad were the tears, that the handkerchief had almost reached saturation point, with the monarch having to turn away for fear of flooding the entire floor. To his credit, the young dragon had skipped over a few dubious volumes as he worked his way down the shelf. Among the titles he'd avoided pulling out were 'Tang with a Bang', 'Stink in Pink', 'Seek the Reek', 'Stench of a Wench' and 'The Pong Song of Hong Kong'. His eyes bulged at the one he really liked the look of: 'The Scent of a Dragon'. However, they were mysteriously drawn to the book beside it, 'Bums that Hum'. Looking carefully from side to side, and feeling more guilty than a child waiting outside the headmaster's office, his tiny human shaped fingers darted forward and with amazing precision and grace, gently, but very quickly, pulled the book out into his, by now, very sweaty hands. Carefully, he turned the old leather covered book over to look at the back. Unusually, there was an inscription written in gold leaf.

'Twenty iconic dragons of the age leave their buttock burping aromas for future generations.'

"A must have, must smell, for the serious collector." Socrates.

"The rich smell of success, from the bottom to the very top." Plato.

"A book not to be sniffed at." Aristotle.

Peter's tears splashed onto the ornate marble floor, in much the same way as the king's own had only a short time ago. Gently, he placed the volume back, knowing that opening it up would only create more hilarity and he was just too sensible for that, fully aware he'd seen more than enough.

'What a wonderful place,' he thought, moving away from the shelf, turning into the next aisle, all the time looking for more amazing manuscripts, aware of the king's footsteps echoing quietly behind him.

Abruptly, he heard Gee Tee scream excitedly. A cross between a roar, a snort and a squawk, the noise was quickly followed by the sound of running feet. Making a quick note of where he'd got to, Peter took off in the wake of the monarch, both of them heading for the old shopkeeper.

When he finally arrived a few minutes later, after having made two wrong turnings, Gee Tee stood in the middle of an aisle, brandishing a thick scroll, an expression of pure wonder on his face, watched by Tank and their host. Wondering how the king had beaten him, Peter's thoughts were suddenly interrupted as the old shopkeeper spoke up.

"Come quickly child, I've found it, I've found it," he squealed in delight.

"What have you found?" replied Peter, intrigued.

"We don't know yet," observed the king, frustrated.

Tank took hold of the master mantra maker's wings in an effort to calm him down, but he wasn't having any of it and shook him off instantly, no mean feat for someone that old, not considering Tank's impressive strength, whatever form he was in.

"What is it you've found?" demanded the ruler.

Gee Tee took deep, measured breaths, trying hard to calm himself.

"I've found something that I've been searching for, for over three centuries."

Peter and Tank were visibly shaken, the king... not so much.

'What on earth has he been looking for that has taken that amount of time to find?' wondered Peter.

"And?" stated the king, losing more patience with every second that passed.

"I've found the instructions for creating '*Elixir of fundo vita*'," he said excitedly.

"Ahhh," sighed George, nodding his head in understanding.

Meanwhile Peter was busy doing the translation in his mind, knowing the others were already well ahead of him. Languages were definitely his weakest link. Tank turned to his friend, recognised the trouble he was having and whispered,

"Elixir of extended life."

Peter mouthed a silent, "Thank you."

Both pals and the king all looked at Gee Tee, waiting for what he had to say next.

"Don't you know what this is?" uttered the old shopkeeper. Tank and Peter of course weren't sure, but could have taken a pretty good guess given its name. On the other hand, the king knew all there was to know about everything in the library. It was part of his remit.

"Do I have to spell it out to you? barked the increasingly frustrated shopkeeper. "The clue's in the title."

"I know exactly what it is, and more importantly, what it's supposed to do," announced the monarch.

"Why didn't you tell me it was here?" demanded Gee Tee angrily. "You knew an awful long time ago that I was searching for it."

Both Peter and Tank could feel the heat rising throughout their bodies, the young hockey player especially. The very last thing he would have wanted was for their host and the master mantra maker to have a full scale row, here inside his private chambers.

'This is supposed to be my day,' he thought, understanding just a little too late how selfish it sounded, even inside his head.

"I should have realised when you shot off like a jet plane from a carrier, exactly what you were looking for. I'm so very sorry."

"Why exactly are you sorry?" asked the Emporium owner, folding the scroll up inside his right wing, a suspicious look etched across his scaly face.

"Because I'm afraid you can't have it," uttered the king, apologetically.

"You owe me!" screamed the old shopkeeper, flame crackling from either side of his jaw as he did so.

"I know."

"I've helped you dozens of times, probably even saved your life. You wouldn't be here if not for me."

"I know."

Looking on, Peter and Tank felt shell shocked, not knowing what to do or say. Clearly this was something between the two of them, something from the past, and something everyone else was better keeping out of.

"Why?" asked Gee Tee, gloomily.

"It's not mine to give you. If it was, you'd have it in an instant."

"Piffle!" spat the master mantra maker, steam rising from behind his ears.

Abruptly the sound of somebody shouting far below echoed throughout the residence. Peter stood watching as the king's normally, kind, caring and responsible face visibly flinched, albeit for just a split second.

"Stay here," he ordered the trio. "Whatever you do, don't reveal your presence. No one is supposed to have access to the library at the moment. Do you understand? If you're caught, you'll be in massive amounts of trouble, and so will I." Shaking his head, turning to leave, this time his voice was softer. "Please don't reveal yourself" and with that, he ran off, pretty quickly for someone of his age, heading for the staircase.

The shouting grew steadily louder with real panic etched into whoever the voice belonged to. Clearly surprised at the turn of events, the three friends stood looking at each other. After a few uncomfortable moments, Gee Tee, still with the scroll tucked neatly under his wing, headed off towards the balcony.

Instinctively, Tank grabbed him by the shoulder, before Peter even had a chance to move.

"What do you think you're doing?" declared the strapping rugby player.

"More to the point, what is it you think you're doing... apprentice?"

The very unsubtle reminder from the master mantra maker about who employed whom would at the very least slow down most people or dragons; not Tank though, who was in no mood to play one of his employer's silly games. Keeping a vice like grip on his boss, not easy whilst being loomed over, he looked him firmly in the eyes, adding steel to his words.

"This is the king we're talking about. He asked us to do something, and by God we're going to do just that. I won't have you getting us and him in trouble. Do you understand?"

Peter's jaw was almost scraping the ground. It wasn't so much what his friend had said, it was the way in which he'd said it that was so shocking. Gee Tee's mouth twitched slightly, but before he had a chance to say anything, Tank let rip once more.

"You should also remember why we're here. This is Peter's day. It is only because of him that we were invited, and I will not have you ruining it."

A tense silence shrouded the three of them as the apprentice continued to hold on to his boss, the old shopkeeper glaring daggers at the outspoken youngster, while Peter stood, too shocked and surprised to speak. Off in the distance, the sound of footfalls floating up from the twisting staircase could be heard. With the yelling having stopped, all three, using their enhanced senses, could just make out a few desperate words.

"Sire, sire... come quickly."

"What is it Madeline?" asked the king, all businesslike.

"I'm really sorry to disturb you on your day off, but it's... it's... one of the Crimson Guards. He's in a really bad way, close to death we think, but he says he has information that he will only pass on to you in person."

High above in the library, Gee Tee shook off his apprentice's grip, and keeping his voice to a whisper, addressed both youngsters.

"I wasn't going to ruin things for either us or the king. It's good to know that you do at least have a little steel in your soul, though, apprentice," quipped the shopkeeper, giving the two of them a little smile. "What I was going to do though, something I recommend that we all do now, is move a little closer to the balcony, so that we can see and hear exactly what's going on. I get the distinct impression that it might well be of great importance, and that the king just might need our help."

Creeping through the array of bookcases, making virtually no noise, Peter was relieved to know that the master mantra maker had no intention of spoiling things, or getting the monarch into trouble. Sneaking round the final giant bookshelf, all three of them crawled along the polished floor, before sitting up against the side of the balcony. No longer the faint whisper they were, the voices from below were much crisper and clearer. Closing his eyes, Peter tried to imagine exactly what George was going through. Three more sets of footsteps came across clearly from the direction of the entrance. If Peter wasn't mistaken, it sounded as though someone was either being supported or dragged along.

"Get him up on the plinth," ordered the king.

"Yes sire," came two identical replies.

"And just who are you?" asked the ruler suspiciously.

"My name is Yoyo Baines, sire, a healer from Perth, Australia."

"You seem vaguely familiar."

"I once served in the council's med centre, a very long time ago."

"Ahhh," sighed the king. "And how is it that you find yourself here today?"

"Your Crimson Guard. I found him beneath Perth, struggling for life. He convinced me to bring him straight here, against my better judgement, it has to be said."

Standing deep in thought, George eventually spoke.

"Couldn't you have just healed him?"

As Yoyo was about to reply, the unconscious Flash started to come round, flailing his limbs about on the plinth as he did so. Sweat poured off his brow as he tried to sit up and swing his legs over the side. Both guards who'd accompanied Yoyo and Flash into the private residence stepped forward to help, only to be waved away. Sitting up despite the pain, the Crimson Guard swayed delicately from side to side. Yoyo stepped in close, just in case Flash lost consciousness again.

Upstairs, next to the balcony that overlooked the plinth, the three friends listened intently to what was taking place down below. In an effort to remain concealed just as the king had wished, Gee Tee had cast a mantra that was now masking all their life signs. It was of course something from ancient times, but the master mantra maker had remembered it in barely an instant. Both friends had been amazed at the change in the old proprietor since they'd entered the library. It was almost as if he'd been infused with energy and had cast off about three hundred years. As the two of them glanced across at each other, hidden from view, they both wondered how long Gee Tee could remain so full of power and, more importantly, how long he could, or would, behave himself.

Down below, in the vast open circle with the plinth in the middle, Flash anxiously looked around at everyone there, before whispering to the king.

"Yoyo saved my life, sire. Please let him stay. He's the only reason I've managed to get back to you with this information."

Like most people and dragons, the king thought himself a good judge of character, and made an instant decision, knowing he could always undo it later on.

"Alright Flash, he can stay... for now."

Flash nodded.

"The others though, they have to go," he whispered.

Thinking hard about what to do, it didn't take him long to reach a decision.

"Guards, Madeline... please leave us," ordered the king.

"Sire?" replied Madeline, his personal assistant, politely.

"Do the three of you not understand a direct command? Leave at once, and don't come back until I order you to do so. Yoyo and Flash will be staying at my behest."

"Yes sire," answered Madeline and the guards simultaneously, before turning around and strutting back out through the entrance.

With a quick flick of his head, the king glanced up at the balcony on the library floor, certain he knew what was going on, despite not sensing anyone up there. A gut feeling told him that the shopkeeper had once again employed his craftiness, and that his guests were indeed taking everything in.

"Sire," announced Yoyo. "Before we go any further, I must tell you that Flash's injuries are very serious, fatal in fact, from what I've seen."

A worried frown creased the king's brow as he eyed the brave dragon agent.

"Is this true Flash?" he asked softly.

"I don't know for sure, Majesty, but I suspect it is. All I really know, is that if not for Yoyo, then I would have died a long time ago, without anyone being any the wiser."

"I see," said the king." Then I suppose you better tell me what's so important."

As Peter, Tank and Gee Tee listened from behind the balcony, Flash began to reel off his adventure in

Antarctica, describing everything down to the finest detail, interrupted only occasionally by the searing pain that racked his fatally wounded body. Yoyo stood by, listening to the story along with the king, doing his best to support the Crimson Guard, casting mantra after mantra, giving his all to relieve the pain when the naga inflicted wound flared up. Some parts of the tale sounded like complete and utter fiction to Peter, while others were so sad it made him want to cry. Of course he couldn't, otherwise it might well have given away the fact that the king, Flash and Yoyo weren't alone. When he heard about the prisoners and the conditions of their incarceration, trapped below the ice, it was all he could do to stifle a sob. On the other hand, the king reacted in quite a different way. Up until then, he'd let Flash get on with it, not once interrupting or asking a question, but while Peter thought his interest may lie in the naga leader himself, he was in fact more interested in the other dragon prisoners, particularly the one who'd helped Flash escape. Listening carefully, Peter heard the dragon agent mention a birthmark on the captive's chest, the description of which caused the head of state to take a deep breath and shake uncontrollably. Reluctantly, he let it go. Continuing on, the injured agent failed to notice the reigned in look of thunder smothered across the ruler's face as talk turned to the memories that had leaked into him from the dying naga. At the mere mention of what had happened, Peter felt physically sick. Surely stealing magic from a being about to kick the bucket was wrong... wasn't it? But the revelation of a corrupt councillor and the existence of some kind of plot that involved nagas disguising themselves as humans across the world, made him forget about any scruples he may have had.

After a few more questions and another painful episode for Flash, the story moved on. Everyone listened intently, intrigued by the Crimson Guard's bravery and ingenuity. With the defeat of the naga disguised as a human at Perth hospital, Flash ended his tale and slumped down hard on the stone plinth. Yoyo took a good look at him while the king stood and watched.

For Peter the compulsion was just too great, and much to the surprise of his two cohorts, he poked his head above the railing, sneaking a peek down at the stone plinth. Luckily for him, Flash and Yoyo were facing the other way, and the king, although looking almost straight at him, didn't flinch at all. The sight of Flash lying on the stone tablet was almost too much for him to bear. Never before in his life had a seen a dragon in such a sorry state. Even from as far away as he was, he could tell just how much pain and despair the brave agent was suffering. Following Peter's lead, Tank snuck a quick look, while Gee Tee's giant, scaly head slowly rose above the rail, much like a submarine surfacing.

Nothing Yoyo did seemed to make any difference to the pain searing throughout the Crimson Guard's body which writhed and flailed about, longing to embrace death now that he'd fulfilled his objective. With one last effort, Flash turned his head towards the monarch and whispered,

"I'm sorry Majesty. I've failed you."

Lowering himself so that he could look directly into Flash's steely blue eyes, the king spoke from his heart.

"On the contrary Flash, it seems that I've failed you. But perhaps all is not quite lost." An expression that suggested he was very sorry for what he was about to do took hold of the ruler's face, as he got to his feet and craned his neck, all the time shaking his head.

"Master Mantra Maker! I need your help once again," he shouted as loud as he could, startling Yoyo and even the semi lucid Flash.

Standing up to their full height, revealing their presence to all down below, Peter, Tank and Gee Tee all made their way around to the staircase that led down towards the unexpected scene of tragedy. Yoyo wondered what was going on, while Flash just continued to wriggle about on the plinth, muttering gibberish as he did so.

Following in Gee Tee's footsteps as they wove their way down the spiral stairs, Tank and Peter finally stopped in front of the king.

"Can you help him?" the sovereign asked Gee Tee.

With the scroll still firmly tucked beneath his wing, the master mantra maker stepped over to the plinth and began examining Flash. Everyone else looked on.

"Beg your pardon Majesty, but I've done everything that I can to render assistance," prompted Yoyo, quietly.

From beside Flash, Gee Tee scoffed and snorted on hearing the healer's words. Ignoring the shopkeeper, the king replied.

"Your work in getting him here is beyond comparison, and I will try to reward your efforts when an opportunity arises. Until then, there may be... other ways. The bravery of this particular Crimson Guard has helped keep our domain safe from many a threat more times than I care to remember. I think if there's anything, anything at all that can be done to save him, then we should at least try, don't you?"

"Of course, sire," replied Yoyo, bowing.

Everyone stood back, watching Gee Tee examine Flash.

"Well, Master Mantra Maker?" demanded the king.

Gee Tee straightened up, a thoughtful expression crossing his scaly face.

"There's something that just might work, but... it's dangerous, very dangerous in fact."

"Then do it," ordered the monarch. "I will take full responsibility."

"Not so quickly. There's the small matter of my... fee," added the old shopkeeper, looking down at the scroll he hadn't let go of since finding it.

Peter stood aghast at what the Emporium owner had just said, watching as the king's face turned purple with rage.

"You dare say that to me, here in this place?"

Gee Tee didn't look phased at all, quite the opposite in fact.

"Yes I dare," he announced, his eyes glinting mischievously through the square plastic glasses that sat on his leathery old nose. "As we've already discussed, I've helped save your life on numerous occasions, and exactly how have you ever repaid me? Stopped the visits from the Guards that bitter old Councillor Rosebloom sends on a regular basis...? No! Given my shop back its royal licence, so that maybe I might win back the custom of just a few of those that I lost when Rosebloom stabbed me in the back for not getting that job...? No! Have I ever received payment of any sort, monetary or otherwise for all the potions, mantras and artefacts that I provided you with, on all your knightly adventures...? No! That's not to mention the knowledge and advice I freely gave. During everything, you had this," the master mantra maker withdrew the scroll from within his wing and waved it in the air, "and all this time you knew that I've spent centuries looking for it. You didn't have the decency to tell me that you had it, but wouldn't give it to me. Well, it all stops here. If you want my help once again, then here's your price," he spluttered, repeatedly waving the scroll above his head. "And let me guess what's next. You can't possibly let a brave dragon die. You're the one chance he's got to live. Yes, I know all these things, but the price of my help is the scroll, full stop!"

There and then, Peter wanted to leave. None of this should be happening. This was supposed to be such a special day, meeting the king with both his friends, having a great time learning some more about his grandfather and finding out exactly what had been left for him. This just wasn't it, he kept telling himself over and over again.

Tank felt thoroughly disgusted and ashamed at what he was seeing.

'This monster,' he thought, 'is not the dragon that I work and care for day in and day out. Why on earth is he doing this? Aside from the morality of helping a brave and badly wounded dragon which if you have the ability and power to do so, you just should. Mirroring his friend's thoughts, he knew none of this ought to be happening. What have we got ourselves into?'

The colour in the king's face started to return to normal, as the small group stood around the stone plinth watching Flash try and manage his pain with as much dignity as he could given the circumstances. Gee Tee and the king had clearly reached an impasse; how it was going to be resolved, nobody seemed to know.

"You would watch this dragon die, knowing that you can prevent it?" roared the ruler, his voice filled to the brim with passion. Clearly he was trying to contain his anger and temper.

"I've told you... it's your responsibility. You've done nothing for me after all I've done for you. It's time for a change. The cost of helping him, and you, is this scroll."

Shaking his head as beads of sweat glistened around the sides of his long, grey hair, the sovereign was finding it hard not to lose control.

"YOU may be the only being on the planet with the ability to help him. Did you not hear everything that he's been through? Everything that he's given? Don't you think you should help him if you have the knowledge to do so?" he stressed, trembling ever so slightly.

The old shopkeeper didn't answer, preferring instead to cross his wings stubbornly in front of his body and gaze dead ahead.

'This is it,' thought Peter. 'We're all going to be sent to jail.'

"Don't you understand?" declared the king more forcefully this time. "That scroll is not mine to give to you. If it were, I would hand it over in a heartbeat, not to save Flash's life, but because I believe after all you've been through that you should have it. But I cannot, not even to save this brave dragon's life. Whatever you say, however much you plead, I cannot let you have that scroll. I'm sorry."

Peter thought that this just might do the trick and persuade the stubborn old shopkeeper to change his mind. Tank, however, knew better. His boss was one of, if not the most, pigheaded beings on the planet, and it wasn't in his nature to change his mind for anyone, not even the king.

'What is needed,' thought the apprentice, 'is another way, a third option, something for... everyone.'

As Gee Tee and the king stood glaring at each other, with Flash mumbling incoherently to himself on the plinth, inspiration suddenly struck the rugby player.

"What if you were to... loan the scroll to Gee Tee, Your Majesty?" Tank blurted out, suddenly.

Simultaneously, both the king and the Emporium owner turned to gaze at Tank, making him feel about a centimetre tall under such scrutiny.

"It wouldn't work I'm afraid. I don't believe for a second that I'd ever get it back again." The master mantra maker nodded in agreement. Clearly the king was right, and the old shopkeeper had no plans to return it. Sudden optimism provided by Tank's outburst regressed back to tension and silence, until a cunning smile snaked its way across the rugby player's misshapen face.

"How about loaning the scroll to *me,* sire? I would guarantee that you'd get it back, and could help Gee Tee work with it," he offered, knowing that it might just be enough to convince him.

Scratching his chin, the king thought about the proposal.

"Definitely not," raved the master mantra maker.

Before the monarch could open his mouth to respond, Tank jumped in.

"It makes sense for everyone, and you know it. Clearly the king can't give you the scroll, otherwise he would. Can't you see how desperate he is to save that young dragon over there? You should be ashamed of yourself."

"Watch your tongue, apprentice," threatened his boss.

"No more watching tongues. I've had to do that for long enough," countered Tank, suddenly. "And we'll be having a little chat about the apprentice thing as well, quite soon, but back to the here and now. Clearly the only way you're going to get your talons on that scroll you so desperately want, is for the king to loan it to me, and for me to grant you access to it. What do you say?"

While Gee Tee considered Tank's question, Peter and Yoyo held their breath, whilst Tank turned to look at the king. Sighing, and with no other option available, George nodded in response to the youngster's question.

"So what will it be? Make up your mind now, for everyone's sake, but most of all for that brave dragon lying there, contorted in pain."

Tank wasn't one to blow his own trumpet. Of course there were things that he just excelled at, plant and animal physiology, rugby and mantras amongst them, but here and now he knew beyond a doubt that he'd achieved his goal, realising that the old shopkeeper would accede to the deal and would therefore help Flash. He was in fact just playing for time, trying to save face.

With Peter and Yoyo still holding their breaths, Gee Tee threw the scroll to Tank, while at the same time saying,

"Agreed."

Releasing a long breath, Peter closed his eyes and thanked the heavens for his friend. If not for Tank, then he hated to think what might have happened. As he did so, the master mantra maker whirled into action, a mini tornado, completely unstoppable, with an unending supply of energy.

"There are some things I'm going to need," stated the old shopkeeper to no one in particular. "Firstly, two clownfish... alive. Secondly, a large quantity of bark from a silver birch, dragon bone, sea salt and a large pestle and mortar." Pointing to the king's hand, Gee Tee made his final request.

"I'll also require that," he said nonchalantly.

Peter and Tank's eyes nearly popped out. Gee Tee had just told the king that he needed the unique magical ring that he wore, the one that held a limitless supply of mana, or magic if you like.

"I see," said the sovereign gruffly. "Anything else?" he added sarcastically, before closing his eyes and telepathically sending the list of ingredients to the head of the guards on duty in the council building. "They know it's urgent, but it still may take a while. Is there anything we can do in the meantime?"

"Hmmm... I suppose we really need to make him more comfortable, as this could all take some time. Do you have anywhere that we can use?"

"There's a dragon sized sofa in the living room."

"Good, good, we'll move him there if that's okay."

The king nodded a reply.

"Come on then you two. Make yourselves useful instead of just standing there gawping. Bring young Flash over to the living room," Gee Tee ordered Peter and Tank.

As carefully as possible, the two friends picked up the barely conscious Crimson Guard, with the rugby player taking his head, since he was by far the stronger, and the hockey player taking his legs. Following the king, the Emporium owner and Yoyo into the living room, they carefully placed Flash down on a very bright red fabric sofa, pretty much the size of a tennis court, making sure he was as comfortable as possible.

'It's amazing,' Peter thought, gobsmacked by not only the size of the room, about a football pitch by the look of things, but also by the style of it. Well stocked shelves full of human literature littered most of two walls, with photos of various places, people and dragons scattered in front of the books. Fantastic works of art, from both above and below ground, adorned the other couple of walls, while ancient looking tapestries fluttered slightly in the very light breeze that ran throughout the place. Peter turned to see Tank and Yoyo as astonished as he was with Gee Tee stroking his huge prehistoric jaw as he took in the entire room.

"Not bad," admitted the old shopkeeper, blowing out a small jet of flame from his nose. "It's a bit ostentatious though."

Shaking his head, Peter wondered how the king would react. To his surprise, George just smiled and wandered off through a doorway to yet another part of this intriguing building. Gee Tee, in the meantime, had commandeered Yoyo and Tank and was busy dishing out instructions.

"Apprentice, when the first items arrive I want you to start preparing everything," grunted the old shopkeeper, still gazing around the room they all found themselves in. Lacking the normally quick response from his apprentice that he was used to, the master mantra maker whirled round to face him. Tank stood, hands on hips, a defiant look scrawled across his face.

'Things,' Peter thought, 'seem to have changed significantly between the two of them.'

Tank and Gee Tee continued to stare at each other from a few metres away, Yoyo standing uncomfortably between them. Flash let out a low moan from the sofa, which was ignored by everyone.

"Is there a problem... apprentice?" enquired Gee Tee, poking his plastic glasses as far up his nose as they would go.

Tank just stood there in silence, refusing to budge or speak.

'I've never seen him like this before,' thought Peter. 'I really hope he knows what he's doing.'

Flash let out another groan, this time longer and much harsher. Slipping out from between the two colleagues, Yoyo rushed over to the sickly dragon with all the speed of someone much younger. Peter watched as the healer turned Flash onto his side, trying to ascertain the state of the lethal wound that ran diagonally across his back. Not sure whether to go and try and help, as it would mean getting in between the warring pair, Peter hoped desperately for a quick resolution to whatever was going on. Surprisingly, he got his wish almost straight away.

Squinting through his glasses, Gee Tee let out a short sigh.

"Please would you start the preparations when things begin to arrive... Tank?"

Peter's eyes widened like never before. Tank's stern look disappeared immediately.

"I would be happy to... Gee Tee," replied the rugby player with a fondness in his voice that nobody in the room missed.

Another moan from the Crimson Guard grabbed everybody's attention.

"You'd better come and take a look at this," Yoyo commanded from the sofa. "His wound is getting steadily worse."

Gee Tee plodded over and, leaning down, inspected the lesion that ran across the dragon agent's back.

"You're right," whispered the old shopkeeper quietly. "It's deteriorating at quite a rate. Unless we do something soon, he'll be dead before everything arrives."

Looking to Gee Tee for guidance, Peter, Tank and Yoyo watched as the master mantra maker stood up straight, head to one side, apparently thinking about the next course of action. You could have heard a pin drop, the silence was so loud. However, it wasn't the Emporium owner who interrupted it.

"Got it!" exclaimed Tank. "At least, I think I have."

The others turned to look at him inquisitively, particularly his employer.

Gathering his thoughts, the rugby player started to pace back and forth on the lush carpet while his friends watched. Turning to face Gee Tee, he tried to explain what he had in mind.

"About two years ago, a European dragon came into the shop to have a mantra repaired."

His employer was about to interrupt, but Tank held up one of his huge fingers and stopped him.

"He was a long, tall dragon, dark yellow all over, except for some red markings that looked like honeysuckle running down his back. He spoke with either a Spanish or Portuguese accent. The mantra he needed fixing was... was... ummmm... let me see. It was something to do with shipping something... plants or animals... or something. Ahh, that's it. Shipping giant squid... *architeuthis,* which I'm sure Peter knows, means dominant squid," he said, turning and smiling at his friend.

Returning the smile, the hockey player, even after all this time, marvelled at his friend's ability to know practically everything related to nature.

"So," interrupted Gee Tee softly, "what has this got to do with...? Ahhh... I see. Good work appr... Tank. The mantra he brought in to be repaired froze the squid right down to the cellular level for a short period of time if I remember correctly."

Tank nodded wholeheartedly.

"So we freeze Flash until everything we need arrives and then... bang, unfreeze him and hit him with the cure. Okay..." muttered Gee Tee to himself. "Let's see if I can remember that spell. It was... it was... Sumerian if I'm not mistaken... um... yes, I think I have it. Right, let's give it a go. Stand back please Yoyo, there's a good dragon."

The healer, ignoring the dripping condescension, and not knowing what to make of everything, did as he was told. In all his time he'd never met a dragon like the shopkeeper, and guessed that he wasn't likely to again, anytime soon.

Gee Tee leant over Flash, whose moaning continued at barely a whisper. The noise from the remarks the master mantra maker was uttering seemed seductive to Peter. He could only grasp a few out of context, random words: *murgu* he knew to be 'back,' *lirum* he knew was 'physical strength,' and the only other one he could get a handle on was *mush,* which he was pretty sure was either 'snake' or 'reptile.'

After barely a minute, Gee Tee called Yoyo over to have a look at the very still Flash. It only took a matter of seconds for the physician to confirm that the mantra had indeed frozen him, right down to the cellular level. With that done, they settled down and waited for the requested items to arrive.

All once again taking in the intricacies of the room, the king poked his head around the corner of a doorway and asked Peter to join him.

Tearing himself away from a picture of the ruler in his human guise jamming with the Beatles, the youngster crossed the room and followed the monarch's soft footsteps into the space beyond. A wide twisting corridor, sparsely lit, wound its way up a slight gradient to open out into a very plain bedroom. Upon entering, Peter was taken aback by the sight of the wooden floor, which was made from the most amazing oak floorboards. The colouring and grain were remarkable, but that wasn't what had caught his attention. There were hundreds, if not thousands, of intricate carvings across all the boards throughout the room. Kneeling down, running his hand across an engraved scene that depicted an almighty battle of some sort, he was hardly able to believe the quality of the craftsmanship that had gone into making them.

"Nice, aren't they?" chirped the king from the far end of the room.

"Magnificent," answered Peter, momentarily lost for words.

"A very famous dragon artist by the name of Flirty Downdraft, probably a little before your time, owed me a favour for saving his life. Anyway, when I became ruler, Flirty offered to make me something that he said would 'make me change the way I think every day.' He spent nearly five years designing and crafting those boards. It took a whole month and five artisans to fit them. Oh the council kicked up a fuss about the cost of putting them in here, but in the end I got my own way, despite making one or two more enemies because of it."

"Why would dragons become your enemy over something like this?" asked the youngster. "It seems so petty and... small."

A low chuckle rumbled from the king's mouth as he sat down on the edge of what could only be described as a proper 'king sized' bed, because it was, in human terms, more like the ground-floor-of-a-house sized bed, with a duvet that could have covered streets, and pillows the size of cars.

"Contrary to popular belief, we as a race are not nearly so far removed from the humans as we'd like to think. Pettiness, squabbles, bickering, scheming, one-upmanship, plotting other dragons' downfalls... it all goes on I'm afraid to say. If you asked most of our kind in the outlying suburbs, they'd tell you that we're above all that and we leave it to the humans and their politicians above ground. But it's simply not true. It goes on in the council and in a lot of other parts of the domain."

Stunned, that's how Peter felt. In the fifty years he'd spent studying in the nursery ring, there'd been no mention of anything like that, and he'd had no cause to believe that dragons didn't live in complete and utter harmony with one another.

"I'm slightly surprised that Gee Tee hasn't put you straight on that front. I'm pretty sure he has a tale to tell on that subject, as well as a few others."

Peter thought for a split second.

"Come to think of it, he did mention... Councillor..."

"Ahh... yes," ventured the monarch, knowing exactly what was coming next, despite the fact that he hadn't finished his sentence. "Bloody Councillor Rosebloom, disappointed about not being employed, does everything in his power to make life hard for the old shopkeeper. I know all about it, from the things his family arranged that led to the royal seal of approval being taken away, to the regular visits from the guards that are supposed to search for anything untoward in his shop."

"You know?"

"Of course," replied the ruler, matter-of-factly. "I am the king after all."

"Why do you let it go on when you know it's wrong?"

"Because I'm constantly fighting battles, many of which I can't possibly win. Not real conflicts of course, but those within the council to affect political decision making, to pass constitutions and to uphold dragon values and our laws. I, much to my disappointment, have to pick and choose which I can win, which I can lose and how much each will cost me in favours, resentment and prestige. I could probably have put a stop to the shop visits by the guards long ago, and believe you me, I wanted to. I really did. But the cost of doing so would diminish what little power I have, control that I need to keep the council in line, to wield when absolutely necessary. Being king is not the be all and end all that it seems. In that, your grandfather had a much greater understanding than I ever did, that is until I gained the position of king, by which time it was more than a little too late. As for Gee Tee, even though he looks a little frail at times due to his age, he's more than capable of looking after himself. I know full well that the guards and captain in charge who go to the Emporium to carry out the searches just sit around and listen to his old stories, something Councillor Rosebloom has absolutely no idea about. Long may it stay that way."

It all seemed pretty complicated to Peter, and sounded a complete nightmare; however, he was glad George had at least one eye on the wellbeing of the old shopkeeper.

'The master mantra maker deserves that at the very least,' he thought, watching the king lean down beside the giant bed and flick a switch of some kind.

A whole section of the wall in front of them swung around one hundred and eighty degrees to reveal a really old and well worn... trunk. Its dark, oily wood was scuffed and scratched, the metal holding it together had started to rust, and numerous dents and knocks had taken their toll.

As Peter sat and stared at it, suddenly it dawned on him what it was.

"My grandfather's trunk," he remarked excitedly.

"I hadn't forgotten," claimed the monarch. "Even with the sudden arrival of Flash, and the urgency of the situation, I still remember why you're here, and since there is a natural lull in proceedings while we wait for everything to arrive, this seems like the perfect opportunity for you to have this," the king said, gesturing towards the haggard old trunk. Peter wandered over to where George was sitting, not once taking his eyes off the chest. Standing up, the king put his hand on the youngster's shoulder.

"I'll leave you to it."

Peter looked perplexed.

"You should open it on your own. Whatever the chest contains is yours. I've done my part in looking after it for you. If you want to tell me after you've looked through it, then that would be great, but I really think you should open it and check it out on your own... in private. I'll make sure you won't be disturbed in here. Come back into the main room when you've finished. I doubt we'll have gone anywhere."

Smiling, the sovereign turned and left, leaving him alone with the trunk.

Sitting on the edge of the bed, he felt reluctant to open it, not having the vaguest idea as to what it might contain. Instead, he chose to study the outside, knowing that his grandfather would have once opened and closed this box all the time by the looks of things. From up close, the chest appeared even more magnificent than when he'd first clapped eyes on it, only a few moments ago. Despite being old and worn, he could see and feel just how sturdy it was. Clearly well made, he found himself tracing the lines of different patterns and initials with his fingers. Something else nagged at the back of his mind as he did so. It was a... feeling. A feeling of... great power. That was the only way to describe it. Something inside the box, or the crate itself had power. Gulping, he knew that he should just get on and open it up.

Carefully avoiding the splinters of wood that surrounded it, he flicked open the old latch, with much less force than he'd thought he'd have to use, and opened the lid right up. Inside, it was a mess. All sorts of one off mantra scrolls littered the top. Pulling out one or two, he couldn't make head nor tail of what was written on them, and that was just the ones where the ink hadn't faded. Working meticulously through the rolled up parchment like a child opening his presents at Christmas, he lost all track of time and his surroundings.

After opening the last scroll and reading something that looked more like a cave man's scrawl than a complicated magical hex, he delved deeper. Reaching in, he pulled out a pair of worn, dark brown, leather boots. They smelt... awful, but looked awesome. Putting them to one side, he grabbed hold of some sort of frame and gently tugged it out. Turning it over in his hands, he gasped... shocked. Inside, lined by dark blue velvet, sat a shimmering golden medal that seemed to quite literally be... on fire! Pretty sure he knew what it was, his eyes read the text that appeared underneath, just to be sure.

The Flaming Cross presented to Fredric Bluewillow on the 6th day of September 1743 for heroic deeds beyond the call of duty, in service to your king.'

Tears splashed onto the smoky glass, racing down its length until they reached the frame and dripped silently onto the oak flooring. For minutes, he just sat and cried, so absorbed that it might as well have been for hours.

Only a handful of dragons throughout history had ever

been decorated with the flaming cross, understandable given it is the highest honour that can be bestowed upon any of their race. It was something dragonlings are taught about in every nursery ring throughout the world. And Peter's grandfather had earned this particular one. Remaining dumbfounded, he cried his eyes out with pride at what little he knew about the grandfather who he'd never met. All the things the king had told him in the hospital shortly after his near fatal encounter with Manson, had made him so proud of his grandfather, but this, this was just... well, words couldn't really describe it.

'Why didn't George tell me about this?' he wondered as he stroked the case that contained the medal. He resolved to ask him about it later. Placing it gently down on the bed, he reached into the trunk and pulled out a set of human shaped robes from near the bottom. Standing up, he unfolded them and let them hang out in front of him. Clean white with a purple trident running from corner to corner across the front, the material they were made from felt scratchy and uncomfortable.

'If these were my grandfather's robes,' he mused, peeking around the front of them, 'then in his human form he must have been nigh on a giant.'

Folding them back up, he placed them carefully on the bed. Leaning over, he looked down into the very bottom of the chest and pulled out a metal canister that sat firmly in the darkest corner. Holding it up to his face, he took a sniff, and immediately wished he hadn't. An overpowering, petrol/cleaning fluid kind of smell that his sensitive nose couldn't quite place threatened to overwhelm him. Turning the canister over, he noticed a small, faded label which read: 'Fox's Igniting Scale Enhancer.' Not knowing exactly what it was, only that it was clearly very old and very flammable, he carefully put it down on the floor, telling himself to safely dispose of it at the earliest available opportunity.

By now, there were only a few things left inside the

trunk. Rolling around next to each other, right at the bottom, were two giant sticks of charcoal, looking very much like sticks of rock from the seaside that the humans were very partial to. It wasn't until he tried to take them out that he realised they ran the whole length of the chest. It took him a minute or so to jiggle them free without breaking them. Once he did, he held them up to the light, admiring them for all they were worth, never having seen charcoal quite like it. Both looked almost too good to eat, despite the gurgled protests of his stomach that told him he should just go for it. Against his better judgement, he put them down on the floor, on the other side of the chest to the flammable liquid in the metal canister, as he was keen to show the king and his friends everything he'd found.

By the look of it, only two things remained: something folded up in a piece of raggedy material, and a half sheet of faded old newspaper. Reaching in, he gently picked up the newspaper. Unfolding it as though his life depended upon it, due to its delicate nature, he glanced down at the very faded picture and the headline that accompanied it.

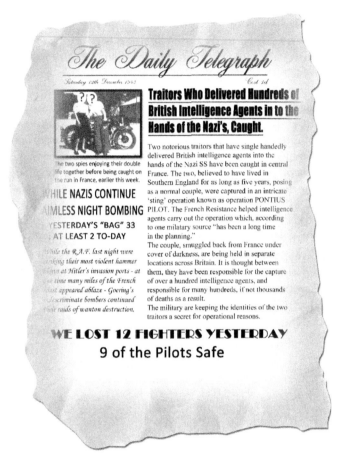

The Daily Telegraph

Saturday 12th December 1943　　　　　　　　　*Cost 1d*

Traitors Who Delivered Hundreds of British Intelligence Agents in to the Hands of the Nazi's, Caught.

The two spies enjoying their double life together before being caught on the run in France, earlier this week.

WHILE NAZIS CONTINUE AIMLESS NIGHT BOMBING

YESTERDAY'S "BAG" 33 AT LEAST 2 TO-DAY

While the R.A.F. last night were striking their most violent hammer blows at Hitler's invasion ports - at the time many miles of the French coast appeared ablaze - Goering's indiscriminate bombers continued their raids of wanton destruction.

Two notorious traitors that have single handedly delivered British intelligence agents into the hands of the Nazi SS have been caught in central France. The two, believed to have lived in Southern England for as long as five years, posing as a normal couple, were captured in an intricate 'sting' operation known as operation PONTIUS PILOT. The French Resistance helped intelligence agents carry out the operation which, according to one military source "has been a long time in the planning."

The couple, smuggled back from France under cover of darkness, are being held in separate locations across Britain. It is thought between them, they have been responsible for the capture of over a hundred intelligence agents, and responsible for many hundreds, if not thousands of deaths as a result.

The military are keeping the identities of the two traitors a secret for operational reasons.

WE LOST 12 FIGHTERS YESTERDAY
9 of the Pilots Safe

Spending a couple of minutes reading the story, its caption, and studying the photo, Peter had no idea who the couple were, or if they were in some way connected with his grandfather.

'Something else to ask George about,' he supposed,

putting the paper gently on top of the folded robes. Taking a deep breath, he wondered how the others were doing in the main room, whether or not Flash had been unfrozen, if the items Gee Tee had asked for had arrived and if everybody had managed to resist the temptation to string the old shopkeeper up from the rafters. Chuckling at that last thought, knowing the master mantra maker had the propensity to get under even the calmest dragon's scales (Tank being the prime example of just that), he started to study the object lying at the bottom of the trunk. Whatever it was wrapped up in the rags, he could feel the power positively oozing from it. Excitement and nervousness tickled his fingers and toes in equal measure as he reached in one last time. It felt heavy as he retrieved it and set it down on his lap, the intensity threatening to consume him, almost as if it were... talking to him, caressing him, at the same time. He could almost taste its electrically charged tang, as if it were coursing through him. Slowly, he unwrapped the grubby material, despite his hands shaking ever so slightly; he was giddy with excitement, awash with energy. After the third turn, a glint of metal caught his eye. Reaching in, he grasped the handle of a... dagger, and pulled it free. Mesmerising beyond words, rubies and emeralds dotted the hilt, but that was not what had him so captivated. Unheard of in fact and only whispered in legend, the whole weapon had been carefully crafted from... laminium! Time disappeared, vowing to never return, as Peter's dragon senses exploded out of his body. In stunning detail he could see Flash lying prone on the king's red sofa, not moving at all, whilst off to one side, the king and Gee Tee argued, with Tank and Yoyo looking on. Reaching out further into the council building, his vision washed over the reception area where two guards had just arrived with a giant fish tank containing the clown fish that the master mantra maker had demanded as part of the mantra to save the Crimson Guard. Suddenly a dragon battle was taking place over a small village, in the...

in the desert. Images and memories assaulted his mind as he sat hunched over on the gigantic bed. Good versus evil, a battle to stay alive, to get vital information back to the council, all played out against the backdrop of the pyramids. It had just the tiniest ring of something familiar. Expanding even further, his mind returned to the present and raced down the steps outside the building, past the lava pools either side and the curious dragon tourists who had now gathered to view this iconic landmark on a Sunday, when it was closed for business.

Struggling now, the dagger's power was threatening to spiral out of control. Knowing he had to wrestle back the initiative, he tried with all his might to ignore the raw intensity that caressed him and the whispered words the weapon knew that he wanted to hear. It was all so... seductive. In a split second of clarity, he dropped the blade onto the bed and instinctively wrapped it back up in the rags. Sweat poured from his face as he placed the weapon in its wrapping on top of the robes and newspaper article, like a nuclear bomb ready to explode. Running both hands through his long black hair, he breathed a huge sigh of relief. And then it hit him, like a boxer's sharp uppercut.

'It's Aviva's dagger, the one she found in the pyramid, the one she used to fight Ptolemy and the two treacherous councillors. How in the name of the laminium ball gods did my grandfather get his wings on that?' he thought, fighting against the exhaustion that threatened to engulf him now that he'd put the blade down.

Standing up to stretch his legs, clear his head and go find the king, a brilliant purple twinkle from the very darkest corner of the still open trunk caught his eye. Leaning right over into it, he was astounded at what lay there. Nestled right in the corner, with the chain strewn across it, was an *alea* exactly the same as the one currently around his neck.

Aleas were the physical embodiment of a mantra from days gone by, albeit in an unstable form. *Alea* itself means 'gamble' or 'last chance.' Used predominantly by dragons fighting in wars of yesteryear, who on finding themselves in an almost certain death situation would break open the *alea*, and amplify the words on them in their mind, to hopefully unleash their power. Because of their instability they had a reputation for going wrong and not achieving what they'd been designed for or were required to do. Sometimes it worked in the dragon's favour, but more often than not it didn't, so they were rare and dangerous artefacts in the present day.

In one swift motion, he slid his right hand down the top of his T-shirt and checked that his *alea* was still there. It was. Cautiously bending down, he scooped up the one in the trunk and sat back on the bed. Holding it up to the light, he once again marvelled at the exquisite craftsmanship, before using his dragon sight to check the inscription on the shaft and forks of the tiny trident. Zooming in with his incredible telescopic dragon vision, he ignored the purple glow, and made straight for the words. They read 'Amplificare... Magicus... Nunc': 'Amplify Magic Now.' The words were an exact match. Peter sighed.

'Gee Tee said *aleas* were incredibly rare,' he mused, twirling it round with his finger tip. 'I wonder what the odds are against me having two exactly the same.'

After a couple of minutes pondering the nature of all this, he took off the *alea* bequeathed to him by Mark Hiscock and replaced it with the one left to him by his grandfather. It felt exactly the same, the weight against his chest, the slight tingling sensation as it brushed against his skin, everything. Putting the spare one safely inside his wallet, unsure of exactly what to do with it, he set off to find the king and see how things were progressing with Flash.

On entering the main room, the first thing that struck Peter was that it was a far cry from the relative quiet he'd left an hour and a half ago. Gee Tee was barking orders at different members of the King's Guards who all seemed to be dropping off one item or another, with Tank doing his very best to control his employer's distinct lack of manners. Yoyo was leant over Flash on the sofa, keeping a sharp eye on the Crimson Guard's condition. All the time the monarch stood watching in disbelief as the once spotless room looked very much like a bomb had gone off in it.

Skirting the edge of the space until he reached George, Peter stood and waited until the king was ready to speak. It didn't take long.

"Never in all my time have I felt like I was going insane, but I do now. Those idiot councillors drive me mad sometimes, but this, this is... just crazy. I swear he's doing it on purpose, no doubt exacting his revenge for me not having gone to see him for all this time."

Not knowing what to say, Peter kept quiet.

"Aaarrgggghhhh," moaned the king under his breath, as across the room, the old shopkeeper found something else to complain about.

Suddenly Peter wished he were anywhere but here.

Shaking his head and wiping his eyes, the king turned to look at him.

"Sorry," he whispered. "It's just that this is my most... private of places. Where I come to when I want to unwind, relax, just think. It's all so hard to take in. Anyway, how did you get on with the... trunk?"

"There are some things I'd really like to ask you about if that's okay," he replied, really not sure if this was a good time.

"Of course, of course," replied the ruler, buoyed. "Let's go and have a look now and you can ask me what you like... lead the way."

Peter headed back through to the bedroom, followed hotly by the king who seemed determined to get away from the chaos of the main room as quickly as possible.

Upon entering, the first thing George noticed was the

small metal canister on the floor by the side of the chest.

"Well I'll be..." he uttered. "It can't be, can it? I haven't seen this stuff in well over fifty years," he recounted, picking up the canister and turning it over and over in his hands. "Ohhh... it is, it is," he cried jubilantly. "'Fox's Igniting Scale Enhancer,'" mused the monarch, a faraway look in his eyes. "This is the stuff of legend Peter. As far as I know, they stopped making it some time ago. If you want your scales to look their best, then this is what you need."

"I've never heard of it."

"Not surprising really," replied the monarch, a little sadly. "Its creator died about half a century ago. Fox, as it states on the bottle, was a genius... oh he had a few other potions and gimmicks on the market, but this was..." reflected the sovereign, holding up the canister, "this was the real deal. I've never seen or heard of anything like it to this very day. Others have tried in vain to recreate it, all with little or no success."

Surprised that such a simple thing could provoke such a passionate reaction, the youngster watched as the monarch unscrewed the cap and inhaled deeply.

"Ahhhh," he sighed. "Reminds me of the good old days." Offering out the canister so that Peter could have a whiff, the youngster shook his head at the invitation.

"Don't know what you're missing," ventured the king. Peter declined once again.

"Anyhow, just so that you know, to use it, you pour a little on, and then work it in until it turns to lather. Covering your whole self like this, you let it dry. Once dried, it's time for the good part. You just simply ignite it with a burst of fire and wwwhumpfffff, the whole thing goes up in flames, eventually burning out. When it does, you'll have the best looking scales in the kingdom, I guarantee."

Nodding, intrigued, Peter wondered if he would have the courage to try using it at any point.

"Anyhow, I take it from the look on your face that this

wasn't what you wanted to ask me about," George uttered, lowering the canister back to the floor.

"Ummmm, no, not exactly."

Picking up the frame containing his grandfather's Flaming Cross, he handed it over.

"I'd hoped you could tell me more about this."

Looking through the smoky glass at the flaming award inside, the king took his time, reading all the words.

"Oh my goodness... I... I... had no idea... but... now it makes... so much sense... of course... it was... him," spluttered the monarch.

Peter sat there shocked, until he engaged his brain.

'Of course,' he thought, 'it was the previous king who awarded it. Why didn't I realise that?'

Turning to the youngster, the king handed him back the frame and said,

"You should be very proud of him. We all knew someone, around that era, had been awarded one of these, but no one seemed to know just who it was. Back then, I spent part of my time on the council, and part with the King's Guards. There were rumours, but the odd thing was, no dragon ever started showing it off. Most would have, believe you me. It was something to be proud of and let others know about, but I suppose your grandfather was different like that, in a good way of course. Thinking back on it now, I really should have guessed it was him and called him out on it. I feel a bit stupid. It seems so obvious now."

"He was a very private dragon then?"

"Private and modest," replied the ruler. "Sorely missed," he added, wiping a tear from his eye. "Anything else you'd like me to have a look at?"

"Two more things if that's okay?"

"Fire away."

Picking up the dagger wrapped in rags and holding it as far out in front of him as possible, he offered it to the king.

"I need to warn you, Majesty, it is incredibly powerful... be careful," he suggested.

The king gave Peter a look.

"What did I tell you? When we're alone, please call me George."

"Sorry I forgot."

"No problem," said the king, smiling. "And don't worry about powerful. The ring," he announced, lifting up his hand to show off the dazzling band, "does more than just store mana, it protects me from almost any magical harm."

Peter looked more than a little sceptical.

"Not convinced I see," he declared. "It's okay, I'll be just fine," he said taking the bundle from Peter and putting it on his lap. Just like the hockey player had earlier, the king carefully unwound the rags until a sliver of metal appeared. And just like his young charge, the sovereign pulled out the dagger as soon as he saw it, his eyes nearly springing out of their sockets once the weapon was fully revealed. Holding it out in one hand, he turned it over and over, inspecting it fully, clearly not affected by its raw, surging power, much to Peter's relief.

Both sat in silence for a matter of minutes, the king taking in every jewel and detail of the blade. Not for the first time, the youngster didn't know what to say, and so decided to say nothing at all, lest he utter something stupid or inappropriate. He was still largely intimidated by the king's presence, despite the time spent with him at Salisbridge hospital and George's best efforts to put him at ease and make him feel welcome.

"This was in the trunk?"

"Yes."

"Your grandfather certainly liked his secrets," he stated, shaking his head. "To think he had this at some point and it's been sitting here for so long is almost laughable. How on earth did he come to have it I wonder? You know what it is, don't you Peter?"

"I assume it's the dagger Aviva had when she fought Ptolemy and the two treacherous councillors."

The king nodded.

"It must be. I can't imagine there could possibly be more than one of these. Laminium in those times was much more of a rarity than it is now, as the methods for extracting it were much cruder. In the present this represents quite a large amount of laminium;, back then, it would probably have amounted to about a tenth of the world's supply. And for you to have inherited it... amazing."

Thinking about what he'd just heard, Peter inferred from his tone that he thought he shouldn't have the dagger. It made little difference to him whether he had it or not, so he concluded that it would be better to give it to the king here and now.

"You can have it Maje... George. It's not like I have a use for it, or anywhere safe to keep it."

The king eyed the young hockey player with suspicion.

"Do you really want to give it away Peter? The history alone that accompanies this item is beyond belief, not to mention its power, which you clearly experienced earlier. When I mentioned you inheriting it, I didn't mean to imply that you shouldn't have it. I just find that with everything that's gone on, with Manson and the like, for you to end up in your possession... well, let's just say that Fate appears to be looking over your shoulder. But what I do know is that you really should keep it. Heaven only knows what your grandfather went through to get it; guessing by the Flaming Cross and everything else we know, he might well have gone to hell and back. But he wouldn't have left it to you if he hadn't wanted you to have it. Keep it, guard it, use it if the need arises. After everything you've been through I trust you implicitly, and if you're even half the dragon your grandfather was, then I would be proud to have you fight by my side."

It was all Peter could do not to cry at the biggest

compliment he'd ever received.

"One piece of advice though," offered the king, interrupting his train of thought. "I would be very careful about telling anyone of its existence, even your friends or the shopkeeper, particularly the shopkeeper. Oh don't get me wrong, I trust Gee Tee, he's saved my life more often than I care to remember, as he's mentioned numerous times today, but with an item like this, something dragons from across the world would kill to acquire, you'd have to be very sure he wouldn't inadvertently tell anyone. One slip of the tongue, and well... you'd be a dragon in demand, for all the wrong reasons."

Reluctantly the king wrapped up the dagger, before carefully handing it back to Peter, who quickly laid it down in the bottom of the trunk, not wanting to hang onto it a second longer than he had to.

"And the final thing is?"

"This," he replied, handing George the faded newspaper article. "I don't know what it is or who the people are. I was wondering if you knew their identities and if perhaps my grandfather brought them to justice?"

Watching the ruler read the article and study the photo, he noticed a look of undeniable anger creep across his face towards the end. It was subtle, and was gone in no time at all, but it had been there, he was sure.

'What would cause that kind of reaction?' he wondered.

Rubbing his forehead nervously, the king thought about what that he had in front of him. So many of his decisions with the council revolved around a certain point of view or concealing part of the truth, things he really didn't want to even consider here and now. But they ran through his mind nevertheless. Knowing that the truth would hurt the young dragon before him, made him not want to be the one to inflict it on him, or to burden him with it. But the core of the matter, he knew, was that Peter would want the truth to come out. Concealment or a partial story wouldn't work here, and anyway, he wouldn't want them to. Only reality would do, he thought, as he looked deep into the young dragon's eyes.

"There's no easy way to say this I'm afraid. So I'll just come straight out with it. Both the spies in the newspaper article are your parents. I'm so sorry Peter."

Feeling like he'd just been hit by a meteorite travelling at full speed from some far flung galaxy, fifty million thoughts and questions whistled round his head, making him feel more than a little giddy.

'It can't be,' was the first thought. 'My parents, spies... working with the Nazis... it's just not possible. There must be a reason... perhaps they were double agents. Yes, that's it, they were double agents and the king's just about to tell me about that part.'

Looking across though, he instantly knew there was no good side to the story. The sadness on the monarch's false human face was more apparent than it ever could have been in his natural dragon form.

"I... I... I... don't understand," he stuttered. "How can they have worked for the Nazis?"

Cold to the core, the king felt Peter's pain, wishing his friend, and Peter's grandfather, Fredric, could be here to explain, as he himself only knew a little of what had happened so long ago.

"I don't know very much, but what little I do know, I will tell you," announced the king, shifting uncomfortably on the living room sized bed. "When your grandfather first revealed your existence to me, I was pleasantly surprised. He seemed so happy, and who could blame him, right up until the point I asked him about your parents. For such a quiet and unassuming dragon, he sure seemed to know a whole range of rather... dubious human words. I listened for a long time as he let off steam, in more ways than one, and once he calmed down I tried to get to the crux of the matter. Even after his out of character explosion, it was very difficult to find out exactly what had gone on. I told you at the hospital that there had been some kind of fallout out or rift. I don't know the details, much as I did try and press your grandfather for them, thinking that I might in some way use my power to influence the situation. I also told you that both your parents had left separate instructions with the nursery ring that he was not allowed to have any contact with you. Why? I don't know, but clearly it had something to do with the falling out that had torn them apart, quite amazing really for both your parents to leave those instructions. Unable to glean any more information from your grandfather, I left matters well alone, not wanting to upset my best friend any more. It wasn't until much later that I learned about the role played by your parents in the war.

Your grandfather had come back from a mission badly injured, unusual for any of our kind. He needed immediate attention and the best physicians were summoned here, eventually working for three days solid, casting mantra after mantra, using all their healing powers and experience. I stayed by his side, listening, helping as best I could, and allowing the physicians to draw magic from my ring. In the end, he survived, but only just. However, over the course of the three days, he became delirious and a little deluded, screaming and shouting, of which we all thought very little. But it wasn't long before he started recounting stories, tales that should probably never be repeated, which appeared at first glance to have been made up, but parts of them seemed all too real, if you know what I mean.

As you can probably guess, the account you see before you in the paper was one your grandfather imparted while he was ill, also disclosing how your parents colluded with the Nazis, how they escaped the British and managed never to reveal that they were dragons. Making their way back to the domain, they survived to live in relative peace before having you and depositing your egg at the nursery ring. Some of the things your grandfather revealed in those three days sounded like pure fiction. But I very subtly checked most of them out, one way or another, and to my surprise, they really did happen. How your parents didn't get caught by other dragons working for British intelligence at the time is beyond me, and we still don't know to this day. As I'm sure you're aware from your history lessons, dark dragons actually started the war and influenced Hitler right up until his death. There were many or our race on both sides, the British ones trying to save lives, the ones allied with the Nazis very happy to take them. But for two prominent dragons like your parents, who were infamous and in the press, to escape undetected is... very unusual indeed. They were there, that's all I really know for sure. I think your grandfather may have suspected or known somehow, and just maybe that's what caused the rift. And as I'm sure you're aware, there's been no record of either of your parents since they deposited your egg at the nursery ring, not in the dragon domain or in the human world above, to my knowledge. If they were to surface above or down here, I would know about it."

Peter tried to make sense of what he'd just been told: his parents working for the Nazis against the Allied Forces, being captured as humans, but not detected as dragons, fleeing back to the domain and blending back in, before mating and then leaving the egg at the nursery ring, with instructions about his grandfather, and then disappearing for good... it was all just too much to take in. Tears streamed down his cheeks, weaving in and out of the thin layer of stubble adorning his chin, before leaping off and diving towards the oak floor, where they began filling up a beautifully carved flying dragon and its roaring flame.

Putting a reassuring arm around the young lad's shoulder, it was the king's turn to stay silent this time, remaining just a comforting presence.

Minutes passed, as tears turned to lonely sniffs, with the worst of it seemingly over. Before either had a chance to break the silence, an echoing voice rang out from the direction of the corridor.

"Majesty... Peter... Gee Tee's just about to begin

making the mantra. Just thought I would let you know," boomed Yoyo nervously.

Wiping his bloodshot eyes with the back of his hand, Peter stood, followed closely by the king. Patting him on the back and ruffling his long, curly, dark hair, the ruler said,

"Leave all the stuff where it is. I'll get someone to deliver the trunk and all its contents over to your house in the next few days. Is that okay?"

"That... that... would be great. Thank you."

"You're welcome. Just make sure you take care of that dagger. I hate to think what would happen if it ever fell into the wrong hands."

"I'll be careful, I promise."

"I know you will," said the king, setting off in the direction of the living room, Peter hot on his tail.

Stepping into the open space from out of the dark corridor, the first thing that grabbed their attention was Tank, sitting in the middle of the room on the floor, a large pestle and mortar between his knees, to which Gee Tee was already adding ingredients.

"Crush the bark and the bones until they become a fine dust," barked the old shopkeeper, from behind him. "Not ultrafine of course, just fine... understood?"

Looking across the room, Tank gave Peter a small smile, shaking his head at his employer's orders as he did so.

"I'll let you know when it becomes fine and you can check it for yourself," replied the rugby player, just a hint of frustration creeping into his voice.

"Ahhhhh welcome back," declared Gee Tee, spotting the king and Peter. "Nice of you to join us. I was just about to restart Flash's cellular structure. I will require the use of the ring, once my apprentice has finished putting all the necessary ingredients together."

Much to Peter's relief, the king chose to ignore the sarcasm and instead, just waved his hand casually and said,

"Carry on," much to the old shopkeeper's annoyance.

'Those two must have been a barrel of laughs when they worked together,' thought Peter. 'Either that, or it must be a getting old kind of thing. Maybe the more mature you get, the more you want to pick a fight. That would certainly explain the master mantra maker's behaviour.'

Gee Tee hovered over Flash's limp form on the sofa, muttering silently. Yoyo stood behind, keeping a close eye on the Crimson Guard, ready to step in at a moment's notice. The 'crunch, crunch, crunch' from Tank's pestle and mortar bounced off the walls, echoing around the room.

A sudden gasp, followed by a painful moan filled the room as the Crimson Guard hurtled back to life. Yoyo was at his side in a split second, mopping his fevered brow with a towel and checking on the state of the rapidly deteriorating wound. Gee Tee turned his attention back to Tank.

"That's just about right," he called from over his co-worker's shoulder. "Now pour in all the sea salt."

Tank followed his employer's instructions, feeling as though a great weight had been lifted from him for the first time in almost... ever. 'Perhaps,' he thought, 'I should have stood up to him a long time ago. Things might have been very different.'

Flash continued to wriggle and squirm uncomfortably, highlighting the sense of urgency.

Gee Tee looked over in Peter's direction and barked,

"Make yourself useful, youngster, and bring the fish tank over to my app... Tank, will you?"

Glad of something to do rather than just standing and watching, Peter raced over to the far side of the room and grabbed the huge tank that contained the clown fish, some coral, their home the anemone, and of course the compulsory open treasure chest on the bottom. Holding it steady, he moved over to his rugby playing pal and placed it gently down beside him.

Plodding over, the Emporium owner motioned with his wings for Peter to get out of the way. Everybody in the room, with the exception of Flash, held their breath as the old shopkeeper captured one of the clownfish and quickly pulled it out of the water. Tank sat back from the pestle and mortar, waiting for his employer to weave his magic. Despite his occasional frustration with the master mantra maker, Tank knew there was no one on the planet more skilled with mantras, magic and spells, and, as usual, looked on with a mixture of awe and admiration. With a firm grip on the first clownfish, Gee Tee, with a gentler touch than anyone in the room would have imagined, carefully scraped off a tiny amount of the slimy mucus that protects it from the sting of the anemone that the fish lives in, letting it drip directly into the centre of the mortar. Peter had to stifle a laugh on noticing the indignant look that had crossed the face of the little creature.

'I bet something that cute has never looked so angry,' he thought, his lips firmly clamped together. Unaware of the animal's objection or discomfort, the old shopkeeper thrust it back into the tank and while that one cautiously swam into the anemone, he scooped up the other one and went through exactly the same process. After finishing with the second, Peter moved the tank out of the way as both Gee Tee and Tank continued mixing all the ingredients, until a gooey looking brown sludge with the consistency of bogies dangled from the pestle. Gee Tee then ordered everyone to hold Flash face down, exposing the wound on his back. With Peter and the king holding a leg each, Tank putting pressure on his shoulders and Yoyo being responsible for both of Flash's arms, the master mantra maker began to apply the gooey mixture to the injury. At the first contact, an undragon-like scream tore out of the Crimson Guard's mouth, as he tried desperately to wriggle free from being restrained.

"Hold him still!" demanded the shopkeeper, spreading

more and more of the concoction on the gaping gash, despite Flash's protests. Once the whole area of the wound was covered, Gee Tee whispered in the king's ear. George whispered back, so quietly that even with their enhanced senses, no one else in the room could hear what had been said. As the king kept a grip on Flash's leg, the master mantra maker placed his left hand against the edge of the ruler's magical ring, and then proceeded to mouth something. Pulsing bright blue light burst forth from the stone encased within the extraordinary band as it sprang to life, running across Gee Tee's entire prehistoric body.

Seemingly content, the old shopkeeper leant forward and cautiously ran one of his talons along the middle of Flash's goo covered gash, all the time remaining connected to the ring via his hand. As the others looked on, blue, pulsing magical energy surged into the goo on the wound, eventually filling it up. Flash, by now, was screaming like a baby that had lost its favourite toy. Gee Tee ignored the noise and, closing his eyes, began to recite a long-forgotten mantra from a much more civilised time. Despite having a near perfect memory, Peter couldn't recall the language that the master mantra maker was speaking, but some of the words were instantly recognisable, "Obliterate," or maybe "raze," was certainly in there, alongside... um... "hazardous," or perhaps "treacherous," and the words "genetic material down to the very last micron." Just when he thought it was over and that it had failed to work, Gee Tee screamed a single word at the top of his voice, a word that Peter thought roughly translated as... "UNLEASH!!!!"

With this thought running through his mind, the pulsing blue of the wound exploded out across the room into the brightest light Peter had ever seen, forcing him to close his eyes and momentarily lose his grip on Flash. Moments later his vision started to return and he immediately reached down to regain his hold on the leg. But it was gone. Using both hands, he felt around the end of the sofa... nothing! Blinking furiously, he wiped his eyes, and upon opening them was astonished to see Flash sitting upright in the middle of the sofa, looking... perfectly okay. With the exception of Gee Tee, who'd known what to expect, the others had all clearly been temporarily blinded too, and were as surprised as Peter to see the Crimson Guard looking so well. Yoyo rocked up and gently slapped Flash on the back in a gesture of goodwill.

"It's good to see you looking so healthy. I haven't lost a patient in many decades, and I'm relieved I can continue with that boast. Well done, well done."

Stepping forward at the same time, Peter and Tank shook hands with the dragon agent before making way for the king.

"Your courage, bravery and sheer refusal to die, continue to astound me Flash... but I'm afraid I will need to quiz you further about what went on in Antarctica," announced the king, a grin etched across his weathered old face.

"Of course, Majesty," replied Flash, nodding.

"But before we do that," declared the sovereign, "I think congratulations are in order. Once again, Shopkeeper, I find myself in your debt."

Unusually, Gee Tee looked less cocky and sure of himself than he had in all the time he'd been in the monarch's company. He looked... nervous, which was indeed very strange for him. Everybody in the room except Flash had picked up on it now, and all were looking in his direction to see what would happen next.

"Well," stated the master mantra maker, scratching the underside of his jaw uncertainly, "perhaps we'll save the back slapping until we make sure everything is okay."

"What's that supposed to mean?" barked the ruler, sternly.

"That particular mantra, Majesty, was extremely old, nearly two thousand years in fact. A mantra of that age, no matter how well delivered, can have unpredictable side effects, something this one would have had even when new. I would suggest we check Flash over fully before we break open the charcoal."

The king looked livid, and to be honest, Peter really couldn't blame him. There'd been no mention of side effects before the mantra had been applied. It was all a bit rushed, Peter supposed, but still, Gee Tee could at least have said something about it.

Through all this Flash looked ultra composed, sitting on the sofa, taking in the vast expanse of the giant living room and everything within it.

The king stood next to Flash as Gee Tee strode over.

"I feel fine, honest," announced the death defying Crimson Guard.

"That remains to be seen, youngster," replied the shopkeeper softly. "Can you scroll through your different visions for me?"

"No problem," replied Flash, with the king looking on. "All works fine... as good as new."

Taking a deep breath, it was then that the Emporium owner asked,

"Can you stand up and transform into your dragon guise... please?"

Tank and Peter swapped glances with each other. The moment Gee Tee used the word 'please,' they both had practically the same thought, which went something along the lines of: 'If he's saying please, then something really bad has happened or is about to.'

Jumping to his feet, Flash closed his eyes, drew in a deep breath and... nothing! Immediately his eyes shot open in shock. Composing himself, he tried once again, with exactly the same result.

Gee Tee wrapped one of his flimsy looking wings around the Crimson Guard and whispered,

"I'm really sorry, I truly am. But I had no choice. I knew there was a chance this might happen, but you were at death's door. If I hadn't tried, we wouldn't be having this conversation right now."

The king stepped in and looked Gee Tee right in the eyes.

"What's happened?"

"My best guess, and that's what it is, is that the mantra has locked Flash's DNA in place, meaning that he can't revert back to his natural dragon form. And before you ask, I don't know of any way to undo, cure or adjust what's happened. I'm sorry."

Flash plopped back down onto the sofa, with everybody else trying to comprehend the turn of events. Losing the ability to change back into his prehistoric, natural form was worse than it would have been for a human to lose all his or her limbs. It was simply unimaginable. Flash, understandably, was crestfallen as he sat with his head in his hands. Against the backdrop of the deafening silence, Yoyo acted first. Squeezing between the king and Gee Tee, he knelt down in front of the Crimson Guard.

"While I understand the frustration shared in this room that the potential side effects should have been made clear from the outset, Gee Tee is right in what he said. You would be dead now if he hadn't acted. How you managed to stave off death for so long is unbelievable in itself, but you were only minutes if not seconds away from losing the battle for life. I know after everything you've been through that you must be devastated, and I can't begin to imagine what you're thinking and feeling. But what I can say is this. In the short time I've known you, only a matter of hours, I've discovered what sort of dragon you are."

Flash looked up from the floor, anger flooding his face as he stared into Yoyo's eyes, as the healer continued.

"And yes, you are still a dragon, no matter what you think. Your DNA maybe locked into place, but that DNA is dragon, not human. You may sit here looking like one of our charges from the surface, but you have the heart and soul of a dragon, a brave, fearless, inventive, warrior dragon... one that I will always be happy to call... my friend, no matter what anyone else may say or do."

With that, Yoyo offered out his hand to Flash and waited to see if he would take it. The anger on the Crimson Guard's face softened, with just a glint of a tear in his right eye as he reached out and shook it. Peter and Tank came over and offered out their hands to the stricken agent, telling him much the same thing Yoyo had. Flash's demeanour changed dramatically over the next few minutes, thanks to the support of his new found friends. It was all a bit different to what he was used to. In the Crimson Guards, you all worked together, sometimes as a team, more often than not as individuals, but you never really counted on any of the others as anything more than colleagues, and certainly not as buddies.

'It's been a long time since I've had a friend,' thought Flash, 'and just like buses or nagas, a whole host have arrived at once.'

Gee Tee was next, telling him that if there was anything he ever needed in the mantra department, he only had to ask or pop into the Emporium. Flash responded by thanking the old shopkeeper for everything he'd done, and that on consideration, he would rather be alive in human form, than dead. Everybody could see how relieved the old shopkeeper was to hear this.

Finally the king approached, looking more than a little uncomfortable.

"Before I ask for your full report on what happened in Antarctica, there are a few things I must say, even though it pains me to do so. I'm afraid it will be simply impossible for you to continue in the Crimson Guards, much as I appreciate all you have done. You and I both know that you could never do THAT job without the ability to take your natural form."

Flash nodded sadly, understanding that the king was right.

"That doesn't mean you can just slope off though. I've got a very specific role in mind for you, something that in many ways will allow you to serve in a much more personal way than you have before."

Flash sat up straight, his interest piqued by what the king had just said.

"Anyway," George continued, "that can wait until it's just the two of us. But I do think it's best you leave the barracks you're stationed in as quickly as possible. The fewer dragons that know about what has transpired, the better. And I bet you can guess what I'm going to say next."

They all could. Unsurprisingly, he asked that everything they'd seen and heard throughout the course of the day's events be treated as top secret and not mentioned to anyone, no matter how trustworthy they seemed. They all agreed without a fuss, even Gee Tee, much to the king's surprise, who thought he might have had to threaten the shopkeeper in some manner. But the old dragon seemed to have been humbled somewhat by the debilitating side effect of Flash's cure.

"Shortly Flash, when our visitors have gone, I'm going to ask you to give me an intricate account of your time in Antarctica, but before that happens I would like to know a little more about one of the prisoners, specifically the dragon that helped you escape. I'd like you to think carefully about what you're telling me. It's important, of course, but it may well have some relevance to those here as well."

Letting out a deep breath and scouring his eidetic memory, Flash recounted everything he could about his brief time in the frozen prison. Yoyo, Peter, Tank and Gee Tee had all taken to sitting in the comfortable chairs which littered the room, while the king hadn't stopped pacing. Once Flash had finished describing that part of his mission, the sovereign continued walking back and forth for a time, until he stopped, deep in thought.

"I want you to think very carefully about the answer to the question I'm about to ask you," he said, looking serious. "The dragon who helped you escape, can you describe in detail the markings on his chest?"

Peter thought this was a really odd question to ask. Flash, having thought about the question for some time, had come up with his answer.

"Majesty, there were some marks on the left hand side of his chest, about level with where his ribs would be."

"Describe them in detail to me," demanded the king, still pacing.

Closing his eyes, Flash concentrated.

"They were dark blue, almost like the kind of birthmark you occasionally see a human carrying. If I had to say they looked like anything, then it would be like a tree with long, spindly branches. Some kind of willow or something I suppose."

Out of nowhere, George let out a thunderous roar, while at the same time, smashing into a thousand pieces a huge ancient vase that had been sitting on a table near to where he'd been standing. As well as being startled, everyone else in the room was stunned at the abrupt outburst. Remaining shrouded in silence, with everybody too afraid to speak, the monarch continued to pace around, anger coiled up inside him, his face flushed. After many minutes of steam pouring off him, he finally spoke, not to Flash, as everyone would have thought, but to Peter.

"The dragon in the prison... I know him. And so do you... it's your grandfather."

"Oh my God," was all that Peter could think to say.

Flash broke the shock, awe and silence with a question.

"Hang on a minute, that dragon... he's... he's not the one who founded the Crimson Guards, is he?"

The king turned and nodded a great big 'yes' to Flash.

"But he's supposed to have died long ago, on a mission."

"Yes, I thought so too, but he's clearly still alive," spat the king angrily.

The stunned room remained quiet and still for nearly a minute before Peter spoke up.

"We have to rescue him," he ventured, approaching George. "Now, this instant! You can send the King's Guard. They'll have him back in no time."

Watching Peter carefully, taking in everything he'd said, the king's measured reply wasn't quite what the young dragon had hoped for.

"I only wish it were that simple. Unfortunately it isn't."

Peter's jaw dropped open ridiculously wide, but before he had a chance to say anything, the king continued.

"Much as it may seem to everyone here that I hold the balance of power, not only in the dragon council, but throughout the whole of the domain as well, it simply isn't true. There was a time, long ago, when that was the case and the head of state's word was practically law, but I'm afraid not now. When I first joined the council all those centuries ago, it was noticeable then just how much control the king wielded, and over time I've seen it diminish beyond belief, mainly due to political wheeling and dealing from the councillors themselves, and some of the very laws and policies they have passed over the course of many, many years. When I agreed to take up this position, I had no illusions about how little power I would have at my disposal, but I thought if I used it only when necessary, and proved to be honest, trustworthy and capable of making the right decisions for the dragon population of the world as a whole, most of the councillors would support me in just about everything.

Alas, that is far from the case. Some of the things that go on in the chamber make the humans look positively naive and honest in their political dealings. Gathering a force to storm the prison and free the captives is now well beyond the political leverage and clout that I wield. If there was any way in which I thought I could sway those who'd make a difference, I would in a heartbeat, even if I had to stand down from my position to make it happen. But I don't see any way in which I can. Everything that Flash has told me I can take to the council in an effort to try and persuade them of the need to rescue the prisoners, but in my heart of hearts I already know what they're going to say... NO! Oh they'll dress it up, maybe even agree to form a subcommittee to look at all the options, which will probably take months. But the long and short of it is, the answer will still be... NO! They'll say it's too costly and requires too many resources that just can't be spared at the moment, particularly as the nagas look like they pose a very serious threat, not just to the dragon domain, but to the human world above. They'll also say that anyone with any sense would have long since moved the captives, so it will almost certainly be a waste of time, something I would tend to agree with."

"On top of all that," piped up Flash, "they'll also say that to trust the word of a dragon who's stuck in human form for the rest of his life, is the wrong thing to do."

The king nodded in agreement.

"Sadly, Flash is right. Most of them would feel him to be tainted at the very least. I know... huh... I know it's wrong, but that's how most of them think," added the king, waving away the protests of the two Salisbridge residents. "I'm sorry Peter, I truly am. I would do anything to get your grandfather back, even give my own life if I could be certain it would work, but at the moment, there are too many other things to take into consideration. This may affect the dragon world in some way, so we have to find out what's going on with the nagas, why they're fighting against us and how we can stop it. Then, and only then, can we consider rescuing your grandfather, and believe me when I say we WILL rescue him, I give you my word as king of this realm.

Peter was lost for words. It was all so much to take in. Tank wrapped one of his huge arms around him and gave him a badly needed hug.

"It'll be alright. The king will get him back, you'll see,"

his friend whispered cheerily, trying his best to look on the bright side.

Peter, however, wasn't convinced and before he had a chance to voice his reservations, the sovereign very politely told them it was time to leave as he wanted to thoroughly debrief Flash and report his findings to the council, his thinking being that the sooner they got the ball rolling, the quicker they'd get Peter's grandfather, Fredric, back. Before they left, he thanked them for everything they'd done, swore them once again to secrecy, and then told Peter that his trunk and its contents would be delivered before the week was out and that he would be in touch. Flash shook their hands and gave each one of them a hug, something that seemed utterly appropriate, and was totally new to him. After Madeline appeared and escorted them back to the main entrance of the council building, the four of them trudged through the doors and down the steps, stopping to reflect on the day's events at the nearest of the two lava pools.

Leaning over the molten magma, watching the bubbles plop, gurgle and fizz, Peter could see his friends' faces reflected in the fiery, molten liquid of the pool.

'They all have pained expressions,' he thought as his mind tried to make sense of the day's events. So far he'd met and made friends with not only Flash, who had nearly died but had been saved by Gee Tee, but Yoyo as well, received the amazing contents of his grandfather's trunk, been told his parents had collaborated with the Nazis, learned of a massive threat to not just the dragon world, but the planet as a whole from the mysterious nagas, found out that his grandfather was still alive, and last but not least, learnt that the king wielded more prestige than power and was really quite toothless in a political sense.

'Whatever happens at work tomorrow will seem quite dull by comparison,' he mused, trying terribly hard to look on the bright side of things.

Yoyo interrupted Peter's train of thought.

"I'm sorry friends, but I really have to go. It's going to take me quite some time to get back to Perth and think up an explanation as to why I've been away. It's been one hell of a day for me, and it's been great to meet all of you, and Flash, and see the king again. Perhaps you could all come and visit me if you get the chance? You would all be very welcome. It would be great to meet up, and if you haven't visited Australia before, you don't know what you're missing. I would be more than happy to be your tour guide."

Peter, Tank and Gee Tee all bade farewell to the healer, wishing him well and promising to keep in touch and even try and arrange a visit, assuring him that they would keep an eye on Flash.

Soon after Yoyo left, the three of them split up, with Tank escorting Gee Tee back to the Mantra Emporium, and Peter heading back home, but not before the old shopkeeper had assured the young hockey player that the king would rescue his grandfather and that he, as the world's foremost mantra expert, would lend his valuable experience and expertise to the cause, putting the outcome beyond any doubt. If nothing else, this put a smile on the young dragon's face for the first time in a little while, something he supposed was the intention of the crafty old shopkeeper. As he strolled slowly towards the nearest monorail station, he had no idea at all of what to make of the most bizarre Sunday of his entire life.

12 SUB-ZERO HERO

Lying against the freezing wall of ice, the human shaped dragon scientist cried constantly, shivering and muttering as he did so. Nearly all his rounded bones were visible through his skin, taut from lack of nourishment. Resembling a waif from a very hot third world country, in dragon terms he was... very ordinary. A model citizen in fact with a mate waiting for him back in Manchester, England. This chained, dirty, filthy, ragged, emaciated and frightened dragon was one of the brightest minds on the whole planet. What he wasn't, however, was a hero. Not brave, steely or tough, he had a low tolerance for pain and wanted nothing more than to live a nice, straightforward, peaceful life. Most certainly he was the wrong dragon in the wrong place at the wrong time, a time that was very nearly at an end.

Night and day blended into one in the icy prison, the lack of daylight making it impossible to know the hour, the only constant, the gurgling of the stream, which slowly chipped away at the captives' sanity.

Curled up in front of the chilly wall, his weight supported by his giant, shiny blue tail that sparkled beautifully, the naga king, as always, had one eye open, resting like this ever since his incarceration, always on the lookout for an opportunity, but in all the time he'd been trapped, the right one had never presented itself... well, not yet anyway.

Lying asleep, flat on the ground, the ancient dragon spluttered and coughed, much as he had for most of his confinement. The only time he woke was when the evil human appeared with food, kicking and beating him awake, only stopping when his thirst for violence had been sated.

Crouching in the flickering light, stretching some of his leg and shoulder muscles, the last prisoner, the dragon shaped as a human with long scraggy hair and a blue birthmark splattered across his chest, was another waiting for a chance to escape and hoping, despite what the evil human had claimed, that the dragon he and the naga king had aided, had indeed made it back to the underground domain.

Hours after the prehistoric detainee had fled, the spiteful human and a naga he'd never seen before appeared from out of nowhere and had inflicted one of the heaviest beatings yet on everyone except the naga king. Afterwards the human jailer had spent a long time explaining how the escapee had been killed in his attempt to gain freedom. For what seemed like an eternity they'd both gone on about it, almost trying a bit too hard. What Fredric Bluewillow, Peter's grandfather, thought, was that he had indeed managed to get away, because if he had been killed, his broken body would almost certainly have been brought back and put on display. A tiny twinkle of hope lit up the back of his mind. All he had to do was survive, like he'd been doing for decades... oh, and not go insane.

Abruptly the freezing monotony was interrupted by the sound of voices carrying over the cold, frosty air from somewhere close by. This was something completely new. In all the time the prisoners had been there, they'd only ever seen the evil human that fed them, or the odd naga or two. On occasions, it had seemed as though there had been another presence flirting in the background somewhere just out of sight, but never had they actually heard anyone talking. And more intriguingly, the voices seemed to be heading in their direction.

Fredric and the naga king instantly became alert, both having the same thoughts.

'The human who feeds us is not long gone. This is something unusual and might be our one and only opportunity. We have to be ready.' Fredric stood poised, his muscles gleaming as quiet determination filled his eyes. Uncurled and risen to his full height, the naga king's serpent-like eyes were alert as he gave off a sense of dignity, quite something given his circumstances.

Suddenly from out of the darkness and the icy mist came the evil little human, followed hot on his heels by a... man. At least, that's what they thought at first.

Cackling and chuckling, the deranged human jailer led this new face up to the row of prisoners. Fredric and the naga king both breathed deeply, not flinching, doing their best to ignore the hated keeper. They were too wise, too well trained, to be provoked into even the smallest of movements. Remaining asleep, the ancient dragon continued to cough and splutter. Hanging limply from the manacles that shackled him to the icy wall, the human shaped boffin shook fiercely as the cold attacked his ill prepared body, startling him awake, still shrouded in fear.

Very slowly, the human shape started to walk up and down the row of prisoners, with it becoming immediately obvious that he had a very pronounced limp. Fredric and the naga king also deduced from his body language that the man was used to relying on something to support his weight, like a stick or a cane. The three prisoners that were aware of the inspection all remained stock still and silent, well... apart from the human shaped dragon scientist who, despite his best efforts, continued to shake and shiver involuntarily.

Although only having limited use of their magical dragon and naga abilities, both Fredric and the naga king could tell that the form before them was much more than he first appeared. They'd both seen human shaped nagas relatively recently and had immediately known what they were. But this was something different. They were able to tell he was something other than human, wearing the form as a type of disguise, if you will, but as to his base identity, they had absolutely no idea whatsoever.

After having walked up the line, inspecting the ancient dragon (still coughing, wheezing and asleep) and Fredric at the very end, the human shaped whatever-he-was turned and limped back to the shivering boffin at the other end, all but ignoring the naga king as he did so. Reaching the scientist who by now was cowering against the icy wall, the large, stocky, human shaped whatever-he-was jutted out his square jaw that had more than a few days growth of stubble on it.

"YOU!" he shouted at the scientist. "What are you doing in Antarctica?" he snarled, "and don't give me all that global warming rubbish."

Shaking and shivering more from fear than cold, the boffin replied.

"I... I... I... I... It... It's... th... th... the global war... warm... warming that we... we... we... were sent to stuuuudy."

"LIAR!" raged the human shaped whatever-he-was, kicking the disguised dragon brutally in the chest.

After the kick landed, an awful CRACK echoed around the cavern accompanied by the being's high pitched scream. In the dark and the cold, Fredric rallied against his chains, pulling them taut, using every ounce of strength he could to try to break free, ready to step in and deliver what he considered justice.

"NOW... tell me the real reason you're here. You're only making things harder for yourself," raved the human shaped whatever-he-was, steam rising from the receding brown hair that dappled his head.

Curled up in a heap, crying like a baby wanting its mother, the scientist had nothing else to say, because he'd only been sent to Antarctica to research the effects of global warming and knew of no other mission, having no idea why he was here, who his captors were, or what would happen next. He just wanted to go home.

"You snivelling, spineless, putrid excuse for a dragon... you're pathetic!" spat the human shaped whatever-he-was. "JOSHIM... here," he ordered.

Slinking forward, the evil, creepy jailer suddenly appeared at his side. With a look of pure malevolence etched across his face, the wicked shaped whatever-he-was gave his command.

"He's no longer of any use. Finish him off... now."

The boffin screamed,

"NOOOOOOO!" as the jailer skulked towards him, sneering menacingly, pleased to be able to show off his talents. Fredric and the naga king strained against their chains in an effort to protect their comrade against the fight, well I say fight, what I really mean is... murder. Joshim the jailer started with a brutal kick straight into the scientist's face. Bright red blood splattered across the shiny, icy surface surrounding him, along with two or three broken teeth. Muffled by the sheer delight of Joshim, the prisoner muttered something, but no one in the deadly cold cavern could make out what had been said, either because of his broken nose, his lost teeth, or the fear that ran through him at the thought of what was to come.

With the scientist babbling incoherently now, Joshim continued his grim task with aplomb, all the time a sadistic smile ingrained on his face. Reaching down, the evil jailer picked up his organic punch bag and head butted him as hard as he could, the sickening noise reverberating up the line of captives. All the time the human shaped whatever-he-was watched in satisfaction, standing just far enough back so as not to get covered in blood, but just close enough to revel in the action. All the while, Fredric and the naga king continued to try and break free from their bonds despite knowing that it was all but impossible.

By now Joshim had rained down another series of blows onto the defenceless human shaped dragon, breaking most of his ribs by the sound of it. Fredric, who hadn't quite given up trying to break free, but had realised the fruitlessness of his efforts, forced himself to watch what was happening. Not because he was a violent being, or got any sort of kick out of it, unlike the human shaped whatever-he-was. No! Fredric forced himself to watch so that the boffin's death would be remembered, his sacrifice would not be in vain and most importantly, so that when his chance came along, and he truly believed it would, he could conjure up what was happening here and use it to power him to freedom, as well as exact revenge on those that had committed the atrocity. They WOULD pay for what they were doing now.

Lying perfectly still on the frozen surface, either unconscious or more probably dead, the scientist's battered and broken body continued to be assaulted by the crazed jailer, who took great pleasure in kicking, punching, slapping and even at one point biting a huge chunk out of the victim's leg. At the sight of this, the naga king let out a piercing scream that had ice and rock tumbling from the ceiling, but still it wasn't enough to distract Joshim from his grim mission. In fact all it managed to do was provoke a smile from the human shaped whatever-he-was.

Half an hour, that's how much longer the sadistic beating lasted, ending only when Joshim lay soaked in sweat and exhausted, next to what was left of the dragon boffin. Wandering over, the human shaped whatever-he-was patted the evil jailer on his sweaty head in much the same way a human would do to a dog that had just done something clever. With pieces of flesh hanging out of his mouth, Joshim looked up at his master appreciatively, grateful for any attention he could get.

Turning away from his wicked little servant, the human shape with the limp strolled past the naga king, grinning from ear to ear as he did so, careful not to get within striking range of the agitated creature. When he reached Fredric, the smug smile had subsided a little, but still remained around the edges of his mouth.

"How did you like the show?"

Fredric knew he was on a hiding to nothing. If he reacted he might get a beating, or worse; with the jailer being in this crazed state things might go a bit too far and bang, there would go the chance of ever being free. The only sensible course of action would be to stay quiet, not react, and hope that it was enough to keep him alive for now.

"Somewhere inside you, the little dragon must be desperate to get out and beat me senseless," mocked the human shaped whatever-he-was, trying to provoke a response.

Focused on his breathing, Fredric tried using what little of his dragon abilities he could access to see if he could fathom anything at all about this mysterious visitor, now that he was standing right in front of him. It wasn't quite instantaneous like it used to be when he was free and at the height of his powers, but his dormant dragon senses awoke at his request, reaching out towards the being in front of him, searching for anything, anything at all. Fredric locked gazes with the stranger across the two metres or so that separated them.

In essence what Fredric was doing would go unnoticed by most, and should certainly not be very taxing. But because of the environment, his incarceration, and having only a smidgen of ethereal energy available, this simple little action was taking its toll. His muscles burned, his head ached, even more than it did constantly. Still he ploughed on, determined to gain what little insight he could, thinking of all the time he'd spent there, the brutality, everything he'd missed in the dragon domain, and how he'd let down his friend the king. All this had the desired effect, spurring his efforts on, washing away some of the tiredness. Through the haze, he caught the tiniest glimpse of something familiar, but for the life of him he couldn't work out what it was.

Shaking his head, and grinning just a little, the human guise in front of him quipped,

"Ohhh... you're good... yes, much better than I'd anticipated. Did you find anything?"

Fredric let his dragon talents drift back down to the place inside him where the cold normally forced them to reside. Sweat trickled down his forehead and his long, matted hair from the exhaustion of using just a fraction of his powers. Reeling a bit from the fact that the human shaped whatever-he-was could tell what he'd been doing, he knew that no ordinary dragon would have been able to sense that, if that's even what he was.

"For someone who's been locked up for so long, you still show a tremendous amount of courage and guile. It's a real shame you couldn't join us. More like you would enhance our forces beyond measure. Unfortunately I sense you'd rather die than take up arms against your kin. Am I right?"

Inside, Fredric was deeply shocked by what he'd just heard, however he remained motionless. Not a flicker of recognition crossed his face.

"I thought so," guessed the human shaped whatever-he-was. "We never did find out what it was you did for your kind. All this time and we still have no idea. I have my suspicions of course, but I don't think there's any way that I could get you to tell me the truth. You'd rather die of course, something that can be arranged, by the way."

Fredric puffed out his well honed chest just slightly in a gesture of defiance. Long ago he'd faced up to the fact that he might die in here without any of his friends or family ever knowing what had happened to him. That's why he was able to take the beatings and the torture, thinking of himself as dead, but never giving up hope that one singular opportunity might present itself to earn back his life.

His captor chuckled as he slowly limped around him, again staying just out of range. Although depleted of dragon magic due to the severe cold, he knew that the prisoner was more than capable of inflicting serious damage with just his physical strength if need be.

"I do respect your bravery and courage. Part of me really does wish it could be different. You're the sort of warrior I would pride myself in fighting alongside."

Fredric gave no reaction at all.

'There's something about this being that's very

dangerous,' he thought. 'And boy, do I know dangerous.'

"Why do you continue, dragon?" asked the human guise in front of him. "Why do you exercise your muscles? Why do you plot and scheme? Why, oh why, do you continue to believe escape or rescue is even possible? Please enlighten me... dragon?"

Every atom in Fredric's body wanted to break free from the chains and snap the human shaped whatever-he-was in half at the way he said 'dragon,' wiping the smug grin off his sneaky looking face forever.

"Ahhhh... you want to hurt me... I can feel how angry you are... dragon."

Still he didn't react.

"I admire your restraint. I don't think I would be able to control myself as you do if our roles were reversed. Perhaps a little reward is in order, particularly in light of the fact that you're not going anywhere any time soon."

Fredric wasn't quite sure what the human shaped whatever-he-was was playing at, but he was pretty certain it was a game of some sort and was determined to remain vigilant against some sort of information trap.

"Do you know where you are?"

Fredric remained totally silent.

"Come now dragon, why so coy? You won't be giving away any information to me. Why not just answer my question? Do you know where you are?"

Against his better judgement, Fredric responded.

"No."

"There, that wasn't so bad was it?"

Fredric had no idea where on earth they were. Oh he could guess, and he had, countless times, but it was just that... conjecture, figuring probably in or around the Arctic Circle somewhere, or maybe deep beneath the Alps in Europe. Realistically though, he could be anywhere in the world where it was cold.

'At least if he's going to reveal where we are, it might help if I ever do manage to escape,' he thought, still more than a little weary of whatever the being in front of him was up to. It was then that his mind shot back decades to the mission he'd been sent on by his friend, the king. In Germany, with two of his trusty comrades, they'd been tasked to retrieve something that had been taken from them. It should have been relatively easy really, certainly with all their dragon powers. But right from the start, little things started to go wrong. Equipment failed... odd in itself. The phones in the hotel they shared would ring for no apparent reason, and when answered, no one would be on the other end, just a cutting silence. Strange noises emanated from the other rooms, and there was just something odd about some of the members of staff there, not least the manager who always seemed to have his eye on them. One of his comrades had expressed doubts, urging him to call off the mission, but stubbornly he'd refused to listen, putting it all down to coincidence and an active imagination on the part of all three of them. As it turned out, he couldn't have been more wrong. They'd walked into a trap, one that had been planned specifically for them, or for dragons at least. In an attempt to fight, his two comrades had been killed, cut down by machine gun fire, not three metres from where he'd stood. Despite overwhelming odds, he'd almost got away, but something, or someone, had surprised him from behind, something he wouldn't have believed possible, and from what little he could remember, had rendered him unconscious.

Looking back now, it was all more than a little hazy, particularly in light of the length of time he'd been stuck in here. But one thing was for sure, and he'd had decades to go over and over it in his mind, whatever it was that had surprised him, he hadn't sensed it... not even a little. A being of some sort had sneaked up on him just when he'd thought he'd escaped, and had knocked him out, without him ever getting a sniff of anyone ever being there. To this day, he still couldn't explain what had happened that night. All that he remembered after that was waking up in this frozen hellhole, and the rest as they say is... history.

A sharp cough startled Fredric out from under the shroud of his dark memories.

"You are in actual fact, deep beneath... Antarctica, the South Pole," boasted the human whatever-he-was. "In part of the very same chamber that your kind entombed those with a radically different view of the world. How ironic don't you think?"

Fredric's control faded as a look of total and utter shock creased his cold and haggard face.

'The South Pole,' he thought to himself. 'But that's where... Troydenn, oh my God... please no... not that, anything but that.'

"You begin to understand now; I can sense it in you. But know this. What you see and what you can guess are just the tip of the iceberg. Your kind will pay for what they did here, pay with their lives and the lives of all the humans on the surface. Events are unfolding even as we speak. In a relatively short space of time, you could be one of only a handful of dragons left alive. A comforting thought, don't you agree?"

Fredric's face was a mixture of anger and puzzlement as he glared at the monster disguised as a human standing before him.

"I sense you have a question... dragon."

In his anger and confusion, Fredric had given up on staying silent, instead deciding to press ahead in the hope of gaining as much information as he could.

"It just isn't possible that anyone could have survived this long in this... environment!" he bellowed.

"Ahhh... but we did survive and now, now it's time to fight back, to reclaim what's rightfully ours and bring scum like you to your knees."

Shaking his head in frustration, his matted, icy hair swaying from side to side as he did so, Fredric refused to believe what he'd just heard, hoping against hope that it was just a desperate ploy to somehow wrangle information out of him. But however hard he tried, he just couldn't see how. With pent up anger threatening to overwhelm him, he lost his cool and screamed at the beast in front of him.

"What part do you play in all of this? You're certainly not a dragon, so don't try and tell me that you were encased in this icy prison all those years ago. Also, if what you say is true, all the dragons here would either be dead, or so old that they would present little or no threat to the king, the council or the dragon domain."

It felt good to Fredric to vent some steam, so to speak, and he could tell by the murderous expression on the being's face that he had provoked a reaction. He just hoped that he hadn't gone too far and signed his own death warrant. Taking stock, he carefully reined in his temper, remembering how important it was to stay alive, while the human shaped whatever-he-was sneered in contempt at him.

"You can be very sure of one thing... dragon. Those that are left here are a very serious threat to everything on the planet. And best of all, your kind have no idea what's going on, and by the time they do... it will all be too late. The world will be ours to do with as we please."

From a distance, the naga king looked on, but had managed to listen in on every single word, thanks to his excellent hearing.

Fredric, meanwhile, was only just starting to grasp the seriousness of the situation. At first he thought the being was all bluster, trying to lure HIM into a trap. But the way he was talking now... that was something different altogether. Not mad as such... Peter's grandfather was sure of that. And it wasn't so much what he said, although that in itself was enough to send shivers down a being's spine, even in a place like this. No, it was the way he'd said those things, with purpose, truth and conviction. Over the course of his career he'd met and defeated enough mad men, women and dragons to distinguish between those deluded about their ideas and those with the strength, conviction and purpose to follow through on what they said. Here was a purely evil being, his orders to put to death the human shaped dragon scientist proved that beyond any doubt, but the way he spoke and carried himself clinched it. Fredric knew a real threat when he saw one, and he was a hundred percent sure that this one was exactly that, even though he only had one small part of the puzzle that formed the whole picture. From whatever madness was being plotted here, the entire dragon domain and the world itself faced a terrible danger, one that couldn't be allowed to go on unchecked. He had to escape... and soon.

"As for my part in all of this... let's just say that if I told you, you wouldn't believe me," bragged the human shaped imposter.

"Try me," prompted Fredric, desperate to find out anything that could be of use.

The human shaped whatever-he-was seemed to consider the request. Moments later, he responded.

"This... place," he said, waving his arm around to signify the whole cavern and beyond, "is all I ever really knew. You see I was born here, and grew up here."

Fredric's legs nearly buckled. It was all he could do to remain upright.

'Impossible,' he thought. 'It's just too damn cold, he must be lying.'

"You don't believe me... dragon, do you?" the human shaped being spat. "But you see... it's true. Look around you. This was my nursery, my school, my playground. It was all I knew. Oh I was told about the outside world. It was described to me in graphic detail, but it might as well have been a fairy story for all it was worth. I knew nothing but this icy, desolate cavern. You think you've had it bad, over decades. That's nothing compared with my time here... NOTHING!" Scratching madly at the stubble occupying most of his face, thoughtful about whether to continue or not, the being eventually decided, much to

Fredric's relief, to carry on.

"I was stuck here, the first of my kind, lonely, helpless and with no chance of escape. Until one day, one of his kind," the human shaped whatever-he-was gestured towards the naga king with his thumb, stopping to glare in the same direction, "one of his kind came out of the stream, just over there. Exploring, or so he claimed, he was shocked to find a whole colony of dragons living under the ice. Ahhh what a day that was... the day we started to take back the planet," mused the human shape.

Fredric looked on in astonishment as his breath froze in front of his face.

"Luckily for us, they're not very intelligent creatures," continued his captor, referring to the nagas. "It took very little ingenuity to convince them to meet with us, spinning them a tale about what dastardly plans the dragon king and his council had for them. With this in mind, a meeting with their ruler was hastily arranged," recalled the being, turning and grinning in the direction of the naga king, who was listening to everything. "As soon as he arrived, we ambushed them, killed the rest of the contingent and captured their beloved king, and he's been here ever since. His loyal subjects do pretty much whatever we want, because if they don't, we'll send him back to them, a piece at a time."

Fredric caught the naga king's gaze out of the corner of one eye, knowing only too well that the serpent-like beast was biding his time, another one waiting for the right opportunity. The human shaped whatever-he-was continued, almost unable to stop boasting about his part in the wicked events of the past.

"Of course the first thing we got them to do was take a couple of us out of this frozen wasteland. It wasn't easy, but it's amazing how quickly they managed to come up with some magic to help us breathe and keep us dry and warm beneath the icy currents, under the threat of violence towards their beloved ruler. After that... well, a quick hop off this continent, up to America and Europe, enlisting a whole host of allies and Bob's your uncle. One ready-made army, fit to take back the planet. Even to this very day, the nagas still do our bidding, disguising themselves as humans, infiltrating every community on the planet. It has taken decades to get ourselves into a position to be able to bring our plan to fruition. But very shortly everything will start to take shape and the world that orbits the sun then, will be very different to how it is now."

With the naga king looking on, Fredric faced the being disguised as a human, the bubbling water of the underground stream almost deafening in volume. Throwing caution to the wind, he bravely pressed on, determined to learn more.

"What I don't understand," he said tugging out ice from part of his matted hair, "is how on earth you can have been born here? Surely that isn't possible. The council built this place as a last refuge, a prison, somewhere no being could thrive."

Drawing back his head, the human shaped whatever-he-was cackled madly, the sound reverberating around the cavern as if it were an exclusive nightclub.

"It was soooo easy. Your king and his council thought they'd planned everything down to the smallest detail, when in fact the scale of their ineptitude was enormous. It was, of course, way too cold for dragons to breed, because for them it has to be positively sweltering. But in their haste to capture and contain those dragons whose ideas they disagreed with, they overlooked something so obvious that at first it was hard for those stuck here to believe that their captors had been so stupid. But oh yes, they had. You see, when Troydenn was originally captured and incapacitated in the city of Salisbridge, the current dragon monarch did something so unbelievably stupid and naive that it's hard to fathom just how he went on to rule your domain. In his haste, he cast a mantra designed to repress any residual magic inside his prisoner. My understanding is that at the time, it left him encompassed by a deep purple glow. Sounds sensible, doesn't it, until you realise just how badly it backfired. What it actually did was lock a miniscule amount of magic deep within Troydenn, something he would go on to use to great effect, much later on. Although it was far too cold for dragons to mate and reproduce in their natural form, what your naive domain idiots overlooked, was the fact that with even a little of their power, the prisoners were still able to manipulate their DNA. Yes, it was difficult and took an amazing amount of time to do, but don't forget, they had centuries to get it right. And they did. With the help of Troydenn's locked away powers and the combined knowledge of all the prisoners, a select few had their DNA manipulated so that they were fully human. Once transformed, what do you think they did? That's right. They did it the old fashioned way... the human way. And what you see in front of you," announced the false human figure, spreading his arms wide and whirling around in a circle, "is the product of that very first union. While the world is full of dragons that can take human form and often do, I'm the very first human able to take dragon guise. And because of who I am and just how I was created, you can't sense me, or my abilities. Tell me... dragon, how does that feel?"

Fredric had thought he couldn't get any colder. It turns out he was wrong. A shiver of epic proportions ran through his innards like a great white shark chasing the scent of blood. Everything that this human hybrid dragon had said kind of made sense. All of it seemed unlikely of course, implausible even, but still entirely possible. And if even a hint of it was true, the danger to his kind and the wider world was much greater than Fredric had thought possible. His friends, the king, his grandson Peter, they were all in incredible peril, from a danger they had little or no idea was coming.

'Human dragons,' he thought. 'Worse still, human

dragons with a grudge, who think they should be ruling the world... how much worse can it get?' he mused, before something rather worrying popped into his cold and foggy brain. Knowing where he was now: trapped here in this holding facility as he'd once heard it described, the place where all those despicable evil dragons had been incarcerated all those years ago, some of whom he'd helped to capture and bring to justice. If, as the human dragon claimed, some were still alive... would they recognise him, and if so... how much worse could things get? More than ever, he wished to escape, or die trying.

'But what can I do?' he wondered, as the human dragon turned round, all the time smiling, and called the evil jailer over, before they both wandered off into the darkness. As he looked across to the naga king, he too wore a grim expression, one that said exactly what Fredric had been thinking. Time was indeed running out.

13 NELLY THE ELEPHANT PACKED HER...?

Sprouting out over the edge of the sink and onto the floor, he'd put too much washing up liquid in the bowl and now the bubbles had a life of their own. Only having gotten home twenty minutes earlier, this was the state he was getting himself into. The trouble was... he was too excited. It was one of those nights to look forward to. It wasn't hockey, or a trip to the pub or a meal, much as he loved all those things. It was something quite literally out of this world. It was of course... laminium ball!

'Yippee,' he thought as he started to gather up all the escaping foam, only to be rudely interrupted by a spark of pain blossoming deep within his shoulder. 'Damn!' After all this time his wounds from fighting Manson should have been fully healed, but they weren't. Regularly a mysterious pain sprang into life somewhere within him. Having been passed fit to return to Cropptech by the dragon physicians, they'd gone on to explain that the pain he was experiencing might well hang about for the rest of his life.

So much remained a mystery about the dreaded ex-army major, if that's even what he'd ever been. No one had been able to explain just how he'd camouflaged his weak spot, or how he could create a fake one on a different part of his body. Another head scratcher was the strange hazy barrier that had surrounded the Astroturf on that fateful November night. Was it created by a mantra or the dragon himself? If a mantra or spell, then where had it come from? A concerted search of the dragon libraries across the world, including the king's own private repository, as well as a gentle quizzing of Gee Tee, had come up blank on a mantra of that type ever having existed. Feeling more than a little selfish in wanting the dark hearted, murderous Manson to be found so that the physicians could cure him fully, he knew deep down that the bigger picture was much more important. Whatever the dangerous deranged dragon was up to, he must be stopped; after all he'd seen firsthand the wanton disregard for life in any form he'd exhibited and knew only too well what he was capable of. The big worry in Peter's mind though, was that the prehistoric monster and whatever he was up to would be put on the back burner so to speak, with everything that Flash had revealed to the king only days earlier.

Wandering through to the living room, he wondered how Flash was doing, hoping to see him again soon. Just then, the doorbell rang. Tentatively, he made his way towards the new front door, the old one having been replaced as part of the security measures designed to keep him safe should Manson return in an act of revenge. Striding down the hallway, he reached out with his magical senses, surprised to find a dragon on the other side. Fear raced around his stomach for a split second, before he realised it definitely wasn't his nemesis out there. Just then, a friendly voice trickled into his subconscious.

"Don't be afraid," it whispered. "I have a delivery for you from the king himself. He said to tell you that Nelly had two of these, but he wouldn't swap either of hers for yours. Does that make any sense?"

Wide eyed, he considered what he'd just heard.

'Nelly? Who the heck was Nelly?' Then it hit him like a bolt of lightning. Of course... Nelly the Elephant. She had two trunks: one like Peter's and the other one attached to her face. Breaking into a smile, he released the normal looking latch on the door that was anything but. Half a dozen mantras had been cast on the apparently standard Yale lock, making it almost impossible for any magical being to gain entry.

Opening the door, he found himself face to face with a very plain looking, dark haired human in brown overalls, holding a small box about the size of a tin of biscuits. His first thought was that it couldn't possibly be his trunk, as it was way too small for that. But then the delivery dragon smiled and said,

"I was ordered to make sure the package was safely inside before I got you to sign for it."

Not able to sense any kind of deception, quite the opposite in fact, he let the very ordinary looking guy into the hallway. On doing so, he glanced over his shoulder and noticed the van parked right outside. In bright white letters on a dark brown background, it read 'Majestic Deliveries.' Peter chuckled to himself.

'The king certainly has a sense of humour, that's for sure,' he thought as he followed the dragon into the living room.

"How are you today sir?" asked the driver, placing the package on the floor, smack bang in the middle of the room.

"Uhhh... fine, thanks for asking."

Taking a step back, the dragon mumbled something Peter couldn't quite make out, and for a split second, a bright white all encompassing light engulfed them. Instinctively he'd closed his eyes. When he opened them, his grandfather's trunk sat there right in front of him. Turning to face the delivery dragon who was sporting a huge grin, Peter said,

"Thanks."

"You're welcome," replied the dragon. "Can I trouble you for a signature please?"

Peter signed for the package, showed the dragon out, and then returned to the trunk, eager to check out its contents once again.

As he opened the lid, the old hinges gave a laboured squeak. Inside the contents had been neatly rearranged, he assumed by the king himself. On top of everything lay a handwritten note. It read:

Everything is here and accounted for. Please keep the item we

talked about 'safe' as mentioned. I apologise for the interruption on Sunday. I was really keen to spend some quality time with you and your friends as I so rarely have visitors but it wasn't to be... sorry. I hope you are recovering well. Your physician constantly updates me on your progress and I know he's working tirelessly to find a cure for the minor ailments that persist in causing you pain. Anyway, as I'm sure you can understand I must go now... there's a lot to do if you know what I mean, and I'm sure you do, especially with regard to your grandfather. By the way, Flash sends his regards. We're still in the process of getting him settled but he says once he is relocated he will drop by and see you and Tank. Any support you can give him would be appreciated because as you well know, he's been through quite an ordeal, much like yourself, and I think it will be some time before everything that's happened has sunk in.

Take care my young friend.

George.

Peter felt a pang of pity for the king. He seemed so... lonely. It was hard to imagine really: all that power, surrounded by all those other dragons and yet so isolated. On that note his thoughts turned inward towards his grandfather. Lonely didn't begin to cover it from Flash's description. How could anyone or anything do that to another sentient being? How had his grandfather survived all this time without going mad? Peter was pretty sure he'd have gone insane a long time ago, but from Flash's description, he'd seemed mentally sharp and had aided in the Crimson Guard's escape. Tears welled up inside him at the thought of a mighty dragon like his grandfather being held somewhere like that.

'Possibly the most brutal place on the planet for one of us,' he reflected, wiping the tears away with the sleeve of his jumper before they dropped into the trunk.

'I will get to meet him,' he vowed through gritted teeth, 'even if I have to take Tank and Richie to Antarctica to rescue him myself.'

A shrill ringing abruptly interrupted all thoughts of a snowy rescue. Following the noise, he picked up his vibrating phone from the kitchen table, pressed the green answer button and said,

"Hello?"

"Where are you then?" asked a familiar voice.

'Pants,' thought Peter.

"I'm really sorry. Where are you?"

"Richie and I are on the platform at Salisbridge, ready to board the monorail," replied Tank, just a hint of frustration in his voice.

Closing his eyes, Peter banged the palm of his free hand against his forehead.

"I'll be there in two minutes," he assured his friend, before hanging up abruptly.

Grabbing everything he needed, he sprinted into the living room, vaulted over his grandfather's trunk, yanked the Galileo thermometer back as far as it would go, and with the piano swinging out towards him, disappeared into the small, dark gap that appeared behind it. Rushing down the winding metal staircase two steps at a time, stubbing his toe in haste, he was in too much of a rush to even let out a curse. Triggering the hidden lock that opened the door to the underground world of the dragons, he sprinted down the path, jumped the wall and continued on at full speed towards the station. Swerving in and out of the other dragons at full pelt, frantically he searched for his friends. Finally he spotted them... sitting on a huge bench on one side of the plaza, stuffing their faces by the looks of things. Peter pulled up abruptly, breathing heavily.

"Sorry I'm late," he puffed.

"That's okay," replied Richie, chewing on a charcoal doughnut.

"We decided to get a bite to eat while we were waiting," added the rugby player, knowing full well that Peter was probably hungry, as he nearly always was.

"Great," ventured their friend, forcing a smile, still out

of breath.

"Don't be like that," declared Richie.

"Yeah," said Tank. "Or we won't let you have this," he added, producing a freshly cooked charcoal fajita from somewhere out of view, before offering it to his friend. Instantly Peter's eyes lit up.

"I don't deserve you two," he said, gratefully accepting the fajita.

"I think he's probably right," stated Richie, turning to Tank and raising her eyebrows.

Tank coughed and spluttered, trying dragonfully not to spit out the huge mouthful of charcoal kebab he'd just taken as he struggled to stifle a laugh. This started the other two off, and within seconds all three of them were splitting their sides with laughter, much to the bemusement of all the dragons around them in the busy plaza.

Ten minutes later, all three boarded the monorail, excited at the prospect of watching a laminium ball match for the first time in ages. Today was a league game against the Colwyn Bay Buccaneers, a team currently in fourth position in the league, compared with a paltry eleventh out of thirteen for the Indigo Warriors. The match was taking place at the amazing Seabed Arena in Porthpean near St Austell in Cornwall. With a massive 150,000 capacity, the newly refurbished stadium was one of the jewels in the crown of the BLB (British Laminium Board).

To get there, the three friends first had to journey to Taunton, and then on to Plymouth, via Exeter. There the monorail would head straight across to St Austell where it was just a short walk to the entrance of the Seabed Arena which was situated below the village of Porthpean. Extending well out across St Austell bay, the arena itself covered an area of approximately thirty square miles.

Squeezing up next to each other in the tightly packed carriage, Richie leant in towards her friends and asked,

"How did it go on Sunday?" This was accompanied by

her usual conspiratorial wink.

Knowing that however quietly he responded, all the other dragons with their enhanced senses would still be able to hear his reply, Peter decided to try and be as cryptic and vague as possible.

"It was a really interesting experience," he replied, offering her a wink of his own.

"Did I miss anything good?" she asked.

'Where to start,' thought Peter, turning to Tank, unsure of what to say, knowing he couldn't mention everything that had happened with regard to Flash, but really not wanting to lie to Richie. He needn't have worried, Tank had it covered.

"Not really," replied the big fella casually. "But the dragon we went to see did... ask after you."

Richie, normally cooler than a cucumber in a Siberian fridge, flinched just a little uncomfortably in her seat, as she thought about this.

"Any particular reason why?" she asked, not fooling either of them.

'Tank,' thought Peter, 'is having a field day tweaking Richie's scales about this. I know he doesn't approve of her seeing Tim, but he really shouldn't mess with her like this.'

"I think in the position he's in, he probably gets to hear just about everything that goes on... everywhere."

"Ahhhh," Richie whispered, thoughtfully. "Well, if there's a problem I'm sure he'll come straight to me and say, rather than pussyfoot around. It's always better that way don't you think... Tank?"

Now it was the plant and animal lover's turn to feel more than a little uneasy, fully understanding her dig at him. Before things could go any further, Peter stepped in to diffuse the situation.

"Guys, we're on our way to a laminium ball match. Let's forget everything else and just enjoy that shall we? I for one am really looking forward to it and have been for a few weeks now. So come on, enough with the petty squabbles... alright?"

Tank and Richie lowered their heads in shame at their childish behaviour. Standing up, Tank offered out one of his giant hands to his female friend in a gesture of goodwill. Standing up, she held her hands back, almost refusing to shake his, that is until she leapt up and gave him what could only be described as the biggest hug in the world. Peter smiled at his two best friends making up, relieved that everything was now alright between them. It was only then though, as he watched Richie enveloped in Tank's giant grasp, that he realised he was slightly... jealous. Not really understanding why, he thought about it for a couple of seconds. He'd had feelings for her forever, but knew on a practical level that nothing was ever going to happen between them as she was way out of his league, something he was the first to admit, at least to himself anyway. Always having known it would take the most amazing dragon in the world to tame... no, that really wasn't the word he was looking for... to... capture Richie's heart. It would be no ordinary being, that much he knew for sure, and that's what made her dalliances with Tim all the more difficult to understand. Richie would be a catch, and a match for almost any living dragon, poor or powerful, but instead she chose to chase after the odd human or two. Unable to get his head around it all, just thinking about it made his brain hurt.

With the momentarily bout of jealousy fading into the background quicker than an X Factor runner up, his thoughts turned to Janice. A shiver of excitement ran down his invisible tail. There was something about her that made him feel... special. Closing his eyes, he imagined being with her and all the things that came with it. Adoring the way she smelled, he remembered the electrifying touch of her hand on his when they'd walked home from the cinema on their first date. Her infectious smile was just mesmerising, as were her gorgeous eyes that always seemed as though they were looking straight into his soul. Speaking of which, his friends seemed to be doing exactly that, eyeing him in a very strange and knowing way.

Coughing awkwardly, he smiled.

"So," he said, "what's the score going to be tonight then?"

"Well," said Richie thoughtfully, scratching her petite chin for effect. "The Buccaneers have been on a winning streak of late, and did win 4-0 last week, hardly allowing the opposition a touch."

Remembering that he'd read about that match in the Daily Telepath, Peter nodded, finding it hard to believe that such a one sided game could happen in the modern day sport. Fifty or sixty years ago it would have been almost commonplace. But since then a huge shakeup had taken place, with things having transformed here and across the world, on a monumental scale. There were four United Kingdom leagues, each comprising of thirteen teams. The bottom two at the end of the season were relegated whilst the top two were promoted, except obviously in the top tier, where there was no promotion, only an outright winner. Aside from the leagues, play offs across the world chose which teams made it into the Global Cup, the competition that the Warriors had almost won last year. With coaching, tactics and facilities constantly improving, the dragons' favourite sport had been revolutionised almost beyond recognition in only half a century or so. What were once very one-sided matches now normally turned out to be too close to call. Of course there were still exceptional teams. Each top tier around the globe normally had two or three, but apart from that, in standard and ability the squads all seemed to be very evenly matched, so much so that even the supposedly elite sides could go without winning for three or four games in a row. Bucking the trend apparent in nearly all the leagues, the Buccaneers had hammered home their victory against a very well drilled and tactically sound Pontypool Pirates side. Not only had it been big news in the Daily Telepath, but it chorused out across all the telepathic papers. Today, weeks later, the story still rumbled on with rumours abounding that the very experienced coach of the Pirates was going to be sacked, something that hadn't ever happened in the history of the team. It was all quite shocking but made for good reading.

"So you think the Buccaneers will win?"

"That's not quite what I said. In theory they should triumph, just purely on form and their league position," she replied.

Tank opened his mouth to pipe up, but before he could get a word out, the lacrosse superstar held up the index finger of her right hand to stop him.

"However, I don't believe they've come up against any team as devious as the Warriors in the league yet, and that could well be their undoing. Silverbonce always has a couple of tricks up his scales and after the double goal with the ball splitting tactic last year, every single side is always gonna believe something like that is possible from the Warriors."

Tank nodded his agreement.

"When she's right, she's right."

"The only thing that worries me at the moment is our lack of a goal scoring threat. Defensively we're fine, but going on the attack we just don't seem to be cutting the mustard, so to speak," announced Peter.

His two friends nodded their agreement as the monorail pulled into St Austell station.

"Our stop, I do believe," declared Tank

"Ours and everybody else's by the look of things," replied Richie, as everyone in the carriage stood up to depart.

Filing off and out onto the platform, the friends followed the LED signs that signalled the way to the arena. As the throng of dragons moved along the lava lined walkway, vendors pulling small carts battled against the tide, trying hard to sell their wares. All the usual things were on display: hats, scarves, flags, banners, and exploding mantras with the name of the team or individual player. It was all there. Richie stopped, keen to look at the merchandise. Tank and Peter were about to continue on but thought better of it. With the crowd so thick, they would probably lose her altogether and in an arena this size the match could well have finished before they found her again, despite them having adjacent seats.

Leaning across the dragon in front of her, the lacrosse player started rifling through the exploding mantra section of the vendor's cart. Tank and Peter stood off to one side, trying hard not to disrupt the steady, one way flow of dragon spectators. Before too long, Richie, clearly delighted with her purchase, zipped in and out of the swarm of spectators and joined her friends. Tank and Peter tried to get a look at what she'd bought, but she was having none of it, telling them both to mind their own business and that they'd find out at the appropriate time. Both friends acknowledged Richie's madness with a familiar look, something they'd used more times than they cared to remember.

Reaching the central plaza in front of the main entrance to the stadium, all three ignored the food stalls which were doing a roaring trade, choosing instead to follow the illuminated signs in the direction of the seat numbers on the tickets that they held. After a long walk, they reached their chairs, halfway along the arena, pretty much level with where the ball enters from the roof, about two thirds of the way up. If it were a human football match, these seats would be considered the best in the house.

As they sat down, the stadium became bathed in light and a happy dragon voice echoed all around.

"Laminium ball lovers, thank you for your attendance today. Before the major event, we have an aerial flying display from the St Austell nursery ring dragonlings display team. So please put your wings and hands together for them as they show you their amazing aerobatic skills."

With that, the lighting dimmed, except in one corner of the arena where it sparkled pink. Moments later, twenty one young dragons shot up into the bright light. Darting in and out of each other, barely a hair's breadth apart, the young dragonlings formed intricate patterns that with every variation turned a different colour.

All three friends sat captivated with the choreography, precision and sheer beauty of the display. Usually there was something like this at every match, but most paid little attention to it. The three friends were as guilty of this as anybody, not normally arriving in their seats until the very last moment, but here and now, were currently having the exact same thought.

'Have we really been missing things like this at every game?'

Continuing for another ten minutes or so, the dragonlings wowed the crowd with daring descents, brilliant barrel rolls, intricate routines and dangerous flybys. Spectators of every age couldn't take their eyes off the youngsters, with late arrivals cursing themselves. Finally the lights flared into life, illuminating the whole group in the middle of the arena, right in front of the three friends, prompting the three quarters full stadium to erupt into a massive round of applause. Bursts of flame in tribute from nearly every dragon in their natural form lit up the scene like a blow torch convention.

Minutes later the lighting died away again, leaving just the lava for illumination. Whispered conversations echoed around the cavern as the final seats filled with latecomers, the electric atmosphere at the prospect of the game almost tangible. It was nearly time.

Once again the smooth voice of the announcer resonated throughout the cavern.

"And now, the moment you've all been waiting for... The Indigo Warriors versus the Colwyn Bay Buccaneers... enjoy!"

Silence fell over the expectant crowd, punctuated only by the gurgling and sloshing of molten magma as they all awaited their heroes. Seconds later, there they were. Abruptly the lights came back on at exactly the same time as a series of small holes opened up in the ceiling, through which dropped each team member, the Warriors at one end, the Buccaneers at the other. Shouting, screaming, breathing flame... the audience went mad. And then the teams were off on their display laps, the Buccaneers forming a tight unit mere centimetres apart, dashing full speed around the edge of the cavern, almost within touching distance of the spectators. Much more spaced out, the Warriors preferred instead to show off their individual prowess. Steel and Flamer ducked, dived, twisted and barrel rolled in and out of each other, with the crowd egging them on to ever more dangerous feats. Cheese, Barf and Silverbonce took it easy, waving, blowing out violent streams of flame while at the same time poking fun at each other. Both teams were a total contrast, as the Buccaneers zoomed around at ridiculous speeds all serious and pent up, while the Warriors pleased the crowd with stunts, all the time making fools of themselves.

After a couple of laps, for the Warriors that is (the Buccaneers had done about twelve) both teams flew up towards the top of the arena, in the middle, where the laminium ball would appear. With both squads hovering high above the middle of the lava pitch, a long sliver of molten lava appeared at exactly the same time on the rock face at both ends of the cavern, beside each goal mouth. A quiet, "Owww," whispered around the crowd. The sliver of lava suddenly shaped the number ten at both ends at exactly the same time, with the crowd joining in.

"Ten." Continuing on its fascinating journey, the lava flowed into the shape of the number nine.

"Nine," screamed the audience. Peter, Tank and Richie had never seen a countdown like it. Normally little lights or crystals lit up as the crowd counted down, but this was all very modern and dramatic. Reaching a crescendo at, "Two," all eyes turned towards both teams, with some of the crowd focusing on the stream of guided lava, just about managing to get out, "One," before in the blink of an eye, out shot the golden ball, just a blur really, quite something given the enhanced senses that every being there possessed.

Wings, tails, bodies and scales all merged into one amidst the mayhem. Both mouth guards swooped round, departing the action, heading back towards their respective mouths to guard the stalagmite and stalactite 'teeth' against breakage from the laminium ball that would mean a goal for their opponents. Hands, wings and tails tried in vain to grasp the ever elusive orb, all to no avail. In the end, Steel came thundering out of the melee with the round prize cunningly trapped under his chin, ducking and dodging the opposition as he did so. As the rest of the outfield Warriors tried desperately to follow him, Barf took an uppercut to the jaw, big time, off the ball, something the referee clearly didn't see, or if he did, refused to acknowledge so early on.

All three friends were literally on the edge of their seats, leaning against the ornamental railing which no dragon thought was really there to protect them from falling over the side. I mean, a dragon falling over the side... they would just fly right back up and into their seat again... obviously!

In the meantime the Buccaneers had forced Steel and his flying honour guard into a dive towards the surface, allowing them only enough room to pull up right at the last second. Droplets of blisteringly hot lava bubbled against Cheese's face as he paced his captain, less than half a metre above the orange lake of danger, weaving in and out of potentially fatal fountains as if they were mere tourist attractions. In one deft motion, Steel transferred the ball from under his chin, to beneath his right wing, feeling the subtle vibration of its power ebbing through him. He always wondered whether the sports men and women on the surface, in anything that involved a ball, felt a buzz or a rush whenever they had possession. If they did, he could relate to their experience... more so really. In his case, with the laminium ball, he really did get a buzz and oh so much more, his magical abilities magnified by the close proximity of the power enhancing metal encased within the shiny sphere. Able to fly just that little bit faster, his awareness was increased, with any stray splashes of lava bouncing off his scales becoming barely noticeable. During this game there was a big difference between being on the ball and off it.

Occasionally players would admit to journalists, fans, or female admirers that in a match all they wanted to do when they received the ball was to play a pass as quickly as possible. Not Steel though, because he knew exactly what it was all about. It had taken its time to dawn on him. Even as a young dragonling he'd had all the necessary raw ability, courage, dexterity, wing eye coordination, etc. But all of that was nothing without the brains and understanding to match. Truth be told, as a youngster, brains were pretty much in short supply, particularly when playing his sport of choice. Even right up until he was chosen to perform professionally it was more down to brawn and courage than thought. But after being selected for the Warriors, it was almost as if a switch had been flicked inside his head, with a giant light surging into life inside his brain. Looking back it was all so obvious, easily recognisable with hindsight, but then most things usually are. It was also pretty easy to see how this insight had come about, mainly due to an individual in the squad, someone he'd always admired and respected for being one of the game's greats, but it was only through playing alongside him that he realised quite how fantastic he really was. Who was that player you ask? Easy... Silverbonce! In Steel's mind he had it all: the courage of ten dragons twice his size, the agility of one of their kind a quarter of his age, brains to match his brawn, coolness under pressure and the trait Steel admired the most... sneakiness, something he'd never really appreciated before meeting the wily old dragon. Bending the rules, stretching them sometimes, right to their very boundaries, the cunning old mouth guard played right on the edge, his mind open to possibilities that no other dragon would even consider. And so it was now, as he whizzed in and out of the scorching hot lava approaching a line of three Buccaneers, that a dozen sneaky thoughts zipped around his head; his only problem was which one to choose.

As the distance closed in the blink of an eye, Steel, flanked by Cheese and Flamer, rolled the ball underneath his body and down onto his tail, all in one seamless move. Together, the entire crowd gasped, all thinking the same thing:

'He's way too far out to have a shot... isn't he?'

Banking hard at the very last second, the courageous captain used all his might and let rip with the ball, then allowed his momentum to carry him way over the head of the opposition. All three Buccaneers did exactly as they should have and concentrated their efforts on the glittering globe, dismissing Steel as no threat whatsoever, as he'd flown out of view way above them. Strangely, when he'd launched the ball, instead of sending it towards the opposition's mouth, he'd angled it down towards the lava, just below the three opposing Buccaneers. Nobody, including the players (on both sides) and the crowd, had any idea what on earth was going on. Well, maybe just one other dragon did. Silverbonce hovered in front of his mouth, nodding in admiration at what he'd just witnessed his leader attempt.

'That,' he thought, 'is very cunning and devious. I like it!'

After the ball left Steel, two things happened. Having spun the ball violently, creating as much rotation as he dared with his tail, he attempted to add something else.

Using every ounce of his concentration, he tried to imbue the ball with a... thought. This was almost unheard of, and if you'd asked any dragon in the crowd, or across the planet in fact, they'd have told you it was beyond impossible. But it wasn't at all, just forgotten. Silverbonce had explained how when he'd first started playing laminium ball, centuries ago, such a thing was commonplace even for youngsters in the nursery ring, going on to explain how the magical qualities of the precious metal provided the potential, if a player retained possession for long enough, to plant a thought in the ball's mind, so to speak. It would only last for a short while, and that decreased immeasurably as the ball left the player, but it was certainly achievable. Talented players back then could bend and swerve the ball at will, on occasion making it stop dead in mid air after having thrown it at speed, with all their might. When Silverbonce had recounted all these feats to him, it had sounded a little far-fetched. At first he'd thought it one of the old mouth guard's renowned practical jokes. Many a laminium ball playing dragon, both team member and opponent, had been on the end of one of the old dragon's famed pranks or warped sense of humour. That, as well as his playing ability and longevity, was why he was one of the public's favourite players in all the leagues throughout the world.

Anyway, Steel had done as Silverbonce had suggested and practised alone with a brand new match ball. After two days, he was convinced it was all a big joke, and was just waiting for the old mouth guard to jump out at him and shout, "Gotcha." Needless to say, that never happened. Very slowly, the valiant leader could sense the ball attempting to carry out a singular thought. At first it was very hit and miss, but at the same time unbelievably exciting. The more he practised, the better at it he got. But he was under no illusion as to how difficult a skill it was to master, let alone use in a match. It was one thing to achieve it while practicing alone, quite another to use the skill against top quality opponents with tens of thousands of spectators watching. Nevertheless, he'd given it his best shot, and Steel's best shot normally far exceeded that of a dozen ordinary dragons combined.

The thought he'd imbued within the fast moving orb was one of a burst of speed, about halfway through its intended flight. Aiming the ball at just such an angle that if it hit the lava's surface, it should in theory, just like a skimming stone on water, bounce right back up off it. The 'if' was whether it got as far as the lava in the first place. Buccaneers players were all swooping towards the rotating sphere, ready to intercept as Steel looked down from high above them. Knowing that if his plan failed, he'd have to double back and defend his mouth as fast as he could, as in essence he would have left the team shorthanded, the momentary sliver of doubt that entered his mind was shattered like a sledgehammer pulverising a pebble, by his razor sharp confidence that returned with a vengeance. Continuing on course, he didn't let the ball leave his sight.

Cheese and Flamer hovered to a halt, unsure of what to do. There'd been no chance of them catching up with the ball once it had left Steel's powerful tail, and they'd been unable to perform the tight turn that had taken their captain high up over their opponents' heads. Both frustrated that Steel had given away possession so cheaply, particularly as any second now the Buccaneers were about to get their claws on it, as they looked on through the haze and the heat of the lava, something unimaginable happened. All three Buccaneers converged on their target at once, competing against each other to see which of them would be the first to get a touch since the start of the game. It seemed to nearly everyone that it would be a close run thing as they all looked as if they'd reach the ball at exactly the same time. A split second before they were due to intercept it on its downward course, abruptly it quadrupled its speed, sending it whizzing past the Buccaneers, rushing on towards the surface. Having smashed into each other, all three opponents couldn't believe what they were seeing.

Steel, high above everybody, shook his head, grinning from ear to ear, hoping that he'd got the next part of his plan just right. Hitting the fiery surface, instead of the expected 'plop,' the sound the spinning globe made was more of a 'twang' as the backspin on it prevented it from being absorbed by the molten magma, sending it soaring off up into the arena and, more importantly, straight into the grinning Steel's flight path. Too stunned by what he'd just seen to put up any resistance, the last Buccaneer defender flailed about haplessly as Steel gathered in the onrushing laminium ball with his tail. Tossing it high up over the player, the sneaky captain swooped around behind him, gathered it in once again and found himself through on the mouth. Tens of thousands of spectators, even the Buccaneers fans, were on the edge of their seats, eager to see if the Warriors' captain could finish what he'd started, what seemed like an eternity ago, straight from the drop off. Putting on the biggest burst of speed possible, Steel headed straight for the middle of the mouth. About a second later, he hit the brakes as hard as he could, bringing himself to an abrupt halt. The forward momentum from his burst of speed brought his tail with the ball nestled in it, up over his head, so unexpected was the sudden stop. Letting the momentum carry his body forward, he rolled tail over head, catapulting the golden ball on its way only when his extremity was at the perfect point in his tumble. Not having a prayer of stopping the ball, all the Buccaneers' mouth guard could do was watch as it smashed perfectly into one of the teeth.

The best part of one hundred and fifty thousand dragons rose from their seats in unison, all cheering and roaring at once, Peter, Tank and Richie among them. Niftily, Richie pulled a small paper packet from the back pocket of her jeans, and in one smooth, fluid motion, ripped open the top and poured a handful of the sparkling dust into the palm of her hand. Sucking in a deep breath, she blew the powder out into the stadium. Instantly, it began to coalesce into recognisable shapes. After only a few seconds, two metre high letters formed and began to make words. This wasn't only happening in front of her... it was happening everywhere, as far as the eye could see. It could only be one name... STEEL! Drifting round the stadium, light from the lava below twinkled off the dust that formed the magical letters.

With the sound and the celebrations having died down, the match could really only go one way after Steel's amazing goal... downhill. Oh don't get me wrong, it was as fine a league match as there'd been all season, but after the stunning start, it could only ever creep back towards mediocrity. Soon after Steel's goal the Buccaneers equalised, before going on to take the lead. After that, things became rather scrappy, with numerous warnings to both sides from the referee. Unfortunately for the three friends, the Buccaneers won 2-1, somewhat taking the edge off the main talking point of the evening... that goal!

As the echo of the giant gong reverberated around the arena to signal the end of the match, Peter, Tank and Richie started to make their way towards the exit. Huge queues meant it took an absolute age to reach the main plaza, where the food stalls were still doing an alarming trade despite the late hour. Throughout their queuing, all the three friends could hear, were dragons raving about Steel's goal. As they joined a line to get a charcoal kebab (Peter, surprise, surprise was starving) only one thing was on their minds.

"If I hadn't seen it for myself, then I would never have believed it," put in Tank.

"That's part of the problem the papers will have in the morning," added Peter. "However well they describe what happened, not everyone will understand. I mean we were that close and I still find it hard to take in exactly what happened."

Nodding in unison, they shuffled steadily forward in the queue.

"I'm still not sure' how he did it," stated Tank, more than a little bemused.

"Me neither," agreed Peter.

Richie paused, her delicate little face screwed up in concentration.

"I," she said, "have a theory about that."

Both males stared at her in disbelief. Finally Tank asked,

"And?"

"Well," said Richie, moving slightly further forward. "I think what Steel did was... suggest to the ball what it should do."

"Suggest... to the... ball?" mocked Peter.

Tank joined in.

"Oh ball, oh ball... I have a suggestion for you," he called out in a stupid voice.

"Very clever," she responded dryly. "I think he planted the suggestion a little more forcibly that that. And yes it's not as ridiculous as you two half-wits seem to think. You wait and see what it says in tomorrow's papers. They normally get to the bottom of stuff like this. Mark my words. If it's not that, then I bet you I'm not a million miles away from what really did happen."

Recognising that they'd been suitably chastised, Peter and Tank knew well enough not to mock her any more, not about the same thing anyway. Tank had reached the head of the queue now and was ordering something called a Super Sumptuous Double Deluxe Charcoal Kebab. Peter slavered with anticipation behind him, just at the mere name, and waited patiently for it to appear. When it did, it lived up to its name... and more. The pitta bread that it came in was the size of a small tent, with Tank barely able to hold it in both his giant hands. Inside, delicious roasted meat tangled with vegetables of all shapes and sizes. Peppers, cucumbers, tomatoes, lettuce, carrot, onion, cabbage, they were all there, interspersed with squash ball sized chunks of steaming hot charcoal. It looked and smelled beyond fantastic, and Peter ordered one before the server even had a chance to open his mouth to ask what he wanted. Richie wasn't quite so taken with the monstrosity that was the kebab and opted instead for pitta bread stuffed with just salad, much to her friends' surprise. Making their way to a vacant table, the three sat down, remaining quiet, choosing to eat rather than talk, as the crowds around them slowly dwindled. Richie of course finished first, followed by Tank, as a determined Peter steadfastly refused to let the kebab get the better of him. As the hockey player wrestled with the last giant chunk of charcoal, a shadow fell sharply across the table. Three of the biggest, meanest looking dragons Peter had ever seen stood side by side, towering over Richie. Tank moved first, his chair scraping across the stone of the courtyard as he leapt to his feet. Richie rose calmly, as did Peter, leaving the remainder of his food strewn across the table. Of course there was no real contest. Tank, even as big and powerful as he was in his dragon form, would still only have been about two thirds the size of the smallest dragon facing them. Suddenly, two of the large dragons parted, making way for someone. The troubled, scared and determined looks of the three friends disappeared as a dragon councillor walked serenely into the gap provided.

"Stand down," ordered the official.

All three of them withdrew just slightly, turning their backs, affording the councillor a degree of privacy.

Peter marvelled at the official's robes which seemed to shimmer and change colour at will; the complex trident design hadn't changed much in hundreds of years and commanded the same respect now as it had back then.

Tank was more interested in the dragon himself. In all his life, he'd never seen one of their kind that was so... slim. Oh he wasn't short, quite the opposite in fact, but he was unbelievably slender and narrow. It didn't help that his stubby little wings were folded behind his back. It gave him the look of a wounded bird rather than a dragon with an air of authority. Also, Tank noted he had very beady little eyes, most strange for a dragon.

Richie had no interest whatsoever in the councillor and now that any potential threat had disappeared, she chose to sit back down in her silver coloured chair.

Casting his beady eyes over all three of them, the councillor asked,

"Are you Richie Rump?"

Surprised, she turned to face him and nodded.

"I am councillor Shady Swampbottom and I need to speak to you, in private please."

A million possibilities ran through her head all at the same time, causing her to smile.

"Anything you have to say to me can be said in front of my friends," she replied nonchalantly.

Forcing his face to remain neutral, the councillor continued,

"It really would be best if we spoke somewhere less public, young dragon," he declared, more than a little patronisingly.

That in itself was enough for Richie to take offence. It seemed that the official had no choice but to accede to her demand that her companions stay.

"Oh well, as you wish," he huffed, his narrow little eyes darting back and forth between all three of them. "It has been brought to the attention of the council that you've been flouting one of its primary rules thereby endangering everything that, we as a race, strive to achieve."

'Wow,' thought Richie. 'Don't beat around the bush... come right out and say what you mean.'

'I hope he's going to be a little more specific about exactly what she's done, otherwise there's the potential for all of this to go very badly. I know at least two primary rules she breaks on a very regular basis,' thought Peter.

Tank breathed a sigh of relief. Despite the fact that he

would never wish either Richie or Peter to get into trouble with the council, he hoped now that she could have some sense talked into her regarding Tim. Nothing good was ever going to come of a dragon and a human having a relationship like that, and it was plain to him that it was only Richie who would suffer in the long run.

As the lacrosse superstar glared frostily at the councillor, she caught Tank's sigh of relief out of the corner of her eye.

"So what exactly is it that you think you know?" she spat, her mood deteriorating by the second.

"There's no 'think' about it," replied the councillor, an edge to his voice. "We know that you've been actively pursuing a relationship with a human on the surface of this planet."

Richie fell silent.

Peter closed his eyes, hoping against hope that common sense would prevail all round and that his friend would agree to stop seeing Tim and just get a slap on the wrist, so to speak. But with the tension around the table rising faster than a thermometer in a supernova, he had visions of it going in quite the opposite direction.

Richie and the official locked gazes in a battle of wills. A resounding silence encompassed the tiny area. Stragglers from the thinned out crowd heading for the monorail station, afforded them only a momentary glance.

Eventually the councillor blinked, causing a small smile to slip across the lacrosse player's delicate face, much to his outrage. Clearly not used to this level of disrespect, he had a face like thunder as he reached into his shimmering robes and pulled out a rolled up scroll. Leaning across the table, he handed it over. Before she had a chance to unfurl it, the councillor interrupted.

"It's a decree, signed by the king himself, ordering you to cease your relationship with the human on pain of being banned from the surface of the planet."

Richie stared open mouthed at the scroll, now that the

tables had been well and truly turned, with the official wearing a smile on his face as he bade them farewell. The shadow lifted as the councillor and the dragons disappeared off in the direction of the monorail station.

Peter was first to break the ice, despite the fact that he didn't want to.

"It's probably for the best Rich. You know full well that it was only a matter of time before they caught up with you. At least now you know instead of having to constantly look over your shoulder, and you can get on with your life. Don't you think?"

Instead of the measured reply he'd been expecting, she turned in the direction of Tank and asked,

"You did this, didn't you? It was you who reported me to the council wasn't it? How dare you?"

Tank looked visibly stunned, and that alone should have told her everything that she needed to know... but it didn't. She was already too far gone to be reasoned with.

"I don't know how you can possibly think it was me, Rich," maintained the big fella, getting to his feet. "I didn't and still don't approve of what you've been doing with Tim as you well know. But I would never jeopardise our friendship over something like that. But since you feel angry enough to speak your mind, so will I. Those rules were put in place for a reason. Dragons and humans are not meant to have that kind of relationship. Think of all the things that could go wrong, and the harm it could do, and not just to the dragons. Think of the pain you could cause to Tim. Think of him growing old and you matching him on the outside with your fancy mantras, but on the inside always being much younger, able to live a longer life. What happens when he dies? You will still have hundreds of years left in front of you. What will happen then? Grab another throwaway human to do with as you will?"

Richie's face contorted so much with anger that she honestly looked as though she might explode. Her cheeks were a brilliant shade of purple while a snarl worthy of the meanest guard dog ran the width of her jaw, her forehead so creased it looked like a range of tiny mountains. Peter had never seen her so upset, and was more than a little frightened. Tank on the other hand, despite his own rage, was much more in control of his own emotions. His top lip quivered a little, more to do with having an argument and hurting his friend than anything else, his kind and caring persona shining through even now, right in the middle of this very dangerous row.

For a split second there was pure silence, Tank and Richie staring menacingly at each other. Peter was sure the argument had run its course and was almost certain Tank would turn around and walk away, leaving Richie alone to calm down in her own time. Not for the first time, he was way off the mark.

Richie took three paces forward towards the rugby player, invading his personal space, easily within striking distance. If Peter had been feeling braver, and he wasn't quite sure how much braver he would have to feel, but he had a fair idea that it would have to be a lot, he would have stepped between the pair. But on consideration, he would almost rather have faced Manson again on that frozen hockey pitch.

"By your own admission, the rules that forbid humans and dragons interacting on such a level were made thousands of years ago," she screeched, poking Tank in the middle of his barrel like chest with the tip of her index finger. "Those same rules clearly cannot be of any relevance today, millennia after they were first dreamt up. Look at how the world has changed in that time, how both races have evolved and advanced. Well I say both races, but in a lot of ways the humans have surpassed us with what they've achieved. The dragon domain has become stagnant not only in what goes on down here but the attitudes of our kind in general. We've become complacent and ignorant of just how far the those on the surface have advanced. You both know dragons who think of humans as almost... pets, something to be tolerated, put up with, looked after if you like. These beings think we're doing the humans a favour but I think it's almost the other way round. They have such short life spans and yet almost all of them live life to the full. With a few exceptions they're tolerant of most things and are becoming more so all the time. Overall they strive for peace and a better life for their entire race, but here we are stuck below ground, hiding away with our mantras, passing ourselves off as one of them on the grounds of guiding and protecting them. What a complete load of dragon dung!"

Richie stopped for a breath, her anger seeming to intensify.

"You two," she continued, indicating Peter and Tank with her finger. "You two can almost see all of this. You with your hockey and your JANICE," she said, pointing fiercely at Peter. "Don't tell me you can't feel it in your soul. You know it and I know it. And as for you Rugby Boy," she observed, turning back to face Tank, "you're fooling no one. The rugby does for you what the hockey does for him. And the only reason you haven't attached yourself to an attractive human yet is because the opportunity hasn't presented itself. If you didn't hang out with those drunken half-wit teammates of yours and more importantly, try and join in with all their antics, then almost certainly you would have had the odd nibble from a female or two. You may try and come across all prim and proper but you fool no one.

Of course it would be easy to believe that the outdated principles of that crazy dragon you call an employer had rubbed off on you, but the three of us know each other too well for all that. It's time the two of you took your heads out of your giant scaly backsides and looked at what's happening now, not what has gone on in the past. The council controls everything for better or worse and I'm here to tell you it's worse. They think they are micromanaging everything but it's the big picture they just can't see. I'm willing to concede that the king might be able to, but he just doesn't have the power any more to make any difference. I like him Peter, I really do. But this isn't a hundred, or even two hundred years ago. Things are different and by his own admission his position just doesn't have the influence it once did. Things are changing not just down here, but on the surface. That whole debacle with Manson should be a warning of what will happen if we don't adapt and integrate with our so-called charges. They can be part of something bigger, something that can encompass the whole planet if only they were given the chance, but we as a race are too caught up in tradition, prophecies, mantras, you name it. Before we know it, it'll be too late. Too late for all of us, the humans, dragons, everything, and I for one will not lie down and roll over for those of our race that can't see what's coming. I won't be dictated to, now or ever, and the two of you are either with me or not. It's time for everyone to choose," and with that she whirled round and stomped off in the direction of the monorail.

Unable to move through absolute shock, it was Peter who spoke first.

"Where on earth did all that come from?" he spluttered.

Tank just shook his head in reply, unable to speak. Eventually he did, but it took more than a minute or so.

"I didn't tell anyone... honest Pete."

"I know," replied his pal. "And deep down, she knows too. She's just angry that she's been caught out. It'll be alright in the end, I'm sure."

"I hope you're right my friend. I've never seen her so worked up about anything," declared Tank, slapping the hockey player playfully on the back.

With that the two of them headed wearily in the direction of the monorail, noting that with the exception of the food vendors who were now busy clearing away and picking up rubbish, they were the last ones to leave.

14 FLASHBACK

During the course of the following day at work, Peter tried to find his friend, but to no avail. Checking her diary, speaking to her colleagues, he searched for her on all the security monitors, but there was simply no sign of her anywhere. She was in the company somewhere, that was for sure. For one thing, he could sense her dragon presence, a little cloudy and still in a rage, but there, blending in. For another thing, she'd clocked in and he'd gone back and checked the security feed from the main entrance. It was her. And still she eluded him. Not willing to blame her workmates, Richie had obviously told them that she didn't want to see him and so they were covering for her, if indeed they really knew where she was. For the last hour or so he'd tried thinking like her, all... sneaky, but that had got him nowhere. She was bloody clever and he was pretty sure wherever she was, smug would have been her overwhelming feeling at the thought of how she'd outwitted him. Determined not to give up though, he needed to speak to her about what had happened last night and resolved to try and patch things up between her and Tank.

That evening, he drove home in a huff, having got virtually no work done, and more importantly, found no sign of his friend. A few times he'd tried ringing Tank on his mobile, only getting a message saying that it wasn't possible to connect, for his troubles, not particularly surprising given that there was no signal in the area of London where the Mantra Emporium was located. Thoughts of travelling up to find him crossed his mind, but he figured it would probably be too late and that Tank would have disappeared off home, and Gee Tee might well have donned his stripy nightcap and sloped off to bed. As he perched on the edge of his sofa contemplating what to do next, the doorbell rang.

'Oh good,' he thought to himself sarcastically, 'a chance to change my energy supplier for only the third time this week... just what I need.' But as he neared the very secure entrance, a tinge of fear ran down the back of his neck, because the presence that he could feel standing outside wasn't human. This of course was nothing new to him, but he couldn't tell exactly what it was, which in turn caused his legs to feel weak and sweat to accrue on his hands and forehead. Reaching the door, he very carefully placed his palm directly in the middle of it and in his mind, shouted one word:

"Patefacere." Immediately the door blurred around the edges, before starting to shimmer. Moments later, the shimmering resolved, having turned the door, from his side anyway, totally transparent. And the face looking through at him was as much a relief as it was a joy. Peter whispered,

"Reverti," and the door instantly returned to its normal state. Opening it up with a huge grin, Peter cried,

"Flash."

"Hello Peter," replied the permanently changed former Crimson Guard. "How are you?"

"I'm fine thanks. Ummm, why don't you come in?"

"Well, if I'm not disturbing you. If you've got other things on I can come back another time."

"No, not at all. Come in," he offered, holding the door open.

Flash walked down the hallway as Peter closed the door.

"It's great to see you again," announced the hockey player excitedly. "How have you been?"

"Ahhh... you know... not too bad. It's still all sinking in... you know, everything that's happened."

"I bet."

"The king's been really great about it all though. I've moved out of the barracks and have been staying with him in his private residence."

"Fantastic."

"Yeah, it's pretty cool."

"Surely it must be a little cramped though?" he joked.

Flash smiled.

"I must admit I struggle with just one floor to myself, but I make do as best I can."

At the thought of Flash wandering all alone around a whole floor of the king's private residence, Peter let out a loud, raucous laugh. It took more than a few seconds for his mouth to stop chuckling so that he could once again use it for talking.

"It's so cool seeing you again. I very rarely get any guests, well... apart from Tank and Richie, and it's great to see another dragon. What brings you this way?"

"Wellllll," said Flash. "It was the king's idea really, he thought I was becoming a little withdrawn and... miserable. In fact, I believe his exact words were 'take your head out of your... scales and go and enjoy yourself.' He suggested I look up some of my friends and well... other than Yoyo, you and Tank would seem to be the only ones I have in the entire world. And rather than spend many hours on the monorail travelling to Australia, I decided to pay you a visit. I hope you don't mind?"

"Do I look as though I mind? As I've said before... it's great to see you and you're welcome any time."

"Thanks."

"In fact," ventured Peter, "I was just thinking about going to find Tank. Fancy a quick trip up to Gee Tee's Mantra Emporium?"

Flash looked more than a little reticent, and then it suddenly dawned on Peter that he'd probably just travelled all the way from London just to see him.

"Sorry. How insensitive of me. You've just come down from there. It's okay, I can catch up with the big fella another time."

Most unusually for him, Flash let out a little sigh.

"It's not that... honest. It's more that I don't want to...

don't want to bump into any of my old workmates... if you get my drift."

"I'm not sure I do."

"The Crimson Guard barracks is based in London. They consider it their patch. If anything goes on there, they know all about it. Just to make matters worse, I had a run in with a couple of them a few days ago."

Peter's face turned serious.

"Go on."

"Promise you won't tell the king?"

Peter thought for a split second before answering.

"I won't tell him... I promise."

"It was just a chance encounter really. I'd been to run a few errands for the monarch, nothing too technical or physically demanding. But after I'd finished, I had nothing else to do. I knew the king had a meeting with the council that would run on long into the night so I decided to do something that I'd never done before: go for a wander. I sauntered around the different districts looking in shops, sampling food, just taking everything in."

"You've never really done that before?" asked Peter, incredulous.

"Not as you'd imagine, no. Oh I've wandered the streets and know London like the back of my hand. But I've only ever strolled along them while following someone, training a squad of dragons or chasing down a shady deal or two. I've never walked them just as an ordinary dragon like you or Tank would have."

"That's one of the saddest things I've ever heard."

"It's not as bad as it sounds. It's what I signed up for. I knew full well what I was getting into when I joined the King's Guards, and even more so when I became a Crimson Guard. Those are the kind of sacrifices that need to be made to guard our domain and way of life."

Peter could feel the passion, commitment and, ultimately, the loss that came through in Flash's words as he spoke. He wouldn't have thought it possible to admire the brave dragon any more than he already did after knowing what he'd been through on that one mission alone, but sitting here listening to him speak, he found a whole new level of respect for the agent.

"Anyway," continued Flash. "While I was just wandering around, I came across two Crimson Guards in a backstreet in central London. I tried to avoid them, but in reality had very little chance of doing so. They cornered me, more in a playful way at first. I wasn't sure exactly what they'd been told, so I just played it cool, put on a bit of bravado. I should have known better. It turned out they knew precisely what had happened. How? I don't know. But they just did. Anyway, the long and the short of it is that they gave me a bit of a beating... well, more than a bit. I managed to use a couple of one off mantra scrolls that I'd kept aside for a rainy day to heal myself up so that the king wasn't any the wiser. But as you can imagine, I'm not particularly keen to repeat the experience."

Peter was flabbergasted.

"But why?" he stammered.

Flash shook his head slowly.

"They said I was *profugus* which as I'm sure you're aware means 'outcast.' It's as simple as that to them. One moment I'm one of the highest ranked among them, carrying out some of the deadliest and most dangerous assignments going. The next, they see me as damaged goods or as one of them said 'something towards the very lowest end of the planet's food chain.' Nearly all of them regard humans as rather... substandard. It's easy to see how I could be held in a much lower contempt, in their view."

"It doesn't make it right though," snapped Peter angrily.

"I know," replied the dragon stuck as a human softly. "But it's just how they are. No excuse I know, but it is what it is."

Both sat in silence contemplating what had just been said. Flash broke it first.

"Can I ask whereabouts Gee Tee's shop is?"

"You don't know?" replied Peter in disbelief.

"No," answered Flash shrugging his shoulders. "Should I?"

"Well it's just... I thought everybody had heard of Gee Tee's Mantra Emporium, that's all."

Flash screwed up his face in concentration.

"It does kind of ring a bell," he said. "But if my altered human or dragon memory, I'm not sure which, serves me correctly, it was a long time ago. Not short of eighty years if I'm correct."

"Phew," Peter whistled. That was quite some time even by dragon standards and although those of his kind in theory had perfect memory recall, it didn't always work that way in practice.

"I seem to remember one of the papers, oh hang on there would only have been one back then, that's right, it must have been the Daily Telepath... there was a big story that lasted for the best part of a week involving... that shop losing... its royal licence I think. Differing versions of events were all across the paper with some suggestions of corruption, while others talked of a deterioration in the quality of the shop's goods. Anyway, it soon blew over, but if I remember correctly, the place was never quite the same again... I think."

"That sounds about right from what little I know."

"So whereabouts is it?"

Peter described the exact location.

"Interesting," was Flash's only response. "It's not where I thought it would be and far enough out not to warrant any interest from the Crimson Guards. I think I'd like to go and see this Emporium if that's okay."

Bursting into a smile, Peter asked,

"Are you sure?"

"Hmmm... let's go."

"Just let me grab my keys and phone," he said, sprinting into the hall. Flash followed, thinking they were going out the front door.

"Uh," uttered Peter. "It's okay, we're not going that way. Let me show you."

Walking back into the living room, closely followed by his new found friend, the home owner made his way over to the piano and, gripping the Galileo thermometer tightly with his right hand, gave it a hefty pull. Flash watched in amusement as the beautifully crafted instrument swung silently back across the floor, revealing one of many secret entrances to the world they both regarded as home. Trotting over, Peter began to step carefully down the winding staircase and into the lightless room below. Flash followed hot on his heels, eager to see more of this little known secret. Making their way through the darkness, dust and cobwebs with Peter instinctively leading the way, eventually they left the underground part of the house, making their way swiftly to the monorail station. Forty seconds too early, they arrived at the London bound platform. About to ask Flash if he'd explored the king's private library yet, Peter was shocked when the ex-Crimson Guard grabbed him firmly by the shoulder and spun him around. Pointing to a river of sizzling molten lava through a gap between two rooftops about a kilometre away, Flash couldn't stop himself from asking,

"What on earth is that?"

Tilting his head while squinting, the young hockey playing dragon let out a low, "Ahhhh...." before answering.

"It's the left nostril."

"What?" exclaimed his stuck-as-a-human shaped friend.

"The left nostril of the 'runny nose'. You must have heard of it... it's famous throughout the domain."

"If you say so."

"It is," assured Peter, going on to explain that the rock formation which the lava floods out of looks like a giant, three hundred metre high nose, with the molten magma continually flowing from two holes that resemble nostrils.

"Dragon tourists come from far and wide just to see it," he added, before they both boarded the silver bullet-like carriage that had just arrived.

Flash just nodded.

During the journey the conversation between the two of them became very mundane, both realising that discussing the king or anything to do with Flash's current predicament would, no doubt, attract unwanted attention.

Before they knew it, they both found themselves embroiled in the shadows of a small arched bridge that supported a walkway above it. A sharp turn later and they were in Camelot Arcade, heading towards the old wooden door of Gee Tee's Mantra Emporium. Stepping up to knock, for no apparent reason Peter tried the handle before he did so. Realistically he knew it was a waste of time, as he was sure establishment had long since closed, but to his surprise, the handle turned and the door creaked open.

Turning to Flash, Peter whispered,

"I thought it would have been locked up for the night, with Gee Tee already having turned in. But it appears not."

Flash raised his eyebrows and followed his friend into the brightly lit shop. As they proceeded, a wave of unusually cold air buffeted their warm faces. Gently closing the door behind him, Flash headed into the labyrinth of tall, wooden bookcases. As they pushed on, the deafening silence was punctuated by a very peculiar humming noise, originating from somewhere towards the front. Tapping his friend gently on the shoulder, as Peter turned round, Flash put his finger over his lips, indicating that they should be quiet. Flash leant in towards the young hockey player and in the quietest of whispers said,

"Something's not quite right here. I'm not sure what, but we should proceed with caution." Peter nodded, and with a sweep of his arm indicated that perhaps his friend should go first. Flash duly obliged.

Creeping stealthily towards the front of the shop, the

two of them rounded the last of the tall bookcases. Out of nowhere shot a giant blur, smashing them into one of the dust covered shelves, causing them to roll back up the aisle from which they'd both come. With the massive weight of the blur crushing his chest, Peter was pinned helplessly to the ground. Flash, not so much. His body had gone onto autopilot and his combat training was a fraction of a second from kicking in. It was only then that the former Crimson Guard's brilliant mind recalled that he'd heard a shout of, "DOWN!" as the speeding blur had smashed into them...

'Odd,' he thought, as he started to slide out from under the breath sapping weight on top of him. Just when it looked as though things couldn't get any weirder, three deadly thick needles of ice shot into the bookcase, behind where they'd been standing only a split second before, quivering there like frosted arrows. The speeding blur had just saved their lives. Both Flash and Peter craned their necks at the same time, trying to get a glimpse of who, or what, had landed on them. As they did so, a thick neck full of muscle swung round, on it a familiar head, with the same inane smile that both had come to know and love.

"Sorry about that," whispered Tank. "We've got something of a situation here," he added quietly, nodding towards the icy bolts embedded in the bookcase.

Flash smiled as the rugby player rolled off the two visitors, and remarked,

"Do tell."

Sitting on the floor, backs against the shelves on the opposite side of the aisle to the ones with the frosty projectiles in them, Tank began to explain.

"Gee Tee and I were working our way through a set of old mantras, trying to determine what they were, if they worked and if they were worth saving. Employing all the usual safeguards, morphic shields, phase resonators, blanket containment mantras, after working our way through five or six in quick succession, we came across a most unusual one written in Inuit. I had no idea what any of it said, and although Smarty Pants claimed he knew, I could sense a lot of nervousness in the old dragon, which is very rare indeed. Anyway, against MY better judgement, he pressed on and cast the mantra, resulting in something akin to one of my nightmares, a creature that's currently residing round the corner there, near the front desk."

"Let me guess," ventured Flash. "An ice salamander?"

Tank nodded his head.

"And not just any of its kind. I've seen them before, and yes, they can be a little bit tricky to handle. But this thing is like the queen of all ice salamanders. She's huge, and you've seen the things she's been firing at us. Gee Tee's trapped in the back of the workshop, where he fled as soon as we realised what happened. I've been out here trying to keep her occupied in the hope that the old dragon will find a way to reverse what he's done. This all started about three hours ago, and we've been doing this ever since, with no luck whatsoever."

"Three hours!" exclaimed Peter incredulously.

Flash's forehead creased deep in concentration, as he considered the sticky circumstances that they all found themselves in.

"Why not simply banish it back to where it came from?" he asked, puzzled.

"That was my thought originally," huffed the plant and animal lover, looking absolutely shattered. "The problem is that the queen seems to be guarding the scroll with the mantra on it, and is currently curled up on top of it, making it all but impossible to banish. I've spent nearly two hours trying to draw it away from the front desk, in the hope that Gee Tee might sneak out, get the scroll, and... waheyyy... banish it. But it's not happening. It will not leave that scroll. It's almost as if it knows what it is and where it's come from."

"That, my friend," said Peter, "is simply not possible."

Tank sighed deeply, wishing that his tired body could

go home and curl up in bed.

"It's not quite as impossible as you seem to think Pete," interrupted Flash, eyes closed, leaning his head back against the dust encrusted book shelves. "In ages past, mantras that summoned creatures with a better understanding of exactly what they were, became almost commonplace. I'm talking of course about a time many, many thousands of years ago, but it did happen. What I struggle to understand is how the magic could have lasted so long, and ended up here. Still... at this moment it's a moot point. We need to banish the ice salamander back to where it came from. If it does have any sort of understanding of what it is, the longer we wait, the harder all this is going to be."

"Uhhh, there's something else as well," whispered the apprentice nervously. "The shields on the building are weaker than they've ever been. The boss has known this for some time, but hasn't got round to having them reenergised."

"Exactly how weak are the shields?" demanded Flash, quietly. "Weak enough for that thing to make a break for it?"

Rather sheepishly, Tank nodded his head.

"And you haven't called the King's Guard?"

Tank shook his head.

"If the King's Guard come, they'll close the whole place down for good. This will be the end of it all. They'll do it, and Rosebloom will make sure that it stays shut," he added, trying desperately to hold back tears. "I know they should have been alerted, and I realise the danger if that thing gets out... but I just couldn't do it. If they locked this place up, it would finish him off. I thought I could distract it and together we could undo everything... oh I can't believe this is happening. What a day!"

Flash slapped Tank playfully on the shoulder.

"Well... now that the cavalry has arrived, there's nothing to worry about is there? I'll create a distraction worthy of note, and you two can get the mantra back to Gee Tee. How does that sound?"

Tank's inane smile reappeared immediately.

"That sounds great. But are you sure you can do it?"

"Do dragons pee in the air?" (And if you'd ever been hit by flying dragon pee, boy you'd know it. Not just hospitalisation, but decontamination as well.) "I'm not called Flash for nothing you know. One very important thing to remember though guys."

"What's that?" mumbled Peter.

"We must avoid those ice bolts at all costs. If one of those hits a dragon, no matter what their form, I think it would be safe to say that the only thing they'd be seeing after that is a great big lake of lava."

Both friends understood his meaning. It brought home to Tank just how much danger he'd been in over the last few hours. Numerous times he'd felt the cold chill of one of the frozen projectiles skimming within inches of a limb. Momentarily, his large, powerful legs wobbled a little at the thought of what he'd narrowly avoided.

"Now," whispered the dragon stuck in the shape of a human, finally seeing what he needed on a belt strapped around Tank's waist. "I need that mantra scalpel my friend, please, and Peter, I need your mobile phone."

Drawing out the sharp blade that was used to repair and reconfigure broken mantras, scrolls and hexes, the tip of which had a brilliant green glow to it, he handed it over, fulfilling the request, as did his friend. Grabbing the touch screen phone, he held it up in the air so that a tiny part of it poked around the end of the bookcase. Glancing into the reflection, Flash gauged exactly where the deadly ice salamander was. After a few moments, he pulled the device back and crouched down with his friends.

"Okay, get as near as you can on the southern side, nearest to the workshop. I'll approach from the north and attempt to lead her out into the depths of the shop that way. When you get the mantra... don't hang about. I'm guessing she's going to be rather mad at me, and I'm not going to have very long. Good luck!"

With that, he turned and headed back up the aisle, in the direction of the front door. Meanwhile, Peter had the startled expression of a bunny caught in the headlights of an onrushing car.

"Come on Pete," whispered Tank, slapping his friend on the back. "What could possibly go wrong?"

Ducking down, the two of them shuffled silently along the exposed cross section of the aisle on all fours. Reaching the welcome cover of the bookcases on the other side, both stood up, relieved that no ice bolts had been fired in their direction. Before Tank could go any further, his pal put a hand on his shoulder.

"Do you think he's going to be alright?"

"He'll be fine," replied the rugby player quietly. "Besides, he's got more experience at this stuff than we'll ever have."

"I know," mouthed Peter. "But he's not done anything like this, since... you know... since he got stuck in human form."

"He'll be okay, we all will if we work together as a team. That's the key to it all... combining our strengths and working as one. You should know that better than most."

Momentarily the youngster's mind flashed back to the hockey, and as it did so a dreamy smile crept across his face. The mere thought of working as a unit sent goose bumps up his arms, at the same time filling him with confidence. Normal service resumed, both made their way past piles of discarded tomes, aiming to get as close as possible to the front counter without being spotted by the mythical creature created out of thin air only a matter of hours earlier.

Meanwhile, Flash had been crawling commando style along the grubby stone floor, with only the phone and Tank's mantra blade for company, knowing he was uncomfortably close to the ice salamander queen's position, a violent humming coming from only a metre or so away, the smell of her icy cold breath a dead giveaway. Lying on his side, snuggled up to one of the small bookcases, he very patiently and very quietly sat up. Slowly, he raised Peter's mobile above the parapet, eyes glued firmly to the reflection on the screen. Nearly frozen with fear at the sight that greeted him, whipping it back down out of sight, his hands and fingers started shaking with fright as he realised she was considerably bigger than he'd first thought. Not only that, but she looked... tough, strong... scary even. He couldn't remember a time when he'd felt so afraid, even his recent adventures in Antarctica hadn't elicited the same terror. Quietly, he took a few deep breaths to calm himself, knowing that, despite the fear, the butterflies zipping around in his stomach and the shakiness of his legs, he was going to do what was necessary, because... because he wasn't going to let his friends down. Peter, Tank... Gee Tee, yes, he even regarded the old shopkeeper as his pal. Now that he thought about it, he recognised he'd never really had any friends before. Ohhh, he'd thought he had, in the Crimson Guards, but looking back with hindsight, he could fully comprehend that they were only really colleagues, most only associating themselves with him because of his talent and reputation, and because he was well thought of by the dragons in charge.

Exhaling the last deep breath, he knew now was the time to act. Using the silent touch screen on Peter's phone, he quickly set the alarm to go off after one minute, while counting down the remaining time in his head. On reaching ten seconds, Flash slid the phone along the floor of the aisle, its dark black shell contrasting harshly with the light coloured stone as it silently spun out of sight. Flash tensed, ready to act, the mantra blade gripped firmly in his right hand. Immediately a loud, telephone style shrill emanated from the direction he'd flung the mobile in. Counting to two, he hoped that the deadly head part of the mythical monster had fallen for the distraction and gone to investigate. As his mouth finished whispering the word, "Two," in a fluid motion, he leapt over the small bookcase he'd been hiding behind and headed at speed towards the front desk, knowing as he leapt that if he'd miscalculated and the salamander hadn't taken the bait, then he was almost certainly dead. It wasn't the first time he'd found himself in this kind of situation, but it had been a little while and he'd forgotten the unmistakable thrill that ran through him at times like this. Counteracting the excitement, somewhere at the back of his mind, a little voice gently whispered,

"One day you're going to do this and it will go horribly wrong... and you'll die."

But not today, at least not yet. The ice salamander had indeed gone to investigate the shrill noise of the phone, well, the front half of it had anyway, with the remaining back half curled tightly around itself on the desk, wisps of cold infusing the air all around it. With no time to lose, Flash pulled back his right arm and buried the mantra blade into the nearest part of the wicked looking creature's tail. An ungodly screech echoed from the direction of the phone, as the huge tail started to jump and flail about. Suddenly the top half of the monster whipped back round the corner of a giant bookcase, its dull white eyes filled with hatred, anger and... revenge. Knowing he'd outstayed his welcome, Flash was already moving in the opposite direction to where he hoped Tank and Peter were hidden, desperately trying to find some sort of cover from what he knew would be an imminent attack. As he hurdled an untidy pile of tomes, the sound of multiple projectiles cutting through the air and heading in his direction assaulted his sensitive ears. Maybe the little voice in his head had been right after all.

Both friends were as close as they dared get when the

phone's alarm had gone off. Peter's reaction had been to try and look over the top of the counter behind which they were hidden. Tank had known better and used one of his giant arms to anchor his friend to the floor, having a fair idea of what was coming next, and wasn't surprised when the hideous screech echoed around the shop. Waiting for a split second after the haunting sound, Gee Tee's young partner popped his head over the parapet of the counter to see the ice salamander, only a few metres away, sitting up like a cobra, firing a seemingly endless bout of bolts, then slithering off in the opposite direction after Flash, its long tail uncurling, freezing cold vapour evaporating into the air all around it. As the last of the tail slithered off in chase of its body, the former apprentice spotted what he was looking for... the scroll with the mantra on it. Ordering Peter to keep an eye out, Tank dashed over to the counter and grabbed the rolled out spell, causing waves of pain to shoot through his fingers and up his arm, forcing him to drop it immediately. Shaking his hand to try and get rid of the pain, the youngster examined the scroll closely. An icy blue grain had formed on the parchment, accompanied by a similarly chilly blue mist, something he was quite sure hadn't been there originally. This, he thought, was far from good. With the crashing of bookcases and the sound of objects and ice bolts flying indiscriminately somewhere off in another part of the Emporium, Tank knew he had to act.

"PETER," he shouted, "open the door to the workshop and then get the hell out of the way."

Although unable to understand what was going on, he did at least recognise the command and urgency in his best friend's voice. Running over to the door, he slid to a halt. Giving it a sharp yank, he continued to hold it open for whatever his pal had in mind. Standing there, a smooth whisper drifted in his direction.

"Hello child. Come to join in the fun?"

It took Peter over a second to find the source of the

voice, but when he did, he smiled. There, poking out from behind one of the oversized dragon chairs, were the distinct, square glasses that could only belong to one being... Gee Tee! With the smile still on his face, he gave the old shopkeeper a 'pleased to see you' nod, and turned back round to see what was going on.

Tank, by now, had decided on a course of action. With his friend holding the workshop door open, he grabbed the mantra and began tossing it from one hand to the other as if it were a hot potato, all the time heading for the workshop at speed. Positively flying past Peter he threw the scroll down onto the nearest workbench, all the time trying to ignore the burning pain running up his hands and arms. Gee Tee stood up, giving his former apprentice a puzzled look. Making to pick up the scroll, one of Tank's powerful arms shot out to stop the master mantra maker.

"There's something wrong with it," he spluttered painfully. "It seems to be imbued with cold."

Shuffling his glasses back along his nose towards his eyes, the shopkeeper leant over to get a better look.

"Fascinating!"

A deafening crash followed by a rumble and a bump, reverberated throughout the shop.

"I don't mean to hurry you, or anything," exclaimed Peter, "but Flash is being chased by that thing, and I'm not sure exactly how long he can last."

Gee Tee glared across at the two friends.

"Why on earth didn't you say so?" With that, he grabbed a couple of mantra pens from a pile on the desk and proceeded to use them to fully unfurl the scroll.

All he could feel was his heart pounding in his chest. It was so loud, he thought he might die. Sprinting around another corner, he grabbed books from shelves on either side of him and flung them as hard as he could back over his shoulder. Sweat dribbled from behind his ears, racing down his neck, flooding his T-shirt with moisture. Instinctively he pushed the top half of his body forward, forcing himself into a roll just as two more deadly ice bolts carved through the air where his head had been only a split second before. He felt exhausted and somehow... different, whether it was something to do with his transformation and being stuck in this ridiculous human form he didn't know, but he was sure that he couldn't go on for much longer. It was almost as if his fuel tank was running on empty. Even in his most desperate state after being attacked by the naga's poison in Antarctica, he'd never once felt like this. With no time to think, he came to a T junction and without knowing any different, turned right... skidding straight into a dead end. His first thought was to clamber up the bookcase he was facing and jump down on the other side. But the bookcases he found himself enclosed by were at least forty metres high, and he knew that the salamander would be on him before he could even get half way up. Turning round, he wondered if he had time to cross over to the aisle that lay directly opposite him in the distance.

Before he could take a step, he had his answer. Steaming with cold and pure, unadulterated rage, the giant ice salamander queen slithered into view, her vicious fangs bared, her stunning blue scales bristling. Instinctively, the ex Crimson Guard threw some more books at her from the shelves, despite the futility of it. Her snarl turned to more of a smile as she realised that her prey had nowhere else to go. Backing up the aisle as far as he could, Flash only stopped when his back rested against one of the giant bookcases. Following him, her head swayed hypnotically from side to side, powered by her injured tail. For his part, the former Crimson Guard racked his brain for anything that would help him out, but nothing sprang to mind. Having done all he could, he hoped, with what he supposed was one of his last thoughts, that he'd bought his friends enough time for them to get out of this safely.

As the frosty queen pulled back her head, baring her icy-white, needle sharp fangs, ready to strike, Flash looked on determinedly, facing his death with strength, pride, dignity and courage. Just as the queen's head darted forward, a look of shock and confusion rippled across her scaly face, before the loudest POP in the world sounded and her whole body disappeared for good in a cloud of water vapour. Slumping down against the bookcase at his back, sweat racing down his arms and legs, Flash had never felt so relieved in his entire life.

Seconds later, two sets of footsteps closed in on the aisle's dead end, as Tank and Peter skidded around the corner, both coming to a direct halt in front of the glittering puddle that only moments earlier had been the ice salamander. Both friends had exactly the same thought at exactly the same time... that Flash looked an absolute mess. Luckily, they had the forethought not to say it out loud.

"Somehow I imagined you'd be a bit fitter," Tank deadpanned.

Flash looked up from his sitting position on the floor.

"You're kidding me... right?"

"Well... you know... all that training and everything... seems to have been wasted, if you ask me."

Not able to contain himself, Peter burst into a fit of laughter as Flash hurled two dust laden tomes in the rugby player's direction with the very last of his energy. Tank dodged out of the way with much more agility than most people, or dragons, would have given him credit for.

Sidestepping the puddle, each offered Flash a hand. Gratefully accepting, he let himself be pulled up by his friends. Tank slapped the exhausted ex-Crimson Guard on the back in admiration.

"Sorry it took so long," he quipped, "but you know what he's like... can't be rushed and all that, even when someone's life's on the line."

Flash just shrugged his shoulders in acceptance. It

wasn't the first time he'd been a bedbug's eyelash away from death and he was pretty sure, the way things were going, that it wouldn't be the last.

Making their way back through the maze of bookcases, stepping over the wreckage as they did so, Tank already had a good idea as to who would be tidying up, and as usual, he was pretty sure it wouldn't be the old shopkeeper. Striding through the gap in the counter, the three of them sauntered into the workshop, just as Gee Tee appeared from behind one of the huge filing cabinets.

"I'm so glad you're okay," he whispered huskily, patting Flash gently on the head. "I would never have forgiven myself if anything had happened to you."

"It was a close run thing," gulped Flash, "but you just managed to reverse the mantra in time. Thanks."

"You're welcome youngster, but it is I who should be thanking you... what happened was a whole lot more than we'd bargained for... and yes, before you say it app... Tank, I've learned a valuable lesson today."

Tank nearly fainted in disbelief. In all the time he'd worked for the shopkeeper, hardly ever had he heard him apologise, let alone in the manner he just had.

'Who's stolen Gee Tee, and what have they done with him?' he thought, only half jokingly.

"I think it might just be about time for a drink, don't you?" announced the master mantra maker.

"I'll put us all on some hot charcoal," declared Peter, trying to be helpful.

"That wasn't quite what I had in mind, child," purred Gee Tee, a mischievous glint in his eye.

Understanding immediately, the hockey player wondered just how his best friend might react to what was about to happen. Dragging his tail in the direction of the nearest filing cabinet, Gee Tee was about to try and reach up when in one leap, Tank beat him to it, jumping up and grabbing something long and silver off the top. Slamming back down onto the floor, he held out the dusty, silver cylinder towards the old shopkeeper.

"Would this be what you're after, by any chance?"

Gritting his teeth, Peter held his breath. Flash stood, bemused by what was going on. Gee Tee turned his gigantic prehistoric head back over his shoulder, giving Peter an icy glare, not realising that he hadn't revealed the old shopkeeper's secret.

"It might be," replied the master mantra maker.

"Hmmm," voiced Tank, clearly enjoying every second of the Emporium owner's discomfort. "I have to ask why you would want some..." Tank took a deep breath and blew off part of the thick layer of dust, "Peruvian Mantra Ink?"

As a single thought circled throughout his mind, Peter's lips creased into a tiny smile... his friend knew about the ink, and what it really was. The follow on thought was: how? Most certainly, he himself had never even so much as hinted at its existence.

"Might I ask how you know?"

"No... you might not," countered Tank, grinning from ear to ear. "But two things. One... Peter didn't tell me, as I assume from your little glance at him, that he knew. And two... you're not nearly as sneaky or clever as you seem to think you are." And with that, in one fluid motion, Tank whipped the cap off the cylinder and let a small sip run gently down his throat. The others there and in particular Flash, who had no idea what was going on, all looked on in anticipation. Rolling his head and neck from side to side, seemingly swirling the liquid round and round inside him, Tank's face changed in an instant, but not how Peter pictured it would. A dreamy quality etched itself across the rugby playing dragon's bold, rugged features, with them all almost able to see the liquid making its way up inside the youngster's neck. Effortlessly, Tank opened his mouth just slightly and exhaled. A long, drawn out, blue flame, tinged around the edges with red and orange, snaked out across the room. Gee Tee, Peter and Flash all looked on in awe.

Just when Peter thought it couldn't get any more amazing, the line of fire started to curl up in the air and form a shape. It then cut off and then started again, in much the same way. All the time the room's occupants stared in disbelief. Four separate lines of flame hung in the air on the far side of the room, as Tank stood making tiny motions with his fingers. Ever so slowly, the constantly swirling fire twisted and turned and... changed.....into four separate letters, spelling out the word T... A... N... K.

Surprisingly, Gee Tee was the first to react.

"Very good. I'm... impressed. Some of my tutoring must have rubbed off after all." Tank grinned and shook his head.

Peter patted his friend on the back gently to get his attention.

"How did you get it to do that?" he asked. "When I had a go, it was like a raging tempest that I couldn't control."

"The raging tempest responsible for that slag heap of a filing cabinet that I spent most of one morning cleaning up?"

"Uhhh... yeah, sorry about that," replied his friend sheepishly.

"You two must think I've got the brains of a politician," he ventured, offering the silver cylinder to Flash.

Still a little behind on the conversation, his experience had enabled him to catch up on a few things. Gripping the dusty cylinder, he put his nose directly above the top and sniffed.

"If I'm not mistaken... *igneus saevio*... very impressive."

"Igneus saevio?" questioned Peter, just beating Tank and Gee Tee to it.

"Yeah, means... 'fiery rage'," remarked the Crimson Guard thoughtfully, "from my least favourite beings on the entire planet... the nagas. Although, to give them credit, this was one of the best things they've ever produced and if memory serves me correctly, it was specially concocted for one of the dragon kings, a gift for the aid he rendered them in some kind of battle they were losing, something that incorporates all their renowned alchemy skills, I might add."

The three others all looked on in astonishment.

"Anyway... bums in the air," Flash announced, taking a slightly bigger sip than Tank had.

"I think you mean... bottoms up," corrected Peter, in a voice that sounded very much like that of a teacher.

"I know what I meant," gurgled Flash, much to Peter's chagrin.

It soon became clear that Flash was also adept at controlling (if that was the right word) the 'drink': it didn't hang around inside him, as it had in Tank, but seemingly using his hands, and his fingers in particular, the ex-Crimson Guard managed to burp, belch and expel all sorts of intricate 3D shapes, his latest being a rather impressive love heart.

After watching Tank and Flash master the art of drinking, or controlling, *igneus saevio,* Gee Tee quickly resumed where they left off, and in no time at all was hurling all sorts of intricate shapes and patterns throughout the workshop. The master mantra maker bowed at the mock applause, and then it was Peter's turn. Having watched his friends work almost miracles, he was more than a little tense, which was totally understandable really, given his previous experience with the disguised Peruvian mantra ink. Grasping the silver cylinder with both hands, he gulped down the tiniest sip he dared, with the three others looking on. Moments later the pleasure from the liquid worked its way down his throat and circled around the top of his stomach like some out of control train. Despite this, he felt more relaxed and in charge of the situation than the last time he'd tried some and was starting, or so he thought, to dominate the drink with some very intricate patterns that his fingers were making.

That was, right up until the point where Tank's oversized head popped up directly in front of his face. Briefly, the young hockey player wondered if he was doing something wrong, but it turned out the animal and plant lover had something else in mind. Instantly the rugby player sucked his cheeks in as far as they would go, while at the same time screwing up his nose and turning cross eyed.

Peter reacted in the only way he could... he laughed. Not just a little laugh, but the mother of all laughs, and couldn't for the life of him remember seeing anything funnier. As the tears started to run down his face, it suddenly dawned on him that the *igneus saevio* had, for all intents and purposes, escaped the clutches of his control. As this registered somewhere deep inside his mixed up DNA, he wondered why Tank's funny face had disappeared, to be replaced by his normal one, crying tears of laughter. It was then that he noticed that Flash, too, had a constant stream running down each of his cheeks, dripping like water from a drainpipe during a storm, onto the floor. Gee Tee, from a sitting position behind Peter, was slightly quicker on the uptake than the youngster himself, and with a speed and agility that belied his age, dived headfirst across the workshop, the tiniest flap of his wings helping him on his way. It was then that it happened. There was nothing Peter could have done to stop it, that was how quick and without warning it was. The single biggest, rip roaring fart in the world exploded out from his arse, forcing a blue and green whistling fireball to rip a hole in the back of his trousers, totally destroying the chair that the old shopkeeper had been sitting in only a split second before.

Howls of laughter echoed around the room, pierced by disapproving sighing and the sound of Peter's feet stamping on the floor as he jumped up and down, clutching his smouldering buttocks. Whirling around in pain, Peter looked for something that might help. Spotting a tiny sink in the far corner of the workshop filled to the brim with a dark liquid, in two quick bounds he was beside it. Turning around to face the others, he plonked his backside firmly into the mass of dark liquid. The look of relief on Peter's face was accompanied by the sound of bubbling and hissing from all around his immersed rear. As the hilarity died down to a manageable level, Gee Tee piped up from the cold, solid floor.

"That's another batch of mantra ink down the drain! If I ever come across a mantra recipe that requires 'roasted rear', I'll be sure to call on your services, child." Not quite sure how to respond, true to form, Peter had no problem seeing the funny side of things as Flash and Tank continued to giggle, despite the presence of Gee Tee. Even the master mantra maker found a smile and a chuckle eventually, especially when it took both Tank and Flash to pull Peter free of the sink. With the festivities over and, more importantly, the steaming great hole in the back of Peter's trousers repaired by one of the Emporium owner's lesser known mantras, the four friends allowed themselves to relax in the remaining oversized chairs in the workshop.

It was only then that Tank went on to explain about the hand and finger movements that helped control the drink, all the time deliberately not revealing how he knew of its existence, much to Gee Tee's annoyance.

Tank told them how he'd become intrigued about what Peter had said Manson had done during the hockey match in which they'd gone head to head. From the plant and animal lover's understanding, it seemed that whatever it was the dark dragon had cast, a mantra or something else, the hand movements played a pivotal role in stunning most of the team. So, Tank being Tank, he'd tried to seek out every last piece of information pertaining to hand gestures and magic. While he hadn't discovered as much as he'd have liked, he had found out that some of the more ancient races had, long ago, been able to cast mantras by very small movements of their limbs or appendages, the Manticores and nagas being but two. As he continued to explain all this, Flash added snippets of information that he'd gleaned over the years in relation to the subject. All of this was new to Peter and, even more surprisingly, most of it was a shock to Gee Tee as well. When Tank had finished talking, the master mantra maker commended him on his work, again suggesting that it was down to his own mentoring. With everything out in the open and the four of them pooling their combined resources (Peter was feeling as though he hadn't brought much to the party so to speak) a wave of optimism rolled across the friends as they sat chatting.

"So you think that Manson may have picked up that trick from one of the nagas?" asked Tank, directing his question towards Flash.

"He could have picked it up almost anywhere. But from what we now know is going on with the slippery serpents, it strikes me as too much of a coincidence for them not to be involved."

"But that's the whole point," interrupted Peter, wriggling uncomfortably in his chair. "We have no idea if they are involved with whatever Manson was doing... I really don't understand how there can be a connection."

"There may not be," reiterated Flash, "but all I was trying to say was that for two things like this to be happening at the same time, and not be connected in some way, sure sounds doubtful to me. I bet right at this very moment the king and his advisors are trying to put the pieces together."

"Hmmmm," hummed Gee Tee softly. "You, young Flash, are wise beyond your years. Both of you," ventured the old shopkeeper, indicating Tank and Peter, "would do well to listen to what this one has to say. I, for one, agree wholeheartedly with him. It is way too much of a coincidence for two things of this magnitude to be going on independently of one another. The three of you need to help the king and start piecing bits of the puzzle together, because something else that I don't doubt is that there's a whole lot more to this than the tiny fragments we know about. The more I hear, the more it makes me think that much darker times lie ahead for all of us."

Sitting in silence, they all considered everything the master mantra maker had just said.

After a few minutes, Gee Tee rose from his chair, more than a little unsteady on his talons.

"Whoa," he uttered, wobbling about. "Hat frink has had more of an feect than I fould have wought."

"I think it's time to get you into bed," declared Tank, making a grab for the old shopkeeper's right wing in a bid to lead him upstairs.

"Before he gets any more of his mucking words fuddled," quipped Peter, trying hard to contain his laughter.

Tank shot the other two his best 'I'll remember this' look from over his shoulder.

Ten minutes later, with Gee Tee firmly tucked up in bed and secured in the shop, the three friends made their way back down Camelot Arcade, heading for the nearest monorail station. On arrival, Peter and Tank bade goodbye to Flash, thanking him for saving their lives. He nodded, shaking their hands and thanking them for a very interesting evening, winking at Peter as he walked away, all the time patting his bottom and laughing. Knowing that he was going to get ribbed about this for quite some time, Peter joined Tank in boarding the monorail, the two friends finding that they had a whole carriage entirely to themselves.

"Do you think both things are connected?" whispered the hockey playing dragon. Tank paused a little before answering.

"I know what they're saying, and why. But I can't for the life of me see how the two events can possibly be linked. The more I think about it, the more implausible it seems."

Peter nodded his agreement, but as he did so, he

realised that the tiny little voice at the back of his mind, the one that seemed to know so much, the one he'd learned to trust in times of need, was screaming out that there was indeed a connection with everything that was happening. As he was about to tell Tank this, the monorail pulled into Salisbridge and the doors to the carriage whooshed open. Both friends exited, walked up the stairs and went their separate ways, all in under a minute. Making his way back home, all Peter could think about was the connection, if any, and just how he could help the king piece it all together as Gee Tee had suggested. Minutes later, with those thoughts still uppermost in his mind, he dozed off, snugly tucked up in bed.

15 BALL PAMPERING

Casually glancing back over his shoulder, he breathed a sigh of relief as he opened the door to his workshop and slipped inside. Standing in the dark for a few seconds, composing himself, he felt like any second now he'd be caught, discovered, that his part in this·plan would come to an abrupt end, meaning his wife would almost certainly fail to see the dawn of a new day.

Wiping sweat from his brow, he switched on the lights and hurried over to his workbench. Slipping off his backpack, he dropped it onto the table and unzipped the main pocket. From inside he retrieved his rather large, dragon sized lunchbox and placed it down on the bench. Tossing the rucksack onto the floor, he slipped into his wheeled seat, letting his tail slide gently into the perfectly formed hole. Knowing time was of the essence, he figured that if he hadn't been caught by now, then the chances were that nobody knew what he was up to. After all, he was one of the single most trusted and respected figures not only in this building, but throughout this part of the dragon kingdom, his work renowned across the world. Why would anyone suspect him of anything untoward? The answer was... they shouldn't, wouldn't, couldn't... it was just too unbelievable.

Opening the lunch box, he ignored the generous slabs of assorted meats that set his stomach rumbling... ham, chicken, beef and lamb. Moving aside all the fruit, he delved beneath the selection of different flavoured sticks of charcoal and pulled out something that was the size of a squash ball, wrapped entirely in silver foil. Carefully he placed it amongst the tools on his workbench and sat back, studying the item, which both terrified and excited him in equal measure. Moments later, he got up from his chair and walked across to the furthest point from the door until he stood in front of a tall, blue, metallic cylinder that rose up from the ground, stopping at about his waist height. The top of the cylinder was flat and about forty centimetres in diameter. Troubled by what he was about to do, he shook his head, knowing that he had absolutely no choice. Reaching out with his mind until he found the tiniest of hidden switches deep inside, he flicked it to the 'on' position and shuffled back just a little. Instantly a circular hole appeared in the flat surface, the slightest of hums reverberating from inside, the delicate movement of air sending shivers along his wing membranes. Again he stretched out with his mind, and on finding a microscopic keypad hidden far below, entered a particular twenty digit number. A buzz replaced the hum as the movement of air changed slightly. Suddenly, as if by magic, a sparkling ball, the size of a football, shot out from the pitch black hole and just hovered a few centimetres above the surface, slowly rotating. Even though he'd done this a thousand times before, he stood in awe for a few seconds as the laminium ball drifted, seemingly of its own accord.

Briefly he recalled the first time he'd ever seen this process... some ninety or so years ago. Cautiously he moved the shiny sphere over to his workbench, before sitting down and double checking that it was the right one, for the right match... this was very important, or so he'd been told. After confirming that it was, he set to work, counting on no one else being around for some time, because of the stupidly early hour. He'd been turning up in the early hours of the morning over the last three weeks or so. The first few times, the King's Guards on duty were a little wary, but he'd spun them a story about having trouble sleeping, the pressure of making sure the balls for all the big matches were flawless and mumbled stuff about 'being a perfectionist', all of which seemed to do the trick. After that, the guards barely gave him a second glance, and tonight, well... he might as well have been invisible, or on duty with them. Figuring he'd be good for four or five hours before anyone else who worked in this room arrived, that was more than enough time to perform the deed he'd been tasked with. Switching on the tiny lamp on his desk, he selected the narrowest, most powerful laser scalpel from the perfectly arranged tools... and got to work. Steam rose as the delicate red laser beam of the scalpel gradually worked its way through the outer layer of the laminium ball in almost complete silence. If anyone had arrived, they would have seen an artisan craftsdragon at work. But they didn't and he was left undisturbed for all the time he needed and beyond. Long before all the other employees arrived, he'd planted the device inside the shiny sphere in such a way that not even the most detailed inspection would show that it had been tampered with.

'Tampered... that's funny,' he thought to himself as he munched through a huge slab of beef. 'More like... pampered,' he told himself. That's right... he'd pampered the ball, much in the same way he did on a regular basis. That was part of his job... to pamper all the balls, and check they were perfect for the matches. At least now his wife would be safe, he mused, as he tore off another hunk of raw meat. Having achieved his objective, life could begin to get back to normal, something he told himself over and over again, all morning and all afternoon. By the end of the day, when his desk was packed up and he was exiting the building with all the other dragon workers, he'd almost totally forgotten about the dreadful deed he'd committed. It was to him... nothing to worry about.

16 A MONOPOLY ON MAGIC

Over the next week Peter tried to get in touch with Richie, but she'd booked some time off work and, so far, he hadn't been able to contact her at home or on her mobile phone. Reluctantly he decided his best plan of action was just to give his friend all the time and space she so clearly desired. So with this in mind, he focused his attention on his day job and the protection of Cropptech.

Used to coming home and chilling out, his evenings had become busier than he could remember; with their lacrosse playing friend deliberately avoiding them, Peter and Tank, joined by Flash, had taken to having a get together a couple of times a week... just to try out some human games. And, unsurprisingly, they had found it immense fun. With it being awkward for Flash to bring anyone back to the king's private residence, the evenings had been hosted alternately by the two Salisbridge residents. The first night at the former apprentice's house was supposed to have been an evening of playing darts. Tank had purchased a board and three sets of arrows. However, the evening hadn't quite panned out as planned. With the board hung carefully on the far wall of the rugby playing dragon's living room, the three started off from the correct distance away and BAM... the correct score every time. Even trying not to use their dragon abilities, the friends were just too good and every throw scored exactly what they needed to get, whether it was 180, or treble 16. It was, for them... just too easy. Whoever started each match won it, just because they were first to throw. So after an hour or so, they all agreed on Flash's idea of moving back a little further than would perhaps be the norm. By the end of the evening, the board had been moved onto a different wall, one visible from the far end of the kitchen, nearly ten metres away from where the three were now standing to throw their darts. This proved much more of a challenge, but even from this distance, their accuracy had still been surprisingly good. After that came an evening of cards at Peter's house, trying all the card games they could... but still, with each having a very high intellect, it was difficult to separate the winners and the losers. Calculating odds and percentages was basic dragon maths taught in the third year of every nursery ring... so the games were frighteningly easy for all three of them. Some adjustment was needed again, just like with the darts, and the friends eventually settled on using four decks of cards. They all had fun, but agreed that other avenues in the way of human pastimes needed to be explored.

Tank chose chess for their next event to be held at his house. At first it seemed like a wise choice, but once again it went pretty much the same way as on the other occasions. It was almost impossible to separate the dragons intellectually and after four and a half hours, only two games had been played... both ending in stalemate.

Tonight it was Peter's turn to host his pals and he was sure he'd found a classic game that would not only offer them something different, but would also throw a large dollop of luck into the mix, which even dragons can't fully account for. Tonight's game was... Monopoly! After overhearing two of his hockey teammates talking about a particularly ill tempered, drunken game of Monopoly that they'd taken part in, Peter had done a little research, and had no hesitation in going out and buying a set. Although there now appeared to be a huge choice of different versions, eventually he'd opted for the classic one, a set that was now laid out in the middle of his living room floor, along with two huge trays... one full of drinks, the other overflowing with food. Right on cue, the tiniest of clicks resounded out from the corner of the room, before the shiny piano began to glide silently across the floor, uncovering a small hole through which the sound of footsteps on metal could just be heard. From out of the darkness a smiling face appeared, albeit covered in a few nasty bruises and the makings of a very serious black eye.

"Evening!" remarked Tank cheerily.

"Have you been chasing parked cars again?" mocked Peter.

Dodging past the piano and into the living room, Tank offered up a sarcastic grin in return. Suddenly, another head appeared.

"Hi guys," called Flash, bounding out of the hole, hot on the rugby player's heels, just as the Galileo thermometer shot back into the upright position and the piano began to swing back into place.

"FLASH!" they both exclaimed. "How are you?"

"Fine thanks, and looking forward to playing... what did you call it again... Monogomy?"

"Monopoly!" asserted both friends simultaneously, their faces creased with laughter.

"Oops... oh yeah... Monopoly. Anyhow, thanks once again for the invite and sorry that I can't return the favour at the moment. With everything that's going on, the king is busier than ever and I don't think, even if I begged, that I could bring the two of you back... sorry!"

"It's okay," replied the big fella, before Peter even had a chance to open his mouth. "We know the situation and it's not a problem for us to take turns in hosting. Anyhow, you have to travel all this way, and we just have to sit in our houses... easy really. So don't mention it again, it's a pleasure to have you come along. Besides, having you here stops me killing Peter when all he goes on about is being clean and tidy. 'Don't put your drink down there... not without a coaster! Use a serviette if you're going to eat one of those! Take care with the ketchup bottle... you don't want to spill any on the carpet!' If I was here on my own with him... I might just end up giving him a head transplant. I often think of ripping it off and mounting it on top of the hoover that's always on standby over there in the corner."

Flash smiled at Tank's little monologue, glancing across at the vacuum cleaner that was indeed standing upright, ready to go in the corner. By now, the home owner was blushing profusely at his buddy's full-on rant.

"It lives in the corner all the time. I've got nowhere else to put it."

"Don't give me that dragon dung," replied Tank smiling. "I know it doesn't live there. And if it did, it most certainly wouldn't be plugged in, with the socket switched on. I know you're a stickler for things like that, Pete, and you'd never let it stay hooked up overnight... so there!"

"Alright, alright," he conceded, holding his hands up. "Let's just get on with... Monogomy... shall we?"

Now it was Tank and Flash's turn to crease up with laughter.

"You know what I mean," he stated, sitting down next to the neatly stacked piles of pretend money on the floor.

"Ahhh... so you're the banker are you?" observed Flash, taking in the game board, the trays of food and drink, as well as all the fake currency.

"How appropriate," chuckled rugby boy, "I've always thought of you as a banker."

Smiling and shaking his head, Flash tried very hard not to laugh as Peter motioned for the two of them to sit, and started giving out the designated amounts. As he did, the doorbell rang. For just a split second the three of them became alert, tense.

"It's alright," declared Peter. "It'll just be someone trying to change my electricity supplier or something like that. I'll get rid of them... back in a mo."

Wandering down the hallway, Peter wondered if Tank and Flash were behaving themselves with the bank's money, so caught up in the moment, he'd already turned the lock and started to open the door before realising that he should at least have looked to see who was on the other side. If he had, he might not have had quite the surprised expression he was now wearing. After a brief, uncomfortable silence, he said,

"Hi Rich. How you doing?"

"Good thanks," the lacrosse superstar replied. "Can I come in?"

The first thing that zipped through his mind was,

'Boy, this has the potential to go badly wrong,' but the word that came out of his mouth was,

"Sure." Before he could mention that Tank and Flash were there, Richie flitted past him and shot through the door into the living room. Securely shutting the front door, he quickly caught up with her, just as she'd discovered the other two. Richie raised an eyebrow at the sight of the Monopoly set.

"I didn't realise you had visitors! I'll come back some other time," she said, turning on her heels.

Bravely, or stupidly, depending on how you looked at it, Peter grabbed her by the elbow, stopping her progress back down the hallway. Instantly he regretted it and let her go.

"Don't go Rich. Stay... please?"

"Please Richie," echoed Tank's voice from the living room floor. "We'd really like that. Besides, it would give us a chance to kick your ass at Monopoly, or Monogamy as these two muppets like it to be known."

Peter knew exactly what his rugby playing pal was doing. Under normal circumstances there was no way she'd let a challenge like that go unheeded, and would undoubtedly make everyone pay by wiping the floor with them.

'But if I know, then so does she,' he thought, as the awkward silence ensued.

Richie gave Peter her... 'look.' He'd seen the 'look' a thousand times and although he didn't know whether things would go badly or not, he was certain that the evening wasn't going to be dull, at the very least.

Strolling back into the living room, Richie sat back down next to the pile of money that was the bank. Peter's mouth opened just a fraction to tell her he was sitting there, when his brain caught up with events and immediately shut it, screaming...

'If she wants to sit there... LET HER!' Walking around to the other side of the board, Peter sat down in between the other two, as far away from the food and drink as possible.

Richie extended her hand in Flash's direction.

"I don't believe we've been introduced?"

Flash reached out with his perfectly formed hands, which encompassed all of Richie's slender little fingers.

"Dendrik Ridge, but you can call me Flash. It's a pleasure to meet you."

Richie's head creased in puzzlement.

"Flash, you say." She looked at Peter and Tank with an odd expression on her face, as her dragon senses stretched out to the max. Tank was the first to catch on.

"It's okay Rich, he is the Flash that we told you about, and yes, he's definitely one of us. It's just since his 'Antarctic adventure', he's very difficult to sense. Whenever I try and check him out, he comes across as more human than dragon... sometimes it's the other way round. It does seem to change."

As she cottoned on, Flash arched his head towards Tank.

"Does it really differ that much?"

Tank nodded.

"Seems to. From my limited experience, you appear more human the later the hour. In the daytime you feel... well not fully dragon... but I can tell you're not human. The later it gets, the more difficult I find it to sense that you're not entirely human... SORRY!"

"Don't be sorry," replied the ex-Crimson Guard. "If nothing else it's an interesting perspective on what's happened to me that I don't know about. Maybe one day it'll come in handy and I can use it to my advantage."

"Well," continued Richie, "it's a pleasure to meet you.

I've heard a lot about you. You sound like my kind of dragon."

Flash bowed his head in acknowledgement.

"I've heard all about you, and it has to be said that by the sound of things, you make everything I've ever done seem quite tame... so it's a pleasure to meet you, finally."

At this point, both Peter and Tank were busy trying to stuff two fingers into their mouths in a mock attempt at making themselves sick. Richie looked at them both and said,

"So Flash, tell me... what makes you want to hang around with these two kids?"

Flash chuckled. It was something he rarely did, or at least used to do. More and more of late he found himself genuinely laughing... and it felt good, despite the fact that he was stuck in this wretched form.

"You of all dragons, Richie, should appreciate there's more to these two, and yourself, than meets the eye. To use your own words... you're all my kind of dragons, so to speak."

And so the fun began, with the game starting, but not before Peter had taken all the fake money back and made Richie (now the banker) count it all out fairly. After only about ninety minutes, it was evident that only one dragon was going to win... Richie, of course. Peter was the first out; at the point where he had to sell all his property back to the bank he gave in, much to the others' disappointment. It was Tank next, and as usual he conceded defeat with the good grace that had always been part of him. Flash lasted the longest, and for a while (well, only really a few moments) it looked like he might give the lacrosse player a run for her money, but simply put, she trounced each and every one of them, something Peter and Tank were used to, and something that Flash was very much starting to get the hang of.

Game over, and with nobody wanting to start again after such a clear cut victory, Flash and Tank kicked back, watching the television. Meanwhile, Richie joined Peter in the kitchen to top up the refreshments. Peter got the distinct impression that there was something on his friend's mind that she wanted to talk to him about. Finishing popping some crisps into a large bowl with a whole load of others of all different flavours, in a kind of crisp Russian roulette, he watched as she walked right up to him.

"Peter," she whispered, "there's something I need to tell you."

"Sure Rich... what's up?" he responded, noticing her gaze fall from his face, down towards his chest. Gently she slipped a finger just inside his open necked shirt and carefully pulled the *alea* he was wearing, out from its hiding place.

"Ohhh... I'd almost forgotten all about this," she said dreamily. "You can almost feel its power, its history, the souls of the dragons that created it."

"Come off it Rich... you're having a laugh aren't you? The souls of the dragons that created it... really?"

"Are you telling me you can't feel anything at all from it? Nothing special?"

Part of him wanted to say yes, wanted to tell her that it was just like any normal modern day accessory, and that he only wore it because it looked good, but he knew in an instant that it was impossible for him to lie, especially to her.

"No... there's certainly something that I can't explain radiating off it... but the souls of the dragons who created it? I'm pretty sure that's not it. And anyway, what makes you think it is? It's an odd thing to even consider, let alone say out loud," he said, trying to make light of the situation.

With that dreamy look on her face, Richie thought for a moment before saying,

"It's just that when I touch it, and look at it at the same time... that's when it screams out at me. I can see the dragons shaping the jewels, heating the metal, composing the mantras. It's almost as if I were there with them, witnessing it all for real. It sends shivers up my spine, my arms, my tail. I don't know how else to describe it."

Gently Peter uncurled Richie's fingers and tucked the *alea* and its chain back down behind his shirt, letting the dreamy look on Richie's face fade away, bringing her back to the present from somewhere in the past.

"The reason I wanted to talk to you..." she started. But before she could continue, Peter put his finger up to her lips.

"Shhhhhh," he whispered, grabbing her by the hand, leading her out into the hallway, without either Tank or Flash noticing. Still holding her hand, he guided her up the stairs and opened the door to his bedroom.

"Gosh Peter," she exclaimed. "This is all so unexpected. What's Janice going to think?"

It was only then that it dawned on him exactly how this could be taken to be something that it wasn't.

"Uhhh... well... ummm... well... I... ummm... errr... well... it's... um... not... er..."

Richie gave him a huge slap on the back.

"I know it's nothing like that! Come on Pete... where's your sense of humour?"

Well aware that he could probably have lit up half the town if his face looked only half as red as it felt, he gave a smile that appeared more like a grimace.

"Sorry Rich... I know. Just wasn't thinking, that's all."

"No harm done," she replied. "So why exactly am I here in this notorious den of iniquity?"

"Ahhhh... hang on a minute."

Clambering over his double bed, he jumped down onto the floor and opened up one of the doors to the wardrobe beyond, proceeding then to rummage around inside. After a little rustling and a few clothes being thrown across the room, he began to pull out something altogether heavier. It was his grandfather's chest.

"Give us a hand will you, Rich?"

She came round to join him, and together they heaved the trunk up onto the bed.

"I really wanted you to see this."

"I bet you use that line on all the laddiieeeesss you bring up here. Is that what worked on Janice? Do you want to come back to my house and see my... CHEST?!!!"

Even Peter thought that was funny, with the two of them laughing until tears rolled down their faces. Wiping away the moisture, he explained what it was and all about the king giving it to him, also telling her that nobody but the monarch knew what it contained, not even Tank or Flash.

One by one, he pulled out all the objects, placing them carefully on the bed, unable to hide the pride he felt for his grandfather when showing Richie the Flaming Cross. It wasn't often that the lacrosse player was lost for words, but she was and gave her friend a big hug, telling him what a wonderful dragon his grandfather must have been.

Skipping through the robes, the canister of *'Fox's Igniting Scale Enhancer'* and the two giant sticks of charcoal, he pulled out the half sheet of newspaper. Reluctantly he explained what George had told him about his parents. Richie sat and listened intently, well aware of how much pain it was causing her friend to even talk about the subject. If she'd been amazed at the revelation about the Flaming Cross, she was shocked to the core about Peter's parents supposedly colluding with the Nazis. More than a few tears were shed by the home owner in telling the story, but it was only when he shared the burden he'd bottled up with one of his best friends that he realised the weight he'd been carrying and just quite how much it had been bothering him. Reaching into the, by now, almost empty box, he pulled out something tiny, wrapped in a clean, but old piece of tissue paper and handed it to his friend.

"For you. I really want you to have it. I haven't had the opportunity to give it to you before now."

Slowly and carefully, Richie unwrapped the tissue

paper, curious to see what it was. Like buses, the surprises were coming all at once today. Letting the paper float to the floor, she held up the *alea* directly in front of her, allowing it to twirl of its own accord from the end of the silvery chain.

"I'm not sure I understand Pete. Why do you have two?"

He went on to explain how the one he was wearing had belonged to his grandfather and was identical in every way to the one that Mark Hiscock had left him in his will.

"Wow... some deity or other must really be watching over you for two of these to end up in your possession. What are the chances?"

"Tell me about it," he replied. "It just seems to be one thing after another... not in a bad way of course... but I do wonder why it all appears to be happening to me. It's like all that stuff with Manson... why me? I'm scared stiff almost every time I walk down the hallway to open the front door, particularly if I think about it too much."

"I'm sorry Pete. That's really not what I meant to say. You do have a lot of things going on though, don't you?"

"That is something of an understatement, I think you'll find Rich. Anyhow, I feel a whole lot better talking to you about my parents. There are so many unanswered questions... it's all so mysterious. If I knew a little more, I might be able to put it all to the back of my mind... but when even the king can't make any headway with it, you have to think there's something very dubious about it all."

Richie nodded her agreement.

"Well, perhaps I can help. You've told me enough to get started, with your permission of course, I'll see what I can dig up."

"Really, would you?"

"I can't make any promises Pete, you know that... but I'll do my best and see what I can find out for you."

"I can't begin to tell you just how much that means to me Rich. Thanks."

"You're welcome, and thank you very much for the... gift," she said, smiling, while at the same time putting the *alea* around her neck, slipping the little ring through the chain's clasp.

"But before we join the others... I have something that I wanted to tell you, in fact the reason for coming to see you tonight." There was a long pause, not quite awkward, just intriguing. Folding her hands together in her lap whilst gazing at the pristine carpet, the lacrosse captain thought long and hard about what she had to say. Eventually, after only a matter of seconds really, she looked up, straight into her friend's eyes.

"I've ditched Tim! There's no other way to say it. I've done what the council demanded. I didn't want to, but... on consideration, it does seem the only way to move forward. So there!"

Of all the things that he'd been expecting to hear, this was right at the bottom of his list, just below... 'I'm setting up a dragon colony on the moon. I think we can fly there under our own steam, and can really make it work.'

"I know it must have been difficult, but I really think it's for the best. Consider Tim's point of view. He'll be growing old, while you will only appear to grow old. I'm sure if he knew he'd never go for that... would he?"

Richie nodded her agreement, two delicate tears sliding effortlessly in and out of the freckles on her cheeks.

"I know," she sniffed. "Anyway... it's done now. So let's just move on."

After a huge hug, both friends parted, about to go back downstairs when all of a sudden she stopped and pointed at the bottom of the chest.

"What's that?"

'Oh crap,' was his first thought, followed swiftly by, 'what to do, what to do?' By now though, it was too late, as Richie's pale, slender hand had already dipped into the trunk and pulled out a much larger object, wrapped in a swathe of old rag. In a blur, Peter swept out his hand as fast as he could in an attempt to grab the object back. Of course she was too quick for him, moving whatever it was just out of his reach.

"What is it?" she asked again.

Shaking his head, knowing there was no way out now, he knew that he was going against pretty much everything he'd told the king.

'Oh well... here goes.' Stretching out his palm upturned, he whispered,

"Let me show you."

Eyeing him suspiciously, eventually she passed over the object.

"You have to promise not to tell another soul about this, Rich. Not anyone... really! He stood and waited, glaring 'daggers' (... you see what happened there!) at his friend.

"You're serious?"

"Deadly."

"Okay."

"Say it," he demanded.

"IT!"

Less than amused, he crossed his arms, the object securely hidden beneath them. After the shortest standoff in history, Richie eventually conceded.

"I promise."

Exhaling, not having realised he'd been holding his breath, part of him was disappointed that she'd complied, hoping that he'd get out of showing her what it was. With nothing else left to do, he laid the object flat on the bed, and started to carefully unwrap it. Having thought there could be nothing left to surprise her, the gasp of disbelief that passed her lips as she recognised what lay amidst the cloth, could almost have blown one of the three little pigs' houses down.

"It... it... it... it... can't be! Can it? Aviva's dagger?"

"It surely is," he replied, trying to sound nonchalant, despite the nerves he felt at revealing its existence.

"Did your grandfather leave you this as well?"

He just nodded.

"Phewwww. He must have been one hell of a dragon. I'd really like to have met him. *Aleas*, the Flaming Cross, and now this... I really don't know what to say."

"Imagine how I feel," declared Peter. "The whole world's gone mad."

"I can see how you'd think that. What's the glow surrounding it?" she asked, holding out her hand to run her fingers along the hilt.

Abruptly he pulled the dagger out of her reach, much to her disappointment.

"What you can see is a mantra designed to contain the power the laminium radiates. It's soooo strong Rich. It makes you feel... invincible, all powerful, invigorated. It's hard to describe. Anyway, the mantra's there to stop all of that leaking into the surrounding environment. I think prolonged exposure would drive you mad."

"I don't suppose..."

"No!" he replied, before she even had a chance to finish.

"Even if I wanted to, I couldn't. It's not that easy to remove the mantra... even temporarily."

"I understand," she replied softly, looking as though she probably didn't. "Anyhow, I'm not sure about you, but I've had enough adventure for one night. Shall we go and see what they're up to downstairs? Unless of course you've got some fully grown dinosaurs in your wardrobe that you were planning on showing me?"

"No... that pretty much covers it!"

"Thank heavens for that. I don't think even I could take much more. And there was me thinking that YOU would find my news shocking. Role reversal or what?" she laughed. "And don't worry, I'll do what I can to look into your parents for you... It might take a while though."

"I know, and thanks. Are you going to tell Tank and Flash about ending things with Tim?"

"Yes, I'll tell them when we go downstairs if that's okay. I just wanted to tell you first."

"You do realise that it wasn't Tank that told the council about you both?"

"Of course I know it wasn't him. I was just angry about being discovered, and lashed out. Don't worry... I'll apologise."

"Brilliant," added Peter.

By the time the two of them made their way back down into the living room, Tank and Flash had finished watching one programme and were now arguing over which of their favourite football teams would finish higher up the league, as they watched the sports news. It was a surprise to Peter that Flash even supported a football team. The ex-Crimson Guard announced that it was a recent development, since he'd become stuck in his new found form, doing all he could to brush up on being human, he'd discovered that he actually quite liked watching Premiership football, despite the fact that so many of the players were actually dragons. Plumping for a team to support that had fewer dragons than most and because he liked the idea of being called a GOONER, he'd chosen... ARSENAL!

Managing to break up the argument with news of her own about the breakup from Tim, Flash told her he genuinely thought it was the best thing to do, while Tank gave her a great big hug as she apologised to him for the things she'd said after the laminium ball match. The three friends... now four... would have found it almost impossible to be much happier. Everything, it seemed, was back to normal, if the word 'normal' could ever be used to describe their lives.

17 A GREMLIN IN THE KREMLIN

Only having had a few hours of sleep after the vast amount of alcohol he'd consumed the previous night, his head felt like it had been hit with a shovel. Nowadays it was very hard to find real Russian vodka, but those guys seemed to have had an endless supply of the very best. The inside of his mouth and both the top and bottom of his tongue felt red raw, just as they should after what he'd imbibed.

When he'd left his flat yesterday, the idea had been to try and drink away his worries. Well, that had been the plan on entering his usual watering hole. Sitting there on the barstool, drinking watered down, cheap vodka, all alone, with only the barman for company in the early afternoon, he was deeply aware that most of the customers wouldn't arrive until much later on, one of the main reasons he frequented that particular bar. Deep down he knew that he was a very sorry drunk... an alcoholic in fact. It wasn't something he'd ever admit to, but somewhere locked deep inside his mind there was the tiniest voice in the darkest corner, afraid and alone, mouthing the word... alcoholic. Because of all this, he liked to drink alone... to just sit on the barstool and knock back drink after drink, all the time staring glassy eyed at the TV on the wall with the sound turned down. Occasionally the bartender would ask if he'd like the volume turned up. But he always refused, preferring his thoughts for company instead.

The previous day had started no differently from countless others. Having drunk enough to make a normal man at least a little unsteady on his feet, he contemplated the future that lay in store for him. His gambling debts... oh his gambling debts. It had only started out as a bit of fun with some of his work mates. But how quickly it had spiralled out of control. First it was just as much as he could afford on a night out... the next month... half his salary... then... oh then! The offer to borrow from The Establishment... well, if you can call a hardcore, gunrunning drug lord's organisation The Establishment. It was just a little at first, enough to win back all he'd previously lost, and the interest on the loan. Or so he'd thought. It was easy really. He was a great gambler... at least that was his opinion, but was just having some bad luck... which as any good gambler knows is bound to change sooner rather than later. At least, that's what he continued to tell himself. Not having been back to The Establishment for over a week now, he knew it was only a matter of time before he got a knock on the door. Having no savings, barely any possessions... save his desktop computer, his laptop and a few other pieces of hardware, there was certainly nothing that would even come close to covering the scale of the arrears he owed to the very scary, and by now 'disappointed' men at The Establishment.

As his feet crunched through the fresh snow, he batted fluttering flakes out of his eyes with one of his gloved hands, feeling the weight of his laden backpack through both his shoulders as he strolled past the awe inspiring Bolshoi theatre. Walking nearly two miles so far since leaving his flat, which although it doesn't sound much, in these temperatures was a gruelling trek. With the weight of history from all the iconic landmarks around threatening to smother him, his mind returned to the previous night.

Things changed dramatically when the other man walked through the door of the bar, and out of all the places he could have sat (don't forget the bar was empty), he sat down right next to me. I sat still, not acknowledging him at first, as he ordered a shot of vodka, and when it arrived he threw it straight down his throat. Immediately he spat it out, followed straight away by every curse I'd ever heard of, essentially telling the bartender exactly what he thought of his watered down excuse for vodka. I smiled at that. Of course it was watered down... name me one bar that doesn't do that? Catching my smile out of the corner of his eye, for a split second I thought his rage might turn on me... but it didn't. Asking what was so funny... I told him. He said he knew somewhere that sold the best original Russian vodka there was, and asked if I'd like to go there with him. I remember thinking about his question for an age. His face appeared friendly, if a little haggard. Dressed roughly, not dissimilar to me, his eyes... there was something about his eyes. Maybe he was wearing contact lenses, but the eyes themselves looked as though they'd seen so much... anguish, so much pain, so much... brutality. But still, at the time it seemed like an offer I couldn't refuse... and so I didn't.

Looking back, the bartender's frightened face should have set alarm bells ringing. It didn't. Whether it was the cold or the watered down vodka that I'd already consumed, who knows... but on our journey, I really started to struggle. It was very unusual. My normally logical brain was having trouble functioning even on the most fundamental level, and it was only once we'd arrived at the building, and made our way down the slippery, cobbled steps, into the basement, that I realised I might have a problem. By then though, it was way too late.

His friends, associates, call them what you will, welcomed me with open arms. It was surreal. There were scantily clad girls, champagne and of course exactly what he'd promised... vodka so smooth and strong that it would have been fit for any Russian king or queen. Time passed in a smoke filled haze. There were dice games, card games, drinking games... scantily clad girl games. I just sat and enjoyed the vodka. All track of time was lost, probably even before I'd arrived there. As quickly as I'd turned up and joined in the fun... everything just stopped. Like that, no warning... nothing! From out of the shadows a man appeared. It was dark, filled with cigarette smoke. The drink made me unsteady on my feet. I remember feeling sick and fighting the urge to puke. I can also recall experiencing genuine fear. I'd suddenly gone from being deliriously happy, to being afraid for my life. It didn't sober me up enough for what happened next. I sat down, not quite of my own free will, but it was a relief not to be swaying about. The man from the shadows limped over to our corner table. I say limped... I think it was limped. I'm sure he had a walking stick. The 'tap, tap, tap' on the wooden floor was the scariest thing in the world at the time. I was boxed in, crowded by so many large figures. They all seemed to know who I was, that I worked at the Kremlin, building computers. They had details about the construction, the guards, the other stuff, my bosses, the shifts we all worked... everything!

Deep, heavy breaths crystallised in front of him as he continued his journey. Glancing over his shoulder at the Metropol hotel that he'd just passed on the other side of the street, its splendour jumped out at him, slapping him around the face, shouting, "You will never be able to afford me!" God he hated that place, with all its well dressed foreign visitors gliding in and out of the... now how did he overhear someone describe it the other day? Oh, that's right... 'amazing art nouveau masterpiece covered with multicoloured mosaics and sculpted stone'. At that very moment in time he despised it all. Despite the freezing cold, the snow and the wind, sweat positively poured off him... down his back, his neck, his legs, under his arms and he could feel his palms sweating like they belonged to an unfit, elderly squash player. By now he'd nearly reached Resurrection Gate; although it wasn't the original structure, it was an exact replica and usually inspired him each and every time he saw it. Not today.

Another lungful of cold air forced him to splutter out a cough, jogging his memory back to thoughts of the previous night. The mysterious man had thrown something down onto the small, round, sticky table. Instantly he recognised it for what it was, despite things being a little... foggy. It was his marker. The marker for the loan that he had with The Establishment. His signature stood out like fireworks in the night sky, that and the amount... 1.5 million Russian Roubles, more than he could save and pay back in many, many years. Although he was scared, something deep down within him squeaked,

'This is your chance; they want something.'

How right that little voice had been, and thinking about things now, how tempting a swift death of his own choosing was, right at this very moment.

Puffing away like he'd run a marathon, he was sure he could smell a tiny hint of vodka from the sweat dripping off his forehead and running down the side of his face. Thinking about cursing, nowhere within him could he find the extra effort or breath required to do so. As he wandered past Kazan Cathedral, he could see the mighty towers of the Kremlin, his eventual destination, dominating the skyline to the west.

With his marker on the table in front of him, and very large, vicious men either side, he sat, waiting for whatever hand fate had dealt him. Death wouldn't have been too much of a surprise, having spent the last week or so contemplating just that, acknowledging that the gambling debt he'd racked up, along with the interest The Establishment were adding on, meant a lifetime of servitude and corruption, something that he'd gone to great lengths to avoid in the past. And now, all of that had been for nothing. As he sat, petrified, the man in the shadows explained how not only could he make his gambling debt disappear, but he could also potentially earn the same amount again, just for making one simple... 'delivery'. The word itself was innocent enough, but the way it was said was something straight out of a Godfather movie. They worded it like they were asking him, like he had a choice, but he was under no illusions. He WOULD be doing it. Nodding, he agreed to what they wanted, just hoping to leave and get away from that place. However... it wasn't that simple, because he was to do it the following day, with only a few hours' notice... now, in fact. That's what he was on his way to do... on his way to work... to make the 'delivery'.

As a hardware technician, he worked inside the Kremlin, building computers from their base components. Hard drives, power supplies, graphics cards, cases, fans, monitors... these were all the tools of his trade; his machines were used by anyone and everyone in the top echelons of the Russian government. And here he was, caught up in God only knows what. The backpack he wore rubbed against his shoulders on the outside of his thick, dark jacket, as he approached the very ordinary looking door, an entrance that was deserted, mainly due to the ungodly early hour of the morning. Only a short time ago he'd been drinking that fine vodka and admiring scantily clad girls... now he was about to commit trea... He was too scared to even think it. Now, he was hoping to make a delivery, one that would, one way or another, shape his future.

Tucked safely away inside his rucksack were half a dozen hard drives and two external desktop drives, all shaped like books, one of which was not entirely as it seemed. This one was the delivery he'd been tasked to make. Taken back to his flat, given the component and very specific instructions about what to do with it, he'd sobered up relatively quickly, and after showering had decided in the hour that he'd been left alone by the very scary men, that he would, against their specific instructions... try and take a peek inside it. Using his highly crafted tools and knowhow, he'd managed to remove a tiny panel. What he'd glimpsed within left him in no doubt as to just how much trouble he was in. A digital display of red numbers counting down could just be viewed behind the circuit board and wiring, with the numbers not seeming to change according to any measurement of time that he was familiar with. Quickly, he put the panel back in place with the utmost care, loading it, with all the other items, carefully into his pack. It wasn't unusual for him to take work home, and the backpack he wore had been specifically designed for the military elite to keep things dry and in particular... warm. As he passed through a very basic security scan (due to the delicate nature of the mechanical and electrical items that he carried) his mind sensed that he was almost the perfect delivery boy for whoever the shadowy man and his colleagues were. Unless anyone actually bothered to disassemble all his equipment, there wasn't a chance in hell that they'd know there was anything odd about it. That didn't stop him from feeling as nervous as a turkey in December.

After mere moments, he'd passed through all the usual checks and probably, knowing his employers, a few more unusual ones along the way. The guards had given him a nudge and a wink, smelling the potent vodka on his breath and from his perspiration. They joked at how much trouble he'd be in, arriving drunk and hung over. Just nodding, he played along... it didn't take much, as it was all true. But his focus remained solely on his delivery. Marching down the short corridor, all the time unzipping his black jacket, he was aware that he was sweating even more than before.

'The heating in this building is ridiculous,' he thought to himself. It was always full on, even during the hottest part of summer. Having unzipped his jacket, he undid the top two buttons of his shirt and opted for the staircase instead of the lift as a means to get to his workshop, despite the fact that his body would rather not make the effort, his reasoning being that he was less likely to bump into anyone else in the staircase, although there were few people about at this time of day; because of the task before him, he felt safer not having contact with anyone at all.

Strolling purposefully into the empty workshop, he quickly checked to make sure it was clear and that all the other technicians who he shared it with were nursing their hangovers somewhere else and would not be in for some time yet.

'Still,' he thought, 'I need to get to work straight away. Better safe than sorry.'

Placing his backpack gently on the floor beside his desk, he took off his coat and threw it over the back of his swivel chair. Undoing the many layers of the pack took about two minutes. (It had been designed to keep out cold, moisture and it would seem... dumb humans as well.) Eventually he retrieved the hard drive and, picking up his small toolbox off the desk, headed out of the door and into the component warehouse. The place was HUGE with racks and shelving over twelve metres high in some places, disappearing off into the distance for as far as the eye could see. Components for computers, printers, faxes, microfiche readers and photocopiers were all there... piled high... quite literally. Now though, he wasn't hunting for any of these. His target was an old workstation right at the back of the underground warehouse. It was in the darkest, dingiest corner, and was said that nobody used it at all, but if they did, it was only if they had to and even then, it was for the shortest time possible. Stories and rumours passed around the departments all the time about what lay on the other side of the wall that the computer sat against. Some said it was weapons, some said experiments were being conducted using strange and wonderful chemicals. Occasional reports of desperate screams and out of this world sounds came back from those few people who used the terminal. This was not a place for the faint hearted. After a journey of only a few seconds short of seven minutes (he'd timed it and counted every second in his head), he'd managed to avoid everyone. Recognising footsteps a couple of times, he'd changed his route to avoid contact with anyone, which at this quiet time in the shift cycle hadn't been too difficult, especially as the whole place was like one giant maze. Reaching his destination, he quietly placed his toolbox on the floor and flicked open the clips, the sound of a lone forklift truck far away in the distance for company.

Positively old and ancient by today's standards, the terminal was the only way to access and search the old stock system that was still occasionally used. Normally it was powered on all the time, but luckily for him it was off. Again, he was counting down the seconds, hoping against hope that he could do what was required in record time. And he did. Twenty three minutes it had taken him to fit two circuit boards and an internal USB adapter, also cutting out part of the back plate of the case, making it look as though it hadn't been tampered with. As he tackled the installation of a new hard drive under a massive pile of wiring covered with dust a few centimetres thick, he was sure no one would stumble across his little addition in a million years, not unless they were specifically looking for it. As he wandered back to his workshop, relief and sweat poured off him in equal amounts. Now all he had to do was act normally and go about his daily routine.

'What's done is done,' he thought, and tried really hard to forget about the little black box counting down, not a million miles away.

Six months ago that had all happened and was now nothing more than a distant memory as he sat in his swivel chair, tiny screwdriver in hand, trying very hard to lever out a stubborn power supply unit. Suddenly his mobile phone vibrated on his desk, causing it to scuttle about like a drunken crab. Looking around to make sure nobody had noticed, phones were supposed to be switched off at all times, something most workers here ignored, though he might get into trouble if caught. Leaving the computer where it was, he picked up his phone and scrolled through the menu to look at the new text. It was from an unknown number and simply said:

'Now is a great time for a vacation. Check out the latest deals to European destinations on our website. Occasionally we have cheap breaks to Madrid... watch this space.'

It was a text he'd dreaded seeing. Everything came flooding back. Having stopped gambling, he'd moved into a slightly better, but not flashy, new flat. But he still drank, every night... to forget. To overlook what he'd done. But now he remembered... he remembered everything. And soon, an offer of a trip to Madrid would appear on that website, and he'd have to take it up, knowing that whatever happened here was now well and truly beyond his control. He got back to work... secretly terrified.

18 THE CHANCE OF ESCAPING...
ABSOLUTE ZERO

Wheezing and spluttering echoes bounced off the reflective white surfaces everywhere as the huge bag of tortured bones slept, if that's what you could call it. To anyone watching, it would have looked more like a self induced nightmare rather than a slumber brought on by exhaustion. Throughout it all, the raggedy old dragon wailed, muttered, screamed and stammered, sometimes names, places and events, occasionally curses, some of them in the ancient dragon language, but always ending in the same way... BETRAYAL!

Fredric Bluewillow, Peter's grandfather, pulled taut the chains holding him against his will and the wall of ice as he listened to the old dragon for what seemed like the millionth time... and perhaps it was. The brutality of this prison was like nothing he'd ever imagined. Not in his worst nightmares could he ever have pictured or dreamed that such a place existed... but it did, and he was trapped here, escape not even a distant possibility. Years, no decades, had passed, of that he was sure. How he hadn't gone insane, he didn't really know. But that was the question wasn't it? Was he still sane, or did he just think that he was? Talk about too much time on your hands... all these questions, and the more he pondered, the more confused he became. Spending the last, what he assumed was about an hour, exercising, he preferred to do that every time 'Bag o' Bones' really started having a bad time of it, often asking himself why, sometimes refusing to admit the real reason, dwelling on it for so long that nothing but the truth mattered now. The real reason he was so uncomfortable was because it could have been him over there now. But for a twist of fate, and a swift promotion to become George's new partner after everything that had gone on during the clean up operation after Troydenn's defeat, he could have been that miserable bag of bones, wailing and moaning, begging to be put out of his misery. After all, he had been scheduled to be on that fateful mission, escorting the prisoners to that icy hellhole in Antarctica... the same hellhole that he assumed he now sat in. Every time the horrific noises started, all he could think about was that it could have been him; he could have been here centuries instead of just decades.

'Just decades...' he smiled to himself. If nothing else, he'd maintained his sense of humour. At times, that was all that seemed to keep him going, that and the memories of his friend... George. In many ways they'd been like brothers, inseparable for the most part, but with very different personalities. His first instinct had always been to fight, not for the joy of it, or the glory... nothing like that. He'd always fought for others... against injustice. For those who couldn't stand up for themselves, his overwhelming impulse being to step in, put himself in harm's way and defeat the perceived evil. That was far from George's way. By no means a coward, the exact opposite in fact, he'd always sought diplomacy first, stepping in harm's way with little or no thought for himself, but always looking to distract, to think things through, to find a non violent solution. On this, the two dragons always disagreed, and often argued vehemently, each sticking to their own point of view. Memories of those disagreements, the long evenings disseminating those very different viewpoints, meant so much and helped him on the odd occasion when his sanity started to slip away, in this bleak desert of white. Desert... there was a word. If he did dream, it was of deserts and... the sun, oh how he missed the sun. To feel its warm kiss one last time he'd give everything he had.

And then there was his grandson... Peter! Barely a moment passed when he didn't wonder what he was doing, whether he was even still alive. Having been stranded here for so long, he had no idea what state the dragon kingdom was in, if it even still existed in the same form at all. Having received no information... nothing. Clearly everything going on here led him to believe some kind of attack had either happened or was in the planning, with the questions asked of him when tortured all the same... all strategic... even after all this time. Decades had passed and they were still asking the same questions... and foolishly or not, he still refused to answer, up until recently, anyway. To him, it was a matter of... PRIDE! There was simply no way he would betray his king, his friend, his grandson and his way of life. Thoughts of Peter brought tears to his eyes, tears that instantly started to freeze as they left the surface of his retinas and slipped onto his sun deprived skin. Anger welled up inside him at being robbed of the company of his grandson for so long. Deep down, he'd known for nearly the entire time that he'd been held captive here that someone had betrayed him. The way he'd been ambushed and so cleverly taken... it could only have been that.

Who? Well, that was the million dollar question, wasn't it? He knew it wasn't George, of that much he was certain. Their friendship was a bond that knew no bounds, a camaraderie forged by flame, flying and from fighting back to back, side by side. But who could have deceived him, and were they still somewhere at large, able to do more harm, especially to his friend... the king? These questions haunted him by the hour. During his torture, that... weasel of a jailer would bellow at him that it was all over, that the dragon kingdom had been burnt to the ground... every last one of them dead. The king, the council... his family! This was the hardest part. At first he'd reacted, screaming and raging against the impossible bonds that held him in place. Cursing, he described in intimate detail exactly what he'd do to the jailer. In his mind anyway. Knowing they were trying to find a weakness, one which they could exploit, he'd been trained by the best, having learnt not to react under the pain of torture or the heart wrenching agony of the most brutal of words, but it had been the hardest thing he'd ever done. However, he'd done it and survived. Not just once, but on hundreds, if not thousands of occasions over the course of decades. At first the filthy warden and the other shadowy visitors that he could feel shrouded in darkness had thought that he'd break... but he hadn't, and in that, the tables had been turned. Although the violence and the scale of the torture increased, he'd known that by some small measure... he'd won. He, Fredric Bluewillow, had beaten them. They could keep him imprisoned until the end of time, but he'd got his victory and that kept him going. Every minute he failed to react, to answer any of their questions, was a triumph, not just for him, but for George, for Peter, for every good, honest and decent free dragon across the globe.

Every emotion he'd ever known raced through his aching, cold body whenever these thoughts crossed his mind, but here and now, it was a miniscule humming that caught his attention.

'Ah... here we go again,' he mused. 'I hope we have more success than last time, and that I'm doing the right thing. I'm ninety-nine percent sure it's not a trap.'

Ramping up substantially, the humming had transformed into more of a buzzing, and become much more pronounced. Fredric concentrated on clearing his mind, not easy given his previous train of thought. His emotions were running high, not exactly ideal for what was about to happen. Still, he lacked the ability to commence contact, and so couldn't control the timing. Initiating that level of communication in these surroundings must be incredibly draining, and could only happen rarely and for very short periods of time, at least that was his assumption. Abruptly, the buzzing was interrupted by a low pitched whistle, and then a harsh, croaky voice rumbled,

"If yoouuu caann heaaarrrr meeee, fleeeexxx yoooouur leeftt armmmm."

Casually as you like, Fredric loosened his neck, rolled

his shoulders twice, and then flexed his left arm, his huge biceps bulging like a giant honeydew melon. Out of the corner of his eye he watched the naga king give an almost imperceptible nod.

"Olllddd Booonnneessss ressstlesss tooodaaaayyy. Whhaaat maakkesss hiimmmm saaadddd maakees yooooou saaaddd tooooooo!"

Focusing his mind intently on the voice, trying his best to weave in and out of all the background noise in his head, he couldn't see any point in denying that he and Bag o' Bones had a connection, albeit slightly tenuous.

"Yes," he replied, hearing it echo off in the distance, which he found more than a little disconcerting.

"Ifff iitttt weerrreee innn myy pooowerrr tooooo doooo soooo I woouuulddd puuutttt himmmmm ouuuuttt offf hissss missssserrrrryyyyy."

"So would I," he answered, with it again echoing off into the void.

There was a short pause, not one of silence, more apprehension. Fredric knew the naga king hadn't finished because the noises in his head remained and were getting louder and more painful by the second.

"Dooooo yoouuuuu thhhinnnkkkk ddraaagggonnn thhaattt waaasssss herrrreee gooootttt awwwaaaayyyy?"

He'd gone over and over this in his mind. The jailer had told them that their unexpected visitor had been caught and executed on the spot, showing them some scales, a few shards of talon and a very ropey looking wing membrane in an effort to make them believe what had happened. But he'd sensed that there was more to that being than had at first been obvious. It was almost as if Fredric had looked into a mirror and seen a younger version of himself. Despite the jailer's claims and the blood splattered evidence to back them up, he was convinced that the dragon had escaped. Escaped to where though? If, as he assumed, they were hidden beneath the Antarctic inside the prison specifically built to hold

Troydenn and his followers so long ago, where on earth could the detainee have fled to? Perhaps things had changed so much in all this time, both in the human world and dragon domain, that there were large cities and thriving communities nearby. Perhaps Antarctica itself had become hugely populated and that's how he'd stumbled across them in the first place. Still... the whole incident had bought some hope, and however small that was, he refused to give up on it.

"That dragon was special. I believe he escaped the custody of our captors," he sent back to the naga king, all the time limbering up for as much exercise as his bonds would allow, just in case they were somehow being watched.

Moments passed before,

"Yessssss, I tooooooo thhhhougghhhttt hiimmmmmm unussssuaaaaalll!"

Above the din in his mind, it suddenly occurred to him to ask a question.

"Have you been able to speak to any of your race?"

Trying desperately not to look in the king's direction, he waited patiently for the answer, despite the overwhelming noise that was now like standing directly beside the speakers at a rock concert.

"I'vvvvveeee trrriieeed mannnnnyyy timmmeeees, buuuut noooo luuucccckkkk. Eeeeveeen thhhooooosssseee thaaatttt I haaavvveee seeennn seeeemmmmm tooo bbeeee shhuuuuuttt offffff frroooommm meeeeee!"

Against the backdrop of the concert assaulting his mind, he let out a string of curses. In the hope of planning some sort of rescue bid, he'd thought the king might be able to get through to members of his race, but as they'd discussed in their previous conversations, there must have been some kind of localised field, probably a mantra or some other magic blocking telepathic communications, which would explain why the short range contact between the two of them was so taxing, both physically and mentally. Before Fredric had a chance to respond, a few last words could be heard before everything went quiet.

"Haaaavvveee tooooooo gooooooo nooooowwwww. Ssssoooorrrryyy!"

A sideways glance showed the king slump to the floor, curling up upon himself. For his part, he wished the monarch a good, dreamless sleep, continuing with his painful exercise, all the time wondering what was going on in the world he knew best... his beloved dragon domain.

19 LIAR, LIAR, TAIL'S ON FIRE

On reflection, the traffic hadn't been nearly as bad as she'd thought it would be, in fact the drive itself could almost be described as enjoyable. It wasn't something that she'd often done, preferring almost always to use the ease, convenience and speed of the monorail, but with the window part way down, the sun shining, and great music on the radio, a little shiver of pleasure pulsed down her arms, despite her feeling a tiny bit claustrophobic. They'd agreed to meet well away from Salisbridge, at her insistence, but with Tim having opted for Swanage as their destination, Richie was feeling decidedly nervous. At the time, she'd been unable to come up with a good reason why they shouldn't convene there, and Tim had been rather understanding about all the cloak and dagger stuff. With Swanage being almost the dead centre of Purbeck Peninsula, the dragon contingent was of course a worry, but by driving there and using a little known mantra that should, if used with the utmost care and control, render her almost undetectable to other dragons for a very short period of time, the lacrosse superstar assumed she would blend in seamlessly. There was always the possibility that her human form could be recognised but the chances of that were so remote, you'd get better odds on Peter, Tank, Flash and Gee Tee forming their own laminium ball team and winning the Global Cup. Just the thought of this brought a smile to her petite, freckly face.

Following the road almost to the sea, she turned left just before the end, parking on an incline just on the right hand side before making her way on foot back along the path and onto the seafront, pausing briefly to look up at the park that towered over her off to her right. It was the same one the three friends had used in the middle of the night to gain access to the dragon domain, the secret entrance ingrained in her eidetic memory, should she ever need to use it. With the wind whipping her hair frantically across her face, she stopped and gazed across at the young human children, toddlers and babies currently playing there.

Something inside her stirred. Something primitive, something unbridled, something forbidden. It was overwhelming, washing over her body in a wave that nearly rendered her unconscious. Recovering almost immediately, she gave a little look around to see if anyone had noticed her momentary wobble. If they had, it didn't show. Slowly exhaling, she set off purposefully towards the venue for their clandestine meeting, glancing at her watch to make sure she was going to be punctual, which to her meant about five minutes after the prearranged time. Well... she was a female dragon, after all, and five minutes was about enough of a delay to make her... fashionably late.

Mooching along the seafront, taking in the beach, the arcades and everything that was going on, she wandered slowly up the main street browsing in the windows of some of the shops. Again, checking her watch, she decided to put Tim out of his misery, so she strolled swiftly into Swanage railway station, the home of the famed steam railway. During the brief walk of only a few hundred metres, she thought about the lies she'd woven for Peter, Tank and Flash. Feeling a little guilty, she reached out instinctively to brush her hand against the *alea* that her friend had given her. At the end of the day, she thought, they just simply wouldn't understand. Well... Peter might, since he was heading on the same rollercoaster journey of his own with Janice, not yet realising it and only just boarding the ride, so to speak. The other two, well... it was her life, and she should be allowed to live it as she saw fit. And no dragon or human was going to dictate how that would be, now or at any time in the future.

Entering the terminus, she glanced down the length of the platform. There, towards the end stood Tim, confident, aware and just a little in awe, Richie could tell. Strolling right up to him, she kissed him passionately, full on the lips, much to the surprise of the other passengers. Tim was neither surprised nor intimidated by this... something that she really, really liked about him. Producing two tickets from his back trouser pocket, he grabbed hold of her left hand and led her towards the waiting Wessex Belle service that would allow them to take the train and dine in style all at the same time. Ironic really, that they'd both driven all this way for a train journey, but what a trip it was... one of the most scenic, beautiful and enjoyable ways to spend an evening, the two of them had decided earlier on in the week. They weren't disappointed. The food was magnificent and fit for a king, another irony considering what the king would do if he had any idea where Richie was, or just who she was with. Tim, had the carrot soup with coriander oil for a starter, followed by roasted, stuffed butternut squash for a main course, with the fruit salad for pudding. Richie, being a dragon (you can count the number of vegetarian dragons on the whole of the planet on one hand) went all out. To start with she had the duck and orange pâté, followed by lamb shank for a main course, which was simply superb. All this was followed by her manically devouring the chocolate challenge which was pleasure personified. The two, very different (in more ways than one) love birds had just the best time and, more importantly for her, not a single prying eye, dragon or otherwise, spotted them on their illicit evening out.

20 THE SORCERER'S APP... FRIEND

Thick, dark charcoal dissolved into the swirling, steamy water. A worn metal spoon that had seen better days pushed the drink around the mug at speed, creating a raging whirlpool at its centre. Beverage created, Tank tossed the dirty spoon into the sink where it rattled against half a dozen others just like it, grabbed both mugs and headed towards the very back of the workshop, where Gee Tee had ensconced himself all morning... up to goodness knows what. Tank knew better than to disrupt the master mantra maker without good reason when things were like this. But lunch had come around and so he figured a good time for them both to have a break, hence the steaming hot offering he held in his hands. Weaving in and out of the huge bookcases, he slipped through the gap in the front desk and stealthily made his way into the workshop. After five minutes of standing very still, smouldering with impatience, the old shopkeeper closed the book he'd been immersed in.

Placing the mug on the desk, Tank slid into the nearest oversized chair, as his employer took a giant slurp of his drink. Knowing better than to jump in, the youngster waited, his patience bristling, for the old dragon to open the conversation.

"I think I may have something."

Puzzled, the former apprentice racked his brains, trying to work out just what the master mantra maker was referring to. Squinting, studying Tank from just out of reach, the old dragon continued where he had left off.

"Your friend... Flash!"

"What about him?" asked Tank, bewildered.

"His condition... I think I understand a little more about it."

Putting down his mug, Tank scooted his chair across the grubby floor, ending up right next to the old dragon.

"You have a cure?"

"No... listen! I didn't say I had a cure, or even that his condition could be alleviated, what I said was that I know a little more about it."

Tank nodded.

"So?"

"The naga poison used on him is a combination of toxins... one part venomous sea snake, one part lion fish, which used in conjunction with the magical power of the mantra I employed to save his life, locked his DNA into place. I think that now I know the type of toxin used, it may be possible to follow the trail back and work out which of his building blocks was affected first. If we can do that and find out where the reaction started, it just may be possible to undo it. And I must stress the 'MAY' part of what I've just said."

"Can I tell him?"

"I don't really know how to answer that app... Tank. Only you can decide. I don't know if we can find a cure or even, if we can, how long it might take. Years or even decades could be a real possibility."

Tank's forehead creased as he thought about his friend's situation. Would it be wrong to get the ex-Crimson Guard's hopes up? How would he feel in those circumstances? Would he want to be told, or would he rather be blissfully unaware of what others were doing on his behalf?

Gee Tee started rummaging around in one of the few remaining filing cabinets, looking for what, only he knew. When his giant head popped up, Tank cleared his throat and promptly announced,

"I can't really decide what to do. I need to give it some more consideration."

Not knowing what to expect from the old shopkeeper, he watched as the master mantra maker pushed his huge square glasses right to the top of his nose and turned to face his friend. A realisation struck the old dragon like a wrecking ball demolishing a building. He now thought of Tank as his friend rather than his employee or apprentice. This was most certainly something he was going to have to give more consideration to.

"I'm glad to hear that, youngster! I think it's the right thing to do. Perhaps in time the solution, or at least another option, might present itself."

Tank nodded.

"Thanks for all the efforts on Flash's behalf... I know he'd appreciate what you're doing, just as I do."

Shuffling over, his long spindly tail dragging across the floor behind him, Gee Tee very gently, and very surprisingly, wrapped his wing around the young rugby playing dragon's massive shoulders (something that had never happened before).

"We need to work together, and give all that we have. My experience is screaming at me that we're reaching a crossroads. Not just us, or your friends, but the dragon race as a whole. Every molecule of my prehistoric blood is shrieking out at me... that the time is fast approaching. You and I, your friends as well, will all have a part to play I'm sure but... we must be ready!"

Gazing up along the shopkeeper's jaw, past his square glasses and into his steely, determined eyes, Tank asked,

"What is it we have to be ready for? And how exactly do we proceed?"

"We must be prepared, as well as we can be, anyway. Trying to rid your friend of his condition would be a good start. Apart from that... well I think we need to research the nagas as much as possible to see if we can find some way to negate the masking field they use to blend in with the humans... their equivalent of the mantras we use. This must become a priority... don't ask me why, but it might well be the key. Also, we need to find a way to disperse whatever we come up with... globally."

Tank thought hard about everything he'd just heard.

"What can I do to help?"

"Brush up on the nagas... anything you can find, anything you can think of, to discover more. You could ask Flash if he can get you access to the king's private library."

"I'll do that when I speak to him next. In the meantime I think I know where to start," and with that Tank wandered off out of the workshop and headed into the deepest, darkest recesses of the Mantra Emporium, slurping on his mug of by now lukewarm charcoal.

Sweat poured down his back and legs as he trudged off the pitch. It had been one of the toughest sessions he'd ever been to. Forty minutes of full-on fitness work followed by twenty minutes of basic skills, in groups of different activities, topped off by a high intensity game. Very much looking forward to a cold drink in the bar, stuffing his stick bag in his car, he grabbed his wallet, watch and phone and headed into the clubhouse. As he jogged across the final part of the car park, his legs started to suffer from that wobbly feeling they only got at certain times. At first he thought it was from the training and maybe part of it was, but as he walked through the double glass doors it became blatantly obvious to him that the feeling was much more than that. Opening the internal door to the bar and stepping through, his fingers tingled, his stomach turned into a butterfly farm and he felt so giddy he thought he might actually faint.

She was there waiting for him on the other side of the deserted bar. Not only that, but a steaming cold pint of diet Pepsi sat on top of the surface in front of her, just waiting to be drunk. Wandering up, red faced and sweaty from his workout, he surprised even himself as he leant across and gave her a full-on kiss on the lips. The smile on her face was sunlight streaming through the clouds on a rainy day. Sliding the drink across in his direction, Janice whispered,

"Have a drink, you look shattered."

Not needing a second invitation, Peter guzzled nearly half of it in one go, only just managing to avoid swallowing the two icebergs that bobbled about inside it.

"Thanks," he sighed. "That hit exactly the right spot."

"Good," she replied. "How are you?"

"Great thanks, but a bit busy at work. Hockey training was fab, if not a little tiring..."

Peter's mouth waffled on, pretty much without his brain, as he gazed across the shiny bar top into Janice's beautiful face. All he could think was how perfect she looked. Suddenly the gorgeous face he'd been lost in became... expectant. It was then that he realised he'd stopped talking and was now just staring, his mouth agape.

"Sorry," was all that he could stutter.

"That's okay," she assured. "Do you fancy going out again?"

"I'd really like that," he just about managed to reply, as the place started filling up.

"I'll catch up with you later," she said, giving him a seductive wink before turning to serve one of the other hockey players.

Resting on the bar, pleased as punch, that warm fuzzy feeling washed over him, making him feel like he'd never felt before. Lost, contented... just happy.

'I really must do some research on these... feelings,' he vowed. 'But who to ask?' Richie would be a little inappropriate given that she'd just finished her relationship with Tim. Tank, again, would be the wrong person to speak to... Flash? Gee Tee? Flash, given what he'd said to Richie, probably wasn't the right individual either, but Gee Tee... There was a thought. Always insightful, the more Peter thought about it, the more he really wanted to hear the old shopkeeper's views on the subject; he would have to make sure Tank was nowhere to be seen though.

A hand on his shoulder brought him back to the present.

"Hi Pete. How's it going?"

"Hi Andy. Uhhh... fine thanks."

"Game on Saturday against Hamble. You okay to play?"

"Sure," he replied.

"Good... see you at 1.30pm. Sorry, gotta dash... date with a lacrosse player," and with that he turned and disappeared into the throng of people now crowding into the bar.

As his captain disappeared, he spotted the familiar hulking frame of Tank heading his way... it was difficult not to.

"Evening," pitched in his friend, a rosy red bruise the colour of an apple spilling across his chin.

"How you doing, big fella?" he replied, attempting something different.

Tank raised his eyebrows. Peter got the message.

"Training any good?" the hockey player asked.

"Not bad," Tank answered. "We're playing much more like a team now... just a shame we're so far into the season. Still, there are at least a few festivals on the horizon."

And so the evening progressed, the former apprentice talking passionately and knowledgeably about rugby, Peter occasionally chipping in with his opinion on hockey, life and the universe. Eventually the two friends were the last remaining customers. Peter feigned tiredness, leaving many awkward pauses in the conversation in the hope that Tank would take the hint and head home, leaving him to talk to Janice alone. However, his huge friend had other ideas and remained seated, nursing the last few drops of his drink... almost determined to make life as difficult as possible.

Having collected all the other empty glasses, Janice came sweeping around the nearby tables and arrived at theirs. Without a second thought she did something that nearly made Tank's eyeballs pop out and roll across the sticky carpet. Plonking herself smack down in Peter's lap, nearly causing him to choke on the ice left in his drink, she

417

wrapped her arms around his neck and kissed him delicately on the cheek.

"So, what are we going to do... tomorrow night?" she asked, hoping he would be free then.

"Weeelllll..." he replied, studiously avoiding Tank's piercing gaze. Before he had a chance to reply, the beautiful young bar worker jumped in.

"What about if you came round to mine and I cooked us a really nice meal? We could watch a film afterwards."

As he nodded his agreement, Tank looked as though he might explode.

"Well, that's settled then," announced Janice, leaping to her feet. "Half seven at mine... just bring yourself." And with that, she scooted off towards the bar, leaving the two friends all alone. To say there was an awkward silence was something of an understatement.

Peter gazed at the table, the floor, his shoes... out of the window. In the end he gave in.

"I know, I know. Please don't say it."

As it turned out, Tank didn't have to say anything... his look alone conveyed it all.

Another awkward silence ensued, before the strapping rugby playing dragon stood, swallowed the remainder of his drink and put a hand on his friend's shoulder.

"Just think about what you're doing, Pete. Remember what happened to Richie. No good can come of all this. I think you know that."

With that, Tank bade his friend farewell and left the building. Peter threw back the last of his drink, got up and returned both empty glasses. Janice popped up from behind the bar, gave him one last kiss and said she would see him tomorrow. With his friend's words ringing in his ears and the taste of Janice's kiss still caressing his lips, he made his way across the dark, deserted car park. Blissfully unaware of the drive home, it was only once he'd showered and was tucked up in bed that he realised exactly how he felt. Despite his pal's warnings, he was ecstatic, feeling as though he were flying with the scorching sun beating down on his natural prehistoric frame, like he'd just scored the winning goal in an important hockey match, like the Warriors had just won the Global Cup. Exhausted from training, his eyes fluttered briefly, before sleep overwhelmed him.

21 GREAT MINDS THINK... ALOUD!

Spitting rivers of molten lava meandered down the outside
of the white, gold-flecked, marble pillars. Occasionally the
brilliant red and orange molten magma would crackle and
hiss, all the while throwing out tiny droplets onto
passersby, or the intricately designed floor. Depicting one
of the most significant moments not just in dragon history,
but in the past full stop, the beautifully crafted solid rock
floor was the bedrock of the most important council
chamber on earth. Dragons depicted in all shades of green,
blue, red and purple stood side by side with the
Manticores, shimmering in their differing shades of white,
complementing the Basilisks' dark, glistening scales,
looking almost neutral about everything that was going on.
Was that how things had really been, or had the artisan
who'd crafted and designed the amazing floor applied
some sort of creative licence? Behind the Basilisks, the
Heretics of Antar could just be seen. 'Seething' was the
only word to describe their expressions, which could just
be made out beneath the colourful hoods that adorned
their heads. However, all that was just background. What
really caught the eye in the scene, especially from
somewhere up above in the guarded cavern that formed
the room, were the figures at the centre, looking majestic,
dignified, regal and... just plain important! The Hydra
Queen herself shone from the water dripping off her,
grasping a document in her hand. Although in the carving
on the floor the record was blank, it was taken for granted
that it was the prophecy agreement. Beside her, looking
very much like a warrior, muscles gleaming, barely clothed,
cloak billowing behind him, staff in hand, Artorius the
Seer stood, overseeing the single most important gathering
of races the world had ever seen. Rumour had it that the
carving had taken nearly thirty years to complete, and that
blood from the different races featured had been used for

the dye that coloured the carving, but it had been done so far in the past, nobody actually knew for certain. It was some floor, that was for sure!

Even without the carving, the room would still have been one of the grandest on the planet. Large, silver, double doors guarded the entrance, delicately designed with images of a nursery ring long in the past, a clear reference to just how much dragons value and respect their young, and how they were as sacred then as they are now.

Hanging across one continuous wall a mosaic, made from dragon scales of all things, depicted a scene familiar to all the council members. A human, neither male nor female, was standing, weapon... maybe a sword or a dagger... in hand, fighting off an unseen enemy, protecting and saving lots and lots of dragons. Mesmerising in detail, it was easy to get sucked in and stare at the work of art for many minutes at a time. Significantly, some of the black scales that had been used to create the effect of the unseen enemy were missing; only a handful, and you'd have to look very closely to notice, which it seemed nobody had.

Rip-roaring fires blazed away in the midst of a gigantic, grey, granite table in the shape of a trident. The table must have been three metres high, with comfy oversized dragon chairs littered along each side of the fork of the trident. At the very end of the shaft, a raised throne made of gold and dotted with every kind of precious gem you could imagine, overlooked everything. Laid out for the dragon councillors who were expected at any minute, the table was scattered with tall vases, filled to the brim with sticks of every conceivable flavour of charcoal, the size of a man's arm. Over the sizzling fires, succulent meat slowly turned on ancient spits, brightly burning chunks of charcoal embedded in each animal. So much care had been taken with their preparation that they could almost be described as works of art, rather than the pre-meeting feast. Gleaming silver plates the size of a car's bonnet were piled high with freshly multi-coloured, charcoal infused, baked bread, chocolate and charcoal pancakes, and of course the king's favourite... doughnuts with a jam and charcoal centre. What little room remained on the actual table itself was taken up by tall, silver flagons of what could only be described as a kind of carbonated metholated spirits... a dragon's drink fit for a king.

Grand and important as any currently in existence, two important features of the room still need to be mentioned. A giant gold coloured abacus, the length and size of a double decker bus, sat along the far wall, its rails made from pure silver, currently reflecting the light from the crackling fires around the cavernous room to great effect. Attached to the rails were balls the size of footballs, crimson in colour, twenty-five in all, one for each of the councillors and the king. Once the council was in session, each ball could be linked to a particular councillor's mind anonymously so that nobody knew who voted which way on an individual motion. Balls were allocated randomly each time telepathically, because the core of each was made from pure laminium. This process had been used for centuries because it was seen to be the fairest, and made sure everything was above board, so to speak. Stunning in its complexity, the whole abacus looked magnificent against the backdrop of the rest of the room.

Finally, one last feature needs a mention, if indeed it could even be regarded as that. A bizarre looking darkened corner of the room, as far away from the table and entrance as possible, had been given over to something far more... chilly. 'Hot' was the best way to describe the chamber in a single word (as that's how dragons like it... the hotter the better), and with lava spitting from pillars all around and the heat from the roaring fires, the large room was scorching... apart from this one corner. Tucked away in this section of the wall, deadly icicles draped down from rustic wooden shelves a fifty centimetres deep and twenty metres high. Individual items could just be made out through the shimmering blue glow that ensconced it all. If you were to look carefully, there were daggers, bows and sets of dragon armour, all carefully laid out. There was even an *alea* that was an exact match to the one Peter and Richie currently both wore. Tucked back against a darkened side wall, about half way up the shelf, almost totally out of sight, sat a black silk bag, containing a dozen tiny, matte black scales... Troydenn's scales from when George incapacitated him during their fight long ago in the city of Salisbridge. A much more valuable prize it would be hard to imagine.

Each shelf was bursting with 'dark' and 'light' outlawed items from ages and wars long since past, protected by the most powerful of mantras, so much so that even the king, should he have wished to, would not have been able to retrieve said items. This cold corner was always avoided by the councillors, well... by almost every one. On very rare occasions, Rosebloom would casually stroll this way, deep in thought about some motion or another. He was the only one that ever ventured near that cold, dark and dangerous part of the room.

With a chilly rush of air and a shudder, the large, silver, double doors slowly opened to reveal a solemn looking line of dragons. Slowly, with the king at its head, the procession made its way into the cavernous room and once the doors closed firmly behind them, the dragons broke off to make their way to the seats they normally occupied, with the monarch giving one powerful flap of his wings, landing perfectly upon his raised throne.

With the sounds of crackling fires, the sizzling fat from the spit roasted meat dripping onto the floor and the molten magma splashing off the pillars for company, the head of state stood and cleared his throat, before uttering the words that have been used to get dragon council meetings started for centuries...

"Before we talk, argue, discuss and chat,
First we must consume, eat and get fat.

Once full to the brim with food,
Our minds and bodies will have attained the right mood.
Thinking and decision making will be right,
And can go on well into the night.
Let the feast begin..."

Well over four hours, that's how long the banquet lasted, with just about everything being consumed. By the end, only a few solitary crumbs of charcoal lay scattered across the floor. As well as gorging themselves, a few of the dragons, mainly the younger ones (still hundreds of years old) wing wrestled each other, faced off in a fire breathing contest, all trying to outdo each other with the latest grooming ideas. Some had intricate tattoos, others had scales painted different colours to form a much bigger and brighter pattern. Rosebloom tried to show off his 'hair', but most of the other councillors just poked fun, thinking this a step too far on the grooming scale. This was the informal part of the process, designed so that those attending could let off steam before they all got down to the business of governing.

Of course, the king was above all this... frivolity. Well, mostly. A small part of him would like to have taken part and he could remember a time when not only would he have joined in, but would almost certainly have been the ringleader... organising crazy competitions, egging on other dragons in stupid stunts... The wildest thing he could remember doing was getting nearly all the other councillors at the time to agree to play a game of... chase! Instead of the chaser having to touch the other dragons to catch them, all he had to do was hit them with a blast of fire from his mouth. The king at the time and a few of the more mature councillors had looked on in disbelief, right in this very room, as those of their kind circled, dived and barrel-rolled, crouched behind the table, hid amongst the tapestries, blowing fire across the room. Of course the whole thing had ended in disaster, pretty much as those who hadn't participated had predicted. In an effort to get away from a dragon chasing him, one councillor dropped down from the roof, as fast as he dared, turned sharply and sped behind the mosaic of scales, glancing over his shoulder to check if his pursuer was still there. He was, and the dragon in front, watching the jet of flame close in on him, panicked, attempted a really tight turn, too tight in fact, and... BAM!... ended up crashing into the mantra protected, ice covered bookshelf. The noise had been earth shattering, not just the sound of the collision, but the blood curdling scream the councillor let out. Try as he might, he would never forget the wickedly chilling sounds from that day. He and a lot of the others learnt a valuable lesson, one of the reasons that he sat back now and let those in front of him get on with things. Plus, council protocol dictated that he should remain aloof and keep his distance, something that as time had gone by, he was happier to do.

But now the feast had come to an end, it was time to get down to the serious business of running the planet. Picking up two of the silver plates in front of him, the king used the full force of his massive limbs to crash them together. Deafening, the clamour bounced off the walls inside the chamber for much longer than its occupants were comfortable with. When all the dragons had stopped stock still, the ruler spoke with all the authority that befitted his position.

"The time for merriment is over. Please be seated."

Instantly the atmosphere changed to one of seriousness, as each councillor took their place at the trident shaped table, all alert, focused and ready to begin. Slowly at first, the matters at hand came and went, as was the dragon norm, starting with the smaller issues of the day, with the much more important topics being saved until last, the theory being that the council would sit until everything was sorted, however long that might be. By having the small matters first, it meant that things wouldn't be rushed. The record for a council sitting currently stood at six days, nine and a half hours, a meeting that had taken place during World War Two, interestingly featuring the escape of two high profile dragon detainees.

Slowly and diligently, the councillors discussed subjects such as the quality of charcoal being provided to under five dragonlings in the nursery rings; whether or not to grant a licence to a dragon entrepreneur for blanket mobile phone coverage below ground, encompassing the entire dragon domain; the enterprise to drill for oil in the Gulf of Mexico which had punctured the subterranean membrane that separates the human/dragon world; and, the most bizarre so far, the problems of charcoal bubblegum! The monarch, up to now, had barely said a word. It was of course his right, to let the others get on with it, but to interrupt and offer his opinion when and where he thought needed. Biding his time, he was saving his influence and energy for the right battles, in the hope that he could win the most important ones. Listening to how the latest craze amongst young dragons was gum, not just any gum, but charcoal bubble gum, you wouldn't have thought this was a subject that would appear before them, but you see... there were problems. The first was the dragonlings chewing while at the same time superheating the gum with their breath. It was all well and good until a bubble was blown, and then the gum exploded across their entire jaw and face, turning into a sort of glue, setting almost immediately, hospitalising many because it blocked their nostrils and jaws simultaneously. Not only that, but they had been blowing bubbles with the gum and then opening their mouths. Filled with superheated air, the gum acted in the same way as a balloon and drifted up into the air. Huge swathes of some dragon cities were dotted with large blobs of sticky gum, and it looked horrendous. There were a lot of unhappy dragons, calling it a disgrace and saying that something like this wouldn't have happened in their day.

Sitting and pretending to listen, the king's mind was on

other matters... primarily Antarctica. Try as he might, he found it hard to piece things together from all he knew, from what Flash had told him, and his other sources. If everything that he'd heard was true, and he had no reason to suspect it wasn't, the one thing which was blatantly obvious was that a traitor, or traitors, existed somewhere close to him, either in the council or one of the other related departments, maybe even in the King's or Crimson Guards... heaven forbid! So, for now, he was isolated. Having no idea who to trust, he felt lonely, tired and racked with guilt... guilt about his friend, the dragon he loved like a brother, being trapped in what could only be described as dragon hell, and for all this time too. All he wished to do was call the dragon world to arms and mount a rescue. But it just wasn't possible... not at the moment.

As his thoughts continued on the same line, the bubble gum debate came to its conclusion around the table in front of him. Suspicious for a while, he hadn't been sure exactly what he'd been sceptical about. Certainly he'd lost some of the power and influence he'd once wielded as king, but for as long as he'd been part of the council there had always been alliances of one sort or another and he'd just assumed that, once again, different friendships and associations had been forged and would at some point split and be reformed all over again. But something was unusual in the council these days... and that worried him beyond belief.

And then there was his ring. For as long as he'd had it (since his coronation), he couldn't decide whether it was a blessing or a curse. Every dragon that had ever lived would have wanted that precious band... well, who wouldn't? It was the source of an almost limitless supply of magical energy... mana... call it what you will. But there was more to it than that. It had a will of its own. It could call to you, act, refuse to act... and just sometimes it would be as though it were giving you a little nudge in the right direction. During council meetings over the last year or so, he'd considered that many of the votes had gone against his wishes, despite his hard work and belief that the decisions in question would go his way. During each of these votes, using the gigantic golden abacus that stood proudly off to his left, the ring had gone nothing short of berserk each time. Waves of spiky energy would wash over him, starting at his finger and racing through his body. It was overwhelming, and most of the time it was all he could do to stay conscious. But the odd thing was, it was only during these important verdicts... the ones he'd saved all his energy and influence for, those he considered he should have rightfully won. For the life of him he couldn't work out what the ring wanted, or was trying to tell him. The abacus was centuries old and was impossible to break, influence or corrupt... that was why it was used. But still, something wasn't right. All this left him with a bad feeling in his stomach. The last vote today was going to be all about Antarctica, and he hoped that no such repeat of the unusual voting patterns would happen on that one. This had been what he'd been saving himself for, and had spent the last week using his contacts, friends and allies on the council, in the hope of influencing the outcome of this vote. He knew he'd done enough, but he'd thought that on previous occasions when the outcome had gone against him. It had to work this time. It just had to.

After the bubblegum debacle, the meeting progressed a little faster, with the king only voicing his opinion on two occasions... the first when the subject of human/dragon relationships was brought to the fore by one of the councillors with regard to the punishments for committing such atrocities. Paying little attention, still mulling over everything in his mind, when the word 'Salisbridge' caught his attention, instantly he became alert, noting that the discussion had turned towards a young, rebellious dragon from that city, who had been apparently involved in a relationship with a human male. Having made it his business to know all about this, George instantly jumped into the conversation, startling almost all them, so quiet had he been previously, making it clear in no uncertain terms that the matter had been dealt with, that he knew for sure that the relationship had ended, the dragon in question had fully learned her lesson, that now was not really the time or place to debate the wider issue of mixed species relationships, and perhaps in the future at some point a committee of council members could be set up to look into it once again with a view to making a full report. This had the desired effect of placating the rest of the councillors, some of whom seemed very keen to discuss the young dragon from Salisbridge. Sensing some mischief making involved somewhere, the head of state returned to his quiet contemplation.

A few more dull issues passed, all of which, in the king's mind at least, took a ludicrous amount of time. It was then that one of the officials stood and addressed him directly. This was the second time the ruler had to voice his opinion, and in his mind he thought the two matters might well be connected, with a little more naughtiness on the cards.

The councillor asked the king about a dragon, formerly a Crimson Guard, who it was rumoured was working for him directly, but who had in fact suffered the worst fate possible... he was, as the councillor so delicately put it, "immutable and stuck in the form of a human... permanently!" Not so hushed whispers echoed around the chamber as this shocking news passed from one dragon to the next, with nearly all of them outraged at the king for employing such a damaged member of their race. Words such as "crossbreed", "mutant" and "monster", could all be heard over the crackle of the almost deceased fires. Barely restraining his temper, the sovereign leapt majestically off his throne, slamming down one of his giant fists on the solid, granite table.

"ENOUGH!" he roared, at the narrow minded beings before him. "The dragon in question is undoubtedly braver and more courageous than any in this room. To say that we all owe him a debt of gratitude is something of an understatement, and I WILL NOT allow the words that I've just heard whispered in such a cowardly fashion, to be associated with him. DO YOU ALL UNDERSTAND?"

A few of the councillors answered the king directly with a, "Yes," while others nodded, slightly ashamed, and one or two (Rosebloom came into this category) sneered and said nothing at all.

"Now," started the monarch, silently seething, "I think it's time to move on to the main reason for this meeting... the problems in Antarctica!"

Most in the room nodded in agreement, while just a few glanced at each other surreptitiously.

"Perhaps Councillor D'Zone would be kind enough to bring us all up to speed with developments before we debate how best to proceed."

"It would be an honour Your Majesty," stated Councillor D'Zone politely, rising from his chair and striding into the space beyond the tips of the trident shaped table, so that he could address everyone.

For the next half an hour or so, he recounted how two Antarctic expeditions of scientists, a month apart, studying global warming and the effect it was having there, had mysteriously gone missing. Also adding that a representative of the council had gone on his own to check things out after the second expedition had failed to report back, and that after he'd arrived at Antarctic Casey Station, a whole series of unexplained events had begun to unfold, including a huge amount of destruction, a missing scientist and two potential murders that were currently under investigation. Councillor D'Zone explained that there had been no sightings of the dragon representative, and that he'd not reported in at all.

Holding on to his stoic look throughout, knowing that he was the only one in the council chamber who knew what had really happened during Flash's trip to Antarctica,

George was determined to keep it that way, at least for the time being. For the ex-Crimson Guard's sake, and maybe even the domain as a whole, it was probably best for now if every councillor was told that the representative hadn't returned. If there was a traitor, and he was sure that was the case, lulling them into thinking that the agent, that is, Flash, hadn't reported back or even survived, might well buy him some well needed time to try and flush them out, although how he was going to do that, even he didn't know.

Wrapping up his update, the councillor stated that he thought unless the entire King's Guard was being deployed (something almost unthinkable and impractical as it was spread too thin as it was) it would be madness to send any more of their kind to Antarctica. It was just too dangerous without knowing exactly what they were dealing with. A close eye should be kept on developments in the human investigation that was underway, and a review of this should take place weekly.

All this sparked off a furious debate, led in the main by Rosebloom who advocated immediate intervention on a massive scale. Speaking passionately about the need to "find answers," to "get to the bottom of what had really happened," and to "finish the scientific work that was the original mission," with each hour that passed, the debate grew more and more rowdy as angry exchanges took place across the massive table. Fists were slammed, insults hurled, chests puffed out and of course flames were blown, each and every dragon there expending massive amounts of steam and heat. The grand old chamber hadn't seen anything like it in decades.

After close to ten hours on this subject alone, with all the dragons irritable, tired, and now starting to get hungry, the wording of the motion to be voted on had almost been agreed. From the king's perspective, it looked as though he had more than a good chance of getting the result he desired. Those who wanted to send a huge dragon task force to Antarctica had, it would seem, been too aggressive in their behaviour towards some of the councillors who were very much neutral in all of this, and if his experience and judgement were any guide, that would drive them to vote against such a force being dispatched. That, combined with the councillors he was sure he could trust to vote his way, would ultimately lead to the motion being overturned. But there was just a tiny, nagging doubt ringing out in the back of his mind.

Councillor Rosebloom stood and, with the agreement of all the dragons there, announced that, "the strongest possible force of dragons will be made ready and sent to Antarctica within one standard month." That would be the proposed motion, and with the golden abacus waiting, the dragons would now vote either in favour of the motion, or against it. The chamber fell deadly silent, with no sounds of fires crackling or smouldering; they'd long gone out and not even the slightest hint of flame dribbled from any of the dragon's noses or mouths. Most sat up straight in their ornate chairs, eyes closed, thinking about the subject, concentrating on linking telepathically with the abacus.

Watching on from his raised throne, the king felt a little tickle in his finger as he was just about to close his eyes. At first he thought he'd just imagined it, but then the tickle became a scratch. Trying hard to control his outward appearance, not wanting to give anything away, he sought to look inside himself in the hope that it was something easily explained. Almost immediately though, as he delved deep down, he became aware that once again it was the ring causing his... discomfort, his anxiety increasing in magnitude by the second. Controlling his breathing and focusing with all his might, he managed to ignore the waves of... not so much pain, but distraction, warning, strange thoughts, almost as if someone or something were screaming a message at him that he just simply could not understand. With what seemed like his last breath, he sent out his command to vote against the motion, after which he just slumped forward, head in hands, eyes closed, pretending to mimic the body language of the other councillors, as he fought inside for his sanity.

Moments later, it was over. Sweat pooled on the floor around his feet, because he'd given so much in his own personal fight.

With his wits about him once more, he sought to find out exactly what was going on. A few of the councillors were still sitting, head in hands, but many had got up and were chatting in groups with each other, something that tended to happen after the last vote. The dragons were a pragmatic race and with the ballot having taken place, they all realised there was nothing else they could do but get on with their normal business and just accept the outcome when it was announced, something that would happen very soon. Sitting back in his chair, trying to look composed and calm, but feeling anything but, the ruler strained his enhanced senses to the limit, trying to listen in on some of the many conversations going on around the room.

"...truly believe it's the right thing to do..." he heard from one corner, sounding very genuine.

"...costly gamble that could prove expensive both in financial and political terms..." growled another voice, just out of sight.

And then just as he was about to give up, he picked up on,

"...so, it's started. The beginning of the end. It was always about getting to this point. It's hard not to be sick and tired of all this... but not long now, not long at all."

It wasn't so much what had been said, although the king struggled to think of a context in which the words that he'd heard would be acceptable. But there was malice and contempt behind the statement that he'd stumbled upon. The threat wasn't even very thinly veiled, but that wasn't the worst part. Whoever had whispered those words (and they had been whispered so quietly that he couldn't identify who'd uttered them) had been very sure of the outcome of the vote they were now waiting to hear the result of. As far as the king was aware, the outcome was still unknown, making the whispered words all the more disconcerting.

A few minutes later, the last of the seated dragons stood, indicating that voting on the motion had finished. As one, all the councillors gathered together and stood in front of the abacus, the king included. It wouldn't be long now, he knew. As they all gazed up at one of the most celebrated relics from a bygone age, very slowly the balls started to move, one at a time at first, almost gathering a will of their own. Some slid across one way, only to falter and then return back to whence they came. It was a nerve-racking moment, especially for George who'd invested so much in the result. Briefly, and it was spectacularly short lived, the monarch thought he'd won. About two thirds of the balls had headed across to the left of the abacus, the 'against' side of the beautifully crafted relic, the amount almost perfectly coinciding with the figures he'd calculated in his head about who would vote which way, thus giving him victory. But in the blink of an eye, the crimson spheres changed, some moving one way, some the other, leaving the result in no doubt, but staggeringly different to the outcome the king had hoped for: an overwhelming majority in favour of sending a force to Antarctica. Still hoping for the balls to slide back his way, the ruler was devastated when terrific jets of flame erupted from almost every part of the abacus to signal the vote had been carried by fourteen votes to eleven. The gathered dragons were silent. This in itself was unusual, as normally there was a group celebrating success, slapping each other on the back or blowing flames halfway across the room. The king had seen enough. Now that the ballot had concluded there was nothing else he could do. With the meeting effectively over, the decision to send troops to Antarctica within the month already made, George, looking a million times more composed than he felt, strolled purposefully over to the huge, heavy doors, swung them back and strolled off in the direction of his private residence, all the time contemplating what had just happened and exactly what he was going to do next. It seemed time was now very much against him.

22 REGRETS 'R' US

As the full length cloak flapped against the heel of his boot, he decided that now was the time to pull the hood up over his face, concealing everything but the tips of his footwear. Darting out of the darkened alleyway, he silently crossed the deserted walkway, ducking into the shadows beneath the archway of the beautifully crafted bridge built from the surrounding rock, all the while looking out for a tail (not his... but someone following him). Under any other circumstances this would be a pointless exercise, as undoubtedly the dragons in the immediate vicinity would sense all the other beings around them, including him. This was where the cape came in, and not just any cloak... Ancient in design, its fibres were imbued with laminium and a very obscure mantra that allowed the power to be redirected and controlled in a very specific way. The mantle was a... CLOAK! Used to mask a user's very presence, the laminium blocked any telepathic search reaching out in its direction. Physically he could, of course, still be seen; masking that would have been all but impossible. No, this cloak shrouded the user's sense of being, so the only way for its wearer to be discovered, was for their physical form to be spotted. No dragon, or any other entity, would be able to sense the user once the cape was fully shrouding them. Armed with this knowledge, its current wearer leapt into the air, found the smallest of finger holds in the rock and scaled it until he reached the bridge above. Once there, he crawled unseen into the deepest shadow, checking for any and all pursuers... there were none. His mission required stealth, secrecy and a dogged determination. It was of the utmost importance.

Twenty minutes later, he breathed a sigh of relief. While he hadn't anywhere near reached his target, he had traversed what he considered the busiest area, the one in which he was most likely to be discovered. Leaning against the wall of an alcove between two dragon houses that looked as though they'd seen better days, he paused to catch his breath. Both walls had crumbled away and from the appearance of tiny flakes of colour, almost microscopic in size, these houses had once been brightly painted... many decades ago! It was the same story the dragon kingdom over, he thought. Much like the humans on the surface, those of his kind now seemed to have little regard for their surroundings and those of their neighbours. Once, long ago, it was possible to walk down streets and streets of colourfully decorated, immaculate dragon houses.

'Not now though,' he mused. Just as on the surface, things had changed, here more than in most parts of the clandestine dragon world. Times were tougher now, even for dragons. Much of it, he thought, rested with the current king. Would a new ruler change things for the better? Quite a lot of him thought the answer to that was YES! Soft, padding footsteps jolted him out of his reverie. Instinctively he flattened himself against the dark wall, just as a dragon wearing a flamboyant hip cloak ambled past. His wandering mind had nearly cost him dear. Silently cursing his lapse and doubling his focus, he set off for his intended target. The sooner he got there, the quicker he just might get some answers to the many questions that had been bugging him for some time.

Nearly an hour later he had his destination in sight. Once again he was concealed by shadows, this time from the furthest recesses of the roof of a small dragon dwelling. His focus, to be sure, was not what it should have been. So many things were going on, and here he was thinking how sad it was that the dragons living below him, and elsewhere in this particular part of London, lived in comparative destitution. Things were far worse than he'd feared and despite knowing that it wasn't really his job to do something about it, he vowed there and then that he would in fact put things right... and not at some far flung point in the future, but very, very soon!

With his head poking just over the edge of the roof, he surveyed the street below him, strategically planning how to reach his target unseen. An elderly male dragon limped along carrying a basket of washing down the garden path of a small dragon house two doors along from his goal.

'He doesn't look a threat... but you never know,' he thought. Once off the roof he would be out of the dragon's sight, but he had to cross a distance of nearly one hundred metres, he estimated, to get to the entrance unseen. A familiar feeling tickled his brain. Instantly he hugged the rooftop, just as two middle aged dragons wandered by below, engaged in casual chitchat about the next round of laminium ball matches. Again, he cursed. While the cloak concealed his very essence brilliantly, the downside of this was the mantra and the laminium in the fibres that in turn hindered his ability to sense other dragons. He felt almost... naked: much like Superman would feel without his powers, or a Jedi Knight without the Force. Steadying himself, he knew he was almost there, after three hours of skulking roof to roof, shadow to shadow. In mere seconds he'd know if all his efforts had been worthwhile.

As quiet as a mouse, he raised his head above the parapet and looked around in every direction. Apart from the elderly dragon now pegging out his washing, there appeared to be no one else around. Sensing it was now or never, he waited until the dragon had his back to him, and as soon as that happened... he pounced. Mirroring a huge graceful cat, he stretched out, bounded three steps, and hurled himself spectacularly off the crumbling roof he'd been hiding on. Mid leap, he threw his weight off to his right, finding himself spinning precariously. With the ground speeding up towards him, he tucked his head between his legs and threw everything he could into rolling left. Hitting the pathway hard, he rolled instantly, his shoulder taking the brunt of the landing. Ignoring the blistering pain from the impact, he rolled three more times before standing and sprinting across to the doorway that he was interested in. Standing against the familiar door in question, he closed his eyes and, with an iron will, commanded the energy required to stave off the pain in his shoulder. In the blink of an eye the blisteringly bad ache had dissipated and he turned his attention back to the door.

Gently he turned the squeaky metal handle and slipped inside. Cool air flooded over him as the familiar sight of bookshelf after bookshelf greeted him. How long had it been...? He tried hard to think. At first he thought it decades, but on reflection he realised it must have been well over a century since he'd last graced this truly magnificent shop. And a lot of it looked as though it hadn't been cleaned in all that time. Strolling softly through the maze of bookcases, careful not to disturb the piles of dusty tomes that littered the floor, he finally found himself at the very front.

'Oh how this brings back memories,' he thought to himself.

A harsh growl from somewhere below the counter nearly startled him back into his natural form.

"Most customers have the common courtesy to show their identities when they enter. You'd do well to take the hint, and the quicker the better if you know what's good for you."

Gee Tee's square spectacles popped up from below the counter, followed by the rest of his head and a ferocious snarl that would have seen almost any dragon proud, and certainly belied his age. Just then the workshop door opened as Tank flew round the corner, chest puffed out, magic crackling from his fingertips, ready to defend his friend and mentor. Standing side by side, Tank and Gee Tee stared intently at their unexpected hooded visitor, as the silence ratcheted up the tension in the room. Deep within the master mantra maker's mind, he was sifting through a list of offensive mantras that could be used as a last resort, while Tank on the other hand was wondering just how long was a reasonable amount of time before it was polite to hurl yourself at a potential enemy, when that particular thought was rendered redundant. Freckled hands, with immaculate nails and 'that ring' swept up and gently pulled down the hood to reveal... THE KING!

"Majesty!" blurted Tank, swiftly dropping to one knee.

"Hmmmmm," growled the old shopkeeper. "It's about time. How long has it been?"

Currently gazing at the floor, head bowed, the rugby player shuddered at the thought of what might happen next. He needn't have worried though, as the ruler let out a huge belly laugh that bore little relation to his actual human size.

"I was just pondering that very question on the way through that poor excuse of a maze you call your shop floor... Proprietor."

"And?" fielded Gee Tee, nonplussed.

"Well over a century by my reckoning."

Tank thought the tension had eased with the monarch's laugh, but hearing the two of them now, he wasn't at all sure, and until told to do so, he had no intention of getting up.

"One hundred and seven years, four months, two weeks, four days and ten hours... give or take," rolled off the old shopkeeper's tongue softly.

So softly in fact that it nearly brought tears to Tank's eyes. So that was it, he thought. The old dragon missed his friend, and felt... let down, lonely... lost. Now that the former apprentice thought about it, it explained so much, including the bad temperedness and tension between them on that fateful day at the king's private residence... things were becoming a little clearer, well... just maybe.

As shell shocked as the youngster on the floor in front of him, it wasn't often the king was lost for words... but this was most definitely one of those times.

"You thought I wouldn't remember? You're surprised that despite my age and senility, I still recall when you were last here... and how we parted."

For but a split second, George's eidetic memory flickered back to the past.

Scurrying along for all he was worth, he slid to a halt in front of the gorgeous new door and, thrusting the handle down with intent, set off at pace into the bowels of the shop, like a youngling with money to burn. Powered by excitement and THE most wonderful news, he felt fit to burst, desperately keen to tell the other of his two best friends. Catching his heel on a precariously stacked pile of books, he nearly stumbled, but righted himself by latching on to the fast approaching shop counter.

"Your haste and reckless abandon will be the death of you if you're not careful," drifted a velvety smooth voice from somewhere unseen off to the side.

Clad in a set of burnished leather armour, sweating buckets and panting profusely, the ex-knight of the realm turned to face his friend who'd just extricated himself from a mountainous array of tomes and magical artefacts, showering his assistant in all things supernatural as he did so.

"What is it I've told you about that... anyway?" he said, pointing and scowling simultaneously at the armour clad warrior in front of him.

"Don't be like that. I didn't have time to change."

"You couldn't spare two seconds?"

"What would I have done with my favourite set of armour? I'm not losing that, and besides... you don't really mind me coming to see you in this form. Do you?"

"Hmmm..." grumbled the master mantra maker, shooing the rest of his staff towards the back of the Emporium to get on with their assigned duties.

"You seem charged full of wonder this morning, youngster."

"And you seem as grumpy as ever. Burnt your egg sacks on the gas again?"

"No I haven't, thank you very much. And I told you that in the strictest of confidence."

"I know, I know. I'm only pulling your leg."

"Which one?" muttered Gee Tee, looking down curiously.

"Never mind," replied George, "never mind."

"So what brings you here today... councillor?"

Unable to contain everything bottled up inside him any longer, he just blurted it out.

"They've voted me to be the next king. I'm the new ruling monarch. How fantastic is that?"

"They've done what?"

"I'm the new head of state," announced George, grinning from ear to ear.

"Why would they vote a dragon as inexperienced as you to be our next leader, I wonder?"

Smile wiped instantly away, George's look immediately mirrored that of the old shopkeeper, only slightly less prehistoric.

"I'm fully capable of stepping up and doing the job."

"I never said you weren't!"

"So what... you're jealous then, is that it?"

Newly crowned or not, he should have known better than to spout those words to the very proud being before him, and regretted them the instant they left his mouth.

"You should leave NOW... Your Majesty," the shopkeeper uttered, laden with sarcasm.

"I... I... I... I didn't... I didn't mean it!"

"OUT! And don't come back!"

"I need to return some of the magical items that you've loaned me. If I don't do it tomorrow, then I might not be able to return them for quite some time."

"You know precisely where you can stick them... RIGHT UP YOUR ROYAL..."

Never having seen the master mantra maker so angry, sensing he should leave, determined to come back and make amends at the earliest available opportunity, George, the dragon domain's brand spanking new king, turned on his heels and left without another word. That was over one hundred years ago, or more accurately, one hundred and seven years, four months, two weeks and four days.

If Tank hadn't been looking at the floor... he would

have seen the king's perfectly formed, fake Adam's apple jump upwards as he swallowed, overcome by this unexpected turn of events. For the strapping great rugby playing dragon, it had got to the point where he now wished the ground would open up and swallow him whole, feeling like such a poignant and personal moment that he really shouldn't be there. Worse still, perhaps the king and Gee Tee had actually forgotten he was still present. Abruptly he cringed with embarrassment as his legs, sore from rugby training last night, twinged just a little.

"What would you have had me do? Oh well, thank you very much for the nice offer councillors, but I don't really think I want to be king... maybe next time...! Is that it? Is that what you'd have wanted...? IS IT?"

Listening to the words, Tank thought the sentiment and meaning behind them would cut him like a knife, crush him like a trash compactor. But that was nothing compared with the excruciating silence that followed. All he wanted to do was rip his ears off and cast a shredding mantra on them. Lasting over a minute, but feeling more like years to the young dragon, the standoff gave him time to think about everything... Peter, Richie, laminium ball and of course... RUGBY!

Finally, the silence was broken as George stroked his top lip, unable to look the old shopkeeper directly in the eye.

"I don't really know what to say. What could possibly make up for all the hurt I've caused you?"

There was a pause, during which Tank, still unable to see either of them, thought the king might actually turn around and leave, but it was really just the monarch gathering his thoughts, searching inside for the truth and how he felt about everything that had happened since he'd been chosen to become leader of the dragon world.

Intelligence, investigations and dubious magical practices subsequently revealed that it had all started around the turn of the twentieth century. Shady alliances, powerful promises and whispers of a new dawn forged a secret dragon sect over the coming years. A decade after its inception, the reigning dragon king unexpectedly died. With peace having prevailed for so long, there was no reason to suspect foul play and so he was, without an autopsy, returned to the earth, via the very private Royal Bereavement Grotto. During the days that followed, councillors argued and bickered, squabbled and shouted, two sides equally matched, unable to find a way ahead, lost in stalemate. After weeks of wrangling, a compromise was found, using an archaic rule of law, long since forgotten. Without his knowledge, George was elected king, both forces confident of bending him to their will. With little choice but to consent, and only able to trust Fredric, he took up the position and over the next two decades, dismantled the sect piece by piece, Fredric and the Crimson Guards instrumental in doing so. Although successful, it did prove to be too little, too late. During the summer of 1914, Archduke Franz Ferdinand (a dragon), heir to the Austrian-Hungarian throne, was murdered by a member of the black hand, a Serbian nationalist secret society, but in reality, the alias by which the dragon sect was known on the surface. This one key event led to the start of World War One, and one of the biggest tragedies the planet has ever seen.

"I can't say I expected to be chosen. Looking back now, I suppose it was obvious. I was the best outcome to both parties, with both thinking they would be able to mould me, and I suppose indirectly do their bidding. They were of course wrong... I am, after all, my own dragon... always have been, always will be. But to be chosen was such a surprise. And once I agreed, not that there was ever really a choice, it was just a whirlwind, one that I became embroiled in, one that refused to let me go, and one I suppose I did my best to stay caught up in for a very long time, much to the detriment of everything else around me. I know better now, of course. I know that what I had back then was much more valuable than I realised at the time. I also know that for about the only time in my life, I'd found a true measure of happiness. Being a knight, being on the council and having friends that I could count on, no matter what... I fail to see, even now, what could be better than that."

Looking up at the old shopkeeper, the king was met with a rather stoic, prehistoric face, his words seemingly having had no impact whatsoever. Feeling a little like he'd taken the top off a badly shaken bottle of fizzy drink, and that it was all likely to come out now, one way or the other... he ploughed on.

"Even once I realised... and it took me a long time... how was I supposed to make amends? I didn't think I could, even with everything in the kingdom at my disposal. You'd already sorted out the trouble with Rosebloom without any help from me."

The frown on Gee Tee's face shifted for just a split second, before returning with interest, but George knew he'd surprised his old friend.

"Did you really think I didn't know? To this day, the dragons of the King's Guard try and change their shift patterns, they barter, deal and cajole, all to be on duty and in the squad that is tasked with coming down here when Rosebloom issues another one of his searches. You, my friend, are something of a... legend. How Rosebloom doesn't know after all this time is quite beyond me. Is there anything you wish to tell me?"

To say this was something of a turnaround was an understatement. Studying his friend, the ruler was well aware that the master mantra maker could now not look him in the eye.

"You do realise casting any sort of mantra on another dragon without their knowledge, in particular a councillor, during peacetime, is a capital offence? The punishment, if proved, would be severe."

"If it could be proved, the sentence would probably be worth it," whispered Gee Tee under his breath, the king choosing to ignore him.

"So, you'd sorted out your own problem; what else could I do? Nothing, really. Like you, I'm almost certainly too proud for my own good at times... something that in this case has definitely let me down, and may have cost me one of my dearest friends, although I hope not. But I have changed, and with experience I now know that I would have done things very differently, but then I suppose we all would. I can only really say that I am sorry, and for what it's worth... I mean it with every atom in my body. Not just for treating you badly, but for being too proud and for taking too long to try and atone for my error. Knowing you as well as I do, I find it unlikely that you'll accept my apology, but I hope in some small way you can realise that it isn't just you that's lost out in all of this, and that I have suffered, maybe not alongside you, but as well as you. While this wasn't the reason I came here today, I have to say it feels something of a relief to get this off my chest, and wish now more than ever that I'd done it a long time ago."

Poking his square spectacles as far up his nose as they'd go, the old shopkeeper stared intently at the king.

"You always were very eloquent with your words, but back then you tended to back them up with your actions."

"Allow me a little time and I'll see what I can do," he shot back.

Nodding slightly, the master mantra maker's reply was abruptly interrupted by the squeaky sound of the shop's door handle. Both had exactly the same thought, at exactly the same time. The moment had come to fight, the king thought, assuming he'd been followed. With Tank still below the shop counter, coming to terms with everything that was going on, Gee Tee stood poised, the deadliest of mantras ready to be unleashed. With quiet footsteps getting ever closer, it was down to him to act.

"STOP!" shouted Tank, bouncing up onto two feet, as the sovereign and his dragon employer both shot him their worst scowls.

"NO... you don't understand," he pleaded. "It's only..."

Reaching the end of the nearest mighty bookcase, the footsteps walked around the corner, revealing... PETER! It was hard to know who was more surprised. The sight that greeted the hockey player was of the king and Gee Tee, almost ready for battle, with Tank standing in front of them, waving his hands frantically. He had no idea what to make of any of it. Before he knew it, the sovereign had swept him up in a great big bear hug, his expression now one of utter excitement.

"Peter, my boy, it's great to see you."

"You too," stuttered Peter. "What's going on?"

"Well," ventured Gee Tee, his wings crossed, still wearing a slight frown, "you were about half a second away from being burnt to a crisp."

"WHAT!!!" he exclaimed, stepping back out of the king's clutches.

"He's exaggerating," announced George with a smile, giving the youngster a playful slap on the shoulder for good measure.

Out of the corner of his eye, Peter caught the expression on Tank's face, and the slight shake of the head that went with it. Only then did he realise the seriousness of the situation.

"Is there something going on that I need to know?"

"It's my fault," stated the king. "I'm on edge, a little too much, truth be told. I've sneaked over here to ask for Gee Tee's assistance, but now that you're here, perhaps you can all help. I don't know who else to trust, and with the exception of Flash, I've no one else to turn to. This, I believe, is of the utmost importance."

Peter and Tank stood aghast but ready to do anything, while the old shopkeeper just rolled his eyes, like the king's request was almost an everyday occurrence.

With the front door to the shop now securely bolted, the four of them sat together in the workshop, sipping hot charcoal with melted marshmallows swirling dangerously on the surface.

"Ahhhh... just being here with the three of you feels so... liberating," exhaled the monarch.

"Your Maj..." started Tank, before getting the royal 'look' from the king. Swiftly he changed tack.

"George," he began again, sheepishly. "We're desperate to help, and I'm pretty sure I speak for all of us," he said, giving the old shopkeeper his sternest look, something that was pretty much ignored. "We'd do anything to assist, even... lay down our lives if need be. But I can't imagine what could be so important, and how we can be of service, so perhaps you could fill us in, as I for one can't wait to find out."

With the master mantra maker studying the cloak held precariously in place by the golden clasp across his chest, the king looked up from the mesmerising circular motion of his drink.

"It's been going on for some time now. So long, I can't even remember when it started. But I can't believe for one minute that it's a coincidence. And if I'm to assume that, then the only logical conclusion is that there's foul play of some sort involved, at the highest level. And that's where I need your help."

During the next half hour the king explained about the crucial council ballots he'd been losing, how the losses were peculiar because the votes he'd been promised always seemed to indicate that things would go his way... most of the time they did, but on the major issues it was always the same. Moving forward by explaining how he felt that his primary opposition, Rosebloom and his cohorts were always particularly smug on these occasions, and never especially bothered when the much smaller, less important ones didn't go their way. He expanded in detail on exactly how the council chamber itself was shielded with some of the oldest, most powerful and incorruptible mantras ever to have been cast, and just how the abacus had been forged by dragon masters of old, and was impossible to either fool, distort or damage. Only the council members and the dragons who worked in and around the chamber were allowed into the actual room itself, with those same mantras also scanning every being for anything potentially dangerous and/or magical, every time they went in or out. And then the matter of the ring! How, on every single occasion that one of these important votes had gone what he considered... the wrong way, the enigmatic band had, well... played up, overwhelmed him almost to the point of passing out, sending a warning of some sort, about what... who knows? But urging caution nevertheless. The three of them listened intently... well, you would, wouldn't you? After all, it was the king. And he was talking about potential traitors, not just to him, but to the whole dragon domain. This was SERIOUS!!!

Attentive changed to sombre once he'd finished, the room becoming shrouded in silence, even the opinionated shopkeeper keeping his counsel.

A weight clearly lifted, the monarch looked like a small child in his human form, enveloped in one of the oversized chairs. Not seeming to mind though, none of the others felt brave enough to point it out.

It was Tank who broke the silence which had almost, but not quite, become uncomfortable.

"From what you've said, the whole process sounds impossible to comprehend. With all the safeguards in place... I just don't see how anything could affect what's going on."

A tiny trickle of flame shot out of Gee Tee's nose as the old shopkeeper let out a snort of derision.

"Could it just be coincidence, or could the councillors whose votes were promised to you have changed their minds or misled you? Or maybe they are in fact in league with Rosebloom and his mates?" continued Tank.

Rubbing his long, straggly, grey hair against the back of the chair, about halfway down, the king thought about the question before answering.

"I don't believe either is a possibility. If the councillors are already on Rosebloom's side, then we're doomed... quite literally. They could easily replace me on a trumped up charge and nothing would be seen or heard from me again... that's how simple it would be. These are honest, hardworking, fiercely loyal dragons who, time and again, have put their lives on the line for the good of the domain. If they had turned against me, I assure you it would all be over by now. Rosebloom doesn't have the power he needs, but he has just the right amount, at just the right time... every time. How is that possible?"

Just as Peter was feeling that he needed to chip in, but didn't quite know what to say, Gee Tee cleared his throat in an attention seeking kind of way that he'd mastered thoroughly over the centuries.

"I know a little about the abacus, the council chamber, and the mantras that protect and shield it. While you claim that it's impossible to sabotage it, I wholeheartedly disagree that it can't be done."

In that instant, the king knew he'd made the right decision in coming to the Mantra Emporium. No other dragon in the kingdom would have stated such a view, and almost certainly if his friend had, he was only seconds away from presenting his ideas on how it was being achieved.

"Hang on a minute," interposed the former apprentice, standing up, "are you telling me there's a mantra powerful enough to penetrate those shields surrounding the chamber? I've always been taught that there are none more impassable. In fact I'm pretty sure I've heard you say the same thing, on more than one occasion."

"Yes, yes... don't get your tail in a twist. Use your BRAIN," commanded the old dragon, pointing to the side of his head with the tip of one wing. "Think like a scheming, devious, desperate dragon. If the shields are impenetrable, how do you influence the abacus?"

It hit Peter like a hockey ball... HARD and FAST.

"From the inside!" he all but shouted.

"Exactly," roared Gee Tee in approval.

"IMPOSSIBLE," maintained the king. "Nothing can

go in or out without being scanned; the mantras would pick it up straight away."

"Then answer me this... child."

Peter cringed at the old shopkeeper referring to the current ruler of everything in that way. Tank did likewise. The monarch paid it no attention.

"How is it that one corner of that room is reserved for... well, how shall we put it... very dark and dangerous, historically significant artefacts?"

"You can't think for one minute that..." observed the ruler, standing up.

Gee Tee looked across the workshop, looking more than a little self-satisfied.

"Okay... so how?" George asked, secretly happy with the way things were progressing, although trying his best not to show it, knowing that he'd get the answers quicker if the shopkeeper thought for them all and presided over events.

"One of the relics... is not what it seems. I mean it might have been, but had a dual purpose, and was activated by the freezing mantra that keeps them all in check. That spell would definitely be beatable, from a mantra maker's point of view. As well, it's close enough to the abacus to exert the kind of influence you're talking about, without readily being noticed."

Scratching his chin, the king thought about the old dragon's words.

"Good," he finally said, "but with just one problem. All the artefacts are inert and are treble checked regularly. None of those items have any power, not even the tiniest inkling. What you're suggesting would need a considerable amount of mana... correct?"

The look on Gee Tee's face couldn't have disappeared faster, not even with the word "abracadabra". Peter and Tank remained silent, fascinated by the level of deep thinking that was going on.

'That,' thought the hockey player, 'must be why the

451

king came, he's playing Gee Tee masterfully, using his ego to see if he can give him what he needs. Truly skilful, and the act of a very worthy and powerful leader.'

"Son of Arctophonos," growled Gee Tee. (Arcotophonos was one of the two giant hunting dogs belonging to the giant Orion in Classical mythology.) "I'm going to string that Rosebloom up by his tail and rip his wings off," the Emporium owner continued.

"You know how?" enquired the king.

"Think about it. Every time this happens, you said the ring does that thing. It might well be a warning... a warning that someone, or something, is tapping into it and using its power. That ring has so much magical energy, an amount like that being taken from it would be positively insignificant."

"And there it is," announced the sovereign, jumping to his feet. "I knew you wouldn't let me down. You are, and always will be... a genius. Thank you."

"You're welcome," replied the old shopkeeper softly.

It was Tank who piped up next.

"What are you going to do about it?"

"That, my young friend," said the monarch, patting Tank on the shoulder and having to stand on tiptoes to do it, "is the 64 million dollar question."

"Is there not some way you could ask for the last vote to be retaken?" posed Peter.

"I could use my power to demand that the motion be voted on again. I don't have to provide a reason, but it's risky. If I were to do that and the ballot turned out the same, it might give Rosebloom and his followers an excuse to challenge my position and call for a vote of no confidence in me. If that were to happen... well, it could change everything. It might open the floodgates for anyone who's ever crossed swords with me to exact revenge, even presenting Rosebloom with the opportunity to become king himself. Perhaps that's what he wants."

"As long as I'm still breathing he bloody well isn't

going to get it. I should have turned that snot nosed little oik into a pile of decomposing dragon dung a long time ago. This is the last straw."

Astonished, Tank and Peter shared a look, having never heard the old shopkeeper use such language. If the situation weren't so dire, it would almost have been funny.

"Be that as it may," stated George purposefully, "even if I did arrange for the vote to be retaken, it would be impossible for me to turn up to the meeting without the ring on, or even with my hand covered up. Each and every one of them would know that something odd was going on, and that too might trigger some sort of rebellion."

"Then we make a copy," stated Tank coolly, a big grin crisscrossing his face. "Think about it. If you go in there, an exact replica on your finger, whatever's affecting the abacus won't be able to draw the power it needs. Rosebloom and his cohorts will have no control, and the vote will go exactly how you predicted it would. Better still, they'll have no idea how you've done it, and they might even try and check whichever dark relic it is, to see where the fault lies, presenting an opportunity to catch them red handed."

Looking pleased with the suggestion, the king replied.

"I'd need to call for a revote within the month, ideally as soon as possible. Do you think you could come up with a quality forgery in such a short space of time?"

Tank glanced across the workshop at the master mantra maker, who was muttering to himself and shaking his head. Striding over, the plant and animal loving dragon spoke up.

"We can do it. You know we can. Those Greek crystal growing mantras that we found last month would help a great deal. We have the resonance die caster to help with the colour. The biggest issue would be forging the metal... but are you really telling me that we can't do that?"

"It's not that we can't do it. It's more about the timeframe. Two months... maybe. Six months... certainly.

But a month? I'm just not sure it's possible."

With his smile having disappeared, sadness and loneliness returned to the George's eyes. It almost broke Peter's heart just to look at him.

"Yes, yes... alright, we can do it. Just put the poor little dragonling eyes away for now. We get the idea," put in the old shopkeeper.

"Are you sure?" asked the ruler sceptically.

"Yes, yes, yes, I'm sure... now, get out of here. The brains of the outfit here," he said, motioning his giant jaw in Tank's direction, "and I have a massive amount of work to do."

Before he turned to go, the king said,

"I'll be waiting."

"I know," replied the old dragon. "Good luck."

"To us both."

With that, George turned and, with Peter beside him, marched off in the direction of the exit, leaving in silence, the already arguing voices of Tank and the shopkeeper echoing eerily down the aisles of bookcases. Reaching the front door to the shop, he turned to Peter.

"Thank you. I know you'd probably like to spend more time here, talking with me, but right now, it simply isn't possible. Every second that I'm missing puts me and anyone else I care about in danger. I really have to go. But don't for one minute think that I don't care, and wouldn't want to spend months or years talking to you about everything. I've been through some scary stuff in my life... but what's happening now far outweighs anything I've ever seen, or even heard about. It's that bad. So for now you'll have to be patient. But know this... I'm thinking of you. I trust you and your friends with my life and more importantly, with the fate of the entire world, because potentially, it's what all this could boil down to. So... for now, it's good to see you. Thanks for the help, and... stay safe." And with that he unlocked the door, disappeared beneath his cloak and, without a sound, vanished into the deserted street. Following an instant later, Peter couldn't find any sign of the monarch.

23 ISN'T IT IRONIC?

Striding purposefully beneath the slender trees that lined the quiet, suburban street filled Peter with a sense of security. Not really knowing quite why, to be honest, it should have been the other way round. When above ground, most dragons feel a little insecure when they can't see the sky for whatever reason. But here the peace, the quiet, the... normality of it all made him long for everything that these people had. Undoubtedly there were mortgages, loans, work problems and those sorts of things, but right here and right now, he'd have swapped all that to live in one of these houses for the rest of his life with... JANICE! At least, that's what he told himself as he turned the corner into the street where she lived.

In the distance he could just make out her bright pink mini in the fading evening light. Smiling as he spotted it, that car seemed to sum her up perfectly. Petite, bright, bubbly, cheerful and full of zooooooooom! Heading for her rented house, he briefly wondered what sort of car he'd be. Ruling out sports cars and 4x4s as far too powerful, and the more flashy ones as far too pretentious, he finally settled on something like a family MPV. Having always had an affinity with babies, children, dragonlings... whatever you like, and the fantasy that had just been playing out in his head, living in one of these houses with the bubbly bar worker of course featured both of them having kids.

"Phewww." He blew out a huge sigh as he reached the gate. Before attempting to open it up, he rolled up the sleeve of his coat and checked his watch. The hands read exactly 7.29pm. Hesitating a little, he found himself sweating profusely despite the cold night air, with his stomach feeling as though he'd been thrown around on a particularly vicious fairground ride. Obsessive about his timekeeping, he glanced again at his watch, and although not quite sporting 7.30 (by only a few seconds), he commanded his wobbling legs to work, very hesitantly opened the gate and strolled up the neat path to the brightly coloured door. With a small bouquet of flowers hidden snugly behind his back, he knocked gently with his, by now, shaking hand. Almost instantly a light appeared in the door's glazed semi circular window, and after the briefest of rattles, it swung open to reveal Janice, looking... STUNNING!! It wasn't in a dressed up kind of way. Tight fitting light coloured jeans together with calf length light brown boots were set off by the cosiest looking, green, chunky knit sweater. Homely but beautiful, plain but gorgeous... that's all that he could think as she waved him inside with her 'light up the room' smile. Once she'd closed the door, he whipped out the flowers from behind his back like a street magician.

"Ohhh Peter you shouldn't have. They're lovely. I'll just put them in water if that's okay."

"Sure," he replied, following her through to the kitchen where he was assaulted by a variety of familiar aromas, one after the other, all equally delicious. If the way to a man's heart is through great food, then it's doubly true of dragons. Even in human form, there's very little better than a really fantastic tasting and smelling meal. This dragon was becoming well and truly smitten.

As she topped up a vase with water, adding the tiny sachet that came with the flowers, Janice told Peter that they were having steak fajitas, 'à la Janice'. Something of a surprise, what with it being almost his preference in the staff canteen at work, all became clear when she revealed that she'd secretly asked Richie what his favourite meal was.

'Wow,' he thought, 'she's gone to some lengths to put on something special.' Before he had time to dwell on it, Janice held out a bottle of wine in one hand and a much smaller bottle of beer in the other.

"Which would you prefer?" she asked meekly.

Silently wondering if his next words were somehow going to impact on the rest of the evening and their relationship as a whole, he reluctantly took the plunge.

"I... uhhh... don't drink, I'm afraid," he managed to stutter.

"OH!" Janice replied. "I don't think I've ever dated anyone who doesn't drink alcohol before."

'Oh... here we go,' thought Peter, fearing that he'd blown what he thought of as one of the best things to ever happen to him. Fortunately, he needn't have worried.

"Well... I'm very proud of you. It must take quite a lot to play hockey like you do and not drink. I bet there are times when it must be almost easier to bow to peer pressure and have a beer?"

He nodded.

"Good for you," she said approvingly, beaming and putting both bottles down next to the flowers. "I see so many people, men and women, acting like idiots every night, week in, week out... all because of alcohol. And it's not just because they've had too much. Sometimes it's because we've run out of their preferred tipple... that's been known to produce the odd violent reaction or two. Oh, and the other good one is when they've not had enough... such as when we're trying to close the bar and they need another drink. And I can't stress 'NEED' enough! I'm sorry I hadn't realised before that you don't drink. I thought it was just because you were driving home all the time... sometimes even that's not enough to dissuade people."

"I... I... don't mind other people drinking... honest," he managed to spout, his mouth by now drier than a grain of sand on a beach, competing in a cracker eating contest.

Just when he thought Janice's smile couldn't get any bigger or brighter... it did!

"Actually, I hardly touch the stuff. And I'm pretty sure I'd be much happier just staying sober, if that's okay with you," she whispered, putting one hand around the back of his neck and giving him the biggest kiss in the world.

"That's fine by me," he spluttered, on finally surfacing for air.

After that, the two of them stayed in the kitchen, Peter helping with the plates and the dips, while Janice tended to the steak and the fajitas, first talking about work, which then naturally progressed onto everything happening at the sports club.

With the food cooked, they moved into the living room, sharing the sofa. For his part, Peter tried hard not to wolf down his food, something he had a bit of a tendency to do, as they continued to talk during the meal. After having finished eating, they stacked the plates neatly in the kitchen before returning to the sofa to watch the film Janice had chosen. Taking a swig of his soft drink at exactly the wrong time, he nearly spat it halfway across the room when she told him what she'd picked.

"How To Train Your Dragon," she announced sweetly. At first, he thought she'd somehow discovered his secret. But as she sat delicately down next to him, he realised it was just a happy coincidence. In fact, it was all he could do to keep the tears of laughter from coming out.

'How ironic,' he thought to himself. "How To Train Your Dragon' indeed. If only you knew the truth. If only you were aware that here and now you're cuddled up with a real one, about to watch a film depicting a stereotypical dragon.' In a way, part of him was aching to tell her, so that she could... accept him for what he really was. But deep down, he knew better. Despite the fact that he was indeed hooked on her, he understood the consequences of those sorts of actions and knew that she could never, ever know. So with that, he sat, arm around her... content, more so than in a long time, and just watched the film, happy that for the here and now all he had to do was be himself... well, almost.

24 SPOIL SPORT... STARS!

Normally this bit wouldn't bother him. I mean really, why would it? Anything that he wanted... WOULD be provided. The only thing that came to mind which wasn't allowed was that under no circumstances could he go to the surface, but other than that pretty much anything he dreamed of would either be brought to him here in these spectacular rooms, or arranged for him. But today... something just wasn't quite right. It was a little under twenty-four hours until the start of the match, and as usual he was being ridiculously pampered, simply spoiled beyond belief. Of course, it was his life, and all that he'd known for almost as long as he could remember. Most of the other players didn't really have a problem with this, in fact for them, this was part of the reason that they'd trained so hard to become professional laminium ball players. The fame, the adulation, never having to work again, female dragons quite literally hurling themselves at you... just a few of the attractions for those who follow this particular path. But for some time now he'd found the whole thing nothing more than a burden.

Quite a while ago he'd become disillusioned by it all, assuming that only he could think like that. Until quite by accident, he'd discovered that one of the few laminium ball players he actually revered, and the only one in his team that he looked up to, felt exactly the same way. In the build up to one of the endless games, some years ago, he'd stupidly taken a wrong turn in the maze of hospitality rooms provided for the players. It was only when he'd stumbled upon Silverbonce angrily ushering away one of the many dragons whose job it was to carry out the player's every wish and command, that he had any inkling things were not quite what they seemed. Hunched over in the shadows of the corridor, he watched his teammate admonish the dragon for trying to bring him the finest food and drink. As the serving dragon sprinted past him, he wandered very casually in to see if the old mouth guard was alright. To his astonishment, his teammate's room was practically bare. There was of course a bed, but other than that... very little. It was then that the famed mouth guard shared his very passionate view about exactly how he felt with regard to all the luxuries afforded to the players... and he did it in quite a vivid way, laced, in fact, with more than a little rage. As he'd stood there taking the heat (in more ways than one) from Silverbonce's anger, he felt more respect for, and a common bond with, the oldest current laminium ball player on the planet. Their views were almost identical, albeit reached by rather different journeys, and were most definitely kept secret from the rest of the squad.

Normally he'd be fine, keep himself to himself before the game, meditate, eat very basic meals (plain charcoal, a lightly roasted hog, a dozen or so chickens... that kind of thing) and of course... REST! But for the hour or so that he'd been here, he just couldn't settle. Something was... well, not exactly wrong, but just not right. And more bothersome was the fact that he just didn't know what was needling him. It wasn't anything he could see, hear, or smell. It was just an underlying feeling... a strong one! Having tried everything he could think of, he'd checked in on the rest of the team; being captain afforded him the opportunity to do that without causing suspicion. All of them were fine, with most partying like only dragons could, with the exception of Silverbonce, who was deep in meditation. Having wandered a little further into the underground complex (he, for very obvious reasons, wasn't permitted anywhere near the opposition's rest and relaxation area) he could sense nothing definitively amiss there, either. Lying back on his very large and comfortable bed (one of the few luxuries he did insist on having) he'd stretched out with all his telepathic senses, up through the three mile thick layer of rock above, scanning for any sort of danger or threat. But still... NOTHING!! Nothing out of the ordinary. Currently situated in New Zealand, on the South Island beneath part of Mount Aspiring National Park, he knew that almost directly above him, magnificent blue pools and rivers flowed throughout the stunning landscape, just north east of Makarora, in a valley that feeds down into Lake Wanaka. And the main laminium ball stadium there, the one that he would be taking to in less than twenty-four hours, sits directly below the surface of the lake, famously separated from it by a very precarious and thin layer of rock. Everything above ground, for all intents and purposes, appeared to be okay. Still... he couldn't shake the nagging feeling that, somewhere close by, danger bubbled away unchecked.

Marvelling at his reflection in the darkened glass of the monorail carriage that had just pulled onto the platform of Salisbridge station, Peter decided that he liked his look. Not many did, but to be honest, he simply didn't care. His faded blue jeans, dark T-shirt and his Merrell walking boots were oh so comfortable, and that was all that mattered to him. Bouncing through the sliding doors as they opened, he slid into the nearest human sized seat, just before they whooshed closed and the carriage sped off in the direction of London.

He was excited. Not just a little excited, but Christmas Eve excited. His legs wobbled, his stomach churned and he couldn't sit still. Currently, there were many reasons for how he felt. His destination and what would happen when he got there were the most immediate, but he couldn't help thinking about the life changing evening he'd spent with Janice earlier in the week. He felt so happy. It was hard to put into words. It reminded him of his first flight, and the first time he'd successfully held human form, all rolled into one. Not entirely sure what the correct word to identify the feeling was, part of him worried that it might be... LOVE! All he really knew at the moment was that he was happier than he could ever remember being, and that was enough for him.

Thoughts returned to the here and now as the dark rock face whizzed by outside the window, his reflection smiling at what was to come. On his way to meet up with Tank and Flash in London, the three of them would then head across the globe to Canterbury, New Zealand. Once there, it would be a short hop south west to Dingle Burn (sounds like something potentially very nasty, or at least that's what he'd thought when the accommodation arrangements had been made) for an overnight stay. The next morning it would be a trip across Lake Hawea, and then a walk that skirted around the edge of Lake Wanaka, before heading up the valley to Makarora. All of this just to see his beloved team compete in the Commonwealth Cup, something that takes place every third year.

The Indigo Warriors had been drawn against the Dunedin Dinosaurs in the competition. Random teams from various Commonwealth countries are selected to face each other in a sudden death cup contest, with only a limited number of places available, so in theory teams may go for years or even decades without qualifying. Twenty-seven years had passed since the Warriors had last played and Tank, using his mysterious connections, had managed to procure three tickets to the match, supposedly one each for himself, Richie and Peter. I say mysterious...the last time the three of them had met up, Tank, Peter and of course Richie, the young lacrosse playing dragon finally managed to wangle out of Tank just where the so valuable tickets had come from. Not quite the detailed description the two of them had hoped for, all the strapping rugby player would say was that he had an acquaintance called Elbow Mudsmear, who he had 'something of a history' with regarding laminium ball. Elbow apparently worked for the company that catered for each of the professional laminium ball players' every need. Using all her charm,

Richie also tried to get Tank to shed more light on what the king had said back in Salisbridge hospital after Peter's battle with Manson, about Tank nearly becoming a professional laminium ball player, but the rugby playing dragon's lips remained firmly sealed on the subject.

Last week, however, the lacrosse superstar had inexplicably cancelled so Tank had offered the ex-Crimson Guard the ticket. Flash's response had been nothing short of priceless, going quite mad... running around in circles, waving his hands above his head and screaming how much he 'loved the big dragon' (hopefully he meant Tank). Surprisingly, Flash had never taken in a laminium ball match... EVER! Both friends were shocked when he'd told them this. His reason... apparently he'd been too busy with his duties and matters of global importance to have time to watch a... GAME! And although laminium ball hadn't featured in the ex-Crimson Guard's life before his accident (the assault in Antarctica by the now deceased naga), it sure did now, due in no small part to the time he had on his hands, having resigned from the elite group of warriors and agents. Of course, the king kept him busy, but dragons generally need little slumber compared with humans, particularly in their natural prehistoric form. More sleep is required in their human disguise mainly due to energy depletion caused by maintaining the shape changing mantras all around the clock, day in, day out. Because Flash didn't use up any magical energy in maintaining his human form, he didn't need to sleep so much and so had, for the first time in his life, a significant amount of free time. Unofficially following up information gleaned about Antarctica and the nagas had been his main priority. Part of his approach had involved scanning past and present copies of the telepathic papers. Of course he didn't know what he was looking for, but if there was a clue to be found, he was sure he would recognise it.

So here Peter was on his way to meet Tank and Flash at London's Pudding Lane complex to board the intercontinental monorail that would transport them straight to New Zealand with only a minimal number of stops.

Without realising it, he'd reached his station. Bounding through the carriage doors, virtually as they whooshed open, he bombed up the steps two at a time, making his way to the furthest platform. Scanning the flickering LCD screens, he could see that his connecting carriage to Pudding Lane was due in twenty seconds. Closing his eyes, he counted down in his head. Sure enough, with a cool current of air washing over him, the monorail arrived exactly on time. Taking his seat, barely able to restrain the excitement pulsing through his forcibly tangled DNA, ninety seconds later he pulled into Pudding Lane. The three platforms that housed the intercontinental part of the station were as far away as possible from where his carriage had pulled in. With a complete disregard for how he looked, he threw his backpack over one shoulder and sprinted as fast as he could up the stairs, all the time weaving in and out of the other commuters, human and dragon shapes alike. Dashing across the concourse and down a set of steep stairs, he finally arrived at the appropriate platform with four minutes to spare. Frantically, he looked around for his friends, who were supposed to meet him here. Panic started to well up inside him, until...

"BOO!!" screamed Tank and Flash, simultaneously leaping out from behind a vertical array of LCD screens. Peter's backpack thudded to the ground, dropped in surprise. Tank and Flash both burst into laughter.

"Blimey you made me jump," protested Peter, retrieving his rucksack from the completely spotless floor.

"Sorry Pete," laughed the rugby player. "We saw you through the windows sprinting across the station and just couldn't resist." Flash nodded his agreement.

"I suppose I'd have done the same," he admitted reluctantly.

Prank over, the three friends thought it best to board their intercontinental ride, rather than risk missing it and having to wait twelve or so hours for the next one.

Luggage stowed, the monorail, all eight carriages of it, pulled out of Pudding Lane station, continuing on its journey across the planet, the friends settling into their seats, imagining how their favourite laminium ball team were furiously preparing for the big game.

By now, he'd normally had a relaxing snooze, but he hadn't slept a wink. Something was deeply wrong. Not knowing what, every molecule in his huge dragon frame screamed out at him. He'd thought about telling someone. But who? Who would believe him? And more importantly, what exactly would he say? "I've got a feeling something's amiss, but I just don't know what"? He'd be a laughing stock. And if it got out, laminium ball fans from teams across the globe would be singing about it for decades to come. No, he had to try and figure it out himself. His search of the facilities had proven fruitless. There had to be something else he could do, another avenue he could explore. Turning the giant car sized pillow over, he tried to find the colder side... it was a habit of his. Even in the middle of the night he'd wake, his head overly hot, often taking a sip from the tankard of ice cold water on his bedside table (the tankard itself was a gift from a fan, and had been carefully imbued with a mantra that kept the liquid inside constantly chilled), before turning his pillow over and dropping back off to sleep. On consideration he supposed it was kind of odd.

Suddenly, there was a knock at the door. He wasn't expecting anyone, and it was unusual to get any visitors before the match.

'Perhaps,' he thought, 'this has something to do with the strange feeling.'

Cautiously he opened it, only to find Silverbonce

standing there, wings on hips.

"It's about time," barked the old mouth guard, dodging past Steel, marching into his room. "Too busy pampering yourself I suppose."

Steel smiled, when most would have taken offence. Knowing the old mouth guard for so many years, he understood this was just his way, and he knew if he waited patiently he'd find out exactly what was on the old dragon's mind.

Standing in the middle of the plush suite, Silverbonce circled like a bird of prey; what he was looking for was anyone's guess. After half a minute or so, he threw open his wings and shouted,

"CAN YOU FEEL IT?"

'Of course,' thought the captain. 'If I can feel it, then Silverbonce, with all his years of experience, is bound to have recognised it. I should have known.'

"Something's wrong," replied Steel to the old dragon's question.

"Exactly. But what?"

"I don't know," answered Steel, hoping the question had been rhetorical.

It had been.

"I've only ever felt like this once before," put in Silverbonce. "It was 1911 and we were playing at the Glockenspiel Arena, just below the town of Söll in Austria."

"Never heard of it," interrupted Steel.

"Wouldn't have expected you to. It doesn't exist anymore. In the days running up to the game, I had the same feeling I have now, the one that you yourself are experiencing. Goodness knows I tried to do something about it, but for the life of me, I didn't know what it meant or what I should do. I searched the arena, talked to everyone I could, even thought about taking human form and going to the surface."

At the very mention of this, Steel's jaws sprang open,

ready to speak. But Silverbonce wouldn't be interrupted.

"Yes, yes... I know. I'm not allowed to take human form... none of us are. But that feeling was so strong, so intense. Very stupidly I told some dragons: the manager of the stadium, some of the other players."

Recalling the events, the expression on the old mouth guard's face became both serious and sad at the same time.

"Of course, they thought I was mad and mocked me mercilessly. So much so that I nearly forgot about the bad feeling. Anyhow, the start of the match came around before I knew it. As I lined up, ready to go out on the display lap, the terrible feeling reasserted itself. I can recall it as if it were only yesterday: pins and needles across my wings, my legs feeling weak, a rolling sickness bobbing up and down inside my stomach. I don't think I've ever felt so bad."

Stood silently listening, Steel couldn't recall his friend ever looking so glum. But sad as he might be, he was determined to carry on.

"The game started and almost immediately we were behind. It was, and still is the quickest goal ever scored in a professional laminium ball match."

Steel exhaled in surprise. Regarding himself as something of a statistics nerd when it came to the game he loved, he was astonished that he'd never heard of that one, and absolutely flabbergasted that the dragon standing before him was involved in a record like that. He vowed to himself to look it up and find out more when he next had some free time.

"Needless to say... it didn't end there. Not only was it my worst performance ever, with us being four down within an hour, despite the outfield players, who, to a dragon, were magnificent."

Silverbonce inhaled deeply and closed his eyes.

"And then... it happened! No warning... NOTHING! A gigantic part of the cavern's ceiling collapsed in one corner of the arena. Hundreds, if not thousands of tons of rock dropped onto the packed stands, full to the brim with spectators. Confusion and chaos ensued. Two of my teammates shot over to help, only to be crushed instantly by falling debris. In all, five hundred dragons were killed that day, including four laminium ball players, two from each side."

By now, Silverbonce had his head in his hands, sobbing gently, tears the size of marbles plopping onto the pristine floor. Steel stood silent, taking everything in, wondering even now if the entire complex was in danger of collapsing. Minutes passed before the famed mouth guard was able to carry on.

"It turned out there had been a fault in the construction. Worse still, the checks by the government department responsible were nothing more than cursory glances at best. And now you're thinking: why haven't I heard of a disaster of that magnitude? Because the authorities covered it up. The information is still out there of course, buried beneath a gazillion other things, but it's still there. Because of their negligence, good dragons died that day. Needless to say there was uproar at the time, most notably from everyone who'd been at the match. But one by one they were all silenced, some bought off, others having pressure applied by councillors themselves. It was a sad day, one I'll never forget, and I wouldn't choose to even if I could. But, back to where I began. That feeling I had then is the exact same one that I'm getting now, the same one you have. What does it mean? I'm not sure. I've checked out the substructure of the complex and all the mantras surrounding it. They're all good. So I don't think we're going to have a repeat of what happened in Austria. But something here is not right. And, my young friend, I think it's our job to try and find out exactly what it is. The thought of another laminium ball match turning to tragedy fills me with dread."

There and then Steel vowed to help the old dragon find out what was wrong and, after a brief hug, they headed out into the complex to see if two minds truly were better than one.

25 WORLDWIDE COUNTDOWN CONUNDRUM

Behind a faded, red coloured brick in a seemingly innocuous wall, in a rarely visited sewer deep beneath Chicago, the numbers on the timer counted down, showing 14 00 00 00 right at this very moment. Fourteen days left. Fourteen days until oblivion.

In the small village of Wang Chan, Thailand, next to the newly opened Cropptech processing plant, an identical parcel counted down right at the bottom of a murky paddy field, the red light from the changing numbers flitting across the passing wildlife, turning their world into something of a disco. The tattered paper surrounding it having long since dissolved, the timer mimicked that of the others deposited across the world, as the tiny creatures continued their daily routines, oblivious to the danger hidden amongst them.

It was supposed to be dark... pitch black in fact. Not that anyone was there to see. But beneath an ordinary pier in Montreal, Canada, red lights flickered and changed against the wall opposite, tucked up amongst the tiniest of air pockets, surrounded by seaweed. Nothing, not even an infinitesimal speck of life was there to watch as fourteen days ticked past. And all the time, above, ordinary people carried on with their lives, unaware of the deadly packets hidden below them.

It had been a long time since he'd felt this... nervous or vulnerable. This wasn't part of the dragon London he was familiar with; nevertheless he recognised a slum when he saw one. As he lay flattened against the roof of a rather run down dragon bakery, he pushed the doubts in his mind to one side. Absolutely convinced something untoward was afoot, he was sure the conniving dragon he was tailing was up to his scales in it. Focusing on controlling his breathing, he waited until his target reached the next intersection and watched him turn right, before bounding to his feet. Taking a small run up, he reached the edge of the roof and pushed off for all he was worth, unable to look down at the eight metre drop below. Flapping in the arid air behind him as he landed, the dark cloak encased him fully from prying eyes in more ways than one. Careful to remain in the shadows, he stalked as close to the edge of the building as he dared. Nagging doubts continued to assert themselves, try as he might to push them aside. Here he was, with no help at hand, which was something of a risk, of that there could be no doubt.

He hadn't told anyone where he was going, quite the opposite, having slipped out of his private residence via a secret entrance only known to him and one other, and that had only been a very recent addition. Knowing he could trust his new temporary tenant with his life, he'd felt it only fair that he clue him in on one of the building's greatest secrets. When he'd taken on the mantle of king, not only had he received the ring and the ostentatious living quarters, but also a sealed trunk containing information from the previous monarch, all for his eyes only. Linked by means of an ancient mantra to the enigmatic band, the trunk was programmed to only open once those items had bonded to him. From his very first day as ruler, he'd tried to open the chest, but to no avail. It wasn't until the twenty ninth day of his reign that the blessed thing had decided to reveal its secrets. Even then he was surprised. Just like every other time, he'd returned from trying to keep everything at the council from falling apart, sat down and tried to open the blessed box. To him, it was going through the motions. To his utter astonishment, on that Sunday evening a satisfying click greeted him when he touched the lock. He then spent the rest of the night devouring the information that had been left behind by his predecessor. To say it was fascinating and insightful was something of an understatement; some of it was simply unbelievable, and all of it was just for him, passed down by the line of monarchs before him, making him feel both honoured and burdened at the same time. Things had never been quite the same since that fateful day. It wasn't often that he'd used that secret entrance, mainly for fear it would be discovered. But tonight he had. And everyone assumed that he was tucked up in his private chambers. No one knew where he was. If anything happened... George was well and truly on his own.

Pretty sure he wasn't being followed, Councillor Rosebloom smiled at the very thought, knowing that he'd gone to great lengths to make it so, having doubled backed on himself numerous times, woven detection webs in his wake, and laid other more formidable traps along his route. None had been set off, so now, sure he wasn't being tracked, he moved with more haste and certainty.

'It won't be long,' he thought, sick and tired of his daily life. It always seemed like such a chore, looking after the interests of other dragons, beings who frankly, he couldn't give a stuff about. 'But soon, when the changes come about, then I'll have real power, proper responsibility, and a land of my own. Then the only interests I'll have to worry about will be... MINE!'

As the king landed softly on another rooftop, the ring on his finger tingled ever so slightly, just as it had done a dozen or so times already this evening. Standing stock still, ever alert, he controlled his breathing, just as he'd been taught. Now was not the time to fall victim to nerves. The slightest mistake could alert Rosebloom to his presence and then everything he'd gone through already tonight would have been for nothing. Not only that, but it might panic the councillor and make him more cautious, something he hoped to avoid. Carefully he held up the enigmatic band in front of him. Silently, a wide, purple beam of light that only he could see erupted out of it. Not worried about being spotted, he was concerned about getting past the intricate web that the stunning loop revealed directly in front of him. Bright blue strands sparkled across rooftops, in alleyways and everywhere in between for as far as he could see. Up to now the tricks, traps and mantras had been relatively easy for him to circumnavigate, with the ring's help of course, but this latest one looked a whole lot tougher than any of those. Aware that with every second he wasted here, the more chance there was of Rosebloom slipping away, the pressure weighed heavy on him as time ticked on.

With only one option, he opened himself up fully to the ancient imbued piece of jewellery on his finger. In the past the circle had helped him during crucial, almost pivotal times and he hoped that this was one of those moments now, when it could find some way for him to get past the intricate mantra driven web that was like nothing he'd ever seen before.

Weird was the only way to describe it. He really should have been used to it by now, but he wasn't. It was like sharing your mind with another being, but one so different that it was almost alien. Numbers, letters and symbols he didn't recognise scrolled throughout his psyche, all the time accompanied by a soft sound like the rush of the wind. Abruptly his hand moved involuntarily, the ring shining the purple beam on a section of the glistening blue web off to one side, on the rooftop he stood on. Watching in awe as the filaments of the web changed colour from blue to purple, it only took a few seconds before a section was big enough for his human shape to pass through. Whispering a silent thank you, his finger tingled vigorously. Needing no further encouragement, he stepped through the purple part of the web sideways and felt nothing, nothing at all. Sure he would have sensed something had he triggered the supernatural trap itself, looking back over his shoulder, the purple strands faded back to the bright blue that had been there before, now waiting for some unsuspecting being to set it off. With no time to lose, he set off in the direction he'd last seen Rosebloom.

This part of the domain sent shivers down his spine. Goodness knows he'd been here often enough that the locals knew to leave him well alone; he felt safe and had no doubt that he wielded a sufficient amount of power to deal with anything thrown at him. Still, he shouldn't have to mix with the kind of low life that called this place their home. Moving swiftly on, he vowed to himself to make this his last trip to this tatty, desperate, run down, scum ridden hellhole.

Drawing the cloak around himself in the shadows as he crouched on one knee, panting, he watched as the councillor surreptitiously glanced back over his shoulder. Of course this wasn't just any cloak, it was the laminium cloak that he'd worn on his last outing to the Mantra Emporium, the one that would stop anyone sensing his presence, yet wouldn't stop anyone from physically spotting him. With his heart beating in his ears, confident that was totally hidden, the king watched to see what would happen as the shady councillor stopped at a darkened entrance to a nondescript alley. Sure enough, after only a few seconds a creature appeared, half obscured by the shadows. George's first thought was that it was another dragon, but on closer inspection he was sure that it wasn't. It was difficult to determine due to the light, or lack of it, and from what he could tell, there was no way to get any closer without revealing himself. Scales were abundant, but something about the way they rippled looked and felt wrong. Plus, he could see no hint of any wings. At first he thought they might have been folded neatly back, just like Rosebloom's were, but the more he looked, the more certain he was that there weren't any there at all. While he wasn't one hundred percent sure, he was confident enough to tell himself that what he was looking at was nothing short of what young Flash had dealt with in Antarctica and Australia... a NAGA! At first he was stunned, too shocked to even move, but it didn't take long for the anger to rise up and fill his veins.

'How dare one of those creatures be living here in MY WORLD!' he thought, before rational thinking started to kick in, and he remembered the fact that he was here, alone, with no back up and no help. He had to be careful. There was no telling who or what else was in that alley. For all he knew, there could be half an army in there.

'Watch, observe and remember,' he told himself.

As he looked on, a rather heated and animated discussion broke out between the councillor and the creature. From what he could make out, Rosebloom had brought something with him, a piece of paper or parchment of some sort, and was about to hand it over. But things weren't going that smoothly for the traitorous councillor. It looked as though he expected something in return, something that clearly wasn't forthcoming.

'The cheater cheated,' thought the king. 'What a shame!'

Standing in animated conversation for another couple of minutes, Rosebloom clearly unhappy at the turn of events, getting more and more agitated as time went on, it turned out that whatever the creature said was more than enough to persuade him in the end. Reluctantly, the councillor handed over the sheet, said a few departing words, then turned and padded away. On turning, the king noticed for the first time a very real fear on the dragon's face, and that frightened him more than seeing a naga here in his domain. Tucked well out of sight beneath his cloak, he remained hidden for quite a while, giving Rosebloom a big head start, not wanting their paths to cross on the way back. During his wait, he watched the mouth of the alley, desperate to know what secrets it held, but too afraid to get any closer. Before setting off, he thought briefly about coming back in force with the King's Guard, but dismissed it out of hand straight away.

'That creature and its cohorts would almost certainly have moved on by the time we got back,' he mused. 'Besides, all it would really do is alert Rosebloom that I'm on to him, something he clearly doesn't know at the moment, but would if I arrived here with a contingent of soldiers. I'll bide my time, but we will meet again, and when we do... they'll be hell to pay,' he promised, getting to his feet, vaulting into the air and off over the rooftops in the direction of home.

26 STEEL YOURSELF!

New Zealand was a stunningly beautiful land, and all three had been having a wonderful time since arriving, but now it was time for the reason that they'd come all this way... LAMINIUM BALL! Following the winding crowd, eager to get to their seats, the three pals couldn't wait for the match to start, with Flash eyeing everything, mouth agape like a small child on Christmas morning, not surprising really given that this was his first laminium ball match and, quite frankly, he'd never seen anything quite like it. Various vendors sold all sorts of mantras, hats, socks, jewellery, flags and plastic laminium balls, as well as every type of food imaginable. Currently he wore an Indigo Warriors hat shaped like a rocket, with a huge cheese shape adorning the top. Having adopted the Warriors as his team, and with Peter's favourite player being Steel, and Tank's being Silverbonce, the ex-Crimson Guard had decided to plump for Cheese as his preference. Unsure why, he liked the name and there seemed to be plenty of Cheese merchandise to choose from. So with his newly bought hat on his head, a new pair of socks tucked into his pocket, a hot dog smothered in charcoal sauce in one hand, and a stack of charcoal covered doughnuts in the other, he tried desperately to keep up with his friends as they moved through the rather excited crowd. Sharing a look, Peter and Tank laughed at the thought of their very tough friend never having been to a match before. Flash had been totally taken in by the atmosphere of the game even before it had begun. Boy was he in for a treat when the sport started in earnest.

Deep below them, the teams lined up. Steel stood at the front, chest puffed out, eyes focused straight ahead, as was his ritual. Looking calm, motivated and ruthless, he felt anything but. Truth be told, he was worried, and not just a little, knowing better than to turn around and look towards the back of the line where Silverbonce was standing, despite feeling the need to do so. Sure the old mouth guard was feeling the same way, and if his account of what had happened in Austria all those years ago was anything to go by, then lives might well be at stake. It was hard to concentrate on going out there and playing laminium ball, even though that was what he was paid to do. It was his job, his profession, his passion and not only did he love it, but he felt honoured and privileged every time he took to the air. He only hoped today that the feeling the two of them shared, turned out to be totally innocent and harmless.

Squeezing past a whole host of other dragons, eventually the three friends found their allocated seats and tried to sit down. It wasn't a quick process though. First they had to sort out their massive beakers of fizzy drinks, align all their snacks... charcoal popcorn, a selection of pencils, crisps, chocolate covered charcoal... the lot. It was a good job there was a great deal of leg room, mainly due to the fact that they'd chosen to attend in their human guises, in a show of solidarity towards their permanently changed friend, while their seats had been configured for huge natural dragon forms. So once done, they reclined, looking a lot like babies in high chairs in the massive oversized dragon seats, trying desperately not to slip through the huge hole at the back. Moments later the lights dimmed and the audience started to clap.

Echoing through the solid rock wall in front of them, the applause did little in the way of disrupting Steel's focus. His mind was well and truly elsewhere. It was too late now, he realised. Between them, he and Silverbonce had found nothing that presented any sort of danger, try as they might. And now he would have to go out into the arena and concentrate on doing his job to the best of his ability, however hard that might be. Attempting one last time to push away the nagging sensation of danger deep inside him, without much luck, he watched as the slightest of rumbles heralded the wall in front of him rolling gently out of the way, revealing the darkened stadium, lit up by only the rolling surface of the lava below. Turning to look at his counterpart on the opposing team who was standing right next to him, he nodded and then they both ran forward and jumped. Immediately Steel veered left, dropping slightly lower than the exit when he did so. It had already been agreed that the Warriors would take the lower plane on the display lap. One by one the team members all flew out of the hexagonal hole in the wall, the Warriors all following Steel, the Dunedin Dinosaurs trailing their captain off to the right, ever so slightly higher up than their opponents. Both teams flew past each other at incredible speed at a point in the arena exactly opposite the entrance from which they'd just come in. After three laps, they all scrambled up into the middle of the stadium, high above the mesmerising molten magma, with the displays at each end starting their countdowns from ten. With that uneasy feeling still threatening to overwhelm him, Steel cleared his mind of everything except... LAMINIUM BALL!

Both teams hovered expectantly, waiting for the glistening globe to come rocketing out of the ceiling as the audience of nearly seventy thousand clapped, whooped and hollered.

"8... 7... 6... 5... 4... 3... 2... 1..." Stunningly bright crystals in the roof sprang into life, illuminating the entire arena. Out shot the ball, at an almost impossible angle. All the Dunedin team had dinosaur related names. There was Raptor, mouth guard; Tri, as in Triceratops; Bronti, as in Brontosaurus; Rex, as in Tyrannosaurus; Terry, as in Dactyl; and Steg, short for Stegosaurus, the substitute. One of the Dunedin Dinosaurs, Rex, by the look of things, took the ball straight in the neck, nose diving off towards the lava, spiralling dangerously out of control. Rebounding around a couple of times, the much sought after orb bounced off Flamer's chest and Barf's shoulder, before ending up in the clutches of Terry, who instantly headed towards the deck and the blindingly hot magma. Flamer and Cheese gave chase, while Barf righted himself from the previous impact. Silverbonce had already retreated back to his mouth, whilst Flamer and Cheese had managed to panic Terry into passing the ball back to his teammate Bronti. This bought the Warriors some time, allowing them to reform their defence and make sure they were now between the ball and their mouth. During all of this, Steel was experiencing some very unusual sensations from the troublesome feelings that he'd tried to put to one side before entering the arena. To some degree he'd pushed them down into his subconscious. What was odd though, was that when the laminium ball had shot out into the arena, the troublesome, nagging sensation that something was wrong, had ripped through him, a thousand times more powerful than it had been at any point over the last few days, so much so that he was barely able to fly, and felt that his balance was all over the place. Gingerly, he made his way back towards the mouth he was trying to defend, as his mind revisited the intensity of what he'd felt.

'What does it all mean?' he wondered, his focus and concentration totally ruined.

Back in the action, the Dinosaurs were on a roll. They'd completed ten passes in a row without the Warriors even getting close, with the only plus point for the three friends' favourite team being that the passes had all taken place in the Dinosaurs' defensive half of the arena. With Steel distracted momentarily, it was down to Cheese, Barf and Flamer to put things right, and they were determined to do exactly that.

Flamer shot towards Tri, who was flying high, not far from the cavern's ceiling, deep within his own half.

'He's looking nervous,' thought Flamer, closing in. He

was right; Tri was indeed edgy, so much so that he was looking to offload the shimmering sphere to one of his teammates. Able to sense this, the Warriors as a squad (minus the otherwise occupied Steel) started to work the opposition. Simultaneously Cheese harried Rex, while Barf was all over Bronti like a rash. With no immediate pass available, Tri continued to fly around in circles, dipping, diving and doubling back, all the while desperate to get rid of the ball. Flamer looked as though he was about to intercept, but Tri was having none of it and banked away at the crucial moment. Sneakily, Flamer had counted on this, and for the fraction of a second that he was in striking range, let go with his trademark jet of flame. A searing blue cone of fire torched the underside of Tri's right wing, forcing him to relinquish the ball. As it tumbled through the air, Flamer swooped down and swept it up with one of his wings. Cheese and Barf immediately shrugged off their defensive duties like a grubby old cape and shot off to offer up some options for their friend and teammate.

Across the arena from all that, Steel was having difficulty flying, looking like he was drunk, weaving all over the place, incapable of moving in a straight line. By now it was clear to everyone that something was up, and Silverbonce had already decided to intervene. Whipping round from beneath the courageous captain, the crafty old mouth guard used his updraft to steady his usually dependable friend.

"What's going on?" he demanded.

Steel shook his head, trying to clear it of the mass of fuzziness, but this only made him more dizzy, not something that was designed to help his current predicament. With Silverbonce twisting and turning in mid-air, trying desperately to keep up, Steel spoke up.

"It's the... baallllllll!!!!!"

"What?" shouted the old mouth guard, barely able to hear over the noise of the crowd, and totally oblivious to what was going on in the game.

"Thhhheeeee baaalllllll!!!!" he yelled, executing a perfect triple somersault, followed by an inverse loop the loop. "Thhheeee feeeeeelling weeee're getttttting itttttt'ssssss cooommming frooooooom thhheee ballllllllllllll!!!!" Neglecting to look where he was going, Steel smashed with great gusto into the rocky lower wall of the arena with a sickening THUD!

Silverbonce watched despairingly as his captain slid comically down the huge stone wall and splattered onto a lower ledge. It was a poor landing by any dragon's standards, and under normal circumstances he'd have gone to check on his friend. But nothing about this was normal, and he'd just worked out what Steel had so frantically been trying to tell him. THE BALL! That was the key. Banking away at speed from his prone captain, the old mouth guard powered his way up the arena, determined to get his wings on that blessed laminium ball, and see for himself what his friend knew, that he didn't.

Wrapped up in their giant oversized chairs, not far away, Peter, Tank and Flash sat glued to the action as the Warriors, deep within the Dinosaurs' half, had finally got their act together and were passing the gleaming globe with a dazzling degree of power and accuracy. None of the Dinosaurs could get near them, but were currently doing just enough to stop their opponents from getting a clear shot at the mouth, much to the friends' annoyance. With all the action to their right as they watched, the three were suddenly equally surprised to hear a gigantic roar from the crowd off to their left. Instinctively, they all turned. Their jaws fell open in unison at the sight of Silverbonce storming over the halfway line, with such phenomenal speed that he was almost a blur, even with their enhanced senses.

'What on earth is he doing this far up the arena?' was the thought that shot through Peter's mind straight away. Tank had pretty much the same idea, with Flash not too far behind.

Silverbonce, meanwhile, only had one intention... to get the ball. Surging forward, he surprised Dunedin's Rex as he swept past at speed. Currently, Flamer had possession of the ball and seemed to be teasing Bronti with it. The look on his face was priceless as the old mouth guard approached. It was practically the last thing he expected. Drawing up short of Flamer, the mouth guard held out his wings in anticipation of receiving the pass. Flamer, momentarily confused as to why Silverbonce was this far up the cavern, hesitated. And that's all it took for Dunedin's Terry to zoom up from beneath him and pinch the prized possession from right out between his wings. Clumsily, Flamer tumbled off to one side, dazed and confused. Cursing under his breath, Silverbonce took off after the reflective orb.

A groggy Steel managed to feebly roll onto his side, back on the ledge deep within his own half. Through slightly blurred vision, he could just make out Silverbonce hurrying after the ball. Closing his eyes, silently he wished the old mouth guard good luck.

THWACK! Terry slapped the burnished sphere down the line with his tail, executing a perfect pass to Rex, who in turn shot up towards the ceiling, all the time twisting and turning. Again, Silverbonce cursed. It was one thing being a mouth guard (normally his experience more than made up for his lack of youth and fitness) but it was something else altogether to go chasing after dragons half his age. Once the Warriors regained possession, he was sure he could reel it in, but as he lagged well behind play, heading back towards his own half, a few doubts presented themselves. Considering letting the Dinosaurs score, knowing that even then there was no guarantee he'd gain possession from the restart, all he really knew as he pumped his wings in frustration, was that things were not going well.

Wondering just where the rest of the team were, Cheese and Barf hurriedly chased back.

'Silverbonce is supposed to be guarding the mouth,' thought Barf, 'and yet there's a great big gaping chasm there. And come to think of it, where in the name of all that's hot is Steel? I haven't seen him since the start of the game.' Roaring flame spat out of Barf's mouth, flicking back down both sides of his jaw as he pursued the Dinosaurs player with the ball, determined to redouble his efforts and stop them getting a shot off.

Having expended a massive amount of energy in putting himself between the object that made the game what it was and the Warriors' mouth, Cheese hovered to a halt, wondering if the rest of the squad would use the valuable seconds he'd bought them... wisely.

Rex had little choice but to pass, with Barf hounding him mercilessly and Cheese blocking him out front. The throw, much to the relief of the Warriors, had to go back, because the rest of the Dinosaurs hadn't managed to keep up with him on the break. Simultaneously, Cheese and Barf both let out sighs of relief, tiny dribbles of orange, yellow and red flame snaking from their nostrils. Meanwhile, Silverbonce would have let out a similar sigh at the sight of the back pass and the slowdown of play, had he had any breath left. Flying at breakneck speed, well... for him anyway, he closed in on Bronti, who currently had hold of the spinning globe. Instinctively, Bronti pummelled the ball with his tail to Tri who'd stormed up to support the rest of his team. Just before it reached his outstretched arms though, up popped Flamer from absolutely nowhere, looking fully recovered from his collision with Terry. Tri lunged forward, trying with all his might to tackle the renowned blower of fire, but the young dragon was too quick, zipping upwards and executing a perfect one hundred and eighty degree flip, before pouring on as much speed as he dare, heading towards the molten magma down below. Silverbonce looked on exasperated. Desperation welled up inside him as the feeling he had got stronger and stronger, more out of control, almost as if on a timer. With every second that passed, the situation became absolutely critical.

All three friends had no idea which way to look. First this way, then that way, the game becoming something of a blur and they, like the rest of the spectators, still had absolutely no idea why Silverbonce was hovering in the middle of the arena instead of guarding his mouth.

Shooting across the bubbling lava, whipping up the roiling magma in his wake, Flamer dodged in and out of steaming pockets of erupting flame as Rex tore towards him from above. Quite quickly it became obvious that because the lava had slowed him down, a challenge from Rex was unavoidable. Searching frantically for one of his teammates, Flamer was lucky that Barf had continued his great work ethic and was now flying parallel to him, some twenty or so metres off to his right, about a metre or so above the bubbling magma. With Rex closing fast, Flamer did the only thing he really could. In one silky smooth move, he flipped the ball up in the air, let his momentum carry it down the length of his tail and once there, braked sharply for all he was worth, transferring all the force in the move to power his tail, and BANG! Off it sped in the direction of Barf, a fraction of a second before Rex slammed into him. Accompanied by the sound of breaking bones and tearing ligaments, both dragons careered off in different directions, before splashing unceremoniously into the searing orange lake.

Silverbonce, meanwhile, tried to breathe first through his nose, then through his mouth.

'At this point,' he thought, 'I'd try breathing through my bottom if I thought it would help me keep up with the action.' Now that play had been reversed and the Warriors had possession, he wasn't far away from the object of his eye, but was still struggling to keep up.

'If only they'd keep still for just a few seconds,' he mused, flapping his burning wings as hard as he could.

Picking up the spinning sphere with the end of his tail,

Barf casually flicked it up into his hands, feeling a tickle of heat from the lava on his bulging belly as he did so. With the laminium from what he carried boosting his senses, he reached out telepathically to his teammates, only to find a muzzy kind of static blocking him. Pulling up sharply, hovering just above the molten magma, so close he could feel the tip of his tail being splattered with tiny droplets, without any opponents nearby, he tried to take in the overall picture of the game. Two dragon medics were currently winging their way towards Rex and Flamer, both of whom were still face down in the scorching lava. Cheese seemed to be catching his breath, right in front of his own mouth. Tri and Terry were zipping across the cavern on an intercept course, while Bronti and Raptor were holding their positions between him and the Dinosaurs' mouth. Strangely, Silverbonce was the closest Warrior to him, something he found odd, but didn't have time to dwell on. Weaving across and then up, hugging the rocks that jutted out of the side of the arena, it suddenly occurred to him that there was no sign of Steel, which in turn made his heart pump furiously.

'Come back,' thought Silverbonce, anxiously trying to project what he was feeling in Barf's direction. It must have worked to some extent as the puking protagonist glanced over his shoulder at the old dragon, giving him a quizzical look, almost colliding with a particularly vicious section of jutting stone for his trouble. Drawing to a halt and projecting a picture of Barf giving the ball to him, Silverbonce used up every last ounce of his willpower. Surprised by the image inside his mind that had all but overwhelmed him, Barf hovered to a halt halfway up the wall. Turning and looking back in the old dragon's direction, he was more than a little puzzled when Silverbonce motioned for him to come back, but knew better than to question his teammate's cunning and experience. After all, the wily old mouth guard had singlehandedly saved them on countless occasions.

Assuming this was just another one of those highly unusual and highly successful ruses, Barf used his mighty talons to push off from the rocky incline, heading swiftly towards his popular friend.

Tri and Terry filled their team's telepathic connection with a sense of puzzlement as they cut through the air at speed towards the lone Warrior with the ball, when unexpectedly he headed back towards the centre of the arena, and the crazy mouth guard who'd long since abandoned his position. Adjusting their trajectories, both sped off accordingly.

A cheer went up from the fans across the stadium as Rex and Flamer emerged from the concealed entrance that the medic dragons used, both patched up and looking more than a little worse for wear.

Just then a snaking smile flitted across Silverbonce's prehistoric jaw, with Barf having nearly reached him with the still glistening globe.

'Things,' he thought, 'are looking up.'

Barf approached at speed, fully aware that Tri and Terry were almost upon him, a fact he was pretty sure his teammate was oblivious to. Holding still, arms outstretched ready to receive the ball, the old mouth guard was about to have all his questions answered. Getting within two metres, Barf threw the ball straight at Silverbonce and then ducked around his teammate, flying head on into the onrushing Tri and Terry. The sound of bones shattering and tendons snapping reverberated around the arena as the crowd turned deathly silent.

Catching the ball, a force the strength of the wildest storm the planet had ever seen ripped through him, that nagging feeling that he'd had for some time now engulfing him totally. Every nerve ending detonated in pain and huge explosions erupted behind his eyes as he tumbled uncontrollably, heading directly for the lake of lava, hands glued to the scorching sphere.

Barf and Terry spiralled frenziedly around in the air,

high above the molten magma, a long tear across the centre of Barf's right wing, the last third of Terry's tail crumpled and broken, the pair locked together in what looked like some bizarre kind of dance. Both were clearly going to play no part in the rest of the match. Once again bounding out of their secluded entrance with a burst of speed, both medic dragons headed towards the two injured players.

Despite overwhelming pain, Silverbonce had managed to arrest his fall somewhat. Currently he was trying to make sense of what he was feeling. Images flashed through his mind, none that he recognised, but all filling him with a sense of terrible dread. Feeling in immediate danger, he had no idea why. What he needed was time... time to figure out exactly what was going on, which he was convinced would come to him... unfortunately not as quickly as one of his opponents.

Tri had taken a glancing blow when the crazy Barf had deliberately flown straight into him and Terry moments before. Cursing himself for not seeing the unconventional attack coming he was, however, proud that he'd managed at the last split second to dive off to one side, limiting the damage somewhat. All this ran through his mind as he watched the medic dragons halt the descent of Barf and Terry, albeit through dark spots that had started to appear in the centre of his vision. Darkness was also starting to form around the edges of his sight, making him realise, along with the searing pain and the fact that he could hardly pull in a single breath, that he'd broken some ribs. (He'd sustained that particular injury before and recognised the familiar sensations.) Also he was reasonably sure that he'd broken the toe phalanges on his left foot, knowing that the next time he had to land would be interesting to say the least, but all this was secondary in his mind. Angry, mad even, he was determined to make up for being suckered into the momentary lapse of judgement that had been the collision. Right at this very moment he had his sights set on retrieving possession of the ball, regardless of his failing vision, breathing problems and the piercing pain. Determined, he tore down towards Silverbonce from directly above, the old dragon not having the faintest idea he was there. In moments he'd have it back for his side. This very thought pleased him no end, even though he knew he'd struggle to last the rest of the match.

Floating above the spitting molten magma, Silverbonce gripped the round prize for all he was worth, frantically trying to unravel what the danger was; he had to know and wouldn't let another disaster take innocent dragon lives. Abruptly his experienced sense of spatial awareness kicked into overdrive. A little rush of air on the back of his neck was his first clue. Craning his head to look up, he got hit full on in the face by the onrushing Tri. SMASH! The old mouth guard's fighting instinct sprang to the fore, enabling him to double grip on the ball, in spite of the pain he found himself in. Instinctively he brought his tail round, catching his opponent fully across the belly. Unbelievably, Tri was still in the mix, having a grip on the ball, determined to regain possession for his side and make up for his earlier error. Both dragons twisted, turned, tumbled and spun, all the while holding onto the incredibly valuable globe. With every moment that passed, the sensation of danger increased.

In a moment of inspiration it came to him. Silverbonce knew what was going to happen. It was a BOMB! And it was about to explode.

Images ravaged the old mouth guard's mind: death, destruction, violence and savagery. Fear coursed through him as he toppled head over heels, all the time trying to pry the ball away from Tri. Spinning out of control, he searched for a solution. None presented itself. Energy sapped, he sobbed as the brilliant orange lake of molten magma rushed up at him, sorry he couldn't prevent the impending disaster that was about to visit itself upon one tiny part of dragonkind. About to let go, a wicked breeze tickled his whole body. With all the energy he had left, he leant back and looked up. A familiar face smiled down at him, albeit something of a blur due to the speed he was travelling. Reluctantly, Silverbonce relinquished his grip on the ball. The doom laden images disappeared. One thought above all others sprang to the forefront of his mind:

'If anyone can save us, he can.'

An impact almost as loud as an explosion streaked across the arena as Steel shot through the two of them from above (quite literally in the case of Tri) and, carrying the ball, plunged head first into the steaming orange mass of superheated, bubbling lava. He hit so hard that the backwash of molten magma covered the wily old mouth guard and Tri from head to tail. Silverbonce caught Tri's broken body as it plummeted towards the orange, superheated lake, the Dunedin dragon barely conscious after Steel's assault. Glancing over at the medics' entrance, the old mouth guard could see no sign of either dragon, so, knowing that the match was well and truly over, he decided to take Tri to them. On doing so, he reached out with his mind, searching for Steel, but any remaining inkling of him had disappeared beyond all recognition.

On fire in more ways than one, he knew what he was holding. Able to envisage the inside, visualise the foreign body inhabiting the ball, take in the red digital lines that formed the numbers, flickering and changing... counting down... he knew that time had all but run out; of course he'd done this before, but under quite different circumstances. Then the lava was of a much stranger consistency, and had been much harder to navigate through. Here and now, it was much... thinner, easier to traverse, but hotter, much, much hotter. Also, last time he hadn't been holding a bomb about to go off, just a normal, everyday laminium ball.

'Oh, how I hope this is going to work,' he thought, as he continued straight down at a colossal rate of knots. His scales were burnt; some even dropping off, with the roiling molten liquid squeezing its way past those that remained, destroying the lining between them and his delicate skin. Epic was the only way to describe the mind numbing agony, but still he carried on, the numbers in his mind all the time counting down. Aware of how many dragons were up there in the arena, he knew he had to get as far down as possible. He had to. Everything depended on it.

Way up above, Silverbonce had managed to get Tri into the hands of one of the medics, the Dunedin Dragon mumbling his thanks to the old mouth guard as he was dragged into the depths of the medical bay. Players from both teams swooped down to surround the Warriors' mouth guard. It had been minutes since Steel had disappeared beneath the lava, with the crowd becoming restless, the players on both sides confused, and the referee helpless. With both squads swarming around him for some answers, the audience's restlessness turned to boos.

Needing everybody's attention, the old mouth guard knew there was only one way to get it done. It was something he'd been taught a long time ago by his then best friend. Searching frantically for the memory, astonishingly he found it, and began waving and weaving his wings in the most intricate of patterns. The booing subsided, with everyone mesmerised by Silverbonce's actions. Only a little chatter flitted around the stadium now, but it was too much.

"SILENCE!" commanded the Warriors mouth guard, putting more than a little magic behind his words. Instantly, the crowd quietened.

"Listen to me... NOW! We need to evacuate the arena... at once!"

"But why?" demanded the referee.

"We don't have time for this," exclaimed the old

mouth guard.

"We're in danger. Every dragon here. I don't know how or why, but there's a BOMB implanted within the ball. And so for everyone's safety, we need to clear the area... RIGHT NOW!"

Nobody needed telling twice. One of the dragon medics listening from just inside the medical bay punched the alarm. A shrill blaring like an air raid siren sounded inside and outside the arena. Dragons of all shapes and sizes started to flee in every direction. Some went on foot in their human form, using their magic to boost their speed, but most took to the skies, flying towards the nearest emergency exit.

Out of time, his last breath was fighting to escape; only the fear of his own death and that of the dragons above prevented him from opening his mouth. Every single part of him burned in excruciating pain. Having closed his eyelids as soon as he'd hit the molten magma, he was now starting to see bright light ahead of him, and knew that his skin had nearly been burnt away. It was time, he thought to himself, feeling lonely and desperate in what seemed like a world away from the laminium ball arena. Gathering all his reserves of energy, he shifted his weight to one side, drew back the arm of the hand carrying the ball, and with all his might threw it further on its way. Instantly he turned and headed in the direction that he thought of as up, putting everything he had into finding as much speed as possible. In reality he had no idea if he was right or wrong, having been under the lava for what seemed like an eternity, and if he'd been off by even a little when he'd dived beneath the scorching liquid, then he'd now be heading in the wrong direction. Kicking what was left of his tail, and pumping the bones in his wings furiously, determined to get as far away from the blast as possible, his thoughts turned to his teammates and the fans, hoping above all else that they'd made their way to safety.

Silverbonce told the players of both teams in no uncertain terms that they had to leave. But not one of them would go. They all steadfastly refused.

'They're all as stubborn as I am,' he thought, knowing that their regard for Steel meant more than their own safety. As they all soared above the lava, just off the entrance to the medical bay, one thought above all others surfaced in Silverbonce's mind.

'Come on my boy... you've had long enough. Make for the surface, make for the surface.'

Having been counting down in his mind, while at the same time racing through the lava for his life, a smile stretched across what remained of his face, as most of the scales there had been either burnt beyond recognition, or just simply destroyed.

'Ha... I'm not sure whether I'm actually flying, or swimming. What a ludicrous thought.' With his mouth clamped firmly shut, his intellect knew that it was being starved of oxygen... hence the rather bizarre notions. But his brain, much like what was left of his body, had little interest in dying. It liked life. It loved laminium ball. It wanted to... play again!

BOOOOMMM!!!! A crushing explosion reverberated far beneath the scorching hot magma, causing the rocky arena to shake uncontrollably. Huge chunks of debris tumbled from the roof. Large masses of the surrounding walls, where dragon families had been sitting only moments earlier, slipped into the blistering lava, causing huge waves to crash around its surface. Massive cracks splintered their way across the unstable ceiling and down the sides. Stone and rubble continued to fall randomly, creating a dust cloud so thick it was barely possible to see the end of your own extremities. Players from both sides, the medics and the officials huddled in the entrance to the bay, all nearly reconsidering their decision not to have left when they had the chance. Suddenly a huge ear splitting rumble rolled around the cavern, shaking more debris from the roof into the rolling lake of lava. By now most fans had made it out of the arena into the surrounding area, only to find themselves packed into adjacent tunnels on their way to the monorail station, all suffering the same panic and fear as those back in the stadium as the ground, ceiling and walls quaked all around them. Individuals and families screamed in terror as the world they knew roared with rage and trembled with dread. To a dragon, they all craved the open, fresh air. But there was just no way they could get there at the moment. Most settled on silent prayers to the Earth Guardian, a long forgotten god from ancient fables, something that was only recalled from the depths of dragon consciousness in times like these.

Minutes passed... slowly for those cowering from the shock waves. Gradually they subsided. The dragon domain in and around New Zealand leapt into action, knowing instantly about the problem and those trapped in and around that area. King's Guards, as well as the usual contingent of emergency services shot into action, immediately heading for the danger zone.

Above the lava, the dust cloud started to dissipate. All the players peeked out from the entrance to the medical bay where they'd taken shelter. Despite gaping cracks in the walls and the ceiling above them, it looked as though the stadium had survived the powerful blast... JUST!

'But what about Steel?' they all thought. 'Has he survived the blast?' Almost as one, they dived off the entrance, swooping up over the choppy molten magma that bubbled and boiled with a ferocity never before seen, searching for the brave and selfless laminium ball player, even those who were carrying injuries.

Elsewhere, those of their kind made their way towards one of the many exits. Disaster management technicians were now on hand, as well as the emergency services and the King's Guard. Tens of thousands of spectators were shepherded to safety out of the badly damaged tunnels, while the monorail was taken out of service until the line could be checked. As the fans left the tunnels, they talked about what they'd seen, with the emergency services and in particular, the King's Guard.

Flooding into the arena, the new arrivals were greeted by the sight of players from both sides, the referee and the medics soaring across the unstable molten magma. Peeling off to explain what had happened, the referee told them that they were searching for any sign of Steel. The leader of the King's Guard thought it utter madness to be looking for someone who'd disappeared beneath the lava so long ago, and said as much. But the referee, like the players, was still of the belief there was a chance that the fearless captain might still somehow be alive. The leader, however, chose to ignore this, and dispatched his contingent to check the structural integrity of the arena and the surrounding area. Rejoining the players, the referee informed them of what had been said. In stark contrast to only minutes ago when the match had been in full swing, the stadium had an eerie feel to it, as the sounds of flapping wings, bubbling and plopping magma and far off muttered mantras echoed throughout. It felt incomplete without the audience it was designed to hold. Continuing their search across the lake's surface, grim reality was starting to become etched on each of the dragon's faces.

Pulling up from the area that he'd been surveying for any sign of his friend, Silverbonce knew in his heart it was time to call it a day. Any hope of him enduring had long since evaporated, realistically. Tears welled up inside him. Trying his best to hold them in check, to no avail, they streamed down the scales on his cheeks, plunging into the smoking hot, orange lava, making a sizzling sound as they made contact. Trying not to let his voice give way, the old mouth guard told the others it was time to call off the search. Of course they were all devastated, but they too knew the moment had come. As a group, they made their way across to the medical bay, as that had been proven by the King's Guard to be the safest and surest way out. As the last dragon landed on the edge of the entrance, a boiling, gurgling, fizzing, bubbling sound whispered up from one of the dark corners of the arena's molten floor. Cheese alone turned to look back as some of the others made their way past him, clearly not having heard the noise. Goose bumps flitted across both his wings and down his tail. Dodging around Raptor, the last of the dragons to come in, instinct and his gut told him there was something out there.

"Wait," he cried, his soft voice echoing down the narrow tunnel. As one, the dragons all turned in his direction. "There's something out there."

Taking a step, he dived off and with one flap of his powerful wings, headed towards the far corner. At first, the others stood and watched. That is, until Silverbonce pushed his way through. He'd been the first to go into the tunnel, wanting to make it easier for them all, but he had no hesitation in following Cheese. The rest of players did the same.

It didn't take long, eight or nine seconds at most, and then Cheese was there, in that darkened corner. Silverbonce arrived next.

"What is it?" he asked urgently.

"I heard something, something over here."

"Are you sure?"

Cheese turned towards his teammate, a look of utter conviction spread across his face. Silverbonce nodded at his friend, sorry for having doubted him. Abruptly, a guttural gurgle boiled up beneath them. Although not an entirely uncommon lava sound, there was something different about this. It seemed almost too loud, too full of air. Then it happened again, only this time much more violently. By now, the remainder of the dragons had arrived and formed a huge ring around the unexplained bubbles in the steaming hot, viscous liquid. Smaller bubbles fizzed to the surface all around the much larger event. Some of the dragons drew back, afraid of what might happen, in case it was some sort of aftershock from the explosion. And then a giant 'SQUELCH' sounding like someone puckering up for a kiss, surprised them all, preceding a lonely grey shape bobbing to the surface. It was impossible for the dragons to make out what it was at first, because of the lava and the damage, but it didn't take them long.

"STEEL!" yelled Silverbonce at the top of his voice, immediately swooping down towards his friend. Joined by his teammates and the medics, Cheese, Barf and Zip all started to lift the sad and lonely dark shape.

"Careful!" screamed one of the medics, appalled at the damage the Warriors' captain had taken.

Barf looked over his shoulder and shot the dragon an evil look. As the limp, wretched body was pulled out of the magma, sighs of dismay echoed around the cavern. Not a single scale remained on the burnt and disjointed body of the brave laminium ball player. But that wasn't the worst part. While the wing carpus and metacarpus bones all appeared intact, the skin, tendons and ligaments of both wings had completely disintegrated; only the outer bone remained. After Steel had been hauled out, the medics moved in to check for any sign of life. None of the dragons there could see how that would even be possible, and after the sight of his wings, or lack of them, most hoped his soul had ascended to a better place. But to the shock and awe of the medics, Steel was still alive, albeit barely. Surprise abounded from them all. Quickly, they ushered those carrying him towards their station, despite protests from the King's Guards, who were still trying desperately to get everyone out of the area. But the medics were having none of it. With what remained of the brave captain in the medical bay, they shooed everyone else off and started their most challenging piece of work ever.

Forced to leave the arena, despite their protests and the fact that the Warriors wanted to remain as close to Steel as possible, it broke Silverbonce's heart not to be at his friend's side, particularly in light of the heroics he'd performed in saving them all. Had that bomb gone off in the stadium itself, the results would have been devastating. As it was though, only a few minor injuries, Steel aside, had been reported during the whole incident. Luck and Steel's bravery had served the dragon community well.

27 THE MAGIC ROUNDABOUT

Blissfully awakened a few minutes earlier, she decided to get up. Quietly, she pulled back the luxurious, Egyptian cotton covers on her side of the bed and brought her small but powerful feet down onto the intricate pattern woven into the expensive carpet.

'This is the life,' she thought, stretching and yawning at the same time. Feeling completely alert, she padded softly across the room to the full sized Venetian window. Twisting the metal handle as gently as possible, she pulled open the old wooden frame and gazed out contentedly, barely able to believe she was there.

It had started out the same as any old week... work, work, work, made even more unbearable knowing that the boys... Peter, Tank and Flash... had all disappeared off to New Zealand to take in the sights and watch the laminium ball match. Of course, she could have gone with them, they had invited her after all. It would have been a mistake though, she'd known that straight away. One little slip and they'd all realise that she'd gone back on her word, gone back to... Tim. Not wanting to put them in that position, she'd declined their offer, citing work commitments as her excuse. That's how her week had started. Two days in, however, things had changed dramatically. There she'd been, sitting in her office, trudging through emails, when the phone had rung. Annoyed at the interruption, she snappily answered the call and was pleasantly surprised to find it was Tim. Her ire at being interrupted disappeared instantly, replaced by curiosity as her love begged her to get the rest of the week off and leave as soon as possible. While something of a rebel in general she was, however, professional in everything she did at Cropptech, and little intention of letting anyone down. Tim though, was very persistent, and despite not telling her what he had planned, all he would allude to was that they would be able to be together without being spotted, and would have the time of their lives. In the end, it proved too much of a temptation. She asked him to phone back in fifteen minutes, which he duly did, by which time she'd booked the days off and arranged for someone to cover all her training commitments. On recounting this to her human love, he told her to get home as quickly as possible, and that he'd pick her up in an hour.

"Oh, and as well," he added, "don't forget to pack your passport." To say this piqued her interest was a massive understatement. Doing exactly as he'd said, not eight hours later they arrived in Florence, Italy. That had been two days ago. The whole thing had been a whirlwind of epic proportions, but as Richie stood, scantily clad, at the window, looking out over the Arno River with all its rich history, it occurred to her just how happy and contented she felt. Like everyone, she'd experienced perfect moments... who hadn't? But most of them had occurred in the middle of frantic lacrosse matches: sprinting down the wing towards the opposition's goal, ball cradled tightly in the head of her stick, hair flying out behind her, the sun shining through the clouds, terrified looks etched across the faces of her onrushing adversaries... PERFECT! Or dropping her shoulder one way and then diving the other, dummying with her stick, her rival falling for it big time. Continuing on her run, beating one, two, three more, until catching sight of the ball and knowing just what to do... Drawing her stick back, picking the exact spot, and then unleashing the single most ferocious shot ever, to win the most important match of her life... PERFECT! She could go on, of course, but you get the idea. Here she was, however, breathing in the refreshing Florentine air, the early morning sounds of the momentous city's hustle and bustle drifting up to greet her ears. Sighing softly, more out of contentment than anything else, she heard the bed rustle behind her, turning to see Tim sitting up, offering her a smile. A serene feeling of peace and tranquillity washed over her. Leaving the window open, she bounded over to the bed and threw herself into his waiting arms, as the bells of The Basilica di Santa Maria del Fiore reverberated around the city.

By the time the friends arrived home, news of what had happened in New Zealand was everywhere. It was the only subject of interest on the monorail carriages that they'd been in, as well as across all the stations, not to mention every single telepathic paper. Questions were supposedly being asked at the highest level... How did it happen? Who would do such a thing? Is it likely to happen again? Can safety be assured at other laminium ball matches? All these, plus the obvious questions about Steel's wellbeing. The outpouring of anger over the incident paled in comparison with the well wishes the Indigo Warriors superstar had received from around the world. Ordinary and famous dragons alike had left messages in telepathic get well books across the planet, some of which had made it into the papers. The mood of the dragon domain was one of shock that something like this could happen, anger and rage at whoever was behind it, and pride at the bravery and selflessness of Steel's heroic deeds.

Sitting on the concourse, enjoying a bite to eat, the friends had just disembarked at Pudding Lane and were waiting for the arrival of their monorail. All three had faraway looks on their faces, due to the fact that each of them was currently reading a different telepathic paper. For Peter, it was his usual 'Daily Telepath'. Tank was enjoying 'Sol', while Flash had taken to 'Speculum'. Each broadcast had its own take on the previous day's events, but none could sum up the terror the three of them had experienced. Again, it was Flash who'd saved them, like the calm in the middle of the storm, like the cool eye of a hurricane. As tons of rock and rubble fell, he, using all his experience and acumen, guided all the dragons around him to safety, once or twice throwing out minor mantras to deflect barrages of stone and debris. As well as his actions, what made it all the more impressive was his humility afterwards, not wanting any thanks from others not seeming to think that he'd done anything special. Both Peter and Tank were glad to be able to call him their friend.

Halfway through a paragraph outlining Steel's current condition, Flash felt the tiniest of niggles towards the back of his mind. Pausing momentarily, he searched for the cause of the interruption. It didn't take long to find it. In another part of his rather open plan brain, an image had appeared and was currently jabbering away. Dispensing with the paper, Flash zoomed over to take a look at this unusual development. On closer inspection, the representation appeared to be the king, albeit in his human form, presented in some kind of hologram, waving this way and that, continuously talking. Scanning the likeness from all sides, it was only when the ex-Crimson Guard dived inside with his psyche that he found the words *'The Date Of The Battle Of Pucallpa'* reading vertically from top to bottom.

'Uhhhh?' was Flash's first thought. But then he recalled one of the long conversations he'd had with the monarch on first arriving at his private residence. It had turned out that the ruler, just like Flash, was something of a history buff and liked nothing more than discussing historic events and battles that had taken place, dissecting them in microscopic detail, even speculating on what would have happened had the outcome been different. They'd both spent many a night doing just that, when George's schedule had allowed, with Flash being more than a little intimidated and nervous at first, but quickly put at ease by the king's pleasant manner and welcoming demeanour, after which both dragons had gone on to express totally opposite points of view. They hadn't done that in a while, with Flash knowing full well it was because of the sovereign's mountain of work that he had to get through. He missed those nights. But his mind, having wandered off a little, returned to the holographic inscription. As he read it again, it was all he could do to keep himself from laughing. And it would look very odd to everyone around if he suddenly burst out laughing in the middle of reading about the laminium ball disaster at the monorail station. Fighting back a smirk, he thought about the words. *The Date Of The Battle Of Pucallpa.'* It had to be a message, something that only he would know, a kind of kingly encryption.

Recalling a conversation on one of those late nights about Pucallpa, there had been no battle there, but the premise had centred around 'if there had been'. Pucallpa, a beautiful city in Peru, almost became the turning point in a South American Crusade in the late 18th century, but for a brilliant seek and capture initiative led by the famous dragon lawmaker, Alvin Comet. Nailed into history as one of the most audacious tactics ever to be played out, the capture of two of the most dangerous rogue dragons to have inhabited the world in centuries led to the cessation of hostilities and in turn spared tens of thousands of lives. Alvin Comet's name will forever be remembered in dragon lore. But Flash and the king had liked to play the 'what if?' game. During those late night discussions, both dragons had begun speculating about what would have happened if the capture of the dark dragons had never occurred. After much argument and disagreement, both reached roughly the same conclusion, albeit they got there in rather different ways, the result being that the war to end all wars would have taken place, in Pucallpa! Hence the cryptic message.

'But,' Flash thought to himself, 'what am I supposed to do with it?' In his mind, he tried moving the letters around. Nothing happened. Next he summoned up the words 'Alvin Comet', thinking that might unlock the hologram and make it talk. Just as he was about to give up and try and contact the king another way... a thought occurred to him. THE DATE! Although both dragons had reached the same conclusion with their speculation, neither could agree exactly when the battle would have happened. Flash had told the king in no uncertain terms that the date would have been 1769. Disagreeing wholeheartedly, the monarch laid out his theory as to why the battle would have taken place much later, in 1791. Both dragons had refused to yield after that, eventually agreeing to disagree.

'I wonder...' thought Flash, thinking about the date he'd suggested to the king. But he knew that wouldn't work. If any date at all was going to unlock the hologram, it would most certainly be the one the ruler had decided on. Instantly he whistled up the numbers 1791 in his head, and tossed them into the middle of the image of the monarch. Numbers and letters collided and then suddenly exploded outwards, causing the ex-Crimson Guard to instinctively squeeze his eyes closed, even though he was sure he couldn't be hurt.

The next thing he knew, the holographic king sprang back to life, only this time... it talked!

"Hello Flash," uttered the perfect likeness of the sovereign, his arms open wide. "If you're listening to this rather marvellous creation straight out of the research and development department, then clearly you've cracked my sneaky, but factually correct, encryption. Well done my boy! I miss our 'what if?' games, and hope that things become a little less hectic soon, so that we can resume playing. And on the subject of hectic, I need your help. I understand you were at the laminium ball match yesterday. To say things have kicked off would be rather an understatement. I'd like you to file a full report as soon as possible, but only to me please, including every last detail you can think of. Also, and here's the tricky bit, I'd like you to start your own investigation into exactly what happened. Currently the King's Guards and the Crimson Guards both have their own enquiries running side by side, but I need someone I can trust to look into things, and I believe your unique perspective would serve me well. I'm sure by now you realise that there's more to this than meets the eye, as well as understanding the danger I'm now placing you in. But if anyone's up to the task, then I know it's you. I would request that you don't tell anyone what you're up to, and I'm sorry to say that must include Peter and the rest of your new found friends. When you have something, anything... get in touch. The usual resources are at your disposal. Good luck. Your King."

Flash, still seemingly studying the telepathic papers, was struck by a confusing mixture of emotions. Delighted that the head of state trusted him to undertake the assignment, he was disappointed that he couldn't tell his friends what was going on, and more than a little afraid of not only what he would find, but also of crossing paths with the Crimson Guards, knowing on that count alone, he'd have to be extremely vigilant. Without hesitation, and knowing time was of the essence, he left the enclave of his mind and let his body overwhelm him. Only a split second later he was back in control, though momentarily it left him a little disorientated. For an instant he expected to be in his dragon form. On finding that he wasn't, a tinge of sadness crept over him like ivy running up the outside of a thatched cottage. Pushing the thought away, despite his anger at being held captive in this falsehood of a body, he leant closer to where Peter and Tank were sitting, both sporting slightly glazed looks. Announcing that he had to leave, his friends' attentiveness returned instantly, so that he could explain that he had a couple of errands to run for the king. Nodding their understanding, something crossed Peter's face for a moment at the mention of the monarch, but it was gone in the blink of an eye. Flash recognised it for what it was... jealousy, and to be honest, he couldn't really blame the youngster, knowing the full story of the king's relationship with him. But George was tied up with important matters, and until those were resolved Flash knew it was unlikely that Peter would be granted the time he so desired with the monarch. Standing, the former Crimson Guard shook both of them by the hand and then disappeared down the concourse, leaving the two friends to catch the monorail back to Salisbridge.

28 ODD BALL

Kneeling down on the slightly sticky floor, she picked up the new bottles from the crate and slid them to the back of the shelf, before placing the old ones in front of them, carefully giving them a little shake as she did so. It was mind numbingly boring sometimes... she knew that, but just supposed every job was like that in some way, shape or form. It was dealing with people and the resulting conversations that she liked the best, well, for the most part. It wasn't pleasant when they were really drunk, but even then they usually weren't too bad. Not as bad as the last couple of places that she'd worked at in the city centre. Scuffles and violence were a nightly occurrence there, and something that she'd learnt to hate. So much so, that she'd had to get away, look for another post... somewhere safer. It had taken the better part of three months to find one, here at the sports club, but she'd known within a matter of days that the move had been the right one for her. Mainly, it was quiet, particularly during the week. Oh, there was the odd event in the function room, the occasional committee meeting and training nights were quite lively, but usually people were courteous, good mannered and polite. She liked them all. The rugby players always showed the most respect, something that she found endearing. Her thoughts turned to Peter's friend Tank... he'd always been very polite and nice to her, but it was as obvious as the nose on her face that he didn't approve of her relationship with his pal. Unable to understand why, she wondered if Peter had in the past suffered a bad break up, with Tank looking out for his friend now in case the same thing should happen again. It wasn't the only thing she supposed. Perhaps it was her job, or perhaps there was something she didn't know, some dark secret that they both shared. A tight little smile flitted across her perfect, pale face at the very thought of her boyfriend having a dark secret.

Although not exactly sure why, the lacrosse girls intimidated her. They were all extremely fit and most were outgoing and confident with it.

'Perhaps,' she thought, as she added yet more bottles, 'it's because I'm so shy and unlike them in almost every way. I've never played a team sport, even at school, and my idea of fit is going to the gym once a week.' Still, she'd never had a problem in serving any of them in the clubhouse. And that left the hockey players. Standing up, stretching her arms high up into the air, something of a ritual after stocking the bar, thoughts of stick wielding sports men and women caused her to gaze out the window across the deserted Astroturf pitch. Peter didn't know it, but sometimes she sneaked out to watch him play. Taking her lunch hour late, or her break early, depending on the time of day, she'd blend seamlessly into the crowd and just focus in on him. Not really understanding much about the sport, as it ebbed and flowed backwards and forwards, she recognised his passion, commitment and regard for his teammates. It made her so proud. She was pretty sure he'd never caught her watching, although his friends almost had on a couple of occasions. Another smile lit up her face. When she thought of the hockey players that frequented this place, all she could think of was him. Hoping he'd had as good a time as he could while working away this week, he'd explained that infrequently, he had to travel overseas for his job to check on the security of the other Cropptech sites. This had been one of those times, and for security reasons he couldn't even tell her where he'd been. She'd just wished him well, and was deeply looking forward to seeing him tonight.

Brought back to the present by the squeal of the door to the bar opening and the soft gust of air that accompanied it, a mass of wiry, copper hair bobbing about with every stride, the chairman of the sports club walked in, his smart grey trousers befitting the dark blue blazer and matching tie.

She smiled, like sunshine on a dark, stormy day, water in a desert.

"Good morning," she remarked as he walked past, only to be greeted by a mumbled reply that she couldn't understand. She stood, stunned.

'How rude,' she thought, only to herself, knowing he'd never been particularly polite. Not only did she find him intimidating, but she always got the impression that she was somehow beneath him.

'Huh,' she reflected, 'well he's not going to ruin my day.' Picking up the empty crates from the floor, she headed through the swing doors at the end of the bar and up the stairs to the stock cupboard, following directly in the chairman's wake. Reaching the top, she strolled purposefully along the corridor, pushed open the cupboard door and stacked the crate on top of several empty ones. Turning to go back down, she just caught a glimpse of the chairman across the function room, sitting at the desk in his office, head in hands... sobbing! For some reason, Janice fought back her instinct to go and see if he was alright, wanting to, but for a tiny little voice deep within that urged her not to. And then her decision was justified. Out of nowhere the chairman bolted to his feet, turned to face the gunship grey metal filing cabinet beside his desk and went berserk, kicking, punching and head butting the defenceless cupboard. Thinking quickly, she pulled the door to, desperate not to be discovered. The chairman's 'moment' lasted longer than a minute, with Janice all the time cowering, too frightened to leave in case he caught a glimpse of her. Steadily, the sound of flesh on metal died away, only to be replaced by the loudest sobbing and coughing she'd ever heard. Peeking through the tiny gap in the door, she noted that he was back at his desk, facing directly away from her. With all the stealth of a stalking tiger, she slipped out, quietly pulled the door closed and padded softly down the stairs back to the bar, determined to be as far away from him as possible.

29 JUST DESSERTS

Just before hitting Paris, the answer came to him. After making his excuses and leaving Tank and Peter to catch the monorail back to Salisbridge, the first thing he did was board the next intercontinental monorail back in the direction of New Zealand. After all, it made sense. That's where events had taken place, that's where the King's and Crimson Guards were conducting their investigations, so that's where he needed to be. But the little voice in the back of his mind, the one he so often listened to, the one that had saved his life on numerous occasions, disagreed. It wouldn't tell him what he should do, only that it was a mistake to head back to the Southern Hemisphere. So he'd sat quietly in the near deserted monorail carriage, and pondered his next course of action. Exactly four minutes after leaving Pudding Lane for the second time in a week, in a flicker of genius, it came to him. The ball! That was the key to everything. Testimonies from all the players confirmed that much, in particular from the Warriors' mouth guard, Silverbonce, having claimed that he could feel the enormity of what was wrong when he held onto the shiny sphere. How this was possible, Flash wasn't entirely sure. But the ball was the place to start, of that he was certain. So with that in mind, just as the monorail pulled into Paris, he stood up and alighted.

In a rush, he sprinted up the stairs onto the station's main plaza, heading for the nearest information terminal. Normally designed to provide basic or local information, deep down all the terminals were hardwired into just three or four mainframes across the world. And he had an array of passwords that would grant him access to anything that he needed. Checking to make sure he wasn't being observed, he entered one of the many secret codes and then started searching for the classified information. It wasn't long before he had his answers. Deleting everything from the screen, he powered the terminal down and eyed the nearest LCD monitor. With his mind working out the number of changes he'd have to make, he scooted off across the plaza in the direction of platform eight, all the time wondering exactly what he'd find at his destination.

A few hours and a couple of monorail changes later, he disembarked, noticing the smell that was like nowhere else on the planet. An enticing concoction of smoky aromas, cooked food and... just plain hard work assaulted his nostrils in waves. It was far from often that he smiled, and he'd tried hard to change that recently, with the addition of his new friends a great help in that department, but on his numerous visits here, he always found himself grinning hugely. Today was no different.

Already having memorised exactly where he was going, he followed the hubbub of his own kind in their various guises exiting the station against the backdrop of bright lit neon adverts. It was crowded, almost like nowhere else. Dragons in their natural form bustled alongside their human shaped counterparts, the homo sapiens shaped ones like Flash, for the most part coming off worse. Wings clipped heads, talons raked shoes and worst of all, tails were everywhere. It was chaos, but in a good way. Tucked in the middle of the long line to leave the station, five or six beings wide, snaking out in front as far as the eye could see, he almost missed the sign that brought back all the memories. But he knew what to look for, sure of where it was. Glancing over to his left, peering through bumbling human and dragon shapes, he could just make out the tattered words on the crumbling old sign. "NEW YORK CITY WELCOMES YOU!"

Gradually the crowd thinned out, meandering off in different directions like the tributaries of a mighty river. Flash continued, all the time marvelling at the superstructures the dragons here lived in. They very much mimicked the sprawling city above in both scale and grandeur. Half an hour later, he arrived at his destination: a tall, nondescript, stone tower, with only one visible entrance, and no name plate or description of what it was. Stepping up, he resembled a dwarf against the oversized metallic door that clearly serviced more ancient prehistoric shapes than the one he currently found himself stuck in. Depressing the buzzer, he waited patiently.

"Can I help you?" answered a silky smooth female voice.

"I'm here on urgent business," announced Flash, sounding all official.

"I think you must be mistaken. This building is not the one you're looking for and you are most certainly not expected. Good day." And with that the intercom cut off.

It wasn't really anything more than he'd expected. Buzzing again, when the voice on the other end crackled into life this time, he didn't bother waiting. Instead he said,

"I'm here at the king's behest. You'd do well to let me in... immediately," putting more than a little menace behind his words.

Ten or so seconds later, a series of clicks erupted and the door silently swung inwards. Flash strolled forward, closing the door behind him. 'Magnificent' was the only word that would have adequately described the lobby. Stunning green and blue marble tiles weaved their way across the floor, as paintings from famous dragon and human artists littered the shimmering walls. Splendid candelabra, studded with precious gems, hung down low from the ceiling. 'Opulent' barely did this place justice.

Through one of the high arched wooden doorways a tall, thin, grey speckled dragon appeared, her tiny beady eyes focusing in on him. The same voice that he'd heard over the intercom drifted across the lobby.

"How do I know you're on the king's business?"

Lifting his left leg up, with his right hand he triggered a microscopic switch on the bottom of the walking boots that he wore. A tiny compartment about the size of a fifty pence piece flipped open. From it, Flash pulled out a sliver of purple metal. Hexagonally shaped, it bore the king's seal. He handed it over to the dragon who studied it carefully, before returning it.

"How can we help you?" she asked politely.

"You can tell me about the balls," Flash shot back.

"I... I... I... don't know what you mean," she stammered nervously.

"The laminium balls. I want to know all about them... NOW!"

Plodding softly up the stairs to his apartment on the eighth floor, all the time sticking to the shadows, both worry and relief coursed through his veins, having done exactly what they'd asked, down to the letter. It wasn't his fault things hadn't gone exactly as planned. Backing up against the wall, he stopped in the darkest point of the landing.

'What was that noise?' he thought, moving forward to sneak a look back down the flights of stairs he'd already climbed. There was nothing there, not that he could see anyway. 'I'm imagining things again,' he thought, not for the first time. The stress of not knowing where his wife was, or even if she was still alive, combined with what he'd done to the ball and the thought that even now the King's Guard might be coming for him, was almost too much. For days he'd waited to hear from the kidnappers, hoping in vain, so far, to get her back. But there'd been no word, nothing, and he had no idea how to contact them... they'd always found him before now. He let out a deep breath, the walk up evidently taking its toll. Reaching the door to his apartment, he scanned the corridor in both directions before inserting both keys in the two door locks, turning them at the same time. Bolting swiftly inside as the door clicked open, he quickly locked it behind him, before leaning against the wall, panting. With a reassuring sense of safety now that he was home, he brushed the wisps of hair that ran down the mottled scales across his jaw line, back behind his head with both hands and traipsed wearily down the corridor and into the living room, nearly jumping out of his skin at the sight of a human male sitting in the middle of the dark brown leather sofa facing him.

"Hhhooow diiiiid yyoooouuu gettt innnn?" he stuttered, suddenly more afraid than ever.

"Does that really matter?"

Breathing heavily again now, he was agitated and off guard.

"Where's my wife? What have you done with her?" he snapped at the intimidating looking being.

"That's why I'm here," the human whispered seductively. "I've brought her back to you."

"Where is she?" he asked excitedly.

"In the bedroom waiting," he answered, motioning to a doorway.

"Oh thank God!" he exclaimed, vaulting across the room to the entrance, before stopping abruptly, some way short. There on the huge expanse of a wooden bed lay his wife, wings spread, her head facing an impossible direction, her neck clearly snapped. A sense of desperation tore through him, like a raging river carving a new path for itself. The dragon he loved, and had done for over a century, was lifeless before him. It was all too much. This all happened in the blink of an eye, and then his sense of danger kicked in. By now though, as you'll have probably worked out, it was far too late. Whirling about, or trying to anyway, something had snaked its way around his throat and was throttling him. Frantically he tried to bat the human shape away with his wings, while at the same time using his hands to pull whatever it was away from his neck. But it was no good. The other being was just too strong, and his own bulky frame was constrained by the wooden doorway he'd been standing in. Abruptly, he thrust back his mighty head as far as it would go, hoping to make contact with his attacker, but it wasn't to be. His assailant had been prepared for this and had made himself as small as possible. Vision failing, he brought his arms around, punching and hitting for all he was worth. Kicking with his powerful legs, hoping to make contact with his razor sharp talons, he gave it all he had in one last effort. At one point, he felt a scratch, as something sharp broke the surface of the scales across his thigh, making him more furious than ever. But by then, the fight was already lost and he'd never really stood a chance. This all came to him as the black spots before his eyes transformed into a much darker, more comprehensive vista. His last thought was of his wife, of how he'd failed her. Darkness engulfed him. His soul left this world.

Flash had taken himself back to the monorail station, and boarded a carriage for the short hop over to the Westchester district of the dragon domain beneath the sleeping city of New York. From the staff at the clandestine facility, he'd gleaned enough information to know that he was looking for a Ball Upkeep Monitor or B.U.M. as they were known in the business, by the name of Professor Cedric Spanner. Married with no children, the lecturer lived in an apartment in Westchester, and had called in sick the last couple of days, unusual in itself for a dragon.

Ten minutes later, the ex-Crimson Guard had the apartment building in sight. It looked no different from any of the others on the street, but he couldn't help but wonder what the place held in store for him, with his mind whizzing through the possibilities. Would he have to fight? Would the professor come quietly? Would there be co-conspirators? That would present a problem if there were a few of them, he thought to himself uneasily.

Standing, clad in shadows, in the entrance to an alleyway directly opposite the high rise, he spent the next few minutes reflecting on the situation. Was it worth calling in some backup? He didn't want to blow the whole thing, and was sure he was in the right place and on the right track of whatever was going on, something the King's and Crimson Guards were clearly not. Scratching the stubble littering his jaw, he ducked back into the darkness as a dragon in human form exited the professor's building, looked around and then headed off in the opposite direction towards the centre of the small community. Somewhere inside him, a buzz of recognition bloomed, but he had no idea why, not recognising the man and from this far away unable to get any sense of him.

'Odd,' he observed.

Casting all thoughts of the stranger to the back of his mind, he made his decision; he was going in. Crossing the street, he strode purposefully up to the building, and with no security, just walked in. A torn sign adorning the lift read 'Out of order', not that he'd had any intention of taking it. Fully committed, he knew he had to act as quickly as possible. Sprinting across to the stairwell, he sprang up the steps three at a time, as silent as a ninja, heading for the eighth floor.

It didn't take long. Poking his head out, he gazed along the corridor. As expected at this time of night, it was empty. Trepidation threatened to overwhelm him, but he pushed his feelings aside. On a mission, a proper one, for the first time in a while, he was a professional, with a job to do. Sucking in a deep breath, he moved silently down the corridor until he found the right door. On spotting the two keyholes, he cursed, well... in his mind anyway. There was more security than he would have thought, so it would take him longer to get in, meaning there was more chance of the occupants noticing. From his back pocket he pulled out a small canvas tool case, and proceeded to take out the relevant sized lock pick, which he gingerly thrust towards the top hole. On making contact with it, the door moved back a fraction, ajar. Heart racing, a thousand questions engulfed his mind, primarily: why was the door open?

Wasting no more time, he put the pick and the tool case back in his pocket, and cautiously entered the apartment.

Stealthily, he made his way along the hallway, glancing into the small, empty kitchen. A cloak of silence shrouded the residence. Reaching the lounge, there was still no sign of anyone. Hugging the wall, he moved silently along to the nearest doorway. Stopping a metre or so short, he spotted the damage to the door frame.

'There's been a fight or a scuffle of some sort, and it looks recent,' he wondered. Prepared for anything, or so he thought, he leapt forward and, using the frame for support, swung around into the room. He thought he'd been primed for almost anything, but clearly that wasn't the case. Most certainly he hadn't been expecting this.

Lying on the bed, a scarlet coloured female dragon looked like some kind of grotesque artwork, her neck most certainly snapped. On the opposite side of the room, a dragon hung suspended from an overhead girder, like a carcass in a butcher's window. It took him a few seconds to process it all. Suddenly, he leapt over the end of the bed, while at the same time pulling his trusty knife from its sheath tucked in the small of his back. With a running jump, he sliced the ultrafine cord that the dragon was hanging from, and watched as the huge mound of a corpse thumped to the ground. Managing to turn him over onto his back was no mean feat for Flash, considering the body was at least four times bigger and heavier than the ex-Crimson Guard. After catching his breath, he set about looking for any sign of life, however unlikely that might have been. It didn't take long for it to become apparent there was none. Resting back against the bed, head in hands, he racked his brain. In all his time he'd never heard of one of their kind committing suicide... NEVER! Moments later he started running through everything he had to do. First he'd have to contact the king. After that, he'd make arrangements for the local authorities to come and deal with the situation.

'Damn,' he thought, 'none of it makes any sense. Perhaps they fought about something, and he accidentally killed her. That would at least explain the damage to the door frame.'

Despondent, he stood and turned to walk back into the living room to call the monarch, when something caught his eye. Crouching back down to floor level, he examined the mark he'd just spotted on the dead dragon's thigh. It was a scratch of some sort, and it looked familiar. And then it came to him. NAGA! Goosebumps raced up his arms and down his back. It was the strike of a naga, he was sure of it, having seen some images of the blow to his back that he'd only just survived.

'The man exiting the building before I came in... that's what the feeling was. He... it... was a naga! Sorting through the pieces of the puzzle deep inside his mind, it all started to make some sort of sense. They killed the professor and tried to make it look like suicide because they're behind the laminium ball explosion at the stadium. And I bet they used the professor's wife as leverage in some way. That would certainly fit with what he now knew.

This was more than just a phone call to the king. He was most definitely going to have to explain this in person. What to do about the crime scene though? That was the question.

30 FALLING... FURTHER AND FURTHER

With a satisfying thwump the fridge door closed. It was the second time she'd checked to see if the bottle of diet Pepsi was chilled. It was. She wanted tonight to be perfect, and knew that was his favourite drink. Pulling in a deep breath, she counted to ten in her mind. Getting as far as three, she gave up, becoming all flustered and a little giddy at the expectation of what was to come. Glancing down at her watch, she then automatically checked the clock on the wall. Both read 6.58pm. Pulse racing, the excitement was tangible, knowing that he would be here in less than two minutes. If nothing else, he was a stickler for punctuality.

During his time away she'd missed him something rotten. It hadn't even been a week, but it felt like forever. Creeping over to the window, she peered round the curtain, looking down the garden path... just as he arrived. Sprinting out into the hall, she undid the lock on the front door, pulled it open and threw herself into his arms. Of course he caught her. It hadn't been totally unexpected. The embrace felt warm, safe, dependable and familiar: think a child's unconditional love for its parent. Peter felt complete, though previously he'd been unaware that anything had been broken or missing. That came as something of a surprise, which he pondered as Janice pulled away slightly and kissed him full on the lips. Tasting sweet, with just a hint of strawberry, he found himself enveloped and smothered with love. Eventually they paused and headed inside.

Dark, effervescent liquid snaked in and out of the polar chunks of ice. Taking the proffered drink, he sat down on the sofa next to her as they waited for their takeaway to arrive.

Their chat was mundane to begin with. Janice asked

about his time away, and once again he explained that he couldn't reveal any details about it. Mentioning that it was okay, that he was glad to be back and had missed her like crazy, brought forth her legendary smile that lit up the room.

Feeling guilty about perjuring himself, he did consider it something of a necessity, given that his whole existence was one big lie. On many occasions he'd contemplated the entire concept of so many untruths: big ones, small ones, necessary ones, little white ones, and had never reached a particular conclusion. In the end he'd given up, because he always found himself going round and round in circles. Looking at it more in terms of doing the right thing and living his life the right way, if he'd have told Janice he was going to New Zealand, he'd have had to answer so many questions... all without revealing the truth. How are you getting there? Oh, didn't you know, there's a vast monorail system deep beneath the surface that zips around at incredible speeds, pulling unbelievable G forces? Oh, and did I mention it was manned (ironic!) solely by and for the use of... DRAGONS! Why are you going to New Zealand? There's this really fantastic sport called laminium ball. Played by, yes you've guessed it... DRAGONS! Two of many enquiries he would have had to answer with lies. So while he did feel a little guilty, deep down he knew he'd done the right thing. On top of all that, he'd never knowingly hurt her, or anyone else for that matter. Kind, thoughtful, selfless, he always tried to put others first and see things from their point of view or perspective. Something else that was important to him, and he hoped underpinned his ethos as a being, was to treat others as he hoped to be treated by them, although more often than not, this seemed to fail spectacularly. Usually he persevered with it anyway.

On enquiring how Janice's week had been, she went on to explain that it had been pretty dull, as usual, with one exception... the chairman of the sports club. Going on to describe his very odd behaviour in graphic detail, Peter was not only surprised to hear this, but completely and utterly shocked. While he wasn't on intimate terms with the chairman, he had played against him and alongside him during training (the chairman being a fellow hockey player), and he'd always got the impression that he was a pretty decent sort of guy. Pulling the cold glass up to his lips, letting the polar ice caps in it clink together, a faded memory surfaced as the fizzy liquid tickled the back of his throat. Goose bumps shuddered across his arms... MANSON! Instantly it hit him in stunning clarity. In the run up to the hockey match in which he'd faced the ex-army major, he'd gone up to the stock cupboard for Janice and, once there, had caught sight of the chairman and Manson together. If his memory served him correctly (which it should have, after all, he was a dragon) the disguised dark dragon and the official were arguing about something. Recalling the chairman's face in excruciating detail, because of his eidetic memory, he certainly didn't look happy, far from it in fact. It was then that Manson had spoken, and although Peter hadn't been able to hear what had been said, the words themselves had caused the chairman to go paler than the lightest mayonnaise. He could remember the evil dragon, in his human form, handing something over, well trying to at least. Whatever it was, the man clearly didn't want to take it, but eventually did, after some whispered words. The chairman had hurried off, after locking the mysterious object securely in his office. Guzzling a little more of his drink, Peter wondered if the official's strange behaviour was somehow related to whatever it was Manson had passed on. Vowing to talk to someone about it, all his thoughts returned instantly to the present as Janice nestled her head against his chest, and for all the world, everything else was forgotten.

31 HI HO, HI HO, IT'S OFF TO WORK WE GO

It had been over three days now, and he was starting to lose his patience, which was unusual for him as in the past it had always seemed like he'd had an unlimited amount. But here and now, it was as if he was being tried like never before. It had started the moment he'd got in on his first day back; instead of the usual cordial greeting, orders had been barked out at him. In a way, it was understandable... so he'd just quietly followed them, hoping that the old dragon would mellow after a few hours and be back to normal. But no. Three days!

Tank knew the master mantra maker didn't like it when he was away. For a start, he was lonely. Of course he'd deny that if challenged, but it was true. In addition, there was the medicine. Undoubtedly he'd failed to take part or all of what he was supposed to, despite him having laid it all out in microscopic detail before he'd left. This too would be part of the grumpiness... because he felt so unwell.

In spite of the awkwardness and how fed up he felt, the rugby player fought back a smile as he rolled up the delicate parchment of an ancient Germanic mantra, carefully placing it back on the shelf in the exact spot he'd taken it from. Deep down, he knew Gee Tee didn't mean any of it, well... not really. Still, it was distracting. They had important work to do and could use their time much more productively.

Giant footsteps with a distinctive shuffling gait thudded across the shop floor towards him. This time, like all the others over the past three days, he hoped that the old shopkeeper had got everything out of his system. Rounding the aisle that Tank was working in, the master mantra maker strolled along it, watching from a distance as his employee picked up yet another scroll and began to cautiously unfurl it. Focused on nothing but his job, he was totally oblivious to the footsteps that traipsed up beside him. There was a tut, followed by a deep sigh, before a pile of books that he'd not quite got round to yet were kicked to the floor, tumbling all over the place.

"Those all need looking at. I expect them sorted by the time you leave tonight," stated the old shopkeeper loudly.

Instantly, Tank jumped to his feet. Wobbling just slightly, Gee Tee instinctively took half a step back.

"ENOUGH!" declared the former apprentice, poking his finger right into the middle of his employer's giant scaly chest, unaware of quite how ridiculous it looked... a human (shape... anyway), standing up to a dragon twice his height.

"You need to take your head out of your scales and stop behaving like a petulant child," growled the plant and animal lover, now in full flow. "I'm sorry that it doesn't suit you that I've had a few days off... but tough! I'm here most of the time, looking after you, and I'm here now. I struggle to believe that there's another dragon in the whole of the kingdom that would put up with the kind of nonsense that I have to take from you. So now, YOU get to make a choice. You can either start behaving with some decorum, some manners and treat me how you'd expect to be treated yourself. Or," continued Tank, throwing the scroll he'd been holding in the direction of the old dragon, "I can leave and never come back. DECIDE!"

The look on the master mantra maker's face was priceless. Shock, terror, sorrow, they were all there in equal amounts, or at least that was the youngster's opinion.

Both stood silently facing each other for minutes, neither willing to give any ground. Looking as angry as he'd ever been, Tank watched as his boss removed his glasses and rubbed his eyes, looking wearier than ever. Knowing how hard the next bit was going to be for the old dragon, he was determined to give no ground and to hold his own.

"You're right... of course. I'm... sorry."

"I'm afraid you'll have to speak up... I can't quite hear you."

"I said, I'm sorry... as you're fully aware," answered the shopkeeper.

"Imagine my surprise that you even know that word," quipped Tank, sarcastically.

"I suppose I deserve that."

"That, and a whole lot more."

"I should know better. It's... it's... it's just that... when you're away, I feel so... so..."

"I know," Tank whispered, putting his arm across the back of the master mantra maker's wing, "but all this isn't fair. How do you think it makes me feel?"

Gee Tee bowed his head.

"I am truly sorry. I will try and make sure it doesn't happen again."

"That would be good. I don't want to fight with you, but occasionally I do need some time off."

"I understand, I do... really. So... how was the laminium ball match? Did I miss anything exciting?"

"You're kidding me, right?" he exclaimed, suddenly realising the old dragon wasn't.

"What on earth are you talking about?"

"You mean to say you don't know about the explosion?"

"I haven't a clue what you're going on about," replied Gee Tee, none the wiser.

Tank went on to explain what had happened and how Flash, at this very moment, was on a mission for the king, almost certainly investigating it in some way, shape or form, at least that was the conclusion that he and Peter had come to on their way home. Gee Tee was so taken aback that the former apprentice had to help him into the workshop so that he could sit down.

Leaning against the wall, he watched the last of them leave, despondently, all looking devastated, broken almost. It was odd. He'd thought that on some level they'd be pleased; after all, it wasn't every day that you got to stay in one of the most upmarket dragon hotels, the bill for everything picked up by the council. But they weren't pleased... far from it in fact. Drawing the only conclusion possible, that they couldn't take any of their belongings with them and that it was the middle of the night, perhaps the cover story, the reason for them having to move, was playing on their minds as well, much as it was on his.

Pretty routine, that's how his evening had been, up until the call anyway. After that, it was a non-stop blur. But when the head of state himself gets in touch, what else can you do? So he'd gotten on over to Westchester as quick as was dragonly possible. It hadn't taken long from the New York office he'd been in. Once at the apartment block, he'd roused all the residents of the eighth floor, all bar one, anyway. On his way there, he'd cast a little mantra. It was nothing fancy, well... not for him. Quite dull in fact, and mainly used as a distraction, with it designed to make random noises, some soft, some loud, banging, clicking, clonking, whizzing... almost every sound imaginable. With this in place, he set about convincing the residents that an infestation of African transmorphic millipedes had taken over the entire floor and that their lives were in very real danger. It hadn't taken long to convince them, not with his credentials. And so they left at a moment's notice, not allowed to take anything with them, escorted to one of the best hotels in the area. Shaking his head knowingly, it wasn't the first time he'd used the old 'African transmorphic millipede' routine. Of course they weren't real... there was no such thing. But if you dug deep enough into the dragon database, it was possible to come up with some information on them, particularly how deadly and relentless they were... even to dragons! Ruses just like that played an important part in backing up some of the necessary cover stories that the King's Guard would occasionally have to put out.

Making sure all the occupants had left, he checked the mantra surrounding the only apartment that had not been evacuated, as he'd been asked to do by the monarch himself. It was solidly sealed.

'Whoever cast this,' he thought, 'certainly knew what they were doing.'

With that, he confirmed that the lift was powered down and then headed off to make sure the guards on the stairwell understood their orders that no one was allowed on the eighth floor, no one but the ruler himself.

It had been quite a dizzying half hour for the old shopkeeper. Laminium ball and bombs... he'd never heard anything quite like it. But given everything that they knew... vote rigging on the council, nagas, dark dragons and prisoners in the Antarctic... nothing should have surprised him. Still... it did! It was a bold move from the slippery serpents, if indeed it was them, and one he considered particularly hard to pull off.

The smell of freshly boiled charcoal preceded Tank into the workshop, forcing Gee Tee to sit up in his chair, his long, discoloured tail wriggling about on the floor behind him as he did so. Tank handed him one of the swirling mugs of steaming hot liquid. Inhaling deeply, the master mantra maker savoured the aroma, before a frown creased his forehead.

"What else is in here?" he enquired quizzically.

Tank looked up at the ceiling as he replied,

"I'm not sure."

"Hmmm," muttered the shopkeeper, sticking a long, scaly finger deep into the dark, churning water.

Tank shook his head at the old dragon's impatience.

"Ahhhhhh," uttered the master mantra maker, pulling

out a perfectly formed, pink marshmallow, the size of a tennis ball. "Lovely!" With one quick flick of his finger, the marshmallow rocketed up into the air, performed a sedate loop just below the ceiling and, once gravity had got hold, headed back towards the gaping chasm that was now the shopkeeper's wide open mouth. As soon as it was in reach, his jaws snapped shut.

"So... what do you think?" reiterated Tank.

Forgetting all about his delicious sugary treat, the old dragon considered the question carefully before he replied.

"From what you've told me, that bomb was clearly designed to cause maximum devastation, and if not for... whatshisname...?"

"Steel," put in Tank.

"If not for Steel's brave actions, then by all accounts it would have succeeded."

Both paused momentarily, taking long draughts from their dragon sized mugs. Tank looked ill at ease in his human form (something Gee Tee had now come to accept in the shop, despite his initial protests), holding in his lap a mug twice the size of his head.

"What I can't understand is why any dragon would do such a thing. The death toll could have been catastrophic."

"To spread confusion, chaos, fear and panic no doubt," replied the old shopkeeper. "Why else?"

"But what sort of dragon *could* do such a thing?"

Waving the index finger of his free hand at his young employee, he began to shake his head.

"Think, my boy. You so nearly had it."

Tank's brow creased fervently, so much so that the lines across it resembled furrows ploughed in a field. Across the room, his boss was still admonishing him.

'What sort of... dragon?' Tank thought to himself. And then it came to him, well... sort of.

"Oh, so if not a dragon... then who?"

"Not necessarily 'who' youngster, but... 'what'?"

Pausing, the rugby player thought hard about what his

boss had just said.

"What on earth could possibly threaten the dragon domain in such a way?" The more he thought about it, the more impossible it seemed.

"Put the pieces together," whispered Gee Tee cryptically. "Your friend is the key."

This practically gave it away.

"PETER! So you think Manson's behind it all?"

Pulling in a shallow breath, the master mantra maker took another slurp from the giant mug in front of him.

"Interestingly, I was talking about Flash. But now that you come to mention it, perhaps the Cropptech traitor is involved."

"I'm not quite sure I follow."

"I was thinking that the whole laminium ball thing seemed so un-dragon-like. And as you so rightly pointed out, why would a member of our race do such a thing? But what if it wasn't a dragon at all? So, if not one of our kind... who, or what, else could it be? I'm inclined to recall Flash's not so happy encounter in the Antarctic."

"You think the nagas were responsible?"

"It does kind of make sense, well... from a certain point of view. But now you've mentioned Manson, I do wonder if they're not in it together."

"How so?"

"Well, think about it. Almost certainly the nagas would have no qualms about using a bomb to wreak havoc on the dragon population. It would probably be relatively easy for them to co-opt one of ours by blackmail or some other means, given that they have little in the way of morals. Once that's done... BOOM!"

"But what about Manson?"

"Remember what Flash told the king, youngster. The naga king is being held against his will in the Antarctic. What if the dreaded dark dragon is in some way blackmailing the nagas in an effort to make them do his bidding, using them as tools to attack us? It wouldn't be totally beyond the realms of possibility."

Picking all the pitch black boulders of charcoal out from the bottom of his mug, Tank slipped them between his lips. Because they'd been in the drink, they dissolved seductively on the journey from his mouth to his stomach, creating a kind of slippery bliss. After much consideration, he turned his attention back to his employer.

"I suppose it does kind of fit. But if that's the case, does it mean that the nagas are here amongst us? Can they take on dragon form as well as human? That seems unlikely at best, doesn't it?"

"I grant you unlikely, but nevertheless... possible. There are areas in and around the larger dragon cities across the world where they could disappear without any real trouble. Given the right contacts and enough money, pretty much anything's possible."

"And if the nagas were behind the laminium ball bomb, shouldn't we contact the king, or at least try and investigate it ourselves?"

"I'd bet a year's supply of top notch charcoal that young Flash is doing exactly that, even as we speak."

Nodding in agreement, the more Tank thought about it, the more everything the old shopkeeper said fitted perfectly into place. Wondering about whatever the former Crimson Guard was up to, he truly hoped his friend was okay.

"Speaking of the king," piped up Gee Tee, totally interrupting his employee's train of thought, "I've had an idea about counteracting the vote rigging that would appear to be going on in the council."

This piqued the youngster's interest as it was something they'd been working on for some time now; creating a forgery of the ring was proving incredibly difficult.

"Go on," suggested Tank, keen to hear what the old dragon had come up with.

"If we are to assume that one of the 'dark' or 'light' outlawed objects in that room is responsible for what is happening, and is stealing the power it needs to operate by hijacking it from the king's ring, then what would happen if another, more powerful item were put on that particular shelf? One that would supersede the object already stealing power, one that would give the ring no choice but to offer up all its power."

"Sounds great. Where on earth are we going to find such an object?"

Bursting into laughter, the shopkeeper's resonant booms bounced off the workshop's walls.

"Look around my boy," he urged, spreading his wings and opening his arms. "We have a veritable treasure trove of magical items, all of which can be adjusted to meet our needs."

Letting out a little chuckle, Tank knew the old dragon was right. However, there was still one particular little problem.

"But how on earth do we get it into the council chamber?" he asked sceptically.

Flashing him a smile that was as wide as it was cunning, the Emporium owner replied,

"I do believe we're long overdue for one of our King's Guard inspections."

Shaking his head more in admiration than anything else, it was at times like this that Tank just sat back and marvelled at the true genius he knew his employer to be.

32 TOUGH AS STEEL

Clear liquid bubbled away inside a huge glass jar on a sterile white table. At the bottom of it lay half a dozen or so unrecognisable objects, looking like tiny black leaves which had been rescued from a forest fire. Where once they would have been flat, thick, strong and slightly pliable, the delicate objects were now curled right up, flimsy and thin. Unbelievably, they were scales... dragon scales! And they were the only ones remaining from the famous, heroic laminium ball playing dragon called... STEEL! Rescued by one of the on duty medics on that fateful day, he'd spotted them drifting on the surface of the furious bubbling lava, alongside the laminium ball star's broken and battered body. Recognising them for what they were, the quick thinking medic had scooped them up and immediately placed them in a sterile container, before helping to cart the barely living hero back to the medical centre. Now the scales remained locked away in this rarely visited space, part of a pioneering new experiment using new and untested mantras by the most eminent scientists from across the globe, under the direct orders of the king himself.

Two rooms down, in another deeply sterile room, what survived of the courageous laminium ball playing dragon clung limply onto life, his body a wreck, despite the ministrations of some of the best dragon physicians in the world. His scalded and burnt frame looked like the charred remains of an animal caught up in a burning building. Only the bones from the wing radius remained; the tissue from the wings themselves had disintegrated completely. Ribs were exposed and warped out of shape, as well as the caudal spade (the end of his tail that controls advanced aerobatics and in his case, used to hold and move the laminium ball) had been totally shattered and was missing. How he was clinging onto life was a mystery to all the medical staff. But somehow, against all odds... he was. And that was enough for now. All of them... surgeons, scientists, nurses, cleaners... were working around the clock, deep inside the secluded London facility that he'd been transferred to only days after the match. Things were looking bleak, bleaker than any of them had ever known. But they were buoyed and impressed with his desire to live and just hoped that they, like him, could live up to his name.

33 IN NEED OF A KING SIZED BED

Soft snoring echoed throughout the aisles in the single most magnificent library of its kind. Sitting slumped at a beautifully carved oak desk, situated in a tiny alcove off one of those aisles, the source's left hand was hanging limply down by his side, while his right hand had the slightest of grips on an exotic looking fountain pen made from brushed laminium, coloured blood red. Once a gift from an emissary to the current writer's predecessor, it had just finished writing the word 'urgent' on an expensive vellum sheet, nestled snugly on the table beneath tousled long grey strands of hair, before the writer had clearly dropped off, exhausted.

An hour or so later, he awoke with a start, the first thought running through his mind being exactly how terrible he felt. Sitting up, he dabbed at the drool that had spilt onto the vellum, with the sleeve of his robe. Rubbing his neck, it felt stiff, tense and knotted. Whispering a curse as he struggled to his feet, the muscles in his back and legs started to spasm. Casting the pain aside as a mere inconvenience, he picked up his precious pen and the beautifully crafted piece of vellum and headed for the nearest staircase. Reaching the ground floor, he headed on through to his living room, briefly considering seeking out his bed. But there was too much to do, doubly so since that dreadful explosion at the laminium ball match. Since then he'd hardly had any sleep, hence his little visit to the land of nod, in the middle of replying to important correspondence.

Entering the expansive kitchen, he flicked the switch on the coffee machine and waited patiently for the caffeine boost that he so desperately needed. Despite everything on his mind, his thoughts turned to one bright light, the one being in all of this he was convinced he could trust... Flash! Despite his rather unfortunate human shaped condition, the ex-Crimson Guard had proved his worth many times over; in the brief period he'd been investigating the stadium bombing, he'd achieved more than the King's and Crimson Guards put together. With the apparent vote rigging, and now this, the world seemed to have turned on its head. Having Flash metaphorically by his side gave George hope, hope for the future, hope that whatever evil was being perpetrated could be summarily defeated and banished for good.

Swigging some of the very strong coffee, he brushed his wavy, grey hair back behind his ears and ran through the list of things he had to do in his head, one that got longer as each hour passed. Deep down inside he longed for the day when the damn thing was but a distant memory, when he could saunter out amongst other dragons, and experience life as it should be.

34 WHISTLE WHILE YOU WORK

Brilliant bright sunshine set against the backdrop of a stunning blue sky, reflected every which way off the windscreen on his rather happy drive to work. For the most part, he liked being behind the wheel, often thinking that if he couldn't do the job he was in, he would have liked to have done something that involved driving. Not anything big, like container lorries or large vans, mind you, just something that meant he could chauffeur a nice car around. On occasion, he'd found himself chatting to the engineer who regularly visited his office to repair and maintain his printer. From the man's description, it sounded like that career would suit Peter down to the ground: a company car, all that travelling, not necessarily being your own boss, but being left to your own devices and able to use your own initiative. He could just see himself cruising along the motorway on a hot summer's day, window down, blazing hot sun warming the skin on his arm as it hung out effortlessly, radio tuned to his favourite station.

Daydream slipping away as he flicked the indicator down to signal a right turn into Cropptech's main entrance, his smile remained as he gently applied the car's brakes, stopping directly in front of the red and white striped barrier. As a burly guard stepped forward, Peter fumbled with one hand for the security pass that had gotten tangled around his neck, while winding down the window with the other. By the time he'd completed those two relatively simple operations, a large grinning head much the same size as a basketball, loomed into view.

"Must be quite tricky, a man of your position, multitasking," stated a very formal voice, noticing Peter's lack of dexterity.

Fingers flapping about in a panic, the hockey player gazed up at his would be inquisitor... and let out a low chuckle.

"Fancy you being out here this morning. Aren't you supposed to be on toilet cleaning duty?" he replied, trying to remain as deadpan as possible.

"Nope! Checked all the toilets earlier. The cling film's all in position as it should be."

Covering his windscreen with spittle, Peter burst out laughing. The 'cling-film-on-the-toilet' trick was a renowned hockey prank, as he'd found to his cost at a house party to which he'd been invited on first joining the club, and he'd been on his guard ever since. At least he'd managed to laugh about it... eventually. On one lonely nightshift that he'd helped to cover, that story and a few others, had come out, with his colleagues finding the whole incident hilarious, and not a week passed when it wasn't mentioned in some way, shape or form, particularly by the individual now leaning halfway through the car window, Peter's friend... OWEN!

Both had started in the security department at exactly the same time, with the young hockey playing dragon grasping the tailor-made opportunities for promotion that came his way more than anyone else's, due to the now deceased, former head of security (and of course dragon) Mark Hiscock. For his part, Owen had never seemed to mind or showed any sort of resentment towards Peter, even though others in the same position might have. So the two had become firm friends, a friendship that in Peter's eyes had increased tenfold when, at the height of the Manson fiasco last year, Owen had stood up to the two goons that had escorted him off the site at gunpoint in front of almost the entire company. At the time, he'd been at the lowest point in his life; having been caught out by the evil ex-army major, who'd unexpectedly turned out to be some sort of new fangled dark dragon in his own right, plus he'd felt as though he'd failed his pals, and as though he had no one to turn to. Owen's brief bout of defiance had buoyed his spirits no end that dark day, and on his return, in his very first meeting with Al Garrett, the first thing Peter had done was arrange for Owen to get a well deserved promotion of his own. So the basketball shaped head, shaven of all but the tiniest amount of fuzz, now poking into the car's interior, belonged to the Assistant Security Coordinator, Peter's deputy.

"I'm glad you checked all the toilets. I'll be sure to mention your thoroughness in your next review. Are you going to let me through now?" enquired Peter, the traffic building up behind him.

"Sure thing... boss!" replied Owen, standing to attention, giving Peter a mock salute, in the style of Benny Hill.

Smiling as the gate lifted up in front of him, Peter zipped off to find a space in the car park nearest to his office.

Once at his desk, tackling those pesky day to day jobs, he'd already figured there would be little or no chance of it happening, but to his surprise, his email offer of lunch in the staff canteen was duly accepted. What started out as a good day, had just got better.

On the cusp of lunchtime, he stood twiddling his thumbs outside the double doors of the staff canteen. Glancing up at the oval shaped clock on the wooden wall opposite, it read 11.51. Richie was late... as always. They'd agreed to meet at ten to twelve, and although only a minute past, he felt the same pent up anger he always did when people weren't punctual. Richie was nearly always the usual suspect on that count. Interestingly, Janice was the only person he could think of who understood his obsession. In the short while that he'd known her, never had she been late for anything... not once. That thought burst into a billion pieces as the lacrosse superstar ambled around the far corner of the corridor and flashed her trademark grin. Instantly he forgot all about her tardiness. Greeting each other with kisses, which seemed to be the norm these days, he commented that she looked absolutely radiant.

With that, the two joined the queue (which was meagre at this relatively early time of day) bought their food and adjourned to a table at the back of the hall. Much of the conversation was left to Richie, with Peter diving straight in. Going on to explain at length about her work, the courses she'd been both on and running, as well as some of the gossip from her part of the building, Peter nodded in all the right places, while paying genuine attention to all the things going on in his friend's life. It hit him while he was chewing on a mouthful of turkey laced with stuffing, just how proud he was of her. So much so, that it almost brought a tear to his eye.

"Are you alright?" she asked.

Thumping his chest, he coughed a little, pretending some of his food had gone down the wrong way.

"That'll teach you to shovel it down so quickly," she laughed.

Nodding in agreement, just as a thought occurred to him, he went on to explain about the chairman of the sports club's odd behaviour, and even reminded her of the little incident he'd seen with the official and Manson. Not able to make head nor tail of it either, she promised to let him know if she heard anything along the same lines from any of the lacrosse girls.

"So how is the lovely Janice?" cross-examined Richie, cutting to the chase.

Peter's coughing fit wasn't exaggerated this time; it was so bad, she thought she might have to perform the Heimlich manoeuvre on him. Waving her away, he washed down his mouthful of food with a large slurp of water.

"Well...?" she remarked, still not willing to give up.

"She's very well, thank you," he replied, blushing profusely.

"Owwww... sweet," teased his friend. "But you know that's not what I want to know."

This was starting to get really uncomfortable for Peter,

and worst of all, he couldn't see any way in which it was going to improve.

"I don't know what you mean."

"I think you do," she replied, loving every minute.

"I don't know what you want me to say, Rich."

Leaning across the table, just to make sure they weren't overheard in the now crowded restaurant, she whispered softly in his ear.

"Is she worth it Pete? Worth the law breaking, and the resulting punishment that'll come your way if you're caught? Would you lay down your life to save her?"

Pulling away, leaning smugly back in her chair as Peter carefully considered her words, the lacrosse player was almost certain she had him. As tables and chairs filled up all around them, the food line got steadily longer and the noise levels increased, she sat there expectantly. Knowing that there was no way to get out of it, he treated her question with the respect it deserved and thought carefully before replying.

Just the image of the stunningly attractive blonde bar worker made him smile, creating a warm, fuzzy feeling throughout the length of his entire falsehood of a form. Try as he might, he just couldn't picture his life without Janice, his bar tending beauty. Was it worth all the potential trouble? Oh yes! Would he lay down his life for her? In an instant! Glancing across at his friend, sitting there smugly, she'd obviously known the answers to the questions before she'd even asked them, even if he hadn't.

"Amazing isn't it?" Richie announced from her position of experience.

"What is?" he replied, slightly afraid of the answer.

"Amazing how quickly it creeps up on you and bites you in the ischium." (That's a dragon's bum to you and I.)

He still looked a little perplexed.

"Humans, Pete," she mouthed, so that only he could hear.

Reluctantly, he nodded in agreement. Once again, his

friend leaned across the table.

"Make the most of it. You deserve it. And... she's lovely."

Of all the things she'd said to him, this brought a lump that felt like the size of a small planet to his throat, but before he had a chance to respond, Richie was out of her seat and up onto her feet.

"Anyhow Pete, gotta dash. Work to do and all that."

Both friends gathered up their dirty plates and cutlery, stacking them neatly in some shelves towards the front of the restaurant. As they did so, Peter whispered in Richie's ear.

"How are things with Tim?"

She froze... for a fraction of a second anyway. Turning slowly, so as to make a point, she gazed purposefully into his eyes.

"You know full well that it's over... I had absolutely no choice. I wish there had been another way, I truly do. So, my friend... make the most of what you have. Who knows when and where it will end?"

And with that she clapped him on the shoulder and vowed to catch up with him on Saturday, when she would be playing lacrosse and he would be playing hockey.

35 ALARM BELLS RINGING

Pulling on the number three shirt he wore so proudly, he gazed in the full length mirror to check out how he looked. Shorts with lycra underneath and double socks on each foot to hold his shin pads in place, set off his white and lime green Astroturf trainers. Trailing down to his shoulders, part of him wondered if it was time to have his dark hair cut into a different style of some sort. He did love it, but very few males carried their hair that way now, and given that he was growing up and held more responsibility at Cropptech, perhaps it was time to bite the bullet. As well, he never really knew what to do with it on the hockey pitch. Quite often it got in his way, and he'd thought on numerous occasions about tying it up, but that seemed far too... girly. Another option he'd considered was a bandana, but whenever he played against somebody wearing one, that particular player always seemed to be a fully fledged, prize muppet, and he certainly didn't want to be cast in that mould. Anyhow, he was ready to wage war... well, on his chosen battlefield anyway, that of the hockey pitch. Satisfied that he at least looked the part, he continued packing his dark green kit bag, making sure to include his towel, shower gel and a full change of clothes. You could almost guarantee one or other of his teammates would forget something, normally one of the younger ones, and for that they would either get fined, or win the dreaded award... the one that involved wearing the pink cowboy hat and matching pink skirt. So far, he'd always done just enough to avoid that dubious honour, and desperately wanted to keep it that way, doing everything he could, on and off the pitch, not to become complacent.

Across the other side of town at the exact same moment, a very different kind of packing was going on.

Inspecting each stud on the bottom of his immaculately clean boots, Tank concluded that they were all fine and proceeded to wrap them in plastic, before placing them gently in the bottom of his wardrobe sized kit bag. Next, his team strip... shirt, shorts, socks... all ironed to within an inch of their lives. Checking that he had the usual strapping for his head and hands, a full water bottle and his very own first aid kit, last of all, he placed a neatly folded towel, some shampoo, shower gel, deodorant and a small bottle of aftershave into the top zipped pocket.

'Rugby players do things right,' he mused, whizzing the zip around the kit bag to seal it up. 'Not like those ungainly hockey and lacrosse jocks who just turn up all scruffy, some already in their kit, some not.' Twisting his dark blue club tie into place, finally he pulled his blazer from the clothes hanger over which it had been draped, slipped it on, checked that he looked perfect, and after picking up his bag, headed downstairs.

In a not too distant flat, it was a whole different story. Somewhere there was a large double bed, but it was impossible to see where at this precise moment, as it looked as though some kind of clothing bomb had gone off, scattering items everywhere. Socks, knickers, a crumpled towel, as well as half a dozen different tops and three or four rain jackets littered the room. Trousers and shoes lay scattered across the fluffy beige carpet; well, the glimpses that could be seen looked beige. Richie Rump's match day preparation differed a great deal from that of her friends. Continuing to root about in one of her drawers, she finally found the tightly fitting red top that she'd been looking for. Grabbing the light coloured jeans that she'd only moments ago flung across the bed, she rolled them up with the top and tossed them casually into her pink and white emblazoned kit bag, adding a scrawny looking towel for good measure. Fleetingly, she checked the large zipped end pocket, making sure she had shampoo and deodorant, and that the prized *alea* that she wore almost all the time was wrapped tightly in a small leather wallet, so that she could put it on after showering. Playing lacrosse was the only time she didn't wear it, as it would stand out and lead to too many awkward questions. But she loved it, because it made her feel powerful, secretive and safe, all at the same time. Picking up a couple of spare balls from behind the door, she lobbed those into the bag from a distance, pleased to see that her aim was its usual... spot on. Grasping the handles of her still open bag, she swept up her two favourite lacrosse sticks from the side of the wardrobe as she passed by and gazed lovingly at the gorgeous linen dress Tim had bought her in Florence. Intricately embroidered with flowers, it looked stunning clinging to a clothes hanger, dangling from the top of her wardrobe door. Clumsily, she headed downstairs, her sports skirt flapping behind her as she did so, the tiniest jolt of excitement running through her, knowing that he'd be at the club at some point today, looking forward to their next sneaky rendezvous. After tying back her hair, she too was ready for the weekly battle. But not just ready to play... ready to WIN! For her, nothing else was imaginable. Failure was not an option.

The clubhouse was relatively empty. One or two people were about... grounds people making sure the rugby and lacrosse pitches were suitably marked out and in the best condition possible, the occasional contingent of players wanting to buy a drink to take with them to their away matches or use the loo before their journeys, and the odd member of staff. Janice usually treasured this particular time on a Saturday, thinking of it as the calm before the storm, as the afternoon and evening were easily the busiest points of the week. But this morning, she felt uncomfortable. The manager had let her in nice and early and to her credit, as always, she'd simply got on with her work: stacking the shelves, checking the pumps and the barrels in the cellar, making the place look clean and respectable, emptying the dishwasher... all those things and more. But about halfway through her long list of jobs, the bar door had swung open, and in had stormed the chairman of the sports club. 'Stormed' was the only way possible to describe it. Taking one long look at him, she knew it would be unwise to make even the friendliest of comments, and so didn't even bother to try. Instead she watched from the other side of the bar as he stomped across the as yet unvacuumed carpet, banged open the door at the bottom of the stairs and trampled all the way up to the first floor, all of which she could hear. Judging from the look on his face, he was in the kind of foul mood that would make Sir Alan Sugar look like a sugar plum fairy on a day out at Disney World. Choosing to ignore what had just happened, she got on with everything else on her list, focusing intently on the thought of seeing her beloved Peter later on in the day. That notion had just the right effect, and not five minutes later she was singing one of her favourite songs as she swerved in and out of all the tables and chairs with the vacuum cleaner.

An hour or so later, with the bar and seating area looking immaculate, though now starting to fill up with customers, one of the female hockey players came running through, covered in sweat and out of breath.

"Please can we have the key to unlock the double side gate to the Astroturf?" she puffed. "One of the opposition has fallen and damaged her ankle rather badly and we've had to call for an ambulance."

Janice knew the only way to get an ambulance anywhere near the pitch was through the double gate, of which there were only three keys to the lock: one each for the hockey men's and ladies' first team captains, both of whom were elsewhere, and one always kept on site, located on a little silver hook on the wall of the chairman of the sports club's office.

(Incidentally this was the key to the same gate that had raised questions on the bonfire night Manson had attempted to flee with the stolen laminium and murdered his cohorts in their van in cold blood. No one had been able to explain to the dragon authority investigators, in their human guises, how the gate had been opened that night, and of only three keys to that particular lock, how two had disappeared. Of course little was made of this at the time amongst the sports club members, due to the fact that the memories of all the spectators from that night having to be quickly and permanently erased by an elite team of King's Guard, put together for just such contingencies.)

With few other bar staff about, and understanding the urgency of the situation, Janice knew what she had to do, despite really not wanting to.

"I'll go and grab the key from the chairman's office and bring it out to you. Shouldn't be too long," she said, smiling reassuringly.

"Thanks," replied the player, turning and sprinting back out to the pitch.

Shaking her head at the thought of what was to come, she headed hastily up the stairwell at the end of the bar, all the while telling herself to be calm and polite whilst dealing with the chairman... after all, it would only be for a few brief moments. Reaching the top of the stairs, she nipped round the first door on the right and into the function room. From where she was she could just make out the door to the chairman's office was ajar. Keen to get on with her urgent quest she strolled over, knocked lightly on the door, and started to push it open, while at the same time politely saying,

"Excuse me." As she entered, the chairman swivelled back round from the wooden desk in his high backed chair, his freckled, bony hands trembling, his narrow face the colour of beetroot, barely able to contain his erupting anger.

"OUT!" he ordered, pointedly, signalling with his arm.

"But, but... I... I... I need the..."

"I DON'T CARE... OUT! NOW!"

Thoughts of the poor injured hockey player out on the pitch, awaiting an ambulance, and Peter's assumption that all hockey players are friends wherever they are in the world, whether you've met them or not and if not, then they're a best mate just waiting to happen, buoyed her spirit and strengthened her resolve.

"The, the... hhhockey pplayers... on the... ppitch need the kkkey to open the bbig gates," she stammered horribly. "Ooone of them has bbbbeen hurt," she announced, managing not to burst into tears, but shaking more than a little.

Deep inside the chairman's world of total and utter madness, the tiniest hint of sanity started to filter back, his breathing slowed to long, ragged breaths, his hands almost having stopped quivering. But still, he looked a state. Janice wouldn't have been at all surprised to learn that he hadn't slept not only last night, but for the last few nights. In fact he looked so bad, she thought he might have been sleeping rough.

With the colour of his forehead having almost turned back to normal and his breathing under control, he dismissed Janice with a casual wave and an overwhelming arrogance.

"The key's on the wall. Take it and go," he commanded.

Turning to look at the key dangling from the hook, because of her diminutive stature, she knew that she'd struggle to reach it, and so with the chairman having already forgotten about her, she got as close to the desk in front of the wall as she could, leant over it and reached for the key. As she did so, the table jarred ever so slightly.

Instantly, the chairman turned with an angst on his face the like of which Janice had never seen. In an instant his whole head had turned pale and clammy, and his eyeballs looked as though they were about to pop right out. This time it was his turn to stutter.

"Ssstop," he whispered, his arm outstretched, his palm turned up.

Janice had gone right the other way now, and didn't have a clue what on earth was going on.

"Okay," she replied, mystified.

Tiptoeing over in a bizarre manner, almost as if walking through a minefield, he carefully leant in front of the beguiling beauty, snatched the key from its hook and handed it to her.

Taking a step back, she gratefully accepted the key. It was only then that she noticed the dark, matte black metal box on his desk, a tiny window adorning the front, through which she could just about see a series of red, digital numbers, counting down by the looks of things, and in the background the most captivating shard of metal she'd ever seen. Slinking over in front of her, strangely, the chairman knelt down and checked the box from that perspective, anxiously making sure it hadn't moved in even the slightest of ways. He didn't touch it mind you, looking too terrified to get his hands or fingers anywhere near it. Janice just stood back and watched, unsure of what she was supposed to do. Once he had determined the container hadn't moved, he got to his feet, visibly relieved, looking deeply uneasy. Momentarily, she thought about questioning him about it, but of all the things in the world she was certain of, right at this very moment, asking about it would be the worst thing she could do. So in a flash, she dangled the key in front of his face, and declared,

"Better get this downstairs and let the ambulance in. Thanks once again," and with that she dashed purposefully across the function room, back into the corridor, down the stairs and across to the hockey pitch, all the while seeking the player that had originally come into the bar. During all this, her inquisitive mind tried to put together all of the preceding events and answer the really big questions. Not only: what was going on in the chairman's office? But also: what was going on in his mind?

Tank was the first of the three friends to arrive, the ever increasing sun glinting off the metallic finish of his car like some kind of 80's disco ball. Appearing dapper in his shirt and tie, the look increased exponentially when he casually slipped on his blazer. Manhandling his huge kit bag from the boot of his car, he headed off towards the changing rooms, pleased to be soaking up the rays from the almost midday sun.

Next, it was Peter who pulled into the crowded car park in his five year old blue Ford Fiesta, carefully weaving in and out of the other vehicles until he found a parking space that he liked the look of. Ideally, there would be just one space left in any car park he found himself in, but very rarely was that the case. Never having had any trouble parking his car in any sort of space... it was simply the choice that bewildered him, always making him wander round and around, ignoring space after space, just because he couldn't choose which one to pull into. Today was no different, and after passing over four different gaps, he finally settled on one, almost identical to the others. Crazy! Pulling the handbrake tight (it had a habit of slipping off), he checked to make sure the car was in gear and got out, snatching his kit bag off the back seat as he did so. Opening the boot, he retrieved his stick bag, turned the key in the lock and strolled casually towards the changing rooms, all the time, like Tank, soaking up the sun's rays. The warmth on his skin reminded him of the first time his animal and plant loving pal had hooked his television up to the buffer of the nodes that carried the telepathic newspapers around the world, and gradually the sandskimming on the new course in the Sahara desert had flickered into view. At the time he could remember feeling so envious of the natural warmth those black and white pictures had conveyed, and had even vowed to save up so that he could holiday there at some point in the future.

"Pete... how are you doing?" called out a voice from behind one of the rows of cars, startling the young dragon from his thoughts of flight and hot skies.

"Hi Andy. I'm fine thanks... how are you?"

"Oh... you know," replied the second team captain, winking. "Bit of a late one last night if you know what I mean. Out nightclubbing with some of the lacrosse girls."

This raised Peter's interest, and his opinion of Andy's drinking ability, if he could keep up with the lacrosse girls on a night out.

"Was Richie there by any chance?" he enquired offhandedly.

"No, didn't see her all night. Some of the girls mentioned she'd been invited, but she claimed to have had something else on," he replied, sounding a bit throaty.

Nodding, he was once again astounded at not just Andy, but at the human propensity for alcohol consumption in general. Never really being able to get his head round it in his relatively short dragon life span so far, he figured there and then that he probably never would. Resigning himself to that, he gave his captain the biggest and friendliest pat on the back he could, and tried not to chuckle too hard at the resulting complaints of going easy, and a headache.

Screeching into the car park in her white Fiat 500, Richie was the last of the three friends to arrive, a good half hour after Peter, despite the fact that their games were all scheduled to start at pretty much the same time. Unlike her friend, the lacrosse goddess had no hesitation in finding a parking space, one adjacent to the clubhouse, almost as if it had been reserved for her. Popping open the driver's door, she slid out deliciously, a movie star at a Cannes premier, showing off her tanned, slender legs, forcing all the males in the immediate area to stop and watch. Conscious of the effect she was having, she gathered up her sports kit and lacrosse sticks, locked her car and headed off to hook up with the rest of her team, already deep in thought about the match itself.

Over the last hour, the bar had gotten considerably busier since the first of the hockey matches had finished, despite the delay caused by the injured player being carted off to hospital in an ambulance. All of the ladies' third XI and their entire opposition sat at various tables, munching eagerly on the hot food provided, keen to replace the energy the match had sapped from them. As well as the female hockey players, regular sports club members were dotted around, some keen on watching whatever matches were taking place on the pitches within view, others trudging out from under the feet of their other halves into the sanctuary of this alcohol oasis. They were easily spotted by how far their noses were buried in the pages of a daily newspaper, or by how glued they were to Sky Sports on the massive LCD televisions surrounding them, that is until the adverts appeared.

As far as Janice was concerned the day was now in full flow, all thoughts of the bizarre happenings in the chairman's office long since pushed to the back of her mind, which was currently being utilised to remember long lists of drinks, numerous bar snacks, the exact amount of change required, and making sure to go the extra mile with a kind word and a smile. While paying strict attention to which customer was next, and to anyone ordering food, in her peripheral vision she was on the lookout for the love of her life, knowing full well that he would already be here somewhere, preparing for his match. Having already arranged with one of her colleagues to have her break during his game so, as on previous occasions, she could sneak out and take a peek at him playing, that single thought helped her to keep her renowned happy demeanour as she went about her work with gusto and pride.

For now at least, the tears had stopped. They'd come in big, sobbing fits throughout the morning but, luckily for him, not while the dumb blonde from behind the bar had invaded his private space. She'd nearly ruined it all, her and her stupid lack of height, and he'd just about managed to stop her in time. How jolting the table hadn't triggered the device, he just didn't know, but was glad it hadn't, well... part of him was at least. Another much smaller part, hidden away deep inside, thought he deserved to be caught in the blast and that, by rights, he should no longer walk the earth. Perhaps it was right, and maybe he did, but that wasn't his intention. Essentially, he was a coward and had unfortunately got himself in so far over his head, that any sort of conscience had long since thrown itself off the tallest building within his mind, disgusted and full of shame.

Slowly, he got to his feet, wary of every little movement now. Earlier he'd thought about placing something over the 'package' to cover it up, after the blonde dwarf had caught a fleeting glimpse of it. But now that it was in its final countdown stage, he'd been assured the merest movement in or around it, in any direction, would cause it to explode. Tiptoeing lightly to the door, ignoring his sports jacket that hung on the coat stand off to one side, ever so quietly he turned the lock and opened the door as gently as he could. Knowing he had to be far away from here when it went off, inexplicably he'd already left it very late to leave. Pulling the door closed behind him, he let out a small sigh of relief on hearing the satisfying click. With his BMW beckoning and no time to lose, he sped off towards the stairs, concerned only with his own wellbeing. On his way down, he tried hard to compose himself, slicking back his dishevelled hair, rolling down the sleeves of his shirt, pulling out his hanky and wiping the sweat from his brow, before opening one of the double doors and heading into what was by now a very busy bar and dining area. All he had to do was make it to the other end. There, his car and all the freedom he craved awaited, but as he focused on the exit... it seemed so distant, so out of reach.

Barely having taken a step, he heard the first shout of his name over the backdrop of all the sports men and women. Turning, he feigned a smile for the approaching male, a sports club representative for the rugby section. And that was the first of many. It seemed lots of people needed to talk to him about all sorts of important and minor matters, and they all seemed to be here... now! He really shouldn't have been surprised. After all, for the last month or so he'd totally ignored all his responsibilities and duties, deliberately not responding to emails and phone calls, as well as only making a few fleeting appearances at the ground, mainly at times when he knew it would be quiet. As the man in front of him started to drone on about an area surrounding the rugby pitch, he tried to listen, but his concentration was elsewhere, mainly on the queue that was forming to speak to him. In his mind, all he could see was time ticking down, the walls around him, closing in, making him feel trapped, claustrophobic and scared. Calmly, he sought the natural charm hidden within that had served him so well throughout the years. It didn't come easy, but a tiny portion of it bubbled to the surface, enough to fob off the first in the queue anyway, with a promise of a meeting the next day. And so he moved onto the next, and the next, all the time members and staff loitered, eager to catch up with him and waste his ever decreasing time. One of them was the bar manager who would no doubt be chasing him up about having a new spare key to his office cut.

'Good luck with that,' he thought, to no one but himself.

Outright lies sorted out the first three, with him claiming that his wife had been seriously ill, explaining his absence and lack of contact. They were each promised a meeting for tomorrow, a meeting which of course would never take place, because this very spot would not exist, well... not in this form anyway, not after the huge wave of devastation. Things, however, were getting no easier. Rapidly running out of patience, he could see in his peripheral vision at least another six people, all wanting to talk to him. First the clock behind the bar swam into view, as his mind twisted and writhed, followed immediately by the minute by minute changing time in the top corner of the sports news on the television. He had to get out, and was starting to panic. Mumbling and stuttering, almost as if drunk, he was able to reassure the next person, but during that encounter, two more of the committee had appeared, hovering with intent. By now, the shaking had returned, not to mention the rivers of perspiration flowing freely down each side of his head. His armpits were lagoons of salty water, while his slicked back ginger hair had sprung out and now looked as though he'd just stuck one of his fingers in an electrical socket.

Finally, he snapped! There and then in the middle of the packed bar he just lost it completely, screaming, yelling, waving his hands around like a mime artist having an epileptic fit, and worst of all were the expletives. There were of course young children with their families nearby, all of whom heard his words, despite desperate attempts by their parents to cover their ears or distract them from what had been said. Each and every person in the bar watched the chairman, who was completely and utterly the centre of attention.

Janice stood, flabbergasted, halfway through pouring a pint of lager for a customer. In all her life, she'd never seen anyone melt down like that. She felt sorry for him, that was until the rude words spewed out of his mouth like sewage from a drainpipe. After that, all she felt was anger and disgust.

Just as some of the more burly adults in the bar were about to step in, the chairman, by now completely out of his mind, shimmied around the surrounding people and stropped (for that was the only word to describe it) off across the bar and out of the main door, leaving the whole building in total and utter silence. Even the tiniest whistle of a trump would have been heard.

Outside in the car park, in his marked bay, the chairman glanced at his watch, got into his car and reversed out, taking one long last look at the building that had been such an important part of his life for so long, before speeding out of the car park, leaving a trail of dust in his wake, glad to finally be free and on his way to safety.

Deep beneath the bonnet of the chairman's black BMW, lodged in a tiny recess below the car's battery, a fist sized lump of what looked like coloured play dough wrapped in a series of wires, connected to a regulator, sat counting down. It had been there for a very long time.

Back at the clubhouse, things had gotten back to normal, with the buzz being all about the chairman's apparent hissy fit, from the staff to the officers, to the players. The day was turning out to be anything but normal. Little did they know that this was just the start.

Charging out of the changing rooms in perfect unison, the home rugby side's choreography was almost up there with the Bolshoi ballet. Three back from the front, Tank looked a sight, his mighty chest puffed out like a proud peacock, his thighs taut, looking like tree trunks, his biceps rippling gently beneath his tight top. Followed by the coach, the team took to one half of the pitch, all going through the same warm up. An expression of utter concentration and a will to win was ingrained in the face of every player. They looked awesome, magnificent, full of unlimited determination, and to the opposition who'd just trotted past them on the way to the other end of the pitch, they looked like all their nightmares rolled into one.

Entering the Astroturf in dribs and drabs, some having come from the changing rooms, others straight from their cars, having arrived fully changed, the men's hockey second XI looked rather messy, especially when compared with the rugby players. Arriving smack bang in the middle of it all, Peter stationed his thick, black stick bag against the dark green wire mesh of the fence, and then began his normal muscle stretching routine. In theory, he didn't have to do any stretching at all; the magic coating, if you like, surrounding his dragon DNA currently maintaining his human form, could withstand a barrage of abuse, and quite literally nothing he could do on a hockey pitch would damage it. But he both wanted and needed to blend in, and that also included making a point of setting a good example to the youngsters in the side whenever he played or trained, showing them how to prepare properly, passing on a very valuable lesson.

Currently the ladies' second XI were playing a humdinger of a league match. While warming up, Peter took note of the crunching tackles, one or two off the ball incidents that the umpires either missed or chose to ignore, and one rather crafty follow through with a stick that nearly took one of the Salisbridge ladies' heads off. In his lowly opinion, the umpires didn't have nearly the kind of control of the game that they should have had. In just the short time he'd been watching, he was sure at least two yellow cards should have been issued, to send off the instrumental player for a minimum of five minutes.

Preparation complete, a smile crept onto his face from noticing two of the younger players mimicking him, one who was playing his first game and whose name he couldn't remember, and one who went by the name of Taibul, the son of the owner of the Indian restaurant the sports club members regularly frequented. Over the last few matches, he'd been impressed with the way young Taibul had performed on and off the pitch. Dedicated and brave in almost every tackle he made on it, the youngster had also started to learn to take in his stride all the friendly banter that came his way off it. A potential star, he was certainly one to watch out for in the future. Just as Peter's smile was about to pack its bags and tuck itself away for the upcoming match, out of the corner of his eye he just caught sight of Janice's gorgeous face pressed firmly against the inside of the clubhouse window, gazing out in his direction. Fervently he hoped she would sneak out again, as she had done on a few other occasions. Of course, she had no idea that he knew, and it would be difficult for him to explain how he did, as she always kept her distance and hid behind others to minimise the risk of being seen. But his highly tuned dragon senses always knew when she was nearby, almost able to perceive her soul vibrating on a frequency only he could hear. Knowing that she was there, he always had to try very hard not to look in her direction and give the game away, that and avoid tapping into his dragon powers to show off in some spectacular fashion, although he did always give more when she was watching, but that more was one hundred percent human, with not an ounce of magic anywhere to be seen. There was simply no way he'd ever give anything from the dragon side of himself when playing hockey; he respected the game, his teammates and everything about it, too much to taint it by doing that. To him, that would just be cheating, and even though he knew he was a long way off being the best hockey player in the club, he considered it his moral responsibility to be the fairest, and most sporting. Looking forward to sensing her presence in the crowd, he craved that tingling sensation that racked his entire body when she was there watching him.

One of the two beleaguered umpires blew their whistle to signal the end of the ladies' game in front of them. Grabbing balls from the plastic white bucket marked 'Second Team', all the players scooted out onto the pitch to continue warming up, weaving around opposing ladies arguing after the previous match. For Peter, now it was game time. He'd been thinking about it all morning, and not even a single thought of Janice or his friends interrupted his train of thought. It was all about holding the stick, feeling the power and a very different kind of magic to the one he was used to, as well as the potential, the ebb and flow of another great chance to line up alongside his teammates. Essentially he was caught up in a small fantasy world, one with sticks and a ball, two umpires, a D, penalty corners, no offside, two goals, and a billion possibilities. Game on!

Strolling calmly out onto the pitch as a group, the home ladies' lacrosse team were focused, determined and unified. It was to some degree quite a scary sight, especially for their opposition, who had been doing all sorts of hakka-like nonsense at the time. In a very precise and controlled manner, the Salisbridge players all started their warm up, ignoring the challengers, throwing the ball with their sticks at what looked like the speed of a bullet, not one being missed, their accuracy was so great. As the young women ran through their drills, blissfully unaware of their opponents, a persistent confidence grew across all the players' faces. They were well and truly in the zone, if such a thing existed. To them, there was nothing else. No clubhouse, no showers, no cars, no money... no nothing!

A penetrating, high-pitched whistle carried across the

pitch, indicating the match was about to start. Quickly the practice balls were put away, as the women lined up ready for their next skirmish.

As the hockey, lacrosse and rugby players outside weaved and darted, dummied and dribbled, Janice found herself crisscrossing the tables filled with customers, picking up empty glasses and plates that were finished with, all the while gazing longingly out of the window and across to the Astroturf. Suddenly she spotted exactly what she'd been looking for. With half a dozen dirty pint glasses piled high in one hand and a stack of dirty plates in the other, she extracted herself from the forest of tables and chairs, scooting quickly back to the kitchen. Once there, and having deposited her load, she swiftly arranged to take her well earned break, and headed outside to see the love of her life doing what he did best.

'It's looking like a great counter attack,' Peter thought as he spurred his body on, determined to catch up with play and offer his teammates another option. Already he could tell things were pretty evenly matched between the two sides, even though the game had only started a few minutes ago. However, at this early stage, Salisbridge had already squandered two half decent attempts at goal and so he figured if he could help them score it would calm the nerves of some of the younger players, settle things down and be a good base to build on for the rest of the half. Just as that thought zigzagged across his mind, the kid on the ball, instead of passing to one of his teammates who'd busted a gut to catch up, tried very stupidly to take on a wily old defender who looked full of experience, if not fitness and pace. Time and time again he'd tried to drill into the younger players that the best way to beat someone was to PASS the ball... But would they listen? Would they

CARK! The teenager, thinking rather highly of his dribbling abilities, had just been dispossessed and now, thanks to his selfishness, the entire team were out of position, himself included. Immediately he turned round and pounded the Astroturf in an attempt to get back into his own half, always keeping an eye on the ball over his shoulder. His breathing was ragged and sweat oozed down his back, as he purposefully blocked out access to his dragon abilities, well... the physical and magical ones anyway.

One of the opposition midfielders played a defence splitting pass through to their centre forward, who was currently trying to take it wide on the open side of the Salisbridge centre back. Gaining ground rapidly, he didn't like the look of what he was seeing as he sprinted for all he was worth. One of the most junior players in the team, the centre back looked as though he was about to pay for his inexperience. Sure he could make it back to cover his teammate, just then Peter's concentration wavered a little as a flicker of recognition and the scent of perfume brushed a tiny part of his mind. Puffing, putting all his effort into returning to his position, the faintest of smiles crossed his face, knowing that she was somewhere nearby, having sneaked out to watch him again. That fact alone was enough to spur him on to greater things, make him more powerful, more dangerous and, for a while, keep him at the top of his game.

Performing THE most outrageous dummy he'd ever seen, the attacker left the young centre back for dead. Peter knew that he'd never have fallen for it in a million years, unlike his out of the equation teammate. Thinking about a shot at goal after having totally written off the centre back, Peter's sprinting form had now entered the frame. If his opponent took his stick off the ball, Peter would win it outright. So the very brazen and cheeky, to say the least, attacker, performed the second most outrageous dummy Peter had ever seen. Or at least, tried to. Peter's experience and instinct told him exactly what was about to happen, and while looking for an instant as though he was going to fall for it, a split second later he laid down his stick strongly on the floor, at a slight angle, with his left hand... and waited. Sure enough, he took the ball cleanly away from his opponent, whose momentum had taken him off to the left somewhere. Inside, a small part of him chuckled at what had just happened, but he knew better than to get cocky. Pulling the ball back onto his open side, he got his head up and looked for the best pass, all the time the end of his stick caressing the orange sphere. The Salisbridge right back had done much the same as Peter and come bombing back from the counter attack that had broken down, so seeing him out wide with no one nearby and with an opposing midfielder threatening to close him down, Peter bent his knees a little more, turned his shoulders, shifted his weight and momentum, and with a flick of his wrist sent the ball hurtling towards his teammate, who picked it up cleanly on the end of his stick, the incoming midfielder sliding to a halt just in front of him, disappointed that he'd been thwarted by a pass. Meanwhile, the right back had played it forward to Andy the captain on the right side of midfield, and the match continued, all the time Peter immersed but also aware of the beautiful bar worker trying incredibly hard to hide her existence on the sideline. 'Thrilling' couldn't begin to describe the feeling running through his bogus body.

Barely two hundred metres away, Tank had just taken a right uppercut to his chin in the front row of the scrum and wasn't happy. It was the second time it had happened, on both occasions from a mean and moody looking giant of a human being... even compared with him, and he was by no means a slouch on that front. But this guy really was built like the proverbial brick outhouse, with not an ounce of fat on him and being over two metres tall. Judging from the punches he'd been throwing, he'd taken an instant dislike to Tank, for what reason the caring and sensitive mountain of a dragon had no idea whatsoever.

Suddenly the mud-ridden oval ball bumbled its way erratically into view, just out of touching distance. Tank fired up all his muscles, not even flirting with the idea of using any of his hidden dragon power. Pushing with all his might, unyielding grunts and groans intermingled with sounds of overwhelming physical exertion and the whispered commands of the referee echoed across the grass. The excitement was off the scale, a bit like the attitude of Mr Moody, the overly physical opponent. Again the former apprentice heaved, the studs on his boots digging in for dear life; his back, neck and legs were the rope in a tug of war. Little by little, Salisbridge edged forward, each player in the scrum winning his own battle. Breathless panting formed the backdrop to all the other scary noises, so great was the effort put in by both sides. Tank's shoulders felt as though they'd been dipped in lava, they burned so much. For the merest instant he thought of Steel and his heroics beneath the boiling magma at the laminium ball stadium. Screwing his eyes up tight, he pushed with all his might, the thought of one of his dragon idols inspiring him to greater deeds. As the scrum advanced faster than previously, one of his teammates grabbed the oddly yet beautifully shaped ball and tossed it with great power, back through his legs. Tank's body automatically eased off, knowing that the scrum was about to break up. It was a shame, because if it hadn't, he might have seen the rather flagrant abuse of the game's law, in the form of another mighty punch, head his way. He didn't, and he hit the muddy ground with such force that some time later, just after the match had finished, the groundsman's son would remark to his daddy while strolling across the grass that he'd found a hole that was, "exactly the same shape as a nose." Dismissing it as the ramblings of an over excited young child, it was a shame the caretaker never checked, because his son was right. And if he'd known what to look for, he might have seen the rest of Tank's face imprinted in the mud as well.

If Tank had been conscious, which at the moment he wasn't, and had looked over in the direction of the lacrosse pitch, he'd have seen his friend weaving her rather special blend of magic, and not the sort the three of them had to keep secret. Running full tilt towards her opponents' goal, ball cradled in the head of her stick which was twisting and turning as though it were cursed, the enigmatic and beautiful Richie Rump was on a mission, as always when playing her favoured sport. Dropping her shoulder one way, and then in an instant cutting back the other, the smallest of openings lay visible before her. A natural calling took over, instinct on its basest level. With a movement that seemed so slight and yet contained so much power, the ball shot towards the goal as if it had been discharged from a cannon. If the opposing keeper had been given all the time in the world, she still wouldn't have saved the shot... it was THAT good. Whirling round, Richie pumped her stick in the air, her teammates slapping her on the back as they all turned to run back towards their own half. It hadn't even reached half time and the Salisbridge team were already cruising at 4-0 up, much to the delight of the spectators, who were mostly regulars and either friends or family of the players. As the gentle breeze whipped her curly brown hair across her freckled cheeks, a sense of freedom and openness engulfed the female dragon. Letting it wash over her, she fed off it. A beaming smile cut her face in half, that is until a slight tinge in the background threatened to burst through. Despite being the star of the show, the one everyone wanted to be... the captain, the leader, the inspiration... it didn't seem to be enough. She wanted more... or was it something different?

At first the feeling was unrecognisable. But it stirred a memory deep within her, a recollection from the previous bonfire night, the one when Peter had nearly died fighting the dark dragon Manson. It had nothing to do with that, or the psychopathic supposed ex-army major. Leaping out at her clear as day, just before the restart, she'd felt the exact same way looking at all the human parents with their children on that fateful night, the night she'd spent snuggled up to Tank, watching the fireworks explode overhead, while Peter was systematically tortured, nearly to death, only metres away. She was feeling... JEALOUS! But of what? The revelation came as something of a body blow, but she had no time to dwell on where or why it had threatened to overwhelm her, now, in the middle of a lacrosse match. Taking a deep breath, and with the determination that was part of her natural make up, she sprinted off in search of the ball, pushing the thoughts from her mind, desperate to make the opposition pay even more than they had already.

Tank had been carried off by two of his team's substitutes, both of whom now felt as though they'd played an entire game, despite not having come on yet. He recovered from his momentary lack of consciousness, something only he seemed aware of, which in his mind was a good thing, because he was determined to go back on and make amends. How, he wasn't sure... but he would, one way or another.

At half time on the synthetic pitch, both teams were enjoying the ancient tradition, which had turned into something of a rarity, of having delicious orange segments to sustain themselves, along with the usual assortment of liquids, of course. It was a nice touch, Andy the captain of the second team thought, and most visiting teams seemed to appreciate harking back to a bygone era.

Having scurried back into the bar as soon as the whistle blew for half time, hoping he hadn't spotted her, Janice was pretty sure she hadn't been caught up until now, and today seemed no different. Having been very careful, she even had an excuse prepared. "Just checking to see if any normal glasses have been taken outside, instead of the usual plastic ones that are supposed to be exclusively used there." That was her justification, and if the need ever arose, that was what she would be sticking to.

Determined to put as much distance between him and it as he could, he'd headed south west on the main road after leaving, believing that to be the best route to get as far away as possible, in the quickest amount of time, and he'd been right. It had been just under an hour since he'd screamed out of the car park, much to the dismay of everyone there, and in that time he'd covered nearly fifty miles. Safe, probably ten times over from what little he knew, that didn't stop his need to keep on driving. Now he was hurtling along a busy dual carriageway, having slowed from ninety miles an hour to a more sedate seventy, for fear of attracting police attention. Even if they pulled him over, there was nothing to find: no incriminating evidence, nothing untoward in the car itself, nothing in his background to suggest anything unusual. With every passing mile, a weight lifted from his chest; the stress blew itself out of the driver's open side window. All in all, things were looking pretty good, he thought, pulling back into the nearside lane, having just overtaken another of those pesky caravans. Flicking the car's indicator back into the off position, thinking about just how pointless caravans actually were, suddenly... BOOOOM!!!!!!!

Watching yet another posh car overtake him as he carefully maintained control of his own and the heavy load it was towing, he could almost see the driver of the BMW thumb his nose up at him as he did so.

'Ahhh... a BMW, what a surprise," he thought, as the sparkling black vehicle cut back in front of him, some two hundred or so metres ahead. In the blink of an eye the pristine black vehicle, without warning, turned from a glinting, speeding beast, into a splintered, ravaged fireball. Depressing the brake pedal hard, causing his wife to spill her drink in the seat next to him and his children in the back to cry out in fear as they lurched forward, their safety belts preventing anything more than a nasty shock, the driver and his family managed to pull up just short of the deadly ball of flaming metal that now encompassed both carriageways, all to the sound of squealing brakes from the traffic behind them. Being a teacher at a primary school, a job he loved dearly, he had of course been educated in both adult and child first aid. But even without that training, just by looking at the blazing mass, the plumes of poisonous black smoke that spiralled into the air from it and the splintered wreckage strewn all around him, he instantly knew that nothing on this or any other planet could have survived what had just happened. In weeks to come, the police would of course investigate. But by then it would be too late. Their resources would be stretched, and they would have more important things to keep them occupied.

On the wooden desk inside the locked chairman's office, red digital numbers continued to count down, in unison with all the other devices across the world. Time was running out. The hour was nearly at hand.

During the half time break, Tank had successfully pleaded his case with the coach and had been allowed to line up for the second half, the other players glad to have him back, particularly for his attitude, the encouragement and belief he gave and his own self control. Little did they know that his renowned willpower had all but got up and left. "Deeply disappointed off," would have been his description of how he currently felt, strong words indeed for such a mild mannered dragon. Worse still was the fact that he was looking to get even with the huge man mountain of a human opponent who'd laid him out only a short time ago. In his mind, it was just a matter of how he went about it. Harking back to something Richie always droned on about, something he normally didn't agree with, her words came flooding back.

"Sometimes," she would say, "you have to take one or two of these humans down a peg or two, purely for their own good."

'Well,' he thought, striding purposefully back into position, 'this one needs taking down, and it'll be more than a couple of pegs by the time I've finished with him.'

Back on the Astroturf, Peter's team were struggling to overcome a 1-0 deficit, with the attack that had led to the goal being almost a carbon copy of the one where Peter had come to the rescue at the last minute, buoyed by Janice's presence on the sideline. Once again, the young, inexperienced, cocksure attacker had been robbed of the ball instead of passing to any number of his teammates, trying to show off with a fancy dribbling move that had ended in embarrassment. Two things made it worse than the first time. One, was the show off's lack of movement after wasting the advantage, not even attempting to run back to try and make amends for his stupidity. Two, was the fact that because so many of his team had been up in support, it had allowed their opponents to counter with speed and relative ease, something Peter had been unable to prevent, ending with the conceded goal. This time even the unflappable, and normally full of praise captain, Andy, had seen enough, immediately substituting the talented youngster with a less gifted but much harder working player, vowing not to bring the moody and selfish teen back on under any circumstances.

Currently feeling more than a little starved of oxygen because of the amount of running he'd been doing, Peter's brain felt very much like his body, as though it were wading through treacle. Along with the rest of the side however, he was determined to get the goal back. It wasn't so much that he minded losing; for him it was more about the manner in which you won or lost. Also, their opponents, while pretty good, were very dirty, with lots of things going on off the ball: stepping on toes during set pieces; following through unnecessarily at times with their sticks; the odd elbow or stick in the ribs, particularly against the younger players. All this made him angry, and determined to address the situation in the only way he knew how... by scoring a victory for his team!

Over on the lacrosse pitch, it was a totally different matter. As a spectacle, the game had long since been over even though the allotted time was not. Salisbridge ladies were now 9-0 up, with their leader and talisman determined to reach double figures. Despite a small part of her still pondering her emotional outburst, she was on fire (ironic really) playing like a demon, her skills sublime and there for all to see. If Peter, Tank or Flash had been watching, they'd all have had serious reservations as to whether or not she'd been dipping into her supernatural abilities... but not so! That's how well she was performing. Not only that, but she would never cheat; her sport meant too much to her. What she was doing on the pitch was pure, unassailable, raw talent, combined with natural ability and just a love of her pastime. It was almost as if she were having a perfect match, if such a thing were possible. Most sportsmen or women have perfect moments... instances they remember forever: scoring a superb goal, making a wonderful save, performing an amazing tackle, block, nutmeg, or just some kind of mazy, dribbling run, but today was Richie's day. Everything she tried came off with spectacular results. It was a joy to watch or be a part of, unless of course you were one of the opposition.

Tank was done, his normally cool, calm, disposition having evaporated entirely, and was just out there now to teach the giant, ignorant, dope of a man mountain a lesson. Up until a few seconds ago, he hadn't been sure of how to do such a thing, not without being sent off in disgrace or worse. But as he'd stood in the line-out, it had hit him like a sledgehammer. He knew just what to do, and it would be nothing short of just desserts for his opponent.

Minutes later, the referee sounded his whistle for an infringement, and Tank had intentionally found himself standing next to the grumpy brick wall of a player who he intended to teach a lesson. Up until now, neither of them had said a word, they'd only locked eyes, particularly in the scrum. All that was about to change. Casually sidling up to the player, Tank, pretending to look in a totally different direction, trod down on the man's left boot with all his might, continuing walking as the player let out an undignified yelp of pain. Striding after the plant and animal loving dragon, the hulk of a player spun him around and barked in a low, threatening voice, asking him what he thought he was doing. Holding out his arms wide in surprise, Tank feigned complete ignorance of what he'd done. Electing to put his face a centimetre or so away from Tank's, the man mountain growled an insult at the young dragon through his cloying breath, hoping to intimidate him. But to the player's surprise, Tank produced his biggest and best smile, before whispering under his breath,

"If that's the best you can do in the scrum sonny, they should replace you with a young child. I've known toddlers that can throw punches harder than that!"

Turning the most fabulous shade of scarlet, with steam rising from his head and ears, Tank's opponent had a face that made him look like the angriest man on the planet. For the merest instant, a flicker of dread raced through the former apprentice, but that was all. Knowing full well his rough and ready dragon body would protect him from almost anything, he had nothing to fear... not from this human anyway. Grabbing the collars of Tank's shirt, the huge angry player lifted him physically off the ground... one of the most impressive feats on any of the pitches at the club during the whole day. By now, almost everybody on or around the match was aware of what was happening between the two players, with men from both sides piling in, pushing, shoving, shouting... swearing. It took all of three or four minutes for the referee to separate the teams and calm things down. All the time, the man mountain glared across at Tank, murder in his eyes.

It didn't take long for the next scrum to come along. Like a pair of star crossed lovers, Tank and his opponent only had eyes for each other as the players came together. Tank had been waiting for exactly this moment. Part of him was sorry for what he was about to do, feeling as though it were cheating. But he'd already made up his mind. This thug deserved everything he got, and besides, HE wouldn't actually be doing anything.

With the scrum locked, all the players' heads were down, darkness engulfing them. Tank refused to look, instead concentrating on holding the pack together and inspiring the rest of his side. From above the panting and heaving of the pack, he could just make out the referee speaking, and then suddenly the ball was THERE! Bracing himself, he knew exactly what was coming. And come it did. There was only one difference this time: Tank had tapped into his well of dragon power, reinforcing his human shape, not shielding it, just reinforcing it. For a few moments, the shell of his outer body was immovable, invincible, unbeatable. Abruptly, the punch hit with a staggering amount of force, so much so that he wouldn't have believed it had come from a human, had he not seen it himself. If it had made contact with another surface dweller, it would most certainly have shattered their cheekbone and left them with a very long stay in hospital. Tank's dragon abilities had shifted the balance and this time he wasn't the one suffering, it was the big fella, who, having just broken every bone in his hand, had stood up in the middle of the scrum, screaming and wailing like a new born baby.

Blowing his whistle because the scrum had broken up, the referee tried to find out what the problem was, but the man mountain was too far gone to be anything close to coherent. Players from both sides were mystified as to what had happened. Nobody had seen anything untoward; Tank had made sure of that with a sneaky, little known, distraction mantra from a small town in Southern Africa.

Looking on with satisfaction as the opponents' physio sprinted on to check out his injured charge, Tank wasn't at all surprised to see the man take one look at the damaged hand, before leading him back off towards the changing rooms, mouthing the word "hospital" to the manager in the process. As the referee looked to restart the match, Tank could just make out the physio in the distance ask his player what on earth he'd done. Wrapping his arms around his teammate's shoulders, Tank sincerely hoped that the very moody thug in question had once and for all learnt his lesson.

Half an hour later it was all wrapped up. Richie's lacrosse team had handed out a crushing defeat, winning

14-0 in the end, the women delighted with their performance, their singing echoing throughout the changing rooms and across the pitches.

For Peter, the hockey hadn't been quite the success he'd hoped for, but the team had managed to fight their way back into the game and for a short time at the end, had looked better placed to go on and win it. But they finally had to settle for a share of the spoils at 1-1.

Despite Tank's run in with their opponents' best player and the confusion that ensued afterwards, Salisbridge were beaten 16-12, only the second time they'd lost all season, the players looking exhausted and demoralised as they trudged off towards the changing rooms and a well earned hot shower.

Being a Saturday afternoon in the league season for all the major winter sports, the bar area of the clubhouse was packed. Janice and three others were working non-stop to serve all the customers, standing two deep. As the lacrosse, hockey and rugby players, as well as the spectators, all started to drift in, the entire place became even busier along its entire fifty metre length. Drink after drink slid their way across the shiny wooden surface, most landing on mats, others being whisked away by a thirsty hand before making it that far. In proportion to the number of new arrivals, the noise rose, with all the tables taken, a queue for food orders and even the smallest of spaces all but filled by either individuals or teams; in all it was noisy, rowdy, crowded, slightly claustrophobic... but WONDERFUL!. There was banter, chit chat, Mickey taking, tactical discussion, game dissections, as well as the usual life, work, and relationship talk. It was BRILLIANT, and something the three friends found magically intoxicating, and an integral part of their deep love for all three of their respective sports.

Currently Peter, his hockey team and their opponents

all sat around a group of tables near the main entrance, sharing some well deserved food, a jug of beer and lively conversation.

In comparison, Tank and the rugby teams all stood next to the furthest part of the bar, just outside the double doors to the stairwell that led to the first floor. They too were sharing a laugh, some food, and significantly more than one jug of beer.

Slap bang in the middle of the clubhouse, making as much noise as both the rugby and the hockey men put together, gathered the lacrosse ladies, who by now were well onto the drinking games, with plenty of clapping, singing, shouting, and of course... drinking. All except for Richie, who despite being their leader and chief cohort, stood well back from the circle of players, nursing an entire pint of lime and soda, the *alea* just visible through the delicate red top she was wearing. For her not to be joining in was very unusual indeed.

Through a crowd of sweaty, heaving bodies, Peter caught Janice's eye (not literally... no ball games in the clubhouse) just as she was filling up a large glass with ice and a light coloured soft drink. On noticing her man, the bubbly blonde winked, instantly melting the hockey playing dragon's heart, causing his knees to go weak and that giddy, excited feeling to start kicking about in his stomach. Holding up five fingers on her left hand, she mouthed the words, "Five minutes," halfway across the bar. He nodded in reply, smitten. With that, a large hand came down firmly in the middle part of his back, forcing him to spill a small part of his drink on the already stained and sticky carpet.

"Alright Pete?" asked the team captain, Andy.

"Ahhh... fine thanks," he replied.

"It's a hot one you've got there my friend," slurred the second team captain, motioning in Janice's direction, with his half finished pint of lager.

Feeling his temperature rapidly rising, Peter started to

blush.

"It's alright me old mate," slurred Andy once again, this time wrapping his free arm around the young hockey playing dragon's shoulders. "I've known for a while there was something going on between the two of you, but don't worry," he announced, really loudly, raising his finger to his lips in an attempt to indicate quiet, following it with a long 'shuuuush,' sound, "I'm almost certainly the most discreet person I know and promise not to tell another soul." With that, he staggered off in the direction of another teammate, Peter relieved to see him go. But before he'd got two paces, he turned back towards the young dragon, a puzzled look etched across his face.

"Terrible thing about the sports club chairman, what with him losing it and all that."

Looking on quizzically, not at all sure what his captain was talking about, before he could ask for some details, Andy turned and continued on his drunken journey, leaving Peter shaking his head, once again wondering what the attraction of alcohol really was.

Mind focused on Janice and the last part of that very weird conversation with Andy, Peter scanned the busy bar, almost instantly finding Richie with his gaze. Watching her for a few seconds in awe of her sheer beauty and the radiance that she exuded, it struck him as odd that she was standing so far back from the rest of her team. Perhaps they'd lost, was his first thought. But that certainly didn't fit in with how the rest of the women were acting. Concern for his friend and an inquisitive nature got the better of him, so he snaked his way through the myriad of bodies, tables and chairs, through the ear splitting laughter and the noise of the football results on the giant television screens. Stalking up behind her, he gently put a soft hand on her exposed shoulder. Surprisingly, she nearly dropped her drink, something of a turnaround particularly given the normal course of events.

"Oh Pete, you startled me," she exclaimed.

"Sorry Rich. Not my intention."

"That's alright," she replied. "I was caught up in my own mind... daydreaming I suppose. So it serves me right."

Feeling a little awkward, he'd never heard his friend talk like this before. Deciding to change the subject, he turned to one he knew she'd be much happier about.

"How was your match today? Did you win?" he asked, having to raise his voice over the din the rest of the lacrosse team were making.

Without even a hint of a smile, something Peter found odd, Richie replied,

"It was okay. We won 14-0."

"Wow... 14-0! That's some score Rich. How many did you get? One, two?" he joked, trying to get a reaction out of his friend.

"I think it was nine in the end," she ventured, glancing over his shoulder towards the main entrance.

"Nice!" he stated, impressed. Just about to ask, as a joke, if she'd been using her SPECIAL abilities, he followed her gaze across the crowded room to... Tim, her so called ex-boyfriend, who'd just walked through the doors with the rest of his hockey team, having no doubt just returned from an away game.

"You two have split up... haven't you?" he asked, his voice taking a more serious tone.

Richie stepped right up to him, a near snarl carved into her freckly face.

"Yes, we have, THANK YOU VERY MUCH! And don't let that fact bother you at all when you're with your cute little barmaid over there," she uttered sarcastically.

People close by had all started to look in their direction. Once again, he started to blush.

"Do as I say, not as I do," she commented, purposefully bumping into him as she stormed past, heading straight for the exit.

With a great many people staring at him, he stuck out like a sore thumb, that is until his knight in shining armour turned up and saved him... JANICE! Tucking one of her slender arms around his waist, she guided him off into a quiet corner. He was so relieved.

Once there, and with nobody paying them any attention at all, she leant up and gave him a lasting kiss, right on the mouth. Most of his worries vanished instantly. Deep down though, he was still troubled by Richie's actions. It was all so unlike her. Splitting up with Tim, if indeed that's what had happened, seemed to have had a profound effect on her, more so than he would ever have thought. Vowing to speak to Tank about it later on in the evening, Janice breaking off the kiss brought him sharply back to the present, and the beaming face that currently smiled up at him. Sitting down, she asked him about the hockey, pretending of course not to have seen any of it. Playing along, he tried to convey some of the match to her, in the most interesting way possible. It was then that he asked how her day had gone. Starting off with some of the mundane stuff, she then recounted the episode with the chairman, which caught his attention, as Andy had mentioned it earlier, albeit in a drunken ramble. Janice explained about the chairman's meltdown in front of everybody, going on to tell Peter about getting the key to the Astroturf from his office earlier that day. For his part, he listened intently, something inside him screaming out that it was important. Nodding in all the right places, wondering what on earth had got into the ginger haired official, all of a sudden Janice mentioned the dark black box and the chairman's fuss surrounding it. But what really got his attention was when she described the metal that she'd glimpsed momentarily inside the package. Her short description of how the metal appeared to shimmer and phase, with just a hint of rainbow colours, started alarm bells ringing deep inside Peter's head. Straight away he closed his eyes, reaching out to the floor above him, searching for anything untoward. Nothing. But he was unconvinced.

"When the chairman had his little... 'moment' in front of everybody," he asked, calmly, "was he carrying anything? Did he have that black box with him?"

Janice thought back, before replying.

"No."

A helpless feeling like he'd never felt before spread out from his gut, threatening to engulf him, given the chairman's known association with the evil dragon Manson's human persona. Janice could see the look of worry running across his usually cheerful face.

"What is it?" she whispered.

Thinking carefully about his response, he wondered what he should tell her. That he thought something odd might be going on because the chairman had something to do with a wanted criminal, who was in fact a dragon? And that the metal she'd caught a glimpse of is practically priceless in the underground world inhabited by millions of dragons, as well as potentially being lethal in the wrong hands?

Staring out of the window for what seemed like a small ice age, he tried to come up with a course of action, as the panic and tension threatened to overwhelm him. Gazing across, he looked directly out at the Astroturf he'd played on earlier, but instead of happy thoughts about hockey, all that came to him were the memories of the bonfire night when Manson had come within a whisker of killing him... the pain, the humiliation, the feelings of helplessness, knowing his friends were nearby but that he couldn't help them, and they couldn't help him.

Although he'd turned away, she could see something was desperately wrong. Perspiration trickled down the side of his neck, his breathing had become heavier and his face had taken on a pale and drawn appearance. The mere mention of the black box and the strange metal inside it had set the change in motion, so she decided to give him space and let him tell her in his own time, if indeed he wanted to. Wrapping her right arm around him, she snuggled up, joining him in gazing out of the window.

Her arm snaking around his waist and her head tucked neatly into his chest, slowed his heart considerably. Up until then, it had been racing full pelt at the thought of all the bad things that could be going on. But still that nagging sensation inside him hadn't gone away. Something was wrong, he was sure of it. But what to do? That was the question. And then his eye caught the slightest movement in the reflection of the glass. It was a strapping rugby player, halfway across the bar, blazer off, in shirt and tie, being cheered on to drink a pint of some horrible concoction down in one. A smile warmed his face, as part of the answer to his problem came to him... TANK!

Leaning forward, he whispered in Janice's ear.

"Do you have a key to the chairman's office?"

"No," she answered firmly. "There was a spare one behind the bar, but it's been missing for some time. The chairman's been promising to get a new one cut for weeks now, but never has, well... not to my knowledge anyway."

'Damn,' he thought. 'It would have been so much easier if Tank and I could have gone up there to take a look. Oh well, at least by telling him I'll be sharing the problem, and just maybe something will occur to him, that hasn't to me.'

Gripping Janice's hand, Peter turned to her.

"Would you do me a small favour and repeat to Tank everything you told me about the black box and the metal inside it?"

"Sure," she replied, all smiley.

"But let's try and do it in some place a bit more... private," he added, trying to pick the big fella out of the rugby crowd.

Approaching, holding hands, Peter and Janice could both see the former apprentice, all animated about something rugby related, his giant hands whipping through the air, whisking up vivid scenes of balls, tries and tackles, his dark blazer balanced precariously on the back of his chair, his white shirt stained with beer, tie dishevelled as though it had been pulled more times than a church bell. Both lovers waited patiently for him to finish explaining something from the game to one of the other coaches, before he politely nodded and took his leave. As Tank turned around, it was only then that Peter noticed the injuries to his face. Janice let out a squeaky little gasp.

"It's alright... I'm fine," he stated. "You should see the other guy!"

"And just where would he be?" asked Peter, more than a little concerned.

"In hospital, as a matter of fact. Broke quite a few bones in his hand, apparently," announced Tank, grinning from ear to ear, or at least trying to. With injuries to both eyes, his nose and lips, he looked like a cross between the Joker out of Batman, and Rocky after twelve rounds in the ring.

"So let me get this straight," exclaimed Peter, incredulously. "He broke his hand on your face?"

Chuckling to himself ever so slightly, Tank nodded.

Turning to Janice, Peter shrugged his shoulders and ventured,

"He's mad. Absolutely mad."

Smiling, Janice did the most unexpected thing. Walking up to Tank, she leaned forward and kissed him gently on the chin.

"Well, I think he's very brave," she said, pulling away. The faces of both young dragons were a picture.

"So anyway, what exactly can I do for you both?" asked Tank, having recovered from the shock somewhat. "Gonna let me buy you both a beer, or have you come to buy me one?"

Peter's thoughts turned back to the matter at hand.

"We couldn't have a quiet word, could we?" he whispered, indicating the double doors leading to the stairwell.

Intrigued, Tank, still holding his pint of beer, squeezed

past the two of them before heading through the doors, Janice and Peter following in his wake.

"I'm all ears," slurred the rugby playing dragon, slightly intoxicated from drinking with all his teammates.

Despite the seriousness of the situation, Peter burst into laughter at the exact same time as Janice. Tank watched them both, with a less than amused look on his face.

"Well, you're not eyes, or a nose, are you?" mocked his pal through a fit of giggles, referring to his rugby inflicted injuries.

A few seconds passed, during which time Peter and Janice shrugged off their sniggers. Peter wanted Janice to tell Tank exactly what she'd told him, but first there was something else he had to do.

"In some ways it's a shame you've had so much alcohol. I could really use you being sober for all of this," he pleaded.

"Well, it's a bit too late for that now," chipped in Janice, wondering why Peter would even mention such a thing. "We could of course make him drink a million cups of coffee, if you like?"

Having turned to face Peter while saying all this, she'd failed to notice Tank's barely audible whispers to himself. Janice turned back just in time for the rugby playing dragon to give her his biggest smile.

"I'll be alright," he announced, clear as a bell. "In fact, I'm already feeling a lot better. What is it that's so important, you needed to drag me out here... all secretly? Engagement announcement?"

Peter started coughing furiously as Janice looked on, Tank just smiling. Fun over, Peter asked Janice to recount exactly what she'd told him, word for word. When she got to the part about the black box and the metal inside, the strapping rugby player stopped her.

"Uhhhh... can you just repeat the last part please?"

She did, and the concerned look on Peter's face

mirrored itself on his friend's.

"Did he take it with him?" asked Tank.

Peter shook his head in response to the question.

"We have to get a look inside his office."

"There are no spare keys, and the chairman's gone off with his," answered the bubbly blonde, wondering what on earth was going on.

"Who said anything about needing a key?" whispered the rugby player, squeezing between the two of them, starting to climb the stairs.

Both Janice and Peter followed.

"What's so important about the box and the metal inside?" asked Janice, all innocently.

Deciding he should take this one, particularly as it was he who'd gotten her involved in all of this, Peter spoke in hushed tones, even though they were the only ones in the stairwell and probably on the whole of the upper level.

"It's probably nothing," he replied, hoping this would be enough. But from the look on her face, it clearly wasn't. In return, she raised her eyebrows at him sceptically, on reaching the top of the stairs.

"It's related to my job at Cropptech. I can't tell you all about it because it's top secret I'm afraid."

It wasn't a lie as such, because the laminium was part of his job at Cropptech, and he couldn't tell her all about it. But the look that she gave him left him in no doubt at all that she really wasn't buying it.

Following Tank's giant strides across the thick, lush carpet of the function room until they arrived at the locked door to the chairman's office, given that there were no windows to see through, it was hard to imagine what was going to happen next. Leaning against the door, Tank quickly came to the conclusion that it was locked and quite sturdy. Turning to Janice, he asked,

"Whereabouts in the office did you say the box was?"

"On a wooden desk on the left hand side, about... hmmm, let me see. About three metres in."

"That's all I need to know," uttered Tank, deep in thought.

Peter had a fair idea what his friend had in mind, but not exactly how he was going to do it though. And he was pretty sure Janice should be as far away as possible.

Leaning into her, the delicate scent of the perfume she was wearing intoxicating him momentarily, he just about recovered before whispering,

"I think perhaps it's better if you leave. I don't want you to get into any trouble."

In response, she jabbed a sharp finger into his chest.

"TROUBLE! I think I'm already in quite deep... don't you? And besides, I want to see exactly what the two of you are up to."

Turning, Tank gave him a look. Peter just shook his head in response.

"Well," announced Tank, "if you're staying, then you'd better stand back." While the other two had been talking, Tank had been busy casting a mantra he was used to working with back at the Emporium. Basically the spell formed a magical shield around anything that was being worked on, which came in handy in his line of work. You wouldn't believe the number of completely unknown or uncategorised mantras, spells and artefacts the old shopkeeper had found himself with over the centuries. Sometimes barely a day passed without an explosion going off that would level a human house. If not for the shield mantra and the other spells and magical hexes crisscrossing the shop's substructure, the whole area would have been decimated many times over. What the dragons living around there thought, goodness only knows.

Anyhow, Tank had cast the relatively simple shield mantra to take shape behind the office door, a metre or so back. It should in theory catch the door itself, and any flying fragments from the wood, lock or hinges. With Peter and Janice both having retreated, Tank took four steps back, turned and... CHARGED! Hitting the door smack bang in the middle with his left shoulder, adding just enough of his dragon power to make sure there was no doubt about the outcome, in an ear splitting CRUNCH the door flew inwards and came to a stop as it hit the invisible wall that was Tank's cunning piece of magic. Janice looked on, astonished, as the animal and plant lover straightened himself up, brushed himself down and set about pulling the door out of the office, placing it up against one of the walls of the much bigger function room.

"Ohhh this is going to be sooo bad," the petite little blonde muttered, hardly able to comprehend what she'd got herself into. It was a good job she didn't know what was really going on.

Walking over, Peter was just about to step through when Tank's huge outstretched arm stopped him.

"One second," he said, muttering something under his breath, the flicker of a faint blue light dispelling the shield mantra, freeing the room of any obstacles. As one, the two friends gazed in and sure enough, sitting exactly where Janice had said, was the black box in question.

Having already decided to keep a look out after the deafening noise of the door coming off, Janice was sure staff would be charging up the stairs at any moment to find out exactly what was going on. She had no idea how on earth she was going to get out of all of this, but it seemed massively important to Peter to go through with it, and she did trust him implicitly. What she didn't know was that as well as the shield mantra, Tank had also added a simple noise suppression spell that any eleventh year nursery ring student could have come up with. Nobody else would have heard the sound of the door coming off, not even if they'd been in the adjacent corridor.

Tiptoeing beneath the threshold of the office, careful not to make any noise at all, Tank and Peter approached the box as if it were a bomb about to go off. It wouldn't be long before they realised the irony.

Putting his hand on his friend's shoulder, Tank

indicated that he should go first, and Peter was in no mood to argue. Carefully, Tank got within an arm's length of it. From where he was, he moved in a semicircle around the dark package, examining it from all angles, mindful of touching the surface it sat on. All the time, Peter stood and watched, holding his breath. Part of him hoped that it had all been a mistake and that on busting the door down, there would be no sign of any box, or the rare metal that it contained. Unfortunately that wasn't the case, and that sinking feeling had once again started to wrap itself around his insides.

There was nothing else for it, Tank thought to himself; he was going to have to go in even closer. It was by no means the best solution, and might well end up getting them all killed, but he needed to examine the object in more detail. All that he'd observed so far concerned him greatly, but it was impossible to see everything from where he stood. Partly concealed digits seemed to be changing all the time indicating, if he was right, a countdown of some sort. Needing to know more, taking a breath, he stepped forward as gently as he could, desperate not to move the table, even a hair's breadth. Nothing happened, apart from his heart beating faster... so much so, he could feel it pounding in his ears. He tried to put that to one side, just to ignore it. But it wasn't easy, particularly given what he could see now that he was a little closer. As well as the metal, which was most certainly laminium, he could just make out the edge of what looked like a gyroscope.

'So no picking it up or touching it in any way, shape or form,' he thought. Cautiously, he leant over the top of it, twisting his neck to get a better angle from which to look through the glass panel. If it was supposed to show the numbers inside, counting down, somebody had done a terrible job on that count. Or perhaps the digital display had slipped across and dropped out of sight of the window. Either way, he needed to know exactly how much time remained. Closing his eyes, he scrolled through all the mantras he knew, to see if anything there could help him.

Behind him, Peter whispered,

"Is it safe to come forward?"

"Slowly and carefully," Tank responded. "I'm pretty sure there's a gyroscope inside. I guess if it moves even a fraction, it'll go off."

"It's a bomb then?"

"That would be my best guess... yes," answered Tank in a hushed tone.

"What are we going to do?"

"First things first. We need to know exactly how long's left on the timer. But it's impossible to see the numbers, as the display looks like it's been dislodged."

Looking at the box close up for the first time, Peter craned his head to see if he could see what Tank meant. Looking closely at the slightly curved edge of the laminium that could be seen, he noticed the tiniest speckle of red light. It changed slightly. And again. It was a mirror image reflection of the countdown, clearly from the light of the numbers bouncing around inside the dark metal frame. Instantly he told his friend. Having a look, the butch rugby player agreed at once and then, with a little of his power, flooded his vision to enhance the sensory capacity of both eyes. Once done, he had little problem zooming in right onto the microscopic image on the rare metal. It was then just a case of working out the numbers, because the image had been mirrored... easy for any dragon. The answer shook him to his very core. Fourteen minutes, twenty seven seconds... and counting!

From the look on his friend's face, Peter knew things were bad, he just didn't know how bad. Tank told him.

"We need to contact the King's Guards... NOW!" cried Peter.

"We need to evacuate the building first," announced Tank.

"You're right of course... but how?"

Just then, Janice appeared at the gap that only minutes

earlier had held an office door, now convinced that no one downstairs had heard what had gone on.

"Well...?" she asked, wanting to know what was happening.

Peter swallowed nervously.

"We need to get everyone out of here... this instant!"

"Why?" she responded. "What is it?"

Turning, he looked in Tank's direction. The huge rugby playing dragon nodded his approval.

"It's a bomb," Peter announced, turning back towards the woman of his dreams.

"A BOMB!" cried Janice. "How the hell can it be a bomb?"

"It would take too long to explain," Peter replied, putting his arm around the petite blonde's waist. "And it's time we really don't have. Do you think you can help?" he pleaded.

"What am I going to tell everybody?"

"You won't have to tell them anything," declared Tank, strolling purposefully to the far end of the function room that overlooked the sports pitches through a majestically curved, giant glass window.

"I'm not sure what you..." Janice's voice trailed off as Tank moved away from the architecturally stunning panes to one of the adjoining walls, stopping right next to a bright red square... one of the fire alarms.

"All you have to do is help get everybody out, and to the far side of the car park, as far away from here as possible. As you go down the stairs, tell them the upper level is clear, but make sure... everyone has left!"

Nodding, making it clear she understood exactly what was expected of her, she still had one last thing to ask, despite the urgency of the situation.

"But what about the two of you?"

"We'll stay a while and see if there's anything we can do. Don't worry," whispered Peter, smiling all the while, "we'll be out in time. You have my word."

Leaning down, he kissed her passionately on the lips. Tank smiled, and then put his fist through the glass of the alarm, a high pitched wail shattering the peace, infusing the whole building with a sense of urgency. Pulling away from Peter, Janice sprinted out into the corridor, heading towards the stairs. Looking at each other for a brief moment, the two friends shared the surreal moment. For Peter, it felt like the whole bonfire night scenario all over again.

In the end, it was Tank who broke the silence (well... not quite).

"Time to contact the King's Guard."

"Do you want to do it?" asked Peter.

"Why don't we both do it? That way they'll get some sense of urgency, and perhaps send the best dragons for the job.

Nodding his agreement at the suggestion, both friends closed their eyes and reached out with their minds.

Approximately twenty minutes ago, it had all started. First in Montreal, Canada, with an initial explosion that was huge and had originated somewhere close to the Old Port. As well as devastating everything within a two mile radius, the blast had unleashed a deadly tidal wave up and down the St Lawrence river, demolishing everything in or around the shore on both sides of the waterway. The Victoria Bridge to the south had been wiped from the face of the earth, while the Concord Bridge, almost at the centre of things, had been decimated instantly. Because the bomb was made from laminium, a psychic wave, fatal to any dragons in an even larger radius, accompanied the original detonation.

Buildings had been reduced to rubble as far as the eye could see. Cars and boats had been flung great distances, as if they were toys discarded by a toddler's tantrum. Fires raged. The earth shook. Stone fell like rain. Thick black smoke littered the sky line. Dead and broken bodies lay everywhere. Dragons in their human guises up to twenty miles away collapsed and died instantaneously. The Montreal part of the dragon domain crumbled in on itself, despite all the mantras supposedly keeping it safe, crushing hundreds of their kind all at once, as well as trapping others in shops, cafes, houses and stricken monorail carriages.

Of course something of that magnitude doesn't go unnoticed. Help from the domain had already turned up, prepared for anything, but not this. Those arriving on the scene had never experienced anything like it. They'd attended a lot of different emergencies, but nothing on this scale.

Immediately the dragon world was put on alert, at the same time as the council was called into session to see if they could make something, anything, of the senseless devastation and wanton destruction. But it didn't stop there.

Six minutes later, thousands of miles away in an ordinary paddy field just outside the small village of Wong Chan in Thailand, a similar device detonated. A remote place by any standards, the carnage should have been only a fraction of that from the Montreal explosion, but for one difference. Less than half a mile away from the epicentre of the blast, a newly completed industrial complex lay pretty much unattended, the staff off for the weekend, most at a specially designed estate some five or so miles away, built at great expense by the company. That company was... Cropptech. And deep inside a small, sterilised room at the heart of the facility, a small amount of laminium (small by dragon standards, but quite significant compared with the amount in the bomb) had been carefully contained inside a state of the art lab, having been recently extracted from a vein quite close by. As easily as tearing tissue paper, the terrific blast wave ripped apart the development, with the power still pretty much at its height when it hit the tucked away laminium. Doing what came naturally to it when extortionate amounts of heat, light, and energy were applied, the magical metal multiplied everything, many times over.

While in Montreal, everything in a two mile radius had been obliterated, here it was much more. A crater nearly four miles wide and over a mile deep sat firmly where the paddy field once had. The village, industrial complex, even the housing estate were all no more, along with every last bit of the surrounding area. Plants, animals, humans... all gone! Everything within a twenty mile radius had been wiped out, incinerated if you like, with a massive ground quake rattling its way along the length of the country in protest.

Much more intense was the psychic wave from this event. Dragons over a hundred miles away were reported to have died instantly. Luckily the spot was a long way from any part of the urbanised dragon domain, much further than either the conventional or psychic blast could reach.

Again, the local dragon authorities responded. Again they were stunned at what had happened on reaching ground zero. It was all fed back to the king and his councillors.

Since then, three more bombs had gone off. One in Melbourne, Australia, one in the Turkish city of Ankara, and one in Macclesfield, England. Blasts in both Melbourne and Ankara had caused carnage and loss of life on the same scale as the Montreal blast, while in Macclesfield something had gone awry, the explosion turning out much smaller than intended, but still causing a lot of damage. Planted in St Michael's church, of which there was nothing left, dozens of houses had been destroyed, along with a few shops, a couple of pubs and part of the famous Macclesfield canal. Again, the loss of life was staggering, but not on the scale of the other sites, with the blast radius of this one measuring only a hundred metres or so. But still, the market town was in disarray, confusion and mourning. Emergency services attended the scene, both dragon and human alike, some even attending in both capacities. It was chaos and mayhem combined. But it could have been worse.

All the bombs were linked to the same timing device, their countdowns all showing the same numerals, all set to blow up together. Well, not quite. Manson, you see, had been both designer and instigator. For a being of his intellectual capacity and motivation it had been easy. Alone in one of the sterile labs at the Cropptech site in Salisbridge, late one night, a thought had occurred to him, just as he'd started working on timer circuit board number eight out of fifteen. The plan had originally been to sow the seeds of chaos and destruction on a global scale... all at the same time, throwing both human and dragon governments into anarchy. But as he sat at the pristine, white desk, his soldering iron smoking like a television character from the 70's, he thought about some of the books he'd read and films he'd watched in the relatively short time he'd been free from the cold. A common theme had always been the dashing hero arriving exactly at the last second as the bomb ticked down, cutting through the right wire just in the nick of time. A smile crossed his malevolent face, his dark, dead eyes twinkling for a moment as the dastardly thought flickered through his mind. It was an idea he liked, one that appealed to him. He would add something to the circuit boards he hadn't built yet... a random algorithm, one that could potentially detonate the bombs before the countdown finished, setting it up so that they could indiscriminately go off at any time during the last half hour. That way, any hero who managed to stumble across one would think they had long enough to do something about it, when in actual fact... BOOM! They wouldn't. Chuckling slightly to himself (something he rarely did) as he pulled some solder off the reel, watching it melt on the tip of his soldering iron, he imagined some poor sucker with time running out, getting the biggest, and most unexpected, surprise of their life.

It was an odd sensation... reaching out with your mind for something a great distance away. It was the ultimate out of body experience. But that's exactly what the two friends were doing, right at this very moment, without much luck it had to be said. All around them chaos ensued, as the blaring wail of the fire alarm accompanied the rush of people exiting the building below them.

Finally, they gave up, after having tried for nearly two whole minutes, not very long I know, unless of course you're in a building that's about to explode.

"Why can't we reach anyone?" ventured Peter, starting to panic.

"I'm not sure," replied Tank, thinking. "But whatever the reason, I think we're on our own."

Peter nodded.

"Do you think everyone will be safe at the far edge of the car park?

Tank swallowed nervously, having already done the calculations in his head, and if the laminium inside the black casing was one of the missing fifteen small, ring sized chunks taken from the Salisbridge Cropptech site, then everyone was in big trouble.

"It's only possible to see a speck of the metal through the window of the box. If that's all the laminium in there, then maybe they will be safe. But if there's more, and I'm thinking of the chunks that went missing when Manson had control over Cropptech, then... no, none of us will be safe."

Now it was Peter's turn to swallow at the thought of all the people outside, his friends, the hockey players... JANICE!

"How not safe are they exactly?" he asked, not quite sure he was ready to hear the answer.

"If we work on the theory that it is in fact one of the missing pieces in there, then I'm guessing the blast wave will cover at least a two mile radius."

"WHAT!" Peter screamed at his friend.

"I've run the numbers three times. I'm not wrong."

Sure that his friend wasn't, Peter wondered how on earth they were going to get everyone far enough away? Not to mention all the other houses, shops, businesses... Cropptech!

"Oh my God Tank," he cried. "If you're right, the blast wave will hit Cropptech. There's enough laminium there to not only level the city, but all the surrounding villages as well."

Although both friends had reined in their emotions up until now, Peter's valid point about the Cropptech laminium really changed things, giving the bomb the potential to cause destruction on an unprecedented scale. If it went off, many tens of thousands of people would lose their lives, not to mention the damage to the city, its infrastructure and the surrounding countryside. There had to be something they could do.

Peter started to talk, but Tank cut him off.

"Let me think for a moment."

Standing stock still, doing exactly as his friend asked, it was then that he remembered Aviva's dagger, stored safely away in his home. That would only enhance the blast wave more, adding to the catastrophic death toll. Since the realisation about the Cropptech laminium, there was a real change in his friend's demeanour. He knew that Tank would lay down his life, just as he would himself, to prevent the bomb from going off. Waiting patiently, he wondered if the Cropptech site was in fact the primary target of the bomb. It would be just like Manson to do something sneaky like this, having a little revenge on all the humans he evidently disliked so much, while at the same time depriving the dragon community of the almost exclusive supplier of the valuable metal, as well as spreading fear and destruction. This was no coincidence, he was sure. They had to come up with a plan to stop it. They had nine minutes and forty six seconds to do just that.

Instantly, the heat and passion from the kiss melted away the cold air of the room. It wasn't the most romantic of places, but neither of them actually cared at the moment. They both just wanted to be together, something that grew more and more difficult with each passing day. Here and now, it was just about finding solace in each other's arms, making the most of the present. Two of his friends had made it easy for them to sneak down here and share a matter of minutes together without being discovered. Although she deplored her current surroundings, there seemed no other way, certain her house was being watched, and probably his as well. So this was it. And it was better than the alternative. But there was always a price to pay with love. Today, that would become more evident than ever before.

Deep inside the Kremlin's very dusty and very dark component warehouse, tucked behind a massive swathe of dirty wiring in the dim recesses of an ancient computer, a red digital display counted down, its numbers glowing brightly in the confined space. It had just dropped below nine minutes when a tiny random signal flared up from one part of the circuit board inside it, setting in motion a catastrophic chain of events. Mere milliseconds later, the explosive and the laminium that it was attached to, detonated.

Instantly everything within the gorgeously coloured red stone walls of the Kremlin was obliterated. The

Archangel's Cathedral, Spasky Tower, the lush trees and the Kremlin Museum (along with Tsar Peter the Great's boots) were all gone, not to mention all the government facilities and offices, some above ground, some below. Continuing on, the shock wave left a trail of destruction in its wake. Great surges of water careered along the Moscow River in both directions, destroying bridges, roads, shops and houses. Ground quakes rattled everything within the city of Moscow itself. Inside the Metropol hotel, valuable mosaics cracked with impunity, while the carefully sculpted marble that it was renowned for, ruptured, tumbling to the floor all around.

Once again, in the blink of an eye, thousands died. But despite the carnage, luck had been on their side. For behind the eerie wall against which the computer containing the bomb had sat, was a dedicated dragon storage base, one in which large amounts of laminium were regularly stockpiled. Up until the day before, a considerable amount had been contained there. It had all been moved to another location the previous afternoon, and that one event alone had probably saved hundreds of thousands of people. At that moment in time, Moscow couldn't possibly know how lucky it had been, but at some point in the future, it would find out.

A silent countdown ticked down in his head, as he stared in awe at the look of sheer concentration on Tank's face. Reaching forty-one, his friend's eyes shot open and he yelled,

"I've got it!"

Just then, the high pitched wail of the fire alarm stopped abruptly.

"What? How?" exclaimed Peter.

Tank turned to face his friend.

"I can't stop the blast, but I think I might know how to contain it."

"Contain it?"

"Yes, contain it. That's the best I can do. It means losing this entire building, but given what we're facing, that seems like quite a small sacrifice. Wouldn't you agree?"

Thinking about it for a split second, he realised that this whole place, the clubhouse, the pitches and especially the Astroturf, were all like a second home to him and he wanted no harm to come to any of them. But the choice was non-existent. At least this way, hopefully nobody would lose their lives, and that was by far the most important concern.

"What do we do?"

"I'm going to put a shield mantra like no other around the whole of the clubhouse, hopefully encasing the blast. IF I get it right, the kinetic power from the explosion SHOULD be channelled up into the sky and down into the ground. However, because of the scale of things, I might need you to lend me some of your magic and strength to help set it up and maybe even to cast it at the end. The only thing that worries me is that there is absolutely no wind at all today. Ideally we'd need a breeze to dissipate the part of the explosion that is focused upwards into the atmosphere, to prevent the contamination just falling straight back down to earth later."

"Well, there's not much we can do about the weather," added Peter. "Where do we start?"

"WE don't," announced Tank. "I need to go to each corner of the building on both floors, starting off on the ground floor. You need to stay here and open yourself up to my thoughts. If you feel me flagging, lend me your strength and magical energy... all you can spare. There should be just enough time to wrap up the entire building, but we'll have to hurry. As well, make sure no one comes back in, otherwise they'll be trapped and caught up in the blast."

Nodding as his friend sprinted past him at breakneck

speed, heading downstairs, Peter, strangely, felt a sense of calm wash over him as the total quiet of the top floor enveloped him. He thought it quite surreal given the situation: bomb, panic, danger, destruction... but quiet. Moving across to the giant curved window, he gazed across to the crowd gathered at the edge of the car park. Enhancing his vision just slightly, he scanned the frightened faces. Richie, it appeared, was long gone, after storming out of the bar earlier. Not happy about falling out with her once again, it appeared that she was the one with the short temper this time, something of an irony given the usual turn of events, but in a sense he felt relieved and glad that it had happened, because she wasn't here now, seeing all this, being so close to the danger that the magically enhanced explosive device presented. Just as he finished scanning the crowd, it dawned on him that he hadn't spotted Janice, the whole point of doing it in the first place. Panic welling up inside threatened to overwhelm him. Hearing the soft sound of small footsteps running up the stairs, he knew instantly it could only be one other... JANICE! Rushing across to the doorway, he was just in time as she turned the corner, and in a running jump, threw herself at him. Surprised, he nearly dropped her, but not quite.

"What are you doing here?" he admonished.

"I wanted to make sure you were safe," she squeaked.

"You have to get back outside with the others.'"

Turning to go, before she did, she mentioned one last thing.

"Oh, the fire brigade are on their way. There was nothing I could do to stop them I'm afraid."

'DAMN!' he thought. 'If they arrive, they'll insist on entering the building, and will all get themselves killed.'

"JANICE!" he shouted after her down the stairs.

"Yes?"

"You have to make sure they don't enter the building. It's really not safe."

"But how?" she answered.

"I don't know," he declared. "Perhaps they won't turn up for a while. But do whatever you have to. They mustn't enter the building at all costs... It's important!"

"I'll try," she yelled, before turning round and running back outside.

'Things could be going... oh, so much better,' he thought. 'I truly hope Tank is having more luck.'

"See... what did I tell you? Nothing to worry about."

Smiling, he gave her a small, knowing nod as they huddled together. She thought he looked magnificent, framed against the stark, white walls of the chilly cellar. With the noise having stopped, the kissing very much resumed.

Tank felt under more pressure than he had in his entire life... and rightly so. The lives of thousands, if not tens of thousands of innocent people were effectively in his hands. Trying not to think about it as he stood in the southernmost corner of the clubhouse on the ground floor, he knew what to do and, in theory at least, it should work and produce a giant invisible cylinder that would contain the blast by feeding it up and down instead of outwards. If only he had more time to check his work and make sure each of the mantra points in the corners of the building were set correctly, and that they lined up above and below. But time was the one thing he didn't have. As he finished uttering the last few words of this particular mantra, he glanced longingly out of the window at the torn up, muddy rugby pitch that he considered his friend. It called to him, sang to him even, the giant white goalposts seeming to smile in his direction. Brushing away all thoughts of the sport he loved, a little synchronised timer remained, counting off the minutes and seconds until the bomb went off. Drained of magical energy, he sprinted off towards the next corner, knowing the cost of any mistake on his part could prove tragic.

Weaving her way through the array of vehicles that littered the car park, Janice ran straight up to the manager of the sports club who'd been marching sternly across towards her.

"Is it safe to return?" he questioned, rather crossly.

"Uhhhh... I'm not entirely sure it is," she answered, a little out of breath.

"Why on earth not? The alarms have stopped, and I'm sure the fire brigade will be here any moment."

Her mind was a whirlwind of thoughts and emotions, and she didn't have the faintest idea of what the hell was going on, but she knew that she trusted Peter implicitly, loved him deeply, and knew that whatever he and Tank were doing was in everyone's best interests. But she hated lying, and had never been any good at it.

'Still, here goes,' she thought, bracing herself.

"I think there might be some kind of gas leak. I'm sure that's what I could smell," she fibbed, mustering up some genuine feeling in her words.

"GAS!" repeated the manager.

"I'm sure," reiterated the diminutive bar worker.

"Ahh... well, in that case, perhaps it's best if we all stay here a while longer and wait for the fire brigade to turn up," stuttered the manager, a little feebly.

"I think that's very wise," replied the bubbly blonde, walking back towards the large crowd of men, women and children gathered as far away from the clubhouse as possible, hoping desperately that she'd bought her friends enough time.

Thousands of miles away across the Atlantic, time had

just run out. The hot, sunny, cloudless day had been rudely interrupted by the mother of all explosions halfway up the oldest skyscraper in the city. Pounding through every floor, the blast incinerated almost everything in its path. Concrete, metal and glass tore off every which way, forming lethal projectiles searching for something to pierce.

The main mass of the building crumpled to the ground, huge chunks of its superstructure impacting the area all around it, spewing lethal clouds of dust and rubble in all directions.

Power and kinetic energy from the mighty detonation assaulted the surrounding skyscrapers, making them all shake. Two toppled and fell, with the same devastating destruction as the first. Thousands died. If it had been a week day, it would have been more.

As the waves of dust and debris continued moving out in a concentric circle, raging fires sprang up as if from nowhere, as in the distance, noisy sirens of the first responders heading towards the emergency, echoed across the rooftops.

Dragons had died too, the psychic wave encompassing the huge underground community, as well as one of the busiest monorail stations on the continent. First responders arrived there as well, but it was far too late to do anything. Perfectly formed dragon corpses littered the pristine underground world for miles and miles around. Immediately the council were informed. Again, there was nothing they could do.

Both above and below ground, the stunning city of Seattle would never be the same again.

Holding each other tight in this most unlikely of meeting places, the dipping temperature had started to bite. She'd never liked the cold, understandable really, but here and now it was a small price to pay to be with HIM!

Just being in his arms felt somehow magical, almost as if she didn't have a care in the world. Despite all the reasons that she should, she never wanted to give that up.

Moving quickly now, Tank had completed all the mantras on the ground floor. For the final one, he'd had little choice but to borrow some of Peter's magical energy, as his reserves were running quite low and the spell required to contain the blast from the imminent explosion was mana intensive, so much so that the rugby playing dragon wasn't entirely sure that they'd have sufficient reserves between them. Focusing intently, he soldiered on towards the top floor.

Hearing his friend approaching, Peter readied himself to part with a little more mana, feeling like a spare part, with his friend doing all the running and casting. Deep down he knew it couldn't be helped... after all, Tank knew the details of the mantra and he didn't, but still, that didn't stop him from feeling utterly redundant, just sitting there, letting his friend draw on his reserves when needed. Briefly he wished he had the dagger... Aviva's laminium dagger. With that, there would be no need to worry about having enough of anything. But stupidly, or sensibly, depending on your perspective, it was safely tucked away deep inside his home, under very stringent safeguards, but it too would be caught in the explosion if his friend's shielding plan didn't work. Sitting nervously at one of the tables in the expansive function room, keeping his mind open to his friend, ready to give everything he had, he tried dreadfully hard not to think about Janice and everyone else from the sports club standing outside, as well as the thousands of innocent people in the surrounding area who were blissfully unaware of the very real danger that right at this very moment was counting down, mere metres away from him.

North America took the brunt of yet another cataclysmic explosion. As the numerals lit up the confined space behind the brick wall deep within the sewer system, on reaching six minutes and three seconds, yet another randomly discharged signal instructed a motherboard that it was time, carrying out its job to perfection.

Below ground, just west of the Fulton River District was the epicentre that the deadly wave rippled out from, reaching as far north as River West, stopping just short of River North on its eastern edge, failing to topple any of the substantial skyscrapers of downtown Chicago. The wreckage stopped some two blocks short of reaching Greektown on its southern edge. Homes, small businesses, shops and car parks were all destroyed, along with a Chicago police department building, numerous police cars and motorbikes. The Kennedy Expressway and the Chicago Edens Expressway were eradicated, along with all the vehicles that had the misfortune to be travelling along them at the time. Next came the Chicago Transit Authority's Green Line which was reduced to practically nothing. Metal support girders were wiped out, along with all the track. Silver carriages of trains travelling along the line lay scattered about the area, most cut open along their entire length, their occupants given absolutely no chance whatsoever. A war zone was the best way to describe the carnage that remained. Producing a tidal wave along the length of the Chicago river which damaged the sluice gates on the waterfront, the explosive blast was heard over one hundred miles away.

In conjunction with the human world above, the dragon domain suffered incredible losses as the psychic wave tore through it, destroying the Chicago monorail station, leaving no dragon standing. Although there were not nearly as many fatalities as in some of the other blast sites, it was dumb luck that the main dragon residential area beneath Chicago was a vast distance away from the city centre above ground. Still, dragon responders in the King's Guard were once again horrified at the scenes that greeted them on arrival. Again, the council were informed. It felt to them as though they were being attacked from all sides.

Sitting overlooking them all, his long fingernails scratching at the white growth on and around his chin, a sense of bewilderment and frustration stabbed at his very soul. For he'd been tasked with keeping them safe... all of them! Dragons, humans, animals, plants... he had failed each and every one of them. It felt as though he was being attacked personally, on all fronts, by invisible forces lurking in the shadows. Random, by all accounts, except for the incredible destruction, the assaults just couldn't be predicted. As dragons scuttled in and out of the chambers, passing flimsy pieces of paper over to the councillors, it seemed inevitable that the human world on the surface would suffer more than the clandestine dragon domain beneath. He knew that, by now, news of the attacks would have disseminated globally; undoubtedly panic, chaos and mayhem were spreading at just the very thought of what was happening. Trying to remain calm... calm and composed, knowing that right now the dragon domain, and the world in general, needed a being with their head screwed on, one that would make the right choices in the cold light of day and not act on an emotional impulse for retribution, should the perpetrators of these despicable deeds ever be discovered, with a grim determination, he set himself to do just that, despite a dark hand squeezing his very heart, urging him to lash out and strike.

Feeling absolutely shattered, nothing to do with the hockey match he'd played in earlier, Peter was tired to his very bones, or more likely, to his very DNA. Tank had drained more of his magical energy to help set up the first two top floor spells, which would all coalesce into one big, giant mantra... hopefully. Knowing there were only two more to go did nothing to reassure him, because he just wasn't sure he could go on, he just didn't seem to have it in him. It sounded as stupid to his mind as it does on this page; after all he was only sitting down, but he'd never really been blessed with an awesome supply of magical energy, or mana as some dragons referred to it. Of course it did recharge at quite a rate, but that was of little comfort in their current situation as it took hours, and not minutes, to go from drained to fully replenished.

A bone weary Tank staggered into the function room, briefly leaning on one wall as he did so, both friends catching each other's eyes. Straight away, Peter's self pity disappeared. Tank looked wasted, ashen, exhausted, almost... frail.

"Two more to go," he huffed, lurching his way towards the far corner, next to the wall that separated the corridor from the function room.

Holding his head in his hands, which were propped up on the wooden table at which he sat, just one thought ran through Peter's head.

'We just haven't got enough in us. The mantra he's using requires too much. We're never gonna make it!'

Outside in the car park, things had just gone from bad to worse. It had been difficult enough trying to assure the gathered members that it wasn't possible to return to the clubhouse just yet, feigning a gas leak. But that paled in comparison with the task that Janice now faced. Not only had the fire brigade arrived, but the rest of the emergency services as well, all at once. Knowing that every second she could stall them was important, and starting to run out of ideas, the petite blonde, being the only one supposedly having any knowledge of the gas leak, decided on a different approach, one that she hoped would work until Peter and Tank finished whatever it was they were doing.

Managing to stand up from the table, but only just, Peter felt so weary. With Tank there in the room, he thought it only proper to go over and stand with him, if for no other reason than to show his support, not that his friend would have any reason to doubt him on that front. With the former apprentice whispering under his breath, while in tandem weaving his hands and fingers through some very strange patterns, Peter gazed out of the squeaky clean window, past the many, many cars, to the far side of the car park. Exhaling in surprise at the sight that greeted him, there, standing directly in front of a fire engine, which had not quite made it through the main gate and into the car park, was... JANICE, looking like she was having some kind of epileptic fit or something, arms waving wildly, head nodding vigorously, her whole body bobbing up and down like a boat in a storm. Firemen on either side looked to be trying to cajole her off out of the way, without much success, but he knew it was only a matter of time before they triumphed over her. Abruptly, a wave of fatigue washed through him, causing him to crumple to his knees, too tired to stand. From out of nowhere a huge hand grabbed him by the collar and pulled him back to his feet. Hugging the all encompassing window, Tank stumbled past him, on his way to the last corner.

"It's nearly over. Last one, and then we're done," he slurred, sounding almost drunk. Seeing the toll this taking on his friend, Peter wondered if Tank would be able to complete the final part of the mantra that would form the invisible barrier and contain the bomb's blast. Even if he did, would the two of them have enough left to get out of the building? Two burning questions, whose answers would only come in time, and on whose outcomes thousands of lives, quite literally, depended.

Despite Tim wanting to go back up, she wasn't having any of it, knowing that these illicit liaisons were becoming more and more infrequent, and were getting harder and harder to arrange. Sooner or later they would have to stop, although she couldn't see how at the moment, or picture her life without him. As they held each other tightly, and kissed some more, he gave in to her every wish. How could he deny her? He loved her, despite her strange ways and all the secrecy that accompanied them. Perhaps one day he'd find out what it was all about; until then he was content just to be with her, even if it meant ending up in strange places like this.

Tank stood, well barely, in the last corner on the first floor. It all came down to this. If he executed the mantra properly, then all the others should join together, forming a perfectly cylindrical invisible shield, capable of containing almost anything. But time was ticking down. Both friends had running timers at the front of their minds, synchronised with the one on the bomb. Both currently stood at one minute, thirty six seconds. And that wasn't their only problem. As was his wont, Peter had been gazing out of the window, trying to keep an eye on developments outside, namely Janice. But the game was up. An instant ago, two police officers from a car blocked in by the fire engine, had crept and physically removed her. Now nothing stood in the way of the emergency services entering the car park and then ultimately... the clubhouse! Immensely proud of her, especially the way she'd played the panic stricken, scared, emotional woman, which had bought them valuable seconds, seconds that might well save the lives of the very personnel that had just manhandled her out of the way, he'd known it was all an act, but confirmation came when she, standing silently, looked in his direction. Beaming, he hoped to be with her in a matter of seconds.

As the smile spread out across his face, his legs buckled in on themselves. Tank collapsed as well. It was a shame really, because if they'd been standing, they'd have noticed a shimmering, curved light sparkle yellow for a fraction of a second, all around the clubhouse, confirming the mantra that the youngster had cast, worked. But at what cost?

Janice had been looking in the direction of the clubhouse hoping, however unlikely it was, that she'd catch a glimpse of Peter or Tank behind the ever so slightly tinted windows now that the policemen had let go of her. But so far, no such luck. As she continued to watch, an eerie yellow light flashed around the building before disappearing. Rubbing her eyes, unsure of what she'd seen, murmurs from those around her confirmed that others in the crowd had witnessed the strange phenomenon, or so all the talking and shouting seemed to indicate, over the sound of the fire engine negotiating the rows of parked cars in and around the entrance. Inside her mind she wished to God that Peter and Tank would come sprinting out from between the double doors of the entrance. Would her wish come true?

Groggy, both friends groaned and muttered as their brief spell of unconsciousness came to an end at exactly the same time. Tank was first on his feet, aware that the timer counting down in his mind showed forty eight seconds. Instantly he yanked Peter upright and the two of them headed clumsily out into the corridor and down the stairs, both clinging onto the handrail for dear life as they did so. Pushing through the double doors into the bar area, through the window they could just make out the bright red of the fire engine, attempting to do a three point turn in the car park. Pulling in long deep breaths, the two ran the length of the bar, both hitting the doors of the entrance in front of them together. Shouts and cries went up from the crowd at the sight of them both emerging from the building they had previously thought empty. Tank muttered a few words in an ancient tongue which allowed them to safely pass through the fully completed shield. Some of the firemen and police officers headed towards them, but Tank and Peter both had the forethought to wave them back, which to their credit, they took heed of.

With everybody, including all the emergency services, corralled in a large group at the far edge of the car park, both friends dodged cars and vans, the muscles in their legs burning, their energy all but spent. In their heads the timer hit nineteen as the two of them pulled up in front of the large crowd. Tank collapsed on all fours, his breathing heavy and strained. Putting his hands behind his head in the hope of taking in more air as he breathed, Peter straightened and turned to face the clubhouse for the imminent arrival of one hell of an explosion. As he did so, just out of the corner of his right eye, he spotted something, something that sent goose bumps up his arms and cold shivers down his tail. RICHIE'S CAR!

'But she's already left,' was his first thought.

'But she can't possibly be in...' was his second.

With his energy waning, he reached out telepathically with everything that he had left. Sure enough, somewhere just below ground level, a dragon presence, all tucked in on itself lurked, along with that of a human. Grabbing his friend, he pulled him to his feet, something of a miracle in itself given the size difference between the two of them.

"She's in there Tank. Richie's in there!" he screamed into his friend's face.

Looking on in utter disbelief, Tank too could now get a sense of a dragon off in that direction. Joy at saving all these people turned to pain, guilt and soul destroying rage at the thought of losing his friend. Deep inside his mind, the timer hit eight seconds. Both friends had the same thought, once again, at exactly the same time. Closing their eyes, they sent out a mental picture, a warning, showing first the clubhouse, and then the imminent explosion, focusing all their efforts on homing in on their friend.

Against the bright, white walls of the clubhouse cellar, Richie broke off mid kiss, gasping sharply, and not because of the chilly, refrigerated air. A series of pictures crashed through her defences, assaulting her strong dragon mind, showing first the clubhouse and then a powerful explosion. Accompanying the images was a sense of utter urgency, desperation and despair from her two best friends. Mouth hanging open, stunned at what she'd just learned, at best, she had but a split second to act. As always she moved faster than she had any right to, her right hand grabbing the *alea* that she wore, the one that Peter had given to her, the one that had originally belonged to Mark Hiscock. Instantly she snapped it in two, while at the exact same time screaming in her mind, with all the willpower she could muster,

"Amplificare Magicus Nunc," which in much plainer language translated as 'Amplify Magic Now'. As a slight afterthought, one hundredth of a second or so later, she popped into existence what can only really be described as a rather primitive personal shield, something all dragons learn to cast in the very first part of their eleventh year in the nursery ring. In doing so, she had the presence of mind to extend it around Tim, who all the while had stood aghast, fearing he'd done something wrong. As the flickering green radiance from the shield encased the two of them, light and darkness encompassed them both, to the accompanying sound of HELL! The world as they knew it... ended!

Starting with a tiny, bright light on the upper floor, instantly it increased to blinding proportions. A rip roaring explosion of the kind which, before today, the earth had rarely seen, tore apart the fairly new clubhouse, shredding every last part of it. The noise was brutal. Violently the earth shook. Fire and magical energy of every different colour swirled inside the invisible barrier that Tank had crafted. On finding no way out to the sides, the raging torrent of destruction flooded downwards into the ground, and upwards into the sky. It must have been more than three miles into the air before the shaft of energy exploded outwards into the relative safety of the atmosphere, at first running over the sides like a cup full to the brim, being constantly topped up, and then forcing its way across the sky, like thunder clouds in a storm. From out of nowhere, a harsh, churning breeze snaked across the heavens, scattering the deadly particles throughout the atmosphere, reducing their concentration to a safe level.

On the ground things were very different. Some of the kinetic energy from the blast had been forced downwards by the mantra, creating a crater the exact diameter of the clubhouse, nearly a quarter of a mile deep. Smoke and fire raged up and out of the fissure, the steamy surface of the bedrock surrounding it looking like an alien landscape from the future. Nothing physical remained of the clubhouse itself. No windows, doors, bricks, furniture... NOTHING! Every last molecule had been obliterated on impact.

Luckily for the two dragon friends, Tank's complicated mantra had contained the deadly psychic wave that was a side effect of all the laminium bombs. That too had been directed harmlessly up into the sky and down into the earth. No part of the dragon domain lay directly below, so no dragons were affected.

Most of the crowd had been knocked to the ground, by the deafening sound and surprise rather than anything else.

But not Tank and Peter. They stood looking on, knowing that nothing, either human or dragon, could have withstood that kind of blast. Their friend was gone. No more. Tears streamed down their cheeks. Fatigue tore at their ravaged bodies. Even if they'd wanted to go into the crater and look for her remains, they couldn't. Understandably, they were spent.

Peter was startled out of thoughts of his friend first, as a face appeared right in front of his. A policeman moving his mouth... talking, but Peter, like most of the others, was having trouble hearing, what with the explosion and all the screaming, shouting and crying going on all around him.

'Odd,' he thought, 'the officer seems mad, angry even.' It made no sense at all to the young dragon. After all, it was he who'd just lost a best friend. Tank as well. All the others had effectively been saved. Just as he was about to tell the man exactly what he could do in a biologically specific way, he felt something grab his hands from behind, forcing them together. Instinctively, he tried to turn round, but a firm pressure on his neck prevented him from doing so. Wondering just what on earth was going on, it was then that he spotted Tank being wrestled to the ground by three of the constabulary.

'Have they all gone mad?' he thought, struggling more than a little. But it was all to no avail. Even the mighty Tank could offer little in the way of resistance, not with practically all his energy depleted.

With their hands cable tied behind their backs, both friends were forcibly marched towards the waiting police cars. As they passed the crowd, angry shouts and jeers assaulted their ears. Neither friend had any idea what was going on, their heads still ringing and their hearing more than a little impaired from the sound of the blast. That is until a lacrosse player carrying an infant in her arms came right up to them and shouted,

"WHY? Why did you do it? Why blow up our lovely

clubhouse? WHY?"

As the mother and infant were pushed out of the way by the heavy handed officers, Tank and Peter exchanged horrified glances. But worse was to come, well, for Peter anyway. While Tank was squeezed forcibly into the back seat of one of the vehicles, a familiar figure approached the edge of the crowd, right next to where the hockey playing dragon stood. The look on her face cut his heart like a knife. The pain he felt there and then was a hundred times worse than anything he'd felt while battling Manson on the artificial pitch less than a year ago. Tears streaked down her beautiful face, smudging what little make up she wore. Her look said it all... betrayal, hurt, injustice... LIES! Opening his mouth to explain, to clarify how they'd both saved them all, it was too late. She'd turned and disappeared back into the crowd, whilst he was now being firmly shoved into the other police car. As the ignition purred into life and the driver spun around and headed out onto the main road, he couldn't help but think about everything he'd just lost.

36 HOUSTON... THERE SEEMS TO BE A PROBLEM!

In all, fourteen laminium bombs had exploded across the world, making it the bloodiest and deadliest day in the planet's history. Places hit included Montreal Canada, Seattle USA, Wong Chan Thailand, Chicago USA, Macclesfield UK, Moscow Russia, Melbourne Australia, Ankara Turkey, Cape Town South Africa, Mumbai India, Balikpapan Indonesia, Shanghai China, Lisbon Portugal and of course the clubhouse in Salisbridge. If the bomb at the laminium ball match, the one that had Steel clinging to life by just a thread, was taken into account, then altogether that made fifteen... the exact number of chunks of metal the evil dragon Manson had stolen from Cropptech. At least, that was the council's assumption, and indeed their hope that there would be no more. No more devastation, no more loss of life. In dragon terms, the death toll was still being revised, but it numbered well into the tens of thousands. For the humans, it was different. Because of where the bombs had been placed, mainly in built up urban areas of highly populated cities, the death toll and casualty count were much higher. At least a hundred thousand people had died across the world, with many more injured and wounded. Significantly, the count was still continuing to grow.

Almost every dragon on the planet, including the king and his councillors, hadn't slept a wink since the terrorism had started. For that's what it was... TERRORISM! As for who'd committed it and what their goal was, the dragon council were still trying to figure that out. To start with, the priority had been to respond to those in need, dragon and human alike, with the King's Guard having been dispatched to each site with instructions to use their abilities to help those both above and below ground.

They'd been warned that it would be unlikely they would find injured dragons, given the power of the psychic blast waves. They would be either dead, killed by the wave, or alive and relatively healthy. And so there was little they could do beneath the surface, in which case they were all instructed to help the human world above in any way that they could. There would also be dragons disguised as humans who'd been killed by the deadly psychic blast wave on the surface, some being well out of the physical radius of the explosion. It was important to recover their bodies before the humans did. While it was almost impossible to distinguish a disguised member of their race from an actual human, the council didn't want to take the chance of autopsies being performed on their kind, just in case the psychic wave had done some molecular damage to the dead dragon's DNA. King's Guards from across the planet scrambled to get to the nearest site, not only to help with the rescue efforts, but to effect the recovery of all the dragon corpses, leaving only a skeleton force left to cope with their normal duties, if anything could be described as 'normal' ever again. At least having agreed on that much, but very little else, the council was as fragmented as it had ever been, holed up inside the chambers. Watching from on high, the king was frustrated beyond belief at the bickering going on below him. Most of the officials were up in wings about something, a couple stressing their point that it must have been one of the many human terrorist groups that had committed the atrocities, and that they should be hunted down and punished. Others argued against, claiming it was highly unlikely. And so it went on. Some claimed that it was the dark dragon Manson; after all, he'd stolen the laminium from which the bombs had supposedly been crafted. There was a further call to round up all the King's Guards across the planet in an attempt to find the deadly dragon and bring him to justice, rather than waste valuable resources and time helping out the humans on the surface. And so it continued, all the time George watching them like a hawk, studying each and every one of them, particularly what they said.

It had taken some fifteen hours for the first dragons to arrive at the site of the Salisbridge explosion, a travesty in dragon terms. Every single witness had long since disappeared, making it impossible to erase their memories of the event. Prehistoric investigators, disguised as government officials, took in the huge, still smouldering, crater from its edge. One or two marvelled at the ingenuity of the mantra used to contain the blast and prevent the same destruction that had occurred elsewhere across the planet. Others scoured the dark, smoky depths for signs of anything at all amongst the rubble and scorched earth.

Five miles away, Peter and Tank were being released from their incarceration, neither of them too happy about how things had played out. They'd endured all sorts of verbal abuse from everyone, officers and prisoners alike. And despite their dragon training against such things, everything that was said... HURT! Words cut like the sharpest chainsaw sliding through butter, the looks felt as though they'd been gutted with a screwdriver, while the small, unnecessary punches and pushes when they'd been moved about, tore at their very being. They'd saved everyone, lost their best friend in the process and then for Peter, there was... JANICE! Regardless of their magical energy recharging, the two friends were devastated, emotional and washed out. Despite being locked up for over fifteen hours, they kept their counsel and waited for what they hoped would be a dragon rescue of some sort. Unable to believe that it had taken this long, that is until they were briefed on what had happed across the world by another prisoner who'd just arrived, to say they were staggered was an understatement. When the chief constable (one of their kind of course) finally got round to signing their release papers, he explained that because of Tank's actions in creating the mantra surrounding the clubhouse, the whole site had been deemed secondary to the other emergencies across the globe, hence the reason why no dragon had attended the scene up until now, and why their fate had only just come to light.

Both friends nodded, glad to be free and leaving this god-awful place. The chief also informed them that a story had been put out that instead of being the perpetrators of this awful crime, they had in fact tried to disarm the bomb, which was pretty much the truth anyway. Either way, they were free to go and shouldn't get any more hassle from anyone, quite the opposite in fact. For Peter, it all felt like déjà vu. People would once again be praising him for something he hadn't really done... it was the Astroturf incident with the dragon Manson, all over again.

Having wasted no time in getting stuck in, the dragon investigators were quick workers. Huge two hundred foot barriers had been erected around the circumference of the bomb blast, with the only way now to see into the crater being from the air, and they'd made sure that all flying privileges in the area had been revoked. Large excavation machinery littered the car park, its purpose clear. But the dragons had no intention of using it. Blanketed by the giant barriers, and with one of their group acting as a lookout, they were free to use the entire range of their magical powers. And so it was that mantra after mantra started to be cast. Huge chunks of rubble magically threw themselves up and over the rim of the crater, as well as tiny, water-like streams of dirt and stone. Ordered to leave no stone unturned (ironic, given what they were doing) in trying to find anything that would aid their investigation, each of the dragons knew that this was just the place to start, given that all the other bombs had exploded over a much larger area.

Across Melbourne, Montreal and Cape Town, it was much the same as in all the other affected cities across the planet. Emergency aid stations were still in operation, with tireless emergency service personnel scouring hundreds of tons of rubble for survivors with specialist equipment. Schools, sports centres, town halls, anything with a large enough capacity, had been set up to accommodate the homeless, of which there were tens of thousands. It was truly a global disaster of epic proportions.

Below ground, it was a little different. In more than a dozen places, the worldwide monorail had been closed for the first time in its history. Bereavement Grottos were working flat out, with the council having passed an emergency mandate, stipulating that dragons would be put to rest without a formal ceremony. Instead, one whole day of mourning would be held, worldwide, exactly one week on from the very first bomb blast. As you can imagine, this caused uproar in most enclaves. Disappointment was widespread. But the dragon council explained their stance in the telepathic papers, by stating that so many of their kind had died, it would take months, if not years, to give them all the personal service they so deserved, something not a single dragon would wish for. On top of that, there were health and safety issues. While dragons, once dead, don't normally decompose, well... not at the rate of a human corpse, they do, ever so slightly, give off a putrid odour that attracts insects from far and wide. So many corpses, all in the same areas, would be something of a nightmare. Finally, the council announced, that with dragon and human kind both suffering tragic attacks on an epic scale, it was time to concentrate on helping the living and safeguard both the underground domain and the world above, against a repeat of these senseless attacks. For most dragons, the council seemed to make sense. But not for all.

As they both walked across the uneven paving slabs towards the waiting police car that had been provided to take them home, Tank pulled his shiny black phone away from his ear, having just listened to a voicemail message. For the first time in what seemed like a week, a small smile snaked its way across the rough features of his face. Peter gave him an enquiring look.

"Everything alright?"

"You have to listen to this," he laughed, handing Peter the phone, the message already starting to replay.

Holding the phone to his ear, Peter listened intently. After a hushed beep, and a few seconds of crackle, a voice he recognised gently hissed into life.

"Ummmmmm... hello? Is that... is that Mr Tank's phone machine? It's... it's his... ummmmm... uncle, that's it! Uncle. It's his uncle here... just checking to see if everything's... um... okay. Perhaps... um... machine, you could tell him to phone. NO! Not phone. You could tell him. I mean ask him to... um... contact me, at his earliest convenience. Thank you so kindly for taking my message. His uncle."

It was all Peter could do not to laugh out loud at the fact that the old shopkeeper had obviously been chasing Tank, because he hadn't turned up to work when he should have, and then the news about the bombs had probably freaked him out, especially the Salisbridge one. Shaking his head, he caught his friend's eye as they both got into the back of the police car, on a very different journey this time. As he handed Tank back his phone, they both had the same thought. Perhaps someone needs to give Gee Tee some human interaction lessons. But who? That was the 64 million dollar question.

"Well?" demanded a silky smooth voice from the shadows of a dark and dreary building somewhere in North America.

"It all went off according to plan, with one exception."

"What exception?" screamed the voice from the shadows. Whoever planted the one that didn't go off would be summarily punished. NO... KILLED, and he'd see to it himself.

In the form of a twenty-something human male, the cowering naga seemed almost too frightened to speak. Once again, the voice asked, only this time with a whole lot of menace behind the words.

"WELL?"

"It was the one in Salisbridge, sire," he nervously volunteered.

"WHAT?" challenged the hidden voice. "You've got to be kidding me."

In response, the human shaped naga shook his head, sorry that he'd been selected to deliver the bad news. A loud CRASH, followed almost immediately by a SMASH, echoed from out of the darkness. The naga had heard tales of this being's temper and had hoped never to experience it firsthand. He had, however, always thought them exaggerated more than a little. I mean, how bad could it really be? Before he had the chance to find out, the PUFF of a silenced gunshot sounded out from somewhere in front of him. Pain from his chest exploded outwards as he crumpled to the floor, vision darkening.

'Pretty bad, as it turns out,' he thought, answering his own question.

With the naga lying dead in a pool of radiant blood, the human shape limped out into the light to inspect his work. Silently he cursed, and thought,

'Of all the bombs not to go off, it would have to be the one I planted. Well, it's not like I'm going to kill myself, is it? I wonder what happened? Was it something that idiot of a chairman did, or maybe a quirk of fate? Typical! That was the one out of all of them that I was most looking forward to savouring. DAMN!'

In his frustration, he took a great big kick at the limp and lifeless body before him on the ground, which only really served to get blood up one side of his immaculate trousers. But despite the relatively minor setback of Salisbridge, things were, for the moment, going as planned. It wouldn't be long now. Not long at all. And then he'd be able to choose when and where to visit retribution. All the residents of Salisbridge had done was buy themselves a little more time. Turning, he climbed the stairs in search of some new clothes.

Climbing out of the police car, he thanked the officer for the lift, before heading along the pavement towards his house. Just before he got to the gate he spotted his own car, parked on the opposite side of the road, just as he'd been told it would be. By all accounts the police had moved it while he'd been in custody, with the car park at the sports club having been cleared, under orders of the so called government agents, who he'd subsequently found out were a dragon squad of specialist King's Guards. Glad his vehicle was back safe and sound, though in the scale of things it mattered little. Richie was dead, Janice had turned away from him, the clubhouse was destroyed and in less than an hour, the planet had been decimated. Meandering up the crazy paving path, the emotional rollercoaster that he'd been on finally came to a halt, hitting him like a rampaging bull. Sitting down on his doorstep, not even bothering to go inside, he felt confused, lonely and sad. Of course he still had Tank, his friend the old shopkeeper, Flash, wherever in the world he was, and the king. But Richie, oh Richie. She was his first ever friend, and he could recall being there with her in the nursery ring when she'd hatched, both of them the tiniest of dragonlings. Even then they seemed inseparable, having grown up together, taken every class together; she'd jumped in and saved him more times than he cared to remember. By now the tears were like a river coming to life in the rainforest at the behest of a newly started monsoon. All sense of time was lost. Images of Richie played through his head, for once, his near perfect memory doing him no favours at all. Passersby on the street gave him strange looks, one even offering to help. He ignored them all, the only thing on his mind was his friend. Turning his thoughts to the future, he couldn't see how he could go on without her. Knowing that losing someone special happened all the time to people and dragons throughout the world, he also knew that eventually, most of them came to terms with it. But not him. NEVER! It would be... impossible.

Carefully, he stood, his legs shaking, partly from his emotional state, partly because he'd been sitting down for so long. Rummaging around in his pocket, eventually he found his keys. Holding them up to undo the door, it was then that a sudden need struck him. He needed to go there... NOW! He needed to see what was being done. He needed to see her one last time. He needed to say... GOODBYE! Turning, he sprinted down the path, vaulted the gate, crossed the road to his car and, sliding into the driver's seat, turned the key in the ignition before shooting off down the road like a Formula One car exiting the pits.

Tank, too, had thanked the police officer politely for the lift, before going straight into his rented house. But he was just passing through. A matter of seconds later, he found himself back in the comforting surroundings of the underground domain, heading towards the monorail station, which would whisk him off to the master mantra maker in no time at all.

Feeling like a powerless teacher in a classroom of badly behaved children, he watched as they still argued, realising that he was starting to lose his temper, never a good thing, particularly when you're aware that it's happening and can do nothing about it. It probably had something to do with the fact that he'd just found out about the bomb in Salisbridge, at some kind of club or other. When the dragon had come in and told him, he nearly went into meltdown. Luckily, the aide had quickly added that the blast had been contained, by a mantra no less, and that there were no reported casualties. On hearing that he'd breathed a huge sigh of relief. Because although he didn't have any offspring (the chance had never really presented itself, and he always seemed to be on one mission or another) getting to know his best friend's grandson in the way he had, made him feel... special. And although he wasn't a father, in a lot of ways he felt much like he imagined a parent would towards the young dragon, even in some regards towards his friends, and was determined to do everything he could to keep them safe from whatever threat their community now faced. After all, hadn't they been through enough already?

Driving in through the gate, that's as far as he got before a very official man wearing a dark suit and grey trench coat stepped out in front of his car, signalling him to stop. Peter did so, knowing that this was one of the King's Guards. As the man headed round to the driver's side, he was staggered to see the huge hoarding screens erected around where the clubhouse had previously stood. Winding down the window, he listened to what the man had to say.

"I'm sorry sir, the whole site is off limits to everyone I'm afraid," declared the dragon in disguise.

"I need to be here. One of my friends, she was caught

up in the blast," he pleaded.

"I think you must be mistaken sir," the guy replied, smiling. "Nobody was caught up in the blast. There were no casualties or fatalities."

Starting to lose his patience, he leant out of the window, to get right up in the dragon's face, feeling the need to clear a few things up.

"Listen to me. I was one of the two that applied the mantra that contained the blast."

That certainly changed the dragon's outlook.

"My friend, the dragon known as Richie Rump, and a human, were here when the explosion occurred, directly beneath the clubhouse... in the cellar I think. They were both caught up in the explosion, of that much I'm sure."

"And you saw this happen?"

"Yes," he replied. "From right over there," he ventured, pointing to a spot at the edge of the car park.

"But the report we had stated that nobody was even hurt, let alone caught up in it. Why didn't you tell us sooner?"

"Because," growled Peter, "both of us were locked up in a police cell, which incidentally is where I've just come from, having spent the best part of fifteen hours there, because the officers on the scene mistakenly thought that we'd blown the damn thing up."

"Oh," was all the disguised dragon could say. Taking a step back, the guard closed his eyes, clearly having a telepathic conversation with somebody. It didn't take long.

"Park over there," he ordered. "Then I'll take you through to my supervisor."

Exiting his car, he was led through a tiny little entrance at the bottom of one of the massive screens, into the sealed off area around the crater. Those dragons who'd been working to move some of the rubble at the bottom of the hole all stopped and were now looking in his direction. Another, who Peter assumed was in charge, came over. Briefly he explained what had happened, down to the last detail, with the dragon in charge thinking long and hard about just what to do, all the time scratching his chin. Moments later, he ordered those around him to redouble their efforts, telling them that the crater was not fit to be the resting place of any dragon, least of all the one he'd heard about.

Standing safely out of the way, Peter watched the impressive rubble moving feats going on all around him, not knowing what to expect. Would there be enough for him to identify? Would there just be the odd body part or two? To some degree it frightened him, but on another level he just knew he had to be here, if for no other reason than to give himself some sort of closure.

Tank, meanwhile, was in the middle of a dressing down, and was loving every minute of it. Ranting and raving in the only way he knew how, the old shopkeeper was still going on about "how worried" he'd been, "how just a short message would have been sufficient," about "who was going to make sure he had the right medication," and how "it was all very inconvenient."

Almost smiling, knowing that this telling off was Gee Tee's way of showing that he cared, yes, he was worried, more so than he was letting on by the looks of things, and not for all the selfish reasons that he proffered. But Tank could see from his body language and the look in his eyes, that what really scared him was the thought that he'd been caught up in that explosion. It was then that he remembered Richie, her brown curly hair, her freckly complexion, her lack of inhibitions and the fun loving way in which she lived her life. His train of thought was interrupted by the old shopkeeper.

"Are you alright? You must know I don't mean everything I say."

Tank nodded, his face full of sorrow.

"Then what is it, youngster?"

"It's Richie, she was caught up in the explosion. She's dead!"

It was all Gee Tee could do to stay on his feet.

"Dead, you say?" he uttered softly.

Tank nodded, the tears welling up in his eyes. He tried to hold it back, but with very little success.

"I'm sorry youngster. I know how close the two of you were."

Tank nodded, unable to speak, while the old shopkeeper thought carefully about what to do. Over the course of his incredibly long life, he'd found himself in this position on a few occasions, and while most thought him uncaring, devoid of emotion and rather self obsessed, those close to him knew otherwise. Wrapping a large, flimsy dragon wing around his former apprentice, the master mantra maker ushered him into a chair in the workshop and asked him to recount exactly what had happened, hoping that this would help unburden his young... friend.

Standing and watching for just over an hour as the mountain of rubble and debris, which would normally have taken days to excavate with human machines, was sifted through carefully and methodically, he wondered just how long he'd have to wait and if they'd find anything recognisable. After all, he'd witnessed the sheer extraordinary raw power of the explosion, enhanced by the laminium. It would have been no real surprise, to him at least, if every last trace of his friend had been wiped from existence. Abruptly, a cry from one of the mantra using dragons startled him out of his thoughts. Others working alongside finished moving material they currently had hold of, before joining their colleague. Skirting around the edge of the crater until he reached the gathering of dragons who were all staring intently down into the large gaping hole, Peter followed their gaze, having to enhance his eyesight with more than a little of his magical power. When he did, he let out an almighty gasp. There, poking out from beneath a huge chunk of rubble, were two arms.

'No, hang on a minute,' he thought. 'Not two arms. Three arms!' By now, the dragons around him had sprung swiftly into action, just like the cohesive unit they were. Two of them held all the debris back on both sides of the area with the bodies in, while at the same time one of the others gently lifted up the rocks on or around the twisted corpses. Once the wreckage had been removed, their leader used his magical abilities to levitate out the two broken, battered and bloodstained carcasses. Gently, he lowered them onto an area of finely cut grass off to one side, as the whole group moved to gather round the two blast victims. It seemed like the right thing to do. Looking down at the two lovers, side by side, for that's who they were, he assumed it had been Tim in the cellar with her, and he was proved right, not that he took any comfort from it. Lying there, perfectly still, their pale faces in total contrast to the blood soaked clothes they wore, they reminded him of the story of Romeo and Juliet. Part of him thought how fitting it was that she'd died with her human lover, sure she'd have thought it a suitable way to go. Swallowing awkwardly, thinking about just how short her life had been cut, it made him sad to his very core.

And then it happened. A racking cough of epic proportions, followed by a huge mouthful of blood, shot out of Richie's bruised and cut mouth. Instinctively they all took a step back, at first anyway. But these were well trained dragons, prepared for nearly anything... any eventuality. Once again, with a professionalism that would put any human to shame, they launched into action. Drawing out his mobile phone, much as a cowboy would his pistol, the leader started speaking into it, telling whoever was on the other end to "initiate medical protocol three, at Salisbridge District hospital." To most it would mean very little, but Peter understood only too well, as the very same thing had been implemented for him after his battle with Manson on that cold November night. Right at this very moment, a room deep in the bowels of the hospital was being readied, shifts and rotas were being changed, dragons of all sorts were being moved like chess pieces on a board, into strategic positions. Just as the leader said the words "dispatch an ambulance," a sickly coughing sound erupted from the other body, followed by a mouthful of vomit.

"NO, make that two ambulances," the leaded screamed into the phone. All the time, Peter stood watching in complete and utter amazement.

'She's alive,' he told himself. 'She's alive!'

Both ambulances duly arrived, each staffed by dragon paramedics. The two survivors were quickly carried on board, having already received the benefit of over a dozen well crafted healing spells. Peter had wanted to travel with Richie, but he hadn't been allowed, so instead followed in his car, breaking the speed limit just trying to keep up. In the end he lost them, but it didn't matter because he knew their final destination.

After parking his car, he sprinted through the main entrance, fairly certain of how to find the obscure area in which they were being treated. As he did so, it suddenly occurred to him that Tank needed to know what had happened. Finding himself a quiet corner of the gleaming white corridor, he phoned his friend. Typically, he couldn't get through.

'He's gone straight to see Gee Tee, I bet,' he thought, not blaming him for one second. Momentarily, he thought about what to do next. Despite sporadic mobile reception areas underground, the coverage was subject to change all the time. In the past he'd managed to reach his friend at the Mantra Emporium, once or twice, but knew that it was more than a little hit and miss. So he decided to send a text, knowing that the instant there was a signal, the message should shoot straight through to his phone. Thoughtfully, he typed in: RICHIE FOUND IN CRATER. BADLY HURT BUT STILL ALIVE. MEET ME AT SALISBRIDGE HOSPITAL ASAP. PETER. Sending the message off into the ether, he tried hard to remember the maze of corridors and passageways that would lead him to where he wanted to go.

It felt good to have let it all out, get it all off his chest, so to speak, knowing full well that's what the old shopkeeper had intended all along. Not only was he mantra smart, but he was people, no... dragon smart as well, thought Tank, waiting for the kettle to boil in the tiny little kitchen off to one side of the shop floor, deep within the famed Emporium. Just as he was about to pour the steaming hot water into both giant mugs, filled a quarter of the way up with the blackest looking charcoal you've ever seen, the back right pocket of his trousers started to vibrate.

'Let me guess,' he mused, pulling out the phone. 'More rugby related nonsense. It's a shame they didn't bother to phone me; at least that way I could tell them that there's now nowhere to coach... that it's all been destroyed.' Phone in one hand, one of the mugs in the other, he depressed the button to read the text with his nose. Tumbling precariously to the floor, spinning like an out of control fair ride, Gee Tee's favourite mug splintered into a thousand pieces across the dirty tiles. Stunned, he was unable to believe what he'd just read, well... for about a second anyway. After that, he moved with all the speed he'd been blessed with, first telling the old shopkeeper what had happened, next making his way back to Salisbridge with all the haste he could muster, all the time silently praying that she'd pull through.

628

Ending up sitting on a blue plastic seat mainly made up of holes, one from a row of four, Peter despised the dark and dreary corridor well beneath the main hospital building. They had refused him entry; this was as far as he'd been allowed to go. Many times over, he'd tried to explain who he was and what had happened, but it had all fallen on deaf ears. Hours had passed, well… that's what it felt like anyway, and still they wouldn't tell him anything. Rubbing his longer than usual stubble with both hands, he gazed aimlessly at the notice board on the wall opposite, wondering what else he could do. It was then that a familiar shape came flying round the corner at the far end of the corridor.

"Tank!" shouted Peter.

Puffing, panting and sweating profusely, Tank doubled up in front of his friend, just about managing to get out a "Hi."

Letting his best mate catch his breath, grateful to have some company in this fruitless situation, Peter sat back, wondering exactly what the doctors were doing.

"How is she?" asked the strapping rugby player, once he'd recovered a little.

"I don't know. They won't tell me anything."

"Why the hell not?" he replied, absolutely furious.

"I don't know. They won't tell me why they won't tell me," explained Peter as best he could.

"Well, we'll soon see about that," announced the big fella firmly, stalking off towards the nearest member of the King's Guard, further down the corridor.

Trailing in his wake, Peter hoped they'd find out more about their friend. In the end though, it didn't happen. It took the appearance of four guards before Tank grudgingly made his way back to the row of blue seats. As the two friends sat in comparative silence, wondering just what was going on, Peter hit on an idea, well… more like an act of desperation. When he'd been alone with him at his private residence, the king had given the young hockey playing dragon a telepathic way to get a message to him, should he ever need to do so. It was extremely private, and only something a few dragons knew about, and he'd been thinking about using it for a while now, but with everything that was going on across the globe, he wasn't sure it was such a good idea to try and disrupt what he knew would be a very busy, stressful and crucial time for the monarch. That and the fact that he felt more than a little selfish, using his connection to George just to see if he could pull a few strings and find out what was going on with Richie. But as time ticked away in the airless corridor where both friends sat, the third of their little trio lying tortuously close in a room nearby, he came to a decision. Using his consciousness in much the same way as he would to download his favourite paper to fire off the message, he kept it short and to the point, hoping it would be enough.

Hours passed, with the two friends still sitting in the same place, only the King's Guards for company. They'd both found it odd that not a single noise had come out from the room that Richie and Tim were supposedly in. Not the hushed tones of a doctor, the sound of equipment being moved around, or the rustling of bed sheets. It was most disconcerting.

Two hours or so later, the guards had a scheduled shift change, and were replaced by much sterner looking, human shaped dragons, with the one in the middle of the corridor nearest to the two friends having a permanent snarl forged across his face. It was hard to take your eyes off him. Peter, fearful of anyone in authority, tried his best not to stare. Tank, not so much. After only a matter of minutes, said guard came swaggering down the corridor towards the pair of them. Peter swallowed uncomfortably. Tank continued to stare.

"What's your problem fella?" growled the snarling guard.

"Nothing!" replied Tank, a little too smugly for the guard's liking. In a move that Peter barely saw, that's how fast it was, the guard picked up Tank by the throat, and held him high above his head, against the shiny wall. Peter stood, panicked, not knowing what to do.

"So you think you're tough do you?" he barked straight into the rugby player's face, while Peter watched helplessly. Tank tried to respond, but the only sound that came out was a rather wet gurgle, the grip on his windpipe was so tight. As his friend's face started turning a rather strange colour, the guard's grip tightened even more, and Peter wondered just what he could do. But before he could act and do something that would no doubt have serious repercussions, a voice accompanied by resounding footsteps boomed down the corridor.

"UNHAND HIM AT ONCE!" it ordered.

Instantly recognising who it belonged to, Peter had never in his life been so grateful to see... FLASH!

Striding towards them with utter purpose and determination, the ex-Crimson Guard watched as the snarling human shaped dragon relinquished his grip on Tank's throat, the young rugby player sliding down the wall, ending up slumped on the floor in a heap.

"Who the hell do you think y... Wait a minute. I know you. You're the one that's stuck... stuck as a human," mocked the guard, chuckling all the time. "Oh... look how afraid I am... Stuck-as-a-human," he taunted. By this time, some of the other guards had moved out of the shadows from their concealed positions, taking a keen interest in what was going on.

"Should I be afraid of you... Stuck-as-a-human? Should I? Why don't you shove off and go mix with your own kind?" the guard scoffed, the snarl on his face long since having bent into a smile. It was so fast in coming, Peter had no idea it had even happened. And he wasn't the only one. Flash had moved so quickly, so gracefully, that now it was the guard who was pinned high up against the wall by the throat, held firmly in place by one of Flash's mighty hands. Some of the guard's colleagues took a step forward, that is, until one of them signalled for them to stand down, which they immediately did, sloping back to the concealment of their former positions. Flash and the rather ignorant individual, meanwhile, had locked steely gazes on each other. As they did so, the guard managed to squeak,

"You'll pay for this, you know."

Flash moved in closer, tightening his already firm grip.

"If I ever hear of you trying to pull a stunt like this again, I'll rip your head off and pee down your neck. Do you understand me?" roared the ex-Crimson Guard, sounding to Peter about as menacing as Manson had on that fateful night.

Taking a few valuable seconds to think, the guard, with his brain being starved of oxygen, had little choice but to nod in agreement. Casually, Flash threw him against the opposite wall, where he destroyed the notice board and everything on it, paying him no more attention. Offering Tank a hand, the grateful rugby player grasped the proffered appendage, and allowed himself to be pulled up. Meanwhile, Peter could see the barely breathing guard now getting up from the floor, thinking about taking Flash from behind, but it must have been the briefest of thoughts, because he very quickly slunk off down the corridor, replaced immediately by one of his colleagues.

Sitting down next to each other, it took nearly forty minutes for the three friends to catch up on what had been going on. Flash had of course been in America when the bombs had started to go off, and at first had been requested to go to Montreal, only then being told as he was about to depart, to change destinations and head towards Seattle. One of the first on the scene, both above and below ground, he left out most of the details, but even so the two friends could see what a heavy toll it had taken on him. Going on to explain how he'd only just arrived back in the country and learned about the Salisbridge bomb, it was then that he'd tried to contact them both, without any luck. So he'd sought out Gee Tee, who'd naturally told him what had happened, and where they could be found. On finding out, he'd come straight to the hospital. Both friends told him how grateful they were, and not just because of the incident with the guard. After that, it was just a case of sitting and waiting. But just like buses, new arrivals never seemed to turn up singly. Peter and Tank had been waiting for over eight hours together, for Peter it was over nine in total. Flash's arrival had been in the last hour, and they were about to be joined by a new visitor.

Confident strides of someone walking resolutely down the corridor adjacent to theirs got them all sitting up. As soon as he walked around the corner, they were all kneeling down on the cold, shiny, unforgiving mezzanine.

"Get up, get up," barked the king.

Peter's surprise at seeing the monarch himself here was palpable. Clearly he'd received the message and had come to intervene personally. Just as he was about to tell the ruler how very grateful he was, the king said something that totally baffled him.

"What on earth are the three of you doing here?"

Momentarily confused about the message he'd sent, Peter remained silent as Tank explained about Richie, and how they were waiting to find out about her condition. The perplexed expression on the head of state's face, led to an even more puzzled one on Peter's.

"Ummm... Your Majesty," he mumbled, remembering to call him that, and not George, with all the other dragons around.

"Yes," responded the king, firmly.

"If you're not here because of Richie, then why exactly are you here?"

"That, I'm afraid Peter, is classified."

"So," ventured the hockey playing dragon, still extremely confused, "you mean to say that you didn't get my message?"

"I'm sorry youngster, but I've not had a chance to check my messages for many days now. But why on earth would you want to send me one anyway?"

"Richie's been in there for over half a day, and no one will tell us how she is, or what's going on. I thought that just maybe you could help. That's what the message was about. And, yes I did realise that you were probably really busy with other important stuff, given everything that's gone on. Sorry!"

The king, almost as confused as the three friends, beckoned over the nearest guard.

"Is this true? Is their friend in there?" he demanded.

Instantly the guard replied.

"Yes, sire," all the time looking straight ahead.

"Get me the physician in charge... NOW!" he ordered.

For his part, the guard didn't even blink, instead, he turned around and disappeared off through a set of ominous looking green double doors.

Turning back to address the three friends, Peter in particular, the king whispered,

"I'm sorry your friend's been hurt. I'm sure she'll be okay. I know for a fact that some of the best dragon doctors in the kingdom are here at the moment."

All three of them nodded, hoping that he was right.

"I checked you know, as soon as I found out about the bomb here. I checked that you were safe and well."

"Thank you," Peter remarked, offering up a little smile.

"And it seems I need to offer the two of you my thanks, since you're both here. By all accounts that was one hell of a mantra you cast around that building son," George said to Tank. "My dragons tell me that they've never seen anything quite like it."

"All it took was a little creativity, Your Majesty,"

replied Tank modestly.

"Hmmmm..." uttered the king. "Well thank you... both, for what you did. If you hadn't, well then I guess you know the consequences better than most. When all this is over, I'll thank you properly. Until then, you're going to have to make do with just a handshake."

Both friends shook the offered hand, both smarting from his grip, much to Flash's amusement. Just then they were interrupted by a female, human shaped dragon wearing a white coat, slamming through the double doors, the ones which guarded the way to Richie and Tim.

"Are you in charge?" demanded the king, steel in his voice.

"I most certainly am," replied the woman.

"Then I demand that you let these three dragons see their friend!"

The wave of relief rolling off Peter, Tank and Flash was palpable. But unfortunately for them, things were never going to be that simple.

"I'm afraid," announced the woman, "that's not going to be possible."

"And why not?" growled the monarch, verging on losing his temper.

"I'm afraid, Your Majesty, we have something of a problem!"

The adventure continues in book 3, A Twisted Prophecy. Lose the stress and instantly escape into a world packed full of dragons hidden in plain sight. Read on for an extract...

A mile away, two sets of eyes shot open at exactly the same time.

"We've been discovered," they both whispered.

With not a moment to spare, they leapt out of bed, quickly pulling on a set of clothes each, eager to be protected from the bitter cold outside. Gloves, boots, and hats followed, and while this was a little time consuming, they both knew the bitter weather had the potential to be as deadly as their attackers. Grabbing a small backpack from a secluded, secret cubbyhole, there for just such an occasion, containing money, jewels to sell, weapons and some chocolate, they opened the back door and silently slipped out into the darkness. Using touch telepathy for fear of being discovered, the two discussed how they would proceed, while swiftly traversing the landscape towards the beach, all the time holding hands.

"We should make a run for it," he said, sending a calm reassurance across their link.

"NO!" Earth replied. "We stand and fight. Give them exactly what they came here for. I'm tired of running, and more than a little disappointed at being discovered here and once again having to give up everything we've worked so hard for."

"But..." he started.

She wasn't having any of it.

"NO MORE! We take them on. Teach them a lesson. Make the cost of them finding us hurt them dearly. So there are three groups... so what! A maximum of three each, that's only nine at most. I don't think we should have any trouble taking care of nine, do you?"

Annoyed because he let her question go unanswered, she could feel him trying hard to shake off the devastation he felt at having to give up this place. It seemed inevitable that their discovery was almost certainly linked to the rather unfortunate accident last week. If only he'd done nothing, or stayed inside the shop a few seconds longer.

Fate, in their bitter experience, had a way of knocking you down flat, just as you thought everything was going along so well.

'It has been so long since I last used it,' she could hear him think to himself, forgetting about the physical link to his wife.

'Are you afraid you won't remember how?'

'It's not that. It's just that I thought this was all behind us. The running, fighting, the taking lives. All I wanted was for us to be left alone.'

Remaining quiet, she abruptly tugged him to a halt. Crouched motionless on a sandy path, masked on either side by tall, wavy grass, some five or so metres above the beach, tears streamed from their eyes as the wind howled viciously around them. With their combined power, their senses extended further, with their physical connection acting as a conduit now, channelling each of their abilities together, making them stronger than the sum of their parts. The five (surprise ran through them at that discovery) dragons were starting to ascend the slope towards their position. With one ancient word, channelled magic cloaked their heat signature, making them all but invisible to their opponents. Before they both rolled to different sides of the path into the long grass, their last words through their physical bridge were to divide up exactly how they were going to launch their attack. Conjuring up her familiar as she hid amongst the long wavy strands, a huge thick serpent with two mighty heads, looking like any dragon's worst nightmare flickered into life. She watched as it slithered off into the darkness, waiting to do her bidding.

Padding along stealthily, the dragon elite ignored the blustery gale they found themselves caught up in, despite the shivers it sent splintering through their false human forms. One had dropped to the back of the group, bringing up the rear. Unable to see how just two of them could possibly outflank his squad, his briefing had stressed how dangerous the fugitives were, and he was determined not to take any unnecessary risks. Cresting the rise, he could just make out the cottage in the distance, showing up as a dark, cold oblong over the shoulders of his troops in front of him. And then without warning, it happened! At first, he thought they'd been struck by lightning because that was the sound that accompanied the blistering surge of magic that had landed amongst them. But he was a professional and trained by the best, and so his survival instincts kicked in instantly, despite the terrible pain behind his eyes from the almost blinding assault. Switching his vision back to normal, an array of attacking mantras from which to choose leapt to the front of his brain as he rolled up onto his feet, after having dived for cover off to one side of the well travelled path.

Others in his group hadn't fared so well. Three, the dragon in front, had taken a huge hit to his back, from the force of whatever had exploded amongst them, falling flat on his face, ears ringing, pain surging down his legs and up his neck. Spitting out the mouthful of sand he'd taken in, his powerful arms pushed himself up, only to be greeted by a dark shadow with a menacing smile standing out in the electrically charged air. Giving everything he had, his reactions were out of this world, but they simply weren't good enough. The shadow (he could just make out it was a woman now) let crackling bolts of bright blue, zigzagging lightning rip from her fingertips. On contact with his body the lightning surged across his skin, burning, flaying and destroying. Like nothing the well trained dragon had ever experienced, the pain was off the scale. In the blink of an eye, he was dead.

In but a few seconds, Earth had unleashed her magic to considerable effect. To her, it was rapture. The feeling was like nothing else. Here and now, she had many beings' lives quite literally in her hands. The power which accompanied that feeling was a rush like no other. Determined to make them pay, she sought out her next victim.

At exactly the same time, Earth's partner in crime had been dealing with Two, who'd been thrown off the path by the force of the explosion, straight into his onrushing enemy. All Two really needed was a split second to get his thoughts together, but his opponent had other ideas. A swift kick to his right knee sent the Crimson Guard flying to the ground, a substantial CRACK the reward for such a well executed attack. Pushing the pain away, the guard tried to focus, but the dark shadow of Earth's husband was on him in an instant. First, a swift, sharp blow to the nose with the side of his hand. Thick red blood spurted everywhere as the guard started to choke. Reaching behind him to the side pocket of the backpack he wore, Earth's husband whipped out a deadly blade that had been secreted there, and plunged it with all his might into his opponent's false heart.

With two of the group dead in only a matter of a few seconds, the odds on the survival of the rest had shortened considerably, despite their leader being back on his feet and ready to join the melee. Four and Five were now both back in the game, with Four looking in desperate need of hospital treatment. Blood flowed freely from a hole in his left thigh, while a massive gash over his right eye left a huge, bloodied sheet of skin flapping about in the frozen wind. Nevertheless, he remained upright, determined to play his part.

The three Crimson Guards approached the two rogue dragons head on in the darkness, on the narrow sandy path. With a vicious snarl on her face and the pent up anger and frustration of having been on the run for years, Earth forced her magic to produce a humungous ball of electricity which she carried in both hands. Blue and purple lightning coursed from the inside to the outer shell, making it look like a child's giant plasma ball. But this one was deadly and her opponents realised it, all

639

simultaneously taking a step back. Bringing her hands round to one side, she thrust the pulsing sphere in the direction of the three stunned agents, who immediately all dived for cover, each missing the murderous, magic filled orb by the merest fraction. With the ball having disappeared over the edge of the rise, One and Five jumped to their feet to once again confront their attackers. Four remained motionless, face down in the long grass. Without a moment to lose, One released an onslaught of bright green filaments in the direction of the husband and wife team. Earth cartwheeled off to the right, but her husband wasn't so lucky, being caught by two of the writhing green tentacles, one piercing his upper right arm, the other holing his stomach. Earth screamed in rage as her husband doubled over in agony. Five, in the meantime, had snuck off to the right, into the grass and, under cover of darkness, launched a blistering attack of poisoned bees at the still raging mad woman, assuming that her all consuming anger had given him the distraction and opening that he needed. But as soon as the toxic bees got to within striking range, they sizzled and burnt, crumbled and fried from the invisible shield that the deranged she-witch in front of them had managed to erect around herself. Still trying to figure out how the hell she'd got a defence up so quickly, Five didn't see the movement in the grass behind him until it was much too late. From out of nowhere the two headed serpent with a body the thickness of the largest human thigh, slithered in behind the distracted dragon, biting both his legs in quick succession before starting to wrap itself around his lower left leg. Five howled in absolute agony as the shiny dark serpent twisted up his torso.

One kept up his onslaught on the male protagonist, determined to even the odds in his favour. With no time to contact the other squads, he knew they must have realised something was wrong by now and be on their way here. All he had to do was buy himself enough time and the odds would become overwhelmingly in his favour. And there would be hell to pay.

Both the inland units had connected with each other as soon as it became apparent that their leader couldn't be reached. A hasty decision was made to get to their last known position with as much haste as possible. So ten dark shapes now rushed as fast as they could towards that point, all thoughts of stealth forgotten. Speed, each of them knew, was the key.

Earth couldn't bear to hear her husband in so much pain. It turned her blood to fire, stoking her rage even more, if that were at all possible. With her serpent peppering the stricken dragon in the long grass with ever more poison, she darted left towards her husband, taking a flying leap, landing directly in front of him. Diverting all her magic towards her shield, she extended it out, cutting off the flying tendrils of bright green, dangerous magic. Exhausted, her husband slumped to the ground. Knowing that time was of the essence, she turned to face a very confident dragon, one she assumed must be their leader.

'Not for much longer,' she thought to herself.

"You will desist and come..." he said, before his voice trailed off.

Desperately, he clutched at his throat, scrabbling at it with his gloved black hands, but the invisible force around it could not be wrestled away.

"I'd give you a message for your precious dragon council," she screamed, "but on reflection, I think your broken bodies might do the trick just as well. What do you think? Cat got your tongue?"

One fought with everything he had, drew on every last resource of magic within him, trying to launch a counterattack, but the oxygen had been forced out of him and his vision was fading fast. In his mind he tried to lash out and unleash a deadly telepathic assault, but he just didn't have the strength.

Turning to her husband, while still choking the life from the dragon force's leader, she urged him to get to his feet and run.

"But I can't leave you here to face such numbers," he babbled.

"GO!" she ordered. "I'll be right behind you, after I've cooked up a little surprise for them."

Seeing little use in arguing, hunched over, he trotted past the upright, blue in the face body of One and headed north, not towards the beach, but the cliff side path. It would be harder work for him but there was more cover, and it would be more difficult for anyone to track him, especially compared with the sandy beach.

One's limp body fell to the ground with a THUMP. Earth revelled in the sick satisfaction of knowing just how much he'd suffered in his last moments. In her mind, she'd planned to conjure up some bombs and booby trap the dragon bodies, knowing full well the other groups would want to recover them. But she'd underestimated them. They were here, almost upon her, and she didn't have nearly enough time to execute her terrible plan. Glancing over her shoulder, she just managed to make out her love staggering up the rise of the cliff top path, hundreds of metres in the distance. Spinning round, she took in her attackers, sprinting across the undergrowth, any hint of subtlety long gone. Fuelled by rage, she called forth everything she had, lighting up the scenery around her like a bonfire night celebration. Hoping to draw all ten of them to her, giving her love half a chance to escape, unfortunately for her, the Crimson Guard were more disciplined than that. Six of them headed straight towards her, while four sprinted off after him. Silently she cursed, but there was little she could do at the moment; she just hoped he could hold on until she could reach him.

They came at her all at once, no holds barred. Streaks of blue tinged flame rocketed out from one dragon, brilliant bright purple bolts of crackling energy ignited the air from another. One of the six had conjured up a golden lattice of pure energy, which hovered steadily in the air, all the time moving towards the, by now, raging mad Earth. This all happened in the blink of an eye, as the other three of the six designated to take her out, closed in for some hand to hand combat, determined to capture her alive and present her to the dragon council.

So many thoughts whizzed through her mind, primarily, how the hell she could catch up with, and save, the love of her life. Instinct and common sense fought off the battle lust that she felt, telling her she had to deal with the six in front of her, and fast. By the look of things, they were all professional and experienced. This was going to be no easy task. Searching her mind for something, anything, that might get her out of this hole, her hunt didn't include anything dragon related. There seemed little point. Clearly her attackers would be able to defend themselves against anything they already knew about, so it had to be something different, something that the nagas had taught her in all the time she'd spent with them.

Off to one side, the Crimson Guard stood still, his eyes closed, concentrating with all his might on the golden net hovering in the air, getting ever closer to his target's position, totally unaware of the tiniest of movements in the long grass beside him. That is until a bite, causing him the most unbelievable pain, made him lose focus and drop to the ground. The sizzling golden trap disintegrated into nothingness, with the overwhelming odds having just turned a little in favour of the rogue dragons.

Earth's husband pulled up, dropping to his knees as he did so, wanting to vomit, but fighting against the urge. Instead, he coughed violently, globules of blood spewing out across the stony path that he found himself on. Knowing they were behind him, he was conscious that he had only moments to act. Before now, he'd never been afraid of dying. Many situations across the years had seen him close to losing his life. In each and every one of those, he'd always faced his destiny with the typical arrogance that was probably a trademark of his old self. But over the years, he'd changed. Whether it was him, or because of her, or just the fact that they were together, he didn't know. But that arrogance was long gone, replaced with love, and regret. He didn't want to lose her; he didn't want to die. For the very first time he was afraid, not only for him, but for her as well. Staggering to his feet, all the while clutching his belly wound, he moved as quickly as he could into the breeze, the salty sea air a constant reminder of what he'd just lost.

Out of the corner of her eye, she glimpsed her serpent taking down another of the hopeless dragons. A twisted smile writhed across her face. Not just because of what she'd just seen, but because she had it. The answer. And now she intended to use it. With the streaks of fire and purple bolts being deflected harmlessly away by her cleverly designed personal shield, she lowered her head to face the attackers who were almost upon her, twisting her finger in a very intricate fashion, putting all her rage, willpower and temper behind but one thought. BOOM! A solid ring of sound erupted out from her. All the Crimson Guards were thrown back, with the closest one smashing his head on a huge chunk of rock jutting up out of the path. The other two charging dragons had fared little better. One twisted his ankle, while the other was out cold, both of his arms twisted in unnatural positions where he lay. Both the Crimson Guards who'd been casting spells stumbled to their feet, blood streaming from their ears and noses. All around, the 'thud', 'thud', 'thud', of birds dropping to the ground, dead, could be heard. In the sea, fish floated to the surface in nearly a half mile radius, while crabs stayed buried beneath the sand, never to move again. Earth strolled purposefully forward, heading straight for the two spell casters, stopping briefly on the way to break the neck of the unconscious dragon, which she accomplished with the ease of a trained professional. It clearly wasn't her first time.

Ignoring the pain they were in, the two Crimson Guards concentrated on channelling their supernatural power. But it was too little, too late. Earth was upon them, gouging the first one's eyes out in an instant, his howling screams carried off into the distance by the squally gusts. The second, despite the severity of his injuries, lunged forward, swivelled and kicked Earth's feet from under her.

Falling brutally to the floor, the wind having been knocked totally out of her, for a moment she was completely at his mercy. Knowing this was his chance and despite decades of training, his anger tore through him, controlling his every action. Leaping upon her, he rained down a torrent of punches into her face and chest, watching as her cheeks erupted in a shower of blood and bone. She tried to mutter some words, but they only came out as an incoherent gurgle. With all consuming rage defining his actions, he'd decided what needed to be done.

'To hell with the council and their judgement,' he thought, still hammering blows into the seemingly helpless woman. 'She deserves to die,' he decided. And so calling forth every last ounce of power within him, he let rip. Purple bolts surged out of him, so lightning fast they looked like one long continuous stream. Her beaten body started to convulse and writhe with pain, making him look like some demonic rodeo rider on the cold, dark, evil winter's night. Thoughts of justice and righteousness consumed the dragon agent, knowing that for once he'd become judge, council and king all at once. It was then that two huge mouths slithered up from nowhere and clamped themselves around his head, causing him to scream out in pain, all thoughts of his previous target forgotten. Rolling off Earth, hoping to shrug off the giant beast, he'd not counted on its teeth having firmly dug into his skull. He tried to get to his feet, but as he got to his knees, powerful muscles wrapped themselves around both his legs, squeezing as hard as they could. Tumbling onto the hard ground, all the time rolling, both his hands searched in the darkness for the slippery serpent's eyes, hoping to jab a finger or two into them. But it was no good, he couldn't find them and the pain was stopping him thinking. By now the evil looking snake had wrapped its entire fifteen metre body around the guard, literally crushing the life out of him. As his vision went dark for the final time, and he expelled his last breath, he smiled, knowing that at least that witch of a rogue dragon would never harm anyone ever again.

A sharp, metallic tang filled her throat and lungs. For all intents and purposes she'd died. But the single thought within her hadn't been told about that. All it cared about was him. And it knew that to keep him safe, this broken and battered body it was concealed within had to get up, get going, and fight. The thought urged the body to roll over and expel its contents. It did. Whacking great mouthfuls of blood coughed up onto the sand beside it. Casting aside the pain it felt, Earth's body lurched to its feet and, avoiding the mass of corpses surrounding it, started to jog in the direction she'd last seen her husband.

'He has to be alright, he just has to,' she thought, over and over again as she followed in his footsteps.

Having never had his wife's skills with familiars, they were, for him, out of the question. But that didn't mean he needed to concede defeat. Resting behind a craggy rock on the cliff's edge, needing to catch his breath and focus his thoughts, the cold wind whipped at his face, keeping unconsciousness at bay. All his eyes wanted to do were close and stay that way. But as with his wife, one singular thought pushed him on. HER. He needed to fight and stay strong for her. They would be together again, he was sure of it. It was meant to be. Over the harsh screaming of the storm, his enhanced senses could just make out noises... no, words. With a great effort he lifted his head up against the rock he had his back to, all the time panting heavily, aware of the precarious drop to his left. The cliff path had mainly headed up, and the rock that he was sitting behind lay at its highest point, some hundred metres above the beach, somewhere below him in the darkness. With a fall like that, he'd definitely be done for, and there would be no time to revert back to his natural dragon form, even if he had the energy to do so, which of course he didn't. Weary and mindful of his enemies approaching, he grabbed a handful of large stones from the ground around him. Ignoring the blood seeping from his stomach wound, he channelled his magic into the pebbles. One by one, they turned the darkest shade of black known to man or dragon. Holding tightly onto what had now become something of an arsenal, he reached out behind him, searching for his ever elusive pursuers.

All the time scratching at her face like some mad, delusional witch, she wobbled up the cliff top path, at times using the fauna around her to pull her up just that little bit further. Sensing them, and of course him, she could tell he was hurt, but not too badly. But they were closing in on his position. She had to move, move faster. But the pain was out of this world, with her face feeling like it had been torn off. Spitting out yet another mouthful of blood, she caught her breath next to a thorny little bush, just for a few seconds, before once again pressing on, knowing time was of the essence.

Eyes firmly closed, he stretched out with his mind... and found them. Now within fifty metres of his position, two were together, two were on their own, wading through the surrounding undergrowth, clear of the path, no doubt fearful of a trap. Taking a breath and then exhaling slowly, he threw a pebble up over the rock he was sitting behind, high up into the air, satisfied with the trajectory it was on. Leaning his chin on his chest, he grabbed another stone and waited for the mayhem to begin.

Eight was stationed directly behind Nine as they moved through the scrub on top of the cliff. Abruptly Nine's closed fist sprang up into the air. They both stopped stock still, tense and on the lookout for danger from every possible angle. They were good, that's for sure. But neither noticed the solid, dark object dropping upon them from directly above as the wind had cancelled out any sound that might have given them a clue. And then it was too late. BOOOOOOMMMMM!!! The explosion tore the ground apart right in between them both. Fire and intense heat scorched the surrounding area, with stones acting as projectiles, peppering the two Crimson Guards with holes, while the kinetic force tossed their ragged bodies metres into the air, both finally landing face down, suffering massive trauma. Just outside the blast radius the two remaining guards looked on in disbelief, a tiny trickle of terror running through them. Both reaching the same conclusion at pretty much the same time, they were sitting ducks for whatever had just taken out two of their comrades. They had to act now. And so, in unison, they did, taking off, heedless of the risks, at full pelt towards the rock which they knew was sheltering their target.

About to throw the next stone that he'd prepared, he realised just a fraction too late that they'd done the last thing they were supposed to. By the time he'd reacted, they were too close to use the stones. He was on his own. Leaping to his feet, ignoring the blossoming pain in his stomach, he prepared to meet them.

Cresting the rise of the adjacent cliff top just in time to see the explosion go off and bits of dragon guard fly everywhere, she smiled at the ingenuity of her husband. The feeling of pride though, soon turned to horror as she watched the two remaining guards break cover and head straight towards him at a sprint. Thrusting out her right arm, she tried to aim her magic somewhere in their path, a series of terrifying electrical charges leaping from her not quite instantaneously. The surrounding air crackled and hummed, filled with electricity, but she was too far away and her desperate efforts were very wide of the mark. Starting to run, her momentum was helped by the slight down slope, but by now the dragons clad only in black had disappeared behind the craggy old rock.

On him in an instant, he blocked an oncoming blow by the first one, surprised at how his body remembered to fight, almost on its own. The second came in, snapping a low kick towards his left leg. Jumping and turning both at the same time, he aimed a well placed punt towards the guard's knee. But he didn't fall for it, instead opting to somersault back out of range. Closing him down, both Crimson Guards knew he had nowhere to go. His back was to the rock that had provided him with cover. To his left, there was a sheer drop into the darkness, with the beach and a quick death waiting. Knowing that if he could get them to commit to an attack, he just might be able to use their momentum to his advantage and force them over the cliff, he put on his best demeaning sneer, almost as if to say, "Bring it on." But these two knew what had happened to the others and recognised a serious threat when they saw it. And so with the coordination and teamwork that comes only with years of experience, they moved as one, launching themselves at him simultaneously. Ducking his head to one side, he let rip with the most powerful punch he could under the circumstances. It wasn't enough. The first Crimson Guard had got well within his defences, while the second had countermanded his punch. After that, it was all over. A head butt struck him first. It wasn't full on, as he'd pulled his face out of the way, but it was a powerful glancing blow, enough to momentarily stun him, making his head ring like a church bell. While blocking the punch, the second guard spun slightly on his heel and then planted the sole of his other foot straight through Earth's husband's knee, causing him to bellow in pain, as the CRACK of snapping bones rose above the gale.

Hurrying down the rise, crashing through bracken, the wind whipping her hair into a Medusa-like appearance, the sound of a loud CRACK resounding over the wind forced her into running faster. Pride in her beloved's work and the thought of yet another dragon badly wounded sent a jolt of excitement through her. During the years that they'd been living in the cottage, she'd missed the thrill of the fight. Often she'd thought about it, those that she'd betrayed, captured, tortured, killed. Not a hint of remorse had ever shown its face, in fact quite the opposite. It thrilled her to think about the power she'd held over others. She missed it. Now... she was making the most of it, living off it, letting it course through her veins, powering her on to something greater.

Spent, he dropped unceremoniously to the ground, the two guards looking like ninjas towering over him in their all black outfits. Instinctively he curled up into a ball, willing his mind to conjure up something in the way of protection as the kicks from each of them smashed into him. It was, however, not going to happen. The absolute agony from his gut wound alone was almost enough to make him black out, and that combined with his fractured knee cap and the onslaught he was now taking left him vulnerable, defenceless, incapable. Leaning down, the first dragon guard grabbed him by the neck, forced his hands away from his face and then hit him with a wild punch, bursting the skin above his right eye, sending blood and bone fragments hurtling up against the craggy rock they all found themselves in front of. Just as another punch was incoming, a bewitching, insane figure, lit up with magic, powered by rage, came flying around from the other side of the rock, forked electricity sizzling from each of her fingertips, death to all written in her eyes.

His good eye caught sight of her. She looked magnificent, and he'd never been prouder. Alright, she appeared to have been in a fight, but just how many dragons had she destroyed this night? After she put these two mutts out of their misery, he looked forward to finding out.

Both Crimson Guards were horrified at what had just skidded to a halt in front of them. Neither had experienced nightmares, but if they had it would be hard to imagine anything worse than that which stood before them. Automatically their training took over. Ignoring the wounded enemy on the ground, the first threw all the magic he had at her, while the second instantly erected a makeshift shield to protect them both.

Despite the run down nature of her invisible defence, the magic thrown at her only tickled. Both dragons were nothing more than insects to her now, able to bite, scratch and sting, but nothing more than that. With her hair dancing around to its own beat in the wind, and spying her battered and beaten up husband curled up in a ball on the ground, right by the cliff's edge, a despairing madness overwhelmed her. She wanted to punish them for what they'd done, make them pay, torture them for days on end before deliciously removing their still beating hearts. Unfortunately she didn't have the luxury of any of that and so instead decided to get it over with. It can only be described as hell being unleashed. Electricity, primarily, with fire, ice and just a hint of pure poison whooshed from her hands, totally filling the gap between her and the two dragons. It ripped apart the childlike shield one of them had erected and then caught both in the chest, forcing them to stagger back towards the pitch black drop behind them. From the floor, he looked up into her eyes, smiling at the power she wielded, proud that she was his. Out of the corner of her eye, she could see him smiling at how well she was doing. It brought forth memories of their early days together, days that were amazing, like no other. Days that would come again, now that they were reunited, standing together against their common enemy.

Unsurprisingly, a wave of tiredness washed over her; she was, after all, using nearly everything she had to continue the onslaught of magic that was burning from her hands. In an instant, she decided to finish it.

ABOUT THE AUTHOR

Paul Cude is a husband, father, field hockey player and aspiring photographer. Lost without his hockey stick, he can often be found in between writing and chauffeuring children, reading anything from comics to sci-fi, fantasy to thrillers. Too often found chained to his computer, it would be little surprise to find him, in his free time, somewhere on the Dorset coastline, chasing over rocks and sand in an effort to capture his wonderful wife and lovely kids with his camera. Paul Cude is also the author of the White Dragon Saga.

Thank you for reading...

If you could take a couple of moments to write a review, it would be much appreciated.

CONNECT WITH PAUL ONLINE:
www.paulcude.com
Twitter: @paul_cude
Facebook: Paul Cude
Instagram: paulcude

BOOKS IN THE SERIES:
A Threat from the Past
A Chilling Revelation
A Twisted Prophecy
Earth's Custodians
A Fiery Farewell
Evil Endeavours
Frozen to the Core
A Selfless Sacrifice
Christmas in Crisis

Printed in Great Britain
by Amazon